FOCUS ON THE FAMILY®
Great Stories

QUO VADIS

A Story of Faith in the Last Days of the Roman Empire

by
Henryk Sienkiewicz

Introduction and Afterword by
Joe Wheeler, Ph.D.

TYNDALE

Tyndale House Publishers, Wheaton, Illinois

QUO VADIS

Copyright © 2000 by Joseph L. Wheeler and Focus on the Family
All rights reserved. International copyright secured.

Sienkiewicz, Henryk, 1846-1916.
   [Quo vadis? English]
   Quo vadis? / by Henryk Sienkiewicz ; introduction and afterword
  by Joe Wheeler.
     p. cm. — (Focus on the Family great stories)
   ISBN 1-56179-795-2
    1. Rome—History—Nero, 54-68—Fiction. 2. Church history—
Primitive and early church, ca. 30-600—Fiction. I Wheeler, Joe L.,
1936- II. Title. III. Series.

PG7158.S4 Q43 2000
891.8'536—dc21   00-036463

Synthesized translation by Jeremiah Curtin, A. Heyman, S.A. Binyon,
S. Malevsky, and Joe Wheeler © 2000.

A Focus on the Family book published by Tyndale House Publishers,
Wheaton, Illinois.

Joe Wheeler is represented by the literary agency of Alive Communications,
7680 Goddard Street, Suite 200, Colorado Springs, CO 80920.

Cover design by Carrie L. Ketcham
Cover photo of Lygia and the Roman soldier by Tim O'Hara Photography, Inc.
Cover photo of the building and the lion © 1999 by PhotoDisc. Inc.
Illustrations are from the Jan Styka edition of *Quo Vadis* (New York: Thomas
D. Crowell, 1905).

Printed in the United States of America

00 01 02 03 04 05 06/10 9 8 7 6 5 4 3 2

A LIFE-CHANGING LETTER

Several years ago I received a letter that changed my life. Sadly, I don't remember who wrote it, only what she said. In essence, this was her plea: Dear Dr. Wheeler,

I have a big favor to ask you. First of all, though, I want you to know how much I enjoy your story collections; they have greatly enriched my life. Now for the favor: I was wondering if you have any interest in doing with books what you are doing with stories.

You see, while I love to read, I haven't the slightest idea of where to start. There are millions of books out there, and most of them— authors too—are just one big blur to me. I want to use my time wisely, to choose books which will not only take me somewhere but also make me a better and kinder person.

I envy you because you know which books are worth reading and which are not. Do you possibly have a list of worthy books that you wouldn't mind sending to me?

I responded to this letter, but most inadequately, for at that time I had no such list. I tried to put the plea behind me, but it dug in its heels and kept me awake at night. Eventually, I concluded that a Higher Power was at work here and that I needed to do something about it. I put together a proposal for a broad reading plan based on books I knew and loved—books that had powerfully affected me, that had opened other worlds and cultures to me, and that had made me a kinder, more empathetic person.

But that letter writer had asked for more than just a list of titles. She wanted me to introduce her to the authors of these books, to their lives and their times. To that end, I've included in the introduction to each story in this series a biographical sketch of the author to help the reader appreciate the historical, geographical, and cultural contexts in which a story was written. Also, as a long-time teacher, I've always found study-guide questions to be indispensable in helping readers to understand more fully the material they're reading; hence my decision to incorporate discussion questions for each chapter in an afterword at the end of the book. Finally, since I love turn-of-the-century woodcut illustrations, I've tried to incorporate as many of these into the text as possible.

There is another reason for this series—perhaps the most important. Our hope is that it will encourage thousands of people to fall in love with reading, as well as help them to discover that a life devoid of emotional, spiritual, and intellectual growth is not worth living.

Welcome to our expanding family of wordsmiths, of people of all ages who wish to grow daily, to develop to the fullest the talents God lends to each of us—people who believe as does Robert Browning's persona in *Andrea del Sarto:*
Ah, but a man's reach should exceed his grasp,
Or what's a heaven for?

Joe Wheeler

Note: The books in this series have been selected because they are among the finest literary works in history. However, you should be aware that some content might not be suitable for all ages, so we recommend you review the material before sharing it with your family.

"Quo vadis, Domine?"

TABLE OF CONTENTS

This has been as tough a book as I can remember in my lifetime. Intertwining three different translations so the language sounds like one voice was by itself a labor of Hercules. So has been the extensive research necessary for the footnoting. My esteemed editor, friend, and toughest critic has been there with me and Connie every step of the six-month way, even consulting with Latin scholars at an area university when we came to a dead end on an obscure item or figure. Thus it gives me great pleasure to dedicate this edition of *Quo Vadis* to Rainey Ratchford.

LIST OF ILLUSTRATIONS

Warning: This book contains graphic portrayal of the persecution of Christians and is not recommended for children under the age of 14.

Introduction

HENRYK SIENKIEWICZ AND
QUO VADIS

Most books that we read barely register in our memory bank—they are there, but only dimly. Rarely does a book dig in its heels and demand that it be taken seriously and that it not be forgotten after you finish it and put it down. *Quo Vadis* is that kind of book.

I first read it many years ago when I was young, and loved it for its excitement and panoramic windows into that long-ago world of the Praetorian Guard; the pomp and opulence of the Roman imperial court; the ludicrous yet malevolent Nero; the fascinating arbiter of elegance, Petronius; the opportunistic and amoral Chilo; the vindictive Tigellinus; the slave girl with a secret love, Eunice; the forgiving physician, Glaucus; the Christian mother-mentor, Pomponia; the evil virago of an empress, Poppaea; the faithful courtesan, Acte; the apostle of love, Paul; the *quo vadis* apostle, Peter; the disillusioned old general, Aulus; the faithful Hercules, Ursus; the ruthless young tribune, Vinitius, and the great love of his life, the beautiful princess, Lygia—this incredibly real cast of characters comes to life as you read, and it never leaves you. In addition there is the kaleidoscopic imagery of racing chariots; decadent imperial banquets; the burning of Rome; torchlight processions into old graveyards; candlelit glimpses into foul, plague-ridden prison cells; Christians burning as living torches in Caesar's gardens, crucified on crosses like their Master, beheaded like Paul, speared by gladiators, pulled apart by horses, gored by bulls and bisons, or savagely attacked by wild dogs, lions, panthers, tigers, and bears. It's almost mind-boggling that Sienkiewicz managed to cram all this between two covers!

It is *not* a book for small children, for it is powerful fare filled with violence. But for the rest of us, it serves as a reality check. Our society has so sanitized events like the bloody lashing of Christ, His falling to the ground under the weight of the cross, His humiliating stripping and public nakedness; the agony resulting from having a crown of thorns driven into His scalp, the nailing of His hands and feet to the cross, the ripping of His muscles as the cross is dropped into the hole, the public taunting, the terrible thirst, the brokenhearted death—yes, we have so sanitized all this that we completely miss the agonizing reality of Christ's sacrifice for mankind.

The same is true of the terrible period of Christian persecution unleashed by Nero, which we quaintly reduce to "the Christians and the lions." Only as we read a realistic book like *Quo Vadis* can we genuinely conceptualize what it was like to be a Christian during those days when death was the probable price you would pay for your convictions. It is a sobering book. It is also about as historically accurate as Sienkiewicz could make it (exceptions noted in the Discussion Questions).

Every book we read is written subjectively from the author's perspective; some more objectively than others. Each of us, after all, writes from the fountain of our selfhood. Sienkiewicz wrote from the Greek Orthodox, Russian Orthodox, Byzantine, and Roman Catholic perspectives; thus we should expect these perspectives to show up as conscious or unconscious bias. They do, but that doesn't diminish the greatness of the book. The most significant historical fact to keep in mind during the reading of the book is this: All these events take place approximately during A.D. 60-69, a period when there were no organized Christian congregations, no church buildings as we know them, no formalized clergy. In periods of persecution—and they continued for centuries, one of the most terrible being under Emperor Diocletion almost four centuries after Nero—the church tended to be underground. The priests of these faithful were called bishops. Not until the fifth and sixth centuries, as Roman imperial power began to wane, did the bishops of Rome gain the ascendancy over the other bishops, and with that came the rise of the mighty Roman Catholic Church that Sienkiewicz repeatedly alludes to in connection with the ministry of the Apostle Peter.

Of all the books I have ever read, I can think of none that incorporate more vivid mental pictures than does *Quo Vadis*. In drama, we would call them scenes, grouped under the heading of an act (Act II, Scene 3, for instance). The first memorable scene is in the garden of Aulus, in which

Lygia draws the sign of the fish in the sand as she speaks with Vinitius. But the first scene of epic proportions is the great banquet of Nero when Lygia, a Christian, is brought into the presence of the most dissolute court of the world and sees for the first time the infamous Caesar and his beautiful but evil empress, Poppaea. Just as biblical writers depicted events with the brush of truth, just so did Sienkiewicz. Had he failed to accurately depict the evil of Nero's court, never could the reader have realized the miracle of Vinitius's escape from that sinkhole of iniquity and journey into the light. Paint a picture of that scene in your mind as I did, for you will rarely see its equal in all literature. Then do the same with each memorable scene that follows.

Perhaps the most daunting challenge facing an author of historical fiction has to do with this question: Can he or she bring the musty past to life? To do so presupposes the author's near total immersion into the history of that period. And it helps mightily if the author has actually been to the places where the story or book is set. Rarely can a story ring with authenticity without that "being there" factor. But even the historians who are world authorities on certain periods often find themselves totally incapable of bringing those times out of the dead past into living Technicolor reality. The author has to have the God-given ability to create a character from a time that the author has never experienced firsthand and then form that character so that the actions, speech, and thoughts are historically true to life (no small challenge!), yet also modern enough so that the reader is able to bridge across the centuries and say, "I like you!" or "You fascinate me!" or "I can't stand you!" or "I could have loved you myself!" or "I can see why you did that." Very few authors can pull it off. Sienkiewicz is one of those few.

How does a story or a book come about? By mere chance? By God's leading? Personally, I believe that stories and books worth reading do not come about by chance but rather because God so choreographs the author's life that the story concept and the author meet face-to-face. It has happened over and over in my own life and writing. We call such experiences epiphanies or life-changing moments. Interestingly enough, we experience our epiphanies and leave them behind without ever knowing what they were; only in retrospect do we realize, in essence: *Do you know, had that day when this took place never been, my life would have been totally different!*

In Sienkiewicz's case, that day occurred during the early 1890s. Just as the "millennial fever" struck at the end of the 1990s, there was a fin de siècle fever during the 1890s, many viewing 1900 through apocalyptic lenses, many feeling that the world had lost its ethical, moral, and spiritual moorings and was adrift on an amoral sea. Sienkiewicz was between stories (or books)—let's face it, each author only has a certain number of stories that she or he can tell within a lifetime—and uncertain about where God was leading him next.

He was walking the streets of one of his most beloved cities, Rome, having experienced the Tiber gilding at sunset; the ancient stones of the world's greatest highway, the Appian Way; the gloomy Mamertine prison, where the Apostles Peter and Paul had been imprisoned; the great columns—still standing after all the long centuries!—of Rome's Forum; the great dome and basilica of St. Peter's dominating the City of Seven Hills; and the Coliseum in the moonlight, eerie and sobering, the only light from distant gas lamps, the only sounds, horses' hooves on cobblestone streets. He shuddered involuntarily as ghosts of long ago—Christian martyrs, lions, tigers, bulls, and gladiators— emerged from the shadows into the arena, above which could be envisioned the roaring crowds and the imperial court. He felt he himself was *there.*

One golden morning, as he walked the Appian Way, on the outskirts of the Eternal City, he came across a small chapel—one of thousands— and a tablet with a faded inscription that he almost passed by. But, for some strange reason, he was impelled to stop and read it. It read "*Quo vadis, Domine?*" Intrigued, he set out to learn the rest of the story. He discovered that it was on this very spot, according to historical chronicles, that the Apostle Peter, fleeing for his life from the bloody sword of persecution and feeling that he had failed in his ministry (for Nero had slain almost all the Christian converts), had met a blinding light and had fallen forward at the sight of his dear Lord, who in answer to Peter's question, "*Quo vadis, Domine?*" ("Where are You going, Lord?"), had told him sorrowfully, "Back to Rome, to be crucified again, since you are deserting the flock I entrusted to you!" Peter turned around, at that very spot, and returned to further ministry, incarceration, and crucifixion. Sienkiewicz was so deeply moved by this story that as he pensively walked back into the heart of Rome, he felt that the tablet had been meant for him, too. And thus was born *Quo Vadis,* one of the reasons for later awarding him the Nobel Prize in literature and, unquestionably, one of the greatest and most deeply moving books ever written.

Quo Vadis hit the Western world like a thunderbolt in 1896, quickly becoming one of the best-selling novels in the world. It was translated into many languages, gradually becoming one of the most beloved books ever written. It has remained in print ever since, although somewhat erratically in the English-speaking world. Hippocrene Books, Inc., advertises it as "World-wide #1 Best-selling Novel of All Time" (on the cover of the 1993 paperback edition). It remained the number one top seller in America for twenty-five years! Nevertheless, in recent years, fewer and fewer people appear to remember it, which is a tragedy, for no one should go through life without reading it at least once. I believe it is one of the ten greatest novels ever written.

So, welcome to one of the most meaningful experiences of your life-time. Turn off the radio or TV, sink deep down into your favorite arm-chair, and prepare to travel—through the magic of Sienkiewicz's pen, mind, heart, and soul—to another time, walking through the streets of Nero's Rome with the unforgettable men and women Sienkiewicz has brought to life for this purpose.

Quo Vadis is such a blockbuster of dramatic scenes that it is very easy not to see the forest for the trees. If you had to reduce the entire epic to one line, it would be this:

The story of the soul of Marcus Vinitius.

This book is about Vinitius and his spiritual journey. It's not about Lygia; she's already a Christian. It's not about Petronius; he changes, but not in seis-mic terms as does Vinitius; the only comparable life-change takes place in the corrupt heart of Chilo, but Chilo is not the protagonist, Vinitius is. Once you realize that Sienkiewicz had in mind the spiritual journey of Vinitius as the book's core, then the reading takes on an entirely different dimension. Few things are more difficult to pull off in literature than a believable transforma-tion of a lead character. You will eventually discover that Sienkiewicz does not leave out one detail in his portrayal of the character evolution of this amoral hedonist, henchman of one of the most dissolute men who ever lived—Nero.

So it is that I urge you, as you climb aboard for one of the wildest roller-coaster rides of your life, not to forget what it all means:
the journey of a soul.

The Wheeler Synthesized Translation

No, I don't know Polish. But yes, I have been heavily involved in this trans-lation. Through the years, I have read *Quo Vadis* several times. Originally, I read the Jeremiah Curtin translation (Boston: Little, Brown & Company, 1896); for my college classes on great books, I used the Stanley F. Conrad translation (New York: Hippocrene Books, 1992). When we decided to include *Quo Vadis* in our first twelve Great Stories collection, the assumption was that we would use the Curtin translation, now long out of print. With that assumption, my wife, Connie, typed out the entire book from a very early text. It took her a long time, for this is no short book!

Well, the time came for me to proof the manuscript. I picked up the first page, and my heart sank. The second page was no better. The Jeremiah Curtin was not only archaic but downright stodgy and unnecessarily verbose. I almost cried. Here we were only days away from the deadline, and we had no manuscript! Connie was even more upset, for it appeared she had spent all that time at the computer for nothing.

I searched for other translations and was able to secure A. Heyman's turn-of-the-century translation (Chicago: J. S. Ogilvie) and S. A. Binyon and S. Malevsky's 1897 translation (Philadelphia: Henry Altemus). William E. Smith's translation I quickly pulled, for it was merely an abridgement. I hoped either the Heyman or the Binion/Malevsky translation would turn out to be just right. Not a chance! Neither of them was satisfactory; neither had the power, the ring, the beauty I was searching for. So I called Larry Weeden at Focus on the Family and shared my frustration with him. He agreed with my conviction that nothing but the best would do and told me not to stop short of that.

Thus it was that I sat down with Heyman and Binion/Malevsky, determined to use the best lines from each one. I wasn't far along before I realized that my synthesis wasn't as good as I'd expected it to be; it was too prosaic. A strange conviction came over me that I should return to Jeremiah Curtin. Incredibly, I discovered that while it wouldn't do by itself, it had the power, beauty, and rhythm the other two translations lacked.

I ended up using the Binyon/Malevsky as a base, then wrote in preferred lines, words, expressions, as well as footnotes from the other two translations. In most cases half of each page or more had to be rewritten to take advantage of the best each translator brought to the table. I belatedly realized something else: A translation must have a coherent style; a hodgepodge cut-and-paste job just won't do! That's when the realization hit me that I had no choice: That missing factor had to be me, *my* style. This intertwining of manuscripts has proved to be one of the toughest tasks I've ever faced. If it turns out to be all that I hoped it would be, much of the credit will have to go to God. Each morning I prayed that God would take away all thoughts of self and grant me, if it be His will, the wisdom He granted Solomon so many years ago. The result of all this intertwining is the Wheeler Synthesized Translation. I will be most interested in readers' reactions to it.

When you are dealing with an author of the stature of Sienkiewicz, extremely knowledgeable in history, literature, music, mythology, and languages, there is going to be a great need to footnote. This part of the job exhausted the resources of my library; in fact, I had to purchase additional Latin-related sourcebooks.

What about the Latin terms that Sienkiewicz incorporated into the original text? Some translators kept them, some did not. I ended up retaining them whenever possible, for several reasons. First, English being a Latin-based language, I was amazed at how many of the terms I recognized because I already used them or their derivatives in my own speech and writing. Second, I found them so fascinating that I hated to deprive readers of the same opportunity to grow that I had. Third, I take a dim view of talking down to anyone—I detest pablumizing. And to my way of thinking, both abridging and taking away opportunities for growth are forms of pablumizing. I am hopeful, therefore, that readers will consider this book to be a treasure hunt into the ancient Latin world. Put together a set of flash cards: Each time an unfamiliar word or term surfaces—in most cases, they'll be footnoted—put it on a card with the definition and usage. Alphabetize these cards and review them daily. This way, if you come to a word like *triclinium,* you'll either already know it, need to look it up in your cards, or fill out a card for it. By the end of the book, you'll be on your way to becoming a Latin scholar.

And let me tell you this: After all that I have gone through to make this book possible, never again will I take a translation for granted! I learned how fluid and inexact translations are, the same phrases and sentences coming out in totally different words, depending on the translator. Several of the translators failed to do their homework and would occasionally come up with the wrong word or words. Some believed in the spirit of a translation rather than a faithful word for word—they tended to abridge—as did Conrad; I was surprised, for I had used Conrad's version in my classes under the assumption that it contained the complete original text. I tend to be a purist, believing wholeheartedly in the sanctity of the text. Every phrase in the original, I have tried to retain in translation. Also, there is a grave danger in over-contemporizing an old book, especially one set almost 2,000 years ago. If one isn't extremely careful, words that are based on modern technology and contemporary culture can jar the reader. To prevent this, I have attempted to stay on middle ground with regard to style. Furthermore, to achieve the unique style for this translation, I was forced to occasionally stray from literal word-for-word transcription in the direction of *feeling* my way into the words I felt Sienkiewicz would have used had English been his native language.

Thank you for being part of this fulfilling journey.

About the Illustrations

Most editions of *Quo Vadis* are either underillustrated or not illustrated at all. For many years now, I have been searching for editions featuring convincing, faithful, and accurate illustrations. At the end, we reduced our candidates to two, both of which are extremely rare today. I just wish we'd had the space to include both sets.

The first was the monumental two-volume work published by Little, Brown and Company in 1897. This illustrated vellum and parchment work was limited to only 250 copies (hence its incredible rarity today) and featured 31 plates. Besides maps of ancient Rome, house plan layouts (Plautius and Petronius), photos (Mamertine prison and Quo Vadis Chapel), and sculpture (Nero, Poppaea, Otho, Galba), it features six paintings by Howard Pyle, six by Edmund H. Garrett, five by Evert Van Muyden, and single paintings by G. Boulanger, Francois Leon Bonouville, and Wilhelm von Kaulbach. It is a wondrous, eclectic mix! *Especially* when you consider how few people have ever seen these illustrations. It must have cost a small fortune for one of these 250 sets.

The other finalist was the almost equally rare Jan Styka edition (New York: Thomas D. Crowell Publishers, 1905). Jan Styka was Polish, like Sienkiewicz, a refugee of divided Poland. Americans know Styka for his great painting "The Crucifixion," which had its birth in Lemberg, Poland, when the young virtuoso Ignace Paderewski conceived of a painting depicting the freedom Poland lacked, the freedom born of Christ's sacrifice on the cross. Paderewski shared this vision with Styka, who decided to make of it his life's masterpiece. After years of study in Rome and the Holy Land, Styka began painting. Year after year (12–14 hour days) passed, and finally, in 1895, it was done—all 43 feet of the height of it and all 195 feet of the length of it! Hundreds of thousands of people from across Europe came to gaze transfixed at it, and it was considered to be one of the greatest spiritual and artistic triumphs of the century. In 1900 the huge painting came to America—and then it was gradually forgotten, for where could a building be found big enough to exhibit it? Finally, Dr. Hubert Eton made of the painting a crusade, and the result was the Great Hall of the Crucifixion at Forest Lawn Cemetery in Glendale, California. And there you may see it today, the largest and most dramatic painting in America (*Ideals Magazine*, vol. 13, no. 2, 1956, special section). The editors of Thomas H. Crowell were so impressed with the great work that they decided to capitalize on all the years of research Styka had done by asking him to illustrate the then-most-popular book in the world, *Quo Vadis*. Since Sienkiewicz was also Polish, the wedding of the two artists between two covers resulted in a unique masterpiece.

In the end, the single-minded artistic vision of Jan Styka won out over the less-focused but magnificent Little, Brown edition. For it Styka painted 17 memorable paintings, as accurate historically as was his great "Crucifixion." Sadly, much is lost in the contraction of these epic panoramas to book-page size.

Movie History

Some of the screen treatments we know very little about.

Year: 1902. *Quo Vadis*, Pathe [Paris] Company, 20 minutes, black and white, silent

Year: 1912. *Quo Vadis*, Cines Company of Italy, 120 minutes, black and white, silent

Cast: Amleto Novelli (Vinitius), Carlo Cattaneo II (Nero), Gustavo Serena (Petronius), Lea Giunghi (Lygia), Bruto Castellini (Ursus), Augusto Mastripietri (Chilo), Cesare Moltini (Tigellinus), Leo Orlandini (Peter), Amelia Cattaneo (Eunice), Olga Brandini (Poppaea), Ignazio Lupi (Aulus)

Director: Enrico Guazzoni

Year: 1924. *Quo Vadis*, Italian movie company, black and white, silent

Cast: Elga Brink, Elena Di Sangio, Lillian Hall-Davis, Emil Jan-
nings (Nero)
Director: Arturo Ambrosio
During filming in Rome, a lion devoured one of the extras!

Year: 1951. *Quo Vadis,* MGM Technicolor, 171 minutes, color
Cast: Robert Taylor (Vinitius), Deborah Kerr (Lygia), Leo Genn
(Petronius), Peter Ustinov (Nero), Patricia Laffan (Poppaea),
Finlay Currie (Peter), Abraham Sofaer (Paul), Marina Berti
(Eunice), Buddy Baer (Ursus), Felix Aylmer (Plautinus), Nora
Swinburne (Pomponia), Ralph Truman (Tigellinus), Norman
Wooland (Nerva), Peter Miles (Nazarius), Geoffrey Dunn
(Terpnos), Nicholas Hannen (Seneca), D. A. Clarke-Smith
(Phaon), Rosalie Crutchley (Acte), John Ruddock (Chilo),
Arthur Walge (Croton), Elspeth March (Miriam), Strelsa
Brown (Rufia), Alfredo Varelli (Lucan), Roberto Ottaviano
(Flavius), Pietro Tordi (Galba), and cameo appearances by
Elizabeth Taylor and Sophia Loren
Producer: Sam Zimbalist
Director: Mervyn LeRoy
Screenplay: John Lee Mahin, S. N. Behrman, Sonya Levien
Musical Score:
Miklos Rozsa
Golden Globe Award:
Best Supporting Actor (Peter Ustinov)
Remade for Italian television in 1985
Twelve years in the making and called "the most elaborate picture ever
made," the film cost around $7.5 million, the largest budget for any
movie ever made (at that time). It brought in $25 million, second only to
Gone with the Wind. (Documentation for this section provided by *M-G-M
Presents* Quo Vadis [New York: Al Greenstone, 1951 movie souvenir
booklet, 1-18].)
The movie did take some liberties with the book, especially in terms of
chronology at the end.

Year: 1981. *Quo Vadis,* Prism Entertainment, 122 minutes (Italy,
200 minutes), color
Cast: Klaus Maria Brandauer (Nero), Frederic Forrest, Christina

Rains, Maria Theres Relin, Francesco Quinn (son of Anthony Quinn), Barbara De Rossi, Philippe LeRoy, Max von Sydow, Gabriele Ferzetti, Massimo Girotti, Leopoldo Grieste
Director: Franco Rossi
(Sources used for this study include Leonard Maltin's 1997 *Movie and Video Guide* [New York: Penguin Books], 1081; *Video Hound's Golden Movie Retriever* [Detroit: Visible Ink Press, 1997], 608; *Variety Movie Guide* [London: Hamlyn Publishing, 1997], 746; and Amazon.com's Internet Movie Database Ltd.)

About the Author
Henryk Sienkiewicz (1846–1916)

Sources consulted and referenced in this short study include the following (code used to avoid wasting so much space on repetition of long titles in references): Catherine B. Avery's *The New Century Classical Handbook* (New York: Appleton-Century-Crofts, 1962) (CBA: *NCCH*); George Albert-Roulhac's "The Life and Works of Henryk Sienkiewicz," included in *Nobel Prize Library: Seferis, Sholokhov, Sienkiewicz, and Spitteler* (New York: Helvetica Press, 1971) (GAR:*LWS*); from the same work are C. D. Af Wirsén's "Presentation Address" for awarding the Nobel Prize to Sienkiewicz (CDW:*NPA*), Gunnar Ahlström's "The 1905 Prize" (GA:*NFP*), and Sienkiewicz's "Acceptance Speech" (HS:*NAS*); Marion Moore Coleman's *Fair Rosalind: The American Career of Helena Modjeska* (Cheshire, Conn.: Cherry Hill Books, 1969) (MC:*FR*); Marion Moore Coleman and Arthur Prudden Coleman's *Wanderers Twain: Modjeska and Sienkiewicz—A View from California* (Cheshire, Conn.: Cherry Hill Books, 1964) (MC/AC:*WT*); Monica M. Gardner's *The Patriot Novelist of Poland: Henryk Sienkiewicz* (New York and London: J. M. Dent and Sons, 1926) (MMG:*PNP*); Monica M. Gardner's "Henryk Sienkiewicz," included in *Great Men and Women of Poland* (New York: The Kosciusko Foundation, 1967) (MMG:*HS*); also included in this collection of short biographies is Eric P. Kelly's "Helena Modjeska: Dramatic Artist—Every Inch a Queen" (EPK:*HM*); Mieczyslaw Giergielewicz's *Henryk Sienkiewicz* (New York: Twayne Publishers, Inc., 1968) (MG:*HS*); Waclaw Lednicki's *Henryk Sienkiewicz* (The Hague, Netherlands: Mouton & Company Publisher,1960) (WL:*HS*); Little, Brown & Company's *Henryk Sienkiewicz: The*

Author of Quo Vadis (Boston: Little, Brown & Company, 1898) (LB:*HS*); and S. C. de Soissons's "Henryk Sienkiewicz," included in his anthology of Sienkiewicz stories: *So Runs the World* (London and New York: F. Tennyson Neely, 1898) (SCS:*HS*). Quotations from Sienkiewicz's own books will be referenced only by book title.

— — —

> *Then suddenly, from overhead came the sound of voices in the distance. I looked up, but the sky was by now so dark that I could see nothing. Then directly above my head came the sound again, the sound of voices. A clamor filled the sky. I recognized it: it was the noisy chattering of the cranes.*
> *. . . I went back to my room . . . but I could not sleep. Scenes from my childhood home crowded into my mind, one after the other. Now the pine forest, now the wide-stretching fields with the Macków pear trees lining the furrows. The thatched cottages of the peasants, the country churches, the white manor-houses nestling in the dense greenery of orchards. For scenes like these my heart was torn with longing the whole night through.*
> (MC/AC:*WT,* 54)

Strange, mused Sienkiewicz as he gazed at the cranes flying overhead, that he could not really see Poland until he had left it—until he lay on a sandbar offshore at Anaheim Landing in 1876 California. His beloved Poland, torn apart eighty-one years ago, now lived only in the broken hearts of a dispossessed people.

Was it perhaps time to return?

A Man Without a Country

Henryk Adam Aleksander Pius Sienkiewicz was born at Wola Okrzejska, the manor house on his mother's estate in Russian Poland, on May 7, 1846. His father was descended from Tartar nobles of Lithuania, and his mother was a member of the Cieciszowska family and thus was of even higher rank than her husband in Polish aristocracy. Diplomats, prelates, and scholars— such as famed historian Joachim Lelewel—graced Henryk's family tree.

Although not far from Warsaw, the province of Podlasie seemed so rural as to almost feel as if it were still the frontier. From the southeast the great River Bug swept around and through, hastening to its eternal tryst with the Vistula. To the north was Lithuania, the ancient heartland of the Polish Slavs, the source of much of their one-time greatness, greater by itself than was the Muscovite empire in those pivotal centuries long gone by.

And Podlasie was a meeting place of three great churches: the Orthodox Church from Byzantium-Constantinople, the Catholic from Rome, and the Greek Catholic from both Byzantium and Rome (MC/AC:*WT*, 2). Part of the very fabric of Henryk's childhood was the great forest, dominated by the towering pines and supported by the weather-beaten oaks, river-worshiping willows, and graceful birches.

His parents and grandmother cooperated to set his sails for life, his education so carefully supervised that he had an abbot for a personal tutor, as well as a French governess. A large and devoted domestic staff watched over him as well. His mother was both gentle and good, always to be counted on wherever there was suffering or trauma. And his father served as a living prototype of "an old Polish nobleman faithful to the codes of honor and religion. The great medieval traditions were so strongly upheld in this family that when a son came of age, he was feted in a ceremony very similar to that of the consecration of a knight in the eighteenth century" (GAR:*LWS*, 257).

Books abounded in the home, and Henryk immersed himself at an early age in the culture, history, literature, and philosophy of Europe, with an emphasis on eastern Europe. Niemcewicz's *Historical Songs* instilled in him a "love of knighthood—'I wanted to be a knight'—and that *Robinson Crusoe* and *The Swiss Family Robinson* fired his imagination to such an extent that his dream was to settle on an uninhabited island" (WL:*HS*, 7). Sir Walter Scott and Alexander Dumas introduced him to historical romance. Then there were living memories: Not far away was the field of Maciejowice, the scene of General Thaddeus Kosciuszko's tragic last stand in Poland's war for independence (Kosciuszko had earlier written himself into American history by his leadership during the Revolutionary War). Many years later, Sienkiewicz would revisit that childhood haunt and experience anew the sorrow of that defeat in a short story he titled "In the Mist."

The scene of the story is a misty, murky day in winter. Two boys from Warsaw are riding along a country road in a sleigh. Suddenly the horses stop dead in their tracks. Total silence envelops the world. The fields are snow-covered and mist-blanketed; the pine trees also are draped with mist. As the sleigh stands there,

> suddenly, and without making the slightest sound, there came from the sheltering gloom of the pines, a column of marching men. In their hands the men carried scythes, and they wore long white coats, the garb of the Krakovian peasant.
>
> "The Scythe-bearers!" the boys breathed, "the men of Kosciuszko's army!"
>
> Though they passed close enough to the sleigh to have touched it, the men in the advancing column gave no sign they had seen it. Like people in a solemn religious procession or at a funeral, they trod heavily forward, eyes lowered, heads bowed on their breasts.
>
> At the head of the column went the priest, wearing his cowl and carrying the cross, while behind him came a division of sharpshooters, led by their commander on his mount. The sharpshooters had their bayonets in readiness on the tips of their rifles, and their banner, with the White Eagle of Poland emblazoned upon it, fluttered in the wind.
>
> Soundlessly the column advanced, row after row making its way out of the forest. The mist accompanied them, half veiling them from view. . . . Soon there was nothing to be seen but the tips of the sharpshooters' bayonets and the steely points of the scythe-bearers' improvised weapons.
>
> (MC/AC: *WT,* 5–6)

Never was he permitted by his family to forget that he was ethnically Lithuanian, nor that the land of his birth, Poland, had been wrenched apart by three rapacious neighbors: Russia, Prussia, and Austria, led by Catherine II of Russia, bent on the utter annihilation of once-grand Poland. In 1772, the infamous triumvirate gobbled up one-fifth of Poland, each from a different direction; in 1793, another gobble left intact but a third of the country, and two years later the last gobble wiped

Poland off the map. To better empathize and understand what it was like, permit me an analogy. Let's say that the United States were suddenly to be attacked from three directions: from the northwest by Russia (which once owned Alaska and lay claim to the Northwest almost to San Francisco); from the north and east by France (which once owned Canada and the vast Louisiana territory—the entire Mississippi basin); and from the south by Spain (which once owned most of what is now the United States from coast to coast). Let's say that Russia, France, and Spain attacked us simultaneously (while we were weak internally) and utterly destroyed our armed forces. The Spanish proceeded to fill one-third of our nation with its military, and its bureaucracy would henceforth make all the top level day-to-day decisions. The schools would be taught in Spanish; the English language and United States history would be regarded officially as if they had never been. Any child or youth who spoke English in public would be severely chastised and beaten into submission. Adults who tried to keep the spirit of U.S. culture alive would be jailed. The most recalcitrant would be hauled south into Central American dungeons, to be heard from no more.

In the third of America governed by the French, the same pattern would be repeated, only French would be the sole tongue permitted, and dissidents would be shipped off to remote bastions such as Devil's Island. Russia would impose the same restrictions on its third: Only Russian could be spoken or taught. Dissidents would be hauled north through Alaska across the straits into Siberia—many would die there. This state of affairs would last for 123 years (comparable timewise to a period beginning with Washington's inauguration in 1789 and lasting until 1912, on the eve of World War I). *That* was the world Henryk Sienkiewicz was born into, lived out his life in, and died in.

But in Poland, the old ways, the old beliefs, died hard. On estates such as Wola Okrzejska, in some respects time appeared to stand still; relationships between master and servants remained almost feudal. In *Hania*, Sienkiewicz's most autobiographical work, there is a wonderful character-sketch prologue titled "The Old Servant" which recreates those growing-up years and relationships. As portrayed, clearly the word *servant,* in this case, appears to be almost a play on words.

> This old servant was called Mikolai Suhovolski; he
> was a noble from the noble village of Suha Vola, which

he mentioned often in his stories. He came to my father from my grandfather of sacred memory, with whom he was an orderly in the time of the Napoleonic wars. . . .

In the house of my parents he fulfilled the most varied duties: he was butler; he was body-servant; in summer he went to the harvest fields in the role of over-seer, in winter to the threshing; he kept the keys of the vodka room, the cellar, the granary; he wound up the clocks; but above all he kept the house in order.

I do not remember this man otherwise than scolding. He scolded my father, he scolded my mother; I feared him as fire, though I liked him. In the kitchen he worked off a whole breviary on the cook, he pulled the pantry boys by the ears through the house, and never was he content with anything. Whenever he got tipsy, which happened once a week, all avoided him, not because he permitted himself to have words with his master or mistress, but because whenever he fastened on any one, he followed that person all day, nagging and scolding without end.

During dinner, he stood behind my father's chair, and though he did not serve, he watched the man who served, and poisoned life for him with a most particular passion.

"Take care, take care!" muttered he, "or I will take care of thee. Look at him! He cannot serve quickly, but drags his legs after him, like an old cow on the march. Take care again! He does not hear that his master is calling. Change her plate for the lady. Why art thou gaping? Why? Look at him! Look at him!"

He interfered in conversation carried on at table, and opposed everything always. Frequently it happened that my father would turn during dinner and say to him:

"Mikolai, tell Mateush after dinner to harness the horses; we will drive to such and such a place."

"Drive! Why not drive? Oi yei! But are not horses

for driving? Let the poor horses break their legs on such
a road. If there is a visit to be made, it must be made.
Of course their lordships are free; do I prevent them? I
do not prevent. Why not visit? The accounts can wait,
and the threshing can wait. The visit is more urgent."

. . . We, that is, I and my younger brother, feared
him, as I have said . . . he was more polite towards my
sisters. He said "Panienka" [i.e., "Lord's daughter" or
"young lady"] to each of them, though they were
younger than we; but to us he said "thou" [used only
by those on most intimate terms of familiarity] without ceremony. For me he had a special charm: he
always carried gun caps in his pocket. It happened
often that after lessons I would slip into the pantry,
smile as nicely as I could, be as friendly as possible, and
say timidly:

"Mikolai! A good day to Mikolai. Will Mikolai
clean pistols today?"

"What does Henryk want here? I'll get ready a dish-
cloth, that is all."

Then he would mock me, saying:

"'Mikolai! Mikolai!' When gun caps are wanted,
Mikolai is good, and when not, let the wolves eat him.
Thou wouldst do better to study; thou'lt never gain
wit from shooting."

"I have finished my lessons," said I, half crying.

"Finished his lessons! Hum! Finished. He is studying and studying, but his head is like an empty canis-
ter. I won't give caps, and that's the end of it." (While
talking, he searched through his pockets.) "But if the
cap goes into his eye, Mikolai will catch it. Who is to
blame? Mikolai. Who let the boy shoot? Mikolai."

Scolding in this fashion, he went to my father's
room, took down the pistols, blew the dust off them,
declared a hundred times more that all this was not
worth a deuce; then he lighted a candle, put a cap on
the nipple of the pistol, and let me aim. Meanwhile I
had often to bear heavy crosses.

"How the boy holds the pistol!" said he. "Hum! Like a barber. How couldst thou quench a candle, unless as an old man quenches it in church? Thou shouldst be a priest to repeat Hail Marys, and not be a soldier."

In his own way he taught us his military art of other days. Often after dinner I and my brother learned to march under his eye, and with us marched Father Ludvik, who marched very ridiculously.

Then Mikolai looked at him with a frown, and, though he feared the priest more than any one, he could not restrain himself.

"Hei!" said he, "but his grace marches just like an old cow."

I, as the elder, was oftener under his command, so I suffered most. But when I was sent to school old Mikolai cried as if the greatest misfortune had happened. My father and mother said that he became more peevish, and annoyed them two weeks.

"They took the child and carried him away," said he. "And if he dies! Uu! U! But what does he want of schools? Isn't he the heir? Will he study Latin? They want to turn him into a Solomon. What folly! The child has gone off, gone off, and crawl, thou old man, into corners and look for what thou hast not lost. The deuce knows why 't is done."

I remember when I came home for the holidays. All in the house were sleeping. It was just dawning; the morning was cold and snowy. The squeaking of the well-sweep in the farm-yard and the barking of dogs interrupted the silence. The blinds of the house were closed, but the windows in the kitchen were gleaming with a bright light which gave a rosy color to the snow near the wall. I had come home tired and gloomy with fear in my soul, since the first rank which I had received was nothing in particular. This happened because I was helpless till I had found my place, till I had grown accustomed to routine and school discipline. I feared my father; I feared the severe, silent face of the priest, who had brought me from Warsaw. There was no consolation from any side. At last I saw the door of the kitchen open and old Mikolai, with his nose red from cold, wading through the snow with pots of steaming cream on a tray. When he saw me he cried:

"Oh, golden Panich! ["heir," very respectful] My dearest!"

And then he put down the tray quickly, turned over both pots, caught me around the neck and began to press and kiss me. Thenceforward he always called me Panich.

For two entire weeks after that he could not forgive me that cream: "A man is carrying cream for himself quietly, and the boy comes along. He picked out his hour accurately," etc. (*Hania*, 3–7)

Living in the extended household was also beautiful Marynia, Henryk's aunt beloved by all for her goodness and kindness—but especially by the local physician, Dr. Stanislav. At first Mikolai liked the genial man, but when it became apparent that the doctor loved Marynia and she him, Mikolai turned cold and stony-faced when the doctor was around. When Mikolai caught the doctor proposing, he rushed to his master and demanded that he step in and stop the match. But the doctor married Marynia anyhow. The years passed, yet Mikolai, in his jealousy, remained cold to the doctor.

There was one person Mikolai loved above all others, lovely Hania, his only grandchild. Suddenly, typhus struck her—in those days typhus was, as often as not, fatal. Dr. Stanislav hardly left her room for three days. Her grandfather neither ate nor drank during that period—just sat brokenly at the door of her room. And then . . . "at last, after many days of mortal fear, Doctor Stanislav opened the door of the sick girl's room quietly, and with a face beaming with happiness, whispered to those awaiting his sentence in the next room, one little phrase: 'Saved.' The old man could not endure; he bellowed like a bison and threw himself at the doctor's feet, merely repeating with sobs: 'Benefactor, my benefactor!' Hania recovered quickly. After that it was clear that to her grateful grandfather, Doctor Stanislav could do no wrong" (*Hania*, 17–18).

A year or so later, the old man, now almost ninety, began to fail—but not even Dr. Stanislav could save him from that ultimate enemy, Death. Mikolai's heretofore straight and powerful figure crumpled, and he became weak and childish. Henryk, sixteen at the time, was there at the end:

> Some days before death he did not recognize people; but on the very day of his decease the dying lamp of his mind gleamed up once more with bright light. I remember this because my parents were abroad then, for my mother's health. On a certain evening I was sitting before the fire with my younger brother, Kazio, and the priest, who had also grown old. The winter wind with clouds of snow was striking at the window. Father Ludvik was praying; I, with Kazio's help, was preparing weapons for the morrow's hunt on fresh snow. All at once they told us that old Mikolai was dying. Father Ludvik went immediately to the domestic chapel for the sacrament. I hurried with all speed to the old man. He was lying on the bed, very pale, yellow, and almost stiffening, but calm and with presence of mind.
>
> That bald head was beautiful, adorned with two scars: the head of an old soldier and an honest man. The candle cast a funereal gleam on the walls of the room. In the corners chirped tame titmice. With one hand the old man pressed the crucifix to his breast; his other was held by Hania, who was as pale as a lily, and she covered it with kisses.
>
> Father Ludvik came in and the confession began; then the dying man asked for me.
>
> "My master is not here, nor my beloved mistress," whispered he, "therefore it is grievous for me to die. But you, my golden Panich, the heir—be a guardian to this orphan—God will reward you. Be not angry—if I have offended—forgive me. I was bitter, but I was faithful."
>
> Roused again suddenly he called in a strange voice, and in haste, as if breath failed him:

"Pan!—Heir!—My orphan!—O God—into Thy—"
"Hands I commend the soul of this valiant soldier,
this faithful servant and honest man!" said Father Ludvik, solemnly.
The old man was no longer alive.
We knelt down, and the priest began to repeat
prayers for the dead, aloud.
Nearly twenty years have passed since that time.
On the tomb of the honest servant the heather of the
cemetery has grown vigorously.
Gloomy times came. A storm swept away the sacred
and quiet fire of my village. Today Father Ludvik is in
the grave, Aunt Marynia is in the grave; I earn with the
pen my bitter daily bread, and Hania—
Hei! Tears are flowing!"(*Hania*, 18–20)

Henryk's years in the country were destined to be short, for his parents
sold their estate in order to educate their children in Warsaw. Their bank-
ing on an apartment house as an investment for the future proved to be a
mistake, for its income fell far short of their expectations. And much of
what money remained was earmarked for dowries for their four daughters.
Thus it was that when Henryk began preparations for entrance into the
University of Warsaw, it became clear that he would have to help earn his
way. He began by serving as a tutor to the children of relatives, the Prince
and Princess Woroniekis.

But this period from preparatory school to university was interrupted
by an event that would change the rest of Henryk's life: the Warsaw Insurrection of 1863. This revolution was ill prepared, yet lasted two years.
Napoleon III of France had promised aid to the insurrection leaders; his aid
never came. Perhaps if it had, Bismarck would have respected him more
and not invaded France seven years later. Everywhere, idealistic and patriotic youth enlisted in the cause and fought for freedom. The end was the
end of more than just the insurrection, for the three occupying powers
unleashed their vengeance in wholesale executions, confiscations, and
deportations. The gentry paid the highest price, for, in all three areas, they
lost their remaining privileges, and many were ruined financially. Russian
Poland was hurt the most, becoming a virtual police state; Prussian Poland
was almost as brutal and dehumanizing; Austrian Poland was hurt the least.

Sienkiewicz's father fought in the uprising—and as a citizen of Russian Poland, he paid a heavy price for it. It was *not* a good time for Henryk to be entering the university in Warsaw. The iron rod of Russia smashed the resistance to a pulp, executed the insurrection leaders (as well as many of the participants), exiled many others to Siberia, and tightened the screws on those who remained. The life and joie de vivre of a generation flickered into almost total darkness. After 1863, "every high-spirited Pole felt a sense of constriction, and as a corollary to this, a desire to escape" (MC/AC: *WT,* 1). Fifteen years before, in 1848, revolution against autocracy had spread like wildfire across Europe. Each revolution ended in a bloodbath. When a given ruler was unable to put down the revolt, he called in troops from other autocratic regimes. The result was that liberty and democracy had to wait seventy more long years. But another result was a widespread feeling of powerlessness and disillusion that settled like a miasmic mist over the continent. Now, in Poland, it seemed as though life was no longer worth living.

Nevertheless, Sienkiewicz enrolled at the university. When he began his studies, the university was Polish/Russian; before he was halfway through, it had become totally Russian, with all use of the Polish language now strictly forbidden. Apparently, Sienkiewicz did not know initially what he really wanted to study: He started out in law, changed to medicine, then changed again to history and literature. His teachers tried their best to weaken his faith and patriotism, but all their rhetoric broke apart on the rock of his childhood training and study. Instead of turning him into an agnostic, the experience proved to be the trial by fire, the crucible, from which he emerged stronger than when he went in.

And women came into his life. None, it appears, with a greater impact than his childhood friend Hania. Apparently, when Hania's grandfather died, Sienkiewicz promised him that he would always look after her. He honored that promise. As he and Hania grew older, she blossomed into a great beauty. Being rather immature still, the boy/man Henryk was long in realizing that his feelings for Hania had evolved from protective friendship into romantic love. A close friend, neighbor, and fellow student at the university, Selim, had fallen in love with Hania. Honorably, Selim asked Henryk if there was any reason he could not court her—in other words, Did Henryk love her himself? Henryk confusedly answered by assuring his friend that he did *not* love Hania; the field was wide open. Selim took him at his word and pressed his suit. But Hania truly loved Henryk, and he her. The two erstwhile friends fought a duel over her—both survived it. Selim later abducted Hania, but was forced to return her to the Sienkiewicz family. Then she was stricken with the dreaded smallpox, which usually resulted in death or a face disfigured with terrible pockmarks; only a blessed few survived with unblemished skin. Both young men were appalled—one look at her terrible sores was enough to drive all thoughts of romantic love out of their heads. Both dutifully proposed anyhow—their code of honor required nothing less—but she promptly rejected both of them, recognizing their obvious insincerity and declaring her intention to take the veil and enter a nunnery, which she did.

Some years later, unable to sublimate the experience in his subconscious, Sienkiewicz wrote the autobiographical *Hania,* concluding it with this remarkable O. Henry ending:

> The first storm of life had broken that beautiful flower when it had barely opened. Poor girl! She needed now after the tempest some holy and peaceful harbor, where she could pacify her conscience, and bring her heart to rest.
>
> She found that quiet and holy harbor. She became a Sister of Charity.
>
> Later on, new events and one terrible storm caused me for a long time to lose sight of her. But after a number of years I saw her unexpectedly. Peace and calm were depicted on those angelic features; all traces of the terrible disease had disappeared. In the black robe and white head-dress of the cloister she was beautiful as never before; but it was a beauty not of earth, beauty more angelic than human. (*Hania,* 167)

Sienkiewicz withdrew from the university without graduating and entered the workaday world—his chosen career: journalism. His output was broad, consisting of articles, short stories, and reviews, and he used the pseudonym of Litwos ("the Lithuanian"). His first novel, *In Vain,* was published in the Warsaw paper *Korona Warszawska.* The plot dealt with student life in Kiev, which was in reality his Warsaw experiences transposed outside the Russian zone so that the manuscript would pass the Russian censors. The protagonist, Yosuf, is a thinly disguised Sienkiewicz. His closest friend and fellow student is Gustav, who is in love with a beautiful widow, Helena. She, however, is in love with Yosuf, who reminds her of her dead husband. Yosuf initially responds to that love but then falls in love with Lula, an entrancing young countess fallen upon hard times. So here he is, torn between the woman he has blindly pledged his life to and a woman who wakes his very soul.

In the end, Yosuf realizes he is afflicted with the fatal disease of his disillusioned generation: the incapacity to seize a moment, of arriving at a firm conclusion. He longs for an object until he gains possession of it; once he gains possession of it, he is no longer interested in it. In his later work, Sienkiewicz returns again and again to this rootless and decisionless intellectual protagonist.

Sienkiewicz was restless, too. Somewhere, somehow, he needed to find an answer to the question: *What was he to do with his life?*

Modjeska

Enter another woman into his life, Helena Jadwiga Opid, who in the end became simply Modjeska. She was born October 12, 1840, in the ancient royal city of Krakow. She was named Helena Opid, but in truth she was the unacknowledged daughter of Prince Wladyslaw Sanguszko, a member of one of Poland's illustrious "Nine Families." Her widowed mother married Szymond Benda when Helena was still a child. Eric Kelly notes that Helena was supremely fortunate to grow up in "one of the most artistic and delightful cities in the world. Krakow is one of the few cities in which the culture of all ages is embodied in some lasting and living form.....Music, literature, art, ideas from every remote corner of the world, somehow find a forum here" (EPK:*HM,* 254).

Out of this wondrous city flowered Helena Jadwiga Ophid Benda, who was destined to cast a long shadow on her age. As she moved from childhood into adolescence, her tutor, Gustaw Modrzejewski, immersed her into the study of music, art, and literature. She was seventeen when she first saw Shakespeare's *Hamlet* performed on stage, and from that moment on, Shakespeare took center stage in her life and career. At length she married her loving tutor and, with him and his acting company, barnstormed all over Galicia. After the untimely death of her husband, she dared the big time: Poland's greatest theater in Warsaw. She and her art took it by storm—and she became its prima donna.

Love came again in the person of Karol (later Americanized to Charles) Bozenta Chlapowski, member of Poland's nobility. She was introduced to him by Charles's cousin Tadeusz, son of General Dezydery Chlapowski, who had served under Napoleon and was a brother-in-law of Grand Duke Constantine, brother of Czar Alexander and Czar Nicholas and a viceroy of Poland. Charles and Helena married, and she never had cause to regret it. Helena's last name was later changed, for stage purposes, to Modjeska. By that name she has been known ever since.

Meanwhile, the 1863 insurrection changed everything. Supplanting the old nobility was the new moneyed class that emerged out of the peasantry and the middle class. Sienkiewicz felt keenly that "the times were truly out of joint" and continued his search for people who felt as he did. He found them at the home of Dr. Edward Leo, where he met Modjeska; from that time on he became a regular at Modjeska's famous Tuesday evening salons. "I can see him now," Modjeska recalls in her memoirs, "sitting in a cozy corner of the room, his handsome, expressive face leaning against his hand, silent, for he rarely spoke, but his brilliant, half-veiled eyes saw everything, and his ears drank in every word. The whole room, with its contents—men, women, and objects—was unconsciously yielding fruit for his acute observation." After most of the other guests had drifted out into the night, Sienkiewicz would remain, reluctant to leave the magic presence of his adored hostess. Now, with this smaller circle, he would enter into scintillating conversation, often throwing out leading or provocative questions, prodding the other guests to prove their points, and sometimes injecting his own unique brand of sarcasm. "He would stay on, with the favored few, until the candles were all burnt out," Modjeska recalls, "and the white light of dawn was beginning to peep across the window-blinds."

Inside that closed circle, there was happiness, fulfillment, and deep friendship. Outside, the terrible Franco-Prussian War was raging—in France, thousands of Poles died as Bismarck's terrible war machine rumbled over France like a juggernaut and left its glory in ruins.

Four years later, Sienkiewicz moved to Paris, where he experienced the aftermath of the terrible war—then returned to Poland and the hospitality of the Chlapowskis. But Sienkiewicz was restless still, and Modjeska was finding life in Warsaw more difficult, thanks to the venomous jealousy of her associates and the increasingly constrictive controls ordered by Russia. Thus the time was ripe to discuss a trip out of all this turmoil to a place that appeared—at least from a distance—to be heaven on earth: America. Should they all (there were five in the group) actually emigrate there? Or should they merely travel across the country and decide later? The group concluded that if everything proved to be as positive as they anticipated it would be, they'd settle down together as a Blithedale or Brook Farm experiment in communal living. Modjeska dreamed that California would be "sunshine and gold, food growing in wild abundance; Indian braves fashioned in the magnificent mold of the 'noble savage' of the romantics; 'charming Indian maidens, our maidens, our neighbors, making wreaths of luxurious wild flowers for us'" (MC/AC: *WT,* 1–42).

It was decided to send out a scout, a Joshua, to spy out the land. Litwos (Modjeska called Sienkiewicz by his pseudonym) was chosen for the task. In 1876 he left for America. From New York, he took that new mode of transportation—the train—across the recently completed transcontinental route to the Pacific. The vast midsection of America, especially the West, was still wild, and Indians still disputed the loss of their ancient hunting grounds. It was the time of Custer, Little Big Horn, and the senseless slaughter of millions of buffalo. He recorded in his mind and in his notebooks the experiences he had and the people he observed and met. Truly it was like nothing else he had ever seen or experienced. He was not very impressed by Americans, considering all too many of them to be crude and relatively uncultured. Here, too, he saw to his chagrin the deification of money and the discrediting of the finer things of life.

This Polish Joshua arrived in southern California in late spring, when all nature was ablaze with flowers, the air was fragrant and balmy, the streams crystal clear, and the ocean beaches a perpetual source of serenity. "Litwos is there," Modjeska wrote on July 13, 1876, ". . . and his letters tell wonders about the climate, scenery, and vegetation of that promised land, so that we are all crazy to go." She was less entranced by an exclamation one of the group made: "And Madame Helena will do the cooking, she will wash the dishes and instead of violets and heliotrope her perfume will be the fragrance of dishwater" (MC/AC: *WT,* 1–43).

When it finally came time for her to leave, Helena gave a farewell performance in Warsaw to her disbelieving public. At the end of one of the great performances of her life, "the audience rose as a single person, to form a double line from the back door of the theater through the whole length of the park, up to the main gate." After waiting a while, the star walked majestically down through the guard of honor. As she left the gate, the people all began to wave their handkerchiefs and implore her to "come back to us! Come back!" (MC/AC: *WT,* 48–49).

Meanwhile, waiting for them in Anaheim Landing, south of Los Angeles, was Sienkiewicz. Here on the beach, in a room next to a tavern, he had found a place to sleep and write. Max Nebelung, the freight clerk and man in charge of virtually everything at the Landing, soon became his friend. Max had been all over the world, knew many languages, and had an endless supply of stories to tell. Through the thin wall of his room, Sienkiewicz could hear the constant noise, laughter, card games, and so on of the Norwegian fisherman—all of which he loved, for he wrote best when surrounded by the cacophony of life.

Whenever Nebelung could spare the time, he'd take his Polish friend on excursions into the Santa Ana Mountains. Here they'd make a fire and watch the glowing eyes of animals through the campfire flames. Afraid, Sienkiewicz had a hard time sleeping. In these mysterious and wild mountains—there were still outlaws, cougars, bears, and other wild animals then—he began to find himself, to discover who he really was: "Everywhere else he had just been something carried around, like an old trunk. One person could be replaced by any other, for none were truly persons. But here you were something. If you were not, you died, for you had nothing between you and death save your own wits and your rifle. For transportation . . . you had only yourself. . . . The utter loneliness of the mountains, especially of the almost impenetrable canyons with their walls towering straight up, a crystal stream gushing at the bottom, and no light getting in at all, a mountain eagle or hawk looking like a speck above," all made images and impressions Sienkiewicz would never forget (MC/AC: *WT,* 49–50). He became a man in those mountains.

But it was the Pacific Ocean and Anaheim Landing that did more, that gave him a destiny. Here each day the thirty-year-old traveler would sit at the edge of the sea or would row out to a sandbar, where he would lie down, watch the thousands of seabirds, and dream. Out farther, he could see stingrays and the fins of prowling sharks. But it was the cranes that transformed him. One of the most beloved Polish folktales has to do with a youth imprisoned in an impregnable fortress far from home. Despairing of ever escaping and seeing his beloved homeland again, he prays and begs God to help him return to his country before he dies. Not long afterward, he looks up into the sky and notices a flock of cranes flying over his prison. A feather falls down to him from one of the birds, then another, and another; the next day, the cranes fly over again, and other feathers fall to him. Day after day, feathers fall until he has enough feathers to fashion wings for himself, as did Icarus long before. Eventually, he makes his winged escape and returns joyfully home.

All this ran through Sienkiewicz's mind as he watched the cranes far overhead. He wondered if there might be any significance to their appearance in the soft blue coastal sky. Was it time for him to return?

Modjeska, Charles, her son Rudolph, and servants, meanwhile, had taken the long way around—across the Isthmus of Panama—and finally disembarked in bustling San Francisco. Here they found many Poles who had fled Europe in hopes of finding a better life in America. (During the nineteenth century, four million Poles emigrated to the United States.) After three weeks or so, the party headed south to Anaheim. Here they rented a house and purchased an orange grove and vineyard, then settled down to watch the money roll in. Never was a group of immigrants more poorly prepared for a life of farming!

One day Modjeska's friend from San Francisco, Captain Piotrowski, a Polish veteran of the 1830–31 uprising, came to visit. Modjeska and her maid prepared a meal. A turkey was to be killed, but none of the male settlers wished to kill it. Eventually three of them managed to decapitate the poor bird (MC/AC: *WT,* 50–62). Sienkiewicz was assigned the task of carrying out the manure; Paprocki milked the cows and took care of the chickens. Anusia, the pretty maid they brought over, tricked the dignified but amorous Piotrowski into falling into an irrigation ditch! Later on, Sienkiewicz would visit Piotrowski and another Polish veteran, Captain Franciszek Wojciechowski—as tall and thin as Piotrowski was tall and fat. It was as the diminutive Sienkiewicz strode along the beach between the two tall veterans that he first dreamed up his inseparable trio (akin to Dumas's *The Three Musketeers*) who would be immortalized in his monumental *Trilogy.*

Time passed in the little colony, but the money bullheadedly refused to flow in, much preferring to gush out. Finally, Modjeska took stock of the situation and realized that if their grand experiment was to survive much longer, it would be up to her to do something about it. So she bade her adieus and headed north to San Francisco, there to begin a crash course in English so that she could audition for the stage. Her son Rudolph (now Americanized to Ralph) went with her. Charles remained in Anaheim to help keep the colony going. Sienkiewicz soon followed Modjeska north. He was going through a difficult time, not only in the sense of being an exile, but also being plagued with feelings of self-doubt. In an almost despairing letter to Edward Leo, he took stock of his talents and failure to achieve much: "Sometimes I think, too, that there is in me some thread of poetic talent, and yet I was born to be a pamphleteer, and I'm afraid a pamphlet is all I'll ever produce. I really do not know myself. Besides this, I am not fecund. I don't know how to hurry . . . and very often I have the feeling I'm only, as a writer, an artificial zero."

Modjeska finally got an audition about six months later, and though her English still had a *long* way to go, she was given her chance. Only around two hundred people showed up at her subsequent theater debut. But incredibly, as word about the occasion spread across the city, more and more came to the theater. Before the curtain fell that opening night, more than a thousand had arrived! Sienkiewicz euphorically recorded her success for the newspapers back in Poland.

Sienkiewicz would remain her devoted friend and admirer all her life, and their paths continued to cross from time to time. He would remain two years in America, gathering stories, insights into life, and models for characters that would dramatically change his life and career. Finally, he concluded that it was time to return to his divided Poland. Only this time, he'd take Modjeska's advice and return via Panama—there was a remarkable story tied up in a lighthouse along the shores of Panama that he had to track down.

"The Light-House Keeper of Aspinwall" would become one of his most famous stories. The old lighthouse keeper in the story, who had wandered the world for forty long years, is sent some books written in Polish. One of them featured verses by Poland's greatest poet, Adam Mickiewicz (1798-1855), himself forced to walk about the world as an exile. The opening lines of Mickiewicz's most famous poem, *Pan Tadeusz*, are these:

> Lithuania, my country, thou art like health.
> How much to prize thee can only be told
> By him who hath lost thee. All thy beauty to-day
> I see, and I sigh, for I pine after thee.

Then came the lines

> So thou shalt grant us to return by a miracle
> To our land.

The rising wave burst the barrier of will. The old
man uttered a loud cry, and flung himself on the
ground; his milk-white hair mingled with the sand of
the seashore. Forty years had passed by since he had
seen his country, and God knows how many since he
had heard his native language, yet here at this actual
moment that language had come to him of its own
accord; it had crossed the ocean, and found the lonely
recluse in the other hemisphere; that language so
beloved, so dear, so beautiful! In the sobbing which
shook him there was no grief, but only a suddenly
awakened, infinite love, besides which all else was as
naught. (GAR:*LWS*, 246–47)

These lines were instrumental, later in Sienkiewicz's career, in bringing
to him in 1905 the ultimate accolade humans can bestow on a writer: the
Nobel Prize in literature.

Intermezzo

Sienkiewicz boarded a steamer for Panama. Once across the isthmus,
he boarded another ship for New York and then another for France. Paris
and its sidewalk cafés represented a thinking limbo for him, a time in
which to put things together, write stories, conceptualize, and plan for the
future. As an international correspondent for *Gazeta Polska*, he could live
and write anywhere he wished. From Paris, he wandered across western
Europe, drinking deeply from many fountains and spending most of 1879
in Italy.

Along the way, he penned *American Letters* and some of his most significant early short stories, prophetic of longer works to come. "Charcoal
Sketches" is a hard-hitting story about a village secretary who uses his education and communication skills to gain ascendancy over the illiterate
community leaders. He also uses his position as an opportunity to seduce
a beautiful young peasant wife. To break through her resistance, he threatens to ruin her husband, then carries out his threat. The story is a major
work of realism, a tragedy. "Memoirs of a Poznan Tutor" ostensibly is an
attack on the Germanization of the Polish people, specifically addressing
the terrible pressures placed on Polish children by inflexible German

instructors. In reality, the story is about Russia's domination in its area of Poland, but to get the story past the censors, Sienkiewicz had to attack the German system. "Yanko the Musician" is about a music-loving child who yearns to create music, to master the violin. But his mother is too poor to help make the dream come true. The end is tragic and leaves the reader with more questions than answers.

"Bartek the Conqueror" is the story of a Polish peasant, a giant of a man, who is forced to fight France for Prussia during the Franco-Prussian War. Like Yanko, Bartek is incapable of comprehending complexity. Bartek becomes a war hero and returns to his village, confident that the Germans will treat him as a hero back in Poland. The story deals with the disillusion and heartbreak that follow, "the Conqueror" turning out to be an ironic play on words.

Sienkiewicz also wrote, during this period, some of his finest stories set in America. "Orso" is about a giant of a man and a tiny girl—a combination he was to use often in his writing—both circus performers. The circus owner frequently beats Orso just to exhibit his authority. The story relates what happens when the owner turns on the little girl with his whip. Some years later, Sienkiewicz would build on this theme in *Quo Vadis* (Ursus and Lygia), and still later, with his boy and girl protagonists in *In Desert and Wilderness*.

"After Bread" presents the dark side of Polish immigrant life in America. It's the story of what happens to those who have no one to fight for them, no one to network with them, no one to help them get jobs, no one to help them make friends, no one to help them learn English. It, too, is a tragedy—a riveting one. "Sachem" has to do with a descendant of an Indian tribe that Texas settlers massacred to gain control of their lands. Sachem might well have planned revenge when he heard his circus troupe was going to be performing in that ill-fated town. Sienkiewicz, as a Pole, strongly empathized with the Indians in American history, clearly finding common cause with them in their long, sad saga of mistreatment and dehumanization.

In 1881, now thirty-five years old, Sienkiewicz clearly felt it was time for him to sink some roots into his native soil. He married Maria Szetkiewicz and one year later began editing *Slowo*, a Warsaw daily newspaper. He was beginning to gain recognition for his writing. His son, Henryk, was born in 1882, and his daughter, Jadwiga, late in 1883 (MG:*HS,* 17–18).

Meanwhile, he had begun to tackle his perceived destiny. To accomplish it, he immersed himself ever deeper into Poland's past, into all the tortuous journeys of his people. Much of this history he already knew from his childhood reading, but now he wanted to study original sources and dig so deeply that no one would be able to challenge his conclusions. Out of nine hundred years of Polish history, he chose certain eras, certain men and women, as jumping-off points for prodigious research that would form the foundation of his masterpiece, *Trilogy*.

The Great *Trilogy*

Westerners may know Sienkiewicz as the author of *Quo Vadis;* Poles know him first and foremost as the author of the *Trilogy*. Only in recent years have non-Poles begun to realize that unquestionably *Trilogy* is one of the greatest works of historical fiction ever written, comparable to, and perhaps even surpassing, Tolstoy's monumental *War and Peace*.

It was no easy task he set for himself, for many other writers of his time had taken the historical novel genre and raised it to new heights. Kraszenski alone (the Polish Sir Walter Scott, author of an astounding eight hundred volumes) was generally perceived as having achieved all that was achievable in that type of writing. Complicating his task immeasurably was the ever-present reality: "Writing under the oppressive Russian regime, he was not free in the choice of his historical themes; he was fatally obliged to avoid using the Russian-Polish problem, which certainly has been of crucial importance through the entire course of Polish history" (WL:*HS*, 37). Of course Sienkiewicz would have had a similar problem in each of the other two zones.

On May 2, 1883, the phenomenon of the *Trilogy* began in the pages of a Warsaw newspaper: the first installment of a new novel, *With Fire and Sword,* by an author who had yet to really win his spurs. Each installment attracted more readers so that before long it became the rage of the day. Then came the second book, *The Deluge,* and finally *Pan Michael* (or *The Little Knight*). By this time the Polish people had elevated both the *Trilogy* and its author to superstardom. For a century now, the *Trilogy* has retained its bestsellerdom in Poland, with every new edition selling out the day it has appeared in bookstores. And so Sienkiewicz came into his own.

For book 1, *With Fire and Sword,* Sienkiewicz chose the terrible Cossack rebellion stirred up by the disgruntled Hmnelnitski, hetman of the

Zaporijian Cossacks. Almost immediately this firebrand rides into the story, and into our very presence. We are *there.*

Towering over the novel is Prince Yeremi Vishnyevetski (an actual historical figure), who alone in all Poland had the military sagacity to hold his own against the wily Hmnelnitski and his Cossack and Tartar forces. The love story is provided by another actual historical figure, Pan Yan Skshetuski, a young Polish officer on Prince Yeremi's staff, who falls in love with Princess Helena Kurtsevich (clearly modeled after Helena Modjeska). Bogun, a wild Cossack chieftain, is also in love with Helena and sets in motion plans to thwart Pan Yan's romance, stopping not even at murder to attain his ends. One of Pan Yan's inseparable friends is a lovable rascal named Zagloba, who is a cross between Homer's wily Ulysses and Shakespeare's bombastic Falstaff. Zagloba is a mixture of psychologist, salesman, confidant, general, organizer, true friend, and strategist, with qualities that include vainglory, braggadocio, hyperbole, humor, love of the bottle, loyalty, and an infinite capacity for turning defeat into victory—even when running from his enemies. The giant Pan Login, who vows not to marry until he has cut off three heads with one slash of his two-edged sword, is the third of Sienkiewicz's three musketeers; and Pan Michael, the little knight, is the fourth.

As with each book in the *Trilogy,* a siege is at the heart of it. In *With Fire and Sword,* it is the great siege of Zbaraz, where Prince Yeremi gained his undying fame. The suspense is unrelenting. And the slaughter and gore strain the imagination—yet it all happened as Sienkiewicz tells it. Pan Yan yearns to spend his time searching out the whereabouts of the abducted Helena, but his sense of patriotic duty takes precedence, and he remains faithful to his country. By the end of the book, the reader is left drained.

Incorporated into book 2, *The Deluge,* are two parallel stories: first, villain Andrei Kmita's doomed love for the beautiful Olenka and the tortuous path his misdeeds take him on, and second, the patriotic struggle to regain the commonwealth from the invading Charles X of Sweden.

The heart of the book is the great siege of the monastery of Czestochowa during the winter of 1655. Once again Pan Michael appears, along with Zagloba and Pan Yan. But Kmita runs away with the book—it is the story of his redemption. And Olenka is one of Sienkiewicz's great heroines: more resourceful and self-reliant by far than Helena (again, more than a little of Modjeska in her). There are real-life historical characters such as the traitorous Prince Radizvill of Lithuania and his equally unprincipled relative, Prince Boguslav; of course the opportunistic Swedish invader; and the great Polish general Charnyetski.

Thrilling indeed is Prior Kordetski's legendary defense of the besieged monastery and Kmita's heroic part in that defense. But that siege merely served as the wake-up call to the nation. The Swedes had yet to be driven out, and the exiled Casimir had to somehow safely reenter the occupied kingdom and gather his people around him. The three inseparables are in the midst of it all, with Zagloba managing to extricate himself from blind alleys, always discovering somehow a way out. The ending is a moving one!

And, finally, the third book in the trilogy: *Pan Michael.* In the beginning, Pan Michael has retired from the world in a monastery, and his friends are near despair, trying to figure out how to get him to change his mind. True, his young wife is dead—but he hardly knew her! Zagloba, convinced that he can get Michael to change his mind, enters the monastery with a letter from a high prelate and quickly discovers that Michael has not yet taken vows. The dialogue that follows—a mixture of a little truth and much fiction—is pure Zagloba:

> "Ai, Michael! You and I have gone through the world of evil and of good. Have you found consolation behind these bars?"
>
> "I have," replied Pan Michael. "In those words which I hear in this place daily, and repeat, and which I desire to repeat till my death, *memento mori.* In death is consolation for me."
>
> "H'm! Death is more easily found on the battlefield than in the cloister, where life passes as if someone were unwinding thread from a ball, slowly."
>
> "There is no life here, for there are no earthly questions; and before the soul leaves the body, it lives, as it were, in another world."
>
> "If that is true, I will not tell you that the Belgrod horde are mustering in great force against the Commonwealth; for what interest can that have for you?"
>
> Pan Michael's mustaches suddenly quivered, and he stretched his right hand unwittingly to his left side; but not finding a sword there, he put both hands

under his habit, dropped his head, and repeated, "*Memento mori!*"

"Justly, justly!" answered Zagloba, blinking his sound eye with a certain impatience. "No longer ago than yesterday Pan Sobieski, the hetman, said: 'Only let Volodyovski serve even through this one storm, and then let him go to whatever cloister he likes. God would not be angry for the deed; on the contrary, such a monk would have all the greater merit.' But there is no reason to wonder that you put your own peace above the happiness of the country, for *prima charitas abego* [the first love is of self]."

A long interval of silence followed; only Pan Michael's mustaches stood out somewhat and began to move quickly, though lightly. (*Pan Michael,* 31)

And so Zagloba wore Michael down—that was one of Zagloba's gifts. Michael left with him, which was appropriate since this is *his* book.

Zagloba then plays matchmaker, with disastrous results: Michael proposes to the wrong girl, Krystia, beautiful, ornamental, and rather passive. Zagloba has in mind that roguish golden-haired Basia. Finally, Basia as good as proposes herself and gets her man. Sobieski sends Michael out to a remote outpost in the steppes—and Basia declares that he won't go without her! Basia is a thoroughly modern woman, even by today's standards, and has been taken to heart by generations of adoring readers. Almost the entire book is permeated by the magic of the wild steppes and the great love Basia and Michael have for each other.

It is a somber book in many ways and reveals the sad truth that many Polish women during these turbulent centuries were carried away by the Turks, placed in harems, and never seen again; the men were either killed outright or chained in galleys until they died. Yet the book is also joyful; no book with both Zagloba and Basia in it could be gloomy for long. The villain, Azya, has designs on Basia and finds a way of carrying her off, thus producing much of the book's excitement.

Then comes the war with the Tartar and Turkish hordes—and the inevitable siege—this time of the border fort of Kamieniec (also true, historically). Sobieski orders Michael to hold the fort at *all costs*—and the end reveals just what those two words meant. The little knight was one of

Sienkiewicz's favorite characters—perhaps because the author himself was mighty, yet short (only five foot two).

As the *Trilogy* was appearing, no conversation in all occupied Poland failed to begin and end with it. People spoke and thought of the heroes of the novel as of living persons; children in their letters, after giving details about the health of themselves and their brothers and sisters, told what Skrzetuski had done or what Zagloba had said.

Sienkiewicz labored long on these novels, researching, writing, and editing the almost-two-million-word epic (2,566 pages), day after day, week after week, month after month, and year after year; the copy was snatched away for serialization almost as fast as he could write it. Incredibly, he managed to keep the entire *Trilogy* in his head without getting mixed up or losing his concept of the whole. He succeeded beyond his wildest dreams in his determination to reach disenfranchised Poles everywhere, give them pride again in their rich history, and—most important of all—give them *hope!* He encouraged them to believe in a golden future, which appeared to be the unlikeliest of daydreams when the three colossal powers seemed so invincible that few believed their sovereignty would ever end.

In Polish homes for more than a century now, the *Trilogy* has been considered so sacred that Poles value it next to the Bible. Not only did it speak during all those terrible years of partition, but it also spoke during the horrors of the Nazi oppression when Poland suffered more than any other victim of Hitler's wrath, for half of the world's Jews once lived in Poland. But it speaks to more than Poles. In its pages Sienkiewicz reminds us that no civilization can long survive if its people lose sight of, and respect for, moral and spiritual values.

The *Trilogy* was one of the main stated reasons for awarding the Nobel Prize to Sienkiewicz. It's considered to be one of the greatest historical novels ever written, on a par with the works of Scott and Dumas (LB:*HB*, 2:3–4).

Out of the Past, Into the Present

Sienkiewicz's wife was plagued by poor health; consequently, even while researching and writing the *Trilogy* (most of it was published simultaneously in Warsaw, Krakow, and Poznan), the little family traveled a great deal, in hopes that Maria would improve faster in a different climate. It was not to be: Maria died October 19, 1885, leaving her husband with Henryk (age three) and Jadwiga (age two) to raise alone.

After Maria's death, Sienkiewicz restlessly moved here and there, residing for a time in Romania, then Bulgaria, then Turkey, and then Greece, writing continually on *Pan Michael* wherever he was. By now he did not need the income as editor of *Slowo*, so he resigned that position in 1887. For six long years the *Trilogy* had consumed him—what was he to do now? Perhaps the answer would come to him in Spain.

While in Spain, he concluded that since he was exhausted from his long visit to Poland's past, why not write a novel set in contemporary times? As a result, in 1889, he began *Without Dogma* (original title: *In Shackles*). He could hardly have found a more different subject from the *Trilogy*. For starters, the men and women he peopled the *Trilogy* with were almost all creatures of action, Zagloba being the key exception, for he *thought* much. In *Dogma,* there is a new kind of protagonist—he cannot be called a hero—Leon Ploszowski, a wealthy Polish dilettante who is the son of another (apparently neither father nor son is capable of decision-making anymore). As for the son, not only is he reluctant to act, but he also does not really have a core belief system on which he can base decisions. In his many peregrinations, Sienkiewicz had seen thousands of Ploszowskis fluttering around from hotel to hotel, resort to resort, languidly seeking thrills but accomplishing virtually *nothing.*

To study fresh cross sections, Sienkiewicz began the novel in Heligoland, then continued it during his sojourns in Ostend, Zakopane, and Vienna. The story is told in the form of a diary.

Leon, because he has no beliefs and his values are fluid and not based on God (or dogma), can be as amoral as he wishes; for him, aestheticism—love of the beautiful—substitutes for religion. Aniela is the person he ought to marry, and she loves him; however, he is unable to bring the moment to a decision. Only when she sadly marries someone else does he pursue her, and then he pursues her with the intent to break her, with a fierce energy he failed to show in productive endeavors. All she has to fall back on is her faith (or dogma). The book portrays this almost mythic struggle between the forces of amoralism and forces based upon dogma (or belief).

The book is just as relevant today as it was when Sienkiewicz wrote it—perhaps more so, for in today's society, dogma is discredited; in its place is permissiveness (one may do *anything,* no matter how cruel, evil, or destructive, in the name of "freedom"). Our media are full of it: evil without penalties, results, or responsibilities. And children who are free to flit through life without effort or work are merely Ploszowskis who are likely to end up very unhappy, disillusioned, and cynical. According to *The Boston Times, Without Dogma* is "worthy of study by all who seek to understand the human soul" (LB:*HS*, 5).

Sienkiewicz completed *Without Dogma* in 1890, then departed for a prolonged stay in Africa. While there, he traveled extensively through countries such as Egypt and Zanzibar and eventually came down with malaria. He returned to Europe in 1891. In 1892, he wrote "Let Us Follow Him," which would eventually grow into *Quo Vadis;* even so, the story is powerful and can stand alone. Also during this year he began *Children of the Soil* (or *The Polaniecki Family* or *The Irony of Life*).

While it is a powerful novel, it is difficult to get into. Perhaps one reason is that the marriage of Stanislav and Marynia takes place one-third of the way into the book. Since love stories usually end with marriage, it is disconcerting to come to a marriage with two-thirds of the book yet to go. But Sienkiewicz knew what he was doing: He was writing a different kind of love story. Stanislav is a successful businessman who prides himself on his moral excellence. He is not particularly religious and takes his perceived goodness to be proof that one doesn't need religion—or dogma, if you will—to be morally upright. After marriage, he begins to take his bride for granted. As the story proceeds, the reader begins to dislike him, for he is opinionated, self-righteous, and unwilling to admit his mistakes or learn from them. Marynia, meanwhile, captures our hearts. Right when Stanislav feels the world is his, a friend's wife causes his self-standing tower of moral rectitude to crack at the seams and crumble into dust. Where does he go from there? That is what he must decide.

Obviously, Sienkiewicz is making his point from a different slant: No one—without the aid of a Higher Power—is capable of remaining moral. Hormones are not ruled by abstract theories that guarantee rectitude on the basis of reason alone. But Sienkiewicz goes beyond moral frailties: When we fall, is it all over? If we profit from our mistakes, humble ourselves, and welcome God into our hearts, can our lives be turned around? These are tough questions he deals with in this book—and there are no easy answers.

Another theme is the land itself. What role does land or home ownership play in our lives? Can we really be happy without physically owning land (as opposed to merely renting it)? What kind of impact does separation from land and home owned for generations by the same family have on a person? Does the land have anything to do with our relationship to God and to our values? These questions, too, Sienkiewicz wrestles with in this provocative book.

Quo Vadis and The Knights of the Cross

During the writing of *Children of the Soil,* Sienkiewicz married Maria Romanowska, but they separated shortly after, and the marriage was later annulled. *Children of the Soil* was completed in 1894. A few years earlier, when he wrote "The Verdict of Zeus" (1890) and "Let Us Follow Him" (1892), Sienkiewicz's thoughts and interests were reaching far, far back— back to the ancient world. He immersed himself in the classics of Greece and Rome. His frequent journeys to Italy and a trip to Greece helped him to gain a sound knowledge of the region. But it was in Nice on the French Riviera, in 1895, that he finally put it all together and began *Quo Vadis.* During the same year, he began an equally daunting writing project: *The Knights of the Cross,* a task that would take him four years to complete.

Ever since the discovery of the buried ruins of Pompeii and Herculaneum (buried under the ashes spewed out by Vesuvius in A.D. 79), in the late sixteenth century, there had been worldwide renewed interest in the world of Greece and Rome. Serious excavation at Herculaneum first took place in 1709, and at Pompeii in 1748. Taking advantage of this renewed interest in those two civilizations, and interest especially in the early years of Christianity, a number of authors penned novels set during the first century or so after Christ. Chief among these works were Edward Bulwer-Lytton's *The Last Days of Pompeii* (1834), Zygmunt Krasinski's *Iridion* (1838), Nicholas Wiseman's *Fabiola* (1854), and John Henry Newman's *Callista.* The age of Nero was especially attractive to historical romance writers and dramatists.

Prodigious research went into *Quo Vadis.* Sienkiewicz conducted his research not only in ancient books and manuscripts, but also on the actual sites being depicted in the book. The cast of characters was superbly chosen: the mercurial Nero, the engaging Petronius, the opportunistic Chilo, the Herculean Ursus, the decadent Vinitius, the unforgettable Lygia, the Apostles Paul and Peter, the amoral Poppaea, the sycophantic Tigellinus, all help the story sizzle—*especially* Petronius. Perhaps that is why Sienkiewicz opens the book with him (MG:*HS,* 127–46).

The book pits the dying pagan world against that of the Christian, Rome being defeated both by its own degeneration and by the vitality of the gospel. Lednicki postulates that the evolving Vinitius is in a way a reverse of Oscar Wilde's protagonist in *The Portrait of Dorian Grey*, who grows ever more degenerate as Sienkiewicz's grows ever more regenerate— transformed into a new creature (WL:*HS*, 55–56).

The book proved to be one of those rarities, an instant success that has remained popular and in print for more than a hundred years—with no sign of ever going away. It certainly didn't harm the author's candidacy for the Nobel Prize.

Even while he was researching and writing *Quo Vadis*, Sienkiewicz was also gathering information for another project, *The Knights of the Cross*. This book would tell the story of Christianity gone wrong, as demonstrated by the Teutonic Knights, who permitted the lust for power to twist their earlier evangelistic missionary fervor into an evil thing. The fuse for this project was lit in 1891, serious preparation commenced in 1895, and the actual writing began in 1896. Unlike the rich treasure trove of Roman and Greek scholarship he had accessed in researching the world of *Quo Vadis*, Sienkiewicz found the pickings lean when it came to fourteenth- and fifteenth-century Poland. But he didn't let that discourage him. Not only did he study modern historians, but he also burrowed into old chronicles, documents, and letters. Real historical figures incorporated into the fabric of *The Knights of the Cross* include Prince Witold, King Jagiello, and Queen Jadwiga. The Battle of Grünwald is the pivotal event in the book, just as it was in actual Polish history. If there be a person in any way shortchanged in the novel, it would probably be Prince Witold, as great a strategist and warrior as early Poland ever knew.

The novel depicts with great power, faithfulness, and brilliance, a broad cross section of Polish life: the royal court, the nobles, the lesser gentry, the hired knights (or soldiers of fortune), the common soldiers, the burghers, the peddlers and merchants, the monks, the peasant farmers, and those outside the law. It is nigh unto incredible how Sienkiewicz manages to bring the time and people out of obscurity and into vibrant Technicolor (MG:*HS*, 147–56).

Historians confirm the essential truth of Sienkiewicz's thesis: that lies, deceit, hypocrisy, treachery, perjury, and blackmail were standard methods employed by the order against those they sought to overcome. Rome itself was unable to control them; even their grand masters felt themselves powerless to reform them. Sienkiewicz could not but be somewhat affected by bias where the order was concerned, for thanks to several Polish kings' failure to totally destroy the order, it later regrouped in Prussia, became a recognized ducal vassal, subsequently declared its independence from all control, and then gradually became the base upon which the Prusso-German empire was built. Like it or not, the order was amazingly resilient and persistent, having more lives than a barnful of cats.

At 757 pages, *The Knights of the Cross* is a monumental tour de force, second only to the *Trilogy* in scope and research effort. Had Sienkiewicz not written the *Trilogy*, chances are that the fame of this later work would be much greater. It represents Sienkiewicz's literary high tide: Never did he write as great a novel again. The fictional characters that make the book live include Zbysko, the fledgling knight; his memorable and resourceful Zaglobian uncle, Matso; Danusia, the beautiful child heiress; Yagenka, the Basia of the book; Danveld, one of Sienkiewicz's most thoroughly evil villains; the King Lear-like Prince Yurand; and the loyal Bohemian Hlava.

The Nobel Prize for Literature

By 1898, so famous around the world had Sienkiewicz become that there was organized a Twenty-fifth Anniversary Jubilee for him. Because of other pressing involvements on his part, that Jubilee was postponed two years. In 1900, both the partitioned Polish people and the world celebrated the life and works of Poland's most famous author with great fanfare. The Polish people even gave him the Oblegorek estate, complete with mansion, which had belonged to ancestors of his.

Although he signed the contract for *On the Fields of Glory* in 1901, he did not complete it until 1905. Meanwhile, he had married Maria Babska in 1904. He never really did justice to the subject of this new book: King John Sobieski and his great victory over the Turks at Vienna (1682–83). One reason Sienkiewicz failed to complete his book (originally he had planned to include the great Sobieski victory over the Turks at Vienna) was his preoccupation with the Russo-Japanese War—as were all Poles, but *especially* those in Russian Poland. It was a bloody war and a fateful one. The Japanese shattered Russia's myth of invincibility and thoroughly humiliated it before the world. This had far-reaching results, for it sowed the seeds of the Russian Revolution against the

1 Quo Vadis

Romanovs—and with it, later on, the emancipation of Russian Poland. From 1901 on, word trickled around in discussions about who might be awarded the next Nobel Prize in literature—and speculation had it that Sienkiewicz was at least one of the nominees. For 1905, fifteen names had been proposed, including Leo Tolstoy, Giosuè Carducci, Selma Lagerlöff, Algernon Charles Swinburne, and Rudyard Kipling. Sienkiewicz was the eventual choice for 1905, but the prize was not awarded purely on his works. Civil rights abuses had reached the point where the Nobel committee welcomed the opportunity to send Russia a message of worldwide displeasure with the way it treated men and women in areas it controlled. There were clear parallels between Nero's Rome and Nicholas II's Russia. Gunnar Ahlstrom noted that

> it was hardly a propitious moment at which to honor the champion of a nation suffering under the oppressive autocracy of the Czar. The Russian part of Poland was in the throes of trouble and strikes, and a state of siege had been declared there. The postal service had ceased to function and normal communication with Warsaw had been interrupted. The Swedish Academy was obliged to send a special emissary, Alfred Jensen, to Kracow via Vienna with instructions to contact the laureate through Austrian Poland to deliver the happy news. Jensen managed to get a telegram sent across the Russian frontier, asking Sienkiewicz to come to Kracow on important business. A few days later, when railway communications had been restored, Sienkiewicz appeared.

On November 29, Sienkiewicz wrote the Swedish Academy, apologizing for the delay in responding to the good news. He had been summoned to Warsaw and did not wish to respond from there, knowing that whatever he wrote would be opened by Russian censors. But now that he was outside the Russian zone, in Krakow, he could safely respond (GA:*NPF,* 262–63).

Sienkiewicz managed to be there in Oslo for the presentation, and his acceptance speech was typically modest—always, it seems, he deflected personal praise and credited the Polish people. In this case, he noted that "Nations are represented by their poets and their writers in the open competition for the Nobel Prize. Consequently the award of the Prize by the Academy glorifies not only the author but the people whose son he is. . . . If this honor is precious to all, it is infinitely more so to Poland. It has been said that Poland is dead, exhausted, enslaved, but here is the proof of her life and triumph. . . . This homage has been rendered not to me—for the Polish soil is fertile and does not lack better writers than me—but to the Polish achievement, the Polish genius" (HS:*NAS*, 182).

C. C. Af Wirsén, permanent secretary of the Swedish Academy, presented the Nobel Prize to Sienkiewicz. Among the reasons he gave for its being awarded to him are these:

> In every nation there are some rare geniuses who concentrate in themselves the spirit of the nation; they represent the national character to the world. Although they cherish the memories of the past of that people, they do so only to strengthen its hope for the future. . . .
>
> Another distinctive trait is Sienkiewicz's habit of never shutting his eyes to the faults of his compatriots; rather he exposes them mercilessly, while he renders justice to the abilities and courage of the enemies of Poland. Like the old prophets of Israel he often tells his people strong truths. . . .
>
> All of these descriptions are distinguished by great historical truthfulness. Because of Sienkiewicz's extensive researches and his sense of history, his characters speak and act in the style of the period. It is significant that among the many people who suggested Henryk Sienkiewicz for the Nobel Prize there were eminent historians. . . .
>
> His own poetic career has indeed unfolded on the path of glory. (CDW:*NPA*, 173–81)

Unquestionably, the awarding of the Nobel Prize to Sienkiewicz lifted for a moment the dark cloud of heartbreak from every Pole, in every place—it gave each of them *hope*.

The Afterglow

Somehow, in the midst of all this turn-of-the-century turmoil, Sienkiewicz found a way to bring *On the Field of Glory* to a close. The novel depicting events occurring in Poland during 1682–83 disappointed many readers. Surprisingly, there is no warfare in the story; rather, the core of the book has to do with the drawn-out love story of an impoverished noble, Yatsek Tachevski, and Anulka Sieninski, last of a once-famous noble house. Father Voynovski, the priest who loves Yatsek as a son, and the four incorrigible Bukoyemski brothers add zest to the story. Had Sienkiewicz's readers been willing to wait until the author, in his own good time, was able to complete his Sobieski research, the book could have been one of his great ones, for what is already in the book has significant power. Had the book been advertised as a love story rather than a Sobieski epic, readers no doubt would have loved it.

In 1906, Sienkiewicz wrote an open protest against a Prussian plan to dispossess Polish landowners and had it published. But most of the next three years was dedicated to the writing of *Whirlpools*, a novel of contemporary Poland wherein he postulated that Poland was imploding. In the book, socialists appear determined to destroy the privileged class even if they have to destroy society to do it. Without strong religious fervor, with a shattered state, with no great war or cause to join or espouse, the wealthy and idle young are portrayed as self-indulgent and rudderless. None of the romances in the book flower into happiness and fulfillment; instead, each ends up twisted, seared, poisoned, and bitter. It is a scathing indictment of hollow modern society, and the statement is made that "knowledge without religion breeds only thieves and bandits." The conclusion Sienkiewicz reaches is this: Without God, society can only self-destruct (*Whirlpools*, 386). The following quotation reflects the overall tone of hollowness and cynicism:

> "Mankind," mused Grouski, "possesses at the same time too much and too little intelligence. For, after all, to simply believe one must unreservedly shut the blinds of his intellectual windows and not permit himself to peer through them; and when he does open them he discovers only a starless night." For this reason he envied those middle-aged persons, whose intelligence reared mental

edifices upon unshaken dogmas, just as lighthouses are
built upon rocks in the sea. (*Whirlpools*, 54–55)

Sienkiewicz especially felt the onslaught of the years when the telegram
reached him that his cherished friend Modjeska was dead. Funeral services
were held in Los Angeles, Modjeska's old friend Bishop Conaty delivering
the sermon. Her body was taken to Krakow to be interred among her
ancestors. Emilia Benda, Modjeska's niece, remembered well that day:

> It was July 17th. The remains of the wanderer who
> had returned home at last [but not to Warsaw!] lay on
> the catafalque in the Church of the Holy Cross. The
> church was crowded to overflowing, with many
> famous people present: Sienkiewicz, Paderewski [a
> dear friend of both Sienkiewicz and Modjeska], the
> artist Witkiewicz, the poet Tetmajer, the playwright
> Ryde. Following the service everyone walked to the
> cemetery.
> Practically all the town did, but we, the family, had
> police and firemen keeping us from being crushed.
> (MC:*FR*, 873)

Modjeska's play was over, and the curtain had come down. Sienkiewicz
wrote, read, and published her eulogy.

In Desert and Wilderness

Sienkiewicz had always been a devoted father. In all his many enter-
prises during his long and productive lifetime, his children were always
his number one priority. Every illness of each child greatly worried him.
Throughout his work are a number of memorable stories involving
children.

Very late in his life, after his own children were grown, Sienkiewicz
conceived the book *In Desert and Wilderness*. A favorite correspondent of
his was thirteen-year-old Wanda Ulanowska, daughter of Krakow
friends. In one of his 1910 letters to her, he told her about his new literary venture:

As in my opinion every novelist should write something for children at least once in his lifetime, I decided
to begin and to finish next New Year's [1911] a novel
bearing the title *Adventures of Two Children in Central
Africa* [later changed]. A Polish boy and an English girl
will appear in it, and besides them Bedouins, Arabs, and
Negro cannibals, plus elephants, crocodiles, lions, hippopotami, etc. I wish to write it in such a way that not
only children but thirteen-year-old teen-agers and even
grown-ups could read it with interest. (MG:*HS*, 158–59)

The book captures the reader from first page to last, with a kidnapping, a near-miraculous escape, and one desperate predicament after
another. Stas is fourteen and little Nell is eight when they are kidnapped
and carried into the heart of war-torn Africa about the time that General
Gordon and his men are being massacred at Khartoum. Also memorable
is the history of Kali, the faithful African prince—clearly modeled after
Robinson Crusoe's Friday; Saba, the lionlike dog; and the giant elephant,
King, who adores tiny Nell above all others. Even reading the book as an
adult, I found the epic mesmerizing. Graphic evidence of Sienkiewicz's
phenomenal memory is the fact that it was written almost twenty years
after his trip to Africa—yet it reads as if written on the spot.

Not coincidentally, the book's writing coincides timewise with the
period during which the worldwide Scout movement was born, for Stas is
almost the quintessential prototype of all that a true Scout stood for.

One would hardly believe that the following introductory paragraphs
were written by the same author as the previous entries:

"Do you know, Nell," said Stas Tarkowski to his
friend, a little English girl, "that yesterday the police
came and arrested the wife of Smain, the overseer, and
her three children—that Fatma who several times
called at the office to see your father and mine."

And little Nell, resembling a beautiful picture,
raised her greenish eyes to Stas and asked with mingled
surprise and fright:

"Did they take her to prison?"

"No, but they will not let her go to the Sudân and

an official has arrived who will see that she does not
move a step out of Port Said."

"Why?"

Stas, who was fourteen years old and who loved his
eight-year-old companion very much, but looked
upon her as a mere child, said with a conceited air:

"When you reach my age, you will know everything which happens, not only along the Canal from
Port Said to the Suez, but in all Egypt. Have you heard
of the Mahdi?"

"I heard that he is ugly and naughty."

The boy smiled compassionately.

"I do not know whether he is ugly. The Sudânese
claim that he is handsome. But the word 'naughty'
about a man who has murdered so many people, could
be used only by a little girl, eight years old, in
dresses—oh—reaching the knees."

"Papa told me so and Papa knows best." (*In Desert
and Wilderness*, 1)

A Patriot Goes Home

In 1911, Sienkiewicz began work on a novel on the Polish legions that
fought for Napoleon, but then World War I broke out and totally threw
him off that track. He was never to finish it. As the winds of war once more
swept across the plains and steppes of Europe, Sienkiewicz left Krakow for
Vienna, then went on to Vevey on the Franco-Swiss border, where he stayed
during the rest of the long and bloody war. He moved there, not to spare
himself, but to lead a worldwide relief program on behalf of the millions of
Poles caught in the firestorm. It was from Vevey that he issued his famous
appeal on behalf of the Polish people: "Gunfire destroys our towns and villages. From the banks of the Niemen to the peaks of the Carpathians, across
the length and breadth of our plains, we see the spectre of famine. [At the
height of this famine it was reported by the press around the world that not
one child eight years old or younger was left alive in all occupied Poland.]
Has not my country Poland a right to your help?" (GAR:*HS*, 261).

Sienkiewicz was not to see the war's conclusion, for he died on November 15, 1916. He was not to know that after the war was over, Poland would

rise again, thanks in no small part to the selfless efforts and example of artists like him, Modjeska, and Paderewski. The Polish people, scattered as they had been around the world, remembering when Sienkiewicz's voice was almost the only one to remind them that so long as they kept Poland alive in their hearts, Poland could never die, held his life and memory as almost sacred.

It is fitting that we close with words penned by Monica M. Gardner, author of *The Patriot Novelist of Poland:*

> Although he died in a foreign land, his funeral at Vevey was the scene of a nation's mourning. His exiled compatriots crowded around his coffin: a guard of honour of young Poles stood at the bier, and for hours after his remains had been committed to the grave the spectacle might be seen of his fellow Poles returning again and again to the church, for the simple reason that they were unable to tear themselves away from the spot where he had spoken to their hearts, who had been to them a loved and living force in life as he remained after death. . . .
>
> Eight years later, in October 1924, the body of Sienkiewicz was carried back to his native land and laid in the cathedral of Warsaw. That journey resembled a triumphal progress. The countries through which the coffin passed received it as an honoured guest. At the moment it crossed the Polish frontier every bell in Poland rang, cannon fired, and there was a minute of general silence in every Polish street. Solemn commemorative ceremonies were observed throughout the length and breadth of Poland: the writers and poets of Poland united in paying in the Polish press a magnificent tribute to the great patriot-novelist; and perhaps the most touching act of devotion in his memory was a scene in central fields on the railway-line in a Polish country district where crowds of Polish peasants, gathered from miles distant, waited merely to fling flowers at the train that carried Sienkiewicz's coffin as it passed by. (MG:*PNP,* 275–76)

Henryk Sienkiewicz had come home.

The Works of Henryk Sienkiewicz

Sienkiewicz's works number more than sixty, so obviously the following listing is incomplete. Since he wrote in Polish, many of his works have not been translated into English, although all the seminal works have. Most of his prolific writing for newspapers and magazines has not been translated either.

Regarding the titles themselves, translators have seemingly gone out of their way to confuse the reading public by publishing stories under titles different from those under which they first appeared. In such cases, one has to go back to the original Polish title to get them straight. Other translations exist of many of the following.

Dates First Published in the United States

Novels

1889   *In Vain* (Boston: Little, Brown & Company; translated by Jeremiah Curtin; first serialized in Poland in 1872)

1890   *With Fire and Sword*, book 1 of *Trilogy* (Boston: Little, Brown & Company; translated by Jeremiah Curtin)

1893   *The Deluge*, Vols. I, II, book 2 of *Trilogy* (Boston: Little, Brown & Company; translated by Jeremiah Curtin)

   Pan Michael [also known as *Pan Wolodyjowski* and *The Little Knight*, book 3 of *Trilogy*] (Boston: Little, Brown & Company; translated by Jeremiah Curtin)

   Without Dogma (Boston: Little, Brown & Company; translated by Iza Young)

1896   *Quo Vadis: A Narrative of the Times of Nero* (Boston: Little, Brown & Company; translated by Jeremiah Curtin)

1897   *Children of the Soil* [also known as *Rodzina Polanieckich* and *The Irony of Life*] (Boston: Little, Brown & Company; translated by Jeremiah Curtin)

1900   *The Knights of the Cross,* Vols. I, II [also known as *The Teutonic Knights*] (Boston: Little, Brown & Company; translated by Jeremiah Curtin)

1906   *On the Field of Glory* (Boston: Little, Brown & Company; translated by Jeremiah Curtin)

1910   *Whirlpools* (Boston: Little, Brown & Company; translated by Max A. Drezmal)

1912   *In Desert and Wilderness* (Boston: Little, Brown & Company; translated by Max A. Drezmal)

Tales and Short Stories
Following are collections I have been able to secure personally; there are others.

1893   *Yanko the Musician and Other Stories* (Boston: Little, Brown & Company; translated by Jeremiah Curtin)

1894   *Lillian Morris and Other Stories* (Boston: Little, Brown & Company; translated by Jeremiah Curtin)

1896   *For Daily Bread and Other Stories* (Philadelphia: Henry Altemus Company)

        Let Us Follow Him and Other Stories (Philadelphia: Henry Altemus Company)

1897   *Hania* (Boston: Little, Brown & Company; translated by Jeremiah Curtin)

        After Bread: A Short Story of Polish Emigrant Life in America (New York: R. F. Fenno & Company; translated by Vatslaf A. Hlasko and Thomas H. Bullick)

1898   *Sielanka: A Forest Picture and Other Stories* (Boston: Little, Brown & Company; translated by Jeremiah Curtin)

So Runs the World (London and New York: F. Tennyson Neely; translated and edited by S. C. de Soissons)

1899   *Tales from Sienkiewicz* (London and New York: James Pott & Co.; translated by S. C. de Soissons)

1904   *Life and Death and Other Stories and Legends* (Boston: Little, Brown & Company; translated by Jeremiah Curtin)

PART I

Chapter I

It was about noon when Petronius awoke, wearied as usual. The evening before he had been at Nero's feast, which lasted far into the night. For some time now, his health had been failing. He said of himself that he usually felt like a block of wood in the mornings and had barely enough strength to collect his thoughts. However, a bath and a thorough massage administered by skilled slaves gradually quickened the flow of his sluggish blood, refreshed and restored his strength. When he left the last portion of the bath, the *elaeothesium*,[1] he appeared as one risen from the dead. His eyes sparkled with wit and merriment. In fact, he became so rejuvenated, animated, and vivacious that even Otho[2] himself could not compare with him, making it clear that Petronius fully deserved his popular sobriquet, the *arbiter elegantiarum*.[3]

Petronius seldom went to the public baths, and then only to hear some speaker whose reputation had aroused the gossip of the city, or when there were games of particular interest going on in the great hall. In ordinary circumstances he preferred his private baths on his own estate, which Celer, the renowned companion of Severus, had enlarged and rebuilt for him. With so much taste were they equipped, that in spite of the fact that the imperial baths were larger and immeasurably more luxuriously planned, Nero himself admitted that Petronius's were superior to his.

After the nocturnal feast, at which he became wearied by the buffooneries of Vatinius,[4] Petronius engaged with Nero, Lucan,[5] and Seneca[6] in an argument as to whether woman possessed a soul. Rising late, as has

---

1 Oiling room.
2 Marcus Salvius Otho (A.D. 32–69), member of Nero's court, later became emperor for a brief time.
3 Arbiter of elegance.
4 Known for his odious behavior.
5 Marcus Annaeus Lucan (A.D. 39–65), Roman poet, born in Spain.
6 Nero's tutor early in life, then his chief advisor after he came to power; now he had lost Nero's ear.

been said, he, in accordance with his usual custom, made use of the baths. Two powerful slaves placed him on a cypress table covered with snow-white Egyptian linen. Moistening their hands with perfumed oil, they rubbed his shapely body while with closed eyes he waited until the vapors of the room and the warmth of the hands pressing upon his body had driven away all feeling of fatigue.

After a short time he opened his eyes and asked about the day's weather. Later he inquired concerning the precious stones that Idomeneus, the jeweler, had promised to bring him to examine. As the breeze was from the Alban Hills, the weather promised fair; as for the precious stones they had not yet been sent. Petronius closed his eyes again and had just commanded that he be moved to the *tepidarium*[7] when the slave whose duty it was to announce the names of visitors to the baths appeared from behind the curtain to say that young Marcus Vinitius, who had just returned from Asia Minor, wished to see Petronius.

Petronius ordered the slaves to carry him to the *tepidarium* into which he directed that his guest should be admitted. Vinitius was the son of his eldest sister, who had years before become the wife of Marcus Vinitius, a consul in the reign of Tiberius. Under Corbulo's command, the young Vinitius had been fighting the Parthians[8] and had now, after the close of the war, returned to Rome. Petronius was extremely fond of him, because he was handsome and athletic, also because he had sufficient delicacy of feeling not to exceed a certain moderation in his profligacy—a faculty that Petronius valued above all others.   *extremely immoral/extravagen*

"My greetings to Petronius," said the young man, as with an elastic step he entered the warm room. "May all the gods, and especially Aesculapius[9] and Cypris,[10] be indulgent to you, for under their joint protection nothing can go amiss."

"Welcome to Rome, and may your rest be sweet after the war," answered Petronius, extending his hand from the folds of the soft linen that covered him. "What news from Armenia? And while you were in Asia, did you happen to go to Bithynia?"[11]

---

7   A room used for taking lukewarm baths.
8   From Parthia, an ancient country in northeast modern-day Iran.
9   Ancient Roman god of healing and medicine; also Asklepios.
10 Another name for Venus; also Kypris.
11 Ancient kingdom on the Pontus Exinus (Black Sea), later a Roman province, today part of northern Turkey.

For a period Petronius had himself been the proconsul of Bithynia and had administered the province with firmness and justice. Inasmuch as this activity presented a curious contrast in the character of one noted for indolence and luxurious tastes, Petronius was fond of referring to his services to the state, since they showed not only what he was able to do, but what he might have been, had he so wished.

"I did go to Heraclea,"[12] answered Vinitius. "I was sent there by Corbulo for reinforcements."

"Ah, Heraclea! There it was I knew a girl from Colchis[13] for whom I'd give all the divorced women I know—Poppaea[14] included. But that's ancient history! Let's talk of other things: What news of the Parthians? Just between ourselves, they bore me—the Vologeses, the Tiridates, and the Tigranes—all those barbarians who are in the habit of going on all fours at home, as Arulenus says, and who affect to be human beings only with us. Rome talks much of them, if only for the reason that it's dangerous to talk of anything else."

"This war fares badly, and but for Corbulo it might have ended in defeat."

"Corbulo? By Bacchus, a genuine war god, a veritable Mars. A great general, though an irritable, blunt, thick-witted fellow. In spite of it all I like him—if for nothing else than because Nero fears him."

"Corbulo is no fool."

"Perhaps you're right; but what difference does that make? As Pyrrho[15] says, dullness is no worse than wisdom, and sometimes they're not very far apart."

Vinitius continued to talk of the war, but when Petronius again closed his eyes, and the young man noticed his uncle's weary, drawn face, he changed the subject of conversation, and inquired with solicitude concerning his health.

Petronius opened his eyes again.

How was his health? So-so. Though he was not in perfect health, he certainly wasn't as bad off as young Sissena, who had lost sensation to such a degree that each morning, when he was taken to the bath, he would have

---

12 An ancient Roman city near the Gulf of Taranto; also known as Heraklea.
13 Ancient country on the Black Sea, in the western part of the Republic of Georgia.
14 Poppaea Sabina, second wife of Nero; Nero was her third husband.
15 Greek philosopher (365–275 B.C.).

to ask whether he was sitting or standing. No, he didn't feel well. Vinitius suggested that he consult Aesculapius and Cypris—but Petronius didn't believe in Aesculapius. Vinitius quipped that it was not even known whose son Aesculapius was, whether Arsinoe's[16] or Coronis's;[17] and when the maternity was in dispute, what could possibly be proven as to the paternity? In this age, for that matter, how could anyone be absolutely certain who his father was?

Petronius burst out laughing, and added, "Two years ago I sent three dozen fat live cocks and a golden cup to Epidaurus.[18] Can you imagine why? I said to myself, *Whether this helps or not, it certainly can do no harm.* I'm of the opinion that those who still bring offerings to the gods reason just as I do—with the possible exception of the mule drivers that travelers hire at the Porta Capena. In addition to Aesculapius I accidentally had some business with some of his descendants last year when my kidneys were out of order. They prescribed a night's sleep within the walls of a temple. I knew them for rogues, but even then I asked myself, *What harm can come to me from that? Society rests on deceit, and life itself is an illusion. Even the soul is a dream.* Nevertheless, one ought to have a certain degree of intelligence to be able to distinguish the illusions that are pleasant from those that are not. I tell my slaves that my *laconicum*[19] must be heated with cedar wood sprinkled with ambergris, because while I am alive I prefer perfumes to stenches. As for Cypris, to whose good graces you have also consigned me, I know enough about her protection to have acquired shooting pains in my right foot. But for all that, she's a passable goddess. I foresee the time, sooner or later, when you also will be bringing white doves to her altar."

"You've guessed right," answered Vinitius. "I came away scatheless from the arrows of the Parthians, but Love transfixed me, in a most unforeseen way, not a mile outside the city gate."

"By the white knees of the Graces, you'll tell me about it, if you have time," said Petronius.

"I've come here for that very purpose," answered Vinitius.

The manicures who now began to busy themselves with Petronius

---

16 Mythological wife of Alcmaeon, who continued to love him even after he had been unfaithful to her.
17 Mythological princess killed by Apollo for being unfaithful to him.
18 Aesculapius.
19 Sweat room.

interrupted him, and Vinitius, at Petronius's invitation, cast aside his tunic and plunged into the tepid bath.

"Bless me! I didn't even ask you if your love was returned," said Petronius, as he gazed at Vinitius's youthful figure, which was so finely proportioned it seemed as if chiseled from marble. "If Lissipus[20] had only seen you, you would be gracing at this very moment the Palatine Gate as a statue of the young Hercules."

The young man smiled with satisfaction as he plunged about in the bath and splashed the warm water abundantly on the mosaic that represented Hera at the moment when the goddess was imploring Morpheus to lull Zeus to sleep. Petronius watched him with the satisfied eye of an artist.

When Vinitius came out of the bath and, in turn, had given himself into the hands of the manicures, the lector[21] entered, carrying at his chest a bronze tube containing rolls of papyrus.

"Would you like to listen?" asked Petronius.

"If it's something of your own—with pleasure," answered Vinitius. "Otherwise I'd prefer to talk. Poets, nowadays, waylay you at every street corner."

"Quite right. It's impossible to get past any one of the basilicas or baths or libraries or bookshops, without running into a poet gesticulating like a monkey. When Agrippa came back from the East, he mistook them for lunatics. That's the way things are these days. Caesar is writing verses; therefore everyone is imitating him. Only one thing is forbidden: to write better verses than Caesar's, and for that reason I fear somewhat for Lucan. As for me, I write prose for which I don't seek praise; neither do I desire to inflict it on others. The lector is about to read the lines of the ill-fated Fabricius Veiento."

"Why ill-fated?"

"Because he has been commanded to amuse himself in the character of Odysseus[22] and has been forbidden to return to his household gods till he receives a fresh command. In one respect, however, his odyssey will not be as hard as Odysseus's—his wife is not at all like Penelope. It is, I think, unnecessary to tell you that he acted stupidly. But in this city, appearances are the only things that count. Fabricius wrote a wretched, tiresome book;

---

20 Roman sculptor.
21 A slave who reads aloud.
22 Who was sent into exile.

but for all that, everyone is reading it with rapture, now that the author is exiled. From every quarter all one hears is, 'It's a scandal, a scandal.' Possibly Fabricius has exaggerated a trifle, but I assure you—as one who knows our city and its heads of families and its women so well—that his account is paler than the reality. But that fact doesn't prevent his readers from searching for allusions to themselves with terror and to their friends with delight. At Avirnus's bookstore there are a hundred clerks kept copying the book from dictation—it's an assured success."

"Did any of your escapades get into it?"

"Of course. But the author fooled himself because he didn't see that I'm both much worse and less stupid than he's represented me. You see, here, we have long since lost the faculty of distinguishing what is moral from what is immoral. For my part, I'm of the opinion that no distinction need be made, although Seneca, Musonius, and Trasca pretend to see one. But for me it's a matter of indifference. By Hercules, I speak my mind openly. But I've preserved my place in society because I don't confuse what is ugly with what is beautiful. And this is, for instance, something our Ahenobarbus,[23] poet, charioteer, singer, and buffoon, doesn't understand."

"Nevertheless, I'm sorry for Fabricius; he's a splendid companion."

"Vanity ruined him. Everyone suspected him, yet no one was certain. He couldn't restrain himself and, under pledges of secrecy to many people, admitted everything."

"Did you hear the story about Rufinus?"

"No."

"In that case, let's go into the *frigidarium*.[24] We'll cool off there and I'll tell you the tale."

They entered the *frigidarium*, in the middle of which a light rose-colored fountain played and filled the room with the perfume of violets. Seating themselves in a niche covered with a silken fabric, they began to breathe in the coolness. For a few moments neither spoke. Vinitius dreamily gazed at the statue of a bronze faun who, as he inclined over a nymph's arm, tried eagerly to kiss her on the lips.

After an interval he said, "He's right. That certainly is the best that life has to give."

---

23   Nero. His name was originally Lucius Domitius Ahenobarbus. Ahenobarbus, meaning "Bronzebeard," clung to him as an appropriate sobriquet.
24   The coolest room.

"Yes—to a degree. But that's not the only thing you are fond of—you like war, for instance, to which I'm not drawn, for the reason that in the camp one's fingernails break and lose their rosy tint. However, every one of us has his weakness. Ahenobarbus likes singing—especially his own songs; and old Scaurus his Corinthian vase, which stands near his bed at night and which he kisses when he cannot sleep. He has kissed the edges off. Tell me, don't you write verses?"

"No, I've never been able to write so much as a single hexameter."

"And do you play the kithara and sing?"

"No."

"Nor drive a chariot?"

"Once I competed in the hippodrome at Antioch, but unsuccessfully."

"In that case, I'll make my mind easy on your account. Which faction did you belong to in the Circus?"

"To the green."

"Now I am perfectly at ease about your safety, the more so since, although you're not as rich as Pallus or Seneca, you're nevertheless well off. Don't you see that with us at present, while it's good if one can write verses, sing to the kithara, declaim, or compete in the Circus, it's still better—and immeasurably safer—for one *not* to write verses, nor to play, nor to sing, nor to compete in the Circus. The most useful thing of all is to know how to be enthusiastic when Ahenobarbus is enthusiastic. But you're a handsome young fellow; therefore, the only thing that threatens you is that Poppaea may fall in love with you. But she's had too much experience. She learned quite enough of love with her first two husbands; with her third she has other plans. By the way, did you know that Otho—that fool!—still loves her insanely. Far away upon the Spanish cliffs he walks and sighs. He has so lost his former grooming habits that it doesn't take him more than three hours a day to dress his hair. Who could have expected such a thing—*especially* of Otho?"

"I understand that," answered Vinitius, "but in his place I'd do something else."

"What?"

"I'd have formed a devoted legion of mountaineers. The Iberians make excellent soldiers."

"Vinitius, Vinitius, I must tell you the truth: You'd have been incapable of such a thing. And do you know why? Because though such things are possible, it's not safe to even hint at them, even when such statements are qualified. As for me, had I been in his place, I would have laughed at Poppaea, laughed at Ahenobarbus, and should have formed a legion, not of Iberian men, but of Iberian women. But more particularly, I would have written epigrams, but unlike that unfortunate Rufinus, I would have read them to no one."

"By the way, you were going to tell me about him."

"I'll do that in the *unctorium*."[25]

But in the *unctorium*, Vinitius's attention was diverted by other matters, particularly by the beauty of the slave women who attended the bathers. Two of them, black women who reminded one of ebony statues, began at once to anoint the men's bodies with delicate Arabian perfumes. Meanwhile, the Phrygians,[26] experts in hairdressing, held combs and polished mirrors of steel in hands that were as soft and flexible as serpents. Two others, Greek women from Cos,[27] who were as beautiful as goddesses, waited till the time should come to arrange the gentlemen's togas in graceful folds.

"By Zeus, the cloud-scatterer!" exclaimed Marcus Vinitius. "What a group to choose from!"

"I prefer quality to quantity," answered Petronius. "My whole household in Rome does not exceed four hundred, and I presume that, for personal needs, no one but an upstart would require more than that."

"More beautiful bodies Ahenobarbus himself does not possess," admitted Vinitius, distending his nostrils.

Petronius answered with a suggestion of good-natured indifference, "You're my relative, but I'm neither as hard-hearted as Barsus nor as pedantic as Aulus Plautius."

At the sound of the last name Vinitius forgot the maidens from Cos and, raising his head, asked, "What made you think of Aulus Plautius? Can it be you don't know that when I dislocated my arm outside the city, I spent more than two weeks in his house? Fortunately, Aulus happened to be passing at the time of the accident, and when he saw how much I was suffering, he had me carried to his house, where his slave, the physician Merien, cured me. I wanted to talk with you about this very thing."

"Why? Are my fears correct that you're in love with Pomponia? If that

---

25 Anointing room.
26 Ancient people who lived on the Black Sea.
27 Kos, Greek island near Turkey.

be true, I'm sorry for you. She's not young, and she's very virtuous. I cannot imagine a worse combination. Brrr."

"I didn't fall in love with Pomponia—alas," sighed Vinitius.

"With whom then?"

"Would that I knew myself. But I don't even know her name, whether it be Lygia or Callina. In the house they call her Lygia, because she's a Lygian by descent, but she also bears the barbarous name of Callina. What a strange place is this house of Aulus. It's filled with people, yet it's as quiet as the groves of Subiacum. In the course of the whole two weeks I was there I didn't suspect that a divinity dwelt there. But once, at dawn, I caught sight of her bathing in the garden fountain. By the foam from which Venus rose, the morning light passed right through her body. It seemed to me that let the sun but rise and she would vanish in its light, as the gleam of the morning stars. After this I saw her twice, and since then I've been unable to find rest. I know no other desires, I care for nothing that Rome can give me. I want no women, gold, nor Corinthian bronze, nor amber, pearls, wine, nor feasting. One thing alone I eagerly long for: Lygia. I confess to you, Petronius, sincerely, that I'm yearning for her as that god imaged on the mosaic of your *tepidarium* yearned for Paisythea. Ceaselessly, day and night I yearn."

"If she's a slave, then buy her."

"She's not a slave."

"Then who is she? One of Aulus's freedwomen?"

"Never having been a slave, she could not be a freedwoman."

"What, then, is she?"

"I don't know; a king's daughter, or something like it."

"Vinitius, your story intrigues me. Go on."

"If you'll listen to me, I'll soon satisfy your curiosity. It won't take long to tell the story. You may perhaps have known personally Vannius, the king of the Suevi,[28] who, when he was banished from his own country, lived for many years in Rome, where he made himself a reputation for his luck at dice and his skill in chariot racing. Drusus[29] restored him again to his throne. Vannius, who was actually a man of many gifts, began by ruling well and was successful in war, but later he gradually began to swindle

---

28 People from what is now central Germany.

29 Nero Claudius Drusus, son of Livia Drusilla and Tiberius Claudius Nero (15 B.C.–A.D. 23).

not only his neighbors, but his own Suevi. At this, Vangio and Sido, two of his nephews, sons of Vibilius, king of the Hermunduri,[30] determined to force him to go back to Rome—to try his luck at the dice."

"I remember, it wasn't that long ago—in the time of Claudius, if I'm not mistaken."

"Correct. War broke out. Vannius sought the aid of the Yazygi; his fond nephews turned to the Lygians,[31] who, having heard of Vannius's great wealth and been tempted by the hope of a rich booty, came in such multitudes that Claudius Caesar himself began to fear for the safety of his frontier. Claudius, not wishing to get involved in a foreign war, wrote to Atelius Hister, commander of the Danubian legions, to follow closely the course of the war and not permit it to disturb our peace. Then Hister exacted of the Lygians a solemn compact that they should leave our territories inviolate. Not only did they agree to this, but they also gave hostages, among whom were the wife and daughter of their ruler. You're undoubtedly aware that the barbarians take their wives and children with them to war. My Lygia is the daughter of that monarch."

"Where did you learn all this?"

"Aulus Plautius himself told me. As a matter of fact, the Lygians didn't cross the frontier, but barbarians come like a hurricane and disappear with the same speed. Just so vanished the Lygians with their wild ox horns on their heads. They completely routed the Vanniusian Suevi, but their own king fell. In consequence, they disappeared with their booty and left their hostages in Hister's power. The queen died soon after, and the daughter was sent by Hister to the ruler of all Germany, Pomponius, because he didn't know what else to do with her. At the close of the war with Catti, Pomponius returned to Rome, where, as you know, Claudius allowed him to have a triumphal entry. At that time, the girl walked behind the conqueror's chariot; but then, in his turn, Pomponius became perplexed, not knowing what to do with the girl since a royal hostage cannot be regarded as a captive. Finally, he placed her with his sister, Pomponia Graecina, the wife of Aulus. In that house, where everything from the host to the chickens in the hennery are virtuous, this girl grew to maidenhood—alas, virtuous as Graecina herself and so beautiful that in comparison to her even Poppaea seems like an autumn fig beside an apple of the Hesperides."

---

30   A Germanic tribe.
31   From modern-day Poland.

"And so?"

"I repeat, that from the instant I saw her at the fountain, when the sun rays passed through her body, I at once fell desperately in love with her."

"She then is as transparent as a sea lamprey or a young sardine?"

"Don't laugh, Petronius. But if you're misled by the freedom with which I speak of my passion, know that the brightest garment often hides the deepest wounds. I must tell you that when I was returning from Asia, I slept a night in the temple of Mopsus[32] in the hope that a revelation might come to me in my slumber. And indeed while I slept, Mopsus himself appeared to me and declared that love would work a great change in my life."

"I've heard that Pliny says he doesn't believe in the gods, but does believe in dreams—and perhaps he's right. My jesting doesn't prevent my thinking, at times, that there exists only one divinity—eternal, omnipotent, and creative—Venus Genirix. She unites souls and bodies—everything. Eros it was who called the world from chaos. Whether he did well, is another question, but since it's so, we must of necessity acknowledge his might, although one need not be thankful for it."

"Alas! Petronius, it's easier to find philosophy in the world than wise counsel."

"Tell me, what is it you really want?"

"I want Lygia. I wish that these hands of mine, which at present embrace only the air, might hold her and press her to me in their embrace. I wish to breathe with her breath. Were she a slave, I'd give Aulus a hundred maidens with feet whiter than chalk[33] in exchange for Lygia. I want to keep her in my home till my head's as white as the summit of Soracte in winter."

"She's not a slave, yet because she belongs to Aulus's family and because she's been forsaken by her parents, she may be regarded as a foster daughter. If he so desired, Aulus might give her to you."

"Clearly you don't know Pomponia Graecina. Both love her as though she were their own daughter."

"Indeed, I know Pomponia—a veritable cypress tree.[34] Were she not the wife of Aulus, she might have been hired as a professional mourner.

---

32 A mythological seer who founded the famous oracle in Cilicia (Southeast Asia).
33 A sign that they were offered for sale for the very first time.
34 A symbol of mourning.

Ever since Julius's death, she hasn't put aside her dark robes; in a word, she looks as if while still living, she were wandering over the asphodel-strewn meadow.[35] Moreover, she's a one-man woman—which makes her a phoenix among our much-divorced women. By the way, did you hear that a phoenix has actually appeared in Upper Egypt? The thing happens not oftener than once in five hundred years."

"Petronius! Petronius! Let's talk of the phoenix some other time."

"Then listen to me, dear Marcus. I know Aulus Plautius. Although he disapproves of my manner of life, yet he regards me with a certain attachment and, perhaps, rates me above others, for he knows that I've never been an informer—as were, for instance, Domitius Afer, Tigellinus, and a whole gang of Ahenobarbus's friends. While making no pretensions of being a Stoic, more than once I've turned away in disgust from certain acts of Nero's on which Seneca and Burrus have looked with indulgence. If you think I can win favor for you with Aulus, I'm at your service."

"I believe you can. You know how to influence him, and your resources are inexhaustible. Think it over and speak with Aulus."

"You've exaggerated both my influence and my resourcefulness. However, if that's all you want of me, I'll speak to Aulus when he returns to Rome."

"They returned two days ago."

"That being the case, let's go into the *triclinium*,[36] where our breakfast is waiting, and when we've restored our strength, we'll command that we be taken to Aulus."

"You've always been good to me," exclaimed Vinitius with fervor, "but now there's nothing left for me but to set up your statue among my household deities—a fine one, like that over there—and make offerings to it."

He turned to the statues that adorned one of the walls of the perfumed chamber and pointed to the one that represented Petronius as Hermes with a staff in his hand. "By the light of Helios," he added, "if the godlike Alexander resembled you, I don't wonder at Helen."

This he said with as much sincerity as flattery, for although Petronius was older and physically not so well developed as Vinitius, his face seemed

---

35 Meadow of the dead where the shades of heroes wandered disconsolately. In Greek mythology, the asphodel is considered to be the plant of the dead.
36 Dining room.
37 Bathing masters.

handsomer. The Roman women not only went into ecstasies over the delicacy of his mind and taste, for which reason they called him the *arbiter elegantiarum*, but also over his figure. This admiration was reflected even on the faces of the two maidens of Cos, who were now arranging the folds in his toga. One of them, Eunice by name, cherished a secret passion for Petronius and now gazed at him with tenderness and adoration.

But Petronius, without even looking at her, smiled at Vinitius and began to quote to him by way of reply Seneca's epigram about women: "Women are all fickle."

When he had finished, Petronius, laying his hand on the young man's shoulder, led him into the *triclinium*.

In the *unctorium*, the two Greek girls, the Phrygians, and the two black women began to put away the vessels of perfume. But at that moment, the heads of the *balneatores*[37] appeared from behind the drawn curtains of the *frigidarium*, and a cautious "Psst!" was heard. At the call, one of the Greeks, the Phrygians, and the Ethiopians sprang up quickly and vanished behind the curtain. The time of mirth and revelry had come in the baths. The superintendent did not restrain them, because he himself had not infrequently taken part in similar orgies. Petronius had his doubts about them, but being an indulgent man and one not fond of criticizing, looked upon the revels through his fingers.

Eunice alone remained in the *unctorium*. She listened for a time to the sound of the voices and laughter retreating towards the *laconicum*; then she took the bench ornamented with amber and ivory, on which Petronius had just been sitting, and carefully moved it over to his statue. The *unctorium* was filled with sunlight and the bright reflection of the many-colored marble slabs with which the walls were covered. Eunice stood on the bench. When she found herself on a level with the statue, she threw her arms impetuously around its neck; then, throwing back her golden hair and pressing her rosy body against the white marble, she ardently covered Petronius's cold mouth with kisses.

Chapter II

Afulter breakfast, as Petronius called it, in spite of the fact that the friends sat down at table when simple mortals had long finished their noonday meal, Petronius proposed a short nap, it being still much too early for visiting. As an aside he noted that there are, to be sure, persons who begin to visit their friends at sunrise, holding that the custom is sanctioned by antiquity and is truly Roman. But he, Petronius, considered it barbarous. The best of all times for visiting is afternoon, but not earlier than when the sun sinks towards the temple of Jupiter Capitolinus,[1] and begins to throw oblique shadows on the Forum. It's usually still very hot and sultry in the autumn, and people are fond of sleeping after eating. In the meantime, it was pleasant to listen to the murmuring of the fountain in the great atrium, after taking the thousand obligatory steps,[2] and to doze in the purplish light filtered through the half-drawn *velarium*.[3]

Vinitius agreed with him. They walked up and down, talking in an off-hand way of the gossip from the palace on the Palatine and from the city, and carelessly philosophizing about life. After a time Petronius retired into the *cubiculum*,[4] but he didn't sleep long. Half an hour later, he returned and, when he had ordered verbena to be brought to him, he began to inhale it and to rub it on his hands and temples.

"You won't believe," he exclaimed, "how stimulating and refreshing this is. Now I'm ready."

The litters had already been waiting for some time. They took their seats, and Petronius commanded that they should be borne to the Patrician Quarter, to the house of Aulus. Petronius's villa was located on the southern slope

---

1 Jupiter was the chief Roman male god (in Greece, Zeus). The central seat of the Jupiter cult was on Capitoline Hill; hence the temple designation.
2 Roman custom; aided digestion.
3 Awning.
4 Sleeping room.

of the Palatine Hill near what is called the Carinae. The shortest route lay through the Forum; however, as Petronius wished to visit Master Idomeneus's jewelry shop first, he gave directions that they should carry them through the Apollinis Quarter and the Forum in the direction of the Sceleratus Quarter, on the corner of which there were all sorts of booths.

The powerful Negroes raised the litters and started on the way, preceded by slaves called *pedisequii*.[5] For a time Petronius was silent; he kept raising his verbena-perfumed palms to his nostrils and was evidently deliberating about something serious.

Finally, he said, "It occurs to me that if your forest nymph is not a slave, nothing prevents her from leaving Aulus's house and taking up her abode with you. You would surround her with love and shower riches upon her, just as I do my adored Chrysothemis, with whom, just between ourselves, I'm satisfied—at least, as well pleased as she is with me."

Vinitius shook his head disapprovingly.

"Why not?" asked Petronius. "If worse came to worst, the case would go to Caesar, and you can be certain that, irrespective of my influence, our Ahenobarbus would take your side."

"You don't know Lygia," answered Vinitius.

"In that case, permit me to ask, if you yourself know anything about her, other than her appearance? Have you told her that you love her?"

"I saw her first at the fountain, and since then I've met her twice. Don't forget that while I was in Aulus's house, I stayed in a separate villa intended for guests—and that with my dislocated arm I wasn't able to be present at the family table. Only on the eve of the day I announced my departure did I find myself with Lygia at supper, but I didn't succeed in exchanging even a word with her. I was forced to listen while Aulus told stories of his victories in Britain, and after that to a discussion of the overthrow of small estates in Italy, which Licinius Stolo sought to prevent. In fact, I don't know whether Aulus is capable of talking about anything else; and don't delude yourself that we'll be able to escape it, unless you prefer to hear about the effeminacy of these times. They raise pheasants in their birdhouse, but they do not eat them, being convinced that with every pheasant eaten, the downfall of Roman power is brought that much nearer. The second time, I met her by the cistern in the garden. She had a freshly plucked reed in her hand, the end of which she was dipping in

---

5 Runners.

the water and sprinkling with it the iris growing about. Look at my knees! By Hercules' shield, they did not shake when the Parthians rushed with howls upon our ranks—but at the cistern they quaked. And, embarrassed as a boy who still wears a *bulla*[6] on his neck, my eyes alone begged for mercy, as for a long while I was incapable of uttering a single word."

Petronius gazed at him with an expression almost of envy, then said, "Fortunate one! No matter how bad the world or life may be, there's one thing that remains eternally beautiful—youth." Then he asked, "So you didn't speak to her?"

"Oh, no! When I had got myself a little under control, I told her that on my way back from Asia I had dislocated my arm outside the city gates, but now that the time had come when I must leave this hospitable roof, I was persuaded that to suffer under it was more delightful than to divert oneself elsewhere, and to be ill there more consoling than to be in health away from it. She became confused, listening to my words, her head bent down, all the while tracing something in the saffron-colored sand with her reed. Then she raised her eyes, looked again at the lines she had drawn, as if preparing herself to ask me something—and then suddenly ran away, like a dryad from a stupid faun."

"She must have beautiful eyes."

"Like the sea—and I was drowned in them exactly as if in the sea. Believe me, the Archipelago[7] is not so blue as her eyes. Shortly afterward, Aulus's little boy ran up and asked me something, but I didn't understand a word he said."

"O Minerva," exclaimed Petronius, "take from this youth's eyes the bandage with which Eros has bound them—lest he dash his head on the columns of the temple of Venus!" Then he turned to Vinitius. "Listen, you springtime bud on the tree of life, you first green branch in the vineyard. Instead of taking you to Aulus, I ought to have carried you to the house of Gelotius, where there's a school for young men who know nothing of life."

"I don't understand you."

"What did she write on the sand? Was it not the name of Amor? Or a heart pierced with a dart, or something of the kind by which you might have inferred that the Satyrs had already whispered the secrets of life in the nymph's ear? Is it possible you didn't examine the marks?"

---

6 Amulet, a symbol of a boy's coming of age.
7 Mediterranean Sea.

"I've worn the toga[8] much longer than you think," answered Vinitius. "Before little Aulus ran up I carefully examined the marks, for well I know that the girls of Greece and Rome frequently write on the sand what their lips know not how to speak. However, guess—guess what she had drawn?"

"If it wasn't what I've supposed, then I have no idea."

"A fish."

"A *what?*"

"I say—a fish. What did that mean? That cold blood is running in her veins? I don't know. But you, who have labeled me a springtime bud on the tree of life, certainly must know better than I how to interpret that sign."

"*Carissime!*[9] Ask Pliny about that. He knows everything about fish. Old Apicius, if he were still alive, might have been able to tell you something about it. Not for nothing did he, during his life, eat more fish than could be gathered together in the Bay of Naples."

Further conversation was precluded by the litters arriving in a crowded street where the noise of the multitude prevented further talk. Passing the Apollinis Quarter, they turned to the *boarium*[10] and thence to the Roman Forum. The Forum, on clear days before sunset, was filled with loiterers who assembled in multitudes to saunter among the columns, to relate and learn the news of the hour, to stare at the litters borne past with their distinguished occupants, and finally to rub shoulders in the jewelers' shops and the bookstalls, in the places where money was exchanged, in the shops where were sold silk, bronze, and every possible sort of thing. The houses occupying a part of the market extending towards the Capitol were filled with these shops. Half of the Forum, immediately under the cliffs of the Capitol, was already plunged in darkness, while the columns that adorned the temples above were drowned in a splendor of gold and blue. The columns on a lower level cast their long shadows on the marble slabs. So great indeed was the number of columns standing about everywhere that the eye lost itself among them as in a forest.

These buildings and columns seemed to have jammed themselves together. They were piled one on the other, they ran right and left, they ascended the hills, took refuge on the walls of the Capitol, or clung to

---

8   Been a mature adult.

9   "Beloved!" (addressed to a male).

10   Cattle market.

each other like trees—large and small, thick and thin, golden or white—now blooming under the architrave with acanthus blossoms, now ornamented with Ionic spirals, now capped with a simple Doric square. Above that forest glistened colored triglyphs; out of tympans stepped the sculptured figures of gods; winged and golden four-horse chariots struggled as it were to fly from their pediments into the air—into the azure blue sky that crowned this city of crowded temples.

In the midst of the marketplace and along the edges flowed a river of people. They wandered under the arches of the basilica of Julius Caesar, or sat on the steps of the temple of Castor and Pollux, or surged about the little temple of Vesta. These crowds resembled, as they moved against this extensive marble background, a variegated swarm of butterflies or beetles. Above, on the enormous stairways leading from the side of the temple dedicated to Jupiter Optimus Maximus,[11] new waves began to surge; some people were listening to orators on the rostrum. Here and there were heard the calls of peddlers as they sold fruit, wine, or water mixed with fig juice; of fakirs praising wonder-working nostrums; of soothsayers seeking out hidden treasure; of the interpreters of dreams. Somewhere above the noise of the conversation and the hawkers' cries were to be distinguished the sound of the *sistra*,[12] the Egyptian *sambuca*,[13] or Grecian flutes. In other places, the sick, the pious, and the afflicted were bringing offerings to the temples.

Amid the multitudes of people, flocks of doves flew down on the marble pavement and threw themselves eagerly on the proffered grain; like variegated or dusky spots in motion, these flocks now rose in the air, then with a loud flutter of wings, again alighted in a place vacated by the crowd. From time to time the people stood aside to make way for the litters in which were to be seen the painted faces of women or the heads of senators and warriors, rigid and almost lifeless. The polyglot multitudes repeated names and nicknames, sometimes sneeringly and sometimes in ridicule and sometimes in praise. Among this disordered crowd, at times, companies of soldiers or guards, enforcing order in the streets, forced their way, proceeding with measured tread. On all sides Greek was heard quite as frequently as Latin.

---

11   As god of the state, Jupiter had this title, which meant, "the best and the greatest."
12   *Sistrum.* A sort of rattle used in the worship of the goddess Isis.
13   *Sambuké.* A sort of harp.

Vinitius, who had not been in the city for a long time, gazed with a certain curiosity on the human anthill and on the famous Roman Forum, which seemed to be lording it over this multitude hailing from the four corners of the earth while at the same time submerged in it. Petronius, guessing his companion's thoughts, called the Forum "the nest of Quirites without the Quirites."[14] Indeed, the real Romans were completely lost in that throng, composed of the representatives of every race and nationality. In it there appeared inhabitants of Ethiopia; enormous, light-haired settlers of the far North—Britons, Gauls, and Germans; slant-eyed immigrants from Seres;[15] people from the Euphrates and from India, with brick-stained beards; Syrians from the banks of the Orontes, with black, insinuating eyes and dried out like bones; nomads from the Arabian deserts; Jews with sunken breasts; Egyptians with changeless, indifferent smiles on their faces; Numidians and Africans; Greeks from Hellas, who governed the city on an equality with the Romans and held sway through science, art, wisdom, and knavery; Greeks from the islands, from Asia Minor, Egypt, Italy, and Gaul. Among the throng of slaves with pierced ears were not a few freedmen, idle people whom Caesar amused, clothed, and even fed at his own expense; not a few voluntary immigrants had flocked here, attracted to the huge city by the possibility of living without labor, and by expectations of success; and usurers, priests of Serapis[16] with palm branches in their hands, priests of Isis to whose altars were brought more offerings than to the temple of the Capitoline Jupiter, priests of Cybele[17] carrying in their hands the golden fruit of the maize, and priests of wandering divinities; Eastern dancers in shining mitres, vendors of amulets, snake charmers, and Chaldean soothsayers; and finally, a considerable number of vagrants without any occupation, who weekly turned to the storehouse on the other side of the Tiber for bread, who fought for lottery tickets in the Circus, who spent their nights in rickety houses in the districts beyond the Tiber, and sunny, warm days under covered porticos, and in filthy taverns of the Suburra, on the Milvian bridge, or before the villas of the distinguished Romans, whence, from time to time, the leavings from the slaves' table were thrown to them.

---

14 "The Knights without the Knights." *Knight* is used interchangeably with *patrician*.
15 China.
16 An Egyptian deity, like Isis.
17 A Phrygian goddess.

Petronius was well known to these crowds. From every quarter the cry, "It is *he!*" reached Vinitius's ear. Petronius was beloved for his liberality. His popularity increased after the Romans learned that he had appealed to Caesar for an annulment of the death sentence pronounced against all the slaves of the prefect Pedanius Secundus, without distinction of age or sex, because one of their number, driven to desperation, had killed the monster. Petronius, to be sure, had stated in public that the case concerned him personally not at all and that he had gone before the emperor in his private capacity as the *arbiter elegantiarum*, because, while a barbarous slaughter of that kind was worthy of the Scythians,[18] it was not worthy of Romans, and it offended his aesthetic sensibilities. Nevertheless, the multitudes, outraged at the punishment, adored Petronius from that time on.

But he did not care for this popularity. Petronius did not forget that Britannicus,[19] whom Nero poisoned, was also beloved of the mob. The same was true of Agrippina, assassinated at Caesar's command; Octavia,[20] who, after her veins had been opened, had been suffocated in hot steam on the Pandataria;[21] Rubellius Plautus, who had been banished; and Thrasea,[22] who lived in daily expectation of a sentence of death. The love of the mob might therefore be a cause for concern, an ill omen, and, skeptic that he was, Petronius was nevertheless superstitious. His contempt for the crowd was twofold: He detested it both as an aristocrat and as a man of culture. In his opinion, those who smelled of dry beans carried in their shirts, who were always hoarse and sweating from playing *mora*[23] on the street corners and in the *peristyles*,[24] did not deserve to be called human beings. For this reason, Petronius, giving no heed to the applause and the

---

18   Syrian nomadic tribe that roved and raided north of the Black and Caspian seas.

19   Britannicus was the real heir to the throne, so Nero had him murdered.

20   Nero's wife (daughter of Emperor Claudius); thanks to Poppaea, Nero divorced and banished her and then had her murdered.

21   An island place of imprisonment and exile in the Tyrrhenian sea.

22   Thrasea Paetus, Publius Clodius, Roman senator and Stoic philosopher. Became consul in A.D. 56. Resigned from the Senate rather than approve Nero's letter justifying the murder of his mother, Agrippina. Even though he was in retirement, Nero kept bringing charges against him to the Senate, which finally, cowed into submission by a large contingent of Praetorian Guard, condemned Thrasea to death. Accepting the inevitable, in the presence of friends he had his veins opened and died.

23   A popular game in which one player guesses how many fingers another player is holding up.

24   Colonnades.

kisses wafted to him, told Vinitius the story of the killing of Pedanius, and he ridiculed the fickleness of the street shouters who applauded Nero as he was going to the temple of Jupiter Stator the very day after they had expressed their indignation at his tyranny. At Avirnus's bookshop, he ordered the litter to halt and, descending, bought an illuminated manuscript, which he gave to Vinitius.

"Here's a gift for you," he said.

"Thank you," answered Vinitius. When he had examined the title, he asked, "*The Satiricon?*[25] Is it something new? Who wrote it?"

"It's mine. But I'm not of a mind to follow in Rufinus's tracks, whose story I was about to tell you; nor in the tracks of Fabricius Veiento; therefore no one knows of this. Tell no one of it."

"But you've maintained that you didn't write verses," said Vinitius, looking over the manuscript, "and here I observe prose and verse side by side."

"When you read it, pay attention to the description of the feast of Trimalchion.[26] As for verses, they disgust me since Nero began to write them. When Vitelius wants to ease his stomach,[27] he uses little ivory sticks that he thrusts down his throat; others for the same purpose use flamingo feathers steeped either in olive oil or boiled in wild thyme; but my unique remedy is to read Nero's verses and the effect is immediate. Afterward I can praise them, if not with a clear conscience, at least with a clean stomach."

Having said this, he again stopped the litter at the jeweler Idomeneus, and when he had settled the question about the precious stones, directed that they proceed straight to Aulus's house.

"On the way, I'll tell you the story of an author's self-love; the story of Rufinus," he said.

But before he began his story, the litters turned into the Patrician Quarter, and they found themselves before Aulus's dwelling. A young and muscular gatekeeper opened the door leading to the *ostium*,[28] over which a caged magpie received the guests with a piercing "*Salve!*"[29]

On the way from the *ostium* to the atrium itself, Vinitius asked, "Did you notice that the doorkeepers here are unchained?"

---

25 Or *Satyricon*, generally attributed to Petronius.
26 Sometimes published as a separate book.
27 Many Roman gluttons would gorge themselves, then induce themselves to vomit.
28 Main entrance (second antechamber or vestibule).
29 A greeting.

"It's a strange house," answered Petronius in an undertone. "You probably know that Pomponia Graecina has been suspected of belonging to a superstitious sect of the East that worships a person called Christus. It appears that Crispinilla, who cannot forgive Pomponia for being satisfied during her life with a single husband, rendered her the kindness of an accusation. A woman with a single husband! At present in Rome it is easier to find a plate of Noricum mushrooms. They tried her before a domestic court."

"You're right, it is truly a strange house. Afterward I'll tell you what I saw and heard here."

They entered the great atrium. The *atriensis*[30] sent the *nomenclator*[31] to announce the visitors. Meanwhile, servants brought them chairs and placed stools under their feet. Petronius, who had never been in the house and had imagined that in it there reigned eternal gloom, consequently looked about himself with surprise and even with a feeling of disappointment, as he observed that the atrium made, on the contrary, a pleasing and happy impression. From above, through a large opening, fell a shaft of bright light, which broke into a thousand rays in the fountain. A four-sided pool, with a fountain in the center, designed to catch rain in bad weather, was surrounded by anemones and lilies. It was evident that the people in the house loved lilies; they grew in thick clumps of white and red blossoms; there were also many sapphire-colored irises whose tender leaves were silvered by the spray. Among the moist moss that concealed the lily pots, and amid the profusion of leaves, bronze statues of children and seabirds could be seen. In one corner a bronze fawn inclined her greenish head, turned gray by the moisture, to the water as if about to quench her thirst. The floor of the atrium was laid with mosaic tiles. The walls, partly faced with reddish marble and partly with wood, on which were paintings representing trees, fishes, birds, and griffins, attracted the eye by the play of colors. The doorways to the side rooms were adorned with tortoiseshell and ivory. Beside the doors, against the walls, stood the statues of Aulus's forefathers. Everywhere a calm plenty was evident, far removed from excess, but noble and possessed of dignity.

Petronius, who lived in a style immeasurably more luxurious, could not find a single thing that offended his taste. He had just pointed this out

30 Slave who stands at the entrance.
31 Butler.

to Vinitius when the doorkeeper suddenly pulled aside the curtain separating the atrium from the *tablinium*,[32] and Aulus Plautius appeared in the distance, approaching rapidly.

He was a man nearing the evening of his life, his head whitened with frost, but still hale. His face was full of energy, but somewhat small, resembling to a certain degree the head of an eagle. At the same time there was depicted on it an expression of surprise; the unexpected visit of Nero's friend, companion, and confidant clearly alarmed him more than a little.

Petronius was a man too observant and worldly not to notice this. Therefore, after the first greetings, he declared with all the eloquence and amiability he could summon that he came to express his gratitude for the hospitality shown in this house to his sister's son; that gratitude alone had prompted the visit, and his long acquaintance with Aulus had inspired him with this audacity.

Aulus in return assured him that he was welcome. As for the gratitude, he, Aulus, considered himself in his debt, although Petronius of a truth could not guess what possible service he could have rendered him.

In fact, Petronius did not guess. To no purpose did he raise his nut-brown eyes, did he strain his mind in an effort to recall the slightest service he had shown Aulus. He could remember none—except that it might be the one that he was about to render Vinitius. Perhaps something of the kind had happened in spite of himself and without his knowing it.

"I love and admire Vespasian,"[33] said Aulus, "and you saved his life when he was unfortunate enough to fall asleep during one of Caesar's recitals."

"It was his good fortune that he didn't hear those verses," replied Petronius. "I'll not deny, however, that this blessing might have turned out unfortunately. Ahenobarbus was wholeheartedly in favor of dispatching a centurion to him at once to advise him in a friendly way to open his veins."[34]

"And you, Petronius, laughed him out of it."

"Yes, or to be more truthful, I did the contrary. I told him that Orpheus knew how to lull the wild beasts to slumber—consequently his triumph would have been still more complete if he had succeeded in

---

32 Terrace.

33 Roman emperor (A.D. 69–79).

34 Die voluntarily so that the Praetorian Guard didn't have to kill him. Rulers in those days kindly offered this alternative to death at the hands of their guards.

putting Vespasian to sleep. It's possible to chide Ahenobarbus, provided that to a modicum of reproof there be added a large amount of flattery. Our gracious Augusta, Poppaea, understands this very well."

"Alas, such are the times," observed Aulus. "Two of my front teeth are missing—knocked out by a stone thrown by a British slinger. On this account I whistle when I speak. Nevertheless, I consider the days spent by me in Britain the happiest of my life."

"Because they were victorious," Vinitius hastened to add.

But Petronius, fearing that the veteran might begin his long tales of the wars, changed the topic of conversation. He remarked, "In the vicinity of Praeneste the inhabitants have found a dead wolf cub with two heads, and three days ago, during the storm, the lightning knocked off a corner of the temple of Luna—an unusual phenomenon so late in the fall. One Cotta, who told me this, went on to say that the priests of the temple of Luna regard this as a sign of the fall of the city, or at least the ruin of a great house, a calamity that may be averted only by extraordinary sacrificial offerings."

Aulus, when he heard what Petronius said, remarked that portents of that kind ought not to be disregarded. The gods might be angered by an excess of wickedness; and in such cases one must offer propitiatory sacrifices.

To this Petronius objected.

"Your house, Aulus, is not particularly large, although therein lives a great man; and my house, although indeed much too large for so unworthy an owner, is equally small. But if ruin threatens as great a house as, for instance, the Domus Transitoria,[35] is it not worth our while to make offerings to save it?"

Aulus made no answer to this question. And his silence offended Petronius because, although he had lost the capacity of distinguishing good from evil, he had never been a spy—and it was possible to speak to him without fear. Therefore he again changed the conversation and started to praise Aulus's house and the excellent taste displayed in all the details.

"It's an ancient seat," answered Aulus. "I've altered nothing in it since I inherited it."

The curtain separating the hall from the *velarium* was thrown aside and the house was open to view through its entire extent, so that, looking through the terrace and the *peristylium*[36] and hall behind it, the gaze

---

35   Apparently, the state or nation itself.
36   A court with a colonnade around it.

reached to the garden itself, which, as seen from a distance, looked like a brilliant picture in a dark frame. From the garden the sound of happy children's voices reached the atrium.

"Ah, General," cried Petronius, "allow us to enjoy at shorter range this genuine laughter, which nowadays it is given to one to hear but rarely."

"Willingly," answered Aulus, rising from his chair. "Those are my little Aulus and Lygia playing ball. As for the laughter, I suppose, Petronius, that your entire life is spent in it."

"Life deserves to be laughed at, therefore I laugh at it," replied Petronius. "That laughter, however, sounds different."

"As for that," added Vinitius, "Petronius doesn't laugh during the day; rather he laughs all night."

Talking thus, they passed through the whole extent of the house and found themselves in the garden, where Lygia and little Aulus were playing ball. Slaves, called *spheristae*, were especially appointed for this game, and they picked the balls up from the ground and handed them to the players. Petronius cast a passing glance at Lygia. Little Aulus, seeing Vinitius, ran up to ask if he was fully recovered. The young man inclined his head as he passed the beautiful girl, who stood with a ball in her hand, her hair slightly disordered, flushed, and somewhat out of breath.

In the garden *triclinium*, upon which the ivy, vines, and honeysuckle threw their shade, sat Pomponia Graecina. The visitors hastened to greet her. Petronius, although he had never visited Aulus's house, knew her, as he had met her at Antistia's, the daughter of Rubelius Plautus, and also in the houses of Seneca and Polion. He could not conceal a certain admiration that her sad but agreeable face, the nobility of her bearing, her movements and speech, inspired in him. To such a degree did Pomponia contradict his ideas of women, that even this man, corrupt to the marrow, self-confident as no one else in Rome—this man not only felt a certain admiration for her, but even lost, when at times he was in her presence, his self-confidence. And now, as he was thanking her for her care of Vinitius, he involuntarily addressed her as "lady"—a title that never came to his mind when conversing with Calvia, Crispinilla, Scribonia, Valeria, Solona, or with other women of high society. When he had greeted her and expressed his gratitude, Petronius fell to complaining that Pomponia so seldom left her home and that she was not to be seen either in the Circus or in the amphitheater.

Laying her hand on her husband's, she answered him calmly. "We are both growing old and are beginning to appreciate more and more the quiet of our home."

Petronius was about to reply when Aulus added in his whistling voice, "And we feel ourselves becoming more and more strangers among people who call even our Roman gods by Greek names."

"For some time past the gods have been converted into mere figures of speech," replied Petronius carelessly. "So, since the Greeks have taught us rhetoric, it's easier for me to say, for instance, Hera than Juno."

When he said this, he turned his gaze towards Pomponia, as if to explain that in her presence he could think of no other divinity. Then he started to complain of what she had said about old age. "To be sure people grow old quickly—but not those who lead a different kind of life. Besides, there are faces of which Saturn seems to remember nothing."

Petronius spoke with a certain degree of sincerity, for Pomponia Graecina, although she had already passed the meridian of life, nevertheless retained an unusual freshness of complexion. And as she possessed a small head and delicate features, she left the impression at times, in spite of her somber dress, sedateness, and pensiveness, of being a quite young woman.

In the meantime, little Aulus, who had become extraordinarily attached to Vinitius while he was in the house, came up to the young patrician to invite him to play ball. Lygia herself followed the boy into the *triclinium.* Under the ivy shade, with the light sparkling and quivering on her face, she seemed to Petronius to be much more beautiful than when he had first seen her and, in very fact, nymphlike.

Still, without exchanging a word with her, he rose and, bowing, began to quote in place of the customary greeting, the words with which Odysseus saluted Nausicaa: "'If thou art one of the gods, queen of the broad heaven, then only from Artemis, the great daughter of Zeus, can come the beauty of that face, and the dignity of that stature. If thou art born of mortals, if thou art under the power of the destiny of the living, then blessed beyond words thy father and thy mother, and blessed be thy brothers.'"

Even Pomponia was delighted with the exquisite courtesy of this man of the world. Lygia listened, confused and blushing, not daring to raise her eyes. But little by little, a mischievous smile began to play about the corners of her mouth, and her face reflected the struggle going on within between maiden modesty and a desire to answer. The latter evidently won, for, suddenly looking up at Petronius, she answered him in the very words of Nausicaa. She spoke without taking breath and in a tone of voice suggestive of the classroom.

"'Stranger, thou art neither wicked nor dull.'"

Then, turning quickly, she ran away like a frightened bird.

Now came Petronius's turn to be surprised. He had not expected to hear Homer's verses from the lips of a girl who, according to Vinitius, was of barbarian birth. He glanced in perplexity at Pomponia, but she could not give any explanation, for she herself smilingly observed only the pride with which the elder Aulus's face was illuminated.

Aulus could not hide his satisfaction. In the first place, he loved Lygia as his own daughter; in the second, despite his ancient Roman prejudices, which compelled him to thunder against the new fashion of using the Greek language, he nonetheless counted a knowledge of it a crown of social refinement. He himself had never been able to learn Greek well, a fact that he secretly mourned. Therefore he was overjoyed that this grand gentleman and writer, who was prepared to consider his house as little more than barbarian, had been answered in the language and verses of Homer.

"We have a teacher—a Greek pedagogue," said Aulus, turning to Petronius. "He instructs our little one, and the girl overhears the lessons. She is a mere wagtail,[37] but a worthy one, and my wife and I have become very fond of her."

Petronius looked through the green of the ivy and the honeysuckle at the young people playing ball. Having laid off his toga, retaining only his single tunic, Vinitius was throwing a ball that Lygia caught as she stood opposite, with uplifted hands. At first she had not impressed Petronius, to whom she appeared too slender. But from the moment when he looked at her more closely in the *triclinium*, she impressed him quite differently. She would, he thought, make a good model for Aurora, and this he, as a connoisseur, understood to be something uncommon.

He observed her in detail and appraised everything on its merits: the rosy, transparent face; the fresh mouth, created as it were, for kissing; the eyes blue as the azure sea; the alabaster whiteness of her forehead; the sumptuousness of her dark hair, with its coils giving forth a reflection of amber or Corinthian bronze; the delicate neck; the divine formation of her shoulders; and the litheness, the posture, of her whole body that

---

37 Small, slender bird, such as a thrush.

breathed the youth of May and freshly blooming flowers. There was awakened in him the artist and lover of beauty who felt that under the statue of this maiden might well be written, "Spring." Suddenly he remembered Chrysothemis, and Petronius was seized with a hollow laugh. She seemed to him strangely faded, with her hair besprinkled with golden powder, with her blackened eyebrows, like a yellow tree shedding its leaves. Yet all Rome envied him that Chrysothemis. Then he compared Poppaea to Lygia, and likewise that renowned beauty suddenly seemed to him soulless as a waxen mask. In this girl with her Tanagrian[38] features was embodied not only spring, but also the radiance of Psyche, which shone through her rosy body as the flame gleams through the lamp.

Vinitius is right, he reflected, *and my Chrysothemis is old, old—old as Troy.*

Then, turning to Pomponia Graecina and pointing to the garden, he said, "I now understand, lady, that with two such companions, home seems dearer than the Circus or the feasts in the palace on the Palatine."

"Yes," answered she, looking aside at little Aulus and Lygia.

The old commander began to tell the girl's history and what he had heard many years ago from Atelius Hister about the Lygian nation that lived in the dark north.

The young people, having finished their game, had been for some time walking along the sandy paths of the garden. Against the background of myrtles and cypresses they seemed like three white statues. Lygia held little Aulus by the hand. When they had strolled for a short time, they sat down on a bench beside the fishpond in the center of the garden. Little Aulus almost immediately ran away to frighten the fish in the transparent water, and Vinitius resumed the conversation begun while they were walking.

"Yes," he said in a low, hesitating voice, "scarcely had I thrown aside the robe that the children of freeborn citizens wear till they are seventeen, than they sent me to the legions of Asia. I had no knowledge of Rome, of life, or of love. I had learned by heart a few verses of Anacreon[39] and Horace, but could not, like Petronius, quote verses when the mind is mute from admiration and cannot express itself in words. When I was a boy I was sent to the school of Musonius, who used to tell us that happiness consists in desiring what the gods wish—and therefore depends upon our

---

38   From Boeotia, in central Greece.
39   Greek poet of Teos (lived about 540 B.C.).

own wills. But I think that there is another more sublime and sweeter happiness that does not depend on our wills, which love alone can give. The gods themselves seek that happiness. Therefore, I who have not yet put love to the test, follow their example, Lygia, and I also seek that one who would desire to give me happiness."

He paused. For a time nothing was heard save the gentle splashing of the water into which little Aulus was throwing stones to frighten the fish. But after a while Vinitius spoke again, in a voice still softer and lower.

"You've probably heard of Titus, the son of Vespasian? It's related of him that when little more than a boy, he fell so deeply in love with Berenice, that grief almost brought him to the grave. I am capable of such love, Lygia. Wealth, glory, power—all are smoke, vanity, emptiness. A rich man can find another still richer; the famous man is cast in the shadow by the greater glory of another; the mighty may be conquered by one more mighty. But can Caesar himself, or one of the gods, seek to know greater delight, can he feel happier than a mere mortal when close to his breast breathes the breast of his dear one, or when kissing her lips? Therefore love makes us equal with the gods—oh, Lygia—"

She heard him in alarm and astonishment, and yet at the same time appeared as if she were hearkening to the sounds of a Grecian flute or a lyre. At certain moments it seemed to her that Vinitius was singing a marvelous song, which poured itself into her ear, set her blood surging, and filled her heart with faintness, fear, and a kind of uncomprehended delight. But in addition it seemed to her that he spoke of something that was already latent in her, but which she could not explain. She felt that he was awakening in her something that had been sleeping in her heart and that, in that instant, a hazy dream was changing itself into a form more and more definite, more lovable and more beautiful.

Meanwhile the sun had long since passed the Tiber and stood low over the Janiculum Hill. A purple light illuminated the motionless cypresses, as if permeating the whole air. Lygia raised her blue eyes—eyes that seemed to have just been awakened from a dream—to Vinitius, and all at once, in the glow of the sunset he bent over her with an entreaty trembling in his gaze, and appeared to her more handsome and noble than any human being or any of the gods of Greece or Rome whose statues she had seen on the pediment of the temple.

Gently taking her hand, he asked, "Can you not guess, Lygia, why I tell you this?"

"No," she whispered, so low that Vinitius could scarcely hear her.

But he didn't believe her, and seizing her arm more tightly, he would have drawn her to his heart, which, in the glow of passion awakened by the beauty of the girl, was beating like a hammer; he would have spoken burning words, had not old Aulus appeared on the myrtle-framed path. On coming nearer he said, "The sun is setting, be careful of the evening cold, and do not trifle with Libitina."[40]

"No," answered Vinitius, "although I haven't yet put on my toga, I don't feel cold."

"But over the hill even now one sees but half the sun's disk," continued the old warrior in a warning voice. "We have not here the favorable climate of Sicily, where at evening the people assemble in the market square so that they may salute the setting Phoebus with a parting song."

Forgetting that but a moment before he had warned them against Libitina, Aulus began to speak about Sicily, where he had estates and extensive farms to which he was much attached. He mentioned also that he had thought many times of moving to Sicily and there spending the remainder of his life in quietness. "He whose head has been whitened by many winters has no further need of frosts. The leaves are not yet falling from the trees, and the sky smiles on the city lovingly, but when the grapevine grows sere, when the snow falls on the Alban Hills and the gods with piercing winds visit the Campania, who knows but that I might transfer my whole household to that quiet countryseat."

"Can it be that you wish to leave Rome, Aulus?" asked Vinitius in sudden alarm.

"That desire I've had for a long time," answered Aulus, "for it is safer and more peaceful there."

He began again to praise his garden, his herds, his house hidden in the verdant hills, where buzzed swarms of bees. Vinitius, however, was not tempted by the bucolic picture and, thinking only that he would be deprived of Lygia, looked aside towards Petronius, as if salvation could come from him alone.

Meanwhile Petronius, seated near Pomponia, was admiring the view of the setting sun, the garden, and the people standing in the garden. Against the dark background of the myrtles, their white garments were bathed with the golden reflection of the sunset. The evening light, which had previously

---

40   Goddess of funerals.

empurpled the horizon, began to change to violet, and then to opal; a portion of the heavens became lilac-colored. The dark silhouettes of the cypresses grew still more pronounced than during the bright day. Among the people, the trees, and the entire garden an evening calm prevailed.

Petronius was impressed with this calm—especially by the serenity of the people. There passed over the features of Pomponia, of Aulus their son, and of Lygia a something that he had never noticed on the faces that surrounded him daily, or more correctly—nightly. The life led by everyone here filled, as it were, the whole soul with light and instilled in it a certain peace and tranquility. He reflected with a degree of amazement that there existed a beauty and delight that he—who was continually seeking for beauty and delight—might never discover.

He could hardly hide these thoughts, and, turning to Pomponia, he said, "I was considering within my soul how different your world is to that which Nero rules."

She turned her delicate face towards the evening light and replied with simplicity, "The world is ruled, not by Nero—but by God."

A moment of silence followed. Near the *triclinium* were heard in the alley the footsteps of the old general, Vinitius, Lygia, and little Aulus. But before they arrived, Petronius had posed another question.

"But do you believe in the gods then, Pomponia?"

"I believe in God who is one, just, and all-powerful," answered the wife of Aulus Plautius.

Chapter III

"**S**he believes in one God, all-powerful and just," repeated Petronius, when he found himself again with Vinitius in the litter. "If her God be all-powerful, life and death are in His power; and if He is just, He sends death justly. Why then does Pomponia wear mourning for Julius? By mourning for Julius, she rebukes her God. I will repeat this course of reasoning to our bronze-bearded ape, since I deem myself the equal of Socrates in dialectics. As regards women, I agree that each of them has three or four souls, but not one of them has a reasoning one. Pomponia ought to debate with Seneca or Cornutus as to what their great Logos is. Let them summon at once the shades of Xenophanes, Parmenides, Zeno,[1] and Plato, who are as wearied in the Cimmerian regions as a green finch in a cage. I wanted to speak to her and Aulus about something else! By the sacred belly of the Egyptian Isis! If I should have told them frankly the purpose of our coming, their virtue would surely have begun to thunder like a copper shield struck with a stick. And I didn't dare to tell! Would you believe, Vinitius, that I dared not? Peacocks are very beautiful birds, but their shriek is disagreeable. I feared a shriek. But I must praise your taste. A genuine 'rosy-fingered Aurora.' And do you know what she reminded me of besides? Spring! Not our Italian spring, when apple trees are rarely covered with blossoms, and olive trees are unchangingly gray, but that spring that I happened to see in Helvetia[2]—young, fresh, vividly green. By that pale moon, I don't wonder at you, Marcus. Be assured that you have fallen in love with Diana and that Aulus and Pomponia are ready to tear you, as once in ancient times the hounds tore Actaeon."

Vinitius bowed his head in silence for a time. Then, in a voice husky with passion, he began.

"I desired her before, but now my desire is still greater. When I

---

1 Founder of Stoic school of thought.
2 Switzerland.

touched her arm, a flame swept through me. I must have her. Were I Zeus, I would surround her with a cloud, as he did Io, or I would descend on her in the form of rain, as he did on Danaë. I would kiss her lips until they became sore. I would hear her scream in my arms! I am ready to kill Aulus and Pomponia and capture her and carry her away to my house. I will not sleep tonight. I'll order that one of my slaves be beaten, and I'll listen to his groans—"

"Calm yourself," said Petronius. "What desires! Like those of a carpenter from the Suburra."

"It matters not to me what you say. I must possess her! I've come to you for aid, but if you can do nothing, I'll do what I have to do myself. Aulus considers Lygia his daughter; then why should I look upon her as a slave? And since there's no other way, let her ornament the door of my house; let her anoint it with wolf's fat,[3] and let her sit at my hearth as my wife."

"Calm yourself, insane descendant of consuls! We do not lead in barbarians bound behind our carts to make wives of their daughters. Beware of extreme measures. Exhaust first the simple, honorable methods and give yourself and me time for reflection. There was a time when Chrysothemis seemed to me a daughter of Jupiter, yet I didn't marry her. Nero didn't marry Acte,[4] though she is the daughter of King Attalus.[5] Calm yourself! Don't forget that Aulus and his wife have no right to retain Lygia if she's willing to leave their house for yours. And know you're not burning alone, for Eros has roused in her the flame too. This I saw, and I'm an observer to be trusted. Be patient. There's a way to do everything, but today I've thought too much already, and it tires me. But I promise you that I'll think about your love tomorrow, and unless Petronius is not Petronius, he'll find a way."

Again there was silence. At length Vinitius said more calmly, "I thank you, and may Fortune bless you."

"Be patient."

"Where did you order them to take us?"

"To Chrysothemis."

---

3 Part of the Roman marriage ceremony.
4 Nero had passionately loved her for a time, beginning in A.D. 55. The relationship was encouraged by Seneca, who was trying to pry Nero from his murderous mother, Agrippina.
5 King of Pergamum (now western Turkey).

"Happy man, to possess the woman you love."

"*I?* Do you know what still amuses me in Chrysothemis? This: that she is untrue to me with my own freedman—Theocles, who plays the kithara—and deludes herself by assuming I don't notice it. There was a time when I loved her; now I'm merely amused by her lies and her silliness. Let's go together to her. Should she try to seduce you or write letters on the table with wine-steeped fingers, know that I'm not jealous."

And he ordered that the litter be carried to the house of Chrysothemis. But in the vestibule, Petronius placed his hand on Vinitius's shoulder.

"Wait, it seems to me I've found a way."

"May all the gods reward you!"

"I have it! Yes! I think it will go without a hitch. Do you know what, Marcus?"

"I hear you, my source of wisdom."

"Well, in a few days the divine Lygia will be yours."

"You are greater than Caesar!" exclaimed Vinitius.

Chapter IV

Petronius was as good as his word. The day after his visit to Chrysothemis, he slept till evening. Then he directed that he should be carried to the Palatine Hill, where he had a private conversation with Nero. The results of this conversation were not long in coming to light. On the third day, a centurion with a small legion of Praetorian soldiers appeared before Aulus's house.

In that period of lawless and bloody deeds, such messengers were generally heralds of death. From the moment when the centurion knocked with his hammer at Aulus's gate, and the *atriensis* announced the presence of soldiers in the vestibule, sudden terror filled the entire house. The family surrounded the old general. No one doubted but that he was the one whose life was in peril. Pomponia, throwing her arms about his neck, clung to him with all her might while she whispered words that were almost unintelligible. Lygia, her face white as a sheet, kissed his hand; little Aulus clung to his toga. From the corridors, from the apartments on the lower floor reserved for the servants, from the baths, and from the arches of the lower dwelling, from the whole house, in short, crowds of slaves of both sexes began to pour forth. Cries of "Alas! Alas!" and "*Me miserum! Me miserum!*"[1] were heard repeatedly. The women began to cry; some of the slaves were already scratching their cheeks, while others covered their heads with their handkerchiefs.

Only the old general, who had accustomed himself for many years to look death in the face, preserved his self-composure. His small, aquiline face was like stone. After he had ordered his servants to cease weeping and to return to their rooms, Aulus said, "Let me go, Pomponia. If my end has come, we'll have time to bid each other farewell."

He pushed her gently aside, but she cried, "I pray to God I may share death with you, Aulus."

---

1 "Woe is me!"

37

Then kneeling, she began to pray with the fervor that could be inspired only by fear on behalf of one beloved.

Aulus went into the hall where the centurion was waiting for him. It was old Caius Hasta, his former subordinate and companion in arms in the wars in Britain.

"I greet you, General," he said. "I bring you a command and a greeting from Caesar. Here are the tablets and the signet certifying that I come in his name."

"My thanks to Caesar for his greeting, and I shall fulfill his commands," answered Aulus. "I greet you, Hasta; tell me your mission."

"Aulus Plautius," began Hasta, "Caesar has learned that living in your house is the daughter of the Lygian king, who during the time of the divine Claudius was given to the Romans as a pledge that the boundaries of the empire should never be violated by the Lygians. The divine Nero is thankful to you, General, for the hospitality shown her for so many years, but not desiring to burden your house any longer, and considering that this maiden, as a hostage, ought to be under the protection of Caesar himself, and the Senate, he commands that you deliver her into my hands."

Aulus was too hardened a warrior and too valiant a man to permit himself to answer a command by lamentations, useless words, and complaints. Yet on his forehead there appeared a wrinkle of sudden anger and sadness. Years ago the British legions had trembled before Aulus's eyebrows contracted in this way. For a moment fear was reflected in Hasta's face. But now, before Caesar's command, Aulus felt defenseless.

He looked for a time at the tablets and signet and, raising his eyes towards the old centurion, said calmly, "Wait in the atrium, Hasta, until the hostage is delivered to you."

When he had said this, he went to the other end of the house, into the chamber where Pomponia, Lygia, and little Aulus were waiting apprehensively.

"Death threatens none, nor banishment into far-off islands. Nevertheless, Caesar's messenger is a herald of misfortune. Lygia, it concerns you."

"*Lygia?*" exclaimed Pomponia, perplexed.

"Yes," returned Aulus.

Turning to Lygia, he began, "Lygia, you have been brought up in our house as our child. Both Pomponia and I love you as our own daughter, but you are a hostage, entrusted by your nation to Rome; and the guardianship over you belongs to Caesar, and now Caesar takes you from our house."

The general spoke calmly but in a strained, changed voice. Lygia listened to his words, blinking in bewilderment, not at all understanding what the real meaning of all this was. Pomponia's cheeks turned pale. At the door leading from the corridor to the chamber appeared the terrified faces of the slaves.

"The will of Caesar must be accomplished," declared Aulus.

"Oh, Aulus!" exclaimed Pomponia, throwing her arms about the girl as if to protect her. "It would be better for her to die!"

Lygia, leaning on Pomponia's breast, brokenly repeated, "Mother, Mother," unable in her heartbreak to find any other words.

Aulus's face contracted again with wrath and pain.

"If I were alone in the world," he said gloomily, "I would not surrender her alive, and my relatives would have this very day to bring offerings to Jupiter Liberator. But I've no right to ruin you and our son, who may live to see happier days, so I will go this day to Caesar and implore him to change his mind. Whether he'll listen or not, I know not. Meanwhile, Lygia, farewell. Know that both Pomponia and I have always blessed the day when you first came to our fireside."

Thus speaking, he placed his hand on her head, but despite all his efforts to preserve his calm, when Lygia turned her tearful eyes to him and, catching his hand, pressed it to her lips, Aulus's voice vibrated with the deep grief of a father.

"Farewell, our joy and light of our eyes!" he cried. Turning quickly, he went into the hall so as not to surrender to an emotion unworthy of a Roman and a general.

Meanwhile, Pomponia, after conducting Lygia to her *cubiculum*, began to comfort, console, and encourage her with words that sounded strangely in this house, where in an adjoining room stood the *lararium*[2] and the altar on which Aulus Plautius, faithful to ancient custom, made offerings to the household gods. Pomponia, struggling for composure, armed Lygia with these words:

"The hour of trial has come. Virginius stabbed his daughter[3] to save

---

2 Sanctuary for the lares, household deities.

3 Around 450 B.C., a commission of ten (the Decemvirate), led by Appius Claudius, ruled over Rome. Appius Claudius determined to violate Virginia, the daughter of the centurion Virginius. Rather than permit that to happen, Virginius stabbed his daughter. The Roman people were so enraged that they overthrew the Decemvirate.

her from Appius; Lucretia[4] redeemed her shame with the price of her life. Caesar's house is a den of corruption, vice, and crime. But we, Lygia, have no right to commit suicide. We submit to another law, more sublime and more holy, and this law permits us to defend ourselves from shame and infamy, even if we have to pay the price of death and torture. It is a great glory for a person to come out pure from a house of infamy. Our world is such a house, but our life is short; the happiness of life lasts but the twinkling of the eye, and the real life begins after the resurrection from the dead, beyond which not Nero rules, but Mercy, and where pain is effaced by delight; and then there will be joy instead of pain, happiness instead of tears."

Then she began to speak of herself. Yes, she was quite resigned, but there were painful wounds in her heart. Her husband's moral vision was yet clouded; his soul did not yet glow with a single ray of eternal light. She could not even bring up her son in the spirit of Truth. And when she reflected that this condition of things might be prolonged to the end of her life, and that then might come a moment of separation a hundred times more terrible than that temporary one over which they were lamenting, she could not imagine herself happy without them even in heaven. And she had already wept many nights; many nights she spent in prayer, imploring pardon and grace. But she brought her sufferings to God; she waited and trusted. Even now, when this new blow struck her, when the command of the tyrant deprived her of her dearest one, whom Aulus called the light of their eyes, Pomponia still hoped, believing that there was a power above Nero's, and a mercy greater than his wrath.

She pressed the girl's head still more closely to her breast. Lygia dropped to her knees and, hiding her face in the folds of Pomponia's garment, was silent for a long time. When she finally raised her head, her face appeared more serene.

"Mother, I grieve for you, Father, and little Aulus, yet I know that resistance would not only be useless, but end in ruin for us all. I promise that I shall never forget your words, your counsel, while in the house of Caesar."

---

4 Lucretia, wife of Tarquinius Collatinus, was considered to be both the most virtuous and beautiful wife in ancient Rome (around 500 B.C.). The unscrupulous ruling tyrant, Tarquinius Sextus, violated Lucretia while her husband was away. Brokenhearted, Lucretia took her life. The outraged citizenry then overthrew the tyrant. Throughout history, Lucretia has been considered almost the ultimate prototype of the virtuous woman.

"Farewell, our joy and light of our eyes!"

Throwing her arms again around Pomponia's neck, Lygia went with her to take farewell of young Aulus, of the old Greek who was their teacher, of the servant who had nursed her, and all the slaves.

One of these, a huge, broad-shouldered Lygian, who in Aulus's house was called Ursus,[5] and who came to the Roman camp with Lygia, her mother, and their slaves, fell at her feet and then, kneeling before Pomponia, said imploringly, "Oh, lady, permit me to follow my mistress. I will serve her and watch over her in Caesar's house."

"You are Lygia's servant, not mine," answered Pomponia. "But I doubt if you'll be permitted to enter Caesar's gates, so how could you watch over her there?"

"I know not, lady, but this I do know: Iron I can break as if it were wood."

At this moment Aulus Plautius approached them, and when he learned what they were talking about, not only did he not oppose the wishes of Ursus, but he also declared that they had not even the right to detain the Lygian. They were by Caesar's command sending Lygia as a hostage; therefore, they were also bound to send her retinue under Caesar's protection. At this he whispered to Pomponia that, under the guise of a retinue, she might send as many slaves as she deemed proper. The centurion would make no objection.

As there was some comfort to Lygia in this arrangement, Pomponia was pleased that she was able to surround Lygia with servants of her choice. Therefore, she assigned her, in addition to Ursus, an old servant, two Greek women from Cyprus who were expert hairdressers, and two German maidens to tend her at her bath. She chose none but followers of the new faith, which Ursus had professed for several years. For this reason Pomponia felt that she might rely on the servants' fidelity, and at the same time she was delighted with the thought that the seeds of truth would soon be sown in Caesar's house.

Besides this, she wrote a few lines to Caesar's freedwoman, Acte, committing Lygia to her protection. For, although Pomponia had never seen her at the meetings of the adherents of the new faith, she was told that Acte never refused to assist them and read with eagerness the letters of Paul of Tarsus. She also knew that the young freedwoman lived in continual sadness, because she was entirely different from the rest of

---

5   "The Bear."

Nero's women. In a word, she was the good spirit of the palace.

Hasta promised to deliver this letter to Acte in person. And deeming it natural that a king's daughter should be surrounded by her suite, he did not refuse to take the servants to the palace. On the contrary, he was surprised at their small number. He begged them, however, to hurry, as he feared that he might be accused of lack of zeal in executing his order.

The moment of parting came. Pomponia's and Lygia's eyes again filled with tears, and Aulus once more placed his hand on her head. A moment later, followed by the cries of little Aulus, who had been threatening the centurion with his tiny fist in defense of his sister, the soldiers conducted Lygia to Caesar's palace.

When the old general had ordered that a litter should be gotten ready for him, he went into the *pinacotheca*[6] with Pomponia and said, "Listen, Pomponia. I'll apply to Caesar, though I think my effort will be fruitless, and I'll see Seneca, though Seneca's opinion means nothing with Nero now. Today, Sophonius, Tigellinus, Petronius, or Vatinus command more influence. As for Caesar, he probably never in his life heard of the Lygian nation, and if he demanded the surrender of Lygia as a hostage, it was at the instigation of someone else. It's not difficult to guess who that would be."

Pomponia raised her eyes in agitation. "Petronius?"

"Yes."

There was a brief silence, and the general continued, "This comes from allowing people without souls and honor to cross your threshold. Cursed be the moment Vinitius entered our house! He's the one who brought Petronius. Woe to Lygia! It's not a hostage they want, but a mistress."

From helpless rage and sorrow for his adopted daughter, his voice hissed more than usual. He struggled with himself for some time, and only his clenched fist indicated how severe was the struggle within him.

"The gods I have honored so far. But at this moment I think that not they rule over the world, but one mad, malicious monster, and his name is—Nero!"

"Aulus!" exclaimed Pomponia. "In the sight of God, Nero is only a handful of rotten dust."

Aulus strode heavily over the mosaic of the gallery. Many acts of valor he had accomplished, but he had known no great misfortune; therefore he was not prepared for this unforeseen blow. The old soldier had grown

---

6 Picture gallery.

more attached to Lygia than he himself knew. And now he could not be reconciled to the thought that he had lost her. Besides, he felt humiliated. A hand that he despised had smitten him, yet he knew that he was powerless against it.

At length, stifling the anger that had thrown his thoughts into confusion, he said, "I judge that Petronius has not taken her from us for Caesar, since he would fear Poppaea's vengeance. Therefore, he took her either for himself or for Vinitius. I'll investigate the case today."

Shortly afterward, the litter bore him in the direction of the Palatine Palace. Pomponia, left alone, went to comfort little Aulus, who was still crying for his sister and threatening Caesar.

Chapter V

As Aulus had expected, he was denied admittance to Nero's presence. He was told that Caesar was engaged in singing with Terpnos, a kithara player, and that he generally received only such persons as were summoned by him. In other words, Aulus must never even attempt to see him in the future.

But Seneca, even though suffering from fever, received the old commander with due respect.

When he had heard his tale, a mournful smile came to his lips as he said, "One service, noble Aulus, I can render you: I promise not to reveal to Caesar my pity for your pain nor my readiness to assist you. If Caesar had the least suspicion of this, he would never return Lygia to you, even if it were only to spite me."

Seneca further advised him not to apply to Tigellinus,[1] Vatinius, or Vitelius. They were not above bribes, and they might be glad to do an injury to Petronius, whose influence they were trying to undermine. But more likely they would merely tell Caesar how much Lygia was prized by Aulus and his wife. Nero then would become all the more unwilling to return her.

Then the venerable sage, with biting irony, continued. "You have held your tongue, Aulus, held it many years, and Caesar likes not those who are silent. How could you help being carried away by his beauty, his virtue, his singing, his declamations, his chariot driving, and his verses? Why didn't you glorify the death of Britannicus and deliver eulogies on the matricide or offer congratulations after the smothering of Octavia? You

---

1 Burrus, an earlier advisor of Nero and chief of the imperial Praetorian Guard (with Seneca), was poisoned; his place was taken by Poppaea (who had encouraged Nero to assassinate his mother, Agrippina) and Tigellinus, who took command of the Praetorian Guard. Tigellinus was infamous for his open pandering to Nero's sensuality.

are lacking in foresight, Aulus, which we who live happily in the court possess in the required degree."

Saying this, he took a cup he carried at his belt, filled it at the fountain in the *impluvium*,[2] and moistening his lips, added: "Ah, Nero has a grateful heart. He loves you because you've served Rome and made his name glorious in the four corners of the earth. Me he loves because I taught him in his youth. For this reason I know that this water is not poisoned. Wine in my house would be less safe; but if you're thirsty, you may drink this water without fear. The aqueduct brings it from over the Alban Hills, so, were it poisoned, all the fountains in Rome would be as well. As you see, even in this world one may enjoy a peaceful old age in security. I'm truly ill—not in the body, however, but in the soul."

Truly, Seneca did not have the strength of soul of such men as Cornutus and Thrasea. His whole life had been a series of concessions to crime. He felt this himself; he understood that as an adherent to the principles of Zeno, of Citium,[3] that he ought to have chosen another road— and he suffered more from that than from the fear of death itself.

Aulus broke in on his self-recrimination.

"Noble Annaeus,"[4] said he, "I know how Caesar has repaid you for the care you gave him in his youth. But our child has been taken from us at the instigation of Petronius. What kind of methods should I use with him? To what influences is he susceptible? Finally, would you be willing to use upon him all your eloquence, on behalf of your longtime friend?"

"Petronius and I," answered Seneca, "belong to opposing camps. There is no way to persuade him. No one's influence prevails on him. It may very well be that, in spite of his corrupt nature, he's better than the other rascals who surround Nero at present. But to attempt to persuade him that he's done wrong is only a waste of time. Petronius long ago lost the capacity of distinguishing right from wrong. Prove to him that what he does offends good taste, and he'll be ashamed. When I see him I'll tell him his conduct is worthy of a freedman. If that doesn't work, nothing will."

"Thank you even for that," answered the general.

After this Aulus directed that he should be borne to Vinitius, whom he found practicing fencing with his private master. When Aulus saw how

---

2   An opening in the roof of an atrium, or a basin to collect the rainwater below it.
3   City in Cyprus.
4   Name of Seneca's clan.

the young man was calmly occupying himself with athletics after the attempt against Lygia, he was overwhelmed by rage. Scarcely had the curtain fallen on the departing fencing master than his wrath found vent in a torrent of reproaches and recrimination. But as soon as Vinitius heard that Lygia had been carried away, he became so pale that even Aulus could no longer suspect him of being an accomplice. The young man's forehead was moist with sweat. His blood, after surging to his heart, rushed in hot waves back to his face; his eyes flashed; his lips moved in incoherent questioning. Jealousy and rage buffeted him like a hurricane. From the instant Lygia entered Caesar's house, she would likely be lost to him. But when Aulus mentioned Petronius's name, quick as lightning the suspicion flashed across the young man's mind that Petronius had tricked him, thinking either to curry new favors from Nero by giving him Lygia, or to keep the girl for himself. That any man could have once seen Lygia and not desired her for himself, he could not have even imagined. Quick-tempered like other members of his family, Vinitius experienced a paroxysm of rage that deprived him of his reason and carried him away like a wild horse.

"General," he cried in a broken voice, "go home and wait for me. Know that were Petronius my own father, I would revenge myself on him for this insult against Lygia. Go home and await me. Neither Petronius nor Caesar shall have her." Turning to the draped wax statues in the courtyard, he shook his fist and exclaimed, "By the faces of the departed, rather would I kill her and myself!"

Then he repeated, "Wait for me," and running from the courtyard, flew like a madman to Petronius, thrusting pedestrians aside on the way.

Aulus returned home somewhat hopeful that if Petronius had persuaded Caesar to take Lygia away to give her to Vinitius, Vinitius would return her to her foster parents. He was also consoled by the reflection that if he should not succeed in saving Lygia, the insult to her would be avenged by death. He believed Vinitius would fulfill his promises. He was witness to his rage, and he knew the reputation the family had for volatility. Aulus himself, though he loved Lygia as a father, would rather kill her than give her to Caesar, and but for the fear of injuring his son (the last of the old line) he would certainly have done so. Aulus was a soldier and knew of the Stoics only by report; nevertheless he was not unlike them in character: He preferred death to disgrace.

When he reached home he pacified Pomponia, telling her of his hopes, and both waited anxiously for news from Vinitius. At intervals, when the approaching steps of the slaves were heard in the hall, they imagined that Vinitius had come, bringing them their beloved girl, and from the bottom of their hearts they were ready to bless both of them. But time passed, and no news came. Not till evening was a hammer stroke heard on the gate.

A slave delivered a note to Aulus. The old general, although he loved to display his self-control, took the letter with trembling hands and began to read as eagerly as if the fate of his whole house was involved. Suddenly, his face grew dark, as if shadowed by an approaching cloud.

"Read," he commanded, turning to Pomponia.

Pomponia took the letter and read: "Marcus Vinitius greets Aulus Plautius. What has been done was done by Caesar's will, before which you must bow your head, even as do Petronius and I."

A long silence followed.

Chapter VI

Petronius was at home. The *atriensis* did not dare to stop Vinitius, who broke into the atrium like a tempest. Learning that the master of the house was in the *bibliotecha*,[1] he rushed into that room. Finding Petronius writing, Vinitius snatched the reed from his hands, broke it, and threw it on the floor.

Then he laid his hand upon Petronius's shoulders and, thrusting his face into his uncle's, cried in a hoarse voice, "What have you done with her? Where is she?"

Then an astonishing thing happened. The elegant and indolent Petronius seized the young athlete's hand that was grasping his shoulder, then seized the other hand, and holding both in his one hand with the grip of an iron vise, he said, "I am weak only in the morning, but in the evening I regain my former strength. Try to escape. A weaver must have taught you gymnastics, and a blacksmith manners."

He said this without any sign of anger, but in his eyes there was a hint of boldness and energy. After a few moments he dropped the hands of Vinitius, who stood before him, humbled, abashed, yet with furious rage in his heart.

"You have a hand of steel," said the younger man, "but by all the infernal gods, if you've betrayed me, I'll put a knife into your throat, even though I should have to do it in the chambers of Caesar."

"Let's talk calmly," replied Petronius. "Steel, as you see, is stronger than iron; therefore, though from each of your arms both of mine could be made, I'm not afraid of you. On the contrary, I grieve over your rudeness, and if human ingratitude could astonish me, I should be astonished at your ingratitude."

"Where is Lygia?"

"In a house of ill-repute; in other words, in the house of Caesar."

"Petronius!"

"Calm yourself. Sit down. Caesar promised to fulfill two requests of

---

1 Library.

mine: first, to get Lygia out of the house of Aulus, and second, to give her to you. Did you conceal a knife in the folds of your toga? It's possible to stab me, but I advise you to postpone the attempt for a few days; otherwise you'd be thrown into prison, and in the meantime, Lygia would grow lonesome in your house."

Silence ensued. For some time Vinitius looked at Petronius with astonished eyes; then at last he said, "Pardon me. I love her—love blinds my mind."

"Look at me, Marcus. The day before yesterday, I said to Caesar, 'My nephew has fallen so deeply in love with a slender girl in the house of Aulus that his house has been turned by his sighs into a steam bath. Neither you,' said I to Caesar, 'nor I, who understand what real beauty is, would give for her a sestertium, but that lad has always been sort of stupid, and now he's lost his mind entirely.'"

"Petronius!"

"If you don't understand that I said it with the purpose of protecting Lygia, I'm prepared to think that I said the truth. I told Ahenobarbus that a man of his aesthetic tastes could not consider such a girl beautiful. Nero, who so far has not dared to look otherwise than through my eyes, will not find beauty in her. I had to guard her from that monkey and draw him on a cord. Not he, but Poppaea, will discover Lygia's charm and beauty now, and believe me, Poppaea will waste no time in evicting her from the palace.

"Furthermore, I said to Caesar with apparent reluctance, 'Take Lygia and give her to Vinitius. You have the right to do it because she's your hostage; and if you take her, you'll greatly offend Aulus.' So he agreed. He has no reason not to, especially as I gave him the opportunity to inflict suffering on decent people. You'll be appointed official guardian over her. Thus this Lygian treasure will be committed into your hands. Surely you, as an ally to the brave Lygians and a true servant to Caesar, will not waste any of the treasure, but will strive to increase it. Caesar, to preserve appearances, will retain her a few days in his house, and then he will send her to your *insula*.[2] Fortunate man!"

"Is that true? Does nothing threaten her in Caesar's house?"

"Should she have to stay there permanently, Poppaea would mention her name to the poisoner, Locusta, but for a few days she can remain in safety. In Caesar's house live ten thousand people. Nero may not see her at all, which is the more likely because he has left the matter entirely in

---

2   Literally means "island," but in this instance it refers to Vinitius's home.

my hands. Only a few moments ago, a centurion came to me with the information that the maiden had been taken into the palace and delivered into the hands of Acte. Acte is kind and good, and that's why I directed that Lygia be entrusted to her guardianship. Pomponia Graecina evidently thinks the same, as she has sent Acte a letter. There will be a feast tomorrow in Nero's house. I've secured a place for you near Lygia."

"Caius!"[3] said Vinitius. "Forgive my hot temper. I assumed that you'd ordered her to be taken away for yourself or for Caesar."

"I can forgive your temper, but it's more difficult to forgive your rude manners, indecent shouts, and your voice reminding one of players at *mora* games. I like it not, Marcus; and in the future mend your ways. Know that Caesar's pander is Tigellinus. Know also that if I desired this maiden for myself, I would look straight into your eyes and say, 'Vinitius, I've taken Lygia from you, and I'll keep her until I weary of her.'"

With these words he fastened his nutlike eyes on the eyes of Vinitius with a cold and almost insolent expression. The young tribune was utterly abashed.

"The fault is all mine," he said. "You are both good and magnanimous, and I thank you with my whole soul. . . . But please permit me one more question: Why didn't you command that Lygia be brought directly to my house?"

"Because Caesar must preserve appearances. People in Rome will talk about this—that we removed Lygia as a hostage; thus she must remain in Caesar's palace until the talk ceases. Then we shall remove her quietly to your house, and the matter ends. Ahenobarbus is a cowardly whelp. He knows that his power is unlimited, yet he tries to give a color of decency to all his actions. Have you recovered your senses enough to view the situation objectively? Good! I've repeatedly sought to explain why it is that crime—no matter how powerful and secure be the transgressor, as for instance Caesar—invariably tries to justify itself by law, justice, and virtue. Why take the trouble? In my opinion, to murder a brother, a mother, or a wife is an act worthy only of a petty Asiatic king—not of a Roman emperor. But had I done any of these things, I should not write letters of justification to the Senate. Nevertheless, Nero *does* write. He's striving to justify his crimes because he's a coward. On the other hand, Tiberius was not a coward, yet he too always strove to justify himself. Why is this? What a

---

3 Another of Petronius's names.

strange, involuntary homage vice pays to virtue! And do you know what I think? I think it is so because transgression is ugly, and virtue is beautiful. Ergo, a genuine man of taste is also virtuous. Ergo, I am virtuous. Today will I make a libation of wine to the shades of Protagoras,[4] Prodictus, and Gorgias. That proves that Sophists too can be of service. Listen, I'm not through yet. I took Lygia from the Auli to give her to you. Ah, Lysippus would have made marvelous groups[5] of you two! Both of you are beautiful; consequently what I've done is beautiful. Being beautiful, it cannot be evil. Look, Marcus, for before you sits Virtue personified in Caius Petronius! Were Aristides[6] alive, it would be his duty to come to me for a condensed treatise on virtue and pay me a hundred minas[7] for it."

But Vinitius, who was more occupied with reality than with any philosophical treatise on virtue, answered, "I'll see Lygia tomorrow, and after that she'll spend every day in my house, ceaselessly till death."

"You'll have Lygia, and I'll have Aulus on my neck because of you. He'll call down the vengeance of all the gods of the netherworld upon me. Would that the lisping creature would at least take lessons in declamation as a preparation! However, he'll rail against me as my old *atriensis* used to rail against my followers—I banished him to the country."

"Aulus has been to see me. I promised to send him news of Lygia."

"Write him that the will of the godlike Caesar is the law of the gods, and that you'll name your first son Aulus: We must give him some consolation. I'm ready to ask Ahenobarbus to invite Aulus to the banquet. Let him have the pleasure of seeing you next to Lygia!"

"No, don't do that," replied Vinitius. "I feel sorry for them both—especially Pomponia."

Then Vinitius sat down to write the letter that was to deprive the old general of his last hope.

---

4 A famous Athenian Sophist immortalized by Socrates in his *Dialogue of Plato*, which closes with this conclusion: Virtue is knowledge. All three—Protagoras, Prodictus, and Gorgias—were participants in the work.

5 Sculptured groups.

6 Athenian statesman (530-468 B.C.). Aristides as public treasurer accused Themistocles of mishandling public monies; even though the accusation was true, Aristides barely escaped with his life. Later on, having learned his lesson, he closed his eyes to pilfering of the public purse and was loudly praised for this, especially by the pilferers. Then he came to the Athenian populace and said, "I'm more ashamed of the present honor than I was of the former disgrace."

7 Greek coin.

Chapter VII

Before Acte, the former favorite of Nero, even the proudest heads in Rome had once bowed. But even then she had shown no desire to interfere in questions of state. And if sometimes she used her influence over the young emperor, it was only to implore mercy on someone's behalf. Quiet and unassuming, she won the gratitude of many, the enmity of none. Not even Octavia had been able to hate her. Even those who were envious of her admitted that she was incapable of harming anyone. All knew that Acte still cherished a sad, painful passion for Nero, a love sustained not by hope but by the remembrance of a time when Nero was not only younger and more devoted, but was also a better man. It was known that she dwelt only in these memories and expected nothing of the future. And as there was no fear that Caesar would return to her, Acte was regarded as an inoffensive being and consequently was troubled by no one. Poppaea looked upon her merely as a quiet servant, so harmless that she didn't even insist upon her expulsion from the palace.

Out of regard for his former love, and because he had separated from Acte without a quarrel and almost in a friendly fashion, Nero did not deny her a certain respect. When he terminated his relationship with her, he allowed her to remain in the palace and gave her special apartments with a few servants to attend her. And as in their day Pallas and Narcissus—though they were made freedmen by Claudius—were not only invited to that emperor's feasts but, as persons of influence, occupied places of honor, so Acte was sometimes bidden to Caesar's table. Possibly this was done because of her beautiful figure, which was a real ornament to the banquet. But, in fact, in his choice of table companions, Nero had long since ceased to be guided by any considerations of propriety. An impressive variety of persons of all classes and occupations assembled at his feasts, among them senators—especially those who were ready to play the fool; there were also patricians, both young and old, eager for pleasure, luxury, and debauchery. These orgies were attended also by women who,

53

although they bore distinguished names, were not above donning discolored wigs at night and seeking adventures in the dark streets. Beside the eminent senators reclined priests who, at full goblets, found pleasure in ridiculing their own gods. Here thronged a motley multitude of singers, mimics, actors, musicians, dancers of both sexes, poets who thought only of the sesterces that might be thrown to them while reciting verses praising Caesar's verses; underfed philosophers, following with greedy eyes the dishes as they were passed around; famous charioteers, jesters, storytellers, and buffoons—every kind of parasitical knave and cheat brought into momentary notoriety by fashion or folly. Among them were many whose long hair concealed ears that had been pierced, revealing their former slavery.

The most distinguished guests partook of the feast with Caesar; the remainder furnished them with amusement while they ate, eagerly waiting for the moment when the servants would allow them to fall upon the remnants of meat and drink. Such guests were supplied by Tigellinus, Vatinius, and Vitelius, who were frequently obliged to also provide them with clothes befitting Caesar's palace. Feeling more at home in it, the emperor liked society of this kind. The splendor of the court covered this rabble as if it were gilded and illuminated by its brilliance. The high and the low; descendants of glorious families and the scum of the city pavements; famous artists and miserable scrapings of talent, all thronged to the palace to sate their dazzled eyes with a splendor almost surpassing human understanding and to approach the giver of every favor, wealth, and property, whose single glance might, it's true, abase, but might also elevate to immeasurable heights.

And now the day had come when Lygia must take part in such a feast. Fear, uncertainty, agitation, and a dazed feeling, quite natural after such a sudden change in her surroundings, contended in her heart with a wild desire to show resistance. She feared Nero, she feared the people, she feared the palace—whose uproar took away her presence of mind—she feared the feasts whose shamefulness and indecency she had heard of from Aulus, Pomponia Graecina, and their friends. In spite of her youth, Lygia knew what vice was, for in those days knowledge of evil came to children early. She knew that ruin threatened her in the palace. Pomponia had warned her of this when they parted. Having a pure young soul, filled with a lofty faith that was instilled in her by her adopted mother, she determined to defend herself against evil, strengthened by her divine

Teacher, whom she had come to love and trust with her half-child heart, because of the sweetness of His teachings, the bitterness of His death, and the glory of His resurrection.

Assured that neither Aulus nor Pomponia Graecina would now be responsible for her actions, Lygia began to consider whether it wouldn't be better to resist and not go to the feast. On one side, fear and alarm had spoken loudly in her soul; on the other, a desire to display a courage and firmness that might result in torture and death. Had not the divine Teacher so commanded? Did He not Himself give the example? Pomponia had also told her that the most ardent of believers desire with all their souls such a trial and pray for it. While still in Aulus's house, Lygia at times cherished such a desire. She sometimes imagined herself a martyr with wounds on her hands and snow-white feet, transcendently beautiful and borne by white angels into the blue sky. And such visions delighted her imagination. In this there was much that was childish and also something of vanity, which Pomponia discouraged. But now when resistance to Caesar's will would be followed by severe punishment, and the fancied tortures might be turned into realities, there was added to these imaginary tortures a curiosity mingled with fear to know exactly how they would punish and what tortures they'd invent for her.

When Lygia told Acte what was in her heart, Acte stared at her, as astonished as though she had heard the voice of one in delirium. Disobey Caesar's will? Expose oneself at the very outset to his rage? Only a child incapable of understanding what she is doing could act thus. From what Lygia herself had said, it was clear that she was no longer a hostage, but a girl forsaken by her own people. No international law protected her, and even if she had the protection, Caesar was powerful enough in a fit of rage to trample on it. It had pleased Caesar to take her, thus he could dispose of her as he wished. Henceforth she was in his power, a power greater than any other in the world.

"Put your mind to rest on this point," said Acte persuasively to the young girl. "I've also read the letters of Paul of Tarsus; I also know that above the earth is God and a Son of God who rose from the dead—but on the earth Caesar alone rules. Remember this, Lygia. I know that your creed doesn't permit you to become what I was, and that to you as to the Stoics, of whom Epictetus has spoken to me, one is authorized to choose only death when one must choose between death and shame. But how can you know that death, not shame, threatens you? Perhaps you haven't heard of the daughter of Sejanus. She was a virgin, but at the command of Tiberius she had to pass through infamy before her death, in order to comply with the law, which prohibits the execution of virgins. Lygia! Lygia! Don't anger Caesar. When the decisive moment comes, when you must choose between dishonor and death, then act as your faith commands, but don't voluntarily seek your ruin, and don't for a trivial cause irritate an earthly, but at the same time, cruel divinity."

Acte spoke with deep pity and even exaltation. Being nearsighted, she put her gentle face close to Lygia's to see if her words had any effect.

Lygia, with the trustfulness of a child, threw her arms around Acte's neck and exclaimed, "How good you are, Acte!"

Moved by the girl's praise and confidence, Acte pressed her to her bosom. Then freeing herself from Lygia's embrace, she answered, "My happiness and my joy have passed, but I'm not wicked."

She began to move with rapid steps about the room and to speak bitterly as if to herself. "No, and *he* wasn't wicked, either. He considered himself a good man and wanted to be good. I know that better than anyone. All this came afterward—when he stopped loving. Others have made him what he is. Yes, others and . . . Poppaea."

Her eyes filled with tears. For some time Lygia followed her with her soft blue eyes. Finally she said, "Are you sorry for him, Acte?"

"I'm sorry for him," answered the Greek woman in a low voice. And she resumed her walk, her face overshadowed by sadness, wringing her hands as if in pain, her face devoid of all hope.

Lygia continued to probe timidly, "Do you still love him, Acte?"

"I still love him." Then she added, "No one loves him but me."

There followed a moment of silence, in which Acte struggled to suppress the emotions aroused by the memory.

When finally her face resumed its usual expression of repressed grief, she said, "Let's talk about you, Lygia. Drop the idea of resisting Caesar's will. It would be madness. Above all, calm yourself. I know all about this house, and I believe no danger threatens you at Caesar's hands. Had he commanded that you be abducted for himself, you wouldn't have been brought to the Palatine Palace. Poppaea is mistress here, and since she bore him a daughter, Nero is more than ever under her control. Although it was Nero who gave the order that you should attend the feast, he has neither seen nor inquired about you—consequently, he cares nothing for you. Perhaps he took you away from Aulus and Pomponia merely to spite them. Petronius asked me to take care of you, and as you know, Pomponia asked the same in her letter—undoubtedly they must have talked the case over together. Perhaps he did so at her request. If so, if Petronius at Pomponia's request takes you under his protection, nothing can befall you. Who knows? He may even have asked Nero to send you back to Aulus's house. I don't know whether Caesar loves him overmuch, but I can assure you Caesar rarely disagrees with him."

"Ah, Acte," answered Lygia, "Petronius was at our house just before I was carried away, and my mother is convinced that Caesar demanded my surrender at his instigation."

"If that is true, one ought, to be afraid," said Acte.

After a moment's thought, she continued. "Perhaps at a supper Petronius unwittingly mentioned in Nero's presence that there was a Lygian hostage in Aulus's house, and Nero, who guards his prerogatives jealously, demanded that they surrender you for the simple reason that hostages belong to Caesar. Besides, he doesn't like Aulus and Pomponia. No, I doubt whether Petronius would have resorted to such a method had he wished to take you from Aulus's house. I don't say that Petronius is better than the others that surround Caesar, but he *is* different from them. Finally, isn't there anyone who would intercede for you? Did you become acquainted at Aulus's with any of those near to Caesar?"

"I happened to see Vespasian and Titus."

"Caesar likes them not."

"And Seneca."

"It's enough that Seneca advises, for Caesar to do the opposite."

At this juncture, lovely Lygia began to blush, and she spoke hesitantly. "And Vinitius?" she asked.

"I don't know him."

"He's just returned from Armenia and is a relative of Petronius's."

"Do you suppose that Nero favors him?"

"Vinitius is liked by everyone."

"And would he wish to intercede for you?"

"Yes."

Acte, smiling tenderly, said, "Then you'll undoubtedly see him at the feast. At all events, you *must* be there. Only a child like you could think otherwise. Besides, if you wish to return to Aulus's house, then you'll have an opportunity to ask Petronius and Vinitius to intercede for you and gain permission for you to return home. If they were here, both would assure you that it would be madness and ruin to attempt resistance. Caesar, we may suppose, might not notice your absence, but if he did notice it and thought you had dared to disobey his will, nothing could save you, Lygia! Do you hear the noise in the palace? The sun is near setting, and the guests will begin to arrive soon."

"You're right, Acte," answered Lygia. "I'll follow your counsel."

Probably Lygia could not herself explain how much her decision was influenced by the desire to see Vinitius and Petronius, apart from a womanly curiosity to be present at least once in her life at such a feast, to see Caesar and the court and the famous Poppaea and the other beauties and all the luxury concerning which wonders were told in Rome. But Acte was right, and the girl acknowledged it. Go to the feast she must. Lygia no longer hesitated; necessity and common sense had united themselves to this hidden temptation.

Acte took her to her private *unctorium* to anoint and dress her. Although there was no lack of slave women in Caesar's house, and although Acte had many servants of her own, she decided out of sympathy for the girl whose innocence and beauty had touched her, to dress her herself. In spite of her bereavement and her admiration for the letters of Paul of Tarsus, it was evident that this young Greek woman had retained the old Hellenic spirit that set physical beauty above anything else in the world. As she undressed Lygia, she could not refrain from expressing her delight at the lines of her figure, at once delicate and full, as if created from a mass of roses and mother-of-pearl. Stepping back a few paces she gazed with rapture on that matchless springlike form.

"Lygia," she finally exclaimed, "you're a hundred times more beautiful than Poppaea!"

Brought up strictly in Pomponia's house, where a modest reserve was observed even when the women were alone, the girl stood beautiful as a charmed dream, harmonious as a work of Praxiteles or a poem, but embarrassed and blushing from mortification like a rose, her knees pressed together, her hands covering her breasts, her eyes closed. Finally, raising her arms with a sudden movement, she pulled out the pins that held her hair, and with one shake of her head, she covered herself with it as with a mantle.

Approaching and touching her dark hair, Acte said, "Oh, what wonderful hair you have! I won't sprinkle it with golden powder, for where the braids overlap it gleams itself like gold. Only here and there I'll sprinkle a little on, but lightly, lightly, as if a ray had freshened it. Wonderful must be your Lygian country where such maidens are born!"

"I don't remember it," answered Lygia. "But Ursus has told me that there's nothing there but forests, forests, forests."

"But flowers bloom in the forests," said Acte as she dipped her hand in the vase filled with verbena and moistened Lygia's hair with it.

After finishing this task, Acte anointed Lygia's entire body with perfumed oils from Arabia, and when she had finished, Acte put upon her a soft, gold-colored, sleeveless tunic, over which was to go the *peplum*. But since it was necessary to first comb her hair, she wrapped her in a loose garment called a *synthesis* and, seating her in an armchair, gave her for a time into the hands of slave women, then stepped aside to observe the process from a distance. Two women put white sandals embroidered with purple onto her feet, fastening them to the alabaster ankles with golden laces drawn crosswise. When at last the combing was over, they put upon her a *peplum* with beautiful soft folds. Then Acte, when she had hung pearls about Lygia's neck and touched her hair with gold powder, gave orders to begin her own toilet, all the while not ceasing to gaze rapturously at Lygia.

But she was soon ready, and by the time the first litter arrived at the main gate, Lygia and Acte entered from the side *criptoportium*[1] from which might be seen the chief entrance and the inner galleries and courtyard surrounded by porticos of Numidian marble.

Gradually, more and more people passed under the lofty arch of the gate over which the beautiful four-horse chariot of Lysias seemed to bear Apollo and Diana into space. Lygia was astounded by the magnificence of the scene, of which the modest house of Aulus could give her no conception. The last rays of the setting sun illumined the yellow Numidian marble, which in those gleams shone like gold and, at the same time, changed into a rosy color. Under the columns near the statues of the Danaides, of gods and heroes, passed a throng of men and women, themselves resembling statues draped in their togas, state robes, and gowns that fell with grace and beauty to the earth in soft folds, on which glowed the light of the setting sun. The gigantic Hercules, with his head still in light, yet from the chest down sunk in shadows cast by the columns, looked down on the multitude from aloft.

Acte pointed out to Lygia the senators in broad-bordered togas and colored tunics, with crescents embroidered on their sandals; knights,

---

1 Side portico.

patricians, and famous artists; Roman ladies dressed in Roman, Greek, or
fantastic Oriental costumes, with their hair arranged in the form of towers
or pyramids or combed after the fashion of the statues of the goddesses—
low on the head and ornamented with flowers. Many of the men and
women Acte identified by name, adding to their names short and sometimes terrible stories, which filled Lygia with fear, admiration, or amazement. A strange world opened before her; its beauty enchanted her eyes,
but her young mind could not grasp the contradictions it presented. In
the purple sunset of the sky, in those rows of motionless columns vanishing in the distance, and in those statuelike people there was a certain
grand repose. It seemed that among those marbles of straight lines, half-
gods might live free of care, at peace and happy.

Meanwhile, Acte's low voice revealed new and terrible secrets of the
palace. There in the distance was a portico, its columns and pavement still
spotted with the blood that splashed upon the white marble when
Caligula fell under the knife of Cassius Cheraea;[2] there was his wife killed,
and there his child's head was smashed against a stone; under that wing a
dungeon is hidden in which the younger Drusus[3] gnawed his hand
because he was starved to death; there the elder Drusus was poisoned, and
there Gemellus writhed in terror; there Claudius[4] died in convulsions; and
here Germanicus[5] suffered—everywhere, these walls have heard the cries

---

2 Slain in A.D. 41 by this centurion of the Praetorian Guard.

3 Drusus Caesar (born around 13 B.C. and died A.D. 23), son of Emperor Tiberius and
   Vipsania.   As heir apparent to the throne, he lived an exceedingly dissolute life.
   Tiberius's wife Livilla, in conjunction with her lover Sejanus (commander of the
   Praetorian Guard), who coveted the throne himself, had Drusus imprisoned and poi-
   soned. When Tiberius found out, he ordered the death of Sejanus.

4 Roman emperor (A.D. 42–54). After executing his third and unfaithful wife
   Messalina, Claudius caused a scandal by marrying his evil niece, Agrippina, who per-
   suaded him to pass over his own son Britannicus and adopt as son and heir her son
   Nero. Claudius died suddenly in A.D. 54, poisoned by Agrippina.

5 Son of Nero Claudius Drusus and Antonia the Younger, and nephew of Emperor
   Tiberius. Of all the Romans, Germanicus Julius Caesar was the most loved, the most
   deservedly honored. He was handsome, brave, kind, and skilled in Greek and Roman
   oratory and literature. As a general, he was one of the greatest of his time. His life
   was short (15 B.C.–A.D.19). The people so adored him that his Uncle Tiberius grew
   jealous and apparently had him poisoned by secret imperial command in Antioch. By
   his wife Agrippina the Elder, he had nine children, including Agrippina the Younger,
   Nero's mother; Emperor Caligula was his son.

and groans of the dying, and these very people who are now hurrying to the feast clad in bright tunics, flowers, and jewels may be tomorrow condemned to death; on more than one face, perhaps, a smile conceals terror, uncertainty even of the next day. Perhaps at this very moment feverishness, avidity, and jealousy are gnawing into the hearts of these crowned half-gods, apparently free from care.

Agitated, Lygia's frightened thoughts could not keep pace with Acte's commentary. Thus, while this strange world more and more delighted her eyes, terror oppressed the girl's heart, and her soul was suddenly filled with an inexpressible, boundless longing for her beloved Pomponia Graecina, for Aulus's peaceful home, where ruled not crime, but love.

Meanwhile the throng of invited guests continued to pour in from the Apollinis Quarter. The uproar and the cries of those who escorted their patrons could be heard from behind the gate. The courtyard and the colonnades swarmed with Caesar's slaves—men and women and small boys—and Praetorian soldiers who were guarding the palace. Here and there among the white and swarthy could be seen the black faces of the Numidians wearing their feathered helmets and large gold rings in their ears. Kitharas and, despite the lateness of the autumn, bunches of hothouse flowers, and hand lamps of gold, silver, and copper were carried by. The ever-increasing hum of voices mingled with the splashing of the fountain, whose roseate jets of water fell and broke on the marble flagging with a sound as of sobbing.

Acte ceased to speak, but Lygia continued to stare about her as if searching for someone in the crowd. Suddenly her face was covered with a blush. From among the columns appeared Vinitius and Petronius. Beautiful, calm as gods in their white togas, they walked into the great *triclinium.* To Lygia, discovering these two known and friendly faces—especially that of Vinitius—among these strange people, it seemed that a great weight suddenly fell off her heart. She felt less alone. The great longing for Aulus's house that a moment before had overwhelmed her, all at once ebbed away. The desire to see Vinitius and to talk with him drowned out all other voices within her. In vain did she remember all the evil that she had heard of Caesar's house, Acte's words and Pomponia's warnings; in spite of everything she had heard she now felt that she should go to the feast, not only because she must, but also because she wished to, for the simple reason that she would soon hear the dear and charming voice that spoke to her of love and happiness fit for the gods, that still sounded like music in her ears. At the very thought, her heart fluttered with joy.

But suddenly she became afraid of that joy, for it seemed that she was thereby being false to those plain, simple teachings in which she had been brought up, as well as to Pomponia Graecina and to herself. To go to the feast of necessity, and to be glad that such necessity exists, were two quite different things. She felt guilty, sinful, ruined. Despair seized her; tears came into her eyes. Had she been alone she would have knelt down and beaten her breast as she repeated, "I'm guilty; I'm guilty." But Acte, seizing her by the arm, led her through the interior apartments to the grand *triclinium* where the banquet was to take place, and it dimmed her eyes, it roared in her ears from internal emotions, and the beating of her heart stopped her breath. She saw as in a dream the thousands of lamps gleaming on the tables and the walls; as in a dream she heard the shouts that greeted Caesar, whom she saw as through a mist. The shouting deafened her; the bright light blinded her; the perfumes intoxicated her, and in her bewilderment she barely noticed Acte as she seated her at the table and sat beside her.

But after a moment, a low, known voice called to her from the other side: "I greet you, fairest of earthly maidens and of the skies. I greet you, divine Callina."

Lygia, recovering herself somewhat, looked around. At her other side was Vinitius.

He was without his toga, as both convenience and custom required that it be laid aside before the feast. He was dressed simply in a sleeveless scarlet tunic embroidered in silver palms. His shoulders were bare, ornamented in Oriental fashion with two broad, golden shoulder bands wound above the elbows. From his forearms the hair had been carefully removed—smooth but exceedingly muscular they were, the arms of a seasoned warrior, made for the sword and shield. On his head he wore a garland of roses. With his eyebrows meeting across his brow and his beautiful eyes and smooth complexion, he was the personification of youth and vigor. His beauty so impressed Lygia that though the confusion she had at first felt had vanished, she was scarcely able to answer.

"I greet you, Marcus."

"Happy are my eyes that behold you," he said, "happy my ears that hear your voice, more delightful to me than the notes of flute or kithara. If I were ordered to choose who should sit at my side—you or Venus— you would I choose, my divine maiden."

Vinitius gazed at her as if hurrying to satiate his eyes with her beauty; he consumed her with his gaze. His glance glided from her face to her neck and her bare arms and lingered lovingly on the beauty of her figure; he admired her, enfolded her, devoured her, but with his desire there was mingled happiness, admiration, and ecstasy.

"I knew that I'd meet you in Caesar's house," he continued. "Nevertheless, when I saw you, such joy filled my soul that I felt as if I'd fallen upon an unexpected fortune."

Lygia, having recovered herself somewhat, and feeling that in that throng and in that house, he was the only being near her, began to converse with him and to inquire about everything that frightened or perplexed her. How did he know that he would see her at Caesar's house? And why was she brought here? Why did Caesar take her away from Pomponia? She was frightened here and wanted to go home. She should die of anxiety and yearning but for the hope that he and Petronius would intercede for her with Caesar.

Vinitius explained that he'd learned of her having been carried away from Aulus himself. He didn't know why she'd been brought here. Caesar didn't account for his actions or his orders to anyone. But she must have no fear, for he, Vinitius, was at her side and would remain by her. He'd rather lose his sight than not see her; he'd rather give up his life than desert her. She had become his soul; therefore he would guard her as his own soul. He would build in his house an altar to her as to a divinity, and he would offer myrrh and aloes and, in the springtime, apple blossoms and early flowers. If she were afraid to stay in Caesar's house, he could assure her she would not remain there.

Although he spoke evasively and at times prevaricated, yet there was a ring of truth in his words because his feelings for her were sincere. He truly pitied her, and her words penetrated his soul so, that when she began to thank him and assure him that Pomponia would love him for his kindness, and that she herself would be grateful to him all her life, he could not master his emotion, and it seemed to him that never in his life would he be able to resist her prayer. His heart began to melt within him. Her beauty intoxicated his senses, and he desired to possess her, but he was conscious that she was also very dear to him and that, like a goddess, he might do homage to her. Besides, he felt an uncontrollable desire to talk of her beauty and of his love for her. As the noise of the feast increased, he drew nearer to her and began to whisper words of tenderness and flattery, which, coming from the depths of his soul, had the sound of music and the intoxication of wine.

And he intoxicated her. Surrounded by these strangers, he seemed ever nearer and ever dearer to her, and deserving of her complete devotion and confidence. He soothed her, he promised to rescue her from Caesar's house, he promised that he would not leave her and would fulfill her wishes. He had, moreover, in Aulus's house spoken of love and the happiness it could bring. Now he confessed frankly that he loved her, and that she was dearer to him than all others. For the first time in her life, Lygia heard words like these from a man. The more she listened, the more she felt that something that had been slumbering in her was waking, and that her whole being was flooded by a happiness she could not explain—a happiness in which boundless joy mingled with boundless apprehension. Her cheeks began to burn, her pulse to race; her lips parted with wonder. Though she was alarmed at hearing such avowals, she could not reconcile herself to losing a single word. At times she dropped her eyes, at times she turned her radiant face towards Vinitius timidly, as if beseeching him to say on. The noise of conversation, the music, the perfume of the flowers, the Arabian scents—all intoxicated her. It was the habit in Rome to recline at the table, but at home Lygia occupied a place between Pomponia and little Aulus. Now at her side was reclining Vinitius, young, immense, enamored, burning, and she—aware that he was consumed with passion for her—felt at once shame and pleasure. A delicious weakness possessed her; a kind of faintness and forgetfulness overcame her—it was as though she were falling into a dream.

His face grew pale, his nostrils dilated like those of an Arabian steed. It was evident that his heart was beating with unusual force under his tunic; his breath came short and heavy, and his voice was broken. For the first time he felt how near he was to her. His thoughts became confused; in his veins raged a fire that he had in vain tried to extinguish with wine. It was not wine that intoxicated him, but the beauty of her face, her bare arms, her girlish bosom moving under her gilt tunic, her shapely body concealed under the folds of her robe—these intoxicated him more and more.

At length he seized her by the arm, as he had already done once before at Aulus's, and drawing her near to him, whispered with trembling lips, "I love you, Callina, my divine one!"

"Marcus, let me go," said Lygia.

But still gazing at her with eyes mist-covered with passion, he continued, "My goddess, love me—"

At that instant the voice of Acte, who was reclining at the other side of Lygia, was heard saying, "Caesar is looking at you two."

A sudden anger at both Caesar and Acte possessed him. Her words had broken the charm. Even a friend's voice at such a moment would have offended him, but Acte, as he thought, had intentionally tried to interrupt his declaration of love.

Raising his head and looking over Lygia's arm at the young freed-woman, he said, malice and venom dripping from every word, "The time has passed when you used to rest near Caesar's side at banquets, and they say you're growing blind. How, then, can you see him?"

Sadly Acte answered him, "Nevertheless, I can see him. He, too, is nearsighted and is looking at you through his emerald."[6]

Everything that Nero did roused attention, even in those nearest him. Vinitius, alarmed in turn, recovered himself and fixed his gaze steadily on Caesar. As for Lygia, so overwhelmed had she been by the magnetism of Vinitius that she'd paid slight attention to the emperor, but now she turned towards Caesar her frightened and curious eyes.

Acte had told the truth. Nero, leaning on the table, with one eye closed, was holding before the other a polished round emerald that he habitually used and was looking at them. For an instant his glance met Lygia's, and the maiden's heart contracted with terror. As a child she had lived on Aulus's Sicilian estate and had heard from an old Egyptian slave woman of the dragons that dwelt in the caves of the mountains, and now it seemed to her that the green eyes of such a monster were gazing at her. Like a frightened child she grasped Vinitius's arm, and in her head fearful and quick impressions began to crowd. So *that* was he? The terrible and all-powerful Caesar? Lygia had never seen him before, but she had imagined him to be quite different. She had imagined some kind of ghastly face with malignity petrified in its features. But now she saw a large head posted on a thick neck—terrible, it's true, but almost ridiculous, for it looked like a child's head from a distance. A tunic of the amethyst color, forbidden to all other mortals except his empress, was throwing a bluish reflection upon his wide and short face. His hair was dark, dressed in a fashion originated by Otho, in four rows of curls. He had no beard, as he

---

6 Nero was famous for his emerald eyeglass, perhaps an early form of a lorgnette.

had recently sacrificed it to Jove, for which all Rome thanked him, although it was whispered discreetly that he did so because his beard, as was true of his whole family, was red. There was, however, something Olympian about his forehead, which protruded over his brows. Consciousness of supreme power was reflected in his contracted eyebrows. Under that forehead of a demigod was the face of a monkey, a drunkard, a mountebank—a face vain, ever reflecting his changing desires, swollen with fat, and notwithstanding his youthful years, sickly and foul. To Lygia, he seemed ominous, but above all, repulsive.

After a while Nero laid the emerald on the table and ceased looking at her. Then the young girl saw his blue eyes clearly. They were prominent, blinking in the strong light, glassy, without thought, like those of a dead man.

Turning to Petronius, Caesar said, "Is that the hostage with whom Vinitius is in love?"

"Yes, that's she," answered Petronius.

"What are her people called?"

"The Lygians."

"Does Vinitius consider her beautiful?"

"Dress a rotten olive root in a woman's peplos, and Vinitius will think her beautiful. But on your face, matchless connoisseur of beauty, already have I read your opinion of her. You don't even need to proclaim it! Yes, you're right. She is too dry, thin, a mere poppy head on a stalk, and you, O godlike aesthete, esteem the stalk in a woman, and three, four times are you right. The face alone does not mean anything. I've learned much in your company, but have not yet attained so true a vision, and I'm ready to bet Tullius Senecio his sweetheart that—although at a feast, where all are in a reclining posture and it's difficult to judge the entire figure—nevertheless you've already said to yourself, *She's too narrow in the hips.*"

"Too narrow in the hips," repeated Nero, blinking his eyes. A faint smile hovered on the lips of Petronius.

Tullius Senecio, who up to this moment had been conversing with Vestinius, or rather laughing at dreams in which Vestinius believed, now turned to Petronius, and though he had no idea of what they were talking about, broke in, saying, "You're wrong; I agree with Caesar."

"Good," answered Petronius. "I've been arguing that you have a glimmer of sense, but Caesar insists that you're an unmitigated ass."

"*Habet!*" said Caesar, laughing and turning down his thumb, as was the custom in the Circus to indicate that the gladiator had received a blow and was to be put to death.

Vestinius, thinking that the conversation pertained to dreams, exclaimed, "But I believe in dreams, and Seneca once told me that he believed in them, too."

"Last night I dreamed that I had become a vestal virgin," said Calvia Crispinilla, bending over the table.

At this, Nero clapped his hands and all followed his example, for Crispinilla had been divorced several times and was infamous throughout Rome for her debauchery.

But she was not disconcerted in the least, but calmly added, "What's there to laugh at? They're all old and ugly. Rubria alone looks like a human being, so there'd be two of us, though Rubria gets freckled in summertime."

"But admit, O pure Calvia," said Petronius, "that you could become a vestal only in dreams."

"But if Caesar commanded?"

"Then I would believe that even the most improbable dreams might come true."

"But they do come true," said Vestinius. "I can conceive that one may not believe in the gods, but how is it possible not to believe in dreams?"

"But predictions?" inquired Nero. "It was predicted once that Rome should fall and that I should reign over the entire Orient."

"Predictions and dreams are closely connected," answered Vestinius. "Once a proconsul, an utter skeptic, sent a slave to the Temple of Mopsus with a sealed letter that he forbade anyone to open. He wished to see whether the god could answer the question contained in the letter. The slave slept in the temple in order that a revelation might come to him in a dream. When he returned he related his dream as follows: 'I saw a youth bright as the sun, and he spoke but one word, "Black."' The proconsul, hearing this, grew pale, and turning to his guests, doubters like himself, he said, 'Do you know what was written in the letter?'"

Vestinius paused for a second, raised a goblet filled with wine to his lips, and began to drink.

"But what was in the letter?" asked Senecio.

"The letter contained this question: 'Which bull must I sacrifice, a white or a black one?'"

But the interest aroused by this narrative was interrupted by Vitelius, who had come to the feast drunk, and who now without reason suddenly burst into senseless laughter.

"What is that keg of tallow laughing at?" asked Nero.

"Laughter distinguishes men from animals," said Petronius, "and he can furnish no other proof that he's not a wild boar."

Vitelius suddenly stopped his laughter. Smacking his lips, greasy from fatty dishes and sauces, he looked inquiringly around among the guests as though he'd never seen them before and, raising his cushionlike hands, said in a hoarse voice, "I've lost from my finger the knightly ring that I inherited from my father."

"Who was a cobbler," added Nero.

Again Vitelius burst out in uncontrollable laughter and began searching for the ring in the robe of Calvia Crispinilla. Whereupon Vestinius began to imitate the screams of a frightened woman. And Nigidia, a friend of Calvia, a young widow with the face of a child and the eyes of a wanton, said in a loud voice, "He's searching for what he hasn't lost."

"And for what would be of no use to him, even if he should find it," finished the poet Lucan.

The uproar increased. Crowds of slaves passed around new courses every moment. From great vases, filled with snow and wreathed with ivy, smaller vessels containing various kinds of wine were brought forth. All drank freely. Upon the table and on the guests, roses fell at intervals from the ceiling.

Petronius urged Nero to ennoble the feast with his singing. A chorus of voices supported this request. Nero at first refused. It was not a question of courage alone, he explained, though it failed him always. The gods knew what the effort cost him each time he appeared before the public. But he was sustained by the consciousness that something must be done for the sake of art. Besides, if Apollo had gifted him with a voice, it was not proper to permit divine gifts to be wasted. He understood, even, that his duty to the state forbade them to be wasted. But today he was really hoarse. Last night he had placed leaden weights on his chest, but all to no avail. He was even thinking of repairing to Antium to breathe fresh sea air. Then Lucan implored him to sing in the name of art and humanity. It was known to all present that the divine poet and musician had composed a new hymn in honor of Venus, in comparison with which the hymn of Lucretius was as the howl of a yearling wolf. Let this feast be a genuine feast. So kind a ruler shouldn't inflict such a cruel disappointment on his subjects.

"Be not cruel, O Caesar."

"Be not cruel," repeated all seated near.

Nero spread out his hands as a sign that he was compelled to yield. All faces immediately assumed an expression of gratitude, and all eyes were turned towards Caesar. But first he commanded that Poppaea should be notified that he was about to sing. He informed his auditors that she had not appeared at the feast because she was indisposed. But as no medicine brought her such relief as did his singing, he would not wish to deprive her of this opportunity.

Poppaea came immediately. She ruled Nero as if he were her subject. Nevertheless, she didn't dare to wound his self-love when he appeared in the character of a singer, a charioteer, or a poet. Beautiful as a goddess, she entered the room dressed, like Caesar, in a robe of amethyst color and wearing a necklace of large pearls stolen from Massinissa. She was golden-haired and dainty. Though she'd been divorced from two husbands, she had the face and manner of a virgin.

She was received with applause and shouts of "Divine Augusta!" Lygia had never in her life seen so wondrous a beauty. She could scarce believe her eyes, for she knew that Poppaea Sabina was one of the most corrupt women in the world. She had heard from Pomponia that Poppaea had induced Caesar to murder his mother and his wife. She knew something of her terrible deeds from listening to the gossiping guests who visited Aulus. She had heard that Poppaea's statues had been overthrown at night-time in the city. She had heard of inscriptions whose authors had been condemned to severest punishment, which nevertheless still appeared every morning on the walls or buildings in the city. But in spite of all this the notorious Poppaea, who was looked upon by the Christians as the embodiment of evil and crime, appeared so sweet and beautiful to the maiden that she thought the angels in Heaven could not look more angelic than she.

Lygia could not take her eyes from the lovely vision, and an involuntary question slipped from her lips: "Oh, Marcus, can it be possible?"

But he, roused by wine and evidently impatient because her attention was distracted from him and his fervent words, retorted, "Yes, she is beautiful, but you are a hundredfold more beautiful. You don't know yourself or you would fall in love with yourself like Narcissus. Poppaea bathes in she-asses' milk, but you, I believe, Venus has bathed in her own milk. You don't appreciate your value, my sweet one. Look not at her; turn your eyes towards me, *Ocelle mi!*[7] Touch this goblet of wine with your lips, and I'll place mine on the same spot."

Then Vinitius began to push himself closer and closer to Lygia, but she moved nearer to Acte. At this moment silence was commanded because Caesar had risen. The singer Diodorus had given him a kithara of the kind called delta; Terpnos, who was to accompany Caesar, came forward with an instrument called a *nablium*.[8] Nero, resting the delta on the table, raised his eyes. A hush of silence fell in the *triclinium*, broken only by the rustle of roses as they continued to fall from the ceiling. Caesar then began to sing, or rather to declaim, his hymn to Venus, to the accompaniment of two kitharas. Neither his voice, though somewhat worn, nor his verses were bad. Lygia's conscience began to reproach her again, for the hymn, though in praise of the impure and pagan Venus, seemed beautiful to her, and Caesar himself, with a crown of laurel on his head and his eyes raised to the heavens, appeared to her more majestic and far less terrible and repulsive than at the beginning of the banquet.

The hymn was received with thunders of applause. Exclamations of "O wonderful, divine voice!" rose on all sides. Some of the women raised their hands and held them up until the end of the singing, as if they had been petrified with delight. Others wiped tears from their eyes. The entire hall buzzed like a beehive. Poppaea, bending her golden-haired head, pressed Nero's hand to her lips and held it for some time in silence. Pythagoras, a young Greek of wonderful beauty,[9] the same to whom the half-insane Nero later commanded the priests to marry him with the observance of all the rites, now knelt at his feet.

Nero, however, looked attentively at Petronius, whose praises he esteemed above all. The latter said, "As to the music, I believe that Orpheus must be at this moment as green from envy as Lucan, who is present. As for the verses, I regret that they are not worse, that I might find words fitting to praise them."

Lucan did not feel offended at being charged with envy. On the contrary, he cast a grateful glance at Petronius and, feigning ill-humor, began to murmur, "O cursed Fate, that destined me to live as a contemporary with such a poet. I might have had a place in the memory of man and on

---

7   "My heart's delight."
8   A stringed instrument with some resemblance to a harp or lyre.
9   *Not* the famous Greek philosopher.

Parnassus, but now I'm quenched like a lantern near the sun."

Petronius, who had an astonishing memory, began to repeat portions of the hymn, recite single lines, and to praise and discuss the more beautiful expressions. Lucan, as if forgetting his envy, added his ecstasy to the words of Petronius. On Nero's face were reflected delight and fathomless vanity, not only resembling stupidity, but equal to it. Nero then indicated which verses he considered the most beautiful, and finally he began to comfort Lucan, advising him not to lose heart, for though a man remains what he was born, still the honor shown by men to Jove does not exclude honors for other gods.

Then Nero rose to escort Poppaea, who being really ill, desired to withdraw. But Caesar commanded the guests not to leave their places and promised to return. In fact, he returned very shortly to stupify himself with the smoke of incense and to gaze at the further spectacles prepared for the feast by himself, Petronius, and Tigellinus.

The guests were constrained to listen to more verses and dialogues in which extravagance took the place of wit. After that, Paris, the celebrated mime, silently dramatized the adventures of Io, the daughter of Imachus. To the guests and especially to Lygia, who was unused to such spectacles, it seemed that they were beholding miracles and enchantments. Paris, by gestures of his hands and body, succeeded in expressing things that seemed impossible in a dance. His hands dimmed the air, creating a bright cloud, living, trembling with voluptuousness, encircling the half-fainting form of a maiden, thrilled with a spasm of delight. It was not a dance, but a picture, disclosing the secrets of love, bewitching and shameless. When at the end of the dance Corybantes, with a crowd of Syrian dancing girls, began a Bacchic dance of unbridled license to the accompaniment of harps, kitharas, cymbals, and tambourines, Lygia began to tremble with fear. It seemed to her that a living fire was burning her into ashes and that a thunderbolt ought to strike the palace, or that the ceiling should fall down upon the heads of the revelers.

But from the golden net fastened to the ceiling the roses were still falling, and now drunken Vinitius said to her, "I saw you at the fountain in the house of Aulus and fell in love with you. It was at dawn, and I can see you yet, though that robe conceals you from my eyes. Cast aside your *peplum*, as Crispinilla has done. Behold! Gods and men are thirsting for love. There's nothing else in the world. Lay your head on my breast and close your eyes."

The pulse beat oppressively in Lygia's hands and temples. She felt as if she were crawling into a pit, and as if Vinitius, who before had appeared so devoted and so worthy of all trust, instead of saving her was drawing her down towards the abyss. She felt angry with him. She began to fear the feast and Vinitius and herself. A voice like that of Pomponia rang imploringly in her ears: *Oh, Lygia, save yourself!* But at the same moment something told her that it was already too late, and that whoever was surrounded by such a flame, who saw all that was done at this feast, whose heart beat as hers did when she listened to the words of Vinitius, and who shivered as she did when he came near her, was lost forever. Her strength left her. It seemed to her that she must faint and that something terrible must follow. She knew that, under penalty of Caesar's wrath, no one might rise until he rose; but even had this prohibition not existed, she did not now have strength enough to leave.

It was far yet to the end of the feast. Every now and then, slaves brought on new courses and filled the goblets unceasingly with wine. On a platform there appeared two athletes to give the guests an exhibition of wrestling.

The contest began. The powerful bodies of the wrestlers, shining with olive oil, blended in one mass; bones cracked in their iron arms, their teeth gritted ominously between their set jaws. At times the quick, dull thump of their feet beat on the saffron-strewn floor; again, the athletes became motionless, silent, so that it seemed to the spectators that they saw before them a group chiseled from stone. The eyes of the Romans followed with delight the motions of terribly exerted backs, thighs, and arms. But the struggle was soon ended. Croto, the master and founder of the school of gladiators, was rightly considered the strongest man in the empire. His opponent began to breathe quickly, then his breathing became choked, his face assumed a blue tint, and finally blood spurted from his mouth, and he fell. A thunderous applause greeted the ending of the struggle. Croto, placing his feet on his opponent's breast, crossed his great arms and looked about himself with the eyes of a conqueror.

After the athletes appeared men who mimicked beasts and their voices— conjurers and buffoons, to whom little attention was paid, for wine had dimmed the eyes of the spectators. The feast gradually became a drunken and dissolute orgy. The Syrian damsels who had participated in the Bacchic dance now mingled with the guests. The music changed to wild and disordered outbursts of harps, kitharas, Armenian cymbals, Egyptian cymbals, trumpets, and horns. Some of the guests, desiring to speak, ordered the musicians to withdraw. The air was saturated with the odor of flowers and the perfume of oils, with which beautiful boys were anointing the feet of the guests; it was permeated also with the odor of saffron and the exhalations of the guests, and it became stifling. The lamps burned with a dim flame; the wreaths drooped on the heads of the guests; their perspiring faces grew pale.

Vitelius dropped under the table. Nigidia, stripping herself half naked, dropped her drunken, childish face on the breast of Lucan, who was also drunk. He began to blow the golden powder from her hair and followed, with delighted eyes, the particles as they floated upward. Vestinius, with the stubbornness of a drunkard, repeated for the tenth time the answer of Mopsus to the proconsul's sealed letter.

Tullius, who was mocking the gods, said in a voice broken by hiccups, "If the *spheros* of Xenophanes[10] is round, then such a god might be kicked along like a barrel."

But Domitius Afer, a hardened criminal and spy, was indignant at all this and, in his wrath, poured Falernian wine over Tullius's tunic. He'd always believed in the gods. People might say that Rome would perish; there were, in fact, some who said it was perishing now. And no wonder, but if this should come to pass it would be only because the youth were without faith, and without faith there can be no virtue. The stern virtues of former days having been abandoned, it never occurs to anyone that Epicureans could not stand against barbarians. And as for himself, he grieved that he lived in such times and that he was compelled to seek forgetfulness in pleasures, otherwise his grief would kill him.

After moralizing thus, he drew towards himself a Syrian dancer and showered kisses upon her neck and shoulders with his toothless mouth.

Seeing this, the consul Memmius Regulus laughed and, raising his bald head with his wreath all awry, exclaimed, "Who says that Rome is perishing? Nonsense! I, a consul, know better. The consuls are watchful. Thirty legions are guarding our *pax Romana!*"

Placing his hands upon his temples, he began to shout in a voice that filled the whole hall: "Thirty legions! Thirty legions from Britain to the Parthian boundaries!" Then suddenly he stopped, absorbed in thought, and touching his forehead with his finger said, "As I live, I think there are thirty-two."

---

10 Greek philosopher (570–480 B.C.). One of the earliest critics of ascribing human frailties to the gods, he believed in a single God.

At last he rolled under the table and was soon engaged in vomiting up flamingo tongues, roast and chilled mushrooms, locusts in honey, fish, meat, and everything that he had eaten or drunk.

But the number of the legions who guarded the safety of Rome did not pacify Domitius. "No, no!" he cried. "Rome must perish, for faith is lost, and so are the old stern virtues. Rome must perish, and it's a pity, for its life is pleasant, Caesar is the greatest of Caesars, the wine is good! Oh, how sad!" And dropping his head on a Syrian girl's shoulder he burst into tears. "What is a future life? Achilles was right—it's better to be a slave in this world, lighted by the sun, than a king in the Cimmerian gloom. Besides, it's a question still whether there be any gods, though unbelief ruins our youth."

Lucan meanwhile had blown all the golden powder from the hair of Nigidia, who had fallen into a drunken sleep. Then he took garlands of ivy from a vase before him and wound them about her, after which he looked about himself with a pleased and inquiring glance. He decked himself with ivy also and repeated in a voice of deep conviction: "I am no man, but a faun."

Petronius was not drunk, but Nero, who had drunk moderately at first to spare his divine voice, drank goblet after goblet towards the end and had become drunk. He wanted to sing more of his verses, this time in Greek, but he had forgotten them and by mistake sang an ode to Anacreon. Pythagoras, Diodorus, and Terpnos accompanied him, but as they could not keep time, they ceased. Nero, as a critic and an aesthete, was enchanted with the beauty of Pythagoras and began to kiss his hands.

Such beautiful hands, he thought, *I've seen but once, and whose were they?* Then his face blanched with terror: *They were those of my mother, Agrippina!*

Nightmarish visions followed.

"They say," he cried apprehensively, "that she wanders by moonlight along the sea around Baiae[11] and Bauli,[12] and ever she walks, walks, walks, and appears to be seeking for something. And when a boat approaches, she looks at it and disappears, but the fisherman on whom she has fixed that look dies immediately."

"Not a bad theme for a poem," said Petronius.

---

11 A town on the Campania coast, a favorite Roman resort.
12 A town between Baiae and Misenum.

Vestinius, stretching his neck like a crane, whispered mysteriously, "I believe not in gods, but I do believe in spirits. Oh!"

Nero paid no attention to their words and continued: "I celebrated the Lemuria.[13] But I have no wish to see her. It's now five years ago—I had to condemn her, for she sent an assassin to murder me, and had I not been the quicker, you would not have heard my song tonight."

"We thank you in the name of Rome and of the whole world," exclaimed Domitius Afer. "Wine! And let the tympans resound."

The uproar was renewed. Lucan, entwined with ivy, arose and began to shout, "I am not a man! I am a faun, and I live in the woods! Echo-o-o-o-o!"

Caesar was completely drunk, and so were most of the other men and women. Vinitius was no soberer than the other guests. Besides passionate desire, there arose in him a determination to quarrel. This always happened when he drank too much. His dark face paled. He stuttered when he spoke, though his voice was loud and commanding.

"Kiss me! Today, tomorrow, it's all the same. I'm tired of waiting. Caesar took you from Aulus to give you to me. Do you understand? Tomorrow, about dusk, I'll send for you. You must be mine! Kiss me! I won't wait for tomorrow. Give me your lips at once."

He attempted to embrace Lygia, but Acte defended her, and she herself resisted, exerting the remnant of her strength, for she felt she was on the brink of ruin. In vain did she attempt with both hands to remove his hairless arm; in vain did she implore him, in a voice trembling with grief and fear, to take compassion on her. Sated with wine, his breath blew about her, and his face was pressed close to hers. This was no longer the kind Vinitius, almost dear to her heart, but a foul and drunken satyr, who filled her with repulsion and fear. But she was no match for him. In vain did she writhe and turn away her face to escape his kisses. He rose and caught her in both arms, and pressing her head to his chest, he began, panting heavily, to press her paled lips to his. But at this moment, some invincible power uncoiled his arms from her neck, as easily as though they'd been the arms of a child, and shoved him aside like a dry twig or a withered leaf. What had happened? Vinitius rubbed his astonished eyes. Before him stood the gigantic figure of the Lygian, Ursus, whom he had met at the house of Aulus.

The Lygian stood calmly, but his blue eyes gazed so strangely at

---

13 A festival held in May to expel ghosts.

Vinitius that the blood congealed in the latter's veins. Then Ursus, with a measured step, quietly conducted the king's daughter out of the *triclinium*. Acte followed him.

Vinitius sat for a moment as if petrified. Then, springing towards the entrance, he shouted, "Lygia! Lygia!"

But desire, astonishment, rage, and wine combined to cut his legs from under him. Staggering, he seized the bare arm of one of the bacchanals and, with blinking eyes, asked her what had happened. She, with a smile in her eyes, handed him a goblet of wine and said, "Drink!"

Vinitius drank and fell down upon the floor.

The majority of the guests were now lying under the table. Others were walking in tottering tread through the *triclinium*, while others were sleeping on couches or on tables, snoring or vomiting up excess wine. And still, upon the drunken consuls and senators, upon the poets and philosophers, and upon the dancing damsels and patrician ladies, upon the members of a society still dominant, but whose soul was dead and whose end was near, roses fell continually from the golden net fastened to the ceiling.

It had begun to dawn outside.

Chapter VIII

No one stopped Ursus, nor did anyone even inquire what he was doing. Such guests as had not fallen under the table, no longer retained their places. Therefore, the servants, seeing the giant carrying out a guest in his arms, mistook him for a slave in charge of a drunken mistress. Moreover, Acte followed him, and her presence removed all suspicion.

Thus they made their way from the *triclinium* into the adjoining chamber, and from there into the gallery that led to Acte's room. Fighting off Vinitius had taken Lygia's last reserves; consequently she hung as if dead from the arms of Ursus. But when the cool, fresh morning air blew on her face, she opened her eyes. It was growing brighter and brighter. After they had passed along the porticoes a while, they turned to a side portico, leading out, not into the courtyard, but into the palace gardens, where the tips of the pines and the cypresses were reddening in the morning light. This section of the building was entirely empty, and the echoes of the music and sounds of the revel gradually became indistinct. It seemed to Lygia that she had been carried from Hell up into the bright light of God above. There was something else in the world then, besides that *triclinium* of horrors: There were the sky, the morning stars, light, and peace.

The maiden suddenly burst into tears. Pressing herself against the shoulder of the giant, she repeated between her sobs, "Take me home, Ursus, home to the house of Aulus."

"Let's go," answered Ursus.

They had now reached the small atrium of Acte's apartments. Ursus placed Lygia on a marble bench near a fountain while Acte strove to calm her and urged her to go to sleep. She assured her that there was no longer any danger, as the drunken guests would sleep till evening.

But Lygia could not calm herself for a long time and, pressing both hands against her temples, repeated like a child, "Let's go home to the house of Aulus. Let's go home!"

Ursus was ready to carry out her wish. Although Praetorians stood at the gates, they would not keep them from passing, for they rarely halted outgoing guests. The space before the arch was crowded with litters. Guests were now swarming out. Nobody would detain them. They could pass out with the crowd and go directly home. At any rate, he must not question: What the queen commands must be done. He was there to execute her orders.

And Lygia repeated, "Yes, yes, Ursus, let's go."

But Acte talked sense to them both. True, they could go away; nobody would detain them. But it was forbidden to flee from Caesar's house, and anyone who did so was guilty of insulting the majesty of Caesar. They might go away, but at evening a centurion would carry a sentence of death to Aulus and Pomponia Graecina, and Lygia would be brought back to the palace. Then nothing could save her. Should Aulus and his wife receive her in their house, nothing could be more certain than their death.

Lygia's arms dropped. There was no other alternative. She must choose between her own ruin or that of Plautius. In going to the banquet she had hoped that Vinitius and Petronius would intercede for her with Caesar and return her to Pomponia. Now she realized that it was they who had induced Caesar to take her away from the house of Aulus. There was no help. Only a miracle could save her from the abyss—a miracle and the power of God.

"Acte," she cried in despair, "did you hear what Vinitius said, that Caesar had given me to him, and that he would send slaves this evening to carry me to his house?"

"I heard," said Acte, and dropping her hands to her side, she became silent. The despair that expressed itself in Lygia's words found no echo in her breast. She herself had been Nero's favorite. Her heart, though sympathetic, was not able to appreciate the shame of such a relationship. A former slave, she had become too accustomed to the law of slavery. Besides, she still loved Nero. Should he desire to return to her, she would stretch out her arms to him and rejoice in her good fortune. Seeing clearly that Lygia must become the mistress of the young and handsome Vinitius or expose the family who had raised her to ruin, she could not understand how the maiden could hesitate.

"In Caesar's house," she warned, "you'll be no safer than in that of Vinitius." And it didn't occur to her that though her words were true, they meant, *Be reconciled with your lot and become Vinitius's concubine.*

Lygia, who still felt upon her lips his kisses burning with desire and glowing like coals, flushed with shame at the very remembrance. "Never!" she burst out. "Never will I remain here, nor in the home of Vinitius!"

Acte was astonished by that outburst. "Is Vinitius so hateful to you?" she questioned.

Tears so choked Lygia that she could not answer. Acte drew her to her breast and strove to soothe her. Ursus breathed heavily and clenched his enormous fists, for loving his queen with a doglike fidelity, he could not bear to see her weeping. In his wild Lygian heart arose a desire to return to the *triclinium* and strangle Vinitius and, if need be, Caesar himself; but he was afraid lest he should sacrifice his mistress in the process. Nor was he certain in his mind that such an act, which seemed to him quite natural, was entirely befitting a follower of the Crucified Lamb.

But Acte, while caressing Lygia, repeated her question: "Is he so hateful to you?"

"No," answered Lygia. "I cannot hate him because I'm a Christian."

"I know, Lygia. I learned also from the letters of Paul of Tarsus that you are forbidden to defile yourself or to fear death more than sin, but tell me, does your faith permit you to cause the death of others?"

"No."

"How, then, can you bring Caesar's vengeance on the house of Aulus?"

There was a moment of silence. The bottomless abyss yawned before Lygia again.

Then the freedwoman added, "I ask because I'm sorry for you, and because I'm sorry for Pomponia and Aulus and their son. I've lived long enough in this house to know what the wrath of Caesar means. No, you mustn't flee from here. There is but one recourse left for you: Beg Vinitius to return you to Pomponia."

But Lygia fell on her knees to implore Someone else. Ursus followed her example, and they united in prayer in the house of Caesar as the dawn broke through the windows.

Acte for the first time witnessed such a prayer. She could not tear her eyes away from Lygia, who, with profile turned towards her, with outstretched hands and eyes raised towards the sky, seemed to seek safety. The morning rays touching her dark hair and white robe were reflected in her eyes. In the glory of the dawn she seemed herself transformed by the light. In her pale face, in her parted lips, in her uplifted hands and eyes shone a

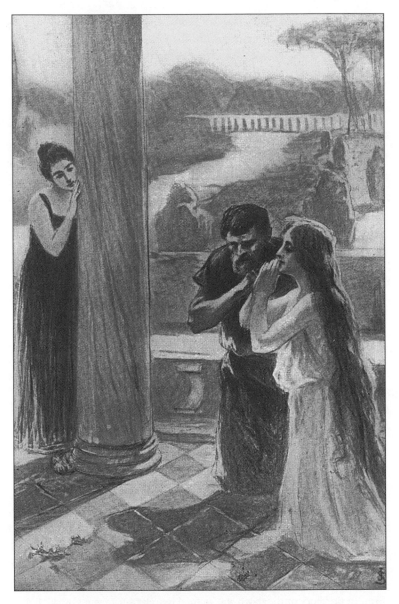

They united in prayer in the house of Caesar.

supernatural exaltation. By now Acte comprehended why Lygia could not become the concubine of any man. Before the face of Nero's former favorite the corner of a veil was drawn aside, as it were, that concealed a world entirely different from the one she knew. She was touched by that prayer offered up in that house of crime and infamy. A moment before she had felt there was no help for Lygia. Now she began to believe that some unlooked-for thing would happen, that aid would come, so powerful that Caesar himself could not resist it; that a winged army would descend from heaven to rescue the maiden, or that the sun would spread its rays under her and draw her up to itself. She had heard of many miracles that had occurred among the Christians, and Lygia's prayer somehow implied that all the stories were true.

At length Lygia rose with a face brightened by hope. Ursus rose also and, sitting on the bench, looked at his lady, waiting for her to speak.

Lygia's eyes grew misty, and two large tears rolled slowly down her cheeks. "May God bless Pomponia and Aulus," she said, "but since I mustn't expose them to danger, I'll never see them again."

Turning to Ursus, she told him that he alone was left her in the world, that he would take the place of father, guardian, and protector. They could not seek shelter in the house of Aulus, for he would thus be exposed to the wrath of Caesar. On the other hand, she could not remain in the house either of Caesar or of Vinitius. Let Ursus take her; let him conduct her out of Rome and hide her somewhere where she could not be found by Vinitius or his slaves. She would follow him anywhere, even beyond the seas, beyond the mountains to the barbarians, where the name of Rome was unheard and where the power of Caesar did not reach. Let him take her and save her, for besides him nobody was left to her.

The Lygian, in sign of his readiness and obedience, knelt and embraced her feet. Disappointment was evident on the face of Acte, who had looked for a miracle. Was it possible that this was all that would come out of the prayer? To escape from the house of Caesar was to commit a crime against his majesty. Such a crime must be avenged. Even should Lygia succeed in escaping, Caesar's wrath would fall on Aulus and Pomponia. If Lygia desired to escape, let her escape from the house of Vinitius. Then Caesar, who was averse to busying himself with the affairs of others, might not wish to help Vinitius in pursuing her. In any case, such a proceeding would not be a crime against the majesty of Caesar.

Lygia's thoughts were as follows: Aulus would not even know where she'd gone; neither would Pomponia. She would escape, not from the house of Vinitius, but on the way to it. While drunk, Vinitius had told her that in the evening he'd send his slaves for her. Undoubtedly he'd told the truth, which wouldn't have escaped him had he been sober.

It was evident that he himself, or perhaps Petronius, had spoken to Caesar and had secured his promise to deliver her on the following evening. If they forgot to send for her today, they'd send tomorrow. But Ursus would save her. He'd come and take her out of the litter as he had borne her from the *triclinium*, and together they would wander over the whole world. Ursus was invincible; not even that terrible gladiator who yesterday had wrestled at the banquet hall would be able to overcome him. But, as Vinitius might send a number of slaves, it would be better for Ursus to go at once to Bishop Linus for aid and counsel. The bishop, undoubtedly, would take compassion on her; he wouldn't leave her in the hands of Vinitius. He'd command Christians to go with Ursus to rescue her and conduct her to a place of safety. Then Ursus could take her out of the city and hide her from the power of Rome.

Her face flushed and wreathed itself in smiles; she was consoled, as though the hope of rescue had already turned into reality. Throwing herself on Acte's neck and pressing her beautiful lips to the Greek woman's cheek, she murmured, "You will not betray me, Acte, will you?"

"By the shade of my mother," answered the freedwoman, "I will not betray you. But pray to your God that Ursus may succeed in rescuing you."

The blue eyes of the giant, simple as a child's, grew bright with happiness. He had not been able to form a definite plan, though he had put all his simple mind to the task. But he would follow such orders as were given him—whether by day or by night made no difference to him. He would go to the bishop, for the bishop read in the sky what should and should not be done. Even without the bishop's aid he could summon a party of Christians. Had he not plenty of acquaintances among slaves, gladiators, and free people, both in the Suburra and beyond the mountains? He could collect a thousand or two, if need be. He would rescue his mistress, take her out of the city, and go away with her. They would go to the end of the world, even to his native land, where no one had ever heard of Rome.

Here he gazed into space, as if looking into the far distant future, and exclaimed, "To the forest! Ah, what a forest! What a forest!"

But he shook his dreams from him. Yes, he would go immediately to the bishop, and in the evening he, with a hundred followers, would watch for the litter. What difference if she be escorted by slaves or by Praetorians? Better for no man, even if clad in armor, to feel the weight of his fist. Iron is not so strong. Should he strike the iron heavily, death would enter the skull beneath.

But Lygia, raising her finger, said with childlike earnestness, "Ursus, do not kill!"

The giant put his huge fist to the back of his head and, rubbing his neck with great seriousness, began to mutter. He must rescue her—his light! She herself had said that it was now his turn. He would do his best. But if anything should happen, he would repent, he would pray to the Innocent Lamb for pardon, he would implore the mercy of the Crucified Lamb. He did not wish to offend the Lamb—but who could tell? His fists were so powerful! Infinite tenderness beamed from his face, but wishing to conceal his emotion, he knelt and said, "Now I will go to the bishop."

Acte embraced Lygia and began to weep. Again she understood that there was a world where even suffering resulted in more happiness than all the excesses and luxuries in the house of Caesar. Once more a door opened, revealing light, but at the same time she felt that she was unworthy to cross the threshold. And two tears glistened upon her drooping eyelids.

Chapter IX

L ygia was deeply grieved to lose Pomponia Graecina, whom she loved with her whole heart, and also the entire household of Aulus. Yet her grief ebbed over time. She took a certain pleasure in the very thought that she was sacrificing plenty and comfort for the Truth; that she was about to expose herself to hardships and uncertainties. Blended with this feeling was, perhaps, an alloy of childish curiosity as to what life was like in remote regions, among barbarians and wild beasts. But, for the most part, she was inspired by deep and earnest faith, convinced as she was that she was following the precepts of the divine Master, and that henceforward He would watch over her as over an obedient and faithful child. In such a case, what harm could possibly befall her? Should sufferings come, she'd endure them for His sake; should death overtake her, He would receive her. When Pomponia died, they'd be reunited forever.

Many a time in the house of Aulus she'd worried her childish brain with thoughts that she, a Christian, had made no sacrifices for the Crucified One, of whom Ursus spoke so tenderly. But now that the time had come to make those sacrifices, Lygia felt truly happy and attempted to tell Acte of her joy, but the Greek woman couldn't understand her. To leave everything behind, to abandon home, affluence, the city, gardens, temples, porticoes, all that was beautiful; to leave a sunny land, and the loved ones therein, and for what purpose? To run away from the love of a young and handsome nobleman? Acte's mind could not comprehend this. There were times when she scented some concealed purpose in Lygia's actions, perhaps some great, mysterious happiness; but the matter wasn't at all clear in her mind, especially as the dangers that threatened Lygia might take her life. Acte was naturally timid, and she thought with dread of what the evening might bring. But she didn't wish to burden Lygia with her fears. As the day was clear and the sun shone into the hall, she began to coax the maiden to rest after her sleepless night. Lygia agreed, and they entered a spacious bedchamber, whose luxurious furniture was a reminder of Acte's former relations with Caesar. Here they lay down, one near the other, but Acte, despite her weariness, couldn't sleep. She'd long been unhappy, but now she was possessed by a new uneasiness. Hitherto, her life had seemed to her merely sad and hopeless. Now, all at once, it seemed shameful.

She became more and more confused. Again the door that revealed light began to open and close. But even when it opened, her eyes, unused to the light, were dazzled, and she could distinguish nothing clearly. She divined that in the light there was unbounded happiness, compared with which all else was of small value, so that even if Caesar, for example, should set aside Poppaea and love her again, this would no longer bring her unalloyed happiness. Then the thought struck her that Caesar, whom she loved and regarded as a demigod, was in reality no better than any slave, and his palace, with its columns of Numidian marble, no better than a heap of stones. Thoughts such as these, which she could scarcely comprehend, began to torment her. She desired to sleep, but, tormented by doubts, couldn't close her eyes. Then, thinking that Lygia, threatened by so many uncertainties and perils, wouldn't be able to sleep either, she turned to speak to her of her flight, which was to take place in the evening.

But Lygia was sleeping peacefully. Into the darkened room, through a curtain not entirely drawn, stole some bright rays, in which floated golden dust motes. By the light of these rays Acte looked upon Lygia's delicate face, resting on her bare arm, her closed eyes and her lips slightly parted. She was breathing regularly.

She sleeps—she is able to sleep, thought Acte. *She is still a child.*

Nevertheless, it was now crystal clear to her that this child preferred to flee rather than to become the favorite of Vinitius, and that she preferred poverty to infamy, wandering to a luxurious house, robes, beautiful ornaments, feasts, the music of lutes and kitharas.

Why?

Acte looked more closely at Lygia, as if to read an answer in her sleeping face. She looked at her beautiful forehead, her arched eyebrows, her dark lashes, her parted lips, her heaving bosom, and thought, *How different she is from me!*

Lygia appeared a miracle to her, as some divine vision, a creation of the gods, a hundredfold more beautiful than all the flowers in Caesar's garden and all the statues in his palace. But in the Greek woman's heart there was no envy. On the contrary, at thought of the dangers that threatened the maiden, she melted into pity; a mother's love was awakened in her. Lygia appeared to her not only as beautiful as a dream, but also as very dear to her heart. Pressing her lips to the dark hair, she rained kisses upon it.

But Lygia slept on calmly, as if in her own home under the care of Pomponia, and she slept long. It was past noon when she opened her blue eyes and began to look with astonishment about the bedchamber. Evidently she was surprised that she wasn't in the house of Aulus.

"Is it you, Acte?" she asked at last, seeing in the darkness the face of the Greek woman.

"Yes, Lygia."

"Is it evening?"

"No, my child, but noon has passed."

"Hasn't Ursus returned?"

"Ursus didn't promise to return. He said that he'd watch with the Christians for the litter."

"True."

They left the *cubiculum* and went to the bath, where Acte bathed Lygia. After breakfast, the Greek woman conducted Lygia to the gardens of the palace, there being no danger, as Caesar and his guests were still asleep. For the first time in her life Lygia beheld these beautiful gardens, full of cypress, pine, oak, olive, and myrtle trees, amid which rose a profusion of white, motionless statues. Mirrorlike streams gleamed brightly; groves of roses were in bloom, sprinkled with the spray of fountains; entrances to picturesque grottoes were overgrown with ivy and vines; silver-colored swans floated on the waters; amid statues and trees wandered tame gazelles from the deserts of Africa and bright-plumed birds from all the known regions of the world.

The gardens were empty, save that here and there slaves were working, spade in hand, singing in an undertone; others, enjoying a rest, were relaxing by ponds or in the shade of groves, in quivering light produced by the sun's rays breaking through the leaves; still others were watering roses or the pale, lily-colored crocuses. Acte and Lygia walked rather long, looking at all the wonders of the gardens; and though Lygia's mind was not at ease, she was too much a child yet to resist pleasure, curiosity, and wonder. It came to her that, if Caesar were good, he might be very happy in such a palace in such gardens.

Later on, somewhat tired, the two friends sat down on a bench almost hidden by cypresses, and talked of what weighed most on their minds—Lygia's escape that evening. Acte was far less hopeful of success than Lygia. At times it seemed to her a wild and impossible venture. Her pity for Lygia increased. It seemed to her that it would be much safer to appeal to the mercy of Vinitius. She questioned Lygia as to how long she had known Vinitius and whether he might not be persuaded to return her to Pomponia. But Lygia shook her head.

"No," she said, "in the house of Aulus he was very different—he was kind. But since last night's feast I fear him, and I prefer to flee to the Lygians."

"But," inquired Acte, clearly puzzled, "in Aulus's house, he was dear to you, wasn't he?"

"Yes," answered Lygia, hanging her head.

"You're not a slave, as I was," said Acte meditatively. "Vinitius might marry you. You're a hostage and the daughter of a king. Aulus and Pomponia love you as their own child. Without doubt, they'd adopt you. Vinitius may marry you."

But Lygia answered in a low, sad voice, "I'd rather fly to the Lygians."

"Would you like for me to go to Vinitius, awaken him if he sleeps, and tell him what I've just told you? Listen, my dear, I'll go to him and say: 'Vinitius, Lygia is the daughter of a king and a beloved child of Aulus. If you love her, return her to the house of Aulus, and from that house take her as a wife.'"

But the maiden repeated, in a voice so low that Acte could scarcely hear it, "I'd rather fly to the Lygians."

Further conversation was interrupted by the sound of approaching footsteps. Before Acte could see who was coming, Poppaea Sabina made her appearance with a small retinue of female slaves. Two of them held over her head bunches of ostrich feathers fastened to golden wires. These served both to fan her and to shade her from the burning autumn sun. Poppaea, an Ethiopian woman, black as ebony, with breasts swollen from milk, bore in her arms an infant wrapped in purple fringed with gold. Acte and Lygia rose, expecting that Poppaea would pass without paying any attention to them.

But she stopped in front of them and said, "Acte, the bells you sewed on the doll were poorly fastened, and the child tore one of them off and put it into her mouth. Fortunately, Lilith noticed it in time."

"Pardon me, O divine one!" answered Acte, crossing her hands on her breast and bowing her head.

Poppaea gazed at Lygia and inquired, "What slave is this?"

"She's no slave, O divine Augusta, but a foster child of Pomponia Graecina and the daughter of a Lygian king, surrendered as a hostage to Rome."

"Has she come to visit you?"

"No, Augusta, since day before yesterday, she's been staying in the palace."

"Was she at the banquet last night?"

"She was, Augusta."

"At whose command?"

"At Caesar's command."

Poppaea gazed more attentively at Lygia. The maiden stood with bowed head, raising her bright eyes in curiosity and now dropping them again. A frown appeared on the brow of Augusta. Jealously guarding her beauty and power, she lived in constant dread lest some fortunate rival destroy her as she had destroyed Octavia. Therefore, every beautiful face that appeared in the palace roused her suspicion. With the eye of a connoisseur, Poppaea scrutinized Lygia's form, took in every feature at a glance, and became frightened. *She is a nymph*, she mused, *and Venus herself must have given her birth.* Suddenly a new thought came to her, which never before had occurred to her at the sight of a beautiful woman: the thought that she herself was growing old. Wounded vanity and alarm seized Poppaea; many fears flashed through her mind. *What might happen if Caesar met this maiden during the daytime in the sunlight? She's not a slave but the daughter of a king. A barbarian, it is true, but still a king. Immortal gods! She's as beautiful as I, and younger!* The frown on her brow deepened. Beneath their golden lashes her eyes shone with an evil light. Turning to Lygia, she asked in a calm voice, "Have you spoken with Caesar?"

"No, Augusta."

"Why do you prefer to be here rather than in the house of Aulus?"

"It wasn't my choice, lady. Petronius induced Caesar to take me from Pomponia. I'm here against my will."

"Do you wish to return to Pomponia?"

This question Poppaea asked in a softer and milder voice, and Lygia's heart throbbed with a new hope.

"Lady," she said, stretching out her hand, "Caesar promised to give me to Vinitius as a slave. Pray intercede for me and return me to Pomponia."

"Then it was Petronius who induced Caesar to take you from Aulus and give you to Vinitius?"

"Yes, lady. Vinitius will send for me today; but you're kind, so have pity on me!" She knelt and, seizing the border of Poppaea's robe, awaited an answer with a beating heart.

Poppaea looked at her a moment, then her face lit up with a malevolent smile. "I promise," she said, "that you today will become the slave of Vinitius."

Then she went her way, fair as a dream but evil. To the ears of Lygia and Acte came only the wail of the infant, who began to cry without any apparent reason.

Lygia's eyes also dimmed with tears, but she took Acte's hand and said, "Let's return. No help is to be looked for here."

So they returned to Acte's apartments, where they remained until evening. When darkness fell and the slaves brought in lighted torches, the faces of both women were pale. Their conversation ceased, as both were listening so as to hear if anyone approached. Lygia declared repeatedly that, though grieved to part with Acte, she preferred that all should end today, for Ursus without doubt was waiting for her in the darkness. Her breathing quickened from emotion and alarm. Acte feverishly collected all the gems she could find and, wrapping them in a corner of Lygia's peplos, implored her not to refuse this gift and means of escape.

At intervals there fell a deep silence, interrupted only by deceptive sounds. It seemed to both that, at one time, they heard someone whisper behind the curtain, then again the distant cry of an infant arose, and now they seemed to hear the barking of dogs.

Suddenly the curtain of the antechamber moved noiselessly and was then thrust aside. A tall, dark man, his face pitted with smallpox, glided like a phantom into the chamber. Lygia, at first glance, recognized Atacinus, one of Vinitius's freedmen, whom she had seen at the house of Aulus. Acte screamed.

Atacinus bowed his head and said, "Vinitius greets the divine Lygia and bids her to come to a feast in his house, which he has adorned with green."

The lips of the maiden grew white. "I go," she said.

Then, in farewell, she threw herself into the arms of Acte.

Chapter X

The house of Vinitius was, in fact, adorned with the green of myrtle and ivy, garlands of which hung on the walls and doors. The columns were wreathed with grapevine. The great atrium, which was closed above by a purple woolen cloth as a protection from the cool night air, was as bright as daylight. Lamps of eight or twelve flames were burning. These took the forms of vessels, trees, birds, or statues, with flames jutting from receivers full of perfumed oil. They were made of alabaster or gilded Corinthian bronze, not so beautiful as the famous lamp from the temple of Apollo that Nero possessed, but nevertheless with a beauty of their own, fashioned as they all had been by celebrated masters. In some the lights were shaded by Alexandrian glass or by transparent webs from India of red, blue, yellow, or violet, so that the entire hall was filled with multicolored rays. The air was heavy with the odor of tuberoses, to which Vinitius had become accustomed and had grown to love while living in the Orient. The entire house, through which moved male and female slaves, was brilliant with lights. The table in the *triclinium* was laid for four persons, for, besides Vinitius and Lygia, Petronius and Chrysothemis were to attend the feast. Vinitius had taken the advice of Petronius, not to go for Lygia himself, but to send Atacinus with the permission accorded by Caesar and receive her in his own home himself, with friendliness and even with marks of special consideration.

"Yesterday, you were drunk," said Petronius to him sternly. "I had my eyes on you. You behaved to her like a quarryman from the Alban Hills. Be not so demanding, and remember that good wine should be drunk slowly. Know, too, that to desire is sweet, but to be desired is sweeter."

Chrysothemis had her own, somewhat different opinion, but Petronius, calling her his vestal and his dove, began to explain the difference that must exist between an experienced charioteer and a youth who holds the reins for the first time. Then he turned to Vinitius.

"Win her confidence, cheer her up, be magnanimous. I don't care to be present at a gloomy feast. Swear to her, even by Hades, that you'll return her to Pomponia; then see to it that tomorrow she prefers to remain in your house." Then, pointing to Chrysothemis, he added, "For five years I acted thus with this flighty dove, and I can't complain of her fierceness."

Chrysothemis coquettishly tapped him with her fan of peacock feathers and said, "But didn't I resist you, Satyr?"

"Out of consideration for my predecessor."

"But were you not at my feet?"

"To put rings on your toes."

Chrysothemis involuntarily looked at her toes, on which jewels actually glittered. Both she and Petronius laughed. But Vinitius didn't listen to their banter. His heart beat uneasily under the splendidly decorated robe of a Syrian priest, which he had donned for Lygia's reception.

"They must have already left the palace," said he, as if speaking to himself.

"They must," said Petronius in confirmation. "Meanwhile, shall I tell you about the predictions of Apollonius of Tyana, or shall I relate the history of Rufinus, which I have not finished, I know not why."

But Vinitius was interested neither in Apollonius nor in Rufinus. His mind was on Lygia. And though he felt it was more becoming to receive her at home than to go to the palace in the role of a myrmidon, as if he wished to take her by force; still, he regretted that he'd not gone, for then he would have seen her sooner and could have sat in the darkness by her side in a double litter.

Meanwhile slaves brought in a tripod, ornamented with rams' heads, and bronze dishes filled with live coals, over which they sprinkled small bits of myrrh and nard.

"Now they're turning towards the Carinae," said Vinitius, again to himself.

"He won't hold out, but will run to meet her and is likely to pass them!" exclaimed Chrysothemis.

Vinitius smiled distractedly and said, "On the contrary, I'll wait." Nevertheless, his nostrils began to dilate, and he breathed heavily.

Seeing this, Petronius shrugged his shoulders and said, "There's not one sesterce of a philosopher in him. I'll never succeed in making a man out of this son of Mars."

But Vinitius didn't even hear his words. "They're already in the Carinae," he murmured.

Indeed, the litter in which Lygia lay was just then turning towards the Carinae. The *lampadarii*[1] were walking in front, and *pedisequii* walked on both sides of the litter, while Atacinus was close behind it, keeping an eye upon the procession. They moved slowly, for in a city that was not lighted at all, the lanterns hardly sufficed to show the way. Moreover, while the streets near the palace were empty—scarcely a man passing with a lantern—farther on, the streets were unusually crowded. Out of every backstreet, groups of three and four were emerging, all without torches, all in dark mantles. Some of them mingled with the slaves accompanying the litter. Others, in greater numbers, approached from the opposite direction. Some staggered as if drunk, and for some moments the advance grew so difficult that the *lampadarii* began to shout, "Make way for the noble tribune Marcus Vinitius!"

Lygia, throwing aside the curtain, looked upon the people clad in dark mantles and trembled with emotion. Hope and fear mingled in her breast. "That's him! That's Ursus and the Christians! The struggle will begin soon," she murmured with quivering lips. "Help me! Oh, Christ, save me!"

Atacinus, who at first hadn't noticed the uncommon crowds in the streets, now became alarmed. Something unusual was taking place. The *lampadarii* had to shout oftener and oftener: "Make way for the litter of the noble tribune!"

From all sides, unknown people crowded around the litter to such an extent that Atacinus ordered the slaves to drive them away with clubs.

Suddenly, a cry rang out. Immediately all the lights were extinguished. Around the litter a confused struggle began.

Atacinus perceived that an attack had been made upon the litter. This terrified him, for it was known to all that Caesar, with a crowd of attendants, frequently amused himself with such attacks in the Suburra and in other parts of the city. It was known that Nero sometimes returned from these nocturnal adventures with black-and-blue spots himself. But those who defended themselves were condemned to death, even if of senatorial rank. The quarters of the *vigiliae*,[2] whose duty it was to preserve order in the city, were not far away, but on such occasions, the guards feigned to be deaf and blind.

---

1   Lamp bearers.
2   Guards.

Ursus bore Lygia to the Suburra.

Meanwhile, the struggle thickened about the litter; people struck and trampled upon one another. It flashed upon Atacinus that he'd better save Lygia and himself and leave the rest to their fate. Drawing the maiden from the litter, he took her in his arms and attempted to escape in the darkness.

But Lygia began to shout, "Ursus! Ursus!"

She had left the palace in a white robe, hence she was plainly visible. Atacinus, with his free arm, was just covering her with his mantle, when suddenly terrible claws were dug into his neck and a crushing mass, like a stone, came down upon his head. He dropped in an instant, as an ox might drop beneath the butt end of an ax before an altar of Jove.

Most of the slaves were already lying on their backs or had escaped into the darkness. Only the litter, smashed in the uproar, remained. Ursus bore Lygia to the Suburra, his companions following him and dispersing gradually at the street corners.

The slaves soon began to assemble before the house of Vinitius and stood there debating. Not daring to enter, they decided to return to the scene of the attack, where they found a few bodies, among them that of Atacinus. He was still quivering, but after a moment of violent convulsion he stretched out and was motionless.

The slaves lifted him up and carried him towards the house of Vinitius, but they stopped at the gate, dreading to inform their master of what had happened.

"Let Gulo be our spokesman," whispered a few voices. "His face is bloody, as are ours, and our master loves him; he runs less risk than any of us."

Gulo, a German slave who had nursed Vinitius and who had descended to him from his mother, the sister of Petronius, said, "I'll inform him, but let's all go in together. Let not his wrath descend on my head alone."

Meanwhile, the patience of Vinitius was exhausted. Petronius and Chrysothemis jeered at him as he walked with quick steps up and down the room, repeating, "They ought to be here already. They ought to be here already."

He would have gone out to meet them, but Petronius and Chrysothemis held him back.

Suddenly steps were heard in the vestibule, and into the hall there rushed a crowd of slaves, who began to utter mourning cries. "Aaaa!—aa!"

Vinitius rushed towards them. "Where is Lygia?" he cried in a strange and terrible voice.

"Aaaa!—aa!"

Then Gulo came forward, the blood streaming down his face. In a trembling voice he exclaimed, "Behold our blood, master! We defended her. Behold blood, master, blood!"

But before he could finish, Vinitius seized a bronze candelabra and with one blow shattered his skull; then, clutching his own head with both hands, he drove his fingers into his hair and repeated in a hoarse voice, "*Me miserum! Me miserum!*"

Suddenly his face grew livid, his eyes turned in his head, and foam appeared at his mouth. "Whips!" he roared in a terrible voice.

"Master, aaaa—aa! Have mercy on us!" implored the slaves.

Petronius rose, an expression of disgust upon his face.

"Come, Chrysothemis," he said. "If you wish to look upon raw flesh, I'll command a butcher's stall to be opened in the Carinae."

And he left the atrium, while throughout the whole house, adorned with green ivy and prepared for feasting, there rang groans and the whistling of whips. These sounds lasted almost until morning.

Chapter XI

Vinitius did not lie down that night. Sometime after the departure of Petronius, as the groans of the slaves undergoing flagellation could appease neither his grief nor his anger, he collected a crowd of other slaves and, though it was late at night, led them forth in search of Lygia. He searched the Esquiline district, the Suburra, the criminal quarter, and all the adjoining byways. Then, passing the Capitol, he crossed the bridge of Fabricius to the island and from there passed hurriedly through the Trans-Tiber district. But his search was in vain. He himself had little hope of finding Lygia, only he felt he must do *something* during that terrible night. He returned home at daybreak, when the carts and mules of the vegetable dealers had already appeared in the streets and when bakers were opening their shops.

On his return he ordered the removal of Gulo's corpse, which nobody had dared to touch. The slaves who had escorted Lygia he sent to rural *ergastulums*,[1] a punishment considered more terrible even than death. Throwing himself, at last, on a couch in the atrium, he began to think confusedly of how he could find and seize Lygia.

To relinquish her, to lose her, not to see her again, seemed to him an impossibility, and at this thought alone, frenzy took hold of him. Imperious by nature, the young soldier, for the first time in his life, met resistance, met another unyielding will, and he couldn't understand how anyone would dare to thwart his desires. Vinitius would rather the entire world should perish and Rome fall into ruins rather than he should fail to attain the object of his desires. The cup of joy had been snatched from his lips; therefore it seemed to him that an unprecedented something had happened—something that cried aloud for vengeance to all laws, divine and human.

He could not reconcile himself to Fate. Never in his life had he desired

---

1 Dungeons.

anything so totally as he did Lygia. He didn't see how he could live without her. He couldn't imagine what he would do on the morrow without her, how he could survive the days that were to come. At times he was transported by fits of rage against her, fits that approached madness. He wanted to possess her, to drag her by the hair to his *cubiculum*, and there to gloat over her; then again his heart would be stirred by a yearning for her form, her eyes, her voice, and he felt that he'd gladly fall at her feet should she but be restored to him. He called to her, he gnawed his fingers, he clasped his head with his hands. He strove to compel himself to think calmly about continuing his search, but he couldn't. A thousand plans flitted through his head, each more foolish than the one before. Then, when it occurred to him that it must have been Aulus who had rescued the maiden, and that Aulus must know where she was concealed, he sprang up to rush off at once to the general's house.

If Aulus wouldn't return Lygia to him—if he didn't fear his threats—then he'd go to Caesar, accuse the old general of disobedience, and prevail upon Nero to condemn him to death. But, prior to this, he'd compel the old man to reveal Lygia's hiding place. Even if she were returned voluntarily, he would be revenged. True, he'd been sheltered in the house of Aulus, he'd been taken care of—but what of that? This insult had freed him from his debt of gratitude.

In his imagination, the young tribune reveled in the despair of Pomponia when the centurion should bring the death sentence to old Aulus. He was certain that he could secure it. Petronius would assist him; besides, Caesar denied nothing to his intimates, the Augustians, unless the request was antagonistic to his own desires or wishes.

Suddenly his heart almost died within him under the impact of a terrible thought: *Suppose Caesar himself had taken Lygia?*

It was generally known that Caesar, to relieve his ennui, sought amusement by making night attacks. Even Petronius used to take a hand in them. The main object of these escapades was to seize women and toss them on a soldier's blanket until they lost consciousness. Caesar at times called these adventures "pearl hunts," for it sometimes happened that in densely populated districts they found a real pearl of youth and beauty. Then the *sagatio* (the term for this sport) was turned into an actual abduction. The "pearl" was sent either to the Palatine Palace or to one of Caesar's numerous villas, or else Caesar presented the jewel to one of his intimates.

Such a fate might have befallen Lygia. Caesar had seen her at the feast. Vinitius had no doubt that he must have thought her the most beautiful woman he had ever beheld. It was all clear enough now. True, Lygia had been in the Palatine Palace, and Caesar might have kept her openly; but Caesar, as Petronius truly said, had no courage in wrongdoing; having the power to act openly, he preferred to do his evil deeds in secret. In this case, fear lest he should betray himself to Poppaea had probably influenced him to act secretly. It now occurred to Vinitius that Aulus and Pomponia wouldn't dare to rescue the girl given to him by Caesar. Who, indeed, would dare to do this? Would that gigantic Lygian, the one who had entered the *triclinium* and had boldly taken her from the feast in his arms? But where could he hide her? Where could he take her? No, a slave couldn't have done this deed. Hence, no one had taken Lygia except Caesar himself.

At this thought, darkness engulfed him and his eyes, and his forehead, was covered with sweat. If this were the case, then Lygia was lost to him forever. It was possible for him to wrest her from the hands of anyone else, but not from those of Caesar. Now, with all the more reason, he could exclaim, "*El misero mihi!*"[2]

His imagination, allowing him no rest, pictured Lygia in the arms of Nero, and for the first time in his life, he understood that there are thoughts that are beyond human endurance. Lygia's image haunted his mind as the past flashes through the memory of a drowning man. He saw her and heard every word that she had spoken—saw her at the fountain, at the house of Aulus, at the banquet. Again he felt her presence, the fragrance of her hair, the warmth of her body, the sweetness of the kisses that he had imprinted upon her innocent lips. She appeared to him a hundredfold more beautiful than ever, more desirable and dearer to his heart, surpassing all mortal women and all goddesses.

And when he thought that all these aspects of Lygia, which had so deeply stirred his heart and had become mingled with his very blood and life, were now possessed by Nero, he was wracked by anguish so terrible that he was strongly tempted to dash his brains out against the walls of the chamber. He felt that he was losing his mind, and he most surely would have gone mad had it not been for the hope of vengeance. Hitherto he'd felt that he couldn't possibly live without Lygia. Now he was determined

---

2 "Woe, woe be unto me!"

that he would not die until he had avenged her. He found relief in this thought: *I'll be your Cassius, O Caesar!* He repeated this to himself, addressing Nero in his mind. After a time he dug his hands into flower vases surrounding the *impluvium*, and squeezing a handful of earth together, he vowed to Erebus, Hecate, and his household lares that he would execute vengeance.

And he was in a measure consoled. Now at least he had something to live for—something with which to occupy his days and nights. Abandoning his intention of visiting Aulus, Vinitius gave orders that he should be borne to the Palatine. On the way he decided that should he not be admitted to Caesar's presence, or should they search him for concealed weapons, it would be proof that Caesar had carried Lygia away. He took no weapon with him. He had lost his usual presence of mind in general, yet, as is not uncommon with people possessed by a single idea, he retained it in all things that concerned his revenge. He acted with great haste so that his thirst for vengeance should not weaken before he had slaked it. He desired, above everything, to see Acte, for from her he hoped to learn the truth. At times, also, he was consoled with the hope that he might see Lygia, and this thought made him tremble. If Caesar had taken her from the slaves, not knowing who she was, he might return her to him on that day. But he soon cast aside this idea; had Caesar wished to return her to him, he would have sent her on the previous evening. Since Acte alone could explain everything to him, he would go to her first of all.

Having determined on this course of action, he commanded his litter-bearers to make all speed. On the way, his thoughts were disconnected, dwelling now on Lygia, now on his plans for revenge. He had heard that priests of the Egyptian goddess Pacht could bring disease on whomever they wished, and he determined to learn their secret. In the Orient he had been informed, also, that the Jews knew certain invocations by means of which they covered the bodies of their enemies with ulcers. In his household he had about a score of Jewish slaves; hence he decided that on his return he would have them tortured until they gave up the secret. But he found the most delight, however, in thinking of the short sword that let out streams of blood from Caius Caligula and left indelible stains on the columns of the portico. He was ready to bathe all Rome in blood. Had some vengeful gods promised him to destroy all mankind save himself and Lygia, he would even have agreed to that. In front of the arch of the Palatine Palace he recovered his presence of mind. At sight of the Praetorian Guard he thought that if they tried even in the slightest way to detain him, this would be proof that Lygia was in the palace by the will of Caesar. To his surprise, the chief centurion smiled at him in a friendly way and, approaching him, said, "Greetings, noble Tribune. If you desire an audience with Caesar, you've chosen an inopportune time. I don't think that you'll be able to see him."

"What's happened?" asked Vinitius.

"The divine little Augusta was suddenly taken ill yesterday. Caesar and Poppaea are at her bedside with physicians summoned from all parts of the city."

This was a matter of importance. When the infant was born, Caesar had become almost insane from joy and received her with divine honors. Even before the birth, the Senate had solemnly committed the child to the guardianship of the gods. After the birth, splendid games were celebrated and a temple was erected to the two Fortunes. Nero, extreme in everything, loved the child beyond measure. She was dear also to Poppaea, if only because the child strengthened her position and made her influence irresistible. On the health and life of this infant might depend the fate of the whole empire. But Vinitius was so carried away with his own problems that, paying no attention to the news, he answered, "I only wish to see Acte."

But Acte also was in attendance upon the child, and Vinitius had to wait a long time before seeing her. She came in about noon, with a pale and weary face that paled still more at sight of Vinitius.

"Acte!" he cried, grasping her hands and drawing her to the middle of the room. "Where's Lygia?"

"I was going to ask *you* about her," she answered.

Though he had determined to question her calmly, Vinitius now clasped his head in his hands while his face grew distorted with grief and anger, and he cried, "She's disappeared. She was captured on the way to my house."

Then he grew calmer and, bringing his face close to Acte's, hissed through his teeth, "Acte—if your life is dear to you, if you don't wish to be the cause of unimaginable misfortunes, tell me the truth: Did Caesar take her?"

"Caesar was not away from the palace yesterday."

"By the shade of your mother, in the name of all the gods, isn't she hidden in the palace?"

"Marcus, by the shade of my mother, she's not in the palace, and Caesar didn't take her. The infant Augusta has been sick since yesterday, and Caesar hasn't left her cradle."

Vinitius breathed more freely. What had seemed to him the most terrible of possibilities was removed from his path.

"Then," he said, sitting on the bench and clenching his fists, "Aulus and Pomponia have taken her—woe to them!"

"Aulus Plautius was here this morning. I couldn't see him because I was busy with the infant, but he made inquiries of Epaphroditus and other servants of the palace concerning Lygia and told them he would come again to see me."

"He wished to avert suspicion from himself. If he truly didn't know what had become of Lygia, he would have sought her in my house."

"He left a few words for me on a tablet. These will show you that Aulus, knowing Caesar had taken Lygia from him at the request of Petronius and you, feared that the maiden had been sent to your house. This morning he went there and was informed of what had happened."

With these words Acte went to the *cubiculum* and returned with the tablet that Aulus had left for her.

Vinitius read it and became silent. Acte, guessing his thoughts from the gloomy expression of his face, said, "No, Marcus, what Lygia herself desired has happened."

"Did you know that she desired to escape?" demanded Vinitius wrathfully.

Fixing her sad eyes upon him, she answered almost sternly, "I knew that she wouldn't become your concubine."

"And you, what have *you* been all your life?"

"I was first of all a princess—then a slave."

But the anger of Vinitius couldn't be appeased. Caesar had given Lygia to him; consequently her previous station was immaterial. He'd find her even if she were hidden in the bowels of the earth, and he'd do what he pleased with her; she'd be his slave. He'd have her flogged as often as he pleased. When he ceased to love her, he'd bestow her on the lowest of his slaves, or he'd send her to turn a hand mill on his African estates. He would begin his search for her at once and find her that he might punish her, that he might trample upon her and compel her obedience.

As his anger grew, he placed no limits to his vengeance, so that even Acte recognized that he was threatening more than he could perform, under the influence of rage and despair. She'd probably have felt pity for his sufferings had not his uncontrollable fury exhausted her patience.

Finally she asked him, "Why did you come to see me?"

Vinitius couldn't find an immediate answer. He'd come to her because he thought she'd give him some information; but really he'd come to see Caesar, but not being admitted to him he'd asked for her. Lygia's flight had represented disobedience to the will of Caesar; therefore he would petition Nero to command that she be sought over the whole city and over the entire empire, even if this entailed the aid of all the legions and the searching of every house throughout the empire. Petronius would support this petition, and the search would begin at once.

To this Acte said, "Take care lest when she's found you lose her forever—at the command of Caesar."

"What do you mean?" Vinitius asked, with wrinkled brows.

"Listen to me, Marcus. Yesterday I was walking with Lygia in the gardens; we met Poppaea with the infant Augusta, borne by the Ethiopian, Lilith. At evening the infant fell ill. Lilith declares that the child was bewitched and accuses the foreign woman whom they met in the gardens. If the child recovers, they'll forget all about this; if not, Poppaea will be the first to accuse Lygia of witchcraft, and then whenever she's found nothing will be able to save her."

There was a moment of silence, which Vinitius was the first to break. "Perhaps she did bewitch the child and has bewitched me."

"Lilith says that the child began to cry immediately after she passed us. This is true. No doubt the child was ill when they brought her into the garden. Marcus, search for Lygia wherever you please, but until the little one recovers don't mention her name to Caesar, or you'll bring down upon her the vengeance of Poppaea. Her eyes have shed tears enough already on your account. May all the gods protect her now."

"Do you love her, Acte?" asked Vinitius sadly.

Tears sprang to the eyes of the freedwoman. "Yes, I love her."

"But she didn't repay you with hatred as she did me."

Acte looked at him as if hesitating or as if she wished to test his sincerity. Finally, she said, "Oh, blind and passionate man, she *loved* you."

Vinitius sprang up as if possessed. "That's false," he said. "She hates me!"

How could Acte know? It was hardly possible that Lygia, after one day's acquaintance, would make such a confession to her. What kind of love would prefer wandering, poverty, the uncertainty of the morrow, perhaps even a shameful death, to a house bedecked with green wreaths where a lover was in waiting, with a banquet all prepared? Better he shouldn't hear such words lest he go mad. He wouldn't have given that girl away for all the treasures of the Palatine—and she had fled. What kind of love was it that feared delight and courted pain? Who could understand it? Who could explain it? But for his hope of finding her, he would fall upon his sword! Love surrenders, it does not run away. There were moments in the house of Aulus when he'd felt that happiness was near, but now he was convinced that she hated him and would die with that hatred in her heart.

Acte, usually gentle and timid, now burst forth with indignant reproaches. How had he tried to win the love of Lygia? Instead of asking Aulus and Pomponia to give her to him, he had taken her away from her guardians by stealth. He wished not to make her his wife but his concubine—she, the foster daughter of an honorable family and the daughter of a king. He had brought her to an abode of vice and infamy; he had defiled her innocent eyes with the spectacle of a shameful orgy; he had treated her as a harlot. Had he forgotten what sort of man Aulus was and what sort of woman Pomponia—they who'd brought up Lygia? Had he not wit enough to understand that women existed who were quite different from Nigidia or Calvia Crispinilla or Poppaea and from all those whom he met in Caesar's house? Had not a conviction forced itself upon his mind at his first sight of Lygia that so pure a soul would prefer death to shame? Didn't he know that the God she worshiped was better and purer than the dissolute Venus or Isis, who were worshiped by the profligate women of Rome? No, Lygia had made no confession to her. But she *had* said that she hoped Vinitius would save her; she hoped Caesar, through Vinitius's petition, would allow her to return home; she hoped that Vinitius would restore her to Pomponia. While speaking of this, Lygia had blushed like a maiden who loves and trusts. Her heart had beat for him, but he had terrified and insulted her—and now let him seek her with the aid of Caesar's cohorts. But should Nero's child die, suspicion must fall upon her, and her ruin would be inevitable.

In spite of his rage and pain, what Acte had said affected Vinitius. Her assurance that Lygia loved him shook his soul to the very depths. He recalled how she had blushed and how her eyes had become radiant with light when she had listened to his words in the house of Aulus. Yes, at that time she had begun to love him. The thought filled him with delight, and then he saw that he might have won her through peaceful means and have gradually possessed himself of her heart. She might have put twine on his door, rubbed it with wolf's fat, and sat as his wife on a sheepskin by his hearth. He might have heard from her lips the sacramental, "Where thou art Caius, there am I Caia," and she might have belonged to him forever. Why hadn't he done this? Didn't he wish to marry her? But now she'd gone; now he might never again find her or, finding her, might cause her ruin. Or even if he didn't bring ruin upon her, neither Lygia nor Aulus would listen to his proposals.

Again he was enraged. But now it was turned, not against Aulus or Pomponia or Lygia, but against Petronius. Petronius was to blame for everything. Had it not been for him, Lygia wouldn't be wandering about. She would now be his betrothed, and no danger would threaten her life. Now all was over; matters could no longer be mended; it was too late. An abyss seemed to yawn at his feet. What was he to do? What measures could he take?

Like an echo, Acte repeated, "Too late."

Falling from another's lips they sounded like a death sentence. One thing, however, was certain: He must find Lygia; otherwise some terrible evil would befall him. Mechanically wrapping himself in his toga, he was on the point of leaving without even bidding farewell to Acte when suddenly the curtain that separated the vestibule from the atrium was thrust aside, and he saw before him the sad face of Pomponia.

Evidently she also had heard of Lygia's disappearance and, assuming that she could easily gain admittance to Acte, had come for information. Seeing Vinitius, she turned towards him her pale, delicate face and exclaimed, "Marcus, may God forgive you the wrong you've done to us and to Lygia."

He hung his head, feeling both unhappy and guilty, yet not understanding what God it was that could forgive him, nor why Pomponia spoke of forgiveness when she ought to have spoken of revenge. Finally, he departed, tormented by foreboding, anxiety, and sorrow.

In the courtyard and in the gallery were crowds of people. Mingled with slaves of the palace were knights and senators come to inquire after the health of the little Augusta and at the same time to show themselves in the palace and give proof of their devotion in the presence of Caesar's slaves. The news of the illness of the little divinity had evidently spread quickly, for every moment more and more people appeared at the gate, and through the archways crowds of people could be seen. Some of the recent arrivals, noticing Vinitius coming out of the palace, attempted to stop him for news, but he hurried on without answering them until Petronius, who had come for news also, almost ran into him and stopped him.

Beyond doubt, Vinitius would have become enraged at the sight of Petronius and committed some lawless act in Caesar's palace, were it not that when he'd left Acte's chamber he was so crushed and humiliated that for the moment his innate irascibility had left him. Vinitius pushed Petronius aside and was about to continue on his way, but the latter detained him, by force almost.

"How fares the divine infant?"

This forcible detention aroused anew the anger of Vinitius.

"May Hades swallow her and all this house!" he hissed through his teeth.

"Silence, hapless man!" said Petronius, and, looking around, he hastily added, "If you desire to learn something about Lygia, follow me. No, I'll say nothing here! Follow me. I'll explain my surmises in the litter."

And putting his arm about the young man, he led him out of the palace as quickly as possible. This was his main concern, for he had no news at all about Lygia. But, being a man of resources and having, in spite of yesterday's indignation, felt compassion for Vinitius, together with a certain responsibility for what had happened, he had taken some measures already.

When they were seated in the litter, he said, "I've ordered my slaves to watch at every gate, giving them minute descriptions of the maiden and of that giant who carried her out from Caesar's feast, for doubtless he's the one who recaptured her from your slaves. Listen to me! Aulus and Pomponia may have wished to hide her away on one of their estates. If so, we'll find in which direction she was conducted. If she passes none of the gates, then this will be proof that she's still in the city, and we'll begin to search for her in Rome today."

"Aulus and Pomponia don't know where she is," answered Vinitius.

"Are you sure of that?"

"I've seen Pomponia, and she's also searching for her."

"She couldn't have left the city yesterday, for the gates are closed at night. Two of my slaves are watching each gate. One is to follow Lygia and the giant, and the other is to return immediately and inform me. If she's in Rome we'll find her, for the Lygian can easily be recognized by his height and the breadth of his shoulders. It's lucky she wasn't carried away by Caesar. I can assure you that it wasn't he, for I know all the secrets of the palace."

Vinitius now erupted, more in sorrow than in anger. In a voice broken by emotion, he told Petronius all he'd heard from Acte. He explained the new dangers that threatened Lygia; that now, in case they found her, they would need to hide her from Poppaea. Then he reproached Petronius bitterly for his advice. Had it not been for him, everything would have been well: Lygia would have been in the house of Aulus, Vinitius could have seen her every day, and he would now be a happier man than Caesar. Carried away by his own words, he became more and more agitated until tears of sorrow and anger coursed down his cheeks.

Petronius, who hadn't thought the young tribune capable of such passion, beholding his tears, said to himself with wonder, *Oh, Venus, mighty sovereign of Cyprus, you alone are the ruler of gods and men!*

Chapter XII

When they alighted in front of the house of Petronius, the *atriensis* informed him that none of the slaves sent to the gates had as yet returned. He'd given orders that food should be brought to them and that on the penalty of a flogging they should carefully watch all who left the city.

"See!" said Petronius. "They are still within the city, and we cannot fail to find them. Give orders to your slaves also, that they watch the city gates, selecting those especially who formed Lygia's escort, for they'll easily recognize her."

"I've given orders that those slaves should be sent to rural *ergastulums*," answered Vinitius, "but I'll revoke the order right away and send them to the gates."

When he'd written a few words on a tablet covered with wax, he handed the tablet to Petronius, who ordered it sent immediately to the house of Vinitius. Then they entered the inner portico and, sitting on a marble bench, began to converse. Eunice and Iris placed bronze footstools beneath their feet and, moving a table near the bench, poured wine into goblets out of beautiful, long-necked jars imported from Volaterrae[1] and Caecina.

"Do any of your slaves know this gigantic Lygian?" asked Petronius.

"Only Atacinus and Gulo knew him; but Atacinus was killed beside the litter, and I slew Gulo."

"I'm sorry for Gulo," said Petronius. "He carried in his arms not only you, but me also."

"I was going to free him," replied Vinitius, "but let that rest. Let's speak of Lygia. Rome is a sea—"

"But it's a sea where pearls are found. We won't find her today, of course, nor tomorrow, but sooner or later we'll find her. You've accused me

---

1   An old town in Etruria (now Volterra).

just now of being the cause of this trouble, but the advice in itself was good; it became bad because of unfavorable circumstances. Besides, you yourself had heard from Aulus that he intended to go to Sicily with all his family. So Lygia would in any event have been far away from you."

"I would have followed her," replied Vinitius, "and in any case she'd have been out of danger. But now if this infant dies, Poppaea will believe—and will persuade Caesar to believe—that Lygia caused the death."

"True; this thought has alarmed me also. But the little doll may recover. If she dies, we'll find some means of escape."

Petronius, after a moment's thought, added, "Poppaea, it's said, believes in the faith of the Jews and in evil spirits. Caesar is superstitious. If we spread the rumor that Lygia has been carried away by evil spirits, it will be believed, since neither Caesar nor Aulus have carried her off; therefore, it'll be believed that she was spirited away. The Lygian couldn't have rescued her alone. It's evident that others helped him. But how could a slave collect so many people in a day?"

"In Rome, slaves help one another."

"Which they'll pay for with their blood someday. True, they help one another, but not when it's against the interest of other slaves. On this occasion it was known that your slaves would be held responsible and punished. If you suggest to your slaves the possibility that evil spirits may have been involved, they'll assert that they saw them with their own eyes, for this would justify them before you. Ask any one of them if he didn't see Lygia borne through the air, and he'll swear at once by the aegis of Zeus that this was just what happened."

Vinitius, who was himself superstitious, looked with awe at Petronius and said, "If Ursus couldn't get slaves to help him and wasn't able to take her alone, who did take her?"

Petronius laughed. "See?" he said. "How could they doubt when you believe? Such is our world that laughs at the gods. All will believe and cease searching for her, and meantime we'll hide her in one of our villas."

"But who could have helped her?"

"Her coreligionists," answered Petronius.

"*What* coreligionists? What deity do they worship? I ought to know better than you."

"Nearly every Roman woman worships a different deity. Doubtless Pomponia has brought up Lygia to worship the deity that she adores, but what deity this is I don't know. One thing is certain—no one has seen her make offerings to any god in our temples. She was even accused of being a Christian, but that's impossible. A secret domestic court cleared her from that charge. It's said that Christians not only worship the head of an ass, but that they are enemies of the human race and that they commit abominable crimes. Consequently Pomponia can't be a Christian, for she's a good woman. Were she a hater of humanity, she wouldn't treat her slaves so kindly."

"In no house are they so well treated as in that of Aulus," added Vinitius.

"So there you are. By the way, Pomponia once spoke to me about some God that's said to be one, almighty, and merciful. What she's done with all the other gods is her affair. But this Logos of hers can't be very powerful, or rather, He must be a poor kind of a God if He is worshiped only by Pomponia and Lygia and Ursus. It may be that there are more adherents of this God, and they assisted Lygia."

"Their faith commands forgiveness," said Vinitius. "In Acte's chamber I met Pomponia, and she said to me, 'May God forgive you the wrong you've done to Lygia and to us.'"

"Evidently their God is a very mild being. Ha! Let Him forgive you then, and as a sign of His forgiveness, let Him restore the maiden to you."

"I'd offer him a hecatomb tomorrow! I'm sick. I desire neither food nor sleep nor the bath. I shall put on dark raiment and wander through the city. Perhaps I'll find her if I go in disguise."

Petronius gazed at him compassionately. There were dark streaks beneath the eyes of Vinitius; his pupils were bright with fever; his unshaven beard made a bluish shade over his jaw; his hair was disordered; he looked indeed like a sick man. Iris and the golden-haired Eunice gazed at him also with commiseration, but he seemed not to notice them. Neither he nor Petronius paid any more attention to the presence of the slave women than if they were dogs moving about the room.

"Fever is tormenting you," declared Petronius.

"It is."

"Then listen to me. I know not what a physician would prescribe for you, but I know what I would do in your place. Till Lygia is found I'd replace the lost one with a substitute. I've seen beautiful women in your house. No, don't contradict me. I know what love is, and I know that if love is induced by one woman, another can't satisfy it. Nevertheless, a beautiful slave will afford at least a temporary distraction."

She implored him not to send her away.

"I don't wish it," replied Vinitius.

But Petronius, who was sincerely attached to him and anxious to relieve his suffering, began to consider how this might best be done.

"Perhaps your slaves don't possess for you the charm of novelty," he said. He glanced first at Iris and then at Eunice. At last he laid his hand on the hip of the golden-haired Greek and resumed, "Look at this nymph! But a few days ago the young Fonteius Capiton offered for her three beautiful boys from Clazomene. Scopas himself has not chiseled a more beautiful figure. I really can't tell why I've been cold to her, since thoughts of Chrysothemis haven't restrained me. Here, I give her to you—take her."

When Eunice heard these words she grew white as a sheet. Looking with frightened eyes at Vinitius, she seemed benumbed while she awaited his answer.

But the young soldier sprang up from the bench and, pressing his temples with his hands, began to speak hurriedly, as a man who, tormented by pain, doesn't wish to listen to any soothing words.

"No, no, I don't care for her. I don't care for any other woman. I thank you, but I don't want her. I'm going to search for Lygia throughout the city. Have a Gallic cloak with a hood brought to me. I'll go to the Trans-Tiber. Oh, if I can succeed merely in seeing Ursus!"

Then he withdrew hurriedly. Petronius, seeing that he couldn't stay still in any one place, didn't attempt to detain him. Taking his refusal as a manifestation of a temporary aversion towards all women except Lygia, but wishing still to be generous, he turned to Eunice.

"Eunice, bathe yourself, anoint your body with perfumes, then dress and go to the house of Vinitius."

The Greek woman fell on her knees and, stretching out her hands, she implored him not to send her away from his house. She wouldn't go to Vinitius. She'd prefer to carry wood to the furnaces of the baths of Petronius than to be the chief servant in that of Vinitius. She wouldn't—she *couldn't* go. She implored him for pity. Let him have her flogged daily, but let him not send her away from his house.

Trembling like a leaf with fear and excitement, Eunice extended her imploring hands to Petronius, who listened with astonishment. A slave woman who dared to answer a command with a prayer, declaring "I will not" and "I cannot," was something unheard of in Rome, and Petronius couldn't believe his ears. Finally he frowned. He was too refined to be cruel. He gave more freedom to his slaves—especially in their pleasures—

than other masters, demanding only that they render good service and honor his will like that of a god. But if his slaves violated either of these requirements, Petronius had them punished in the usual fashion. Besides, he couldn't endure opposition or anything that ruffled his peace of mind.

So he looked at the kneeling slave and said, "Call Tiresias and return with him." She arose, trembling, with tears in her eyes, and retired, returning soon with the chief of the hall servants, the Cretan Tiresias.

"Take Eunice," said Petronius, "and give her twenty-five lashes, but in such a way as not to disfigure her skin."

Then he went into his library and, sitting at the rose-colored marble table, he commenced work on his "Feast of Trimalchion." But Lygia's escape and the illness of the little Augusta distracted his thoughts so much that he didn't work long. The supremely important question at present was the illness of the infant. Petronius foresaw that if Caesar believed Lygia to have bewitched the young Augusta, the blame might fall on him also, for the maiden had been brought to the palace at his request. But he hoped that as soon as he saw Caesar he'd convince him of the absurdity of such a supposition. He relied somewhat also on a certain weakness that Poppaea had for him—a weakness that she'd not succeeded in concealing from him. After a time he shrugged his shoulders, having convinced himself that his fears were groundless, and he decided to take his meal in the *triclinium.* After that he would go in his litter to the palace, next to the Campus Martius, and finally to Chrysothemis. On his way to the *triclinium,* at the entrance to the corridor assigned to the slaves, Petronius noticed the shapely figure of Eunice. Forgetting that he had given no order to Tiresias beyond that of flogging her, he frowned and looked around for that official. Not seeing Tiresias among the slaves, he turned to Eunice.

"Have you been flogged?"

"Yes, master, I've been flogged. Oh, yes, master!"

Joy and gratitude blended in her voice. She evidently thought that the punishment had been given in place of sending her away from the house and that now she might remain. Petronius, seeing this, marveled at the passionate resistance of the slave; he was too deep a student in human nature not to understand that only love could call forth such a resistance.

"Do you love someone in this house?"

She looked at him with her blue eyes dim with tears and answered in a voice so low that it could scarcely be heard, "Yes, master."

Eunice, with her wonderful eyes, with her golden hair flowing down her back, with an expression of hope and fear upon her face, was so beautiful that Petronius, who as a philosopher, recognized the power of love, and as an aesthete, rendered homage to all beauty, felt pity for the slave.

"Whom of these do you love?" he inquired, turning towards the slaves.

No answer came. Eunice bent her head down to his very feet and remained motionless as a statue.

Petronius looked around at the slaves, among whom were some handsome and muscular youths. None of the faces explained anything to him; he saw only strange smiles. He looked again at Eunice, who was lying at his feet, and then went on in silence to the *triclinium*. When he had eaten, he gave orders that he should be carried to the palace and from there to Chrysothemis, where he remained until late in the night. On his return he summoned Tiresias.

"Did you punish Eunice?"

"Yes, master. But you commanded me not to disfigure her skin."

"Did I give any other command?"

"No, master," answered the slave with alarm.

"Very good. Which of the slaves does she love?"

"None, master."

"What do you know about her?"

Tiresias answered in an uncertain voice. "At night, Eunice never leaves the *cubiculum* in which she lives with old Acrisiona and Ifida. After your bath she never remains in the bathing rooms. Other slaves laugh at her and call her Diana."

"Enough," said Petronius. "My relative Vinitius, to whom I offered her this morning, didn't want her, hence she may remain here. You may go."

"May I speak, master, a few more words concerning Eunice?"

"I commanded you to tell all you know about her."

"The entire household is talking about the escape of the maiden who was to dwell in the house of Vinitius. After your departure Eunice came to me and said that she knew a man who could find this maiden."

"Who is this man?" asked Petronius.

"I don't know him, master, but I thought I ought to tell you about the matter."

"You've done well. Let that man await tomorrow the arrival of the tribune, whom in my name you will request to meet me here."

The *atriensis* bowed and departed. But Petronius's thoughts returned to

Eunice. It was clear to him that the young slave woman wished Vinitius to find Lygia so that she wouldn't be compelled to be her substitute in the house of the tribune. It occurred to him that the man whom she had proposed for the search might be her lover. Somehow this thought hurt him. It wouldn't be difficult to get at the truth; he had only to summon Eunice, but it was now late, and Petronius, feeling weary after his long visit to the house of Chrysothemis, desired to sleep. On the way to his *cubiculum* he recalled for some unknown reason that he had noticed wrinkles that day in the corners of Chrysothemis's eyes. It came to his mind also that her reputation for beauty was greater than she deserved and that Fonteius Capiton wished to buy Eunice too cheaply.

Chapter XIII

The next morning, Petronius had barely finished dressing in the *unctorium* when Vinitius, who had been summoned by Tiresias, appeared. He was aware that no news had come from the gates. This, instead of consoling him as proof that Lygia was still in the city, troubled him, for he feared Ursus had carried her out of the city immediately after her rescue, and consequently before the slaves of Petronius had been sent to watch the gates. True, in autumn the gates were closed earlier on account of the short days, but then they were open for the people going out. Of these there were always a great many. One also could pass out of the city by other means, known, for instance, to slaves who contemplated an escape. Also, Vinitius had dispatched his slaves to all the roads leading to the provinces, instructing them to carry alarms to all the watchmen in the smaller towns and to furnish minute descriptions of Ursus and Lygia, portraying them as fugitive slaves and offering a reward for their capture. It was doubtful, however, whether the fugitives could be overtaken, or, if so, whether the local officials would arrest them at the private request of Vinitius, unsupported by the Praetorian Guard. Vinitius had no time to gain such support. Disguised as a slave, he'd sought Lygia the entire previous day in every corner of the city, but couldn't find any clue. True, he'd met the slaves of Aulus, who were also searching for something, and this confirmed his belief that Aulus and Pomponia hadn't taken Lygia away and that they didn't know what had become of her.

So, when Tiresias informed him that there was a man who would undertake to find Lygia, Vinitius rushed to the house of Petronius and, barely greeting him, began to inquire about him.

"We'll soon see him," said Petronius. "He's an acquaintance of Eunice's. She's even now coming to fold my toga and will give us additional information."

"Is that the slave woman whom you wished to give me yesterday?"

"The one whom you rejected, for which, by the way, I'm grateful, as she's the best robe folder in the city."

He'd barely finished when Eunice entered. Taking the toga that was lying on a chair inlaid with ivory, she opened the garment to throw it over Petronius's shoulders. Her face was clear and calm, and joy was reflected in her eyes.

Petronius looked at her, and she appeared very beautiful to him. While she was wrapping him up in the toga, bending now and again to smooth the folds, he noticed that her arms were of a wonderful pale rose color and that her bosom and shoulders were transparent, like mother-of-pearl or alabaster.

"Eunice," said he, "has the man come whom you mentioned yesterday to Tiresias?"

"Yes, master."

"What's his name?"

"Chilo Chilonides, master."

"Who is he?"

"A physician, sage, and soothsayer who can read the book of Fate and forecast the future."

"Did he forecast your future?"

A rosy blush spread over her ears and neck as she answered. "Yes, master."

"What did he predict?"

"That pain and happiness should be my lot."

"Pain you suffered yesterday at the hands of Tiresias, hence the prediction about happiness should also be realized."

"It's realized already, master."

"What is this happiness?"

"That I remain," she replied in a low voice.

Petronius put his hand on her golden head. "You've arranged the folds well today, and I'm pleased with you, Eunice."

As his hand touched her head, her eyes grew moist and her bosom began to heave.

Petronius and Vinitius went into the antechamber, where Chilo Chilonides was waiting for them. The latter bowed low on their entrance. Petronius smiled at thought of his suspicion yesterday that this man might be Eunice's lover. This man could be no woman's lover. His strange figure was at once repulsive and ridiculous. He was not old: Only a few gray hairs showed in his filthy beard and curled locks. He had a lank stomach and shoulders so stooped that a cursory glance might have mistaken him for a hunchback. Above his bent shoulders was a large head that seemed a cross between the face of a monkey and a fox. His eyes were bright and penetrating. His yellowish face was checkered with pimples, which were concentrated on his nose, suggesting an excessive love for the bottle. His disordered attire, consisting of a dark tunic of goat's wool and a ragged mantle of similar material, indicated poverty, real or pretended.

At sight of him, Petronius was reminded of Homer's Thersites.[1] So, answering Chilo's bow with a wave of his hand, he said, "I greet you, divine Thersites. How are the lumps that Ulysses gave you at Troy, and what's he doing himself in the Elysian fields?"

"Noble lord," answered Chilo, "Ulysses, the wisest of the dead, sends through me to Petronius, the wisest of the living, his greetings and requests that you should cover my lumps with a new mantle."

"By Hecate,"[2] exclaimed Petronius, "the answer merits a new mantle!"

But Vinitius impatiently interrupted the conversation and asked Chilo point-blank, "Do you know clearly what you're undertaking?"

"It's not difficult to learn what the question is," answered Chilo, "when the slaves of two lordly mansions speak of nothing else, and when it's the current gossip of half of Rome. Night before last, a maiden called Lygia, a ward of Aulus Plautius, was carried away while your slaves were bearing her from Caesar's palace to your house. I offer to find her in Rome, or if she's left the city, which seems improbable, I shall discover for you, noble Tribune, whither she has fled and where she's hiding."

"Well said," said Vinitius, pleased with the confidence of the answer. "What means do you have to accomplish this?"

Chilo smiled slyly. "You, master, have the means. I have only the wisdom."

Petronius smiled also, for he was fully satisfied with his visitor. *This man can find the maiden*, thought he.

Vinitius frowned under his knit brows and said, "If you deceive me for gain, I'll have you flogged."

"I'm a philosopher, master, and a philosopher cannot be tempted by gain, especially such as you promise so magnanimously."

"Ah! Are you a philosopher?" asked Petronius. "Eunice told me that

---

1 Son of Agrius, a Greek at the battle of Troy, notorious for his ugliness and scurrilous tongue.

2 Goddess of magic and enchantment, identified with Diane and Luna.

you were a physician and a soothsayer. How did you make Eunice's acquaintance?"

"She came to ask my advice, for my fame had reached her ears."

"What advice did she desire?"

"Master, she desired to be cured of unrequited love."

"Did you cure her?"

"I did more than that. I gave her an amulet that insures reciprocity. In Paphos, on the island of Cyprus, there's a temple wherein a girdle of Venus is preserved. I procured for her two threads from that girdle, enclosed in an almond shell."

"And no doubt you received a good price for it?"

"One can never pay enough for reciprocated love. And I, who have lost two fingers of my right hand, am saving money to buy a slave copyist, that he may write down my thoughts and preserve my wisdom for mankind."

"To what school do you belong, venerable sage?"

"Master, I am a Cynic because I wear a mantle full of holes; I am a Stoic because I bear poverty patiently; I am a Peripatetic because, not owning a litter, I walk from one wineshop to another, teaching on the way those who promise to pay for a pitcher of wine."

"And does the pitcher change you into a rhetorician?"

"Heraclitus[3] maintains that all is fluid, and can you deny, master, that wine is fluid?"

"And he also taught that fire is a divinity; divinity therefore is perched upon your nose."

"And divine Diogenes of Apollonia taught that the universe is created from air and that the warmer the air, the more perfect are the created beings. And as in autumn the air is cold, ergo, a genuine sage ought to warm his soul with wine. For you cannot deny, master, that a pitcher even of the watery wine made in the environs of Capua or Telesia would impart warmth to all the bones of a perishable human body."

"Where is your birthplace, Chilo Chilonides?"

"On the Pontus Euxine.[4] I come from Mesembria."[5]

"O Chilo, you are great!"

---

3 A Greek philosopher of Ephesus, about 500 B.C.
4 Evidently on the Euxine shore.
5 A town in Thrace at the foot of Mount Haemus.

"And unrecognized," said the sage in a mournful tone.

Vinitius's impatience increased. Because of the hope that Chilo had raised, he wished him to begin his search at once; hence he regarded the whole conversation as a waste of time and consequently was angry with Petronius.

"When will you begin the search?" he asked, turning to the Greek.

"I've begun it already," was the answer. "Even here, even in answering your courteous questions, I'm still searching. Only have confidence, noble Tribune. Know that if you were to lose the string from off your sandal, I would find it or him who picked it up on the street."

"Have you ever been used for similar services?" asked Petronius.

The Greek raised his eyes heavenward. "Nowadays wisdom and virtue are so little esteemed that a philosopher is forced to seek other means of earning a livelihood."

"What other means have you?"

"To know everything and to furnish information for those who are in need of it."

"And who pay for it?"

"Ah, master, I need to buy a copyist; otherwise my wisdom will perish with me."

"If you haven't saved enough money to buy a new mantle, your services can't be very valuable."

"Modesty forbids my speaking of them. But, master, take into consideration the fact that there are no longer so many benefactors as of old, for whom it was as great a pleasure to cover a body with gold for services rendered as it was to swallow an oyster from Puteoli.[6] It's not my services that are small, but the gratitude of men. If a slave escapes, who will find him, if not the son of my father? When on the walls appear inscriptions against the divine Poppaea, who else will point out the perpetrators? Who will unearth in the bookshops verses against Caesar? Who will tell of conversations held in the houses of senators and patricians? Who will deliver letters that cannot be entrusted to slaves? Who will listen to the gossip of the barbershops? From whom have the wineshops and bakeshops no secrets? In whom do slaves trust? Who can see at a glance through any house, from the inner chamber to the garden? Who knows every street and byway and hidden den? Who knows what is talked of in the baths, in the Circus, in

---

6 A coastal town in Campania.

the markets, in the gymnasiums, in the stalls of the slave dealers, and even in the arenas?"

"By the gods, enough, noble sage!" exclaimed Petronius. "Otherwise we'll be drowned in your virtues, your wisdom and eloquence. Enough! We wished to know who you are, and now we know."

Vinitius was pleased. *Once put a man like this on the trail,* he thought, *and, houndlike, he would not stop until he had flushed the game.* "I'm satisfied," said he. "Do you need clues?"

"I need arms."

"What kind of arms?" asked Vinitius, perplexed.

Chilo stretched out one hand while with the other he made a motion as if counting money. "Such times as we live in!" he sighed.

"This means that you'll be the ass who wins the fortress by means of gold," remarked Petronius.

"I'm but a poor philosopher, master," answered Chilo with humility. "You have the gold."

Vinitius tossed him a purse. The Greek caught it before it fell, despite his missing fingers. Then he raised his head.

"Master, I know already more than you suspect. I didn't come emptyhanded. I know that Aulus and his wife didn't intercept the maiden, for I've questioned their slaves. I know that she's not in the Palatine Palace, for all there are occupied with the sick child; and perhaps I know also why you prefer my aid in the search for the maiden to that of the guards and soldiers of Caesar. I know that her escape was effected by the cooperation of a slave who came from the same country as she. He couldn't have procured assistance from slaves because slaves who stand together would not have helped him against your slaves. Only his coreligionists could have given him aid."

"Listen to these words, Vinitius," interrupted Petronius. "Have I not said the same thing to you?"

"You do me a great honor," said Chilo. "The maiden, master," he continued, addressing himself again to Vinitius, "worships beyond doubt the same divinity as Pomponia, that most virtuous of all Roman matrons. I've heard that Pomponia was tried in secret for worshiping strange gods, but I couldn't learn from her slaves what kind of divinities these are, and what their adherents are called. If I could learn this I'd go to them and become the most devout among them and win their confidence. But you, master, as is known to me, passed a few weeks in the house of Aulus; can you not give me some information about these gods?"

"I cannot," answered Vinitius.

"You've questioned me long about various matters, and I've answered you. Now allow me to question you. Have you not seen, noble Tribune, some statuette, some sacrifice, some token, or some amulet upon Pomponia or Lygia? Have you not seen them drawing some images intelligible to them alone?"

"Yes, I once saw Lygia draw a fish in the sand."

"A fish? Aha! Oho! Did she draw it once or many times?"

"But once."

"And are you sure that she drew a fish?"

"Yes, I'm sure," answered Vinitius with interest. "Do you know what it means?"

"Do I know!" exclaimed Chilo. Then, bowing in sign of farewell, he said, "May Fortune present you with all gifts, noble masters."

"Order a mantle to be brought to you," said Petronius at parting.

"Ulysses offers to give thanks for Thersites," answered the Greek, and bowing again, he left the room.

"And what do you think of that noble sage?" asked Petronius.

"I think he'll find Lygia," exclaimed Vinitius joyfully. "But I think also that if there were a kingdom of knaves, he would be crowned king there."

"Without doubt. I must get better acquainted with this Stoic. In the meantime, I'll have this atrium disinfected."

Chilo Chilonides, wrapped in his new mantle, felt beneath its folds the purse that Vinitius had given him and rejoiced at its weight and jingle. Walking slowly and looking furtively around to see that he was followed by no one from the house of Petronius, he passed a portico of Livia and, reaching the corner of the Virvius Quarter, turned into the Suburra.

I must go to Sporus, he said to himself, *and pour out a libation to Fortune. I've at last found what I have sought for so long. He's young, passionate, lavish as the mines of Cyprus, and is ready to give half his fortune for this Lygian linnet. I must deal with him carefully, however, for his frowns forebode no good. Oh, the wolf whelps rule the world today! I would be less afraid of Petronius. Oh, gods! To be a procurer pays better in these times than virtue. Ah! She drew a fish in the sand. May I choke myself with goat's cheese if I know the meaning of that symbol, but I shall find out! As fish live under water, and seeking under water is harder than on land, he shall pay me liberally for this fish. One more purse like this and I might cast aside the beggar's wallet and purchase myself a slave. But suppose, O Chilo, if I advised you to*

buy not a male but a female slave? I know you! I'm sure that you'd say yea!
Were she as beautiful as Eunice, for instance, you would grow young at her
side; moreover, you would draw from her a large and certain income. I sold
that poor Eunice two threads from my old mantle. She is dull; nevertheless, if
Petronius would give her to me, I would not reject her. Yes! Yes! Chilo, you've
lost both your father and your mother. You're an orphan; therefore, buy a
female slave to console you. She must have shelter; therefore Vinitius will pay
for a dwelling for her, in which you also may abide. She must have clothing;
therefore Vinitius will pay for it. And she must have food; therefore he'll pro-
vide it. Oh, it's costly to live in this world! Oh, for the times when an obol
would buy as much pork and beans as one could hold in both hands or a piece
of goat's gut filled with blood and as long as the arm of a twelve-year-old boy.
But here's that thief Sporus. It'll be easier to gain some information in the
wineshop.

Chilo entered the shop and ordered a pitcher of wine. Noting the dis-
trustful look of the shopkeeper, he took a gold coin from the purse and
threw it on the table. "Sporus," he cried, "I worked today with Seneca
from dawn until noon, and here, see what my friend has given me along
the way!"

The big eyes of Sporus grew bigger still at sight of the coin.

In a twinkling the wine was placed before Chilo, who, moistening his
fingers, drew a fish on the table and said, "Do you know what that
means?"

"A fish? A fish means a fish."

"You're stupid, though you add so much water to the wine that one
might find a fish in it. It's a symbol, which in the language of philosophers
means 'the smile of Fortune.' Should you understand it, perhaps you, too,
might make a fortune. And look you, honor philosophy or I'll change my
wineshop, which my dear friend Petronius has long urged me to do."

Chapter XIV

For some days Chilo disappeared from sight. The information Vinitius had received from Acte—that Lygia loved him—made him a hundred-fold more eager to find her. Through his slaves he instituted a careful search. He was both unwilling and unable to appeal to Caesar, whose attention was now completely absorbed in the dangerous illness of the little Augusta. Nothing, however, availed to help the child, neither sacrifices in the temples nor prayers, nor vows, nor the skill of physicians, nor the magic spells to which they had recourse when the last hope had vanished.

At the end of a week the infant died. The court and the whole city of Rome were plunged into mourning. Caesar, who'd been wild with delight at the birth of the child, was now equally wild with grief. Shutting himself up in his room, he refused food for two days. The palace swarmed with senators and Augustinians,[1] who hastened there with their condolences. Caesar denied himself to all. The Senate assembled in extraordinary session and proclaimed that the little Augusta was a goddess. The senators decided to dedicate a temple to her and appoint a special priest for the service of the new goddess. In other temples, sacrifices were also offered to her. Statues of her were cast from precious metals. Her funeral was celebrated with unprecedented solemnity, at which the people marveled at Caesar's unrestrained grief. They wept with him, stretched out their hands for gifts, and above all found amusement in the splendid pageant.

The death of the little Augusta alarmed Petronius. All Rome was aware that Poppaea ascribed it to witchcraft. The physicians eagerly caught up her words as a convenient excuse for their unsuccessful efforts. So likewise did the priests whose sacrifices had proved unavailing, the soothsayers who trembled for their lives, and the people in general. Petronius was glad now that Lygia had disappeared, since he wished no evil on the house of

---

1 Nero's cronies.

123

Aulus, and especially he wished good to himself and to Vinitius. As soon as the cypress placed before the Palatine had been removed, he went to the reception appointed for senators and Augustinians, to learn how far Nero had credited the rumors of witchcraft and to neutralize the possible consequences.

Knowing Nero, he was convinced that though he didn't believe in witchcraft he would feign belief, partly through self-deception, partly through a desire for revenge, but especially for the purpose of averting the suspicion that the gods were punishing him for his crimes. Petronius strongly doubted that Caesar had any deep or sincere love even for his own child, though he made a great show of attachment. But he had not the least doubt that Nero would pretend an exaggerated grief. Nor was he mistaken. Nero listened with a stony face and fixed stare to the condolences of patricians and senators. It was evident that even if he were suffering, he was simultaneously thinking what impression his pain was making on others. He was posing as a Niobe and giving a representation of paternal sorrow, such as an actor might give on a stage. Yet even now he could not long retain his attitude of stony and silent sorrow. At times he'd make a gesture as if casting dust upon his head; at other times he groaned deeply. Seeing Petronius, he assumed a tone of tragic pathos, evidently wishing that all should hear him.

"*Eheu!*"[2] he cried. "You're the cause of her death. By your advice an evil spirit was admitted to these walls, which at one glance sucked the life out of her breast. Woe is me! Better that I had never seen the bright face of Helios.[3] Woe is me! *Eheu! Eheu!*"

Gradually raising his voice, he filled the chamber with exclamations of despair. Petronius saw that he must risk everything on one cast of the dice; hence, stretching out his hand, he seized the silk kerchief that was always around Caesar's neck and put it to Nero's lips.

"Caesar," he said solemnly, "let Rome and the whole world perish from grief, but preserve your voice for us!"

All present were amazed. Caesar himself was stricken dumb for a moment. Petronius alone stood unmoved; he well knew what he was doing. He didn't forget that Terpnos and Diodorus had a direct order to close Caesar's mouth whenever his voice might be threatened by overexertion.

---

2 "Alas!" An expression of grief.
3 The sun god.

"Oh, Caesar!" continued Petronius in the same sad and persuasive voice. "We have suffered an immense loss, but let this treasure remain to console us."

Nero's face quivered. Tears stood in his eyes. Placing his arm on Petronius's shoulder, he suddenly bent his head to his breast, and in a voice choked by sobs, he began, "Only you, Petronius, have reminded us of this. Only you, Petronius, only you!"

Tigellinus grew green with envy. Again Petronius turned to Nero.

"Go to Antium. There she came into the world; there joy flowed in on you; there solace will come to you. Let the sea air refresh your divine throat; let your breast breathe in the salt dampness. We, your loving servants, will follow you everywhere, and when we comfort your sorrow with our friendship, you will comfort us with song."

"True," answered Nero sadly. "I'll write a hymn in her honor and compose the music for it."

"And after that, you'll seek the warm sun in Baiae."

And his stony, gloomy state of mind gradually passed away, as clouds covering the sun. Then ensued a conversation, which though still full of signs of sorrow, was nonetheless enlivened by plans for the coming journey. They spoke of the exhibitions that Caesar would make of his artistic skill, of the feasts that would be prepared for the expected arrival of Tiridates, king of Armenia. Not surprisingly, Tigellinus tried to bring up once more the matter of witchcraft, but Petronius took up the challenge with full assurance of victory.

"Tigellinus," he said, "do you believe that witchcraft can harm the gods?"

"Caesar himself has spoken of spells," answered the courtier.

"Grief and pain were speaking through his lips. But tell us what you think of them yourself."

"The gods are too powerful to be influenced by spells."

"Then would you deny divinity to Caesar and his family?"

"Per actum est!"[4] exclaimed Eprius Marcellus, who stood close by, repeating the shout used in the Circus when a gladiator had received a mortal blow.

Tigellinus smothered his rage. Between him and Petronius had long existed a rivalry for the favor of Nero. Tigellinus had an advantage—that

---

4   "It is finished!"

Nero observed no ceremony in his presence—but Petronius hitherto had always vanquished Tigellinus in every encounter of wit and judgment. And so it happened now. Tigellinus grew silent; he occupied himself by impressing upon his memory the names of the senators who crowded around Petronius at the other end of the hall, in the expectation that after this victory he would become the prime favorite of Caesar.

Petronius, on leaving the palace, directed his litter to be borne to the house of Vinitius. He informed his nephew of his encounter with Caesar and Tigellinus and added, "I've removed all danger, not only from Aulus Plautius and Pomponia, but also from ourselves, and more particularly from Lygia. She will not be pursued now because I've persuaded the red-bearded ape to go to Antium and then to Neapolis[5] or Baiae. He will surely go. He hasn't yet made up his mind about an appearance before the Roman public in the theater, but I've known for some time that he intends to do so at Neapolis. Moreover, he's dreaming of a visit to Greece, where he wishes to sing in all the principal cities and then make a triumphal entry into Rome with all the wreaths that the *Graeculi*[6] may bestow upon him. In the meantime, we'll have an opportunity to search for Lygia without hindrance and to hide her in a safe place if we find her. But hasn't our noble philosopher returned yet?"

"Your noble philosopher is a swindler. He hasn't appeared, and we may be certain of never casting eyes upon him again."

"On the contrary. I've a better opinion, if not of his honesty, at least of his sense. He's drawn blood once from your purse; be assured that he'll return, even were it only to draw blood a second time."

"Let him beware lest I draw his own blood."

"Don't do that. Bear with him until you are entirely convinced of his deceit. Give him no more money, but promise him a liberal reward if he brings you certain information. But what about you: What are *you* doing about it?"

"Two of my freedmen, Nimphidius and Demas, with sixty slaves, are in full pursuit. I've promised freedom to him who finds her. Furthermore, I've sent special messengers to inquire of Ursus and the maiden in all the inns on the roads leading to Rome. Day and night, I myself traverse the city in the hopes of a chance meeting."

---

5   Naples.
6   Greeklets.

"Whatever you learn, inform me of it by letter, for I must go to Antium."

"Very well."

"And if some fine morning, on waking, you say to yourself that it's not worthwhile to torment yourself for one girl, then come to Antium, and there we'll have plenty of women and amusement for you."

Vinitius strode with long steps across the floor. Petronius gazed at him for some time before he again broke the silence.

"Tell me frankly," he said at last, "not as a dreamer who conceals something within himself, but as a man of sense answering a friend—are you still carried away by Lygia?"

Vinitius stopped for a moment and gazed at Petronius as intently as if he'd never seen him before. Then he resumed his walk. Evidently he was restraining an outburst. But the sense of his own impotence, the pain, the wrath, and the ceaseless yearning that possessed him moved him to tears. His dim eyes spoke to Petronius with more force than the most eloquent words.

After a moment's thought, the elder said, "It's not Atlas who bears the world on his shoulders, but . . . but . . . women, and sometimes they play with it as with a ball."

"True," answered Vinitius. Then they bade each other farewell. But just then a slave announced that Chilo Chilonides was outside in the antechamber, awaiting permission to enter. Vinitius ordered his instant admittance.

"Behold!" laughed Petronius. "Didn't I tell you so? By Hercules, preserve your calm. Otherwise he'll subdue you; not you him."

"Salutations and honor to the noble soldier and tribune, and to you, O master," said Chilo, entering. "May your good fortune equal your fame, and may your fame resound over the world, from the Pillars of Hercules to the uttermost boundaries."

"A greeting to you, wise and virtuous lawgiver," answered Petronius.

Vinitius asked with assumed calmness, "What news have you brought?"

"Master, on my first visit I brought you hope, and now I bring assurance that the maiden will be found."

"Which means that you haven't found her yet?"

"True, master, but I've discovered the meaning of the sign she drew. I now know who the people are that rescued her, and I also know among what class of religionists she must be sought."

Vinitius was on the point of leaping from his chair, but Petronius laid his hand on the young man's shoulder and, turning to Chilo, said, "Speak on."

"Are you certain, O master, that the maiden drew a fish upon the sand?"

"Yes!" exclaimed Vinitius.

"Then she's a Christian, and Christians have taken her away."

A moment of silence followed.

"Listen, Chilo," said Petronius, "my kinsman has set aside for you a large reward for the finding of Lygia, and no smaller allowances of lashes if you're trying to deceive him. In the first case, you'll be able to buy not merely one, but three copyists; in the second case, not all the philosophy of all the seven sages and your own in addition will serve you as a healing ointment."

"Master, this maiden is a Christian," insisted the Greek.

"Listen, Chilo, you're no fool. We know that Unia Sylana and Calvia Crispinilla accused Pomponia Graecina of professing the Christian superstition. It's also known to us that a private investigation acquitted her from this charge. Do you wish to renew it? Do you think you'll be able to convince us that both Pomponia and Lygia belong among the enemies of the human race, the poisoners of fountains and wells, the worshipers of an ass's head, among a people who murder infants and who give themselves up to the foulest corruptions? Beware, Chilo, lest the thesis announced by you be turned back upon you as an antithesis."

Chilo spread out his hands as a sign that it was not his fault and said, "Master, pronounce the following words in Greek: 'Jesus Christ, Son of God, Savior.'"

"Well, I've done so. But what of it?"

"Now take the first letters of each word, and form them in such a manner as to compose a new word."

"*Fish!*" cried Petronius in astonishment.

"Now you see why the symbol of a fish became the symbol of Christianity."

The argument of the Greek was so convincing that both the friends remained buried in thought.

"Vinitius," asked Petronius, "are you not mistaken? Did she really draw a fish?"

"By all the infernal gods, do you wish to drive me insane?" cried the young man wrathfully. "Had she drawn a bird, I should have said a bird."

"So she's a Christian," repeated Chilo.

"Which means," said Petronius, "that Pomponia and Lygia are poisoning wells, murdering kidnapped children, and giving themselves up to profligacy. Nonsense! You, Vinitius, remained for some time in their house. I wasn't there long, but I know Aulus and Pomponia well enough. If a fish is the symbol of the Christians, which is really difficult to deny, and if they are all Christians, then, by Proserpina, it's evident that Christians are not what we suppose them to be."

"Master, you speak like Socrates," replied Chilo. "Who has ever interrogated a Christian? Who is familiar with that creed? When, three years ago, I passed from Neapolis to Rome (oh, why did I not remain there?), I was joined by one Glaucus, who was said to be a Christian, and in spite of this, I convinced myself that he was a good and virtuous man."

"Did this virtuous man inform you of the meaning of the fish?"

"Master, on the road this honorable man was stabbed in an inn, and his wife and child were taken away from him by slave dealers. In their defense I lost these two fingers. But they say that there is no lack of miracles among Christians, so I hope that these two fingers may grow out again."

"How is that? Have you become a Christian?"

"Since yesterday, O master, since yesterday. This fish has made me a Christian. See what power it has? In a few days I shall become one of the most zealous of believers, so that I may be admitted to all their secrets. But when I'm admitted, I'll learn where the maiden is; then perchance my Christianity will pay me better than my philosophy has. I made a vow to Mercury that if he aided me in finding the maiden, I would sacrifice to him two heifers of the same age and size, whose horns I shall gild."

"Which means that your Christianity of yesterday and your philosophy of the day before allow you to believe in Mercury?"

"I always believe in what I need to believe in. Such is my philosophy, and it ought to especially harmonize with the taste of Mercury. But you, worthy lords, know what a suspicious god he is. He trusts not the vows of the most irreproachable philosophers. Perchance he may desire the heifers in advance, but this involves a large outlay. Not everyone can be a Seneca, and I cannot afford the expense, unless the noble Vinitius be willing to advance a portion of the promised reward."

"Not an obol, Chilo," said Petronius, "not an obol. The liberality of Vinitius will surpass your expectations, but not before you find Lygia or show her place of concealment. Mercury must trust you for the two heifers, though I don't wonder that he does it unwillingly. I see Mercury has intelligence."

"Listen to me, worthy masters. The discovery I've made is very great. For, though I haven't yet found the maiden, I've found the method by which she may be found. You've scattered freedmen and slaves throughout the city. Has anyone given you a clue? No. I'm the only one who has found one. I will say more. Among your slaves may be slaves of whom you know nothing. This superstition has spread itself everywhere. Instead of helping you, they may betray you. It's even dangerous for me to be seen here. Therefore, you, noble Petronius, swear Eunice to silence; and you, noble Vinitius, announce that I'm selling you an ointment that secures certain victory for horses in the Circus. I alone will seek her, and I alone will find the fugitives. But have faith in me, and know that whatever I receive in advance will be only a stimulus, for I'll always hope to receive more and will be more certain that the promised reward will not fail me. Yea, this is true. As a philosopher I have a contempt for money, though it's not scorned by Seneca, nor by Carnutus; yet these philosophers haven't lost two fingers in defense of some unfortunate. They can write their books and memoirs and leave their names to posterity. But, besides the slave whom I wish to buy and Mercury, to whom I've promised two heifers (and you know how expensive cattle are at present), the search itself involves numerous expenses. Listen to me patiently. During these last few days my feet have become sore from continuous walking. I've sought to converse with people in the wineshops, in the bakeries, in the butcher shops, and with oil dealers and fishermen. I've run through all the streets and lanes; I've been in the dens of escaped slaves; I've lost large sums of money playing *mora*; I've been in laundries, in drying sheds, and in lunchrooms; I've met mule drivers and carvers, men who cure troubles of the bladder, and men who pull teeth. I've talked with dealers in dried figs; I've been in cemeteries.

"And know you my object in all this? It was to draw a fish everywhere, to look into people's eyes and to hear what they might say when they saw this sign. For a long time I learned nothing. Then at last I met an old slave at a fountain, drawing water and weeping. Approaching, I asked the cause of his tears. We both took our seats on the steps of the fountain, when he told me that all his lifetime he had been saving up sesterces to redeem his beloved son from slavery; but his master, Pausa by name, on seeing the money, took it and kept the son in slavery anyway. 'And so I weep,' said the old man, 'for though I repeat, "The will of God be done," yet I, a poor sinner, cannot restrain my tears.' Then I moistened my finger in the pail of water and drew the figure of a fish, at which he remarked, 'I also put my trust in Christ.' Then I asked him, 'Did you recognize me by this sign?' and he answered, 'Yea, may peace be with you.' I then began to question him and the old man told me all. His master Pausa is himself a freedman of the great Pausa. He ships stones in boats along the Tiber to Rome, where slaves and hirelings unload the stones and carry them to buildings at night so as not to obstruct the streets during the day. Many Christians are engaged in this work, among them his son; but as the work is beyond his son's strength, he desired to redeem him. But Pausa kept both the money and the slave.

"While relating this, the old man wept again and I followed his example, which wasn't difficult because of my kind heart and the pain in my feet, caused by continual walking. I lamented, likewise, that I had arrived recently from Neapolis, so that I knew none of the brethren, nor where they assembled for prayer. He marveled that the brethren in Neapolis hadn't given me letters of recommendation to the brethren in Rome, but I explained to him that I'd been robbed of my letters on the way. Then he instructed me to come to the river at night, and he would introduce me to the brethren, who would conduct me to the houses of prayer and to the elders who rule this Christian community. I was so overjoyed by this information that I gave him the necessary amount for his son's redemption, feeling confident that the magnanimous Vinitius would return me double the amount."

"Chilo," interrupted Petronius, "in your narrative, falsehood floats on the surface of truth as oil on water. No doubt you've brought important news. I think indeed that a great step has been taken towards finding Lygia; but don't mix falsehood with truth. What's the name of the old man from whom you learned that Christians recognize one another by the sign of a fish?"

"Euritius is his name, master, a poor, unfortunate old man. He reminds me of Glaucus, whom I defended from murderers."

"I believe you did make his acquaintance and that you'll be able to make use of this acquaintance, but you didn't give him any money. You didn't even give him one as,[7] do you understand? You didn't give him anything."

---

7 Very low value coin.

"But I assisted him to lift his pail, and I spoke of his son with the greatest sympathy. Oh, master, what can be concealed from the insight of Petronius? I didn't give him any money, or more correctly, I gave it to him in intention only. This would have sufficed him had he been a true philosopher. I gave it to him because I considered the gift necessary and useful; for think how this will win for me the hearts of all the Christians and how I'll secure access to them and win their confidence."

"True," said Petronius, "but it was to your interest to do it." Then, turning to Vinitius, he said, "Order that five thousand sesterces be counted out to him, but in intention only."

But Vinitius said, "I'll give you a servant who will carry the necessary amount. You'll tell Euritius that the servant is your slave, and you'll count out the money to the old man in the servant's presence. But as you've brought important news, you'll have the same amount for yourself. Call this evening for the servant and the money."

"You're as liberal as Caesar!" cried Chilo. "Permit me, master, to dedicate my work to you, but permit also that I come this evening for my money only, as Euritius informed me that the boats had all been unloaded and that others would not follow from Ostia until a few days have passed. May peace be with you! Thus do Christians greet one another. I shall buy a female slave. No, I mean a male slave. Fish are caught with bait, and Christians with fish. *Pax vobiscum!*[8]. . . *Pax!* . . . *Pax!* . . . *Pax!* . . ."

---

8   "Peace be with you!"

Chapter XV

PETRONIUS TO VINITIUS:

I send this letter to you from Antium by a faithful slave, expecting that you'll return an answer without delay, by the bearer, although your hand is better used to the sword than to the pen. I left you hopeful and on a clear trail. I trust, therefore, that you've already satisfied your sweet desires in the arms of Lygia or that you'll satisfy them before the real winter winds from the summits of Soracte blow on the Campania. Oh, dear Vinitius! May the golden-haired goddess of Cyprus be your instructor, and may you in turn be the instructor of this Lygian morning star, fleeing before the sun of love. But remember that even the most precious marble is nothing in itself and that it obtains real value only when the sculptor makes of it a masterpiece. Be you such a sculptor, *carissime!* To love is not enough; one should know how to love and how to teach love. For even the common people and animals experience sensual delight, but a genuine man differs from them in this: that he transforms love into a noble art and, conscious of its divine meaning, recreates it in his mind so that he satisfies not only his heart, but also his soul. Often when I think of the vanity, the uncertainty, and the tediousness of our lives, it occurs to me that perhaps you've taken the wiser course and that not the court of Caesar, but war and love are the only two things worth being born and living for.

You've been fortunate in war; be fortunate also in love. And if you're curious to know what goes on at the court of Caesar, I'll send you news of everything. We're staying here at Antium and nursing our divine voice, continuing to cherish the same hatred of Rome, and intending to spend the winter at Baiae, in order to make our public appearance in Neapolis, whose citizens, being of Greek descent, will appreciate us better than the wolf brood on the banks of the Tiber. People will hasten there from Baiae, Pompeii, Puteoli, and from Stabiae; there'll be no lack of applause or wreaths, and this will be an encouragement for the intended expedition to Achaea.

As regards the memory of the little Augusta? Yes, we're still lamenting for her. We're singing hymns of our own composition, so beautiful that the Sirens, from envy, have concealed themselves in Amphitrite's[1] deepest caves. The dolphins themselves would listen to us were it not for the noise of the sea. Our[2] grief is not yet over; hence we shall exhibit it in every form of sculpture known to art, and we're careful that our poses shall be beautiful and that the world will recognize this beauty. Oh, my friend, we shall die as clowns, comedians, and buffoons.

All the Augustinians are here, male and female, including five hundred she-asses, in whose milk Poppaea bathes, and ten thousand servants. At times it's even cheerful here. Calvia Crispinilla is growing old. It's said that she petitioned Poppaea to let her take the bath immediately after herself. Lucan slapped Nigidia on the face because he suspected her of having relations with a gladiator. Sporus lost his wife at dice to Senecio. Torquatus Sillanus has offered me for Eunice four chestnut horses that will surely win this year at the races. But I declined the offer. I'm grateful to you that you didn't accept her. As to Torquatus Sillanus, he, poor wretch, doesn't suspect that he's more of a shadow than a man.[3] His fate is decided. Do you know what

---

1   The wife of Neptune, hence goddess of the sea.
2   Nero's, the Augustinians', and the court's.
3   Close to death.

his crime is? He's the great-grandson of the divine Augustus.[4] There's no help for him. Such is our world! As you know, we've been expecting Tiridates, but he has not arrived. Meanwhile, Vologeses has written an offensive letter. Having conquered Armenia, he asks that it be left to him by Tiridates; and if it be not left to him, he declares he will hold onto it anyway. Pure comedy! We've decided on war. Corbulo will be given such power as Pompius Magnus received in the war against the pirates. There was a moment, however, when Nero hesitated. He evidently fears the glory that Corbulo may win by martial deeds. It was even proposed to give the chief command to our Aulus, but Poppaea, to whom Pomponia's virtue is as salt in the eye, opposed it.

Vatinius has promised us some remarkable gladiatorial combat that he's preparing in Beneventum. Behold the height to which cobblers rise in our time, despite the saying, *"Sutor supra crepidum."*[5] Vitelius is the descendant of a cobbler, but Vatinius is the son of one! Perhaps he himself has stitched with the waxed thread! Alituras, the actor, gave a great representation of Oedipus yesterday. He's a Jew, and I asked him whether Jews and Christians were the same? He answered that the Jewish religion is a very ancient one, but that the Christians are a new sect, risen lately in Judea; that in the time of Tiberius, a certain man was crucified, and that the Christians consider him as God. His followers, by the way, are increasing daily. The Christians, it seems, refuse to worship all other gods, especially ours. I fail to see what harm such worship would do them.

Tigellinus openly manifests his enmity to me. As yet he has not prevailed against me, though he's my

4 Translated: Nero and Poppaea will have him murdered, since he would have a legitimate claim to the throne.
5 "Let the cobbler stick to his trade."

superior in that he cares more for life and is at the same
time a greater scoundrel than I, which helps him in
Ahenobarbus's eyes. Sooner or later these two will
come to an understanding, and then my turn will
come. I don't know when this will happen, but it's only
a question of time. Meantime I must enjoy life. Life
would not be a bad thing, if it were not for Ahenobarbus. Thanks to him, men like me can't help but feel
self-disgust.

The struggle for his favor must not be placed upon
the same plane as that of rivals in the Circus, or in
games, where the victory is desired on account of
ambition. True, I often explain it to myself in these
terms; but at other times it seems to me that I'm no
better than Chilo. By the way, when you don't need
him any longer, send him to me. I've taken a fancy to
his edifying conversation. Present my greeting to your
divine Christian maiden or, rather, implore her in my
name not to be a fish to you. Write to me about your
search for Lygia. Know how to love, teach how to
love—and farewell.

VINITIUS TO PETRONIUS:

Lygia has not yet been found. Were it not for the
hope that I should find her before long, you wouldn't
be receiving this answer, for one is not inclined to let-
ter-writing when concerned in a matter of life and
death. I wanted to find out whether Chilo was deceiv-
ing me or not, so on the night that he came to secure
the money for Euritius I wrapped myself in a military
cloak and, unseen by him, followed him and the servant whom I sent with him. When they reached the
appointed place, I watched them from a distance, hiding behind a portico pillar, and I convinced myself that
Euritius had not been invented for the occasion. Below,
by the river, groups of workmen were unloading stones
from a large boat and hoisting them onto the bank. I
saw Chilo approach and enter into conversation with

an old man, who knelt down before him. Others surrounded them, looking on with astonishment. Before
my eyes the servant gave the purse to Euritius, who,
seizing it, began to pray, raising his hands to the sky. At
the old man's side, another was kneeling, evidently his
son. Chilo said something that I couldn't hear and
blessed the kneeling figures and the others about them,
making in the air a sign in the form of a cross, which
evidently they all honor, for all knelt down. I would
have approached them, to promise three such purses to
him who would deliver Lygia to me, but I feared lest I
might spoil Chilo's work; so, after hesitating for a
moment, I departed.

This was some twelve days after your departure.
Chilo has visited me frequently since then. He tells me
that he has gained great influence among the Christians. He explains that if he has not yet found Lygia,
it's because there are such multitudes of Christians in
Rome that they are not all acquainted with one
another and cannot know everything that goes on in
the community. Besides, the Christians are wary and
usually reticent. But he assures me that when he comes
to know the elders, called presbyters, he'll be able to
learn everything from them. He has gained access to
some of them already and has begun to question them,
though with the utmost circumspection, lest he
awaken their suspicions and thus raise difficulties in
his own path. It's hard to wait and I'm impatient, but
I feel that he's right, and I wait.

He has learned, too, that the Christians assemble
for prayer beyond the city gates, in empty houses and
even in sandpits. There, they worship Christ, sing
hymns, and hold feasts. They have many such places of
assembly. Chilo thinks that Lygia goes intentionally to
different places of worship than those frequented by
Pomponia, so that the latter, if questioned by the
authorities, could boldly swear that she didn't know
Lygia's hiding place. Perhaps the presbyters suggested

this precaution. When Chilo discovers these places, I will go with him, and if the gods permit me a sight of Lygia, by Jupiter, this time she won't escape me.

I think continually of those places of prayer. Chilo doesn't want me to go with him. He's afraid. But I can't sit idly at home. I would recognize her at once, even in disguise or veiled. The Christians assemble during the night, but I'd recognize her even at night. I'd know her voice and movements under all possible conditions.

I'll go myself in disguise and scrutinize every person who comes in or goes out. I think of her always and shall certainly recognize her. Chilo is to come for me tomorrow, and we'll go together. I'll take arms with me. Some of my slaves whom I sent to the provinces have returned without any news. I'm certain now that she's here in the city and possibly not far away. I myself have looked through many houses under pretext of renting them. She'll be a hundred times better off with me, for she's now probably dwelling amid poverty. I shall refuse her nothing. You write that I have chosen the happier lot. No, I've chosen only suffering and sorrow. We'll go first to the houses within the city, then to those beyond the gates. Hope is born anew in my breast every morning, otherwise I couldn't live. You say that one should know how to love. I knew once how to speak of love to Lygia, but now I only yearn. I wait only for Chilo, as life at home is unendurable for me. Farewell!

Chapter XVI

Chilo, however, didn't appear for a long time, and Vinitius didn't know what to think. Vainly he repeated to himself that a successful search must be slow and careful. His impetuous nature rebelled against the voice of reason. To do nothing, to wait and sit with folded hands, was so adverse to his nature that he couldn't reconcile himself to it. To run in the disguise of a slave through dark streets and alleys, without result, seemed a useless employment of energy. His freedmen, quick, sagacious, and experienced, whom he'd commanded to make an independent search, proved themselves to be a hundredfold less effective than Chilo. But Vinitius, in addition to his love for Lygia, felt the gambler's craving for victory. This had always been one of his characteristics. From his childhood he had accomplished all his wishes with the passion of one who doesn't understand the word *impossible* or recognize the necessity of surrender. Military discipline had, for a period, curbed his self-will to a certain extent, but it had also engrafted into him a conviction that every command given by him to his subordinates must be carried out at any cost. His long sojourn in the East, among a docile people accustomed to slavish obedience, strengthened him in his belief that there was no "Nay" to his "I will." At present, therefore, his pride, as well as his heart, was wounded. Besides, the resistance and flight of Lygia remained incomprehensible to him, a riddle he hadn't been able to solve. He felt that Acte told the truth—that Lygia was not indifferent to him. Yet, if this were so, why did she prefer vagrancy and misery to his love, to his caresses, and to his luxurious home? He couldn't answer these questions. He only knew that between him and Lygia and Pomponia, between her feelings and his, between the world of Pomponia and that in which he and Petronius lived, there existed a division as deep and impassable as an abyss. Then it seemed to him that he must lose Lygia; but at that thought he lost all the remnants of self-control that Petronius sought to bolster up.

There were times when he didn't know whether he would love Lygia or hate her, should he find her; but one thing he did know, and that was that he *must* find her. Better that she was swallowed up in the bowels of the earth than that he should surrender her. The strength of his imagination often conjured her up visibly before his eyes. He recalled almost every word that he'd ever spoken to her or heard from her; he felt her near him, felt her lying on his chest, in his arms; and pride and passion reawakened in him like flame. He loved her and called upon her, and when he remembered that she loved him in turn and might yield willingly to his desire, an intense and endless sorrow overcame him, and a kind of deep tenderness flooded his heart like an immense wave. But he also had moments in which he grew pale from rage and reveled in the thoughts of the humiliation and tortures that he would inflict on Lygia when he found her—he desired not only to possess her, but to possess her as a trampled slave. Nevertheless, he felt that if the choice were given him to be her slave or never to see her, he'd rather be her slave. He savored the very thought of the scars that his merciless whip would inflict upon her rosy body, but simultaneously a wild desire arose within him to kiss those scars. He even thought that he would be happy if he could kill her.

The torture, torment, excitement, and doubt told upon his health and even upon his manly beauty. He became cruel and unreasonable. Slaves and freedmen approached him trembling. He punished them without mercy and without pretext, and they grew to hate him secretly. He recognized this and felt his isolation still more keenly and wreaked a still bitterer and more unreasonable revenge. With Chilo alone was he on friendly terms, for he feared that Chilo might give up his search. Chilo, noticing this, established greater control over him and grew ever more domineering in his demands. At first he'd assured Vinitius that the task would be easily and speedily accomplished. Now he inwardly exerted himself to invent new difficulties and, although holding out the hope of ultimate success, insisted that time was needed.

Finally, after many days had passed, Chilo arrived with so troubled a look that the young man paled at sight of him. Springing up, he had barely strength to ask him, "Is she not among the Christians?"

"Of course she is," answered Chilo. "But among them I've found a physician, Glaucus."

"What of that? Who's Glaucus?"

"Master, have you forgotten the old man with whom I traveled from Neapolis to Rome, in whose defense I lost these two fingers—a loss that has deprived me of the use of a pen? The robbers who carried off his wife and children stabbed him with a knife. I left him in a dying condition at a tavern in Minturnae[1] and mourned for him a long time. But, alas! I've now ascertained that he's alive and a member of the Christian community in Rome."

Vinitius, who couldn't understand what the problem was—only understanding that Glaucus in some way was an obstacle in his path—suppressed his rising impatience and said, "He should be grateful for your assistance and now aid you in return!"

"Ah, worthy Tribune! But if even the gods themselves are not always grateful, what can we expect from men? Yes, he should be grateful. But, alas! He's an old man. His mind is bowed and darkened by age and disappointment. I learned not only that he's ungrateful, but also that he's accused me to his fellow Christians, saying that I actually conspired with the thieves and thus am the real cause of all his misfortunes. Such is my reward for my two lost fingers."

"Scoundrel! I'm certain that he tells the truth," cried Vinitius.

"Then you know more than he does, master," answered Chilo with dignity, "for he only guesses that it was so. But that guess would suffice for him to call the Christians to aid him in some cruel revenge. He would certainly have done this sooner and found many willing Christians, but that happily he knows not my name. In the house of prayer where we met, he didn't recognize me. But I recognized him at once. My first impulse would have been to throw myself on his neck, but prudence and long habits of self-restraint preserved me from this. On leaving the place I made inquiries and learned from his acquaintances that this was a man who had been betrayed by his companion on the way from Neapolis. And that's how I know what story he is telling."

"What's all this to me? Speak! Tell me what you've seen in the house of prayer."

"It doesn't concern you, master, but it does concern my life. As I wish my wisdom to survive me, rather would I renounce the reward you have offered than sacrifice my life for empty gain. A true philosopher can always live without such remuneration and devote his time to the search for wisdom."

But Vinitius glared at him and said in a voice that trembled with

---

1 A town in Latium, near Campania.

wrath, "Who told you that death was more certain at the hands of Glaucus than at mine? And how do you know, dog, that I won't bury you even
now in my garden?"

Chilo, who was a coward, looked at Vinitius and trembled. He knew
that with one more heedless remark, he was a dead man. "I will seek, master,
and I shall find her!" he cried hastily.

A silence followed. Only the heavy breathing of Vinitius and the far-
off songs of slaves at work in the garden could be heard. Not until Chilo
had assured himself that the young tribune had grown calmer did he
resume the conversation.

"Death has often passed so close as to touch me, but I looked at it with
the coldness of Socrates. No, master, I haven't said that I would renounce
the search for the girl, but only that this search involves much danger for
me. There was a time when you doubted the very existence of a certain
Euritius, but you convinced yourself with your own eyes that the son of
my father told you the truth. Now you think that I've conjured up an
imaginary Glaucus. Alas! Were he really a fiction, and could I walk among
the Christians as safely as of yore, I would cheerfully give up the poor old
slave whom three days ago I purchased for my assistance in my old age
and decrepitude. But, master, Glaucus is alive. Were he to see me, even
once, you'd never see me again. Then who would discover the girl?"

He again became silent, wiping away his tears. Then he continued, "So
long as Glaucus is alive, how can I continue my search for her, when I may
meet him at any moment? If I meet him, I'm lost, and without me the
search is lost."

"What are you aiming at? What do you expect *me* to do about it?"
snarled Vinitius.

"Master, Aristotle teaches that small things must be sacrificed to great.
King Priam always said that old age is a heavy burden. This burden has
oppressed the aged Glaucus for long years, so heavily, indeed, that death
would be a blessing. And, indeed, what is death? According to Seneca, it's
but a release."

"Keep your jesting for Petronius, not for me. What are you trying to
say?"

"If virtue be a jest, may the gods allow me to remain a jester forever. I
wish, master, to put Glaucus out of the way. While he lives, my life and
the search are in the greatest danger."

"Then hire men to beat him to death with clubs. I'll pay the bill."

"They'll rob you, master, and afterward make profit of the secret. There are as many criminals in Rome as grains of sand in the arena; but you wouldn't believe how mercenary they can be when an honest man seeks to employ them. No, worthy Tribune, suppose the watchmen caught the murderers in the act? They would undoubtedly reveal the name of him who had hired them, and great trouble might follow. It's not I that would be denounced, for they know not my name. You're wrong in failing to trust me, for whether you believe in my honesty or not, remember that two things are concerned here: my own life and the reward you've promised me."

"How much do you need?"

"I need a thousand sesterces, master, for I must find honest rascals who won't disappear after taking earnest money, leaving no trace behind them. Good work requires good pay. Something should be added also for me, to wipe away the tears of pity that I'll shed over Glaucus. The gods be my witness how I love him. If I could get the thousand sesterces today, in two days his soul will be wandering in Hades. Then and there, if souls retain the power of memory and of reason, he'll learn how deeply I loved him. I shall find men this very day and tell them that for every day of Glaucus's continued existence one hundred sesterces will be subtracted from their pay. Then there'll be no failure."

Vinitius once more promised him the stipulated sum, forbidding him, however, to speak further of Glaucus. He also questioned him as to what other news he brought, where he'd been in the interval, what he'd seen, and what he'd discovered. But Chilo had little news to tell. He'd been in two more places of prayer, had carefully watched everyone, especially the women, but had seen no one who bore any resemblance to Lygia. The Christians, however, all looked upon him as one of themselves. Ever since he'd ransomed the son of Euritius, they had honored him as one who trod in the ways of Christ. He learned further that their great teacher, Paul of Tarsus, was now in Rome, imprisoned on charges preferred by the Jews, and he'd determined to make his acquaintance. He was most overjoyed with the additional news that the greatest of all the sect, a disciple of Christ, to whom had been confided the administration of the entire Christian world, might arrive in Rome at any moment. All the Christians were anxious to see him and to hear his teachings. There would be great gatherings, at which Chilo himself would be present. He would bring Vinitius there in disguise, and together they would unquestionably find

Lygia. Once Glaucus was out of the way, there would be small peril in all this. The Christians might avenge themselves, but in general, they were usually a quiet and peaceful people.

And now Chilo began to explain with some enthusiasm that he'd never found them to engage in any debauchery, nor to poison wells and fountains, nor to preach enmity to humanity, nor to worship an ass, nor to feed on the flesh of children. No, these things he'd never seen. True, among them might be found persons who would do away with Glaucus, but their teaching, so far as he knew, wouldn't incite them to crime. On the contrary, it commanded forgiveness even to the wronged.

Vinitius recalled what Pomponia Graecina had said to him at Acte's and listened with delight to the words of Chilo. Though sometimes he felt that he hated Lygia, he was relieved to hear that the sect to which she and Pomponia belonged was neither criminal nor disgusting. An indescribable feeling rose within him that these unknown teachings and the mysterious reverence that they paid to Christ created a chasm between him and Lygia. So he began to both hate those teachings and to fear them.

Chapter XVII

For Chilo, it was imperative that he silence Glaucus—permanently—though he lied when he implied to Vinitius that the old man was already near death's door, for while Glaucus *was* advanced in years, by no means was he weak and decrepit. And there was precious little truth in the story Chilo told Vinitius. The truth was that he had indeed known Glaucus—and had betrayed him and sold him to robbers; he had caused the loss of his family and fortune and had delivered him up to murder. He had left him dying, not in a tavern, but on a field near Minturnae. He had not dreamed at the time that Glaucus would ever recover from his wounds and come to Rome. On seeing him in the church, therefore, he had been terrified. His first thought had been to renounce his search for Lygia. But, on the other hand, he feared Vinitius even more. When it came to a choice between his dread of prosecution by Glaucus and of the vengeance of the mighty patrician, who could summon to his aid the still mightier Petronius, he did not long hesitate. He deemed it better to have small enemies than great ones.

His cowardly nature revolted from bloodshed, but when he found that bloodshed a necessity, by shifting the responsibility for the murder to hirelings, he mentally distanced himself from the crime. The important question now was that of choosing the right men for his purpose. He would give them the task of which he had spoken to Vinitius. Passing his nights in taverns among vagrants, men without home or honor or faith, he could readily find men willing to undertake any crime. But it was still easier to find among them men who would accept the money, would promise to do the work, and would then extort still further money from Chilo by threatening to deliver him into the hands of justice. Besides, for some time he had felt a repugnance for these wretched vagrants who lurked in the disreputable houses of the Suburra and the Trans-Tiber. Judging all people by himself, and not having sufficiently fathomed the Christians or their religion, he judged that among them he would also find willing tools, and as they seemed more honest than others, he decided to represent the case to them in such a way that they'd undertake it not only for the money, but also for the good work they were accomplishing.

Therefore he spent his evenings with Euritius, whom he knew to be devoted to him body and soul and would do anything at his bidding. With his native caution, he decided not to reveal anything of the truth to him, which might prove repugnant to one so pious and full of devotion to God. He needed men who were ready for anything and who would both commit the deed without knowing much about why the deed was done and then keep that deed secret forever.

Euritius, after the redemption of his son, had rented a small shop, one among many that surrounded the Circus Maximus. Here he sold olives, beans, fruitcakes, and water sweetened with honey to the people who flocked to the Circus. Chilo found the old man at home, busily arranging his little shop. Greeting him in the name of Christ, he unfolded the reason of his visit, confident that he could depend upon his gratitude for the service he had already extended. He explained that he needed two or three strong, courageous, and fearless men to ward off the dangers that threatened not only himself but all Christians. Poor as he was since he had given his all for Euritius, he still would be able to pay men of this sort for their services, but only on condition that they would trust him and do blindly whatever he commanded.

Euritius and his son, Quartus, listened to him as to their benefactor. They almost dropped upon their knees when they assured him that they were ready to fulfill all his wishes, being convinced that so holy a man would not require from them anything inconsistent with the teachings of Christ.

Chilo assured them that they were right. He lifted up his eyes as if in prayer. In truth he was trying to figure out how he could both accept their offer and keep the thousand sesterces for himself. But after a moment's thought he decided to refuse. Euritius was an old man, burdened not only by his age, but also by sickness and sorrow; and Quartus was but a boy of sixteen. What Chilo needed was strong and dexterous men. As to the thousand sesterces, he hoped that his elaborate scheme would enable him in any event to save the larger portion of it.

The men insisted for some time that he should inform them more specifically of what he needed them to do, but when he refused, finally they yielded.

"Master," said Quartus, "I know a baker called Demas who employs slaves and hired men. There is one among the hired men who is stronger than two or even four ordinary mortals. I myself have seen him lift stones that no four men could have lifted."

"If he be a good and pious man, willing to sacrifice himself for his brethren, you may introduce him to me."

"He's a Christian," said Quartus, "for Demas employs few except Christians. He has both night and day laborers. This man is one of the night laborers. If we go there now, we shall find them at supper, and you'll have a chance to talk freely to him. Demas lives near the Emporium."

Chilo joyfully consented. The Emporium lay at the foot of the Aventine Hill, but a short distance from the Circus Maximus. It could be reached without climbing the hill by passing along the river, through the Porta Aemilia, and this would shorten the journey.

"I'm old," said Chilo when they had arrived under the portico, "and sometimes my memory betrays me. Yes, our Lord was betrayed by one of His disciples, but I can't remember his name."

"It was Judas, master. He who hanged himself," answered Quartus, inwardly astonished at how such a name could escape any memory.

"Oh, yes! Judas! I thank you," answered Chilo.

They continued on their way for a time in silence. When they reached the Emporium, which they found closed, they were obliged to go around the storehouses, from which grain was distributed among the people, and then turn to the left by the houses that stretched along the Via Ostiensis up to the Testaceus Hill and the Forum Pistorium. Here they stopped before a wooden building, from the interior of which they could hear the noise of revolving millstones. Quartus entered, but Chilo remained outside, not wishing to show himself in a crowd and fearing that Fate might bring about a meeting with Glaucus.

I'm curious to see this Hercules who works in a mill, he said to himself, looking up at the radiant moon. *If he's a clever rascal, he may cost me something. But if he's an innocent Christian and a fool, he'll do as I wish for nothing.*

He was interrupted by the return of Quartus, who came out with another man, clad in a shirt cut in such a fashion that his right arm and right chest were exposed, so as to allow him free movement. Such shirts were generally worn by laborers. At sight of this man, Chilo's face revealed his admiration and satisfaction. Never had he seen such an arm and such a chest.

"Master," said Quartus, "here is the brother you wished to see."

"The peace of Christ be with him," was Chilo's greeting. "Tell this brother, O Quartus, that I'm trustworthy, and then return in the name of God, for I see no need that you should leave unprotected the home of your wise old father."

"This is a holy man," said Quartus, "who surrendered his all to redeem me from slavery—me who was unknown to him. May our Lord and Savior prepare a heavenly reward for him."

At these words, the gigantic laborer bent and kissed the hands of Chilo.

"What's your name?" asked the Greek.

"Father, in holy baptism, the name of Urban was given to me."

"Urban, my brother, have you time to speak with me freely?"

"Our work begins at midnight, and at present they're preparing supper for us."

"Ah, then, we have enough time. Let's go over to the river, and there you'll hear my words."

They went and sat down on a stone embankment. The silence was broken only by the far-off turning of the millstones and the rippling of the water. Chilo glanced inquiringly at the face of the laborer. That face was stern and melancholy, as was usual among the barbarians who lived in Rome, yet it was full of kindness and honesty.

How fortunate, thought Chilo. *Here's a kindly fool who'll kill Glaucus for nothing.*

"Urban," he asked, "do you love Christ?"

"I love Him with all my soul and all my heart," answered the laborer.

"And your brethren, your sisters, and all those who taught you the truth and faith in Christ?"

"I love them also, Father."

"Then peace be with you."

"And with you, Father."

There was silence anew, interrupted as before by the sound of the millstones and the water.

Chilo, eyes fixed on the moon, began in low and impressive tones to speak about the death of Christ. He seemed not to be addressing Urban directly, but to be recalling facts that were known to both, for the benefit of the sleeping city. His words seemed so inspired and so holy that they moved the laborer to tears. When Chilo sighed and expressed his sorrow that there had been no one near the dying Christ to defend him, not only from crucifixion, but also from the humiliation inflicted by the Jews and the soldiers, the gigantic fists of the barbarian were clenched in pity and anger. The death of Christ was bad enough, but the thought that the blood of the Lamb was shed amid scoffs and jeers revolted his simple soul and aroused in it a wild desire for vengeance.

Suddenly Chilo asked, "Urban, do you know who Judas was?"

"I know, I know. He hanged himself!" cried the laborer. In his voice was immense sorrow that the traitor had punished himself and was consequently out of his reach.

"But suppose," said Chilo, "that he had *not* hanged himself and that some Christian were to meet him. Would it not be a Christian duty to avenge the sufferings, the death, and the blood of the Savior?"

"Oh, Father, who would not mete out such revenge?"

"Peace be with you, O faithful servant of the Lamb. True, we may forgive wrong done to us, but who has the right to forgive the wrongs done to God? For as serpents breed serpents, as crimes breed crimes, as traitors breed traitors, so from the venom of Judas was born another traitor. As the first Judas betrayed our Savior to the Jews and the soldiers of Rome, so this traitor, who lives among us at present, wishes to betray the lambs of God to the wolf, and if no one prevents this—if no one crushes the head of this serpent—awful destruction awaits us all and with us the destruction of the Holy Lamb."

The laborer glanced at him in wild excitement. He could scarcely believe what he had heard. The Greek covered his face with a corner of his mantle and began to repeat in a deep voice that seemed to come from the depths of the earth: "Woe unto you, servants of the true God. Woe unto you, Christian men and women!"

And again silence followed. Again there was no sound save the revolving millstones, the singing of the millers, and the rippling of the waters below.

"Father," asked the laborer abruptly, "who is this traitor?"

Chilo bowed his head still lower. "Who is this traitor? A son of Judas, the spawn of his venom, who pretends to be a Christian and visits the houses of prayer solely for the purpose of betraying his brethren to Caesar, charging that they don't honor Caesar as a god, that they poison wells, that they murder children, and that they wish to hurl the city into such destruction that not one stone shall remain upon another. Mark my words: In a few days an order will be issued to the Praetorians to imprison

men, women, and children and lead them to death as they led to death
the slaves of Pedanius Secundus. This is the work of our second Judas. But
if the first one was never punished, if nobody took vengeance on him, if
no one defended Christ in the hour of torment, who will now take
vengeance? Who now will destroy him before Caesar can hear his terrible
charges? Who now will put him out of the way and so prevent the ruin of
our brothers in the faith of Christ?"

Urban, who till now had remained seated on the stone, arose immediately and said, "I'll do this, Father."

Chilo also rose. He looked straight in the face of the laborer as he stood
in the rays of the moonlight; then, placing his hands upon his head, he
solemnly said, "Go among the Christians, go to the places of prayer, ask
the brethren to point out Glaucus the physician, and if they show him to
you, kill him!"

"Did you say Glaucus?" repeated the laborer, with an effort of memory
to retain the name.

"Do you know him?"

"I know him not. There are thousands of Christians in Rome, and they
don't all know one another. But tomorrow night at Ostranium there'll be
a general gathering of all the brothers and sisters without a single exception, for a great Apostle of Christ will preach there, and I'll ask the
brethren to point out to me Glaucus."

"In Ostranium?" inquired Chilo. "Why that's outside the gates of the city.
All our brothers and sisters at night? Outside the city gate, in Ostranium?"

"Yes, Father, our cemetery lies there, between the Via Salaria and Via
Nomentana. Didn't you know that the great Apostle is expected there?"

"I've been away for two days; consequently I didn't receive his letter.
And I'm not familiar with Ostranium since I just arrived from Corinth,
where I was the head of a Christian community. But so be it. Christ will
be with you. You'll go tomorrow night, my son, to Ostranium, and there
you'll find Glaucus among the brethren. You'll slay him on his way back
to the city. All your sins will be forgiven you in return. And now, peace be
with you!"

"Father!"

"I hear you, servant of the Lamb."

The laborer's face expressed perplexity. He explained his confusion to
Chilo.

Not long before, he had killed a man, perhaps two, but the religion of

Christ forbade murder. He had not killed them in self-defense, for even this was forbidden. Nor—Christ forbid!—had he killed for the sake of a reward. The bishop himself had given him brethren to help in a certain adventure but had commanded him to take no life. The killing had been through inadvertence, for the Lord had burdened him with extraordinary strength. And now he was doing penance for this. Others might sing while grinding wheat; he could only think on his sins and his offenses against the Lamb. How he had prayed! How he had wept! How often he had sought the Lamb for forgiveness! In spite of everything, he felt that his repentance was not yet sufficient. And now he had promised to kill a traitor! So be it. One may readily forgive trespasses against oneself, but against oneself only. So he would kill Glaucus, even in the presence of all the brothers and sisters gathered at Ostranium. But Glaucus should be tried first, before the elders selected from among the brethren by the bishop or the Apostle. To kill was no great matter, and to kill a traitor was a pleasant duty, like killing a wolf or a bear. But suppose Glaucus was innocent?

At last he asked, "How can I burden myself with a new murder, a new sin, a new offense against the Lamb?"

"There's no time for a trial, my son," answered Chilo, "for the traitor will hurry from Ostranium directly to Caesar in Antium or hide himself in the house of a certain patrician in whose employ he now is. I'll give you a sign; if, after killing Glaucus, you show it to the bishop or the Apostle, they'll bless you and your deed."

With these words, he took from his pocket a coin. Drawing a knife from his belt, he cut the sign of the cross upon the coin and gave it to the laborer.

"Here's a sentence upon Glaucus and a sign for you. When you show this to the bishop, he'll give you absolution, not only for the killing of Glaucus, but also for the involuntary homicides that preceded it."

The laborer hesitantly stretched out his hand for the coin. He recalled his first homicide and couldn't repress a shiver.

"Father!" he exclaimed in a voice of entreaty. "Do you take this upon your own conscience, and are you certain that Glaucus has plotted to slay our brethren?"

Chilo saw that he must give some proof and mention some names; otherwise doubt would arise in the mind of the laborer. A happy thought struck him.

"Listen to me, Urban," he said. "I dwell in Corinth, but I come from

Cos. Here in Rome I'm instructing in the religion of Christ a servant girl, my countrywoman, Eunice by name. She serves as a handmaiden in the house of a certain Petronius, a friend of Caesar. In this house I learned how Glaucus had promised to betray all the Christians and also to betray to a certain Vinitius—another imperial advisor—a certain maiden—"

He stopped abruptly, for he had caught a strange look in the eyes of the laborer. They blazed like the eyes of a wild beast, while the whole face took on a look of wrath and menace. "What's the matter?" he asked in some alarm.

"Nothing, Father. I'll kill Glaucus tomorrow."

The Greek was silent. He took the laborer's arm and turned him so that the moonlight fell full upon his face, which he scrutinized carefully. Evidently he was hesitating whether to inquire further or to be content with the impression he had already made. His habitual caution gained the upper hand.

Twice he sighed deeply, and again placing his hands upon the head of the laborer, he asked in solemn tones, "The name of Urban was given you in holy baptism?"

"Yes, Father, it was."

"Then peace be with you, Urban."

Chapter XVIII

PETRONIUS TO VINITIUS:

It fares badly with you, dear friend. It would seem that Venus has disturbed your mind and deprived you of reason and memory, as well as the power of thinking of anything save love. Reread your answer to my letter, and you'll see how indifferent you are to all except Lygia; how exclusively your mind dwells on her, how it returns to her always and circles above her, as a falcon above a chosen prey. By Pollux! Find her soon! Otherwise the fire within you will turn you to ashes, or you'll transform yourself into an Egyptian sphinx that was enamored of the white Isis, as the story goes, and was turned deaf and dumb and indifferent to all things, awaiting only the night when he could gaze upon her with cold and stony eyes.

Run disguised through the city in the evening; even honor Christian houses of prayer in your philosopher's company. Whatever raises hope and kills time will help you. But, for the sake of my friendship, do this one thing. This Ursus, the slave of Lygia, is a man of rare strength. So hire Croto and go out three together, that will be safe—and wise. The Christians, since Pomponia and Lygia belong to them, are surely not so vile as is believed. But in their capture of Lygia they gave proof that when some lamb of their flock is in danger, they know how to act. When you see Lygia you won't be able to restrain yourself, I'm sure, but will try and carry her away at once. But could you do this with the help of Chilo alone? Croto could manage it, even if there were ten Ursuses to defend Lygia. Therefore,

don't let Chilo plunder you, but lavish money on
Croto. This is the best counsel that I can give you.

The infant Augusta is forgotten here; forgotten also
are the charges of witchcraft. Poppaea mentions her at
times, but Caesar's thoughts are elsewhere. At all
events, if it's true that the divine Augusta is again in a
delicate condition, the memory of the first child will
disappear without leaving any trace. We've already
been more than ten days in Neapolis, or rather, in
Baiae. If you're still capable of thought, surely your ears
must have heard echoes of what occurs here, for it
must be the general subject of talk in Rome.

We came directly to Baiae, where memories of our[1]
mother revived and the voice of conscience was heard
again. But do you know the frame of mind to which
Ahenobarbus is reduced? Simply to this, that the murder
of his mother has become for him only an inspiration for
poetry and tragic themes. The voice of conscience spoke
only to his cowardice. He soon reassured himself with
the thought that the whole world was under his feet and
that no god would wreak vengeance upon him. He
feigns emotion only to move his auditors. Sometimes he
rises at night, crying that the Furies are after him. He
awakens us all, gazes around at us, and assumes the pose
of an actor (and a bad actor at that) in the role of Orestes.
He declaims Greek verses and watches to see if we are
admiring him. And we do admire him, or feign admiration. Instead of saying to him, "Go back to bed, you
clown!" we become tragedians in our turn and defend
this great artist from the furies.

By Castor! You must have heard how he's appeared
in public in Neapolis. From the city itself and from the
surrounding villages, all the Greek rabble were driven
into the arena, filling it with so vile an odor of perspiration and garlic that I thanked the gods that in lieu of
sitting in the first rows with the Augustinians, I was

---

1   Nero's.

behind the scenes with Ahenobarbus. And will you believe it, he was afraid! Truly he was. He seized my hands and placed them upon his heart, which was throbbing violently. He breathed with difficulty. At the moment when he was to appear, he turned pale as parchment, and on his forehead stood huge drops of sweat. Yet he knew that around all the seats were stationed Praetorians armed with clubs, ready to stimulate the necessary enthusiasm. No herd of monkeys could have raised such a clatter as did this multitude. I tell you that the smell of garlic invaded the stage.

Nero bowed, pressed his hand to his heart, threw kisses, and shed tears. He rushed back among us who were waiting behind the scenes and cried like a drunken man, "What are all other triumphs compared with this of mine?"

The rabble howled out their applause, knowing that it was applauding for favors, gifts, free places in the theater, lottery tickets, and a new exhibition by Caesar the clown. I marveled not at this, for I knew that never before had they witnessed such a spectacle.

And every moment, he repeated, "See what the Greeks are! See what the Greeks are!" From that evening it seemed to me that his hatred for Rome increased. As a matter of fact, special messengers were dispatched to Rome to carry the news of his triumph, and we expect at any moment the thanks of the Senate.

Immediately after Nero's first exhibition, a strange thing happened. The theater suddenly collapsed, but fortunately it was after the audience had left. I was there at the time and did not see a single corpse taken from the ruins. Many, even among the Greeks, looked upon this as a sign of anger of the gods over the disgraced imperial dignity.

Caesar asserts the contrary: He declares it to be direct evidence of the favor and protection of the gods, extended not only to his hymns, but also to those who listened to them. Hence thanks and sacrifices were

offered up in all the temples. He desires now to set out
for Achaea. Yet, a few days ago he acknowledged to me
that, should he do so and delay further his return, he had
doubts as to what the people of Rome might say. He
wondered whether they might not rise in revolt out of
love for him and fear that the distribution of bread and
the exhibition of spectacles might cease during his prolonged absence.

We're now ready to start for Beneventum to gaze
upon the cobbler's magnificence that Vatinius will
exhibit, and then on to Greece, under the protection
of the divine brothers of Helen. As for me, I've noted
one thing: When a man is among the mad, he grows
mad himself, and what is more, he finds a certain
charm in mad pranks. So I look forward to Greece and
the voyage there in a thousand ships—a sort of triumphal procession of Bacchus, amid nymphs and bacchantes, crowned with wreaths of myrtle, vine leaves,
and honeysuckle. There'll be women in tiger skins harnessed to chariots, flowers, music, poetry, and applause
for the Greek god. All most entertaining.

But we have more important projects in view: We
wish to create a sort of Oriental empire, a fairyland of
palms, sunshine, poetry, and reality turned into a delicious dream, into a life of luxurious pleasure. We wish
to forget Rome; to place the center of the world somewhere between Greece, Asia, and Egypt; to live the life
not of men, but of gods; to forget the commonplace;
to wander in golden galleries, under the shadow of
purple sails in the Archipelago; to be Apollo, Osiris,
and Baal in one; to be rosy in the dawn, gold in the
sun, and silver in the moon; to act, to sing, to dream.
. . . And will you believe it? I, who possess at least a sestertium's worth of judgment and an ass's worth of
sense, allow myself to be borne away by these fantasies
for the reason that, even if they're impossible, they're at
least grandiose and spectacular. Only when Venus
transforms herself into a Lygia, or even into a slave like
Eunice, only when art beautifies life, is life worth living.

Otherwise it's a grinning ape. But Ahenobarbus will never realize his dream, if only because in that Oriental fairyland he allows no place for treason, iniquity, and death; while in him, in the false guise of poetry, is a common comedian, a stupid charioteer, and a frivolous tyrant. Meanwhile, we are killing people whenever they displease us in any way.

Poor Torquatus Silanus[1] is now a shade. He had to open his veins a few days ago. Lecanius and Licinus accept the consulate with trembling. Old Thrasea cannot escape death, for he was bold enough to be honest. Tigellinus has not yet succeeded in securing an order to make me open my veins. I'm still needed, not only as an *arbiter elegantiarum,* but also as a man whose counsel and taste are vital for the success of the expedition to Achaea. But I often think that sooner or later this must end. And do you know what my chief anxiety is? That Ahenobarbus should not get that Myrrhene goblet that you know and admire. Should you be near me during my last hour, I'll give it to you; but should you be far away, I'll break it. Meanwhile, we have before us the cobbler's Beneventum, Olympian Greece, and Fate, which points out the unknown and unforeseen road.

Take my advice and hire Croto; otherwise Lygia will a second time elude you. When you have no further need for the services of Chilo, send him to me wherever I may be. Perchance I may succeed in making of him a second Vatinius. Consuls and senators will tremble before him yet, as they now tremble before our noted cobbler. Ah, it'd be worthwhile to live to see such a spectacle! When you've found Lygia, let me know, that I may sacrifice a pair of swans and a pair of doves in our round temple of Venus. Once in my dreams I saw Lygia on your knee, seeking for kisses. Try to make that dream a reality. May there be no clouds in your sky, or if some there be, may they have the color and the odor of roses. Be in good health, and farewell!

---

1 Another descendant of Augustus conveniently removed from Nero's path.

Chapter XIX

Barely had Vinitius finished reading this letter when Chilo pushed quietly into the library, cautiously and unannounced, for the slaves had orders to admit him at any hour of the day or night.

"May the divine mother of your noble ancestor show such favor to you as the divine son of Maia[1] has shown to me."

"What do you mean?" exclaimed Vinitius, springing from the table at which he was seated.

"Eureka!" cried Chilo proudly.

The young patrician fell back upon his chair; for some moments, excitement prevented his speaking.

"Have you seen her?" he asked at last.

"Master, I've seen Ursus and have spoken with him."

"Speak then. Do you know where they're living?"

"No, master. Another man might have informed the Lygian that his identity was known to him, might have revealed his own name and sought information as to where the maiden lived. But what would his answer have been? Perchance a blow from that mighty fist, full in the face, which would have made him indifferent to all worldly things. At all events, he would have raised suspicion in the mind of the maiden's guardian, which would have led to an immediate change in her hiding place. Master, I did not act thus. Sufficient was it for me to know that Ursus is a night laborer in the mill of one who bears the same name as that of your freedman Demas. This, I say, sufficed, for now it will be easy for one of your slaves to follow him in the morning and learn their hiding place. I'm certain that if Ursus is here, Lygia is also in Rome. And for further news, I bring assurance that both will be present tonight at a gathering in Ostranium."

"Ostranium! Where's that?" interrupted Vinitius. "I must be there, too!"

---

1 Daughter of Atlas, wife of Jupiter, and mother of Mercury.

"It's an old hypogeum between the Via Salaria and the Via Nomentana. The chief priest of the Christians, of whom I've spoken to you and who has long been expected, has arrived and will teach and baptize in that cemetery tonight. They conceal their religion, for though there's no edict against it, yet the people hate them, and therefore they're cautious. This same Ursus has told me that *all*, even to the last soul, will gather in Ostranium, for all wish to see and hear him who was the foremost disciple of Christ and who is called Apostle. As they consider women equal to men, women will also be there, save only Pomponia, who might find it difficult to explain her absence to Aulus, a believer in the ancient gods. But Lygia, master, who is under the guardianship of Ursus and the elders of the Christian community, will surely be there with the other women."

Vinitius, who had been living in a state of feverish excitement and upheld only by hope, now that this hope seemed about to be realized, was suddenly attacked with weakness such as a man feels after a long journey. Chilo noticed this and resolved to take advantage of it.

"The gates are watched, it's true, by your slaves, and the Christians must know this. But they need no gates. The Tiber has no gates, and though it's far from the river to the appointed place, still for them it's worthwhile to get there to see the great Apostle. Besides, they probably have a thousand ways of reaching the spot. In Ostranium, master, you'll find Lygia. And if she's not there, which I think unlikely, you'll find Ursus, for he has promised to kill Glaucus. He himself told me that he'd be there and that he'd kill him. Do you hear, my golden Tribune? Then you'll either follow Ursus and so come to the place where Lygia dwells, or you'll command your slaves to seize him as a murderer, bind his hands, and make him confess where he has hidden Lygia. I've completed my task. Another, O master, would have told you a story that he had drunk ten *cantars*[2] of the best wine with Ursus before he could get the secret out of him; another would have said that he had lost a thousand sesterces to him in gambling or that he had bought this information for two thousand. I know that you'll pay me doubly, for the noble Petronius has told me that your bounty will exceed my hopes."

Vinitius, who was a soldier gifted with a keen perception, mastered his momentary weakness and said, "You won't be disappointed in my liberality, but first, however, you'll accompany me to Ostranium."

---

2   From *cantharus,* a large goblet or tankard.

"*I* to Ostranium?" asked Chilo, who had not the slightest wish to go there. "Noble Tribune, I engaged to find Lygia for you, but I didn't engage to carry her off for you. Think, master, what would happen to me. If that Lygian bear, after killing Glaucus, should realize that he didn't deserve death, would he not regard me as the cause of an unjust murder? Forget not, master, that the greater the philosopher, the more difficult it is for him to answer the stupid questions of a fool. What should I answer him if he asked me why I slandered Glaucus? If you distrust me, then I say, pay me only when I show you the house where Lygia lives. Give me today but a part of my remuneration, so that if any accident should befall you (may all the gods protect you), I wouldn't be left without any recompense. Your heart couldn't endure that."

Vinitius went to a chest that stood on a marble pedestal, took a purse from it, and flung it at Chilo. "These are *scrupula,*"[3] he said, "and when Lygia shall be in my house, you'll get the same filled with *aurei.*"[4]

"You're a veritable Jove!" exclaimed Chilo.

Vinitius frowned. "Here you'll receive food, after which you may rest. But you must remain here until evening, and when night comes you'll accompany me to Ostranium."

A look of alarm and uncertainty flitted over the face of the Greek. He controlled himself, however, and answered, "Who could oppose you, master! These silver pieces outweigh my services, to say nothing of your society, which to me is a happiness and a delight."

Vinitius interrupted him impatiently and questioned him as to the particulars of his conversation with Ursus. It seemed clear that they would be able to discover Lygia's hiding place that night or to seize her on the way back from Ostranium. This thought filled Vinitius with wild delight. Now that he felt confident of finding Lygia, his anger and vexation against her disappeared. In his joy he forgave her everything. He thought of her only as one dear to him; he felt as if she were returning after a long absence. He was strongly tempted to summon his slaves and command them to deck his house with garlands. In that hour he felt no anger even against Ursus. He was ready to forgive everything to everybody. Chilo, for whom, in spite of his services, he had always felt aversion, seemed to him now an entertaining and unusual person. Joy filled his house. His eyes and

---

3   Coins of silver.
4   Coins of gold.

face grew radiant. He felt again youth and the delight of life. The sufferings he had gone through were not as great as his love for Lygia. This he understood now for the first time, when he hoped to possess her. His desires woke in him as the earth wakes in the springtime beneath the glow of the sun; but now his desires were less wild and blind than formerly, and more joyous and tender. He felt within himself unlimited energy and was confident that once he had Lygia in his sight, all the Christians in the world could not take her from him, nor could Caesar himself.

Chilo, meanwhile, emboldened by the young tribune's delight, began to offer advice. He warned Vinitius that victory was not yet won and that the greatest caution was necessary or the entire undertaking might fail. He urged Vinitius not to attempt to carry off Lygia from Ostranium. They should go there with hoods on their heads and with their faces concealed. They should hide in dark corners and restrict themselves to scrutinizing people as they passed. When they saw Lygia, it would be best to follow her at a distance, to notice the house she entered, and on the morrow to surround it with a large force and take her away at daybreak. Since she belonged to Caesar as a hostage, all this might be done without any fear of the law. Should they not find her in Ostranium, they would follow Ursus. The result would be the same. It would be impracticable to go to the cemetery with a crowd of attendants, for it might attract attention. Then the Christians need only extinguish all the lights as they had done at the time of Lygia's rescue and, scattering in the darkness, conceal themselves in places known only to them. But they should be armed, or better still, take two trusty men to defend them in case of need.

Vinitius acknowledged the wisdom of this advice. Recalling Petronius's counsel, he ordered his slaves to bring Croto to him. Chilo, who knew everybody in Rome, felt greatly relieved on hearing the name of the famous athlete whose superhuman strength he had admired many times in the arena. The purse filled with large *aurei* would be easier to acquire with the aid of Croto.

Hence he sat down in a cheerful mood at the table, to which he was summoned by the *atriensis*. He informed the slaves that he had brought their master a magic ointment, which if rubbed upon the hooves of the worst horses would make them outstrip all others. A certain Christian had shown him how to prepare the ointment—the Christians being better skilled in magic and miracles than even the Thessalians, though Thessaly was renowned for its witches and wonder-workers. The Christians had great confidence in him; anyone who knew the meaning of the sign of the fish would understand the reason for this. While speaking, he looked sharply at the faces of the slaves, in the hope of discovering a Christian and betraying him to Vinitius. But when that mercenary hope failed him, he fell to eating and drinking uncommon quantities, not sparing praises on the cook and declaring that he would try to buy him from Vinitius. His joy was clouded only by the thought that he must go that night to Ostranium, but he took comfort in the fact that he would go in disguise and in the company of two men—one a giant admired by all Rome and the other a patrician, a high officer in the legions.

If they discover Vinitius, he said to himself, *they won't dare to lay hands on him. As for me, they'll be sharp-eyed indeed if they see even the tip of my nose.*

He recalled his conversation with the laborer. The recollection brought much joy to him, for beyond a doubt that laborer was Ursus. From what Vinitius had said and from the account of those who had brought Lygia from Caesar's palace, he knew of the man's wonderful strength. When he had asked Euritius who he knew that possessed exceptional strength, not surprisingly, he had singled out Ursus. The confusion and wrath of Ursus at the mention of Vinitius and Lygia confirmed his suspicion that the giant knew one or both of them. Ursus had mentioned also his penance for killing a man—and Ursus had killed Atacinus. Moreover, the appearance of the laborer corresponded to the account that Vinitius had given of the Lygian. The changed name was the only thing that could raise a doubt, but Chilo knew that Christians often assumed new names at baptism.

Should Ursus kill Glaucus, mused Chilo, *that will be all the better. But should he not kill him, it will be proof of how difficult it is for a Christian to commit murder. I described this Glaucus as a son of Judas and as a betrayer of Christians. I was so eloquent that even a stone would have been moved and would have promised to fall upon the head of Glaucus. But I barely persuaded that Lygian bear to put his paws on him. He hesitated and spoke of penance and compunction. Evidently murder is not pleasing to them. They're obliged to forgive offenses against themselves, and they're not allowed to revenge the wrongs of others. Therefore, stop and think, Chilo, what could possibly threaten you? Glaucus is not permitted to take revenge on you. If Ursus refuses to kill Glaucus for such a heinous crime as the betrayal of all the Christians, he most certainly will not kill you for the small offense of betraying one Christian.*

Moreover, when I've revealed to this lecherous ring pigeon⁵ the nest of the tur-
tledove, I will wash my hands of everything and will betake myself to Neapolis.
The Christians speak also of a kind of washing of the hands—it must be
a ceremony to indicate that when any transaction with them has come to an end,
it is finished definitely. What good people these Christians are, and how they
are maligned! Oh, gods! Such is the justice of the world. I like this religion
because it doesn't permit one to kill. But if to kill is forbidden, to steal, to
cheat, or to bear false witness are also surely forbidden; hence the teachings
must be hard to live up to. Apparently the Christian religion teaches that people
should die honestly, as the Stoics teach, but at the same time it teaches that
they should also live honestly. If ever I acquire a fortune and a house like this,
with as many slaves, perhaps I'll be a Christian for as long as it's convenient
for me. For a rich man can permit himself everything, even virtue. Indeed!
This is a religion for the rich man; consequently I don't understand why so
many poor embrace it. What good will it do them to be honest and thus to tie
their hands? I must think this over sometime! Meanwhile, glory to you,
Mercury, for helping me to find this Lygia! But if you've done so for the two
white yearlings with gilded horns, you're fooled. Shame on you, murderer of
Argos, such a wise god as you are, not to foresee that you'd get nothing. I offer
you my gratitude, and if you prefer two beasts to it, then you're the third beast
yourself. Beware lest I, a philosopher, should prove to the world that you don't
exist; then all would cease to offer sacrifices to you. It's best always to be on
good terms with philosophers.

Speaking thus to himself and to Mercury, he stretched himself on a couch, placed his mantle under his head, and fell asleep while the slaves were clearing the table. He awoke, or rather was awakened by the arrival of Croto. He arose at once, went into the hall, and gazed with delight at the huge figure of the ex-gladiator, who seemed to fill the entire place. Croto was talking to Vinitius.

"By Hercules, it's a good thing, master, that you sent for me today, as tomorrow I start for Beneventum, where the noble Vatinius has summoned me to fight before Caesar with a certain Syphax, the most powerful Negro in Africa. You can't imagine, master, how his spinal column will crack in my hands, and how I shall shatter his black jaw with my fist."

"By Pollux!" answered Vinitius. "I'm sure that you'll do just that!"

"So say I," added Chilo. "Yes, smash his jaw. That's an excellent idea

---

5 Largest and most aggressive of the species.

and a worthy deed. I'm ready to bet that you'll smash his jaw; but rub your limbs today with olive oil, my Hercules, and eat well, and then I'm sure that you can fight even a real Cacus.[6] The man who guards the girl with whom the lordly Vinitius is concerned possesses extraordinary strength."

Chilo spoke thus to rouse Croto's ambition.

And Vinitius added, "So it is—I haven't seen him, but I'm told he can drag a bull by the horns where he pleases."

"*Oh!*" exclaimed Chilo, who had not imagined Ursus was so powerful.

But Croto laughed in scorn. "I undertake, worthy master," said he, "to bear away with this one hand whomever you point out to me—and with this other one to defend you against seven such Lygians and to bring the girl to your home, though all the Christians were pursuing me like Calabrian wolves. If I don't fulfill my promise, may I be beaten with clubs in this very *impluvium*."

"Don't allow that, master," cried Chilo. "If they begin to throw stones at us, what help would his strength be? Wouldn't it be better to abduct the girl from the house without exposing her or ourselves to danger?"

"He speaks wisely, Croto," said Vinitius.

"Your money, your will. Remember only this, master, that tomorrow I go to Beneventum."

"I have five hundred slaves in the city," answered Vinitius. Then he gave a sign to them to retire, and going into the library, he wrote the following note to Petronius:

"Chilo has found the Lygian this evening. I go with him and Croto to Ostranium; I'll take her from her lodging tomorrow. May the gods favor us! Good health to you, dear friend. Joy does not allow me to write further."

Laying aside his pen, he walked up and down with rapid strides, for besides joy, which filled his soul, impatience burned in him like fire. He assured himself that tomorrow Lygia would be in his house. He didn't know exactly what course to take with her, but he felt that he loved her and was ready to be her slave. He called to mind Acte's assurance that Lygia loved him as well, and this excited him greatly. He needed only to conquer her modesty and to go through certain ceremonies that Christian teaching required. And if that were true, once Lygia entered his house, she would yield to persuasion or superior force; then she must tell herself, *It's done*, and after that be submissive and loving.

---

6   Son of Vulcan, a giant cattle robber, slain by Hercules.

The coming of Chilo interrupted his delightful daydream.

"Master," said the Greek, "a solution to a great problem has come to me: Have not the Christians certain passwords, some tessera, without which no one can gain entrance to Ostranium? This is the case I know in the houses of prayer, and I can get those passwords from Euritius. Permit me to go to him, master, to procure such signs as will be necessary."

"Well, noble philosopher," answered Vinitius joyfully, "you speak like a prudent man, and for that you have my thanks. Go then to Euritius or wherever you please, but for security, you'll leave the purse you've received on the table."

Chilo squirmed. Though not at all pleased with the order, he nevertheless complied with it and went out. From the Carinae to the Circus, near which was the shop of Euritius, was not very far, so he returned before evening.

"I've learned all the passwords, master. Without them we would not have been admitted. I inquired minutely also about the road. I explained to Euritius that I needed the passwords for some friends, declaring that I couldn't go myself since the journey was too long for an old man to take, and that, furthermore, I would see the great Apostle on the morrow, and he would repeat to me the more important parts of his sermon."

"How is that? You're not planning to go? You *must* go!" demanded Vinitius.

"I know that, but I'll put a hood on my head, and I advise you to do likewise, lest we frighten the prey."

Soon they began to prepare themselves, for darkness was covering the world. They put on Gallic mantles with hoods and took lanterns. Vinitius armed himself and his companions with short knives; Chilo put on a wig that he had procured from a barber, and they hurried out to reach the Porta Nomentana before it closed.

Chapter XX

They strode through the Patrician Quarter along the Viminal Hill and passed through the former Porta Viminal, near the plain where Diocletian afterward erected magnificent baths. They passed the remains of the wall of Servius Tullius and through other greater ruins until they reached the Via Nomentana. There they turned to the left towards the Via Salaria, to find themselves in the midst of hills full of sandpits and here and there a graveyard.

Meanwhile it had grown quite dark, and since the moon had not yet risen, had it not been for the Christians who showed them the way, it would have been a difficult task for them to find the road, as Chilo had foreseen. At right and left and in front, dark figures were discernible moving towards the sandpits. Some carried lanterns, hiding them as much as possible under their mantles; others, better acquainted with the road, walked in the dark. The trained soldier's eye of Vinitius distinguished by their movements the young from the old ones, who walked with staffs, and men from women, who were carefully wrapped in long mantles. The rural police and the country people returning from the city evidently took these nocturnal wanderers for laborers going to the sandpits or for some brotherhood of gravediggers whose members chose for themselves certain hours to celebrate their nightly ceremonies. But as the young patrician and his companions pushed their way onward, the number of people and gleaming lanterns increased. Some sang hymns in a subdued tone, which appeared to Vinitius full of melancholy longing. At moments his ear caught disconnected words or phrases such as, "Arise, O thou that sleepest," or "Rise from the dead." At times, again, the name of Christ was repeated by men and women.

But Vinitius gave little heed to the words, for it crossed his mind that one of those dark figures might be Lygia. Some passing near him said, "*Pax vobiscum!*" or "Glory to Christ!" But he became increasingly tense, and his heart began to beat more quickly, for it seemed to him that he heard Lygia's voice. Shapes or movements like hers deceived him every moment, but not until after repeated mistakes did he begin to mistrust his own eyes.

But the way appeared long to him. He was well acquainted with the surroundings, yet he could not recognize places in the darkness. Every moment they came upon some narrow passage, some part of a wall, some booth that seemed strange to him. At last the edge of the moon emerged from behind a bank of clouds and illuminated the place better than had the dim lanterns. Something like a fire or the flame of a torch began to glimmer in the distance. Vinitius turned to Chilo and asked whether that might be Ostranium.

Chilo, on whom the night, the distance from the city, and the phantomlike figures had made a deep impression, replied in uncertain tones, "I know not, master. I've never been in Ostranium, but it seems to me that they might find someplace nearer the city."

After a while, feeling the need of conversation and to strengthen his faltering courage, he added, "They assemble like murderers, yet murder is forbidden to them, unless that Lygian giant deceived me scurvily."

Vinirius, who was thinking of Lygia, was astonished at the caution and secrecy with which her fellow worshipers gathered together to listen to their high priest.

"Like all religions," he said, "this also has its followers among us, but the Christians are a Jewish sect. Why, then, do they gather here when in the Trans-Tiber there are temples to which the Jews bring offerings in bright daylight?"

"No, master; the Jews are their most relentless enemies. It has been related to me how, even before the time of the present Caesar, the Jews and Christians almost came to war. These disturbances annoyed Claudius Caesar so much that he expelled all the Jews. But now that edict has been abolished. Still Christians hide themselves from the Jews and from the people, who as you know, accuse them of crimes and hate them."

For a while they walked on in silence. The first to break it was Chilo, whose fear increased the farther the gate was left behind.

"When I returned from Euritius," he said, "I borrowed a wig from a barber, and I inserted two beans in my nostrils. They ought not to be able to recognize me. But even if they do, they won't kill me. They're not bad people and are very upright. I love and esteem them."

"Deal in no premature praise," advised Vinitius.

They came now to a narrow declivity closed in at the four sides by two ditches, over one part of which an aqueduct crossed. Just then the moon peeped out through the clouds. At the end of the declivity they observed a wall covered abundantly with ivy, upon which the moon shed a silvery light. At last—Ostranium.

Vinitius's heart beat more quickly than ever. At the gate two *fossors*[1] accepted the watchwords. The next moment Vinitius and his companions found themselves in a large space entirely surrounded by a wall. Here and there stood individual monuments, and in the center, the entrance to the hypogeum itself. In the lower part of the crypt, underground, were graves. A fountain played in front of the entrance. As the crypt was too small for so large an assemblage, Vinitius soon realized that the ceremony would be held in the open air above, where a great multitude had already gathered. As far as the eye could see, lantern gleamed beside lantern. Many of those present, however, had no light. Save for a few bare heads, all were hooded, as a precaution against treachery or cold. The young patrician grew alarmed at the thought that if they should remain thus to the end, he wouldn't be able to recognize Lygia in such dim light and in such a vast crowd.

Suddenly, near the crypt, some pitch torches were lighted and placed together in a little pile. There was now sufficient light. Soon the crowd began to sing a strange hymn—in low tones at first, and then louder and louder. Never in his life had Vinitius heard such a hymn. The same wild longing that had moved him when he heard the hymns sung by a few of those he passed on the way to the cemetery was heard now in this hymn, only it was far more distinct and powerful, until at last it swelled into so vast a volume that the cemetery, the hills, the pits—in short, the entire region—seemed to have joined the multitude in their yearning.

Almost it seemed as if a cry had gone up from the night, a humble prayer for salvation from a wanderer in the darkness. Eyes lifted heavenward seemed to be fixed upon some being above; outstretched hands implored that being to descend. When the hymn ceased, there followed a moment of hushed expectation so overpowering that Vinitius and his followers unconsciously imitated the Christians in casting their eyes towards the stars as if fearful that something extraordinary would happen and that Someone in reality would descend among them.

---

1 Quarrymen.

In Asia Minor, in Egypt, and in the very city of Rome, Vinitius had seen all varieties of temples. He knew of many religions and had heard many hymns, but now for the first time he beheld people calling upon a divinity with hymns, not because they were fulfilling some established ritual, but from the very depths of their hearts, with such genuine yearning as children might express for a father or mother. One would have to be blind not to be convinced that these people not only adored their God, but loved Him with their whole souls, and this devotion Vinitius had never before witnessed in any land, in any religion, or in any temple. In Rome and in Greece there were those who still worshiped the gods from selfish motives or from fear; but love for the gods never entered their heads.

Though the mind of Vinitius was occupied with looking for Lygia in the crowd, he couldn't help seeing the extraordinary things that were happening about him. Meanwhile the fire, fed by more torches, filled the cemetery with a red glare, darkening the gleam of the lanterns. At that moment a venerable man emerged from the crypt, arrayed in a hooded mantle, but with his head uncovered. He mounted a rock adjacent to the fire.

The crowd swayed at sight of him. About him Vinitius heard voices whispering, "Peter! Peter!" Some knelt down; others stretched out their hands to him. A silence so profound followed that one could hear the falling cinders on the embers, the distant rumbling of wheels on the Via Nomentana, and the soughing of the wind through the sparse pine trees growing near the cemetery.

Chilo leaned towards Vinitius and whispered, "That is *he!* The foremost disciple of Christ—the fisherman!"

The old man lifted up his hands and blessed the assembled crowds with the sign of the cross. All fell upon their knees. Lest they should betray themselves, Vinitius and his companions also fell on their knees. Vinitius could not grasp the situation at once; it seemed to him that the figure he saw before him was simple yet impressive; moreover, it was impressive because of its simplicity. The old man had neither miter nor garland of oak leaves on his head nor palm branch in his hand nor golden tablet on his breast. He wasn't arrayed in a star-embroidered robe of white. In short, he had none of the insignia that distinguished the priests of Egypt and Greece and Rome. Vinitius was again struck by the same difference that he had felt when he listened to the Christian hymns. For the fisherman appeared to him unlike a high priest versed in liturgical ceremonies, but rather like a simple and most vulnerable witness who had traveled from a far-off land that he might tell some truth that he had seen and touched, which he believed with the faith that comes from actual seeing, and which he had come to love on account of his firm belief. The conviction depicted in his face was such as truth alone can possess. The skeptical Vinitius had no intention of being influenced by the teachings of the old man, but he had a feverish curiosity to know what would flow from the lips of that companion of the mysterious Christ and what that teaching was that Lygia and Pomponia Graecina professed.

And now Peter began to speak. First he spoke as a father who points out to his children the way they should live. He commanded them to renounce all excesses and luxurious living, to love poverty, purity, and truth; to suffer wrongs and persecutions with patience; to obey those in authority; to beware of treason, deceit, and calumny; and finally, to give an example to one another, and even to pagans.

Vinitius, for whom good was only that which could restore to him Lygia and bad everything that formed an obstacle between them, was both touched and angered at certain portions of the fisherman's discourse; for it seemed to him that when he enjoined purity and a struggle against natural desires, the old man dared not only to condemn his love, but also to confirm Lygia in her opposition to him. He understood that if she were in the assembly listening to those words, and if she took them to heart, she must regard him as an enemy of that teaching and as an evil man. The thought angered him.

What have I heard that is new? he asked himself. *Is this the unknown religion? Everybody knows these teachings, everybody has heard them. Poverty and limitation of necessities have been taught by the Cynics. Socrates taught virtue; every Stoic, even such a one as Seneca, who has five hundred tables of lemon wood, enjoins moderation and advocates truth, patience in adversity, and endurance in misfortune. All such teachings are like stale grain, fit for mice to eat, but not for men, because it's musty with age.*

Besides being angry, Vinitius was disappointed, for he had expected that some unknown magical secrets would be revealed, and he at least expected to hear some uncommon eloquence. Instead he heard plain, simple speech devoid of all rhetorical display. He was surprised only by the mute attention with which the crowd listened.

The old man continued to address his attentive listeners, admonishing

Peter the Apostle.

them to be good, peaceful, upright, and pure; not that they might have peace in this life, but that after death they might live eternally with Christ, in such joy and glory, and in such health and delight, as none on earth had ever attained. And here Vinitius, though hostile only a moment before, couldn't help but observe that there was a difference between the teachings of the old man and that of the Cynics, Stoics, and other philosophers; for these recommended good and virtue as reasonable qualities and the only practical thing in life, while he promised *immortality*—and not some kind of hapless immortality beneath the earth, in wretchedness, emptiness, and want, but a glorious life equal almost to that of the gods. Moreover, he spoke of it as of a thing of absolute certainty, therefore in the presence of such faith virtue assumed a priceless value, and the misfortunes of this life became trivial. For to suffer temporarily for the sake of endless happiness is something entirely different from suffering only because such is the course of nature. But the old man said further that virtue and truth should be loved for themselves since the highest truth and virtue existing eternally is God Himself; hence the more one loves them, the more he loves God and becomes thus the beloved child of God.

Vinitius didn't comprehend this very well, but he knew from words spoken by Pomponia Graecina to Petronius that according to the Christian belief, God was one and almighty; when, therefore, he now heard that He was also all-good and all-just, he could not help thinking that in the presence of such a God, Jupiter, Saturn, Apollo, Juno, Vesta, and Venus would seem like a vain and quarrelsome crowd, where each one ravages for self and against all the others.

The young man's astonishment was greatest when the old man declared that God is equally universal love; hence whoever loves mankind fulfills God's greatest commandment. But it wasn't enough to simply love the people of one's own nation, for the God-man shed His blood for all and had already found among the pagans such elect as Cornelius the centurion. Again, it wasn't sufficient to love only those who do good to Christians, for Christ forgave the Jews who delivered Him over to death and the Roman soldiers who crucified Him. It behooved Christ's followers, therefore, not only to forgive those who wronged them, but to love them and return them good for evil. It wasn't enough to love those who do good; Christians must love the wicked also, since by love only is it possible to expel evil from them.

At these words Chilo bethought himself that all his work had gone for nothing and that Ursus wouldn't dare to kill Glaucus either on this or any other night. On the other hand, he was comforted by an inference from the old man's words that Glaucus wouldn't kill him even if he were discovered and recognized.

Vinitius no longer thought that there was nothing new in the teachings of the old man. He asked himself in amazement, *What sort of God is this? What sort of religion, what sort of people?* All that he had just heard could not find lodgment at once in his mind; it was a jumble of new ideas. He felt that should he wish, for example, to embrace such a doctrine he would have to sacrifice on a burning pile all his former thoughts, habits, character, and his very nature itself, that they would have to be burned to ashes, so that he might then fill himself with a new life and soul. The teaching that enjoined him to love Parthians, Syrians, Greeks, Egyptians, Gauls, and Britons—to forgive enemies, to love them, and to return good for evil—seemed to him nothing short of madness, yet there was something in that madness greater than all the philosophies he had ever heard. He felt that the doctrine, in spite of its madness, was impracticable; but because impracticable, it was divine. In his soul he rejected it, yet felt as if he were emerging from a meadow full of flowers, breathing a perfume that intoxicated and that, having inhaled it once, he must, as in the land of the lotus, forget all else and yearn for it alone.

It seemed to him that there was nothing real in that religion, but at the same time, that reality, compared with it, seemed insignificant and undeserving of thought. Heights of some kind, unthought of before, certain immensities topped with clouds, engulfed him. The hypogeum seemed to him a rendezvous for madmen, yet also a place mysterious and wonderful where, as on some mystic bed, something was being born, the likes of which the world had never seen before. There passed before his mind everything that the old man had said concerning life, truth, love, and God; and his thoughts were dazzled by them, as are eyes from successive flashes of lightning. As is usual with people absorbed by a single passion, these thoughts came to him through the medium of his love for Lygia, and by these lightning flashes he saw one thing clearly: that if Lygia were present in the cemetery and she professed and obeyed that religion, she would never become his mistress. For the first time since he had met her at Aulus's house, Vinitius felt that though he had now found her, she had not found him. No thought like this had come to him before, and he could not explain it to himself then, for it was not so much an express understanding as a dim feeling of irreparable loss and misfortune. He became alarmed, and his alarm soon turned into a storm of wrath towards all Christians, especially towards the old man. That fisherman, whom at first glance he had considered an ignorant peasant, now filled him with fear almost and seemed to him as some mysterious power who held his fate in his hands—inexorably, and therefore tragically.

The quarrymen again quietly placed fresh torches on the fire. The wind ceased to moan in the pines, and the flames rose evenly, ascending upward towards the stars twinkling in a clear sky. The old man, having recalled the death of Christ, talked now only of Him. All held their breath, and the deepest silence prevailed, so that the beating of hearts could almost be heard. The man had seen, and he narrated as one in whose memory every moment had been so engraved that were he to close his eyes, he would still see. He told them how on their return from the cross he had sat with John for two days and two nights in the supper chamber without eating or sleeping, in suffering, in sorrow, in doubt, in alarm, holding their heads in their hands, convinced that He had died. Oh, how terrible, how awful it was! The third day had dawned, and the morning light illumined the walls, but he and John still were sitting in the chamber, without hope or comfort. How desire for sleep tortured them, for they'd also spent the night preceding the Passion without sleep. But hardly had the sun risen when Mary Magdalene rushed in, panting, her hair disheveled, crying, "They've taken away the Lord!" Hearing this they sprang up and ran towards the sepulchre, but John, who was a younger man, ran faster and was the first to arrive. He saw that the tomb was empty and dared not enter. Only when there were three at the entrance did he—the one now speaking to them—enter; and they found on the stone a shirt with a winding sheet. But the body they found not.

Then fear fell upon them, for they assumed the priests had removed the body of Christ, and thus they returned in greater grief than they had come. Other disciples arrived later and joined in the lamentations, so that the Lord of Hosts might hear them in chorus. They wept until the spirit died within them, for they had hoped that the Master would redeem Israel, and it was now the third day since He died; they therefore didn't understand why the Father had forsaken the Son, and they preferred not to look at the daylight, but to die, so heavy was their burden.

The remembrance of those awful moments caused two tears to flow from the eyes of the venerable man. These were visible in the light of the fire as they trickled down his gray beard. His bald and aged head trembled, and his voice was choked.

Vinitius said in his soul, *That man speaks the truth, and it moves him to tears.* The simple-hearted listeners were greatly affected. They had heard more than once of Christ's Passion, and they knew that joy would follow sorrow; but now that an Apostle, an eyewitness, retold the story, they wrung their hands and sobbed and beat their breasts. But they calmed themselves by degrees, for the desire to hear the rest of the story prevailed over their grief. The old man closed his eyes as if to look more carefully into his soul for the things that had happened in the past; then he continued.

"While the disciples were sorrowing, Mary Magdalene rushed in again, proclaiming that she had seen the Lord. Failing to recognize Him because of a great light that surrounded Him, she had thought Him to be the gardener. But He said, 'Mary,' and she cried, *'Rabboni'* and fell at His feet. He bade her go to His disciples—then He vanished. But we refused to believe her. When she wept for joy, some taunted her; others thought that sorrow had disturbed her mind, for she said also that she had seen angels at the grave. We ran therefore a second time to the grave and found it empty. Later in the evening came Cleopas with another from Emmaus, saying, 'Truly the Lord has arisen from the dead.' From fear of the Jews we discussed the subject within closed doors. Suddenly He stood among us, though there had been no sound at the door, and when we feared, He said, 'Peace be with you.'

"And I saw Him as all did see, and He was like a light and like the joy in our hearts, for we knew that He had risen from the dead and that the seas might dry up and the mountains turn to dust, but His glory would never pass away.

"After eight days Thomas Didymus thrust his finger in the Lord's wounds and touched His side. Then Thomas fell at His feet and cried, 'My Lord and my God!' To whom the Lord answered, 'Because you have seen Me, you have believed; blessed are they who haven't seen, yet have believed.' And we heard those words, and our eyes looked on Him, for He was among us."

Vinitius listened; something strange was taking place in him. He forgot for a moment where he was. He began to lose the feeling of reality, measure, and judgment. He stood in the presence of two impossibilities: He couldn't believe what he heard, and yet he felt that one must be blind or lost to reason if he could maintain that that man who said, "I have seen," was lying.

There was something in his emotions, in his tears, in his whole figure, and in the details of the events, that made it virtually impossible to doubt him. Vinitius felt that perhaps all this was but a dream and that all these things were creatures of his imagination, but then when he looked again at the silent throng around him, he *knew* this was no dream. The odor of smoking lanterns came to his nostrils; in the distance the torches were blazing, and near him on the rock stood this old man on the verge of the grave, his head trembling somewhat, who, while bearing witness, repeated, "I saw."

And he told them everything up to the Ascension into heaven. At moments he paused, for he spoke very minutely, but it was felt that every detail had fixed itself in his memory as though engraved on stone. The listeners were seized with ecstasy; they threw back their hoods from their heads that they might hear him better and miss not a single word of those priceless utterances. To them it seemed that some supernatural power had carried them to Galilee, that with the disciples they were walking through the valleys and upon the waters, that this cemetery had changed into the lake of Tiberius, and that on the bank, in the mist of the morning, stood Christ as He had stood when John, looking up from the boat, said, "It is the Lord"; and when Peter leaped into the water and swam so as to fall sooner at the well-beloved feet, in the faces of all shone boundless joy, forgetfulness of life, happiness, and immeasurable love. It was evident that during Peter's long exhortation some of the listeners had experienced visions. When he began to relate how, at the moment of the Ascension, the clouds closed in beneath the Savior's feet, how they enveloped Him, how they hid Him from the gaze of the Apostles, all eyes were raised involuntarily to the sky, and a moment as of expectation followed—as if all hoped to behold Him there, or as if they expected that He would descend again from the heavens so that He might see how the venerable Apostle was tending the flock that had been entrusted to him and bless both the lambs and him.

And for this people, at that moment, there existed neither Rome, nor the mad Caesar, nor temples of pagan gods. There was only Christ, who filled the land, the sea, the heavens, and the world.

From about the houses scattered along the Via Nomentana, the cocks began to crow, announcing the midnight hour. Just then Chilo tugged at a corner of Vinitius's mantle and whispered, "Master, over there not far from the old man, I see Urban, and by his side is one that looks like a maiden."

Vinitius shook himself as though waking from a dream. He turned in the direction pointed out by the Greek—and beheld Lygia.

Chapter XXI

Every drop of blood in the young patrician quivered at the sight of her. He forgot the crowd, the old man, his own astonishment at the marvelous things he had heard—he saw her alone. At long last, after all his efforts, after long days of alarm, trouble, and suffering, he had found her! For the first time he realized that joy might rush at the heart like a wild beast and constrict it till breath was lost. He, who had maintained that Fortune was duty-bound to fulfill all his desires, now hardly believed his own eyes and his own happiness. Had it not been for this, his unruly nature might have hurried him on to some rash deed. But now he paused to make sure that this wasn't one of those miracles that filled his brain, that it wasn't a dream. No, he could doubt no longer. It was Lygia who stood before him, only fifteen steps away. She stood in the glare of a torch so that her full beauty was revealed to him. Her hood had slipped off from her head and disheveled her hair; her lips were slightly parted, her eyes were raised towards the Apostle, and her whole attitude was one of rapt attention. She was dressed in the cheap garb of the working classes, but never had she seemed more beautiful to Vinitius. Despite the tumult in his soul, he was struck with the contrast between that noble patrician head and that dark mantle of coarse woolen stuff, almost that of a slave. Love burned in him like an immense flame, mingled with a marvelous feeling of yearning, homage, honor, and desire. He felt the delight that the sight of her caused him; he drank of her as life-giving water after a long thirst. Standing by the side of the Lygian giant, she seemed smaller than before, almost a child. He noticed, also, that she had grown more slender. Her complexion was almost transparent; she seemed to him to be a flower or a phantom. But the more he gazed on her, the more he wanted her; she was so different from all the women of Rome or of the East whom he had seen or possessed. Gladly would he have given them all up for her, and given up also Rome and the world besides.

He lost consciousness of his surroundings, but Chilo, fearing that he might do something to betray them, brought him back to reality by a tug at his mantle. And now the Christians lifted up their voices in prayer and the hymn "The Lord Hath Come!" After they had thundered out this "Maranatha," the great Apostle baptized with water from the fountain all whom the presbyters presented as prepared for the rite. To Vinitius, it seemed that the night would never end. His aim was to follow Lygia and to abduct her on the way or at her home.

At last some of the Christians began to leave. Then Chilo whispered, "Master, let's go and wait at the gate, for people look at us distrustfully, seeing that we haven't removed our hoods."

This was true. While the Apostle was preaching, the congregation had cast aside their hoods for convenience of hearing. They alone had not followed the general example. Chilo's advice seemed sound. Standing at the gate they'd see all who passed through, and the huge form of Ursus would be easily recognizable.

"We'll follow them," said Chilo. "We'll see which house they enter, and tomorrow, master, or rather today, you'll surround the house with your slaves and take her."

"No!" cried Vinitius.

"What, then, do you intend to do?"

"We'll enter the house after her, and we'll carry her away immediately, for didn't you undertake this, Croto?"

"Yes, master," replied Croto, "and I give myself up to you as a slave if I don't break the back of that bull."

But Chilo tried to dissuade them and implored them by all the gods not to act so rashly. Croto had accompanied them only to assist in their defense if they were recognized; he had not been employed to capture the girl. To attempt to capture her when they were only three against a multitude was to risk almost certain death. Worse still, she might escape from them and hide elsewhere or flee from Rome. What could they do then? Why not wait until they were certain of success? Why expose themselves to peril and risk the failure of the whole undertaking?

Though it was with great effort that Vinitius restrained himself in the cemetery from taking Lygia then and there, he felt that the Greek was right and might have listened to his counsel had it not been for Croto, whose one thought was of the promised reward.

"Master," he cried, "command silence to that old goat, or let me crush his head with my fist. Once in Buxentum, after a spectacle to which

Lucius Saturninus had taken me, seven drunken gladiators fell upon me at a tavern. Not one of them escaped me with a whole rib. I don't advise the abduction of the girl here in the crowd, for they might pelt us with stones. Wait till she has reached her house. There I'll seize her and carry her off for you."

"By Hercules!" cried Vinitius, delighted with the advice. "So be it. Tomorrow we may not find her at home. If we alarm them they may spirit her away."

Chilo groaned. "This Lygian seems awfully strong to me," he complained.

"You won't be asked to hold his hands," retorted Croto.

There was still a long wait before them. Not until dawn did they catch sight of Ursus and Lygia coming through the gate. A number of people accompanied them. Among these, Chilo thought he recognized the great Apostle. Beside him walked another old man of much smaller stature, two elderly women, and a boy who lighted the way with a lantern. A crowd of about two hundred followed. In this crowd mingled Vinitius, Chilo, and Croto.

"Yes, master," said Chilo, "your maiden is strongly guarded. It's the great Apostle himself who walks before her. See how they kneel as he passes them."

In fact many did kneel. Vinitius, however, paid no attention to them. Never for a moment did he lose sight of Lygia. His one thought was of her capture, and since his military experience had accustomed him to strategizing, he arranged the whole affair in his mind with military precision. He felt that his plan was an audacious one, but he knew that success often crowned audacity.

The way was long. At times his thoughts dwelt upon that strange creed that had opened a gulf between him and Lygia. Now he understood the meaning of everything that had happened. He had penetration enough for that. He knew now that he had never really known Lygia before. He had seen in her a maiden surpassing all others, a maiden who inflamed his passions, but he knew now that her religion made her a different being from other women and recognized the fallacy of his former assumption that feeling, passion, wealth, or luxury could tempt her. Last of all he understood what Petronius and he had never fully understood: that the new creed engrafted upon the soul something entirely foreign to the world in which he lived, and that even if Lygia loved him she would not for the sake of that love sacrifice any of that faith. If she looked forward to happiness, it was a happiness entirely different from that sought by himself, Petronius, Caesar's court, or all Rome. There was no other woman of his acquaintance whom he could not make his mistress; this girl could only be his victim. At this thought, he was filled with rage and a poignant pain, because of the very uselessness of that rage. It might be possible to carry off Lygia; in fact, he was certain that it was possible, but he was equally assured that in the face of her religion, he himself was nothing, his courage was nothing, his power was nothing—all these things would be of no avail. This Roman soldier and tribune, who had believed in the might of sword and fist to conquer the world and dominate it forever, realized for the first time in his life that beyond that might there was a greater might. Puzzled, he asked himself what it was.

He could come up with no clear answer. Confused pictures chased one another through his brain—the cemetery; the vast congregation; the figure of Lygia, listening with all her soul to the words of the old man as he told of the passion, death, and resurrection of the God-man who had redeemed the world and promised it everlasting happiness beyond the Styx.

When he thought of this, chaos engulfed his mind, but he was brought back to earth again by the lamentations of Chilo bewailing his fate.

He'd been hired to find Lygia, he'd found her at the peril of his life, he'd pointed her out—what more could they want of him? Could they expect him to carry her away—he, an old man who had lost two fingers, an old man devoted to philosophy, science, and virtue? Suppose so mighty a lord as Vinitius were to come to grief in the effort to capture the maiden! The gods are indeed expected to watch over their favorites, but doesn't it often appear that the gods give themselves up to dice-playing, forgetting what goes on in the world? We all know that Fortune is blindfolded. It's hard enough for her to see in the daylight; what must it be at nighttime? Let something happen—suppose that Lygian bear were to hurl a millstone, a keg of wine, or worse still, a keg of water, at the noble Vinitius? Who could say whether blame instead of reward might not fall to the lot of the unhappy Chilo? A poor philosopher, he had attached himself to the noble Vinitius, as Aristotle to Alexander of Macedonia. If the noble Vinitius would give him merely the purse that he had thrust into his girdle before starting, that might be of some avail in an extremity, to summon aid or to bribe the Christians. Oh, why do they not listen to the advice of an old man who speaks from prudence and experience?

Vinitius, hearing this, jerked the purse from behind his belt and hurled it at Chilo.

"Take it and hold your tongue!"

The Greek, dexterously catching it, then feeling its weight, grew more cheerful. "My one hope," he said, "lies in the fact that Hercules and Theseus performed still more difficult tasks. And is not Croto, my personal and dearest friend, a Hercules? As to you, master, you're more than a demigod—you're a god. Surely you won't forget in the future your humble and faithful servant, whose needs must occasionally be provided for. When he's deep in his books, he forgets everything else. Some few stadia of garden and a little house, with even the smallest portico for coolness in summer, would be something worthy of such a donor. Meanwhile I'll admire your heroic deeds from afar, invoke Jove's favor for you, and if need be, raise so great a clamor that half of Rome will rush to your aid. What a wretched, difficult, and rough road this is! The oil in the lantern is all but gone. . . . If Croto, whose strength is only equaled by his nobility of character, would carry me to the gate in his arms, he would first be able to satisfy himself that he could carry the maiden easily, and secondly, by imitating Aeneas, he would win over the favor of the honest gods and so assure the success of the undertaking."

"Rather would I carry a sheep that died of the mange a month ago," was the gladiator's ungracious answer. "But hand over that purse given by the wealthy tribune, and I'll carry you to the gate."

"May you forever lose the great toe from your foot!" replied the Greek. "Have you profited nothing from the teachings of that good old man, who spoke of poverty and charity as the greatest of virtues? Did he not expressly command you to love me? Alas! I see that I can never make of you even a poor Christian. Easier would it be for the sun to penetrate the walls of the Mamertine prison than for truth to penetrate that hippopotamus skull of yours."

"Never fear!" cried Croto, who had beastlike strength but no human feelings whatsoever. "I've no intention of becoming a Christian; nor do I wish to lose my bread!"[1]

"Yes, but if you knew even the rudiments of philosophy, you'd know that gold is vanity."

"Away with your philosophy! I'll butt my head into your stomach, and you'll see who'll come out the victor."

---

1 Living.

"An ox might have said the same thing to Aristotle."

The world was growing lighter. Dawn covered the outlines of walls with pale light. The trees that skirted the road, the buildings, and the gravestones scattered here and there emerged from the shadows. The road was no longer empty. Dealers in vegetables hurried their heavily laden asses and mules towards the gates; carts full of provisions creaked along the highway. A light fog lay upon the road and beyond it on both sides, a portent of fair weather. Through that fog, people loomed in the distance like phantoms. Vinitius had his eyes fixed upon the slender figure of Lygia, which seemed to grow more luminous as the light increased.

"Master," said Chilo, "far be it from me to foresee when your bounty will cease. But now that I've been paid you won't suspect me of speaking only for myself. Once more I advise you to go home, to collect your slaves, and to bring a litter as soon as you've discerned the home of the divine Lygia. Don't listen to that mere elephant's trunk, Croto. He promises to carry off the maiden only to squeeze your purse as though it were a bag of curds."

"You'll have from me a blow of the fist to be struck between your shoulder blades, which means that you'll die!" snarled Croto.

"I have a cask of Cephalonian wine, which means that I will live!" retorted the Greek.

Vinitius made no answer. They had now neared the gate, where a strange scene greeted him. Two soldiers knelt as the Apostle passed; he laid his hands upon their helmets and then made the sign of the cross over them. The patrician had not dreamed that there were Christians among the soldiers. Amazed, he thought that just as a great conflagration attacks house after house, so that religion embraces new converts every day, from all classes, and spreads beyond all human comprehension. He now realized that if Lygia desired to escape from the city, she'd find guards to assist her. He thanked the gods that this had not happened.

As they reached vacant spaces outside the walls, the groups of Christians began to scatter. It was necessary, therefore, to follow Lygia from a greater distance and with more care, lest suspicion be aroused. Chilo, complaining of bruises and pains in his legs, fell farther and farther to the rear. Vinitius was content to allow this, as he knew that the cowardly and incompetent Greek would be of little use to him in this enterprise. He wouldn't even have objected if he'd expressed a wish to quit them. But the philosopher still followed, urged on probably by curiosity. Occasionally he approached them to repeat his former counsel. He informed them also that he would have taken the Apostle's companion for Glaucus, except that he was too short.

It took a long time to reach the Trans-Tiber. The sun had almost risen when at last the group around Lygia dispersed. The Apostle, with an old woman and a boy, went up the river; his companion, with Ursus and Lygia, turned into a narrow quarter and, about a hundred yards farther on, entered a house that contained two shops, one for the sale of olives, the other of poultry.

Chilo, lagging about fifty yards behind Vinitius and Croto, stopped and, crouching close to the wall, softly called them back. They did so, wishing to consult as to their next movement.

"Chilo," said Vinitius, "go around and see if this house fronts on some other street."

Chilo forgot his bruises and pains and disappeared around the corner as nimbly as though the wings of Mercury were attached to his ankles. In a moment he returned.

"No," said he, "there's but one entrance. But I implore you," he added, clasping his hands, "by Jupiter, Apollo, Vesta, Cybele, Isis and Osiris, Mithra, Baal, and all the gods of the East and the West, to drop this plan. Listen to me—"

He stopped suddenly, catching sight of the face of Vinitius, pale with agitation, and the wolfish glitter in his eye. One look was enough to convince him that nothing on earth would move him from his purpose. Croto drew air into his Herculean breast and swayed his formless head from side to side, as bears do in confinement. But not an iota of fear was visible in his face.

"I'll enter first," he said.

"You'll follow me," commanded Vinitius imperiously.

Then both vanished through the dark entrance. Chilo found refuge behind the corner of the nearest alley and awaited results.

Chapter XXII

Not till he had reached the hall did Vinitius fully understand the difficulty of the enterprise. The house was large, containing several stories, one of thousands of such buildings erected in Rome for renting to tenants. These houses, for the most part, were so hurriedly and poorly built that rarely a year passed without a number of them collapsing upon the heads of their occupants. Veritable beehives they were, high and narrow, full of little rooms and dens overcrowded by the poor. In a city where many streets were without names, these houses had no numbers. The owners entrusted the collection of rents to slaves, who, not being obliged by the city authorities to report the names of the tenants, often didn't know the names themselves. To find anybody by inquiry in such a house was often a difficult task, especially when there was no doorkeeper.

Vinitius and Croto went through a long passage that was walled in on four sides, forming a kind of common atrium for the entire building, with a fountain in the middle, the water of which sprayed into a stone basin embedded in the ground. Stone or wooden stairways led to galleries from which there were entrances to lodgings. On the ground floor were more lodgings, some provided with doors, others separated from the yard only by woolen curtains. These were, for the most part, torn, ripped, or patched.

The hour was yet early, and there was no one in the yard. Evidently everybody was asleep in the house, except those who had just returned from Ostranium.

"What shall we do, master?" asked Croto, halting.

"Let's wait here; somebody may appear," replied Vinitius.

"It's best that we not be seen in the yard."

He thought that Chilo's advice was practical. Had he with him but a score or so of slaves, nothing would have been easier than to occupy the gate, which apparently was the only exit, and then search all the lodgings. It was necessary to find Lygia's abode at once; otherwise the Christians, who certainly were plentiful in this house, might warn her. On this account it was dangerous to make inquiries of strangers. Vinitius was considering whether it might not be better to return for his slaves, when suddenly, from behind a screen hiding a remote lodging, a man emerged, a sieve in his hand, walking towards the fountain.

The young tribune at once recognized Ursus.

"It's the Lygian," whispered Vinitius.

"Shall I break his bones now?"

"Wait!"

Ursus hadn't seen them, for they stood in the shadow of the entrance. He quietly set to work washing the vegetables that filled the sieve. It was evident that, after an entire night spent in the cemetery, he was getting a meal ready. When he'd finished, he took the wet sieve and disappeared behind the curtain. Croto and Vinitius ran after him, expecting that they would gain immediate access to Lygia's lodgings. They marveled greatly on finding that the curtain divided not lodgings from the courtyard, but another dark passage, at the end of which they beheld a small garden containing a few cypresses and myrtle bushes and a small house attached to the back wall of another stone building. Both understood that this was a favorable circumstance. The tenants might all assemble in the courtyard, but the seclusion of the little house made their project easier. They would overcome the defenders—or rather, Ursus—quickly and would reach the street just as quickly with the captured Lygia. There their troubles would be over. Most likely no one would stop them. If they were questioned they'd say that a hostage of Caesar's had escaped. Vinitius would then declare himself to the guards and would call upon them for help.

Ursus was on the point of entering the little house when the sound of footsteps attracted his attention. He halted and, seeing two men, put down the sieve and turned towards them.

"Whom do you seek?" he asked.

"You," replied Vinitius.

Turning to Croto he said in a low, hurried voice, "Kill!"

Croto sprang upon Ursus like a tiger, and before the Lygian could recover himself or recognize his enemies, he had caught him in his arms of steel.

Vinitius was so certain of Croto's superhuman strength that he didn't even wait to witness the issue of the combat. Passing the two, he sprang to the door of the little house, pushed it open, and found himself in a room lighted only by a fire burning in the hearth. A gleam from this fire fell full upon the face of Lygia. A second person sitting by the fire was the old man who had accompanied the girl and Ursus on the road from Ostranium.

Vinitius rushed in so suddenly that, before Lygia could recognize him, he had seized her around the waist and, lifting her, had gained the door again. The old man attempted to bar the way, but holding the girl with one arm, Vinitius pushed him aside with the other. The hood fell from his head, and at the sight of that face, which was known to her and was at that moment terrible, the blood froze in Lygia's veins and words died in her throat. She would have called for help, but couldn't. Vainly did she attempt to grasp the door frame and to resist. Her fingers slipped along the stone. She would have fainted were it not for a horrible sight that she was compelled to witness when Vinitius had reached the garden.

Ursus was holding in his arms the limp form of a man whose head was hanging down with blood flowing from his mouth. Seeing them, the giant struck the head once more with his fist and instantly sprang towards Vinitius like an infuriated animal.

Death! thought the young tribune.

Then he heard, as in a dream, the cry of Lygia, "Kill not!" Then he felt that something like a thunderbolt opened the arms with which he embraced Lygia; then the earth spun around, and the light of day died in his eyes.

— — —

Chilo, hiding around the corner, was waiting for what would happen. Curiosity and fear fought within him. Should they succeed in kidnapping Lygia, he deemed that he would fare well at the hands of Vinitius. He had no further fear of Ursus, for he was confident that Croto would kill him. He calculated that in case a crowd should gather in the now empty streets, or if Christians or anybody else should offer resistance, he would speak to them as one in authority and a representative of Caesar. If necessary he would summon the guards to help the young patrician against the mob and thus win fresh favor. He felt that the plan of Vinitius was unwise; but when he considered Croto's remarkable strength, he admitted that it might succeed, feeling that if any difficulty arose, the tribune might carry the girl while Croto cleared the way. Time passed slowly, however, and the silence of the entrance where he watched alarmed him.

"If they don't find her hiding place and make a noise, they'll warn her in time," he muttered.

But this thought didn't displease him, for he understood that in such a case he'd again become necessary to Vinitius and could squeeze out of him a goodly number of sesterces.

Whatever they do, he said to himself, *it will accrue to my benefit, though no one perceives it. Gods! O gods! Gods! Permit me only—* he stopped suddenly. It seemed to him that someone was leaning forward from the entrance. Crouching still closer to the wall, he peered out, holding his breath. He hadn't been deceived. A head thrust halfway out of the entrance, looked hastily around. A moment later it disappeared.

That's Vinitius or Croto, thought Chilo, *but if they've captured the girl, why doesn't she cry out, and why are they gazing out upon the street? They're sure to meet people anyway, for before they reach the Carinae there'll be people stirring in the city. What is that? By the immortal gods!*

The remnants of his hair rose suddenly on his head.

In the doorway stood Ursus, the body of Croto hanging on his arm. Warily glancing around, the giant started to run with the body towards the river.

Chilo flattened himself against the wall like a piece of plaster. *I'm gone if he sees me,* was all that he could think.

Ursus ran quickly past the corner and disappeared beyond the next house. Chilo, without more ado, his teeth chattering with fright, ran along the cross street with a swiftness that would have done credit to a youth.

If when coming back he spies me from afar, he'll catch and kill me, he said to himself. *Save me, Zeus! Save me, Apollo! Save me, Mercury! Save me, God of the Christians! I'll leave Rome and return to Mesembria, but save me from the hands of that demon!*

The Lygian, who had slain Croto, seemed to him a superhuman being. Even as Chilo ran he wondered if Ursus were not some god who had assumed the appearance of a barbarian. At that moment he believed in all the gods of the world and in all the myths, which he usually mocked. It passed through his mind also that it might have been the God of the Christians who had killed Croto, and his hair rose again at the thought that he was warring against such a power. Not until he had traversed a number of alleys and seen some workmen approaching him did he recover somewhat. His breath failed him, so he collapsed on the steps of a house and wiped his perspiring forehead with a corner of his mantle.

"An old man like myself needs rest," he said, still panting.

The people coming towards him turned into a side street, and again everything was quiet. The city still slept. In the morning, movement began earlier in the wealthier sections of the city, where the slaves of rich families were made to rise before daylight. In the sections inhabited by the freed population, supported in idleness at the expense of the state, the inhabitants rose late, especially in wintertime. Chilo, after sitting for some time, began to get cold, so he got up and, after feeling for the purse that Vinitius had given him, walked slowly towards the river.

I may see Croto's body somewhere, he said to himself. *Gods! This Lygian, if he be a man, might earn millions of sesterces in one year, for if he strangled Croto like a whelp, who could withstand him? He could get his weight in gold for each appearance in the arena. He guards that girl better than Cerberus does Hades. But may Hades swallow him! I want nothing to do with him. He's too muscular. But what'll I do now? A horrible thing has happened. If he's broken the bones of such a man as Croto, surely the soul of Vinitius is whining over that cursed house, waiting for his burial. By Castor, he's a patrician, a friend of Caesar, a relative of Petronius, a man known throughout Rome, and a military tribune. His death will certainly not be ignored. Should I go to the Praetorian camp or to the city guards?*

He stopped and debated with himself, then after a time he resumed.

Woe is me! Who led him to that house, if not I? His freedmen and his slaves know that I came to him, and some know with what purpose. What will happen to me if they suspect that I purposely pointed out to him the house where he met his death? Although afterward in court I could prove that I didn't desire his death, they'll say I was the cause of it. Besides, he's a patrician, so in any case I'll be punished. But if I steal away from Rome and go far away, I'd expose myself to still greater suspicion.

It was a bad case from any point of view. The only thing to be done was to choose the lesser evil. Rome was a big place, but Chilo felt that it might become too small for him. Another man might have gone straight to the prefect of the guards and informed him of what had happened. Suspicion might indeed fall on him, but he could calmly assist the investigation. But Chilo's whole past was of such a character that a closer acquaintance with the prefect of the city or with the prefect of the guard would cause him serious trouble and confirm any suspicions that might come into the heads of the officers.

On the other hand, to fly would be to convince Petronius that Vinitius had been betrayed and murdered through conspiracy. Petronius was a powerful man who could enlist the police and the whole empire and who would undoubtedly endeavor to find the guilty ones even at the end of the earth. Still, Chilo debated whether he should go to Petronius and tell him the whole story. This might be the best plan to pursue. Petronius was an even-tempered man, and Chilo could be certain at least that he'd hear him out to the end. Petronius, who knew the whole affair, would be more likely to believe in Chilo's innocence than the prefects would.

But before going to him it was necessary to know for certain what had befallen Vinitius, and Chilo didn't know that. He'd seen the Lygian stealing towards the river with Croto's body, but that was all. Vinitius might have been killed, or he might only have been wounded and taken prisoner. Now the thought struck Chilo that the Christians wouldn't dare to kill so powerful a man—an Augustinian and a high military official—for such a deed might cause a general persecution. It was more likely that they'd forcibly detained him to give Lygia time to hide herself in some other place.

This thought filled Chilo with hope. *If that Lygian dragon hasn't torn him to pieces at the first onset, he's still alive; and if he's alive, he himself will testify that I haven't betrayed him, and then not only does nothing menace me, but—O Hermes! Count on two heifers again!—a new field opens before me. I can inform one of the freedmen where to look for his master. It's his business whether he goes to the prefect or not—the point is that I shouldn't go. I may even count on a reward from Petronius. First I searched for Lygia, now I'll search for Vinitius, then for Lygia again. But first of all I must find out whether Vinitius is alive or dead.*

Here it occurred to him that he could go at night to the miller Demas and inquire about Ursus. But he rejected that thought immediately; he preferred to have nothing to do with Ursus. It was more than probable that if Ursus hadn't killed Glaucus, he'd almost certainly been warned by some Christian elder, to whom he'd confessed his purpose, that it was an evil affair to which a traitor had persuaded him. Besides, the very thought of Ursus sent a shiver through Chilo's body. He determined that in the evening he'd send Euritius to the house in which Lygia had been staying and let him bring back the news. Meanwhile he needed refreshment, a bath, and rest. The sleepless night, the journey to Ostranium, and the flight from the Trans-Tiber had fatigued him beyond measure.

One thing gave him great comfort. He now had two purses: one that Vinitius had given to him at home and another that he had flung at him on the way back from the cemetery. In view of this happy circumstance, and because of the excitement through which he had passed, he resolved to eat heartily and drink better wine than he usually drank.

When at length the hour arrived for opening the wineshops, he ate and drank so much that he forgot about the bath. Since he desired sleep above all, he returned with stumbling steps to his abode in the Suburra, where a female slave, bought with Vinitius's money, awaited him.

As soon as he entered the bedroom, dark as a fox's hole, he fell across his bed; almost immediately, he was asleep. Not till evening did he awake, or rather, he was then awakened by the slave woman calling him to get up, for someone was inquiring for him and wished to see him about an urgent matter.

The vigilant Chilo was awake in an instant. Hastily throwing on his mantle and hood, he commanded his slave to stand aside and peered out cautiously. The sight that greeted him almost paralyzed him. Before the door of the sleeping room stood the gigantic form of Ursus.

He felt his feet and head grow cold as ice. His heart ceased to beat, and shivers passed up his spine. For some time he couldn't speak. But at length, with chattering teeth, he said, or rather, groaned, "Syra—I'm not at home—I don't know that—good man—"

"I told him you were home and asleep, master," answered the girl, "but he told me to awaken you."

"Oh, gods! I'll command that you—"

But Ursus, as if impatient with the delay, approached the door of the bedroom and thrust his head inside.

"Chilo Chilonides!" he said.

"*Pax tecum! Pax! Pax!*" replied Chilo. "O best of Christians! Yes, I'm Chilo, but there must be some mistake—I don't know you!"

"Chilo Chilonides," repeated Ursus, "your master, Vinitius, demands that you go with me to him immediately!"

PART II

Chapter XXIII

Vinitius was awakened by a piercing pain. Where was he? What was happening? For a moment he couldn't tell. There was a roaring in his ears, a mist over his eyes. Gradually, however, his consciousness returned, and through that mist he saw three men bending over him, two of whom he recognized. The first was Ursus; the second was the old man whom he'd knocked down as he carried off Lygia. The third, an utter stranger, was holding the tribune's left arm and testing the arm from the elbow to the shoulder blade. This caused such terrible pain that Vinitius, imagining it was some kind of revenge, cried through his set teeth, "Kill me!"

But the men paid no apparent attention to these words, acting as though they hadn't heard them or, hearing, considered them but the meaningless moans of a badly wounded man. Ursus, his face serious yet stern in its strong barbaric lines, held a bundle of white linen rags torn into long strips. The old man was speaking to the stranger.

"Glaucus, are you certain that the wound in the head is not mortal?"

"I'm certain, worthy Crispus," was the reply. "While serving as a slave in the galleys and later, while living in Neapolis, I cured many wounds. With my earnings I purchased my own freedom and that of my family. The wound in the head is a slight one. When this man," he nodded at Ursus, "snatched the girl from the young man, he knocked him against the wall. To save himself, the young man shielded his head with his arm, which he dislocated and broke, but by so doing saved both his head and his life."

"You've had many of my brethren under your care," replied Crispus, "and are renowned as a skillful physician. That's why I sent Ursus for you."

"Ursus? Why, he's the man who, on the way here, confessed that yesterday he was ready to kill me."

"Before he made that confession to you, he'd already shared his intention with me. I, who know you and your love for Christ, explained to him that the traitor was not you, but that stranger who sought to incite him to murder."

193

"That was an evil spirit that I took for an angel," replied Ursus with a sigh.

"Tell me all about it some other time, but now we must care for the patient."

With these words Glaucus proceeded to set the broken arm. Vinitius, notwithstanding the water that Crispus sprinkled over his face, fainted repeatedly because of the excruciating pain. This was fortunate, as it saved him from feeling the setting of the bones and the tightening of the bandages around the two splints between which Glaucus placed the arm so as to render it immovable.

After the operation was over, Vinitius revived. He woke to see Lygia. She stood there by the bed, holding a brass bucket of water, into which Glaucus from time to time dipped his sponge, moistening the head of the patient.

Vinitius stared at her, unable to believe his eyes. Was this but a dream, a delusion induced by the fever? It was some time before he could whisper, "Lygia!"

At the sound of his voice, the pail trembled in her hand, and she turned on him eyes full of sadness. "Peace be with you," she murmured, in a low voice.

She stood there with extended hands, with a face full of pity and sorrow. But he stared at her as though he wished to fasten her image upon his retinas where it might remain even after his eyelids were closed. He studied her face, paler and thinner now than it had been; the dark tresses of her hair; and her cheap, working-girl dress. He stared so fixedly that under the influence of his gaze her snowy forehead flushed rosily. His first thought was that he'd love her always; his second, that her pallor and her poverty were both due to him—he had driven her from a home where she was surrounded by love and comfort and forced her into that squalid hovel and clad her with this threadbare dress of dark wool. Willingly would he have arrayed her in the costliest gold brocade and adorned her with the most precious jewels in the world! Amazement, alarm, and pity overcame him, as well as a sorrow so great that he'd have fallen at her feet had he been able to move.

"Lygia," he said, "you didn't let me be killed!"

In sweet, low tones she replied, "May God restore you to health."

To Vinitius, mindful of all the troubles he'd inflicted on her, these words were as balm. He forgot for a moment that her lips could utter

"Peace be with you."

Christian teachings; he felt only that the speaker was the woman he loved and that her reply was marked by a special tenderness, a superhuman goodness that stirred him to the depths of his being. Once again he grew weak. As shortly before from pain, so now he grew weak from emotion. A faintness, overwhelming yet pleasant, crept over him. It seemed to him as though he were falling into a deep abyss, yet the fall was a delight, and he was happy. At that moment he felt as though he were face-to-face with a divinity.

Glaucus had now finished washing the wound in his head and had applied a healing salve. Ursus took the basin from the hands of Lygia, who, lifting a cup of wine mixed with water from the table, brought it to the lips of the sufferer. Vinitius drank eagerly and felt immediate relief. After the wounds and bruises had been dressed, the pain almost ceased. Complete consciousness returned to him.

"Give me another drink," he asked.

Lygia retired with the empty cup to the next room.

Meanwhile, Crispus, after exchanging a few words with Glaucus, approached the bed and said, "Vinitius, God didn't permit you to accomplish an evil deed, but preserved your life so you might repent. He, in whose sight man is but dust, delivered you defenseless into our hands; but Christ, in whom we believe, commanded us to love even our enemies. And so we've dressed your wounds, and as Lygia has said, we'll pray that God restores your health, but we cannot watch over you any longer. Therefore, remain in peace, but consider whether it becomes you to continue persecuting Lygia, whom you've deprived of home and guardians, and us of a roof, though we've paid you good in exchange for evil."

"Is it your intention to leave me?" asked Vinitius.

"It's our intention to leave this building in which prosecution by the city prefect can reach us. Your companion was killed, and you who are a man of influence among your own people lie here wounded. It was no fault of ours, but we might be made to answer for it before the law."

"Fear not," said Vinitius. "I'll protect you."

Crispus didn't feel it wise to admit that their fear was not solely on account of the prefect and the police, but of Vinitius also, whom they couldn't trust and from whose further pursuit they wished to protect Lygia.

"Master, your right hand is sound," he said. "Here are stylus and tablets. Write to your servants requesting them to come tonight with a litter and carry you to your home, where you'll have more comfort than here amid our poverty. We live here with a poor widow. She'll soon return with her son, who'll carry your letter. As for ourselves, we must all seek another refuge."

Vinitius grew pale, for he understood that they wished to separate him from Lygia, and if he lost sight of her again, he felt that he might lose her forever. He recognized that grave obstacles had intruded themselves between him and her and that he must think up some scheme to gain possession of her. But for this he needed time. He perceived also that whatever he might tell these people, even if he swore that he'd return Lygia to Pomponia Graecina, they wouldn't believe him and would be justified in their distrust of him. Long before, rather than harassing Lygia, he might have gone to Pomponia and sworn to renounce all further pursuit; then Pomponia might have found the girl and taken her back. No, he felt that no promises of this kind would be believed, nor would his solemn oath be accepted, since he was not a Christian and could only swear in the name of the immortal gods, in whom he himself had scant belief and whom they considered evil spirits.

He desired desperately to break down the resistance of Lygia and her guardians—but this required time. For him it was all-important to see her, to look at her, even if only for a few days. As a drowning man sees safety in every fragment of a plank or an oar, so it seemed to him that during these few days he might say some words that would bring her closer to him, that he might come up with some stratagem, or that some lucky accident might occur.

Collecting his thoughts, he said, "Listen to me, O Christians! Yesterday I was with you in Ostranium, and I listened to your teachings. But even had I not heard them, your actions alone would have convinced me that you are honest and good people. Tell the widow who lives in this house to remain here. You remain, too, and allow me to remain as well. Let this man"—here he turned his eyes on Glaucus—"who is a physician, or at least understands the dressing of wounds, say whether it would be wise to carry me elsewhere today. I'm sick and have a broken arm that must remain immobile for at least a few days; therefore, I declare to you that the only way I'll leave this house is if you carry me off by force!" And with that he stopped speaking, out of breath and clearly in deep pain.

Crispus responded, "No one, O master, will use force against you. We alone will take ourselves from here to a place of safety."

To this, the young man, unused to opposition, frowned and said, "Let me recover my breath."

After a while, he began to speak again. "Nobody will ask after Croto, whom Ursus strangled. He intended to go today to Beneventum, whither he was called by Vatinius—everybody will think he's on his way. When we came with Croto to this house, nobody saw us save one man, a Greek, who was with us in Ostranium. I'll tell you where he resides. Bring him here and I'll order him to keep silence, for he's in my pay. I'll write home that I also have gone to Beneventum. If the Greek has already informed the prefect, I'll say that it was I who killed Croto and that it was he who broke my arm. I swear by the ashes of my father and my mother that I'll do this. Therefore, you can remain here without danger; not a hair on any head will be injured. Bring me the Greek who calls himself Chilo Chilonides."

"In that case," said Crispus, "Glaucus will remain with you, O master, and will aid the widow in caring for you."

Vinitius frowned more darkly. "Listen, old man, to what I say!" he cried. "I owe you gratitude, and you seem to be a good and honest man, but you're not telling me what you're really thinking. You're apprehensive that I'll summon my slaves and command them to take Lygia away. Isn't this so?"

"It is so," replied Crispus sternly.

"Then remember this, I shall speak before all of you to Chilo and write home that I've gone to Beneventum. I shall have no messengers hereafter but you. Remember this and don't irritate me any longer."

As he spoke, his face was distorted with anger. A little later he resumed violently. "Think you I'll deny that it's for her sake I wish to remain here? A fool could perceive this, even were I to deny it. But I'll no longer attempt force where she's concerned. To you I'll say one thing more: If she doesn't remain here, with this well hand I will tear away the bandages from my arm. I will take neither food nor drink, and may my death rest upon the heads of you and your brothers. Why did you nurse me? Why didn't you order them to kill me?"

He was now pale with anger and weakness. But Lygia, who'd heard the whole thing from an adjoining room and was certain he'd carry out his threat, was terrified. Not for anything would she have wished his death. Wounded and defenseless, he'd awakened her pity, but not her fear. From the time of her escape she'd lived among religious enthusiasts whose only thoughts were of sacrifices, offerings, and unlimited charity. To such a degree was she imbued with the spirit of her surroundings that it took the place of her home, of her family, of her lost happiness, and transformed her into one of those Christian maidens whose influence was to change the erstwhile soul of the world.

Vinitius was too important a factor in her life; he'd thrown himself too obtrusively in her way to make it possible for her to forget him. For whole days she'd thought of nothing but him. Often she'd begged God to send an opportunity when, following the dictates of her faith, she might return him good for evil, mercy for persecution, break him and win him to Christ, save him.

And now it seemed to her that the opportunity had come, and that her prayers had been answered. She approached Crispus, her face alight as that of one inspired. When she spoke, it was as though some other voice spoke through her.

"Crispus," she said, "permit him to remain among us, and we'll remain with him until Christ has healed him."

To the aged presbyter, accustomed to see in all things the finger of God, Lygia's exaltation took on the aspect of a direct message from on high. He bent his gray head and, with awe in his heart, answered, "Let it be as you say."

On Vinitius, who hadn't once taken his eyes from her face, this immediate obedience of Crispus produced a strange and profound impression. It seemed to him that Lygia was a sibyl or priestess among these Christians, who rendered her honor and obedience. Almost against his will he surrendered himself to that deference. To the love that he felt was now added a kind of awe, before which love itself seemed almost an impertinence. He didn't know how to reconcile himself to the realization that their relations were now changed, that now it was he who was at her mercy, not she at his. Lying there sick and broken, he'd ceased to be the aggressor and the conqueror and was merely a helpless child under her guardianship. To his haughty and domineering nature such a relationship with any other being would have been a humiliation. This time, however, not only did he not feel humiliated, but rather he was grateful to her as to a sovereign. These were new feelings that he could never before have dreamed of even as a possibility and that even now would have astonished him if he could have explained them to himself. But now he didn't ask why this thing had happened. He accepted it as something absolutely natural. He simply felt happy at being allowed to remain where she was.

He wished to thank her with gratitude and some other feeling so little known to him that he couldn't name it, for it was simply humility. But the excitement he'd gone through had so exhausted him that he was unable to speak. He could only thank her with his eyes, wherein shone joy that he could remain with her, could look on her tomorrow and the next day, perhaps for a long time. There was only one fear to spoil his joy—the fear of losing what he'd gained. So great was this fear that when Lygia once more approached him with a cup, he was overcome by a desire to take possession of her hand—but he was afraid. He was *afraid!* He, the same Vinitius who at Nero's banquet had forcibly kissed her lips and after her escape had sworn that he'd drag her by the hair to his *cubiculum* or order her to be flogged.

Chapter XXIV

Nevertheless, he now began to fear that some outside force might ruin his joy. Chilo might already have communicated the news of his disappearance to the prefect or to his own freedmen. This would mean an invasion of the house in which he lay. For a moment, it's true, the temptation came to him that he might give an order to abduct Lygia and lock her up in his house; but the next instant he felt that he couldn't do it. Arrogant, self-willed, and dissolute as he was, merciless enough when need be, he yet was no Tigellinus, no Nero. Military life had imbued him with enough of a perception of justice, good faith, and conscience to enable him to recognize the dastardly nature of such a deed. In a moment of rage, indeed, when in full possession of his strength, he might have done this, but at this moment and under these circumstances, his nerves were unstrung. He was sick at heart, filled with tenderness, and deeply moved. All that he cared for was that no one should stand between him and Lygia.

Astonished, he perceived that from the moment Lygia had pled for him, neither she nor Crispus had demanded any assurances from him, apparently confident that some supernatural force would defend them in case of need.

Vinitius, who, since he'd heard the sermon of the Apostle at Ostranium, had felt the distinction between the possible and the impossible fading away, was inclined to believe that this might be so. But, recovering his former coolness, he reminded them of what he'd said about the Greek and again asked them to bring Chilo to him.

Crispus consented, and it was decided to send Ursus. Vinitius, during the last days before his visit to Ostranium, had often sent his slaves to find Chilo, but they hadn't been successful. He now explained to the Lygian exactly where Chilo resided. Then, writing a few words on the tablet, he addressed himself to Crispus.

"I give you this tablet because this man is suspicious and cunning. Often when I've summoned him he's sent word to my messenger that he was away. This he always did when he had no good news for me and was afraid of my anger."

"If I find him, I'll bring him whether he's willing or not," replied Ursus. Taking his cloak, he hurried out.

It was no easy task to find anyone in Rome, even with the most detailed of directions. Ursus, however, was aided in such cases by the instincts of the semisavage of the forests and his intimate acquaintance with the city, hence he soon found himself in Chilo's dwelling. He failed to recognize him, however. Only once before, and then at night, had he seen him. Besides, that towering and self-possessed old man who had ordered him to murder Glaucus so little resembled the Greek who now bent himself almost double before him in abject fear, that no one would have supposed them to be the same person. Chilo, perceiving that Ursus took him for a stranger, was relieved. The sight of Vinitius's writing on the tablet quieted him still more, for it never occurred to him to think that Vinitius would entrap him into an ambuscade. Nor did he imagine that the Christians could have killed Vinitius, inasmuch as they wouldn't dare to lift their hands against so eminent a person.

And Vinitius will protect me in case of need, he thought. *Surely then he doesn't summon me for the purpose of giving me up to death.*

Regaining courage, he asked, "Good friend, didn't the notable Vinitius send a litter for me? My legs are swollen, so it's impossible for me to walk so far."

"No," replied Ursus, "we'll walk."

"Suppose I decline?"

"Don't, for you *must* go."

"Oh, I'll go, but I go of my own free will. No one can compel me, for I'm a freedman and a friend of the city prefect. As a philosopher I have means against the use of force. I know how to change men into trees and animals. But I'll go, I'll go! But I'll first put on a warmer cloak and a hood so that the slaves in that quarter may not recognize me. If they did, they'd detain me at every step to kiss my hands."

Speaking thus, he put on another mantle, as well as an ample Gallic hood, so that Ursus shouldn't recognize him in clearer light.

"Where are you taking me?" he asked Ursus on the way.

"To the Trans-Tiber."

"I haven't dwelled long in Rome, and I've never been in the Trans-Tiber, but most likely even here there live men who love virtue."

The blunt and outspoken Ursus had already heard Vinitius say that the Greek had been with him in the Ostranium cemetery. Later he'd seen the pair at the portal of the house where Lygia lived. So he halted for a moment.

"Tell no lie, old man. Today you were with Vinitius at Ostranium and under our gate."

"Oh!" said Chilo. "Is your house in the Trans-Tiber? I've been but a short time in Rome and am not familiar with the names of the quarters. That's true, my friend: I stood at your gate today, and I implored Vinitius, in the name of virtue, not to enter. True, also, I was in Ostranium, and do you know why? Because for some time past I've been endeavoring to save Vinitius, and I wished that he could hear the oldest of the Apostles. May the Light gain access to his soul and to yours. Certainly as a Christian you must wish that truth should conquer falsehood."

"Yes," said Ursus humbly.

Chilo had now entirely regained his courage.

"Vinitius is a powerful lord and a friend of Caesar," he said. "He often listens to the suggestions of evil spirits, but if a hair of his head were injured Caesar would revenge himself on all Christians."

"We are protected by a still greater Power."

"True, true, but what do you intend to do with Vinitius?" asked Chilo with renewed uneasiness.

"I don't know. Christ commands mercy."

"You've answered well. Remember this always. Otherwise you'll fry in hell like sausage in a frying pan."

Ursus sighed. Chilo said to himself that he could easily manipulate this man, terrible as he might be in a moment of passion.

Anxious to know how things had gone since the carrying off of Lygia, he asked in the voice of a stern judge, "What have you done with Croto? Speak, and tell no lie."

Ursus sighed a second time. "Vinitius will tell you," he said.

"Which means that you stabbed him with a dagger or killed him with a club."

"I was unarmed," answered Ursus.

The Greek couldn't repress his wonder at the supernatural strength of the barbarian.

"May Pluto—I mean, may Christ forgive you."

For a while they continued their journey in silence.

Then Chilo said, "I'll not betray you, but look out for the watchmen."

"I fear Christ, not watchmen."

"That's right. There's no greater crime than murder. I'll pray for you, but I'm not sure my prayer will help you unless you'll vow you won't raise a finger against anybody else."

"But I didn't kill with premeditation," replied Ursus.

Chilo, who was determined to ensure his own safety, continued to instill in the mind of Ursus a horror of murder and to persuade him to take the vow. He also questioned Ursus about Vinitius, but the Lygian answered him unwillingly, again asserting that he'd hear all that was necessary from the lips of Vinitius himself. Thus conversing, they traversed the long distance from the dwelling of the Greek to the Trans-Tiber and reached the house. Chilo's heart throbbed uneasily. In his terror it appeared to him that Ursus gazed upon him with a look of longing ferocity.

Small comfort it would be to me, he thought, *if he should kill me without premeditation. Would that paralysis might strike him, as well as all his fellow Lygians. Grant this, O Zeus, if you can.*

So thinking, he drew his Gallic mantle more tightly around him, explaining that he was afraid of the cold. At length, after passing the portal and the first courtyard, they found themselves in a corridor leading to the garden of the little house.

Chilo halted suddenly and said, "Let me regain my breath; otherwise I couldn't speak with Vinitius to give him wholesome advice."

Saying this, he stopped short, for though he repeated to himself that no danger threatened him, nevertheless the thought of facing those mysterious people whom he'd seen in Ostranium made his legs tremble. From inside, hymns came floating out to his ears.

"What's that?" he asked.

"You claim to be a Christian, yet don't know that we have a custom after each meal of singing a hymn of praise to the Savior? Miriam and her son must have returned by this time. Perhaps the Apostle is with them, as he's a daily visitor to the widow and Crispus."

"Lead me to Vinitius."

"Vinitius is in the same room as the others, as it's the largest room. The rest are small, dark chambers that we use only for sleeping. Come in and rest yourself."

They went in. The room was somewhat dark; it was a cloudy winter evening, and the flames of several lanterns failed to entirely disperse the darkness. Vinitius felt rather than saw that the hooded man was Chilo. The latter, seeing Vinitius stretched on the bed, went straight to him without looking at the others, as if convinced that with him alone was safety.

"Master, why didn't you take my advice?" he exclaimed, clasping his hands together.

"Hold your tongue," said Vinitius, "and listen." Here he looked sharply into Chilo's eyes, speaking slowly but distinctly, as if he wished every word to be taken as an order to be forever engraved upon Chilo's memory: "Croto assaulted me with intent to kill and rob me, do you understand? So I had to kill him. These people dressed the wounds that I received in the fight."

Chilo understood at once that if Vinitius spoke in this way, it was by some previous arrangement with the Christians and that he wished to be believed. He perceived this in Vinitius's very face, so without expressing either doubt or wonder, he lifted up his eyes and exclaimed, "That faith-breaking ruffian! Remember, I warned you not to put your faith in him. All my teachings rebounded from his head like peas against the wall. There's not torture enough in all Hades for him. But to assault his benefactor and so generous a master, ye gods!"

Here he belatedly remembered that on the way he'd represented himself to Ursus as a Christian, and he stopped short.

Vinitius resumed speaking.

"Had it not been for the *sica*[1] I had with me, he'd have killed me."

"Blessed be the moment when I advised you to take the *sica* with you."

Vinitius, turning on the Greek an inquiring look, asked, "What have you done today?"

"Master, have I not told you that I was offering up vows for your health?"

"And nothing more?"

"I was just making ready to call upon you when that good man came and said you'd sent for me."

"Here's a tablet. Go with it to my house, find my freedman, and give it to him at once. It's here written that I've gone to Beneventum. You'll tell Demas yourself that I went this morning in answer to an urgent call from Petronius." Here he repeated emphatically: "I've gone to Beneventum. Do you understand?"

---

1 Dagger.

"You've gone, master! This morning I bade you farewell at Porta Capena, and since your departure such melancholy has overcome me that, if your magnanimity doesn't soften it, I'll weep myself to death like the unhappy wife of Zethus[2] mourning for Itylus."[3]

Vinitius, despite his sickness and his knowledge of the craftiness of the Greek, couldn't refrain from smiling. It pleased him that Chilo understood him in a flash; hence he said, "I'll add an order that your tears be wiped away at once. Give me the lantern."

Chilo, his self-assurance restored, rose and, stepping to the hearth, took from the mantel one of the burning lamps. As he did this the hood slipped from his head, and the light struck full in his face. Glaucus sprang from his seat; a few quick steps brought him face-to-face with the Greek.

"Don't you recognize me, Cephas?" he asked. There was something so terrible in his voice that a shiver ran through all present.

Chilo raised the lamp and immediately let it drop. Then he bent nearly double in terrified supplication.

"No, I'm not he—I'm not he. Have mercy!"

Glaucus glanced towards the people around the supper table and cried, "Here's the man who betrayed and destroyed me and my family."

The story of Glaucus was known to all the Christians. Vinitius himself had heard it, but he hadn't guessed that Glaucus and the stranger were one. Owing to his continuous fainting spells during the dressing of his wounds, he hadn't heard the man's name.

But to Ursus the words of Glaucus came, in that moment, as lightning out of darkness. With one leap he was at Chilo's side and, seizing his shoulders and shaking him, exclaimed, "This is the man who persuaded me to murder Glaucus!"

"Have mercy!" shrieked Chilo. "I'll return everything," he moaned. "Oh, good master," he cried, turning to Vinitius, "save me! Oh, save me! I confided in you. Be my protector. I'll take your letter—Oh, master! Master!"

But Vinitius was least moved of all the spectators at this strange scene—first, because he knew all the hidden doings of the Greek, and second, because his heart knew not what pity or compassion even were.

---

2 The son of Jupiter and Antiope.
3 In Greek mythology, the only child of Aëdon and Zethus. By mistake Zethus killed Itylus, and Zeus changed Aëdon into a nightingale, forever mourning for her son.

"Bury his carcass in the garden," he said coldly. "Some other messenger will take the letter."

To Chilo these words seemed to be a final sentence. His bones were cracking in the terrible clutch of Ursus; pain filled his eyes with tears.

"For the sake of your God, don't kill me! *Pax vobiscum!* I'm a Christian. If you don't believe me, baptize me at once, twice more, ten times more. Glaucus, this is a terrible mistake. Let me explain. Make me a slave. Don't kill me. Mercy! Mercy!"

His voice, stifled with pain, was growing weaker and weaker when suddenly the Apostle Peter rose from the table. For a moment his white head trembled and drooped. His eyes closed.

Then he opened them again, drew himself up, and amid a hush, said, "The Savior has commanded, if your brother sins against you, chastise him; but if he's repentant, forgive him; and if he has offended seven times in one day against you and has turned to you seven times, saying, 'Have mercy on me,' forgive him."

The silence grew deeper. Glaucus stood for a long time with his face covered by his hands. At length he removed them and said, "Cephas, may God forgive your offenses against me, as I forgive them."

Ursus freed the Greek's arms and added, "May the Savior take mercy upon me even as I take mercy upon you."

Chilo fell to the floor, upon his hands and knees. Shaking his head like a beast caught in a trap, he gazed around in anticipation of immediate death. Even now he couldn't believe his eyes and ears, for he didn't dare to hope for forgiveness. Slowly he recovered himself, his blue lips still trembling from fright.

The Apostle said, "Go in peace."

Chilo rose, but couldn't speak. He approached the bed of Vinitius, as if seeking protection in it still, for he hadn't yet realized that the tribune—though he'd used his services and was his accomplice—had condemned him to death, while those he'd wronged terribly forgave him. This realization was to come to him later. At present, astonishment and incredulity were clearly evident in his face. Though they said he'd been forgiven, he wished to flee immediately from these incomprehensible people whose kindness terrified him almost as much as their cruelty would have.

Chilo felt he couldn't remain in that room another instant; hence, standing above Vinitius, he said in a broken voice, "Give . . . master . . . the letter."

Taking the tablet that Vinitius handed him, he bowed low to the Christians, then to the patient, and edging crabwise along the wall, he hurried out into the darkness of the garden. Fright raised the hair on his head, for he felt certain that Ursus would follow and kill him. Though impelled to put forth his utmost speed, his legs failed him. The next moment he lost control of them completely as he caught sight of Ursus by his side.

Chilo fell to the ground and, with his face pressed to the dirt, pleaded in agony, "Ursus, for Jesus' sake!"

But Ursus said, "Don't be afraid. The Apostle ordered me to lead you beyond the gate so that you don't go astray in the darkness. If you lack strength, I'll lead you to your house."

Chilo raised his face.

"What did you say? What? That you won't kill me?"

"No, I won't kill you, and if I gripped you too strongly and injured a bone of your body, forgive me."

"Help me up," said the Greek. "What? You won't kill me? Lead me to the street and I'll make the rest of the journey alone."

Ursus lifted him as he might have lifted a feather and stood him on his feet. Then he led him through the dark alley to the second courtyard. Here was the exit to the street. In the corridor, Chilo repeated to himself, *I'm lost!* Not until he'd reached the street did he recover and say, "I can now go alone."

"Then peace be with you."

"And with you! And with you! . . . I'll just catch my breath."

After the departure of Ursus, he breathed easier. With his hands he felt all over his legs and hips, as though to convince himself that he was still alive and whole. Then he hurried forward. But after a score of rapid steps he halted and said aloud, "Why didn't they kill me?"

In spite of his long dispute with Euritius about Christian teaching, in spite of his discussion with Ursus by the millpond, and in spite of all he'd heard in Ostranium, he could find no answer to this question.

Chapter XXV

Vinitius also was at a loss for an explanation of what had happened; in fact, in the innermost depths of his soul he was as much astonished as Chilo. That these people had treated him as they had and, rather than avenging his assault, had carefully dressed his wounds, might have been ascribed partly to the doctrines they professed, more to Lygia, and not a little to his eminent position. But their behavior to Chilo was beyond his conception of the human possibilities of forgiveness.

Involuntarily the question forced itself upon him, *Why didn't they kill the Greek?*

They could have done this without fear of punishment. Ursus could have interred the body in the garden or carried it at night to the Tiber, which, in those times of nocturnal homicides (often committed by Caesar himself), cast up human corpses so frequently that few stopped to inquire whose they were or where they came from. Besides, in his personal opinion, the Christians not only had the power, but also the right to kill Chilo. Yet compassion wasn't totally absent from the patrician world in which he belonged. The Athenians had raised an altar to compassion and had long opposed the introduction of gladiatorial shows into Athens. In Rome, the vanquished sometimes received mercy from the victor. In fact, Caractacus, a king of the Britons, taken captive by Claudius and richly provided for by him, was even then living in the city in freedom. But revenge for personal injuries seemed to Vinitius, as to all other Romans, just and right. To renounce it was contrary to all the principles he'd been brought up on.

True, he'd heard in Ostranium that one ought to love one's enemies, but he held it to be a new theory without any application to real life. Even now the thought passed through his mind that possibly Chilo hadn't been killed because the day was a holiday or fell under some phase of the moon when Christians were not allowed to kill. He'd heard that among foreign nations certain days and periods were tabooed even for warfare. But why, then, wasn't the Greek surrendered into the hands of justice? Why, then, had the Apostle said that if someone should offend you seven times, seven times should you forgive him? Why had Glaucus said to Chilo, "May God forgive you, as I forgive you"?

Chilo had inflicted upon Glaucus the most terrible injury man can wreak on man. At the very thought of what he would do to anyone who killed Lygia, the heart of Vinitius seethed like a boiling cauldron. No tortures would be too terrible for such a wrong. And that man had forgiven! And Ursus, too, had forgiven—he who might kill anyone he wished in Rome with entire impunity, for he could escape by simply killing the king of the Nemorian Grove[1] and taking his place. How could the gladiator who held that dignity for the time being—a dignity only held by killing the former king—stand up against the man whom Croto couldn't stand against? There was only one answer to all these questions: They refrained from killing through a goodness so great that the like of it hadn't been seen in the world up to that time, and because of a love for humanity so boundless that the believer forgot himself, his own injuries, his own happiness and sorrows, and lived only for others. What reward these people expected, Vinitius had heard in Ostranium, but it lay beyond his comprehension. Nevertheless, he felt that a life lived in this world with complete renunciation of all wealth and comforts would be a wretched one.

Therefore, in thinking about the Christians, pity and a shade of contempt mingled with his astonishment. In his eyes they were like sheep that sooner or later must be devoured by the wolf. His Roman nature forbade him to respect those who laid themselves open to be devoured.

One point, however, startled him: After the departure of Chilo, some great joy illuminated all faces. The Apostle had approached Glaucus and, placing his hand on his head, said, "Christ has conquered in you."

Glaucus had lifted up a face as radiant as though overflowed by some great and unexpected happiness. Vinitius, who could only understand the joy of accomplished vengeance, stared at him with fever-brightened eyes, as one who gazes upon a lunatic. With some inward indignation, he saw Lygia press her queenly lips to the hands of this man who at first sight had the appearance of a slave, and it seemed to him that the order of the world had been reversed.

Then Ursus returned and related how he'd led Chilo to the street and craved his pardon for any injury he'd inflicted upon his bones, whereupon

---

1   Chief gladiator.

the Apostle blessed him also. Crispus declared that it was the day of a great victory. On hearing the word *victory,* Vinitius was too confused to even follow such a line of reasoning.

When Lygia once again brought him a refreshing drink, he held her hand for a second and asked, "And do you forgive me as well?"

"We are Christians; we are not allowed to nurse anger in our hearts."

"Lygia," he said then, "whoever your God may be, I'll offer Him a hecatomb, only because He's yours."

She replied, "You'll honor Him in your heart only when you love Him."

"Only because He's yours," persisted Vinitius, but his voice had grown faint. He closed his eyes, for weakness had again overcome him.

Lygia left him but shortly returned and, standing by his couch, bent over to see if he were sleeping. Vinitius, feeling that she was close to him, opened his eyes and smiled. She placed her hand softly over his eyes as if to induce him to sleep. A great calm settled down upon him. But now his condition changed: He felt worse. In fact, he *was* worse. With the coming of night had come a violent fever. He couldn't sleep, and his eyes followed Lygia wherever she went.

At times he fell into a half-dream, wherein he saw and heard all that went on around him but in which reality was strangely mingled with feverish visions. It seemed to him that Lygia was a priestess in a tower-shaped temple in an ancient and lovely cemetery. Though he didn't remove his eyes from her, she appeared suddenly to be standing on the summit of the tower, a kithara in her hand, her entire form bathed in light. She resembled those priestesses who at night sang praise to the moon, whom he'd often seen in the Orient. Then he dreamed that by a great effort he climbed the spiral staircase to carry her off. Behind him crawled Chilo, his teeth chattering together with fright, crying, "Master, don't do this, for this is a priestess who'll be avenged by God." Vinitius didn't know who this God was; nevertheless he knew that he was about to commit a sacrilege and felt immeasurable terror. But when he reached the balustrade surrounding the top of the tower, the Apostle with his silvery beard appeared suddenly by the side of the maiden and said, "Raise not your hand against her, for she belongs to me." With these words the pair moved upward as if ascending towards heaven on a pathway formed by moonbeams. Then Vinitius, raising his hands, begged them to take him with them.

At this point he awoke. With regained consciousness he stared about him. The fire in the hearth had burned low but still shed light enough for

limited visibility. The Christians all sat before the fire, warming themselves, for the night was wintry and the room was cold. Vinitius noted the
fog of their breath. In the midst of the group was the Apostle. Lygia sat at
his knees on a low footstool; farther away sat Glaucus, Crispus, Miriam.
On one side of the crescent so formed sat Ursus, on the other Nazarius,
son of Miriam, a young lad with a charming face and long dark hair
falling down to his shoulders.

Lygia, her eyes uplifted to the Apostle, was listening intently, and all
eyes were turned to him while he spoke in a low voice. Vinitius began to
look upon him with a superstitious fear, hardly less than the terror he'd
experienced in his fevered dream. Was his dream at least half true? And
was this wanderer from distant shores really to carry off his Lygia and lead
her away through unknown paths?

He felt certain that the old man was speaking of him, perhaps suggesting how he could be separated from Lygia, for it seemed to him
impossible that any other subject for conversation could come up. Hence,
collecting his presence of mind, he strained to hear the Apostle's words.
But he found himself entirely mistaken. The Apostle was speaking once
more of Christ. *They live only in that name,* thought Vinitius.

The old man was describing the arrest of Christ.

"A detachment of soldiers and servants of the high priest came to take
Him. When the Savior asked whom they were seeking, they replied: 'Jesus
of Nazareth'; but when Jesus said, 'I am He,' they fell to the ground and
didn't dare to raise their hands against Him. Not until after the second
question did they attempt to seize Him."

Here the Apostle paused, stretched out his hands to the fire, and then
continued.

"The night was as cold as this. But my blood so boiled within me that
I drew my sword to defend Him, and I cut off the ear of the servant of the
high priest. I would have defended Him with more than my life had He
not said, 'Put your sword back into the sheath. Shall I not drink the cup
that the Father has given Me?' Then they seized and bound Him."

Having said this, Peter raised his hand to his forehead and stopped short,
as though striving to banish some of the recollections that crowded upon
him before proceeding further. Ursus, unable to bear any more, leaped up
and stirred the fire with an iron, scattering a multitude of golden sparks
around, until the flame shot up with new vigor. Whereupon he sat down
and exclaimed, "If I'd been there, I'd—"

He stopped short, for Lygia had placed her finger on her lips. He breathed loudly, however, and it was evident that his soul was in turmoil. Although he was always ready to kiss the Apostle's feet, Ursus couldn't approve that one act: resheathing his sword. Had anyone in *his* presence raised his hand against the Savior, had *he* been with Him that night, ah, how he would have battled the priests and servants and soldiers and officials! His eyes overflowed with tears at the very thought. He went through a frightful mental struggle. For, on the one hand, he thought how gladly not only would he himself have fought, but also how he would have summoned to the aid of the Savior his fellow Lygians, the very pick of them all. On the other hand, he reflected that this would have been disobedience to the Savior himself—a disobedience that would have hindered the redemption of the world. Hence his tears.

After a while, Peter, withdrawing his hand from his forehead, continued the narrative.

But a new feverish waking dream had now overcome Vinitius. What he'd overheard mingled itself with what he'd previously learned in Ostranium, of that day when Christ appeared on the shores of the Sea of Tiberias. He saw a broad surface of water whereon was a fisherman's boat, and in the boat were Peter and Lygia. Vinitius swam towards them with all his might, but the pain in his broken arm prevented his reaching them. A storm hurled waves into his eyes, and he began to sink below the surface as with a loud voice he cried for help. Lygia knelt imploringly before the Apostle, who turned the boat around and reached out an oar to him. Vinitius clutched it and by its aid succeeded in clambering into the boat and falling prone in the bottom of it.

After a while, it seemed to him, he raised himself to his feet and, gazing back, beheld a vast multitude swimming after the boat. The waves covered their heads with foam; in the gale only the hands of a few could be seen, but Peter saved them from drowning time after time and pulled them into the boat, which miraculously grew larger and larger. Soon great crowds filled it, as great as the crowds at Ostranium, and more and more were added to them. Vinitius wondered how they'd find room and was afraid that the boat should be swamped and all would drown. But Lygia comforted him by showing him a light on the far-off shore towards which they were sailing. Again dreams were mixed with what he'd heard at Ostranium from the lips of the Apostle, as to how Christ had appeared on that sea. In that far-off light he saw a figure towards which Peter steered.

As they drew nearer, the storm diminished, the waters grew calmer, and the light burned with an ever stronger blaze. The crowds began to sing a sweet hymn, the air was pervaded with the odor of nard, and the waters took on the hue of a rainbow, as if lilies and roses were looking up from the bottom of the sea. Finally, the boat's prow struck softly on the sand. Then Lygia gave him her hand and said, "Come, I'll lead you," and she conducted him into the light.

Once more Vinitius awoke, but his dreams were slow to leave; gradually, he regained the full consciousness of reality. For a time it had seemed to him that he was still on the sea, surrounded by the multitude. Unwittingly he'd looked around for Petronius and wondered why he wasn't there. The bright light from the chimney, from which the others had now withdrawn, fully brought him back to reality. Olive sticks smoldered slowly on the rose-colored ashes, while splinters of pine, evidently recently thrown upon the fire, shot up in a bright flame, and in this light Vinitius saw Lygia sitting not far from his bedside.

The sight moved him to his soul's depths. He remembered that she'd spent the entire previous night in Ostranium, and that during the whole of the present day she'd occupied herself in nursing him. Now that all had retired, she alone remained by his bedside. It was evident that she was weary, for while sitting motionless, her eyes were closed. Vinitius knew not whether she slept or was buried in thought. He gazed at her profile, at her drooping eyelashes, at her hands dropped listlessly on her knees. In his pagan brain, the thought began to evolve that besides the beauty of nudity—confident of itself and proud of its Greek and Roman symmetry—there existed in the world another order of beauty, pure and undefiled, in which a soul resides.

He couldn't bring himself to call this strange new thing Christianity. Yet, looking at Lygia, he couldn't separate her from the creed that she professed. He now understood that if all the others had gone to sleep and she alone, whom he'd wronged, had remained awake to keep watch over him, it was undoubtedly because that creed so commanded. Though this thought filled him with wonder, he felt it unbearable. He would have far preferred that Lygia had done this thing out of love for him, for his face, his eyes, his statuesque form—in a word, for all those reasons that had often caused Greek and Roman beauties to wrap their snowy arms around his neck. And then he realized that were she like these other women, something would be lacking in her. He wondered at himself. What was happening to him? He recognized that strange new feelings of some kind were rising in him, new tendencies, new insights, new priorities, strange to the world in which he'd always lived.

She opened her eyes then, and seeing that Vinitius was gazing at her, she approached him and said, "I'm with you."

He replied, "I saw your soul in a dream."

Chapter XXVI

The next morning he awoke weak but with a cool brow and free from fever. It seemed to him that a whispered conversation had aroused him, but when he opened his eyes, Lygia wasn't beside him. Ursus, bending over the fireplace, was raking the gray ashes away from the live coals beneath them. These he blew upon, not merely with his lips, but as if his lungs were a pair of bellows. Vinitius, remembering how yesterday this man had crushed Croto, gazed with the critical interest of a gladiatorial connoisseur at his Cyclopean back and his columnlike thighs.

Thank Mercury that he didn't break my neck! reflected Vinitius. *By Pollux, if all other Lygians are like him, there's a hard task ahead for the legions of the Danube.*

He called aloud, "You there! Slave!"

Ursus withdrew his head from the fireplace. With a friendly smile he said, "God give you a good day, master, a happy day and good health, but I'm a free man, not a slave."

Vinitius, anxious to question Ursus concerning Lygia's native place, was pleased by these words, for conversation with a free man, however simple, brought less humiliation to his Roman and patrician dignity than with a slave, whom neither law nor custom recognized as a human being.

"Don't you belong to Aulus?" he asked.

"No, master. I serve Callina, as I served her mother, but by my own free will." Once more he hid his head in the fireplace, blowing on the coals, on which he placed a bundle of wood. He withdrew his head for a moment to say, "Among us there are no slaves."

"Where's Lygia?" asked Vinitius.

"She's just gone out, and I have to cook your breakfast, master. She stayed awake all night to watch over you."

"Why didn't you take her place?"

"Because she willed it so, and my duty is to obey." Here his brow

216

darkened. The next moment he added, "Had I not obeyed her, you wouldn't now be alive, master."

"Are you sorry you didn't kill me?"

"No, master. Christ has commanded us not to kill."

"And Atacinus and Croto?"

"I couldn't restrain myself," murmured Ursus. He gazed regretfully at his hands, which had evidently remained pagan, though the soul had been baptized. He put a pot on the fireplace. Crouching down beside the fire, he fixed a thoughtful regard on the flame.

"It's your fault, master," he said at length. "Why did you raise your hand against her, the daughter of a king?"

Indignant pride boiled up in Vinitius that a common man and a barbarian dared not merely to address him so familiarly, but even to reprove him. To the uncommon and improbable circumstances that had happened to him since last night a new one had been added. But weak as he was, and without his slaves around him, he restrained his anger, especially since he wished to obtain further particulars of the past life of Lygia.

Recovering himself, he inquired about the war of the Lygians against Vannius and the Suevi. Ursus was more than willing to talk but could add little to what Vinitius had already heard from Aulus Plautius. Ursus hadn't taken part in the battle, for he'd conducted the hostages to the camp of Atelius Hister. He knew only that the Lygians had vanquished the Suevi and the Yazyges,[1] but that their leader and king had fallen beneath the shafts of the Yazyges. News had quickly followed that the Semnones[2] had set fire to the forests on their frontiers. The Lygians returned at once to avenge the injury. The hostages had been left with Atelius, who at first ordered that they should be treated with royal honor. Soon afterward, Lygia's mother had died. The Roman leader didn't know what to do with the child. Ursus had wished to return with her to the fatherland, but the road was infested with wild beasts and savage tribes. So when the news came that a Lygian embassy had waited on Pomponius to propose that they should become allies with him against the Marcomani,[3] Hister sent them to Pomponius.

From him, however, they learned that no ambassadors had arrived, and

---

1 Iazyges, a Sarmatian tribe on the Danube.
2 A people of northern Germany.
3 A powerful Germanic tribe.

thus they remained in the camp. From here Pomponius took them to Rome and, after his triumph, handed the king's daughter over to Pomponia Graecina.

Though few of these details were unknown to him, Vinitius listened with pleasure because his overweening patrician pride was elated that an eyewitness to the royal lineage of Lygia still existed. As a king's daughter, she could take a place in Caesar's court equal to that of the daughters of the first families, all the more so since the people over whom her father ruled had never warred against Rome. It was a barbarian lineage, indeed, but it was formidable, for according to the testimony of Atelius Hister himself, it possessed innumerable warriors. Ursus fully confirmed all this.

Vinitius questioned him about the Lygians.

"We live in the forests, but we possess so much land that no one knows where the end of the forest is, and we are large in number. There are also large towns in the forest built of wood, where there are many rare treasures. For what the Semnones, the Marcomani, the Vandals, and the Quades despoil from the world, we in our turn plunder from them. They dare not invade us. Only, when the wind blows from their quarter they burn our forests. We are afraid neither of them nor of the Roman Caesar."

"The gods gave Rome dominion over the world," said Vinitius severely.

"The gods are evil spirits," said Ursus simply. "Where there are no Romans, there is no sovereignty."

He stirred the fire and continued speaking as if to himself. "When Caesar took Callina to his court and I thought evil might befall her, I wished to go far away to the forests and bring with me a regiment of Lygians to help the king's daughter. Gladly would they have gone to the Danube, for they are good and brave, though pagans, and I would have brought them good news. Even as it is, should Callina ever return to Pomponia Graecina, I'll beg permission to go to the Lygians, for Christ was born in a far-off place, and they've never heard of Him. He knew better than I where it was right that He should be born, but should He have come into the world in our forests, we wouldn't have tortured and crucified Him. We'd have brought up the child and cared for Him so that He never wanted for game, nor mushrooms, nor skins of beaver, nor amber. Whatever we could have plundered from the Suevi or Marcomani we'd have given to Him so that He'd have plenty of comfort and affluence."

As he spoke, he placed on the fire the vessel containing broth for

Vinitius. He paused in the flow of his talk; evidently his mind was wandering in the Lygian forests. When the liquid began to simmer, he poured it into a shallow plate to cool.

"Glaucus advises, master, that you should move your sound arm as little as possible; therefore Callina has asked me to wait on you."

Lygia commanded! Then no contradiction was possible, no thought of opposition to her will crossed Vinitius's brain; he obeyed as implicitly as if she'd been the daughter of a Caesar or a divinity.

Ursus, seating himself by his couch, dished up the broth in a small cup that he lifted to the patient's lips. He did this so carefully, with so kindly a smile in his blue eyes, that Vinitius could hardly accept the testimony of his own senses that this was the same titan who last night, after crushing Croto, fell upon him like a tempest that would have torn him limb from limb but for Lygia's intercession. For the first time in his life, the young patrician began to ponder over the question of what strange emotions and thoughts might be at work in the breast of a simple man, a servant, a barbarian.

Ursus as a nurse was as awkward as he was willing. The cup lost itself so completely among his Herculean fingers that no place remained for the lips of Vinitius. After several vain efforts, the giant lost heart.

"Well! It would be easier to lead an aurochs out from a tangled wilderness."

Vinitius was amused by the crestfallen look of the Lygian, but he was no less interested in his conversation. In the Circus he'd seen the terrible aurochs from the northern wildernesses, whom the bravest *bestiarii*[4] pursued with fear and whom only the elephant exceeded in strength and bulk.

"Have you ever tried to take such beasts by the horn?" he asked in amazement.

"Until twenty winters had passed over me I was afraid, but then I mustered up sufficient courage for the task." Again he strove to feed Vinitius, more awkwardly than ever. At last he said, "I must seek the help of Miriam or Nazarius."

Just then the pale face of Lygia appeared from behind the curtain. "I'll help you now," she said. The next moment she'd come out from the *cubiculum*, where evidently she'd been preparing to sleep, as she was clad

---

4 Hunters of wild animals.

only in a tight-fitting tunic called a *capitium*. Her hair was unbound. Vinitius, whose heart beat more quickly at sight of her, reproached her for not yet having sought her couch, but she replied merrily, "I was just making ready for it, but first I'll replace Ursus."

Taking the cup from Ursus, she seated herself at the edge of the couch and began to feed Vinitius. He experienced a mixture of humiliation and joy. When she bent towards him, he felt the warmth of her body, and her long tresses fell on his chest. He paled with emotion. In the torment and turmoil of passion, he felt that her head was dear and venerated beyond everything; and, in comparison, the whole world was as nothing. Once it had been mere passion that she'd excited; now he felt that he loved her with all his heart. Once, like most people of his time, he was a blind and utter egoist, both in life and in feeling, who cared only for himself; now he cared only for her.

Consequently, he declined any more food. Though he found boundless delight in her presence and in gazing at her, he said, "Enough! Go to rest, my divinity!"

"Don't call me that. I ought not to listen," said Lygia.

Nevertheless, she smiled. She insisted that she'd lost all desire for sleep, that she felt no fatigue, and that she wouldn't retire to rest before the coming of Glaucus. Her words were music in his ears; his heart overflowed with still greater emotion, still greater ecstasy, still greater thankfulness, and he was at a loss as to how to show her his gratitude.

"Lygia," he said after a moment of silence, "I didn't really know you before. But I now know that I would have gained you by wrong means. So now I tell you, go back to Pomponia Graecina, and be assured that henceforward no one will raise a hand against you."

Her face saddened. "It would give me great happiness if I could so much as catch a glimpse of her from afar, but I cannot return to her now."

"Why?" Vinitius questioned in astonishment.

"We Christians know, through Acte, what's done on the Palatine. Have you not heard that Caesar, soon after my escape and before his departure to Neapolis, summoned Aulus and Pomponia and, suspecting that they had assisted me, threatened them with his wrath? Happily, Aulus was able to reply, 'You know, lord, that a lie has never passed my lips. Therefore now I swear to you that we didn't assist her to escape and that we know no more than you what has become of her!' Caesar believed and soon forgot. But, by the advice of the elders, I've never communicated with my mother nor told her where I was, so that she could always boldly swear complete ignorance of my whereabouts. You may not be aware, Vinitius, that we're not allowed to lie, even were our life at stake. Such is the teaching to which we conform our hearts; therefore, I haven't seen Pomponia since I left her abode. From time to time, far-off rumors reached her ears, assuring her that I was alive and . . ."

Here a great longing overcame her, and her eyes filled with tears, but she soon recovered herself and said, "I know that Pomponia is longing for me. But we have consolations unknown to others."

"Yes," answered Vinitius, "your consolation is Christ. But that's something I can't understand."

"Look at us. We have no partings, no sorrows, no sufferings, or if they do come, they're changed into joys. Death itself, which for you is the end of life, for us is only its beginning—the exchange of a lesser happiness for a greater happiness, a happiness less calm in exchange for one calmer and eternal. Imagine a religion that commands us to love even our enemies, forbids lies, cleanses our souls from evil, and promises illimitable happiness after death."

"I heard all this in Ostranium. I've seen how you behaved towards me and Chilo, and when I think of all this, it seems a dream and that I ought to disbelieve my ears and my eyes. But now answer another question: Are you happy?"

"Yes," replied Lygia. "Confessing Christ, I cannot be unhappy."

Vinitius looked at her as if that which she spoke were altogether beyond human understanding. "And wouldn't you wish to go back to Pomponia?"

"I would, with all my heart—and shall do so if such be the will of God."

"Then I say to you, go back. In the name of my lares I swear that I'll never raise my hand against you."

Lygia pondered for a moment and then replied, "No, I cannot expose my dear ones to peril. Caesar doesn't love the family of Aulus. If I go back—you know the slaves scatter news throughout Rome—the fact would soon be rumored within the city. Nero undoubtedly would learn it from his slaves. He'd punish Aulus and Pomponia and would tear me away from them once more."

"Yes," said Vinitius, knitting his brows, "that's possible. It's true that apparently he's forgotten you; after all, the loss wasn't his, but mine. But perhaps if he took you away from Aulus, he'd again bestow you on me. Then I'd return you to Pomponia."

Sorrowfully she asked, "Vinitius, would you wish to see me again on the Palatine?"

He ground his teeth together and replied, "No, you're right. I spoke as a fool! No!"

It seemed to him that a bottomless abyss opened out before him. He was a patrician, a military tribune, a mighty man, but above all the power and the authority of the world to which he belonged stood a madman whose malignity and evil will were impossible to foresee. Not to take him into account, not to dread him, was possible only for people like the Christians, for whom this world with its separations, sufferings, and death itself, were as nothing. All others must tremble before him. The terrors of the times in which they were living presented themselves to Vinitius in all their monstrosity. Therefore he couldn't return Lygia to the Auli, fearful that the monster would remember her and pour out his wrath upon her. For the same reason, should he wed her, he would imperil her, himself, and the Auli. A moment of imperial irritation would suffice to destroy everyone. For the first time in his life, Vinitius felt that the whole world needed a change, a regeneration, or life itself would become impossible. And he also understood that which only a moment before had been obscure to him: In such times only the Christian could be happy.

But, above all, remorse engulfed him as he realized that it was he himself who had so tangled up his own life and Lygia's that no disentanglement seemed possible. Under the influence of this contrition, he began to speak.

"Do you realize that you're happier than I am? In poverty, in this one room, in the midst of baseborn people, you have your creed and your Christ. But I have only you; and when I lost you, I was like a beggar who has neither roof above him, nor bread to eat. You are dearer to me than all the world. I searched for you, for I couldn't live without you. I cared neither for banquets nor for sleep. Had it not been for the hope of finding you I would have thrown myself on my sword. But I'm afraid of death, for if dead, I couldn't see you. I tell you the sincerest truth when I say that I couldn't live without you, and I lived till now only in the hope that I'd find you and see you. Do you remember our conversations at Aulus's house? Once you drew a fish for me on the sand, but I didn't understand what it meant. Do you remember how we played ball? Even then I loved you more than life, and you gradually became aware of that love. And Aulus came, scaring us with talk of the Libitina and interrupting our conversation. When we took leave, Pomponia told Petronius that God is one, almighty, and all-merciful, but it didn't occur to us that your God was Christ. Let Him but give you to me, and I'll love Him—although He seems to be a God of slaves, aliens, and outcasts. You sit near me, but think only of Him. Think of me also, or I'll hate Him. To me you alone are a divinity. Blessed be your father and mother, blessed be the land that produced you. Would that I could cast my arms around your feet and pray to you—render homage, offerings, adoration—you thrice divine. You don't know, you couldn't possibly know, how I love you."

Speaking thus, he passed his hand over his pale forehead and half closed his eyes. His character recognized no limitations to anger or love. He spoke excitedly, as a man who, losing self-mastery, places no check on either his words or his emotions. But he spoke from the depths of his soul, frankly and openly from his heart. It was evident that the pain, ecstasy, passion, and adoration accumulated in his heart had burst forth at last in an irresistible torrent of words.

To Lygia these words seemed sacrilegious; nevertheless, her heart throbbed as though it would rend the tunic that enclosed her bosom. She couldn't help but pity him in his suffering. She was deeply moved by his expressed adoration of her; she felt that she was loved and deified beyond measure, felt that this imperious and terrible man now belonged to her, soul and body, like a slave. This recognition of his submission and her own power filled her with happiness, and her earlier memories revived in all their original force. Again he was the same Vinitius—splendid and handsome as a pagan god—who in the house of the Auli had spoken to her of love and awakened her yet childish heart as from a dream, the same whose kisses she still felt on her lips, the same from whom Ursus had torn her away on the Palatine, as though he were tearing her away from the flames. But now, with mingled pain and ecstasy on his eagle face, with pale forehead and imploring eyes, wounded and crushed by love, full of adoration and humility, he came closer to that ideal that she would have him realize, that ideal that she could love with her whole heart, and therefore he was now dearer to her than ever.

Then she realized that an hour might come when her love for him might carry her off her feet like a whirlwind, and she, too, felt as Vinitius had just felt—that she stood on the edge of a precipice. Wasn't it because of this that she'd left the Auli? Because of this that she'd saved herself by flight? For this that she'd so long lain hidden in the poorer quarters of the city? Who was this Vinitius? An Augustinian, a soldier, one of Nero's courtiers. He participated in Caesar's mad debauches, as was proven by that banquet that Lygia could never forget. He'd gone to the temples with the others and made offerings to depraved gods—in whom, it may be, he had little faith, though he paid them official homage.

Still more, he'd pursued her to make her his slave and his mistress and had cast her into the midst of that terrible world of excess, debauchery, and depravity that called aloud for the wrath and vengeance of God. True, he seemed changed; yet but a moment ago, he'd told her that if she thought more of Christ than of him, he'd hate Christ. To Lygia it seemed that the mere thought of any love other than the love of Christ was in itself a sin against Him and against His teachings. When, therefore, she saw that at the bottom of her soul, other feelings and desires could be awakened, she was almost overcome by fear, fear both of her own future and her own heart.

At this moment of mental turmoil, Glaucus arrived to dress the wounds of the patient and to see how he was progressing. Immediately, anger and impatience flashed in the eyes of Vinitius, for he was furious that his passionate declaration of love to Lygia had been so untimely interrupted. When Glaucus questioned him, he answered almost with contempt. He calmed himself almost instantly, but if Lygia had preserved any faint illusion that what he'd heard in Ostranium would soften his unbending nature, that illusion had at once been dispelled. There was a change only towards her. Behind that single feeling, his heart retained all the old fierceness and egoism, Roman and wolfish, incapable not only of realizing the sweetness of Christianity, but even of common gratitude.

She left the room, full of inner sorrow and inquietude. Hitherto in her prayers, she'd offered to Christ a calm heart, a heart as truly pure as a tear. Now that serenity was disturbed. Within the petals of the flower, a poisonous worm had intruded itself and commenced its ravages. Sleep itself, notwithstanding two sleepless nights, brought her no peace of mind. She dreamed that at Ostranium, Nero, leading a troop of Augustinians, bacchantes, Corybants, and gladiators, was crushing throngs of Christians under the wheels of his rose-covered chariot. In her dream, Vinitius, grasping her in his arms, pulled her into the chariot and, tightening his embrace, whispered, "Come with us."

Chapter XXVII

From that moment on, Lygia appeared more rarely in the common room and still more rarely approached the couch of Vinitius. But peace didn't return to her. She felt the patient's imploring eyes following her every movement. She knew that he accepted every word of hers as a favor, felt that he dared not complain through fear that she'd shun him. Realizing that she alone was joy and health to him, her heart couldn't help but overflow with compassion. But she saw that the more she turned away from him, the more she pitied him, and the more tender were her feelings towards him. Peace forsook her. At times she strove to persuade herself that, in very truth, it was her duty to be with him constantly; first, because God taught that good should be returned for evil, and second, because by her conversation she could draw him towards the true religion. But conscience stepped in to accuse her of self-deception, of being influenced only by his charm and by her love for him. Thus she lived in a constant turmoil, which intensified day by day. At times it seemed as though she were caught in the meshes of a net and that every effort she made to escape only entangled her the more. She also had to admit to herself that every day his face grew more necessary to her, his voice dearer, and that she needed all her strength to battle with the growing desire to sit by his couch. When she approached him and his eyes brightened, joy danced in her heart. One day she observed traces of tears on his lashes. For the first time in her life there came a wild desire to wipe them away with kisses. Frightened at the very thought, apprehensive beyond measure, she wept all through that night.

As for Vinitius, he was so uncharacteristically patient, it was clear that he had determined to be on his best behavior. When at times his eyes flashed with petulance, impatience, self-will, and anger, he repressed those feelings at once and looked anxiously at her as if imploring her pardon. This disarmed her the more. Never before had she had the feeling of being so much beloved. At thought of it she felt at once guilty and happy.

Vinitius also was immensely changed. He showed less haughtiness in his discussions with Glaucus. Often the thought came to him that this poor slave-physician and the old barbarian Miriam, who surrounded him with care, and Crispus, whom he saw constantly immersed in prayer, were human beings, just as he.

These thoughts amazed him; nevertheless they returned again and again. In time he came to appreciate Ursus and conversed with him all day long, because it gave him an opportunity to talk about Lygia. The giant, for his part, was inexhaustible in tales. While rendering the simplest services to him, he became increasingly attached to the young tribune. Though to Vinitius, Lygia seemed like a being belonging to another species, higher a hundredfold than those who surrounded her, nonetheless he began to empathize with poor and simple folk, something he'd never experienced before in all his life. He even discovered in them traits of character—the existence of which he'd never suspected.

Nazarius was the only one he couldn't endure, for he felt that the youth dared to love Lygia. For a time he restrained his aversion, but when Nazarius brought Lygia a pair of quails—purchased in the market with his own earnings—Vinitius's noble Quirite ancestry asserted itself, the heritage that viewed alien wanderers as lower than the worst vermin. Hearing Lygia's thanks, he turned frightfully pale.

When Nazarius went out to get water for the quails, he cried, "Lygia, how can you stoop so far as to accept presents from him? Don't you know that his people are called Jewish dogs by the Greeks?"

"No, I don't know," she replied. "But I know that Nazarius is a Christian and my brother."

Astonishment and regret were in her eyes as she spoke, for she'd grown unused to such outbursts. He set his teeth to keep from telling her that he was strongly inclined to have Nazarius flogged to death or have him sent as a *compeditus*[1] to his Sicilian vineyards. But he restrained himself, throttled his fury, and finally said, "Lygia, forgive me, but for me you are the daughter of kings, the adopted child of Aulus."

He had so fully conquered himself by the time Nazarius reappeared that he promised the young man that when he returned to his villa, he'd present him with a pair of peacocks or flamingos, of which his gardens were full.

---

1 A man who labors with chained feet.

Lygia knew how dearly such self-conquest was purchased, and the more often he achieved it, the more her heart yearned towards him. His merit, in the case of Nazarius, was really smaller than she supposed, for while Vinitius might be momentarily angry with him, he couldn't be jealous. The son of Miriam, in his eyes, was a mere dog. Furthermore, he was still a mere child who, if he loved Lygia, loved her without knowing what love meant. Harder battles must the young tribune fight with himself to submit even in silence to the honor with which these people surrounded the name of Christ and His creed.

In this regard wonderful things happened in Vinitius. It was in any case the religion that Lygia professed, and for this alone he was ready to acknowledge it. The nearer he came to full recovery from his wounds, the more vividly did he recall the series of events that had occurred that night at Ostranium. As a result of the train of ideas, reactions, and questions that had since swirled around in his brain, he marveled at the superhuman power of this religion that regenerated the soul of man down to its very foundations.

He perceived that there was something extraordinary in it, something heretofore unknown on earth, and he felt that if it could conquer the world and engraft into it its own love and charity, an epoch would arise resembling that in which not Jupiter but Saturn ruled.

He dared not doubt the supernatural parentage of Christ, His resurrection, nor the other miracles. The eyewitnesses who related them were too trustworthy and had too firm an aversion to lies for him to believe that these things had never happened. Roman skepticism, which rejected the gods, nevertheless accepted miracles.

Vinitius, therefore, found himself in the presence of a strange and insoluble problem. This religion seemed to him opposed to all the existing state of things, utterly impracticable, and mad beyond any madness he'd ever heard of. In his opinion, the people in Rome and all over the world might be bad, but the order of things was good. If the Caesar of the day were honest, if the Senate of the day were composed not of depraved debauchees, but of men like Thrasea, what more could be desired? No, Roman peace and the Roman rule were good; social inequality was right and just. To Vinitius's mind this new creed must prove subversive of all order and all rule, must abolish all inequality. What would then befall the supremacy of Rome? Could Romans cease to govern? Could they recognize a herd of conquered nations as their equals? This was beyond the reasoning powers of a born patrician. Furthermore, this religion was personally repugnant to all his convictions, his customs, his character, and his ideas of life. He couldn't even imagine how he could exist if he accepted it. He feared and admired it, but he shuddered at the mere thought of accepting it. Nevertheless, he realized at last that nothing but that teaching separated him from Lygia, and whenever he thought about it, he hated Christianity to the very depths of his soul.

Nonetheless, he couldn't help but admit that it had adorned Lygia with that exceptional, inexplicable beauty that had nurtured in his heart not only love, but homage; not only desire, but adoration. It had made Lygia herself dearer to him than any other being in the world. Then the desire to love Christ would rise afresh within him. He saw clearly that he must either love or hate; no middle ground was possible. Two currents drove him from opposite sides; he wavered in his thoughts and feelings. Not knowing what to choose, he bowed his head and paid silent homage to that incomprehensible God, but only because He was Lygia's God.

Lygia perceived what was going on within him—how he strove to humble himself, yet how his whole nature recoiled from the creed of Christ. On the one hand she was mortally grieved by this rejection; on the other hand this unacknowledged respect that he felt for Christ inclined her heart to him with irresistible force, aroused her compassion, gratitude, and pity. She recalled Pomponia Graecina and Aulus. For Pomponia it was a source of constant sorrow and never-drying tears that beyond the grave she wouldn't find Aulus. Lygia now grew into a more complete understanding of this bitterness, this pain, for she too had found a being who was dear to her, and eternal separation threatened them both.

It's true that at times she deluded herself into the belief that he might accept the teachings of Christ, but such illusions couldn't last. Too well did she know and understand him. Vinitius a Christian! Even in her inexperienced head the two conceptions refused to blend. If the thoughtful, considerate, and prudent Aulus hadn't become a Christian under the influence of the wise and near-perfect Pomponia, how could Vinitius ever become one? There was no answer to this, save one—that for him there was neither hope nor salvation.

But she drew back with terror at this sentence of destruction that hung over him, and that realization, rather than estranging her from him, perversely, only made him the dearer. At times she longed to speak to him frankly of his dark future. And once, as she sat beside him, she dared to tell him that there was no life outside of Christianity. He'd now grown stronger. He lifted himself up with his sound arm and suddenly laid his head in her lap, saying: "You are life!" Breath failed her at that moment; presence of mind left her, a shiver of delight running through her from head to foot. Taking his head between her hands, she strove to lift him, but meanwhile bent so that her lips touched his hair. For a moment they were both overcome with the passionate love that drew them to each other.

Lygia rose at last and hurried away. There was fire in her veins and a giddy dizziness in her head, but that was the drop that overflowed the cup filled already to the brim. Vinitius had no inkling of the price he'd have to pay for that one moment of ecstasy, for Lygia now realized that she needed to be rescued from herself. She spent a sleepless night in tears and prayers, feeling that she had no right to pray and that God wouldn't listen to her. Next morning she left her *cubiculum* early and, calling Crispus to the garden summerhouse covered with ivy and withered vines, opened her very soul to him, entreating him to let her leave Miriam's house since she couldn't trust herself any longer, being unable to reject Vinitius—for she loved him.

Crispus—aged, severe, ever immersed in religious ecstasy—assented to her desire for flight, but could find no words of forgiveness for a love that seemed sinful in his eyes. His heart filled with indignation at the very thought that Lygia, whom he'd watched over since the moment of her escape, whom he'd loved, whom he'd confirmed in the faith, and on whom he'd looked as a white lily growing in the soil of the Christian creed, undefiled by any earthly breath, could have found a place in her heart for any but a heavenly love.

He'd thought that in the whole world there didn't exist a heart more purely and sincerely devoted to the glory of Christ. It was his desire to offer her to the Redeemer as a pearl, a jewel, rounded and perfected by his own hands. Hence this disappointment filled him with amazement and bitterness.

"Go, and implore God to pardon your guilt," he said gloomily. "Flee, before the evil spirit who has tempted you brings you down to utter ruin and before you end up renouncing the Savior. God died on the cross for you, shedding His own blood to redeem your soul, but you've elected to love him who plotted to make you his concubine. God miraculously saved you from his hands, and now you open your heart to impure desire and are beginning to love the son of darkness. Who is he? A friend and servant of the antichrist, a participant in his debauchery and crimes. Where will he lead you if not to that abyss, to that Sodom in which he himself abides, but which God Himself will annihilate with the flames of His wrath? I say to you, it would have been better if you'd died, if the walls of this dwelling had fallen upon your head, before this man crept into your heart and besmirched it with the poison of his depravity."

He grew more and more incensed, for Lygia's love filled him not only with wrath, but also with contempt and loathing for human nature in general and for female nature in particular. Even Christian teaching couldn't save woman from Eve's weakness. It meant nothing to him that the maiden remained pure, that she wished to flee from temptation, that she confessed her love with remorse and contrition. Crispus had wished to transform her into an angel, to lift her to heights where no love existed save that of Christ. And worst of all, she'd fallen in love with an Augustinian. The very thought filled his heart with horror intensified by disappointment and disillusion. No, she was beyond pardon. Words of horror burned his lips like live coals; although he stifled his outrage to a limited extent, it was offset by the effect of his shaking his withered hands at the terrified maiden.

Lygia acknowledged her guilt, but not to that degree. She'd felt that her flight from Miriam's dwelling was a victory over temptation and a minimizing of her guilt. But Crispus ground her into the dust, implying that her very soul was base—she'd never suspected that she was *that* depraved! She'd even hoped that the old presbyter, who from the time of her escape from the Palatine had taken the place of a father to her, might show her some compassion, console her, encourage her, and strengthen her; instead he raged on.

"Would that I might offer up to God my disappointment and my pain, but you've cheated the Savior Himself, for you've descended into a quagmire that has poisoned your soul with its miasma. You might have offered it up to Christ as a precious vessel, saying: 'Fill it, O Lord, with grace,' but you've preferred to offer it to the servant of the fiend. May God forgive you and have mercy on you! As to me, until you cast out the serpent, I who deemed you a chosen—"

He stopped short, realizing that they were no longer alone. Through the withered vines and the evergreen ivy, he saw two men, one of whom was the Apostle Peter. The other he failed to recognize, for a mantle of

Lygia, sobbing, nestled closer to Peter's feet.

coarse woven stuff, called *cilicium*, hid a portion of his face; for a moment Crispus thought him to be Chilo.

But the men, having heard the loud voice of Crispus, entered the summerhouse and sat down on a stone bench. Then Peter's companion uncovered his thin face. The sides of his head were covered with curly hair, which grew thinner at the top; his eyelids were red, his nose crooked. In his homely yet inspired countenance, Crispus recognized the features of Paul of Tarsus.

Lygia, falling to her knees, despairingly embraced the feet of Peter and, hiding her tortured head in the folds of his cloak, remained there in silence.

Peter said, "Peace be with your souls." And looking at the child at his feet, he inquired what had happened.

Then Crispus told of Lydia's confession of her sinful love, of her intended flight from Miriam's abode. He told of his sorrow that the soul he'd wished to offer to Christ as pure as a tear had been defiled by earthly feelings for a participant in all those crimes in which the heathen world was sunk, which called for the avenging wrath of God. While he spoke, Lygia clung the more closely to the Apostle's feet, as if seeking a refuge there and supplicating mercy.

The Apostle, after listening till the end, bent down and placed his aged hand on her head, after which he raised his eyes to the old presbyter and said, "Crispus, haven't you heard that our beloved Master was present at the wedding in Cana, where He blessed the love between woman and man?"

Crispus's hands fell, and he stared with amazement at the speaker, unable to utter a word.

After a moment of silence, Peter continued: "Crispus, do you think that Christ, who permitted Mary Magdalene to lie at His feet and forgave the adulteress, would turn from this child who's as pure as a lily of the field?"

Lygia, sobbing, nestled even closer to Peter's feet, understanding that she hadn't sought a refuge in vain.

The Apostle, lifting up her tearstained face, said, "Until the eyes of him you love are opened to the light of truth, avoid him, lest he induce you to sin; but pray for him and know that there's no guilt in your love. And since you wish to flee temptation, this will be accounted as merit to you. Grieve not, weep not. I say to you that the grace of the Redeemer has not left you, that your prayers will be heard, and that after sorrow will come days of joy."

With these words he again laid his hands on her head, and lifting up his eyes to heaven, he blessed her. From his face radiated a goodness beyond that of earth.

Crispus, repentant, now sought humbly to justify himself. "I've sinned against mercy," he said, "but I presumed that the admission of an earthly love in her heart was a denial of Christ—"

"Thrice I denied Him," interrupted Peter, "yet He forgave me and commanded me to feed His sheep."

"And because Vinitius is an Augustinian—" continued Crispus.

"Christ has softened stonier hearts than his," said Peter.

Then Paul of Tarsus, who had been silent up till then, placed his finger on his breast, pointing to himself, and said, "I am he that persecuted and harried to death the servants of Christ. I am he who at the stoning of Stephen kept guard over the garments of those who stoned him. I am he who would have rooted out the Truth in all parts of the inhabited earth, yet nonetheless the Lord predestined me to announce it all over the world. I've preached it in Judea, in Greece, on islands, and in this godless city, where on my first visit I was cast into prison. And now when Peter, my superior, has summoned me, I'll enter this house to bow this haughty head before the feet of Christ and sow the seed within that stony soil, which the Lord will fertilize so that it may yield an abundant harvest."

He raised himself to his full height. To Crispus, this little hunchback seemed at that moment what he was in reality—a giant who was to shake the world to its foundations and win over nations and peoples everywhere.

Chapter XXVIII

PETRONIUS TO VINITIUS:

Have pity, *carissime*. Imitate not in your letters the Laconians[1] or Julius Caesar! Of course, could you, like him, write, *"Veni, vidi, vici,"*[2] I might understand your brevity. But your letter means only this: *"Veni, vidi, fugi."*[3] Since such a conclusion of the affair is directly contrary to your nature, since you're wounded, and since strange things are happening to you, I seek a fuller explanation.

Scarce could I believe my eyes when I read that the Lygian had strangled Croto as easily as a Caledonian dog[4] would kill a wolf in the ravines of Hibernia. That man is worth his weight in gold, and if he so desired, he might easily become a favorite with Caesar. When I return to the city, I must make his acquaintance and have a bronze statue of him made for myself. Ahenobarbus will burst with curiosity when I tell him the figure has been cast from nature.[5] Really athletic bodies are becoming rare in Italy and Greece, to say nothing of the Orient. The Germans, though of large stature, have muscles covered with fat and are bulky rather than strong. Ask the Lygian if he's an exception or if there are other men like him in his own country. If you or I were ever officially entrusted with the organization of the public games, it would be

---

1 People of Sparta.
2 "I came, I saw, I conquered."
3 "I came, I saw, I fled."
4 Perhaps the ancestor of our modern-day Irish wolfhound.
5 Real life.

well to know where to seek the best bodies.

But praise the gods, both of the East and of the West, that you've escaped alive from such hands. Of course, you escaped because you're a patrician and a consul's son; nevertheless, all that's happened to you amazes me in the highest degree—that cemetery where you were among the Christians, they themselves, their behavior towards you, the escape of Lygia, and finally, that strange melancholy and disquiet that your short letter breathes. Explain, for there are many things I can't understand; and if you want the candid truth, I'll tell you plainly that I understand neither the Christians nor you nor Lygia. Marvel not that I, who find interest in few things on earth save myself, question you so eagerly. Since I contributed to all that has happened, it's therefore partly my affair as well as yours.

Write at once, for I'm not certain when we'll meet again. Ahenobarbus's plans are as uncertain as autumn breezes. Here in Beneventum, he announces that he'll go straight to Greece and not return to Rome. Tigellinus, however, advises him to return, even if for but a brief period, as the people, yearning for his presence (read "for games and bread"), may revolt. So I know not what may happen. Should we decide on Achaia, we may then want to see Egypt. I should insist with all my might on your coming, for I think, in your state of mind, traveling and our amusements would be a medicine, but you might not find us. Consider, therefore, whether it might not be better for you to seek rest in your Sicilian estates than to remain in Rome. Write me the fullest details about yourself. Farewell! I add no wishes this time except for health, because, by Pollux, I don't know what to wish you.

Vinitius, on receiving this letter, at first felt no desire to reply to it. An answer seemed useless; it would benefit no one, would explain nothing. Discouragement and a sense of the utter futility of human life weighed him down. Furthermore, he felt that in any case Petronius would be utterly incapable of understanding him. A great gulf seemed to have opened between them. Since he couldn't even come to an understanding in his own mind, how could Petronius possibly help? After his return from the Trans-Tiber to his beautiful *insula* in the Carinae, he was still weak and exhausted. For the first few days he'd found some enjoyment in mere rest amid the comfort and affluence that surrounded him, but that satisfaction was short-lived. Again he felt the emptiness of his life. All that had formerly interested him had either ceased to exist for him or had shrunk to infinitesimal proportions. He felt too that all the soul ties that had bound him to life had been cut and that no new ones were possible.

At the mere thought of going to Beneventum and then to Achaia, to immerse himself in that life of luxury and mad excess, he experienced revulsion. *What's the use? What can I gain from it?*

These were the first questions that came to mind. And for the first time in his life the thought of the conversation of Petronius, his wit, his brilliance, his exquisite precision of thought and phrase, failed to attract him—more than that, he wondered if he'd be annoyed instead.

But solitude also wearied him. All his friends were with Nero in Beneventum; hence he was condemned to loneliness at home, with a head full of thoughts and a heart full of feelings he could neither analyze nor explain. There were times when he longed for someone to whom he might pour out all these thoughts and sensations in the hope that he might be able to grasp them, structure them, and make some sort of sense of them. Under this pretext, after some days of hesitation, he decided to answer Petronius, and though uncertain whether another letter would come in return, he put his thoughts into the following words:

> It's your wish that I should answer you more fully. So be it. But as to whether I can do this clearly I know not, for there are many snarls that I find impossible to untangle. I've told you of my stay among the Christians, of their treatment of their enemies— among whom they had the right to count me and Chilo—finally, of the kindness with which they cared for me, and of the disappearance of Lygia. No, dear friend, I was spared, but not because I'm a consul's son. Such considerations have no weight with them, for they pardoned even Chilo, although I'd encouraged

them to bury him in the garden. They're people whose like the world has never seen—and so it is with their creed. I cannot tell you any more except to say that he who measures them with our measures will fail. Why, I tell you that had I been lying with a broken arm in my own home, nursed by my own people, or even by my own family, I might certainly have enjoyed greater comfort, but not half the care that I received from them.

Know this also, that Lygia is such as they. Were she my sister or my wife, she couldn't possibly have nursed me with greater tenderness. More than once joy filled my heart, for I assumed that love, and love alone, could inspire such tenderness. More than once I've read it in her face and glances, and then, will you believe that among these common people, in that poverty-stricken chamber—*culina*[6] and *triclinium* at once—I felt more happiness than I'd ever known.

No! Her feeling towards me was not one of indifference. To this day I cannot think it, and yet that same Lygia escaped secretly from Miriam's house on my account. I sit all day with my head buried in my hands, pondering why she did this. Have I told you that I myself offered to return her to the Auli? She answered that this was now impossible, as the Auli had gone to Sicily, and because the news of her return, carried from house to house by the slaves, would finally reach the Palatine, so Caesar might demand her again from the Auli. But she well knew that I'd make no further attempts on her, that I'd abandoned all thought of force, and that, unable to cease from loving her, unable also to live without her, I would willingly lead her to my house through a garlanded door and seat her on a sacred skin at my hearth.[7] And still she ran away. Why? Nothing threatens her now. Had she not loved me, she

---

6 Kitchen.
7 Marry her.

could have rejected me. Only the previous day I'd met an extraordinary man, one Paul of Tarsus, who spoke to me of Christ and His creed and spoke with such forcefulness that it seemed to me that every word would unwittingly reduce to ashes the very foundations of our world. The same man visited me after her flight and said to me, "When God opens your eyes to the light and removes the scales from them, as he removed them from mine, then you'll see that what she did was right, and then perhaps you'll find her again."

And now my head is splitting as I try to make sense of those words. It's as though I'd heard them from the lips of the Pythoness at Delphi.[8] Sometimes glimmers of understanding come to me. These people, though loving humanity, hate our life, our gods, and our crimes. So she fled from me as a man belonging to this world and one with whom she could at best share a life that Christians would consider both criminal and evil. You'll counter by saying that since she had it in her power to reject me, she had no need to withdraw from me. But suppose she loves me? In that case she sought to flee from love. At the very thought of this, I feel like sending my slaves into every alley in Rome, crying in every house, "Lygia, come back!"

But, again, I fail to understand why she did it. I wouldn't have forbidden her to worship Christ; in fact, I would have erected an altar to Him in the atrium. One more God—what harm could He do me? Why might I not believe in Him, I who have little faith in the old gods? I'm certain that the Christians never lie, and yet they maintain that He rose from the dead. No mere man could do this. Paul of Tarsus, who is a Roman citizen, but who as a Jew is conversant with the

---

8   In Greek mythology, a huge female dragon or serpent born from the mud of the flood. As guardian of the cave and chasm at Delphi, she was killed by Apollo in order that he might subsequently control the messages that originated from the oracle at Delphi. During Roman times, the term *Pythoness* was synonymous with *soothsayer*.

ancient Hebrew writings, has declared to me that the advent of Christ was foretold for thousands of years by the prophets. All these are wonderful things, but doesn't the wonderful surround us on all sides? People haven't ceased talking yet of Apollonius of Tyana.[9] What Paul affirms—that there is but one God, and not a crowd of them—seems rational to me. Seneca probably holds the same opinion, as did many others before him.

Christ lived, gave Himself to be crucified for the salvation of the world, and rose from the dead. All this is certain. I see no reason, therefore, why I should stubbornly insist on a contrary opinion, why I shouldn't erect an altar to Him when I'm quite ready to erect one, for example, to Serapis. Nor would it be difficult for me to renounce all the other gods, for no rational mind now accepts them. But all this, it seems, doesn't suffice for the Christians. It's not enough to render homage to Christ; one must live in accordance with His teachings—and His alone. And so one stands as on the shore of a sea that one is ordered to walk on afoot.

Should I promise to do so, they themselves would consider the promise to be a mere empty sound upon my lips. Paul openly acknowledged this. Well you know how I love Lygia and that there's nothing I wouldn't do for her. But even at her bidding, I couldn't lift Soracte[10] or Vesuvius upon my shoulders, nor hold Lake Thrasymene in my palm, nor change my eyes from black to blue, like those of the Lygians. If she desired me to, I might be willing, but these things are beyond my powers. I'm no philosopher, but I'm not stupid either, though I may have appeared so to you. But I know this: Where Christian teaching begins,

---

9 First-century Greek who claimed to be a philosopher, magician, and wonder-worker. Like Saul, he was born and raised in Tarsus. In travels to Babylon, Persia, and India, he immersed himself in Eastern mysticism, then returned to set up a school in Ephesus. He claimed to be a miracle worker like Christ. Most everything he said, did, or claimed has since been discredited.
10 A mountain in Etruria (now Mount Oresta) on which stood a temple of Apollo.

Rome's dominion ends; Rome itself ends; our mode of life ends; the distinction between vanquished and victor, between rich and poor, between master and slave, ends; government ends; Caesar, law, and the order of the world ends. And in place of all this comes Christ, with a certain mercy that never existed before and a kindness contrary to all human and Roman instincts.

True, I care more for Lygia than for Rome and all its dominions. Let the whole world crumble so long as I possess her in my own home! But that's another thing: For the Christians, it's not enough just to agree in words; it's necessary to feel that their teachings are truth and to have nothing else in one's soul. And, the gods be my witness, this to me is impossible. Do you understand what that means? There's something in my nature that flinches from this creed. Though my lips praised it, though I conformed my life to its precepts, my mind and my soul would tell me that I did so for love's sake, for Lygia's sake, and were it not for her, nothing in the world would be more abhorrent to me. Strange to say, Paul of Tarsus understands this. And Peter understands this—Peter, who despite his simplicity and his lowly origin, is the greatest among them—Peter who was the disciple of Christ.

Do you know what they're doing? They're praying for me and calling down something they call grace, yet nothing comes from it at all, so far as I am concerned, save a strange unrest and a wilder longing for Lygia.

I told you she fled secretly. But she left behind her a cross that she'd made for me out of two bits of boxwood. On awaking, I found it by my bed. I now keep it in my *lararium*, and I cannot account for the strange feelings of awe and reverence that come over me when I approach it. I love it because her hands bound it. I hate it because it divides us. At times it seems as though there were some sorcery at the bottom of this whole affair, that this Peter, though he styles himself a simple fisherman, is mightier than Apollo and all his predecessors, and that it was he who cast a spell upon all of us—upon Lygia, Pomponia, and myself.

You wrote that disquiet and sadness are visible in my previous letter. Sadness there must be because I've lost her again, and disquiet because a great change has come over me. I tell you sincerely that nothing can be more repugnant to my nature than this creed, yet from the time I first encountered it, I've found it virtually impossible to return to my old self, what I once was.

Is this sorcery or is it love? Circe transformed human bodies by a touch; but by a touch my very soul has been transformed. Only Lygia could do this, or, rather, Lygia acting through the strange creed that she professes. When I returned home from the Christians, no one expected me. The slaves thought I was in Beneventum and would be away for a long while. Thus I found disorder at home, drunken slaves, and a feast they were giving in my *triclinium!* Death was sooner expected than I and would have terrified them less. Well you know that I rule my house with a strong hand. All, to the last one, threw themselves on their knees, and some fainted from terror. Can you guess what I did? My first inclination was to call for rods and hot irons, but immediately a kind of shame seized me, and—will you believe it?—a certain pity for those wretches. Among them are old slaves, whom my grandfather Martius Vinitius brought from the banks of the Rhine in the days of Augustus. I locked myself up alone in the library, and still stranger thoughts visited me— namely, that after all I'd heard and seen among the Christians it didn't become me to act as formerly I had towards my slaves—for slaves, too, are human beings.

For several days they moved around in mortal fear, convinced that I had suspended punishment merely because I was devising an even more ingeniously cruel one. But I didn't punish them—I didn't, because I couldn't.

On the third day I summoned them to my presence.

"I forgive you," I said. "Strive now with loyal service to make amends for your offense."

With streaming eyes, they fell upon their knees. Moaning, they stretched out their hands. They called me master and father. And I—I say this with shame— I was equally moved. At that moment it seemed as if I saw the sweet face of Lygia. Her eyes were moist with tears, thanking me for that deed. And *proh pudor!*[11]— if I didn't feel my eyes moisten in turn. Can you guess what I'm about to confess to you? That I'm lost without her, that I find myself ill all alone, that I'm simply unhappy, and that my sadness is greater than you can possibly conceive. As for my slaves, one thing struck me: The forgiveness they'd received didn't make them insolent, nor weaken discipline among them—on the contrary, fear had never roused them to such willing service as gratitude. They don't merely serve now; they seem to vie with one another in the effort to divine my every wish. I mention this for the reason that on the day prior to my departure from the Christians, I told Paul that society would fall apart as a result of his teachings, like a cask without hoops, and he answered, "Love is a stronger hoop than fear." And now I realize that in certain cases he may be right. I have verified it in the case of clients who flocked to greet me on my return. You know I have never been stingy with my clients, but my father on principle acted arrogantly towards them and taught me the same behavior. But now, taking note of their threadbare cloaks and hungry faces, I had a feeling for them akin to compassion. I ordered food to be brought them, I conversed familiarly with them, called some by name. I asked about the welfare of their wives and children. I saw tears spring to their eyes. And again I felt that Lygia saw all this, that it gave her pleasure, that she praised it. Am I losing my mind or is love bewildering me? I don't

---

11 "May I be not ashamed to admit it!"

know. I only know I have a constant feeling that she's gazing on me from afar, and I'm afraid to do anything that might sadden or offend her.

Yes, Caius, my soul is changed. Sometimes I'm glad of it. Sometimes I torment myself with the fear that I'm losing my old-time manliness, my old-time energy, and that perchance I'm already unfit, not only for counsel, for judgment, for feasts, but even for war. Doubtless here is some strange sorcery. So greatly am I changed that I'll even admit to you what passed through my mind as I lay sick: If Lygia were like Nigidia, Poppaea, Calvia Crispinilla, or others of our divorced women—were she equally vile, merciless, and cheap—I couldn't love her as I do. But when I love her for the sake of that which separates us, you can see what chaos is rising in my soul, in what darkness I live, how hidden is the path before me, how uncertain my future. If my life could be compared to a spring, unrest instead of water flows from that spring. I live only in the hope of seeing her. Sometimes it seems to me that she must surely come. But what will happen during the next year or two, I don't know, nor can I guess.

I won't leave Rome. I couldn't stand the society of the Augustinians, and besides, the only comfort in my sadness and unrest is the thought that I'm near Lygia and that through Glaucus, who promised to visit me, or through Paul of Tarsus, I may occasionally gain some news of her. No! I wouldn't leave Rome even were you to offer me the governorship of all Egypt.

Know also that I ordered a sculptor to carve a stone monument for Gulo, whom I killed in my anger. Too late came the thought that he'd borne me in his arms and had been the first to teach me how to put an arrow to the bow. I don't know why the memory of him rises in me now, a memory resembling sorrow and remorse. If what I write astonishes you, I reply that it astonishes me no less—but I write the pure truth. Farewell!

Chapter XXIX

No reply came to this letter. Petronius didn't write, apparently expecting that Nero at any moment might command a return to Rome. In fact, the rumor of a contemplated return spread throughout the metropolis, awakening a lively joy in the hearts of the mob, eager for games and the distribution of corn and olive oil, great supplies of which had accumulated in Ostia. Helius, Nero's freedman, finally announced the return to the Senate; but Nero, having embarked with his court at the promontory of Misenum, returned slowly, landing at every city along the coast to rest or to exhibit himself in the theaters. In Minturnae, where he sang in public, he spent more than ten days. He even thought of returning to Neapolis to enjoy the spring, which had come early and was warmer than usual.

During all this time, Vinitius remained shut up in his home, thinking of Lygia and of all the new things that now occupied his soul, and with them a host of unknown sensations and ideas. Glaucus called upon him from time to time; his visits filled Vinitius with joy, for he could speak with the physician of Lygia. Glaucus, it's true, knew not her hiding place, but he assured Vinitius that the elders surrounded her with protecting care. Once, moved by the evident sadness of the young patrician, he told how the Apostle Peter had rebuked Crispus for reproaching Lygia for her earthly love. Vinitius, hearing this, paled with emotion. More than once it had seemed to him that Lygia wasn't indifferent to him, but quite as often he fell into doubt and uncertainty. Now for the first time, he heard from other lips—the lips of a Christian—the confirmation of his hopes. In the first moment of gratitude he would have run to Peter. Learning, however, that he wasn't in the city but was preaching in the country, he implored Glaucus to bring him back, promising to make liberal donations to the poor of the community. It seemed to him also that if Lygia loved, all obstacles were removed, as he was ready at any moment to do homage to Christ. But though Glaucus strongly urged him to receive baptism, he refused to assure him that thereby he'd win Lygia at once, telling him he

244

must desire baptism for its own sake and for the sake of Christ and not for ulterior motives.

"One needs also a Christian soul," he said.

And Vinitius, though he grew angry at every obstacle, had now begun to understand that Glaucus, as a Christian, said only what he ought to say. He didn't yet fully realize that one of the most radical changes in his own nature was that previously he'd measured men and things only through his own egoism. Now, without fully realizing it, he was gradually becoming accustomed to the thought that the eyes of others might see differently, that the hearts of others might feel differently, that personal rights didn't always mean personal gain.

He often yearned to see Paul of Tarsus again, whose words had astonished and moved him. He conjured up arguments against Paul's creed, he strove against him in thought; nevertheless he wished to see and hear him again. But Paul had gone to Aricium.[1] As the visits of Glaucus grew rarer, Vinitius found himself in utter solitude. Again he began to traverse the alleys near the Suburra and the narrow streets of the Trans-Tiber in the hope of catching even a far-off glimpse of Lygia. When even that hope failed him, weariness and impatience began to rise within him.

At last the time came when his old nature reasserted itself. It was like the onslaught of a wave to the shore from which it had receded. It seemed to him that he'd made a fool of himself to no purpose, that he'd filled his mind with things that brought only sorrow in their wake, that he ought to make life yield him all it had. He resolved to forget Lygia, or at least to seek joy and delight from other sources. He felt, however, that this was the last trial. Therefore he threw himself into the whirlpool of life with all the blind energy of his impulsive nature. Life itself seemed to invite and encourage him to do so.

Rome, half dead and deserted during the winter months, had begun to revive with the hope of Caesar's speedy return. Preparations were going on for his solemn reception. Spring had come. The snow on the crests of the Alban Hills had melted away under the breath of African winds; violets covered the lawns in the gardens; the Forum and the Field of Mars swarmed with people basking in the growing heat of the sun. On the Via Appia,[2] the usual place for drives outside the city, a stream of chariots,

---

1 A town on the Via Appia.
2 The famed Appian Way.

richly ornamented, passed to and fro. The usual excursions to the Alban Hills had begun. Young women, under pretext of worshiping Juno in Lanuvium or Diana in Aricium, stole away from home in search of new adventures, of society reunions, and of pleasures outside the city walls.

Here one day Vinitius, among the splendid chariots that crowded the way, caught sight of one more magnificent than all the others, the splendid carriage of Chrysothemis, Petronius's mistress. Two Molossian dogs[3] preceded it. A crowd of young men and aged senators, detained by their duties in the city, surrounded it. Chrysothemis, driving four Corsican ponies, scattered smiles promiscuously and gaily cracked her golden whip. Noticing Vinitius, she reined in her horses and took him into her carriage. She drove him to a banquet that lasted all night. Vinitius got so drunk he didn't even remember being brought home. But he could remember that when Chrysothemis mentioned the name of Lygia, he was indignant and in his drunken wrath emptied a vessel of Falernian wine upon her head. Recalling this in his sober state, his anger returned.

Next day Chrysothemis, evidently forgetting the insult, called at his house and once more drove him along the Via Appia. She supped with him that night and confessed that she'd wearied not only of Petronius, but also of his kithara player, and that her heart was now free. All that week they appeared together, but the relationship didn't seem likely to last. After the incident of the Falernian wine, Lygia's name was never mentioned again; nevertheless, Vinitius couldn't banish the thought of her. He still retained the feeling that her eyes were ever gazing upon him, and that feeling made his heart sink. Discontented with himself, he couldn't free himself from the consciousness that he was causing Lygia pain, nor from the remorse with which this consciousness afflicted him. After the first scene of jealousy raised by Chrysothemis on account of two Syrian girls whom he'd bought, he rudely dismissed her. Not yet, it's true, did he cease to wallow in pleasures and debaucheries, but now he seemed to be urged on by a perverse desire to spite Lygia. At last he realized that the thought of Lygia never left him for a moment, that she was the motive at once of his bad actions and his good, that he cared for nothing in the world save for her.

Then weariness and disgust overcame him. Pleasure became abhorrent to him and left only remorse behind it. It seemed to him that he was a

---

3   These hounds from Molossia, a district of Epirus, were greatly prized as sporting dogs.

villain, and that perception filled him with measureless astonishment, for formerly he'd accepted as good everything that brought him pleasure.

In the end he fell into an utter apathy, from which even the news of Nero's approach couldn't rouse him. Nothing interested him. He didn't even call on Petronius until the latter sent him an invitation and his own litter.

Though Petronius greeted him joyfully, Vinitius responded unwillingly to his questions. But at last his long-repressed thoughts and emotions burst their bounds and rushed from his lips in a torrent of words. Once more he told in full detail the story of his search for Lygia, of his stay with the Christians, of all that he'd seen and heard among them, and of all that had passed through his head and his heart.

And finally he admitted that he'd plunged into a chaos of mind where all peace had abandoned him, together with all faculty of judgment and discernment. Nothing attracted him, nothing pleased him, everything had lost its savor. He knew not what to think, nor how to act. He was ready both to honor Christ and to persecute Him. He recognized the sublimity of His creed, yet at the same time he felt towards it an overpowering aversion. He understood that even if he possessed Lygia, he wouldn't possess her entirely, for he'd have to share her with Christ. In short, in the midst of life he wasn't living at all. Without hope, without a morrow, without a belief in happiness, he was engulfed by darkness and groping for an exit that he couldn't find.

Petronius, during all this narration, gazed at his changed face, at his hands that he stretched out with a strange gesture, as if he really *were* groping his way, and pondered deeply. He rose and, approaching Vinitius, began to run his fingers through the hair above his nephew's ears.

"Are you aware," he asked, "that there are several gray hairs on your temple?"

"That may well be," was the reply. "I wouldn't be surprised if *all* of my hair should turn white."

Silence followed. Petronius was a sensible man and more than once had pondered on life and the human soul. In general, life in the world wherein they both lived could be outwardly happy or unhappy, but inwardly its usual state was quiet. Just as lightning or an earthquake might overthrow a temple, so unhappiness could crush a life. In itself, however, it consisted of simple and harmonious lines, free from all entanglements. But something altogether different was hinted at by the words of Vinitius.

For the first time Petronius stood face-to-face with a complication of spiritual snarls that no one heretofore had unraveled. He was sufficiently a man of reason to feel their importance, but even with all his mental agility and cunning, he found himself incapable of providing solutions. So, finally, after a long silence, he merely stalled for time.

"All this may be mere sorcery or enchantments."

"So I've thought. More than once has it seemed to me that both of us were under a spell."

"Suppose you were to go, for instance, to the priests of Serapis? Doubtless among them, as is generally true among priests, there are many tricksters. Nevertheless, there may be others who possess wonderful secrets."

But he spoke without faith and in a halting voice, for he knew how hollow and even ridiculous these words must sound on his lips.

Vinitius rubbed his forehead. "Sorceries!" he cried. "I've seen sorcerers who wrestled unknown and subterranean forces for profit. I've seen sorcerers who used these forces to harm their enemies. But Christians live in poverty, forgive their enemies, and proclaim humility, virtue, and mercy. So what could they possibly gain from sorceries? And why in the world would they resort to them?"

Petronius was piqued that all his wit could find no adequate reply. Unwilling to confess this, however, he jumped at the first thought that came to him.

"It's a new sect," he said. After a pause he added: "By the divine dwellers in Paphian[4] groves, how all this would spoil life! You admire the purity and the virtue of those people, but I tell you that they are evil, for they are enemies of life, even like diseases or death itself. We already have our fill of these enemies; thus, we need no addition from the Christians. Count them up: diseases, Caesar, Tigellinus, Caesar's poems, cobblers who rule over the descendants of the old Quirites, freedmen who sit in the Senate. By Castor, enough of it! This is a pernicious and disgusting sect! Have you made any effort to cast off this melancholy and make some use, even if small, out of life?"

"I've tried."

Petronius laughed. "Traitor!" he cried. "Gossip flies quickly among slaves. You've seduced Chrysothemis and stolen her away from me."

---

4 Paphos in Cyprus, sacred to Venus.

Vinitius waved his hand in disgust.

"In any case, I thank you," said Petronius. "I'll send her a pair of slippers embroidered with pearls. In my language that means 'Go away!' I owe you a double gratitude: first, that you didn't steal Eunice; second, that you've freed me from Chrysothemis. Listen to me: You see before you a man who rose early, bathed, banqueted, possessed Chrysothemis, wrote satires, and even sometimes interwove poetry with prose, but who was as frightfully bored as Caesar himself and often knew not how to unfetter himself from gloomy thoughts. And do you know why that was so? Merely because I was seeking afar what was right next to me.

"A beautiful woman is always worth her weight in gold, but if such a woman loves, she's beyond all price. The treasures of Verres[5] couldn't purchase her. So now I set for myself this rule of action: I shall fill my life with happiness, as a goblet with the finest wine produced on earth, and drink till my hand becomes numb and my lips pale. What may come later, I care not, and this is my newest philosophy."

"It's the same one you've always professed; there's nothing new in it."

"It has substance, something previously lacking."

He called for Eunice, who entered clad in white drapery, golden-haired, a slave no longer, but a goddess of love and joy.

He opened his arms, saying, "Come!"

She ran up to him and, sitting on his lap, threw her arms around his neck and nestled her head upon his chest. Vinitius watched her cheeks grow crimson and her eyes melt slowly in mist. Together they formed a wonderful tableau of love and happiness. Petronius reached his hand to a shallow vase standing on the nearby table and, taking a handful of violets, sprinkled them on the head, bosom, and robe of Eunice.

Then he pushed the tunic from her shoulders and said, "Happy is he who, like me, has found love enclosed in so lovely a form. At times I deem we are two divinities. Look at her yourself. Has Praxiteles or Miron[6] or Scopas[7] or Lysias himself carved more marvelous lines? Is there

---

5 Praetor in Sicily who was prosecuted by Cicero for extortion.

6 Greek sculptor (ca. 450 B.C.). He worked exclusively in bronze, which freed him to depict action with subjects such as athletes.

7 Fourth-century B.C. sculptor and architect, born on the island of Paros. Superintended the Mausoleum of Halicarnassus (one of the Seven Wonders of the ancient world). Supposed to have pioneered the departure from serenity to strong emotion in the faces of his figures.

in Paros[8] or in Pentelicus[9] marble like this—warm, rosy, pulsating with love? There are men who kiss the edges of vases, but I prefer to seek delight where it can be truly found."

And he passed his lips over Eunice's shoulders and neck. She trembled visibly; her eyes closed and then opened with an expression of ineffable joy.

Petronius, after a while, lifted her exquisite head and said, turning to Vinitius, "Think, now, what are your gloomy Christians compared with this? And if you can't see the difference, go to them. But this sight will cure you."

Vinitius distended his nostrils, which were invaded by the perfume of violets that pervaded the room. His face paled. Oh, if he could only press his lips on the shoulders of Lygia in that way, it would be a kind of sacrilegious delight so great that the world might then pass away, and he wouldn't care. But accustomed now to a ready analysis of his own emotions, he noticed that even at that moment he thought of Lygia and of her alone.

After a while Petronius said, "Eunice, divine one, order garlands for our heads and a good breakfast."

When she'd left, he turned to Vinitius. "I would have set her free, but do you know what she answered? 'I'd rather be your slave than be Caesar's wife.' And she refused to accept her liberty. I freed her without her knowledge. The praetor did this for me without insisting on her presence. But she knows nothing of it, nor does she know that this home, with all my jewels, save only the family gems, will belong to her in case of my death."

He rose and took a few steps up and down the room. "Love," he resumed, "changes some more and others less, but it has greatly changed me. Once I loved the odor of verbenas, but as Eunice prefers violets, I now love them above all other flowers, and since spring arrived we have breathed nothing but violets."

Here he stopped in front of Vinitius and said, "And you—do you still remain true to the perfume of nard?"

"Give me peace!" retorted his nephew.

"I wished you to look on Eunice and mentioned her to you because you, perhaps, are also seeking at a distance what is near. Maybe for you, too, is beating somewhere in the *cubiculums* of your slaves a true and simple heart. Apply such a balm to your wounds. You say Lygia loves you? Perhaps she

---

8 An island in the Aegean Sea famous for its marble.
9 A mountain near Athens, celebrated for its marble quarries.

does, but what kind of love is it that renounces itself? Doesn't it signify that there's something stronger than that love? No, my dear boy, Lygia isn't Eunice."

To this, Vinitius answered, "It's all but one long torment. I saw you kissing Eunice's shoulders, and I thought then that if Lygia would bare her shoulders to me, the ground might open next minute under our feet, and I wouldn't care. But an awful fear seized me at the very thought, as though I'd assaulted a vestal virgin or debauched a goddess. True, Lygia isn't Eunice. But I see the difference in another way than you do. Love has changed your nostrils so as to make you prefer violets to verbenas. In me the change is in my soul, despite my fears and my desires, so that I prefer Lygia to be such as she is rather than to resemble others."

Petronius shrugged his shoulders. "If that's so, no wrong has been done you, but I fail to understand."

"Alas, too true!" answered Vinitius. "We understand each other no longer."

There was silence once more. Then Petronius resumed violently.

"May Hades swallow your Christians! They've filled you with unrest and destroyed your sense of life. May Hades devour them! You're mistaken in thinking their creed is good, for good is only that which gives people happiness—namely, beauty, love, power; but these they call vanity. You're mistaken in thinking they are just, for if we must return good for evil, what shall we return for good? And besides, if the same return be made for good and evil, why should people be good?"

"No, the return isn't the same. According to their creed, it begins in a future life, which is eternal."

"The future life doesn't interest me, for we have yet to find whether we can see without eyes. In this life the Christians are mere weaklings. Ursus strangled Croto because he has limbs of iron, but they're dreamers, and the future cannot belong to dreamers."

"For them, life begins with death."

"That's like saying, 'Day begins with night.' Do you propose to carry off the girl?"

"No; I cannot return evil for good. Moreover, I've sworn not to do so."

"Do you intend to accept the religion of Christ?"

"I wish to do so, but my nature can't endure the thought."

"Will you be able to forget Lygia?"

"No."

"Then travel."

Breakfast was announced by the slaves. Petronius, who thought he'd hit upon a good idea, said on the way to the *triclinium*, "You've traveled over a large part of the world, but only as a soldier hurrying to his destination who doesn't stop on the way. Come with us to Achaia. Caesar hasn't given up the journey. He'll stop everywhere along the way, sing, receive garlands, plunder temples, and in the end will return in triumph to Italy. It will be like a procession of Bacchus and Apollo in one person. Augustinians, male and female, and a thousand kithara players. By Castor, it'll be well worth seeing, for the world has never seen anything like it!"

He stretched himself out beside Eunice on a couch before the table. A slave placed a garland of anemones upon his head.

"What did you see in the service of Corbulo?" he resumed. "Nothing! Did you visit the Greek temples as did I, who for two years passed from guide to guide? Did you visit Rhodes to view the site of the Colossus? Did you see in Panopeus, in Phocis, the clay from which Prometheus shaped man? In Sparta, the eggs that Leda laid? In Athens, the famed Sarmatian armor made of horse hooves? In Euboea, the ship of Agamemnon? The goblet that was modeled over the left breast of Helen? Did you see Alexandria, Memphis, the Pyramids, the hair Isis tore out of her head in bewailing Osiris? Did you hear the moaning music of Memnon? The world is wide and doesn't end at the Trans-Tiber. I shall accompany Caesar, and then when he returns, I'll leave him and go to Cyprus, for my little golden-haired goddess desires that we should together offer up doves to Venus. For you must know that what she wishes must be done."

"I'm your slave," whispered Eunice.

But he leaned his wreathed head upon her bosom and smiled. "If so, I'm the slave of a slave," he said. "From your feet to your head, my divinity! I love you."

Turning to Vinitius he said, "Go with us to Cyprus, but remember that you must first call on Caesar. It's too bad you haven't already been to see him. Tigellinus is only too ready to use this to your harm, though he has no personal hatred against you. Still, as my sister's son, he cannot love you. We'll explain that you were unwell. We must think over what reply to give if Nero asks about Lygia. It might be best for you to make a gesture with your hands and say that she was with you until she wearied you. This he understands. And tell him sickness detained you at home; the fever was augmented by sorrow that you were unable to be in Neapolis and hear his song, and that you were restored to health only by the hope that you'll hear him. Fear no lie, no exaggeration. Tigellinus promises to invent not only something great for Caesar, but also something enormous. I'm afraid he'll undermine me—I'm also afraid of your disposition."

"Do you realize," said Vinitius, "that there are men who don't fear Caesar and who live as calmly as though he were not in the same world?"

"I know whom you're talking about—the Christians."

"Yes. They alone. But our life—what is it if not continuous terror?"

"Mention not your Christians to me. They don't fear Caesar because it's possible he's never heard of them. In any case, he knows nothing of their creed, and they interest him no more than withered leaves. But I tell you they're incompetent. You feel that way yourself. If your nature revolts at their creed, it's because you feel their impotence. You're a man of different clay; therefore don't trouble yourself with them. We can live and die; what more they can do, no one knows."

Vinitius was struck by these words. On his return home he wondered whether after all it might not be true that the goodness and mercy of the Christians was but the evidence of their powerlessness. Surely men of virility and character couldn't forgive in this way. Wasn't this the real secret of the aversion that his Roman soul felt towards this creed?

"We'll be able to live and die," said Petronius. "But they! They know only how to forgive, but they don't understand either a real love or a real hatred."

Chapter XXX

Nero soon wearied of Rome, regretted his return, and decided on a new visit to Achaia. He issued an edict explaining that his absence wouldn't be a long one and that public affairs wouldn't suffer in any way. Accompanied by the Augustinians, among whom was Vinitius, he went to the Capitol to offer sacrifices for an auspicious journey. But the next day, at the temple of Vesta, an event took place that changed all his plans. Nero had no belief in the gods, but he feared them. The mysterious Vesta, especially, filled him with such dread that in the presence of the goddess and her sacred fire, his hair rose on end, his teeth chattered, a shiver ran through his lips, and he fainted in the arms of Vinitius, who happened to be standing behind him.

They carried him out of the temple and bore him to the Palatine. Though he soon recovered consciousness, he didn't leave his bed all that day. To the astonishment of all present, he announced that he'd deferred his journey, for the goddess had secretly warned him against undue haste. An hour later it was publicly announced in Rome that Caesar, noting the saddened faces of his people, towards whom he felt as a father to his children, would remain to share their joys and their fate. The mob rejoiced at this decision that assured them a continuance of the games and bread; they assembled in large numbers before the Palatine gate and shouted loud and long in honor of divine Caesar.

The latter, pausing a moment from the game of dice with which he was amusing himself with the Augustinians, said, "Yes, it was right to defer the journey. It's been prophesied that Egypt and the Orient cannot escape from my dominion; therefore I won't lose Achaia. I'll order a canal to be cut through the Isthmus of Corinth, and we'll erect monuments in Egypt that'll make the Pyramids seem like childish toys. I'll build a sphinx seven times larger than the one that gazes at the desert from Memphis and will command that my face be put upon it. Coming ages will talk only of this monument and of me."

"In your verses you've already erected a monument, not seven times merely, but thrice seven times greater than the Pyramid of Cheops," said Petronius.

"And what of my singing?" asked Nero.

"Ah, could men only raise to you a statue like that of Memnon, to resound with your voice at sunrise! For all ages to come, the seas adjoining Egypt would swarm with ships in which crowds from the three parts of the world would come to listen to your song."

"Alas! Who could do that?" Nero asked plaintively.

"But you can give the command to cut out of granite a representation of yourself driving a quadriga.

"True! I'll do it!"

"That will, indeed, be a gift to all humanity."

"In Egypt I'll wed with the moon, who's now a widow, and be a god in fact."

"And you'll give us stars for wives, and we'll make a new constellation, which shall be known as the constellation of Nero. Wed Vitelius with the Nile so that he may breed hippopotamuses. Give the desert to Tigellinus and let him become the king of the jackals."

"And what shall I have?" asked Vatinius.

"May Apis[1] bless you! You've arranged for us such magnificent games in Beneventum that I can wish you no evil. Make a pair of boots for the Sphinx, whose paws must grow cold in the night dews, and sandals for the Colossi that line the ways leading to the temples. So each may find a suitable occupation. For instance, Domitius Afer, famed for his honesty, will be the treasurer. I rejoice, O Caesar, when you dream of Egypt, and I'm saddened because you've postponed your journey."

"Your mortal eyes saw not," answered Nero, "for the goddess becomes invisible to whom she wills. Know that when I was in the temple of Vesta, she herself stood beside me and said in my ear, 'Postpone your departure.' That happened so unexpectedly that I was terrified, though I ought to be grateful for so marked a sign of protection of the gods."

"We were all terrified," said Tigellinus, "and the vestal Rubria fainted."

"Rubria!" cried Nero. "What a snowy neck she has!"

"But she blushes at sight of you, divine Caesar."

"True! I noticed that myself. It's astonishing. There's something divine

---

1 A sacred bull worshiped by the Egyptians as a god.

in every vestal, and Rubria is the most beautiful."

He pondered for a moment, then asked, "Tell me, why is it that people fear Vesta more than other gods? What does this fear mean? I'm the high priest. I was filled with fear today myself. I can just remember that I was falling backward and should have struck the ground had not someone caught me in time. Who was he?"

"I," answered Vinitius.

"You, O fierce Ares? Why weren't you in Beneventum? I was told that you were sick. In truth your face has changed. But I heard that Croto sought to kill you. Is that true?"

"Yes, it is. He broke my arm, but I succeeded in defending myself."

"With a broken arm?"

"A barbarian helped me, who was stronger than Croto."

Nero stared with astonishment. "Stronger than Croto? Surely you're joking. Croto was the strongest of men, but now Syphax from Ethiopia is."

"I only tell you, Caesar, what my own eyes have seen."

"Where is the pearl? Has he become the king of Nemi?"[2]

"I know not, Caesar. I lost sight of him."

"But you know at least to what nation he belongs?"

"No. I had a broken arm and no heart for questioning."

"Seek and find him for me."

"I'll take that upon myself," said Tigellinus.

Nero continued, still addressing Vinitius. "I thank you for having supported me. A fall might have broken my head. Once you were a good companion, but since your campaign with Corbulo you have become wild and unsociable, and I seldom see you." He paused, then resumed: "How is that maiden with the narrow hips whom you loved and whom I took away from Aulus for you?"

Vinitius grew confused, but fortunately Petronius stepped in to rescue him.

"I'll wager you, lord, that he's forgotten her. See how confused he is. Ask him how many successors that maiden has had and I guarantee he'll be unable to answer. The Vinitii are good soldiers, but still better breeders; they must have a retinue of women. Punish him for this, lord! Invite him not to the banquet that Tigellinus has promised to prepare in your honor on the Pond of Agrippa."

---

2 Chief gladiator.

"No, not that. I trust that Tigellinus will not allow us to lack for beautiful women."

"How could the Graces be absent where Cupid is present," answered Tigellinus.

"Weariness torments me," sighed Nero. "I've remained in Rome at the bidding of the goddess, but I cannot endure it. I'll go to Antium. I'm stifling in these narrow streets, amid these stinking houses and filthy backstreets. Stenches of all sorts reach even here to my house and gardens. Would that an earthquake might destroy Rome, or that some angry god might level it to the ground. Then I'd show you how a city ought to be built that's worthy to be the head of the world and my capital."

"Caesar," answered Tigellinus, "you say, 'If some angry god would destroy the city,' is that so?"

"Yes, but what of it?"

"Are you not a god?"

Nero waved his hand with a gesture of weariness and sighed, "We'll see what you'll arrange for us on the Pond of Agrippa. Afterward I'll go to Antium. You're all small, and therefore you don't understand what great things I need."

Then he closed his eyes as an indication that he needed rest. The Augustinians withdrew, Petronius accompanying Vinitius from the imperial presence.

"So it appears that you're invited to take part in our amusements. Ahenobarbus has renounced his journey, but on that account he'll be madder than ever. He'll treat the city as though it were simply his own house. It would be a good time for you to seek distraction and oblivion in the outcome of that madness. Well, by Pluto, we've conquered the whole world and thus have a right to amuse ourselves. You, Marcus, are a very comely fellow; that's one reason why I'm so partial to you. By Diana of Ephesus, could you only see your manly brow, your face in which shines the ancient blood of the Quirites! Others look like freedmen beside you. In truth, were it not for her wild teaching, Lygia would be today in your house. Attempt no further argument with me that the Christians are not enemies of life and of humanity. They behaved well to you, therefore you can be grateful to them. But in your place I'd hate their teachings and seek pleasure wherever it can be found. I repeat that you're a good-looking fellow, and Rome is swarming with divorced women."

"My only wonder is that this state of affairs doesn't bother you."

"Who says so? I've long been annoyed by it, but I'm not of your age. And I've tastes that are lacking in you. I love books, which you don't; I love poetry, gems, and multitudes of things to which you wouldn't even spare a glance; I have back trouble, which you don't have; and finally, I've found Eunice, but you've found nothing like her. I feel pleasure in my own home, among works of art, but I'll never make an aesthete out of you. I know that in life I'll find nothing beyond what I've already found; but as for you, you're continually expecting and seeking something. Should death come to you, notwithstanding all your courage and melancholy, you'd die with astonishment that it was necessary to part from the world; I, on the other hand, would accept it as a necessity, satisfied that there was no fruit in this world that I hadn't tasted. I don't hurry, but neither will I linger; I shall try merely to enjoy myself to the last. The world is full of cheerful skeptics.

"I look on the Stoics as fools, but Stoicism at least gives fortitude to men, while your Christians bring gloom into the world, and gloom in life is like rain in nature.

"Do you know what I've learned? That during the festivities Tigellinus is preparing on the Pond of Agrippa, *lupanarias*³ will be erected, and in them will be assembled women from the first families of Rome. Certainly you ought to find someone beautiful enough to console you. There'll be virgins even, making their first steps into the world—as nymphs. Such is our Roman Caesardom! The weather is still pleasant; the south wind will warm the water, yet not bring out pimples on nude bodies. And you, Narcissus, must know full well that not one of them will be able to resist you—not one, even if she were a vestal virgin."

Vinitius tapped his head with his palm, like a man possessed by one thought. "I should need luck to find such a one."

"It happened to you among the Christians. But then, people whose emblem is a cross cannot be other than they are. Listen. Greece was beautiful and created the wisdom of the world; we created power. And what do you think this religion can possibly create? If you know the answer, explain it to me, for by Pollux, I cannot even imagine what it might be."

Vinitius shrugged his shoulders. "One might think that you're afraid I might become a Christian."

---

3 Temporary houses of assignation.

Chapter XXXI

The Praetorian Guard surrounded the groves by the Pond of Agrippa, lest the multitude of spectators annoy Nero and his guests. Everybody in Rome distinguished for wit, beauty, or intellect thronged to the banquet, which had no equal in the history of the city. Tigellinus wished to thereby recompense Caesar for postponing the journey to Achaia, to surpass all who'd ever feasted Nero, and to prove that no one could amuse and entertain as he could.

To this end, while still with Caesar at Neapolis and later at Beneventum, he'd made his preparations. He'd sent orders to the remotest parts of the world for beasts, birds, rare fishes, and plants, and for such vessels and cloths as would increase the splendor of the occasion. The revenues of entire provinces were lavished on mad projects such as this one. The all-powerful favorite had nothing to restrain him, for his influence waxed greater every day. Tigellinus was not yet more beloved by Nero than others, but he had grown indispensable.

Petronius incomparably excelled him in culture, intellect, and wit, and his conversation was far more amusing to Caesar. Unfortunately, however, he surpassed even Caesar in these respects and thus awoke the tyrant's jealousy. Furthermore, he knew not how to be a willing tool in all things. When it came to matters of taste, Caesar feared his opinion. With Tigellinus, on the other hand, Nero felt no constraint. The very title, *arbiter elegantiarum*, bestowed by the general public upon Petronius, piqued Nero's vanity, for who save himself deserved the title?

Tigellinus had sense enough to recognize his own limitations. Knowing that he couldn't compete with Petronius or Lucan or others who were conspicuous either by lineage, talents, or knowledge, he made up his mind to surpass them by the loyalty of his services and by such a scale of luxury, grandeur, and excess that even the imagination of Nero would be dazzled.

For the banquet itself, he'd prepared a monster raft built of gilded beams. Its edges were decorated with exquisite shells from the Red Sea and

259

the Indian Ocean, which glittered with all the colors of the rainbow. On every side were groups of palms, groves of lotus, and roses in full bloom. Amid these were hidden fountains that sprinkled perfumes, statues of gods, and gold and silver cages full of birds of brilliantly varied plumage. A tent, or rather the top of a tent, of Syrian purple, rested on silver columns. Within, the tables prepared for the guests sparkled like miniature suns with Alexandrian glass, crystals, and priceless vessels, all plundered from Italy, Greece, and Asia Minor. The raft, which looked like an island garden, was tied by ropes of purple and gold to boats fashioned like fishes, swans, seagulls, and flamingos, in which sat naked male and female rowers with forms and faces of marvelous beauty, their hair dressed in Oriental fashion or caught in golden nets.

Upon Nero's arrival with Poppaea and his Augustinians on the main raft, where they seated themselves under the tent roof, the boats began to move; the oars splashed into the water, the golden ropes grew taut, and the raft bearing the banquet and the guests described circles in the pond. Surrounding it were other boats and other rafts, filled with nude female kithara players and harpists, whose pink bodies—against the blue background of the heaven and the waters and in the reflections from golden instruments—seemed to absorb into themselves this blue and those reflections, ever changing and blooming like flowers.

From the groves on the banks, from the fantastic buildings erected for the day and hidden in the dense foliage, resounded music and song, the echoes interwoven with the sounds of horns and trumpets. Caesar himself, with Poppaea on one side and Pythagoras on the other, marveled at the sight and marveled the more when, among the boats, young slave maids appeared, masquerading as sirens and covered with green netting in imitation of scales. He was effusive in his praises to Tigellinus, but he glanced up at Petronius from habit, anxious for the opinion of the *arbiter elegantiarum.* The latter bore himself indifferently and only when directly questioned made answer.

"It seems to me, O Lord, that ten thousand nude maidens make less impression than one."

Nonetheless the floating banquet pleased Nero, as it was something totally new. Besides, such exquisite dishes were served that even the imagination of Apicius would have failed at sight of them; and there were wines of so many kinds that Otho, who used to serve eighty, would have hidden under the waters for shame, could he have witnessed the luxury of this feast. Besides the women, there were only Augustinians at the tables, among whom Vinitius eclipsed all as the most handsome. Formerly his face and figure had indicated too much the soldier, but now pain and sorrow had chiseled his features, as if the delicate hand of a master sculptor had passed over them. His skin had lost its former swarthiness, but the golden tinge of Numidian marble remained in it. His eyes had grown large and more pensive. But his body retained the powerful lines that had always made it seem as if created for armor; but above the body of a soldier sat the head of a Greek god, or at least a refined patrician, at once subtle and splendid. When Petronius had told Vinitius that none of the ladies of the court either could or would resist him, he spoke as a man of experience. All eyes turned to him, not excepting Poppaea or the vestal Rubria, whom Caesar had wished to see at the feast.

Wines, chilled in mountain snows, soon warmed the hearts and heads of the guests. From out of the thickets overhanging the shores, at every moment, shot new boats fashioned like grasshoppers and dragonflies. The blue surface of the water seemed as if strewn with the petals of flowers or sprinkled with butterflies. Here and there above the boats floated doves and other birds from India and Africa, held fast by threads of silver and blue. The sun had already overrun the greater part of the sky, and though it was now only the beginning of May, its rays were warm, even hot. The waters rippled with the splash of oars moving in time with the music, but no breath of air was stirring, the groves standing motionless, as if lost in contemplation of the sounds and scenes in the water. The raft circled continuously on the pond, bearing guests who were becoming drunker and noisier.

Before the banquet was half over, the order in which the guests had been seated at the table was utterly disrupted. Nero himself had set the example. Rising from his couch, he ordered Vinitius to yield his place, which was beside the vestal Rubria. Into the ears of the vestal, Nero whispered in soft tones. Vinitius found himself next to Poppaea, who stretched out her arm to him and asked him to fasten her loosened bracelet. When he did so, with hands trembling somewhat, she cast at him from beneath her long lashes a glance as it were of modesty and shook her golden head as if denying something.

Meanwhile, the sun, grown larger and redder, slowly sank behind the crests of the groves. Most of the guests were now thoroughly intoxicated.

The raft now circled nearer the shore, on which, among trees and clusters of flowers, were seen groups of people attired as fauns or satyrs, playing on flutes, bagpipes, and drums, with groups of maidens representing nymphs, dryads, and hamadryads. Darkness fell at last amid drunken shouts from the tent, shouts raised in honor of Luna. Meanwhile the groves were lighted with a thousand lamps. From the *lupanarias* on the shore shone bright flashes of lights, and on the terraces appeared new groups, also naked, consisting of wives and daughters of the first Roman houses. These, with voices and unrestrained voluptuous movements, began to call enticingly to the feasters.

At last the raft touched the banks. Caesar and the Augustinians vanished into the groves and scattered themselves through the shameful houses, in tents hidden in thickets, and in grottoes artificially made among the springs and fountains. All controls and proprieties ceased. No one knew Caesar's whereabouts; no one knew who was a senator, who a knight, who a dancer, who a musician. Satyrs and fauns pursued the nymphs, and with their bacchic staffs they struck at the lamps to extinguish them. Darkness fell on many parts of the groves. Everywhere was heard the sound of laughter, shouts, whisperings, or the panting of both sexes. Rome had never seen its like.

Vinitius wasn't drunk, as he had been at the feast in Caesar's palace where Lygia had appeared. But he was roused and intoxicated by all that was going on around him, and at last even he succumbed to the fever of pleasure, sensation, and lust. Rushing into the forest, he ran with the others, seeking the dryad that might seem to him most beautiful. New groups of naked women fled by him with songs and shouts, pursued by fauns, satyrs, senators, and knights. Music was everywhere. Noticing at last a band of maidens led by one clad as Diana, he sprang forward, seeking a closer look at the goddess. And then his heart stopped in his breast! It seemed to him that in that goddess, with the crescent moon in her hair, he recognized Lygia.

Maidens danced around him in a circling whirl and seemed almost frenzied in expressing their desires. Then as if they wished him to pursue, they scampered away like a herd of antelopes. But he stood rooted to the spot, his heart throbbing wildly, for though he belatedly realized that Diana was not Lygia and at close sight didn't even resemble her, that powerful first impression deprived him of strength. Suddenly he was overpowered by an intense yearning for Lygia, far greater than he'd ever experienced before. A tremendous wave of love surged into his heart, and never had she seemed to him dearer, purer, and more beloved than in this moment of madness and debauchery. A moment before, he himself could have drunk from this cup and taken part in this dissipation and shameless sensuality, but now disgust and abhorrence mastered him. He felt himself stifling. He needed air and the sight of the stars hidden by these infamous groves.

He determined to flee, but before he could move, a veiled figure appeared before him who, resting her hands upon his shoulders and pouring her passionate breath in his face, whispered, "I love you. . . . Come! Nobody will see us."

Vinitius awoke as from a dream. "Who are you?"

She leaned her breast against him and repeated, "Hurry! We're alone, and I love you. Come!"

"Who are you?"

"Guess."

And through her veil she pressed her lips to his, drawing his face to hers, till at length breath failed her, and she snatched her face away.

"Night of love! Night of madness!" she cried, catching her breath with an effort. "Tonight everything is permitted. Take me!"

That kiss burned into Vinitius like acid. It filled him with renewed aversion. His soul and heart were elsewhere, and nothing existed for him in all the world except Lygia. He thrust the veiled figure aside.

"Whoever you are, I love someone else. I don't want you."

But she merely lowered her head and whispered a command: "Remove the veil!"

At that moment, the leaves of a nearby myrtle rustled, and the figure vanished like a dream; but as she escaped in the distance, her laugh rang back with a strangely ominous mocking sound.

Petronius appeared from the thickets.

"I've heard and seen everything," he said.

"Let's get away from here!" urged Vinitius.

They passed the *lupanarias*, all gleaming with lights, passed the groves and the line of mounted Praetorians. Reaching their litters, Petronius said, "I'll go with you to your house."

They got into a litter together, and both were silent until they reached the great atrium in Vinitius's house. Then Petronius spoke.

"Do you know who that was?" he asked.

"Rubria?" queried Vinitius, with a shudder at the very thought, for Rubria was a vestal.[1]

"No."

"Who was it, then?"

Petronius lowered his voice. "The fire of Vesta has been defiled, for Rubria was with Caesar. But she who spoke to you"—and he spoke still lower—"was the divine Augusta."

A hush fell upon them.

"Caesar," resumed Petronius, "failed to conceal from her his passion for Rubria, so she may have wished to revenge herself. But I interrupted you for the reason that had you refused the Augusta after recognizing her, nothing could have saved you, nor Lygia, nor perhaps even me."

Vinitius broke out fiercely: "Enough of Rome, enough of Caesar, of banquets, of the Augusta, of Tigellinus, and the rest of you. I'm suffocating. I can't live in this way. I cannot! Do you understand?"

"Vinitius, you're losing sense, judgment, moderation."

"I love only her in the world."

"Well, what of it?"

"Just this—I want no other love. I have no wish for your life, your feasts, your shamelessness, your crimes!"

"What ails you? Are you a Christian?"

The young man grasped his head with both hands and cried in despair, "Not yet! Not yet!"

---

1 Vestal virgins were expected to retain their virginity and were worshiped because they were undefiled.

Chapter XXXII

Petronius went home shrugging his shoulders, greatly displeased. He saw clearly that he and Vinitius no longer understood each other, that a gulf yawned between them. Once he had wielded an immense influence over the young soldier, being for him a model in everything, and often it took only a few ironic or sarcastic words from Petronius to sway him one way or the other. Now all was changed so completely that Petronius dared not fall back on his old methods. Wit and irony, he felt, would glance off ineffectually from the new layers deposited in the mind of Vinitius by contact with the incomprehensible Christians.

The experienced skeptic knew that he'd lost the key to that soul. Discontent and even fear followed, aggravated by the events of that night.

Should it be no passing whim in the mind of Augusta, he thought, *but a permanent passion, one of two things will happen: Either Vinitius will yield and possibly be ruined by some "accident,"*[1] *or, what's more probable, he'll resist, and then he'll almost certainly perish. And I, as his relative, may perish with him, because Augusta, including the whole family in her wrath, will throw her entire influence on the side of Tigellinus. Both horns of the dilemma are unpleasant.*

Petronius was a brave man and had no fear of death, but as he expected nothing from death, he had no wish to invite it ahead of time. After long thought he at last concluded that the safest course would be to send Vinitius away from Rome on a journey. Ah, could he only add Lygia as a traveling companion, how gladly would he have done it! Still, he hoped it wouldn't prove too difficult to induce him to go alone. He would spread the report in the Palatine that Vinitius was sick and thus save both the nephew and the uncle. Augusta couldn't be sure she'd been recognized by Vinitius; in fact, she might suppose she hadn't, and in that case her sense of being spurned wouldn't drive her to extreme measures. But the future

---

1 Fatal "accidents" were frequent in those days, and no inquests followed.

might open her eyes in that respect. That was the danger most to be avoided.

Above all, Petronius wished to gain time. He foresaw that if Nero went to Achaia, Tigellinus, who had no understanding of art, would descend to a secondary place. In Greece, Petronius knew himself certain of victory over all rivals.

Meanwhile, he resolved to keep his eye on Vinitius and urge him to leave Rome on a journey. For several days he pondered over a scheme to obtain from Caesar an edict banishing all Christians from Rome. Then Lygia would depart with the other confessors of Christ, and after her would go Vinitius, thus there'd be no further need for persuasion. The thing itself was possible. In fact, it wasn't so long since the Jews had raised disturbances against the Christians. Claudius, unable to distinguish one from the other, had ejected the Jews. Why shouldn't Nero eject the Christians? Rome would be less crowded without them.

After the floating banquet, Petronius saw Nero daily, either in the Palatine or other houses. It would be easy to suggest this idea to him, for Nero never resented suggestions that would bring pain or ruin to others. After considerable reflection, Petronius hit upon a plan: He'd give a feast in his own home and at that feast persuade Caesar to issue the edict. He had a well-founded hope that Caesar might entrust him with its execution. Then he'd send Lygia out of Rome with all the consideration due to the mistress of Vinitius—to Baiae, if she and his nephew chose, and let them amuse themselves there with love and Christianity to their hearts' content.

Meanwhile, he made frequent visits to Vinitius, first because with all his Roman egoism, he couldn't rid himself of attachment to his young kinsman; second, to persuade him to take the journey. Vinitius was now feigning sickness and never showed himself upon the Palatine, where new plans surfaced every day. At last Petronius heard definitely, from Caesar's own lips, that in three days he'd set out for Antium. The next day he reported the news to Vinitius, who'd already heard it, for that very morning a freedman had brought him a list of the people invited by Caesar.

"My name is among them, and so is yours," he said. "You'll find the same list at your home when you return."

"Were not I among the invited guests," mused Petronius, "it would mean I'd been selected for death. But I hardly expected that such an omission would occur before the journey to Achaia, for there I'll be too indispensable to Nero."

Petronius examined the list.

"Barely have we returned to Rome," he complained, "but we must leave again and drag ourselves to Antium. There's no alternative, for this is no mere invitation. It's a command."

"And . . . suppose one didn't obey?"

"He'd receive an invitation to quite a different journey, one from which no traveler ever returns. What a pity you didn't take my advice and escape from Rome in time. Now there's no help for it: You *have* to go to Antium."

"I *have* to go to Antium? See in what times we live and what vile slaves we are!"

"Is this the first time you've noticed it?"

"No. But your argument has it that Christianity is an enemy to life, since it puts chains on us—could they possibly be any heavier than these we are wearing? You've said, 'Greece created wisdom and beauty, and Rome power.' Where is our power?"

"Call for Chilo; talk to him. I haven't the slightest inclination to philosophize today. By Hercules! It wasn't I who created these times, nor am I responsible for them. Let's talk of Antium. Beware, for great danger awaits you there. It might be safer to try a fall with that barbarian who strangled Croto, but still you've no choice in the matter. Refusal is not an option."

Vinitius carelessly waved his hand. "Danger?" he sniffed. "We're all wandering—groping, if you will—under the shadowy *velarium* of death, and every moment another of us plunges into that ultimate darkness."

"Shall I remind you of all those, who, possessing a little sense, made it safely through the times of Tiberius, Caligula, Claudius, and Nero, for eighty or ninety years? For starters, let's take as an example Domitius Afer; he has grown old undisturbed, though all his long life he's been a thief and a scoundrel."

"Perhaps that was the reason," quipped Vinitius. He glanced over the list and read, "Tigellinus, Vatinius, Sextus Africanus, Aguilinus Regulus, Suilius Nerulinus, Eprius Marcellus, and so on, and so on. What a precious lot of blackguards and scoundrels! And these men govern the world! Wouldn't they be better employed in carrying some Egyptian or Syrian divinity through the towns for public exhibition, or in earning their bread by fortune-telling or dancing?"

"Or by exhibiting educated monkeys, calculating dogs, or flute-playing donkeys," added Petronius. "True enough! But let's talk of something more important. Collect your wits and listen to me. On the Palatine, I've reported that you're sick and unable to leave the house. But still your name's on this list, which proves that somebody doesn't believe me and has done this on purpose. The matter is of no importance to Nero, for you're only a soldier, with whom at best he could only converse about the races in the Circus. And you haven't the slightest conception of poetry and music. So it's Poppaea who's had your name placed on this list, which means that her passion for you is no passing fancy, and that she intends to have her way with you."

"She's a daring Augusta!"

"Daring indeed! For she may ruin both herself and you beyond redemption. May Venus inspire her with some other love as speedily as possible! But as she's cast a wanton eye upon you, we must exercise the greatest caution. Ahenobarbus is beginning to weary of her. He prefers Rubria or Pythagoras, but his self-love will impel him to wreak the most hideous vengeance upon you both."

"I didn't know it was she who addressed me in the grove, but you were listening and heard my answer: I love another and wished her to leave me alone."

"By all the Plutonian gods! I implore you not to lose whatever shreds of intelligence the Christians have left you with! How can one hesitate when the choice lies between probable and certain ruin? Haven't I already explained that if you'd wounded the Augusta's vanity, no rescue would have been possible? By Hades! If you're tired of life, it would be better to open your veins or throw yourself upon your sword, for if you offend Poppaea, no such easy death will be open to you. May Jove be my witness, it's tough to talk sense to you these days!

"Come now, be honest with me: Where are we here? How are you planning to respond? Should you give in, would such an affair hurt you in any way or stop you from loving Lygia? And don't forget for a moment that Poppaea saw Lygia on the Palatine, and it most certainly won't take her long to guess who it is you prefer over her! If you reject her, believe me, she'll drag Lygia forth, even if from the very bowels of the earth. Thus, in the end, you'll not only destroy yourself, but Lygia as well. Have I made myself clear?"

Vinitius listened, though his thoughts were elsewhere.

"I must see her," he said at last.

"Whom—Lygia?"

"Lygia."

"Do you know where she is?"

"No."

"And will you resume your search for her in old cemeteries and beyond the Tiber?"

"I don't know, but I must see her."

"Well, though she's a Christian she may have more sense than you. She may have sense enough not to wish your destruction."

Vinitius shrugged his shoulders. "She saved me from the hands of Ursus."

"Then hurry, for Ahenobarbus won't delay his departure, and he can issue sentences of death in Antium just as well as here."

Vinitius wasn't listening. One thought alone obsessed him: to obtain an interview with Lygia. He pondered ways and means.

Then something happened that seemed to remove all obstacles. Chilo called upon him unexpectedly next morning.

He entered wretched and ragged, signs of hunger in his face. But as the servants had received orders to admit him at all hours of the day or night, they dared not deny him admittance. He went straight to the atrium and saluted Vinitius.

"May the gods give you immortality and share with you the dominion of the world."

Vinitius's first impulse was to have him thrown out the door. His next was that the Greek might know something about Lygia. Curiosity conquered disgust.

"Is that you?" he asked. "What's happened to you?"

"Evil things, O son of Jupiter! Genuine virtue is a ware that nobody prizes nowadays. The true philosopher must be content if only once in five days he's able to procure a sheep's head from the butcher and gnaw it in his garret, washing it down with tears. Master, what you gave me, I spent on books. And I was robbed and ruined. And the slave who should have written down the wisdom I was ready to dictate fled with the remnant of your generosity. I'm destitute. But I thought to myself, to whom could I go, save to you, O Serapis, whom I love and adore and for whom I've jeopardized my life?"

"Why have you come, and what do you bring?"

"To seek help, O Baal! I bring you my wretchedness, my tears, my love, and finally, news that I've gathered out of love for you. Do you remember, master, that I once told you I'd given to a slave of the divine Petronius a thread from the girdle of Venus of Paphos? I sought to discover if it had helped her. You, O son of the sun, who knows all that goes on in that house, know what position Eunice holds there. One other such thread do I possess. I've preserved it for you, master!"

He stopped short, seeing the wrath gathering upon the brow of Vinitius. Chilo, wishing to appease the rising storm, resumed quickly.

"I know where the divine Lygia resides. I'll show you, master, the alley and the house."

Vinitius suppressed the emotion that this news caused him. "Where is she?" he asked.

"With Linus, the oldest of the Christian priests. She's there with Ursus, who goes as formerly to the miller—the namesake of your *dispensator,*[2] Demas. Yes, Demas! Ursus works at night, so if you surround the house after dark, he won't be there. Linus is old. Besides him there are only two women, still older, in the house."

"How do you know all this?"

"You'll remember, master, that the Christians had me in their power and spared me. It's true that Glaucus was mistaken in imagining that I was the cause of his misfortune, but the poor devil believed this and still believes it. And, in spite of all, they spared me. No wonder, master, that gratitude filled my heart. I'm a man of better times. So I thought to myself, *Why should I desert my friends and benefactors? Wouldn't it be ungrateful on my part not to ask about them, not to learn how they're getting along, whether they're sick or well, where and how they live?* By Cybele of Pessinunt![3] It's not in me to act thus. But I feared at first that they might possibly misconstrue my motives. Affection proved stronger than fear— all the more so, since I was encouraged by the readiness with which they forgive injuries. And, above all, master, I thought of you. Our last adventure ended unhappily. But can a son of Fortune reconcile himself to defeat? With this in mind I prepared victory for you in advance. The house stands apart. Slaves at your order can surround it so completely that not a mouse could escape. Oh, master, master, it depends only on you whether this magnanimous king's daughter spends this night in your house. If this should happen, remember that it was the poor and hungry son of my father who made your happiness possible."

---

2 Overseer.
3 A town in Galatea, famous for its worship of Cybele, a Phrygian goddess.

The blood rushed to Vinitius's head. Temptation once more shook his whole being. Yes, that was the way, a certain way. Once Lygia was in his house, who could take her away? Once his mistress, what would be left her save to remain so forever? Let religions perish. What could the Christians do for him, with their mercy and their gloomy creed? Hadn't the time come for him to shake off those illusions? Why shouldn't he live as others lived? Lygia might find it difficult to reconcile her faith with what had befallen her, but what of it? The only important thing was that she would be his—and his this very night! Doubtless her faith wouldn't hold out against this new world, against the delights of the passion to which she would surrender herself. And today was the day! He had but to detain Chilo and give orders at nightfall—then would come joys without end.

What has my life been, thought Vinitius, *save gloom, unsatisfied passion, and an endless propounding of unanswerable questions?*

Now he had the chance to end his misery. True, he'd sworn not to raise a hand against Lygia. But in whose name had he sworn? Not by the gods, for he no longer believed in them. Not by Christ, for as yet he didn't believe in Him. For the rest, if she felt that she was wronged, he'd marry her and so wipe out the wrong. Yes, he must do that much, for he owed his life to her.

He recalled the day when he and Croto had invaded her retreat. He recalled the fist of Ursus raised above him and all that had happened thereafter. Again he saw her bending over his couch, clad in the garb of a slave, beautiful as a goddess, merciful and adorable. Unconsciously his glance fell on the lares and on the cross that she'd left behind her. Should he repay her for all that by a renewed attack? Should he drag her by the hair like a slave to his bed? How could he do this, when he not only desired, but loved her, and when he loved her for the very reason that she was what she was?

Then he knew that it wouldn't be enough for him to merely have her in his house, not enough to seize her in his arms by force. His love needed something more—her consent, her love, her soul. Blessed would be that roof if she came under it of her own free will, blessed the moment, the day, life itself. Then the happiness of both would be as inexhaustible as the sea and the sun. But to possess her by force would be to destroy that happiness forever and at the same time to destroy, defile, and make loathsome the only precious and beloved thing in life.

Horror seized him at the very thought. He glanced at Chilo, who, staring back, hid his hands under his rags and scratched himself uneasily.

In a frenzy of unspeakable disgust, Vinitius wished to crush underfoot this former ally of his, as one crushes a foul worm or a poisonous serpent. In an instant he made up his mind. But knowing no middle ground in anything and yielding to his fierce Roman nature, he cried, "I won't do what you advise, but so you may not go forth without the reward that you've earned, I'll order three hundred lashes[4] to be given you in my *ergastulum.*"

Chilo paled. The handsome face of Vinitius glowed with such stern determination that he couldn't hope the promised reward was merely a cruel jest. He cast himself on his knees and, bending himself almost double, moaned in a broken voice, "For what? O king of Persia, *for what?* Pyramid of mercy! Colossus of charity! For what? I'm old, hungry, wretched, and I've done you a service. Is this your reward?"

"Such is the reward you'd give to the Christians," snarled Vinitius. He summoned the *dispensator.*

Chilo fell prostrate at his feet and, embracing them convulsively, cried with deathly pallor in his face, "Master, master! I'm old. Fifty, not three hundred! Fifty are enough. A hundred, not three hundred! Mercy, mercy!"

Vinitius thrust him away with his foot and gave the order. In but seconds, two powerful Quadi[5] appeared from behind the dispensator. Seizing Chilo by the remnants of his hair, they wound his cloak around his head and dragged him off to the *ergastulum.*

"For the sake of Christ!" moaned the Greek as they reached the door of the corridor.

Vinitius was left alone. The order he'd given raised his spirits. He strove to collect and order his scattered thoughts. The victory he'd gained over himself elated him, for it seemed to him that he thereby had made a long stride towards Lygia and that great reward was thus due him. Initially, it didn't occur to him that he'd been guilty of grievous injustice to Chilo in ordering him to be flogged for the very thing for which formerly he had rewarded him. As yet he was too much of a Roman to feel compunction for the pain of another or to concern himself with what happened to a wretched Greek. Had he even thought of Chilo's suffering, he would have felt totally justified in punishing such a

---

4 More than enough to kill a man.
5 North Germanic slaves.

monster. But his only thought was of Lygia. He imagined himself saying to her, *"I will not return evil for good. When you learn what I've done to this man who would have persuaded me to raise a hand against you, you'll be grateful."*

Then followed the thought, *Would Lygia approve of my treatment of Chilo?*

No; her creed commanded forgiveness. In fact, the Christians forgave the scoundrel, though they'd had far greater reasons for revenge than he did. Then for the first time there rang through his soul the cry, *For the sake of Christ!* He remembered that with this cry Chilo had rescued himself from the hands of the Lygians. He resolved to remit the rest of the punishment.

He was on the point of summoning the *dispensator* when that individual appeared before him.

"Master, the old man has fainted, and perhaps he's dead. Shall I command further flogging?"

"Revive him and bring him here."

The *dispensator* disappeared behind the curtain. But the revival couldn't have been easy, for Vinitius waited for a long time and was growing impatient when the slaves finally led in the Greek and at a given signal retired.

Chilo was pale as a sheet. Down his legs and upon the mosaic pavement trickled streams of blood. He was conscious, however, and throwing himself on his knees, he stretched out imploring hands.

"Thanks to you, master," he cried. "You are great and merciful."

"Dog! Know that I forgave you for the sake of that Christ, to whom I myself have owed my life."

"Master, I'll serve Him and you."

"Hold your tongue and listen. Rise! You shall accompany me to the house where Lygia dwells."

Chilo rose, but scarcely had he stood on his feet, when he paled with a deadlier pallor and moaned in a broken voice, "Master, I'm truly hungry. I'd go, master, but I'm too weak. . . . Let me have but the remnants from your dog's plate, and I'll go."

Vinitius ordered that he should have food, a piece of gold, and a cloak. Chilo, weakened by the lashes and by hunger, couldn't even totter after food. Terror struck him lest Vinitius might construe his weakness as obstinacy and order him flogged again.

"Only let wine warm me," he cried, his teeth chattering, "and I'll be able to go—even to *magna Graecia.* "[6]

In fact, after a time he recovered some of his strength, and they went out.

The road was long, for Linus, like most Christians, lived in the Trans-Tiber, not far from Miriam's house. Finally Chilo indicated to Vinitius a small house standing apart, surrounded by an ivy-covered wall.

"This is the house, master," he said.

"Good!" said Vinitius. "And now, begone! But first listen to what I tell you. Forget that you've served me. Forget also where Miriam, Peter, and Glaucus live. Forget also this house, forget the Christians. Every month you may come to my house, and Demas will pay you two pieces of gold. But if you spy on the Christians any further, I'll order you flogged to death or hand you over to the prefect of the city."

Chilo bowed low and said, "I'll forget."

But when Vinitius had disappeared around the corner of the alley, he stretched out his threatening hands and cried, "By Actes[7] and the Furies! I will *not* forget!"

And then he collapsed.

---

6   Great Greece.

7   Daughter of Zeus, the goddess of mischief who supposedly caused mortals to act rashly and unreasonably.

Chapter XXXIII

Vinitius went straight to Miriam's house. At the gate he met Nazarius, who turned pale at sight of him. Vinitius greeted him cordially and asked to be led to his mother's lodgings.

In the room, besides Miriam he found Peter, Glaucus, Crispus, and Paul of Tarsus. The latter had recently returned from Fregellae.[1] The sight of the young tribune astonished everyone.

"I greet you in the name of Christ, whom you honor," said Vinitius.

"Blessed be His name forever," was the reply.

"I know your virtues and have received your kindness; therefore, I come as a friend."

"And we greet you as a friend," returned Peter. "Sit down, master, and partake of our meal as a guest."

"I will gladly sit down and eat with you, but first give me a hearing, Peter and Paul of Tarsus, so that you may trust me. I know where Lygia is. I've come here from before the house of Linus, which is close to this dwelling. Caesar has given me the right to possess her. I have nearly five hundred slaves in my house and thus could easily surround her abode and carry her off, but I haven't done this, and I won't do it."

"Then may the blessing of the Lord descend upon you and purify your heart," said Peter.

"I thank you. But listen to me further. I didn't do so, though I live in a torment of longing. Before I came among you, I would surely have carried her off and kept her by force. But your virtue and your creed, though I profess neither one, have changed something in my soul, so that I dare not use force. I myself cannot comprehend it, but so it is. That's why I come to you, for you stand to Lygia in the place of father and mother, and I say to you: Give me Lygia for my wife, and I swear that not only will I allow her to confess Christ, but also I myself will begin to learn the principles of your faith."

---

1 A town of the Volsci in Latinium.

275

He held his head erect, and his voice was firm; nevertheless, he was moved and his legs trembled beneath his striped mantle. When he noticed the hush that followed his words, he continued, as if anticipating a refusal.

"I know that obstacles still stand in the way, but I love her as my own eyes. Though I'm not your enemy—neither yours nor Christ's—I wish to meet you truthfully, so that you may trust me. I'm staking my whole life on this issue, but I tell you the truth. Another might perhaps tell you, 'Baptize me.' But I say, 'Give me light, enlighten me.' I believe in Christ's resurrection, for truthful witnesses have testified to me of it, witnesses who have the courage of their convictions and saw Him after death. I believe, for I've seen it, that your religion teaches virtue, justice, and mercy, but not the crimes of which you're suspected. Still, I fail to understand it as a whole. Something I've learned from your works, something from Lygia, and something from my discussions with you. I claim that a change has been wrought within me. Once I ruled my servants with a rod of iron; I can do this no longer. I once knew no mercy, now I know it. Once I loved pleasure; the other night I ran from the pond of Agrippa because it disgusted me. Once I believed in violence; now I renounce it. Know that I cannot recognize myself. I revolt at banquets, at songs, at cymbals, at garlands, at Caesar's court, at nude bodies, at every crime. When I think that Lygia is pure as the snow in the mountains, I love her all the more. When I realize that she is what she is because of her beliefs, I love that faith and desire it. But since I don't fully understand it, since I don't know if I'm capable of really practicing it or if my nature will endure it, I live in uncertainty and torment, as though in some dark prison."

Here his brows knitted with pain and a flush appeared on his cheeks. Then he spoke with growing haste and greater emotion.

"You see, I'm tortured with love and doubt. I've been told that in your religion there's no room for life, for human joy, for happiness, for order, for government, for the Roman dominion. Is that true? I've been told that you're insane, but tell me yourselves what your objectives are. Is it sin to love, is it sin to experience pleasure, is it sin to wish for happiness? Are you enemies of life? Need a Christian be miserable? Should I renounce Lygia? What is your view of truth? Your acts and your words are as transparent water, but what lies at the bottom of that water? You see that I'm sincere. Scatter away the darkness, for I've been told this: 'Greece created wisdom and beauty, Rome power,' but what have the Christians brought forth?

Therefore, tell me what it is that you intend to bring forth? If there's light beyond your doors, open them that I may see it."

"We bring love," said Peter.

Paul of Tarsus added, "If I speak with the tongues of men and angels and have not love, I am as sounding brass."

But the heart of the old Apostle yearned to that soul in torment, which like a bird beating against its bars, strove towards the air and the sun, so Peter stretched out his hand to Vinitius and said, "Whoever knocks, to him shall be opened. The favor and grace of the Lord is upon you; therefore, I bless you, your soul, and your love, in the name of the Savior of the world."

Vinitius, who reacted with unbelieving joy on hearing this blessing, sprang towards Peter. Then a strange thing happened. That descendant of the Quirites, who until recently had failed to recognize any common humanity in a foreigner, knelt down, respectfully reached out for the hands of the old Galilean, and pressed them gratefully to his lips.

Peter was filled with joy. He saw that once more the seed had fallen on good soil, that his fishing net had gathered in another soul.

All present were no less rejoiced at this sign of homage to God's Apostle. With one voice they exclaimed, "Glory to God in the highest!"

Vinitius arose with a radiant face.

"I see," he cried, "that happiness *can* dwell among you, for I myself am happy, and I'm confident that you'll be able to convince me in all other things. But I'll say more. This can't happen in Rome, for Caesar goes to Antium, and I must accompany him, for he's commanded it. And you of course are aware that to refuse is certain death. But if I've found favor in your eyes, go with me and teach me your faith. You'll be safer than I. In that vast concourse of people you'll find opportunity to proclaim the truth in the very court of Caesar. Acte, they say, is a Christian. Among the Praetorians are many Christians, for I myself have seen soldiers kneeling before you, O Peter, at the Porta Nomentana. I have a villa at Antium where we may assemble at the very side of Caesar to listen to your teachings. Glaucus has told me that for the sake of a single soul you're willing to travel to the ends of the world. Indeed, that it's for that very purpose that you've journeyed here all the way from Judea. So please accept my heartfelt invitation, and desert not my soul."

Hearing this, they deliberated among themselves. With joy they thought of the victory of their teaching and the impact that the conversion

of this Augustinian—the scion of one of the oldest families in Rome—
would have on a pagan world. It was true indeed that they would have
wandered to the ends of the world for the sake of a single soul. Since the
death of the Master, they had done nothing else. Therefore, a refusal was
the furthest thing from their minds. But Peter was at that time the pastor
of a great multitude; hence, he couldn't go. Paul of Tarsus, however, who'd
recently been in Aricium and in Fregellae and was preparing for another
long journey into the Orient to visit the churches and inspire them with
new zeal, consented to accompany the young tribune to Antium. It would
be easy to find a ship there bound for Greek waters.

Vinitius regretted that Peter, to whom he owed so much, couldn't
accompany him, but he thanked Paul heartily. Then he turned to the old
Apostle with a final request.

"Knowing Lygia's dwelling," he said, "I might myself go there and ask,
as is only proper, whether she would accept me as a husband if my soul
turned to Christ. But I prefer to ask you, O Apostle! Let me see her or lead
me to her. I know not how long I shall remain in Antium. Remember, by
Caesar's side no one is sure of the morrow. Petronius himself has already
assured me that there may be danger for me there. Let me see her before
I go, let me feast my eyes upon her, let me ask her to forgive the evil I've
done to her, and let her help me to a better life."

Peter the Apostle smiled kindly and said, "My son, who would deny
you a just joy?"

Vinitius again bowed low over his hand, for he couldn't suppress the
joy that flooded his heart. The Apostle took his head between his hands
and said, "Be not afraid of Caesar, for I tell you that not a hair on your
head will be harmed."

Then he sent Miriam for Lygia, but asked her not to tell her that a visitor was waiting to see her, so that her joy might be the greater.

In a little while those assembled in the chamber saw Miriam leading
Lygia by the hand through the myrtles in the garden.

Vinitius wished to rush forth to meet her, but at sight of that beloved
figure, happiness deprived him of his strength. He just stood breathless,
with throbbing heart, barely able to keep his equilibrium, a hundred times
more excited than when for the first time in his life he'd heard the shafts
of the Parthians whizzing around his head.

She ran in, totally unsuspecting, but at sight of him she stopped as if
rooted to the spot. Her face flushed and then paled, and she looked with

astonished and frightened eyes at those present in the room.

But only bright and kindly eyes met hers.

Peter approached her and asked, "Lygia, do you still love him?"

There was a sudden hush. Her lips began to tremble like those of a child who is about to weep, who feels that she is guilty, but sees that she must confess that guilt.

"Answer," said the Apostle.

Then with humility, obedience, and fear in her voice, she whispered, slowly falling at the feet of Peter, "I do."

Vinitius at the same moment knelt beside her. Peter placed his hands on their heads and said, "Love each other in the Lord and for His glory, for there's no sin in your love."

Chapter XXXIV

Walking in the garden, Vinitius poured out to Lygia in burning words all he'd previously confessed to the Apostle—the unrest of his soul, the changes that had taken place in him, and finally all the immense longing that had haunted him since he'd left Miriam's house. He confessed to Lygia that he'd tried to forget her but couldn't. For whole days and nights he could think of nothing but her. The little cross of boxwood branches that she'd left for him and that he'd placed in his *lararium*, to be adored against his will as something sacred, had been a constant reminder of her. And the longing had increased with every moment, for love was stronger than he and had possessed his soul, even from his first sight of her at the house of the Auli.

The Fates spun the thread of life for others, but for him love and melancholy had spun it. Even his evil actions had their origins in love. He'd loved her at the Auli's and on the Palatine; he'd loved her when he saw her at Ostranium listening to Peter, when with Croto's help he'd sought to carry her off, when she'd watched at his bedside, and when she'd fled from him. Then Chilo had come with news that he'd discovered where she lived and suggested that he once more try to carry her off; but he preferred to punish Chilo and seek the Apostles to ask them for light and for Lygia. Blessed be the moment when he entertained that thought, for now he was by her side, and no more would she flee from him as she'd fled from the house of Miriam.

"I didn't flee from you," said Lygia.

"Then why did you leave me?"

She lifted her beautiful eyes to his, then hid her blushing face and murmured, "You know why."

Vinitius was silent from a very excess of joy. Then he sought to explain to her how his eyes had slowly opened to the fact that she was entirely different from Roman women, with the single exception of Pomponia. Yet he couldn't express this fully, for he couldn't fully define his own feelings: In her

"You know why."

person a new strange beauty had entered the world, a beauty that wasn't a mere statue, but a soul. He told her something, however, that filled her with delight—that he loved her just because she'd fled from him and that she'd be sacred to him at his hearth. Then, taking her hand in his, he found it impossible to continue. He could only look at her with rapture, as at the source of his regained happiness, and repeated her name over and over, as if to reassure himself that he'd found her at last and she was there at his side.

Later, he began to question her as to all that had gone on in her soul. She confessed that she'd loved him from the time she first met him at the Auli and that, had he restored her to them from the Palatine, she would have confessed that love and tried to soften their anger against him.

"I swear to you," said Vinitius, "that it never entered my mind to take you from the Auli. Petronius will tell you that, even then, I informed him that I loved you and wished to marry you. 'Let her anoint my door with wolf grease,' I said to him, 'and take her seat at my hearth.'

"But he laughed at me and suggested to Caesar that he demand you as a hostage and hand you over to me. Often have I cursed him in my anguish, but it may have been a favoring star that ordained it thus, for otherwise I should never have known the Christians nor understood you."

"Believe me, Marcus," answered Lygia, "it was Christ who so ordained it to lead you to Himself."

Vinitius lifted his head in some astonishment.

"It's true," he said with animation, "for all things worked themselves out so strangely that in seeking you I found the Christians. In Ostranium I listened thunderstruck to the Apostle, for never had I heard such words before. And you were praying for me there?"

"Yes."

They passed the ivy-covered arbor, approaching the spot where Ursus, after strangling Croto, had fallen upon Vinitius.

"Here I should have perished but for you," said the young man.

"Forget all that, and don't be angry at Ursus for it."

"Could I seek vengeance on him for his defense of you? Were he a slave, I'd free him immediately."

"Had he been a slave, the Auli would have freed him long ago."

"Do you remember," continued Vinitius, "that I would have restored you to the Auli? But you replied that you feared Caesar might hear of it and wreak his vengeance on the Auli. Take thought of this, that now you may see them as often as you wish."

"How, Marcus?"

"I say now, for I think that you may without danger see them once we're married. For should Caesar hear of this and ask what I've done with the hostage he entrusted to me, I'll answer him, 'She's my wife and visits the Auli at my wish.' His stay in Antium will be short, for he wishes to go to Achaia. But even should he remain longer, I won't have to call on him every day. After Paul of Tarsus has completed my instruction in your religion, I'll receive baptism, then return here and receive the friendship of the Auli. There'll be no further obstacles in our way. I'll set you by my hearth. Oh, *carissima!*[1] *Carissima!*" He raised his hand heavenward as if to make God a witness to his love.

Lygia, lifting her shining eyes to him, said, "And then I shall say, 'Where you are, Caius, there am I, Caia.'"

"Oh, Lygia! I swear that never was a woman so honored in her husband's home as you shall be in mine."

They walked in silence, as though unable to realize fully their own happiness. In their deep love, they seemed a pair of gods, as beautiful as though spring had brought them forth into the world with the flowers.

At length they halted under the cypress growing by the door of the dwelling. Lygia leaned against its trunk, and Vinitius implored her with a trembling voice, "Tell Ursus to go to the Auli's home for your belongings and childhood toys."

But she, blushing like a rose or like the dawn, replied, "Custom dictates otherwise."

"I know that. It's customary for a *pronuba*[2] to bear these behind a bride, but please do this for me. I'll take them with me to my villa in Antium, and they'll serve as constant reminders of you."

Here he clasped his hands together and, with the manner of a child begging for something, repeated, "Pomponia will soon return. Therefore do this, my divinity; do this, my *carissima.*"

"Let Pomponia do as she wishes," answered Lygia, blushing still further at the mention of a bridal ceremony.

Again they were silent, rapture depriving them of speech. Lygia still leaned against the cypress, her face whitening in the shadow like a flower,

---

1 "Beloved." Spoken to a woman.
2 Matron that attends the bride during the marriage ceremony and explains wifely duties to her.

her eyes downcast, her bosom heaving more rapidly. Vinitius's face changed and grew pale. In the noonday stillness they heard only the throbbing of their own hearts; and in their mutual ecstasy, the cypress, the myrtle bushes, and the ivy of the arbor were strangely transformed as though this were in truth a garden of love.

Miriam, standing in the threshold, awoke them to reality by her call to the midday meal. The pair sat down with the Apostles, who gazed on them with joy, as representatives of the young generation that, after their death, should preserve and spread still further the seeds of the new faith. Peter broke and blessed the bread. Peace shone in every face, and a great happiness seemed to pervade the whole room.

"See," said Paul, turning to Vinitius. "Are we enemies of love and joy?"

"I know the truth now," answered Vinitius, "for never have I been so happy as among you."

Chapter XXXV

Returning home through the Forum that evening, Vinitius perceived at the entrance to the Tuscus Quarter the gilded litter of Petronius, borne by eight Bithynians. He halted it by a signal of his hand and approached the curtains.

"May your dreams be pleasant," he exclaimed, with a laugh at the sight of Petronius asleep.

"Oh, is it you?" asked Petronius, awakening. "True, I'd just dropped into a dream, for I've spent the night at the Palatine. I merely came to purchase something to read at Antium. What's the news?"

"Are you shopping in the bookstores?" asked Vinitius.

"Yes. I wish to leave no disorder in my library, so I'm providing myself with a special supply for the journey. Some new works by Musonius or Seneca may have come out. I'm seeking also for Persius and a certain edition of Virgil's *Eclogues* I've long searched for. Oh, how weary I am! How my hands ache from unrolling parchments. When one's in a bookstore, his curiosity rushes him on from book to book, from this to that. I've been to the shops of Avirnus and of Atractus on the Argiletum, and before that I visited the Sozii at Vicus Sandalarius. By Castor! How sleepy I am."

"You were at the Palatine? Then I must ask you, what's the news? Or do you know? Here, send your litter home with the books and come to my house. We'll talk of Antium or other things."

"Gladly!" said Petronius, emerging from the litter. "You must know that day after tomorrow we set out for Antium."

"How could I know that?"

"In what world are you living? So I'm the first to announce this news? Yes; be ready the morning of the day after tomorrow. Neither peas in olive oil nor a handkerchief around his neck helped any, and Ahenobarbus has grown hoarse. So delay is no longer to be thought of. He curses Rome and its air by the foundations of the world. Gladly would he raze the city or destroy it with fire, and he longs for the sea as soon as possible. He maintains

285

that the stenches that the wind blows from the narrow alleys will drive him into the grave. Today huge sacrifices were offered up in all the temples for the restoration of his voice. Woe to Rome, and especially to the Senate, if the gods don't grant this soon."

"Then why should he go to Achaia?"

"But is that the only talent possessed by our divine Caesar?" laughed Petronius. "He would like to exhibit himself in the Olympic Games, as a poet with his verses on the burning of Troy, as a charioteer, as a musician, as an athlete—even as a dancer—and in every role he'll win all the garlands destined for the victors. Do you know why that ape grew hoarse? Because so eaten up with jealousy of Paris's dancing is he, that yesterday he danced for us the adventures of Leda. He perspired too freely and caught cold. He was as wet and slimy as an eel just taken from the water. He changed masks one after another, wriggling like a spindle, and waved his arms like a drunken sailor. It made me sick to gaze on that big belly and those thin legs. Paris had taught him for two weeks, but just try to imagine the sight: Ahenobarbus as Leda or as a divine swan. That was a swan indeed! Now he wants to come out in public with this pantomime, first in Antium and afterward in Rome."

"People have already been shocked by his singing in public, but to even think, a Roman emperor coming out as a mime! No, that at least Rome won't stand!"

"*Carissime*, Rome will stand anything. The Senate will even pass a vote of thanks to the father of his country." Then he added, "And the mob will be proud that Caesar is its buffoon."

"Tell me," cried Vinitius, "is it possible to be more debased?"

Petronius shrugged his shoulders. "You've buried yourself so much in your own home with your thoughts of Lygia and of the Christians, that you evidently haven't heard what happened two days ago: Nero publicly married Pythagoras. Nero was the bride. Doesn't it seem that the full measure of insanity has been surpassed? The priests were invited, and they came and solemnly performed the ceremony. I was present. I can stand a good deal, but I confess that I felt that the gods, if they exist, should have given a sign of their outrage. But Caesar believes not in the gods, and he's right."

"So, in one and the same person, he's the high priest, a god, and an atheist."

Petronius laughed. "True, but that thought hadn't occurred to me. It's a combination never yet seen in the world." Then, stopping a moment, he said, "But it must be added that this high priest who does not believe in the gods, and this god who jests at gods is afraid of them in his character of atheist."

"That is proved by what happened in the temple of Vesta."

"What a world!"

"As the world is, so is Caesar. But this can't last."

They had now entered the house of Vinitius, who cheerily called for supper. Then he turned to Petronius.

"No, my beloved uncle," he said, "the world just regenerates."

"We at least won't regenerate it, if but for this reason: that man, in these days of Nero, is but a butterfly—he lives in the sunshine of favor and perishes at the first breath of cold, even against his will. By the son of Maia, more than once have I asked myself, *By what marvel has Lucius Saturninus, for example, been able to reach the age of ninety-three and outlive Tiberius, Caligula, and Claudius?* But let that go. Will you permit me to send your litter for Eunice? My desire for sleep has passed away somehow, and I'd like to enjoy myself. Order the kithara players to come to supper, and afterward we'll talk of Antium. It's necessary to think of it, and especially of you."

Vinitius sent for Eunice but declared that he wouldn't bother his head about the Antium matter.

"Let those bother themselves who know no other way of living than in the sunshine of Caesar's favor. The world doesn't end in the Palatine, especially for those who have something else in their heart and soul."

He said this so carelessly, with such animation and gladness, that Petronius was alarmed. Staring at his nephew, he asked, "What's happened to you? Today you are as one who wears a golden *bulla*[1] around his neck."

"I'm happy," said Vinitius, "and invited you here to tell you so."

"What's happened?"

"Something I wouldn't exchange for the entire Roman Empire." He seated himself. Placing his arm around the back of the chair and leaning his head on it, he spoke with a face wreathed in smiles and a bright light in his eyes. "Do you remember when we were together at the house of Aulus Plautius and when for the first time you saw the divine maiden whom you yourself called the morning star and Aurora? Do you remember

---

1 Worn by triumphant generals.

that Psyche, that incomparable one, the most beautiful among virgins and among all your goddesses?"

Petronius could only stare at him, wondering if the youth's wits had forsaken him.

"How you do run on!" he said at last. "Of *course* I remember Lygia."

"I'm her betrothed," said Vinitius.

"*What?*"

Vinitius sprang up and called his *dispensator.*

"Summon the slaves to the last soul, and be quick about it."

"You're her betrothed?" repeated Petronius, in utter disbelief.

But before he could recover from his astonishment, the great atrium of Vinitius swarmed with men and women. Panting old men ran in, together with men in the prime of life, women, boys, and girls. More were seeking to push their way in. In the corridors were heard voices, calling in many languages. At length, all formed themselves in rows along the walls and among the columns.

Vinitius, standing by the *impluvium*, turned to Demas. "All those who have served twenty years in this house will present themselves tomorrow before the praetor, where they will obtain their freedom. All who have not served that long will receive three pieces of gold and double rations during the week. Send orders to the *ergastulums* in my villas that all punishments be remitted, that the shackles be stricken from all prisoners, and that everyone be sufficiently fed. Know that this is a happy day for me, and I wish joy to pervade the house."

For a moment the slaves stood in awed silence, as if not believing their own ears. Then all hands were uplifted simultaneously and a cry went up from all lips: "Ah, master! Ah—ah—ah!"

Vinitius waved them away with his hand. Though they each desired to fall at his feet and thank him, they hurried away at the signal and filled the house from basement to roof with their joyous voices.

"Tomorrow," said Vinitius, "I will summon them all into the garden, where they will draw such figures as they choose in the ground. Those who draw a fish will receive their freedom at the hands of Lygia."

Petronius, who never wondered long at anything, now asked indifferently, "A fish? Ah yes! I remember Chilo told us that it's a Christian symbol." He stretched out his hand to Vinitius and said, "Happiness always exists wherever a man sees it. May Flora strew flowers before your feet for long years. I wish you all you could wish for yourself."

"I thank you for those wishes. I had feared that you'd seek to dissuade me, and that, as you see, would be to no avail."

"*I* dissuade you? Not in the least. On the contrary, I tell you that you're doing the right thing."

"Ha, turncoat!" cried Vinitius joyously. "Have you forgotten what you told me when we were turning from Pomponia's house?"

Petronius answered coolly, "No, but I have changed my opinion." Then he added, "*Carissime,* everything changes in Rome. Husbands change wives, wives change husbands—why shouldn't I change my opinion? It was a mere accident that Nero didn't marry Acte, for whom a royal lineage was drawn up for the purpose. And why not? He would have had an honest wife, we an honest Augusta. By Proteus and his barren wastes in the sea! I'll change my opinion as often as I find it right or convenient. As to Lygia, doubtless her royal lineage is more certain than that of Acte. But when you're in Antium, watch out for Poppaea, who is ruthless in her revenges."

"I fear nothing. Not a hair of my head will fall in Antium."

"If you're seeking to astonish me once more, you're mistaken, but whence comes that certainty?"

"The Apostle Peter told me so."

"Ah! The Apostle told you this! There's no argument against that. But at least let me take certain precautions, if only for the purpose of preventing the Apostle Peter from proving a false prophet; for should the Apostle Peter, by some mischance be mistaken, he might lose your confidence, which will probably be useful to him in the future."

"Do as you wish, but I believe in him. If you think that you'll sway me by scoffing repetitions of his name, you're mistaken."

"Well, one more question. Have you become a Christian?"

"Not yet. But Paul of Tarsus accompanies me, to explain the teachings of Christ, and afterward I'll be baptized, for your statement that they're enemies of life and joy isn't true."

"So much the better for you and Lygia," returned Petronius. Then, shrugging his shoulders, he added as though to himself, "It's marvelous how clever these people are in making proselytes, and how their sect is spreading."

"True," replied Vinitius, as if he'd already been baptized. "There are thousands and tens of thousands in Rome, in other Italian cities, in Greece, and in Asia. There are Christians in the legions and among the

Praetorians, and in the very palace of Caesar. Slaves and citizens profess the creed, poor and rich, plebian and patrician. Are you aware that some of the Cornelii are Christians, Pomponia Graecina is a Christian, that most likely Octavia was, that Acte is one? Yes, it's a creed that's spreading across the world. It's the only thing that can regenerate it. Shrug not your shoulders, for who knows but that in a month or a year you also may accept it."

"*I?*" said Petronius. "No, by the son of Lethe, I will not—not even if it contains all human and divine truth and wisdom. It would involve trouble, and I hate trouble. It would require self-denial, and I wouldn't deny myself anything in life. In a nature like yours, which resembles boiling water over a fire, something of this sort should be expected. But I? I have my gems, my cameos, my vases, and my Eunice. I have no belief in Olympus, but I make one of my own on this earth. I will blossom until the shafts of the divine archer pierce me, or until Caesar orders me to open my veins. I'm too fond of the odor of violets and the comforts of the *triclinium*. I even have a fondness for our gods, as rhetorical figures, and for Achaia, where I'm preparing to go with our corpulent, thin-legged, incomparable, godlike Caesar, the August, the ever victorious, the Hercules of our time—Nero himself."

He grew hilarious at the very idea that it would be possible for him to accept the teachings of the Galilean fisherman and hummed to himself:

> With the green of the myrtle
> I will entwine my bright sword
> After the example of Harmodius and Aristogiton.[2]

He stopped short, for Eunice's arrival was now announced. Immediately after her coming, supper was served, during which the kithara players provided music. Vinitius then told Petronius about Chilo's visit and how the idea of going directly to the Apostles came to him while Chilo was being flogged.

Petronius, who'd grown drowsy again, woke up at this and said, "The

---

2   Two Athenian young men who killed Hipparchus (Tyrant of Athens) in 514 B.C. Both were tortured to death. Hippias, brother of the slain Hipparchus, proved to be so repressive that gradually Athenians changed their minds about the two young men, and they were elevated to the status of folk heroes.

suggestion was a good one. As for Chilo, I'd have given him five pieces of gold. But if your choice was to flog him, you should have flogged him to death, for who knows whether the time may not come when the senators will bow before him as now they bow before our cobbler-knight, Vatinius. Good night."

And removing his garland, he and Eunice made their preparations for departure. When they'd left, Vinitius went up into the library and wrote the following to Lygia:

> Would that when you open your beautiful eyes, O divinity, this letter might say to you, "Good morning." It's with this hope I write, though I'll see you tomorrow.
>
> Caesar goes to Antium the day after tomorrow, and I, alas! must accompany him. I've already explained to you that not to obey would cost me my life—and at present I wouldn't have the courage to die. But if you don't want me to go, write me only a word, and I'll remain and leave it up to Petronius to save my life by well-chosen words.
>
> Today, the day of joy, I scattered guerdons among all my slaves. Those who have served twenty years in my house I'll lead tomorrow to the praetor to give them their freedom. You, *carissima*, must commend me for this, because it seems to me that this will conform to that kindly creed that you profess, and also because I've done this for your sake. I'll tell them tomorrow that they owe their freedom to you, so that they may know whom to thank and may praise your name. I yield myself up to the bondage of joy and you. God grant that I never know freedom.
>
> May Antium be cursed, together with Ahenobarbus's journey. Thrice and four times happy am I that I'm not as wise as Petronius, for then I should certainly be obliged to go to Achaia as well.

Chapter XXXVI

It was known in Rome that, on his way, Caesar would stop at Ostia to see the largest ship in the world, which had recently brought wheat from Alexandria, and from there he would go to Antium by the shore road. The orders had already been given; therefore, at the Porta Ostia, there assembled at early morn a great multitude, consisting of the rabble of Rome and of all the nations of the world, come to feast their eyes on the sight of Caesar's retinue, of which the Roman plebeians could never get their fill. The road to Antium was neither long nor difficult, and the city itself was filled with palaces and villas sumptuously furnished. One could find there everything required for comfort, even the most exquisite luxury of the time. It was Caesar's custom, however, to take with him all the things in which he delighted, from musical instruments and artistic furniture to the statues and mosaics that he would arrange in order, even where he stopped but a short while for rest or bodily refreshment. Therefore, multitudes of servants accompanied him on every journey, as well as detachments of Praetorians and Augustinians, each of whom had his individual following of slaves.

At early dawn of that day, pastors[1] from the Campania, their legs swathed with goatskins, their faces sunburned, drove five hundred she-asses through the gates so that Poppaea might have her customary bath in their milk on the morrow at Antium. The mob found hilarious delight in watching the long ears swaying amid clouds of dust and in listening to the whistle of the whips and the wild cries of the pastors.

When the she-asses had passed, crowds of boys rushed out upon the road, swept it clean, and strewed it with flowers and pine needles. Word ran through the crowd, and swelled it with a sense of local pride, that the entire road to Antium would be covered with flowers plucked from private gardens in the neighborhood or purchased at high prices from hucksters at

---

1 Herdsmen.

292

the Porta Mugionis. As the morning hours passed, the crowds increased. Many had brought their entire families, and to temper the tedium of waiting, they spread provisions on stones intended for the new temple of Ceres and ate their *prandium*[2] under the glowing sun. Here and there were groups in which the lead was taken by those who had traveled; they talked learnedly of Caesar's present trip, of his future journeys, and of journeys in general. Sailors and veterans told strange tales that they'd heard during foreign campaigns, about countries where Roman feet had never been planted. Townspeople who had never gone beyond the Via Appia listened openmouthed to the marvels related of India, of Arabia, and of archipelagoes surrounding Britain (where Briareus[3] had chained the sleeping Saturn on a certain haunted island), of hyperborean seas whose waters were like jelly, and of the hissing and roaring that the ocean emitted when the setting sun descended into its waters. Such stories found ready credence among the rabble, as they'd already found credence even with such men as Pliny and Tacitus. They spoke also of that ship that Caesar was to stop to gaze at, a ship that had brought grain enough for two years, besides four hundred passengers, the same number in the crew, and a multitude of wild beasts to be used at the summer games. All this created a general goodwill towards Caesar, who not only fed his people, but also amused them. Everybody prepared to give him an enthusiastic greeting.

A detachment of Numidian horsemen belonging to the Praetorian Guard were the first to arrive. Their uniforms were yellow, girt at the waist with crimson. In their ears were huge earrings that reflected a golden gleam upon their burnished black faces. The points of their bamboo spears shone in the sun like flames. After them came a brilliant procession. The multitude pressed forward for a closer look, but a detachment of Praetorian infantry lined both sides of the road from the gateway, to keep them from blocking progress. Then passed wagons bearing tents of purple, red, and violet; snowy white tents of muslin, interwoven with golden threads; Oriental carpets; tables of lemon wood; pieces of mosaic; kitchen utensils; and cages with birds from the East, South, and West, whose brains and tongues were destined for Caesar's table; amphoras of wine; and baskets of fruit. Such objects as might be bruised or broken in the wagons were borne by slaves on foot; hence there were hundreds of men

---

2 Late breakfast or lunch.
3 A mythical giant (also called Aegaeon) with a hundred arms.

carrying vessels and statuettes of Corinthian bronze. To special bands of slaves were assigned Etruscan or Grecian vases, to others golden or silver vessels or goblets of Alexandrian crystal. Each band was separated from the next one by a detachment of Praetorians, on horseback or on foot, and each had overseers armed with whips with lashes that ended in lumps of lead or iron. The procession, consisting of men bearing all these different objects with intense care and preoccupation, seemed much like a solemn religious function, and the resemblance grew still more vivid when the musical instruments of Caesar and his court followed. Harps; Grecian lutes; lyres; kitharas; flutes; fifes; trumpets; long, winding buffalo horns; and cymbals passed by in bewildering profusion.

That sea of instruments with all the gold, bronze, precious stones, and mother-of-pearl gleaming in the sun might well have given the impression that Apollo or Bacchus was journeying through the world. After the instruments came lordly chariots full of acrobats and dancers, male and female, picturesquely grouped with wands in their hands. Then came slaves devoted not to service, but to shameful uses: children—male and female—selected from throughout Greece and Asia Minor, with long tresses or curly hair gathered in golden nets, whose lovely faces resembled cupids and were thickly covered with cosmetics, so their delicate complexions might not be tanned by the winds of the Campania.

And now came a Praetorian detachment of gigantic Sicambrians,[4] bearded, with red and flaxen hair and blue eyes. Roman eagles were borne in front of them by *imaginarii*,[5] together with inscribed tablets, statues of German and Roman gods, and finally statues and busts of Caesar. From beneath the cloaks and armor of the soldiers appeared massive sunburned arms and shoulders, like machines of war fit to wield the mighty weapons that they bore. The earth seemed to bend beneath their measured and heavy tread. Conscious of the strength that, if need be, they could turn against Caesar himself, they glanced contemptuously at the rabble in the street, evidently forgetting that many of them had come to that city in chains. But few of the soldiers were in the procession, for the main body of the Praetorians remained encamped to watch over the city and preserve order there. When they'd marched past, Nero's chained lions and tigers were led by, so that if at any moment the urge to imitate Dionysius should

---

4   The people who later became known as the Franks.
5   Standard-bearers.

come, he might attach them to his chariots. Arabs and Hindus led them in chains of steel that were so fully concealed by encircling flowers that it seemed as though the animals were led in garlands. Tamed by skillful *bestiarii*, they gazed at the crowd through green and sleepy eyes, but from time to time they lifted their giant heads and breathed through wheezing nostrils the exhalations of the surrounding humanity, licking their chops the while with rasping tongues.

Now came Caesar's chariots and litters, large and small, gold or purple, inlaid with ivory and mother-of-pearl or sparkling with diamonds and other precious stones; then another small detachment of Praetorians in Roman armor, consisting entirely of Italian volunteers;[6] then crowds of gorgeously clad servants and boys. At last, Caesar's approach was heralded from afar by the shouts of thousands.

In the throng was Peter the Apostle, who wished, once in his lifetime, to catch a glimpse of Caesar. He was accompanied by Lygia, her face covered by a thick veil, and Ursus, whose strength afforded the surest protection for the young girl in the midst of that disorderly and dissolute crowd. The Lygian hoisted up a great stone destined for the temple and brought it to the Apostle, so that by ascending it he could see better than the others.

The crowd murmured at first when Ursus pushed it apart as a ship cleaves through the waves, but when they noticed the size of the stone, which four of the strongest athletes could not have lifted, the muttering changed into shouts of admiration. "*Macte! Macte!*"[7] resounded from all sides.

But now Caesar appeared. He sat in a tentlike chariot drawn by six white Idumean[8] stallions shod with gold. The sides of the tent were purposely left open so that the crowds could see Caesar. Others might have found places in the chariot, but Nero, wishing to center all attention upon himself, passed through the streets alone, save for two deformed dwarfs lying at his feet. He wore a white tunic and an amethyst-colored toga that cast a bluish tint upon his face. A laurel wreath was on his head. His body had grown considerably in bulk since his departure from Neapolis. His face had become bloated; beneath his lower jaw hung a double chin so

---

6 Since the inhabitants of Italy were freed from military service by Augustus, the *cohors Italica*, generally stationed in Asia, was composed of volunteers. The Praetorian Guard was composed of both these volunteers and foreigners.

7 An expression of goodwill, congratulation, glory, honor.

8 A district in Palestine.

that his mouth, always too close to his nose, now seemed to be just under his nostrils. His thick neck, as usual, was wrapped by a silk handkerchief, which he rearranged every few moments with his fat, white hand, grown over with red hair forming what looked like bloody stains. He wouldn't permit the *epilatores*[9] to pluck this hair, since he'd been told that to do so would bring trembling of the fingers and injure his kithara playing. Infinite vanity, as always, was depicted on his face, tempered by tedium and suffering. It was the face at once of a tyrant and a fool. While riding, he turned his head from one side to the other, blinking at times, and listened intently to the manner in which the crowd greeted him.

A storm of shouts and applause came first. "Hail, godlike Caesar! Hail, Emperor! Hail, Conqueror! Peerless One! Son of Apollo! Apollo himself!"

Listening to these words, he smiled, but occasionally a scowl flitted across his face, for the Roman rabble, fond of jesting and confident in their own numbers, always had their sarcasm, even against the triumphal heroes, whom they loved and honored. At one of Julius Caesar's entrances into Rome, they'd shouted, "Citizens, hide your wives! The baldheaded libertine is approaching!"

But Nero's monstrous self-love couldn't brook the least jesting or criticism. Nevertheless, the shouts of applause were mingled with cries of, "Ahenobarbus! What have you done with your flaming beard? Are you afraid it would set fire to Rome?" Men who so shouted little knew what a prophecy lay hidden in their jest. Caesar was not much disturbed by their cries, as he no longer wore a beard. He'd sacrificed it some years ago to place it in a golden cylinder and dedicate it to Jupiter in the Capitol. But there were others in the mob who, hidden behind heaps of stones and the corners of temples, shouted, "Matricide! Nero! Orestes! Alcmaeon!" and others still, "Where is Octavia?" "Yield up your purple!"

Poppaea, who followed immediately after him, attracted howls of "Yellow Hair!" (a nickname for public prostitutes). Nero's trained ear caught all these various exclamations, and he lifted his polished emerald to his eye as though wishing to discover and remember those who uttered them. In this act, his glance rested upon the Apostle Peter, standing on the huge stone.

For a moment, the two men looked at each other, and it occurred to no one in all that magnificent retinue, nor to all those innumerable people in

---

9 Manicurists.

the crowd, to have imagined that in that instant, two rulers of the earth looked at each other, one of whom would soon pass away like a bloody dream, while the other, the old man in coarse cloth, would seize in eternal possession the city and the world.

And now Caesar had passed. Poppaea, whom the people loathed, followed him in a sumptuous litter borne by eight Africans. Arrayed, as Nero was arrayed, in amethyst-colored robes, with a thick layer of cosmetics on her face, motionless, pensive, indifferent, she looked like some beautiful and wicked divinity. In her wake followed a whole court of servants, male and female, and lines of wagons filled with articles for comfort and dressing.

The sun had already passed the noonday hour when the procession of the Augustinians began—a resplendent, glittering line, changing like a serpent and apparently endless. The indolent Petronius, saluted with kindly indulgence by the crowd, was carried in an open litter with his goddesslike slave. Tigellinus rode in a chariot drawn by ponies adorned with white and purple feathers. The people noticed him rising repeatedly, stretching his neck to see if Caesar was ready to give him the longed-for signal to take a seat in the imperial chariot. Among the others, Licinianus Piso was greeted with applause, Vitelius with laughter, Vatinius with hissing. Towards the consuls, Licinus and Lecanius, the crowd behaved with indifference, but Tullius Senecio, whom for some unknown reason they loved, and Vestinius got their plaudits.

The court was innumerable. It seemed as if all that was richest, most brilliant, or most illustrious in Rome was migrating to Antium. Nero never traveled otherwise than with thousands of vehicles, and the number accompanying him nearly always exceeded the number of soldiers in a legion.[10] Hence the crowd could point to Domitius Afer and the decrepit Lucius Saturninus and Vespasian—who hadn't yet gone on his campaign against Judea (whence he'd return to receive Caesar's crown)—and his sons, and young Nerva and Lucan and Annius Gallo and Quintianus, and a multitude of women renowned for wealth, beauty, luxury, and debauchery.

The eyes of the multitude turned from these familiar faces to the harness, the chariots, the horses, the strange livery of the servants, all of which had been selected from all the nations of the world. In that flood of splendor and grandeur, one hardly knew what to look at—not only the eye, but also the mind was dazzled by the gleaming of gold, purple, and violet, by the

---

10 One thousand two hundred.

The two men looked at each other.

sparkling of precious stones and the glitter of brocade, mother-of-pearl, and ivory. It seemed that the very rays of the sun were dissolving in that abyss of splendor. And though wretched beings, with sunken stomachs and hunger-smitten eyes, were not lacking in the crowd, the spectacle not only inflamed their envy and their greed, but also filled them with delight and pride, as a manifestation of the power and invincibility of Rome, to which the world contributed and before whom the world knelt. And indeed, there was not on earth anyone who ventured to doubt that that power would endure for all ages and outlast all nations, or that in the whole world there was anything with strength enough to resist it.

Vinitius, riding in the rear of the procession, caught sight of the Apostle and Lygia, whom he didn't expect to see. Leaping down from his chariot, he was quickly at their side, greeting them with a radiant face. He spoke hurriedly, as one who had no time to lose.

"You *came!* I don't know how to thank you, Lygia! God couldn't have sent me a better omen. I greet you again, even while bidding you farewell, but the farewell won't be for long. I'll place relays of Parthian horses all along the way, and every free day I'll come to see you, until I get leave to return. Farewell!"

"Farewell, Marcus!" answered Lygia, then added in an undertone, "May Christ go with you and open your soul to Paul's words."

Overjoyed that she took thought for his speedy conversion, he replied, "Be it as you say! Paul prefers to travel with my people, but he's with me and will be my companion and master. Lift your veil, *carissima*, that I may see you once more before my journey. Why are you so thickly veiled?"

She lifted her veil. Her bright face and wonderfully smiling eyes were turned full upon him. "Don't you like my veil?" she mischievously asked.

Vinitius delightedly retorted, "Bad for my eyes. They wish to gaze on you forever until death. Ursus!" he added, turning to the Lygian. "Watch her as the pupil of your eye, for she's my *domina*[11] as well as yours."

He then took the maiden's hand and pressed it to his lips, to the great astonishment of the crowd, who couldn't understand such signs of honor from a resplendent Augustinian to a maiden arrayed in simple garments, almost those of a slave.

"Farewell!"

He departed quickly, to catch up with the now disappearing rear of the

---

11 Mistress of a household.

procession. The Apostle Peter blessed him with an unseen sign of the cross, but the kindly Ursus began at once to praise him, glad to see his young mistress listening with pleasure and beaming gratitude upon him.

The retinue moved on, disappearing in clouds of golden dust. They gazed long after it, however, until Demas the miller approached, the same who employed Ursus in nightly toil. After kissing the hand of the Apostle, he urged them to break bread with him, explaining that his house was near the Emporium.

"You must be hungry and weary," he said, "after spending the greater part of the day at the gate."

So they went with him and, after rest and refreshments in his house, returned to the Trans-Tiber in the evening, having the intention of crossing the Aemilian Bridge, passing through the Clivus Publicus, and going over the Aventine Hill between the temples of Diana and Mercury. From that height, the Apostle Peter looked down upon the buildings surrounding him and on the others vanishing far away in the gloom. Silently he pondered over the power and the immensity of this city, to which he'd come to preach the word of God.

Up to this time he'd seen the Roman legions and governors in the many lands through which he'd wandered, but they had been merely single limbs of that power, which today for the first time he'd seen personified in Nero.

That city was immense, predatory, rapacious, unrestrained, dissolute, rotten to the marrow of its bones, and unassailable in its superhuman power. Caesar himself was a fratricide, a matricide, a uxoricide, followed by a retinue of bloody specters, no less in number than his court. That profligate, that buffoon, was yet lord of thirty legions and through them of the whole earth; those courtiers covered with gold and purple, uncertain of the morrow, but today more powerful than kings—all these things together seemed to him to make up a hellish kingdom of injustice and depravity. His simple heart marveled how God could bestow such inconceivable might upon Satan, that he should have given him the earth to knead it as he willed, to turn it over and trample on it, to squeeze tears and blood out of it, to wrench it as with a whirlwind, to storm it like a tempest, to consume it like flames.

His Apostle's heart was alarmed by these thoughts. In spirit he spoke to the Master. *O Lord!* he cried. *What shall I do in this city to which You have sent me? Seas and lands belong to it, the beasts of the field and the living creatures in the water belong to it, other kingdoms and cities belong to it, and the thirty legions that guard them. I, O Lord, am but a fisherman from a lake. How shall I begin? How shall I overcome its malice?*

Thus speaking, he raised his gray, trembling head towards heaven, praying and calling from the depths of his heart to his divine Master, full of sadness and fear.

Meanwhile, his prayer was interrupted by Lygia. "The whole city is as if on fire!" she observed.

And in very truth the sun set strangely that day. Its enormous shield had now sunk halfway behind the Janiculum Hill, and the entire expanse of heaven was filled with a fiery glow. From the place where they stood, their eyes took in a vast view. A little to the right they saw the long extending walls of the Circus Maximus, above it the towering palaces of the Palatine, and in front of them, the Forum Boarium and Velabrum, the summit of the Capitol with the temple of Jupiter. But the walls, columns, and summits of the temples were flooded in that golden and purple light. Such of the river as could be seen from a distance seemed to flow as with blood, and as the sun sank lower behind the mountains, the glow flushed redder, like the reflection of a conflagration, and increased and widened until finally it embraced the seven hills, from which it poured over the whole surrounding country.

"The entire city seems to be on fire," repeated Lygia.

Peter shaded his eyes with his hand and said, "The wrath of God is upon it."

Chapter XXXVII

VINITIUS TO LYGIA:

The slave Phlegon, by whom I send you this letter, is a Christian; therefore he's one of those who are to receive freedom at your hands, *carissima!* He's an old servant of our house; therefore I can place full confidence in him and have no fear that the letter will fall into hands other than yours. I'm writing from Laurentum, where we've stopped on account of the heat. Otho, former husband of Poppaea, possessed here a splendid villa, which he donated to her, and she, although divorced from him, refused to give it back. When I think of those women who surround me now and then of you, it seems to me that from the stones thrown by Deucalion[1] must have arisen various species of people altogether unlike each other and that you belong to the species born of crystal.

I admire and love you with all my soul, so that I wish to speak only of you. But I must restrain myself in order to tell you about the journey, how I am faring, and news of the court. Well, Caesar was the guest of Poppaea, who had secretly prepared for him a splendid reception. She invited but a few of the Augustinians, but Petronius and I were summoned. After the noonday meal we sailed in golden boats over the sea, which was as calm as though it were sleeping and as blue as your eyes, my divinity. We rowed ourselves, for it evidently flattered Augusta to feel

---

1 Son of Prometheus, king of Pthia. He and his wife Pyrrha were said to have been saved in an ark from a great flood. Together they repeopled the world by throwing stones behind their backs.

302

that she was rowed by men of consular dignity or their sons. Caesar, standing by the rudder in a purple toga, sang a hymn, which he had composed last night in honor of the sea. He and Diodorus arranged the music.

Indian slaves in the other boats accompanied him on seashells, while all around appeared numerous dolphins, as if really enticed from the depths of Amphitrite by the music. Do you know what I did? I thought of you and longed for you. I wanted to grasp the sea, the calm weather, and the music and give it all to you.

Would you like to someday live on the shores of the sea far from Rome, my Augusta? I have an estate in Sicily, whereon there's a forest of almonds that are covered with rose-colored blossoms in spring. The forest is so near to the sea that the branches almost touch the water. There I will love you and revere Paul's teachings, for I know now that it is not opposed to love and happiness.

Do you wish this? But before I hear the answer from your beloved lips, let me tell you more about what happened in the boat.

Soon the shore was left far behind us, and we saw a sail before us in the distance. A discussion arose as to whether it was a mere fisherman's boat or the great vessel from Ostia. I recognized it first; then Augusta said that it was evident nothing could be hidden from my eyes and, suddenly lowering her veil, asked whether I could recognize her even thus. Petronius answered at once that even the sun cannot be recognized behind a cloud, but she laughingly retorted that so keen a glance as mine could be blinded by love alone. Naming different ladies of the court, she asked me which I loved. I answered calmly enough until she mentioned your name. When she got to your name, she uncovered her face and studied me with evil and inquiring eyes.

I feel true gratitude to Petronius, who at that moment nearly tipped over the boat and so drew general attention away from me. I swear that if I'd heard your name mentioned in a slighting or sneering tone, I wouldn't have been able to hide my wrath, but would have had to struggle with the impulse to break the head of this wicked and treacherous woman with my oar. You will recall, of course, what I told you just before I left, about the incident on the Pond of Agrippa.

Petronius is alarmed on my account, and even today he implored me not to trifle with the vanity of the Augusta. But Petronius doesn't understand me fully and doesn't realize that apart from you I know neither pleasure, nor beauty, nor love, and that for Poppaea I feel only disgust and contempt. You've greatly changed my soul—so greatly that it would now be impossible for me to go back to my former life. But do not fear that harm may reach me here. Poppaea doesn't love me, for she's incapable of love. Her caprices arise only from her anger against Caesar, who's still under her influence and who may even still love her. Yet he, on his part, no longer spares her or hides from her his shamelessness and his crimes.

Let me tell you something else that should reassure you. Peter, when I parted from him, told me not to fear Caesar, as not a hair of my head would be injured, and I believe him. Some voice in my soul tells me that every word of his must be fulfilled. Since he blessed our love, neither Caesar nor all the powers of Hades, nor fate itself, can take you away from me. Oh, Lygia! When I think of this, I'm as happy as though I were in heaven, which alone is peaceful and happy. But you, as a Christian, may be hurt by what I say of heaven and fate. If so, forgive me, for I sin against my will. Baptism has not yet washed me, but my heart is as an empty goblet that Paul of Tarsus will fill with your sweet teaching, so much sweeter to me because it's yours. May you, my divinity, count to my merit that from this goblet I have emptied the liquid that formerly filled it and that I withhold it not, but stretch it forth as a thirsty man standing by a pure spring. Let me find favor in your eyes.

In Antium my days and nights will pass in listening to Paul, who already on the first day of the journey acquired such influence over my people that they surround him continuously, seeing in him not merely a wonder-worker, but an almost supernatural being. Yesterday I saw joy on his face, and when I asked him what he was doing, he answered, "I'm sowing." Petronius knows that he's among my people and wishes to see him. So does Seneca, who heard of him from Gallo.

But the stars are now paling, O Lygia, while the morning star glows still brighter. Soon the dawn will make a rose of the sea—the whole world sleeps, but I am thinking of you and loving you. I salute you as well as the dawn, O *sponsa mea!*[2]

---

2 "O my betrothed!"

Chapter XXXVIII

VINITIUS TO LYGIA:

Dearest, have you ever accompanied the Auli to Antium? If not, it will give me happiness sometime to show it to you. All along the seashore since we left Laurentum are rows and rows of villas, and Antium is itself an endless succession of palaces and porticoes, whose columns are reflected in the water during clear weather. I, too, have a villa on the water, with an olive grove and a forest of cypress trees behind the villa. When I remember that this villa will some day be yours, its marble seems to me even whiter, its gardens more shady, and the sea more deeply azure.

Oh, Lygia! How good it is to live and love! Old Menikles, who has charge of the villa, has planted great bunches of irises under the myrtles on the lawns. At sight of them the home of the Auli, the *impluvium*, and the garden in which I sat by you came to my mind. And, to you too, these irises will remind you of your childhood home; therefore, I'm certain you'll love Antium and this villa.

Immediately after our arrival, I had a long talk with Paul at the noonday meal. We spoke of you, and afterward he began to teach me. I listened for a long time and I can only say to you that, even had I the pen of a Petronius, I couldn't explain to you all that passed through my mind and soul. I hadn't supposed that there could be such happiness, such beauty, and such peace, of which people heretofore have had no knowledge. But all these things I keep until I can share them with you in person, next time I can get back to Rome.

306

Tell me, how can the world find room at once for such men as the Apostles Peter and Paul and such a man as Caesar? I ask this because the evening of that same day I passed at Nero's palace, and do you know what I heard there? First, Caesar read his poem on the destruction of Troy and complained because he'd never seen a burning city. He envied Priam and he called him a happy man just because he'd witnessed the burning and destruction of his native city.

To this Tigellinus replied, "Say but the word, O divine one, and before night passes you'll see Antium in flames."

Caesar in turn called him a fool. "Where," he asked, "would I come to breathe the air of the sea and preserve this voice that the gods have gifted me and that men tell me I should carefully preserve for the benefit of humanity? Is it not Rome that harms me? Are not the stenches of the Suburra and the Esquiline responsible for the hoarseness in my throat? Would not burning Rome present a spectacle a hundredfold more splendid and tragic than Antium?"

Here all broke in with exclamations about what an unspeakable tragedy it would be should the city that had conquered the world be reduced to a heap of gray ashes.

Caesar insisted that his poem would, in that case, surpass the songs of Homer and afterward explained how he would rebuild the city and how future generations would admire the work, which would throw all other human achievements into the shade.

The drunken feasters joined in with shouts of, "Do it!"

"No," he replied. "First it would be necessary to find friends truer and more loyal to me than you are."

On hearing this, I confess I grew uneasy; for you, O beloved, are in Rome. Now I laugh at those fears and believe that no matter how mad they may be, Caesar and his courtiers wouldn't dare to reach that level of insanity. But see how love unnerves a man! I'd prefer that the house of Linus wasn't in that narrow alley of the Trans-Tiber, nor in a quarter inhabited by aliens who would receive the least consideration of all in case of any disaster. Since I contend that even the palace on the Palatine is not worthy of you, you shouldn't be surprised by my desire to restore to you all the comforts and luxuries you've been accustomed to from childhood.

Go to the house of Aulus, Lygia! I've given a great deal of thought to this matter. Were Caesar in Rome, news of your return might readily reach the Palatine through the slaves. This might turn attention to you and renew your persecution for daring to act against the will of Caesar. But his stay in Antium will be a long one, and before his return the gossip of the slaves will have ceased. Linus and Ursus might dwell with you. I live with the hope that before the Palatine again beholds Caesar, you, my divinity, will be dwelling with me in your own house on the Carinae. Blessed be the day, hour, and minute when you cross my threshold; and if Christ, whom I'm learning to accept, will accomplish this, may His name also be blessed. I'll serve Him and give my life and my blood for Him. But I speak incorrectly; we'll both serve Him as long as the thread of our lives endures.

I love you and salute you with my whole soul.

Chapter XXXIX

Ursus was drawing up an amphora of water from the cistern, singing in an undertone a wondrous Lygian song and casting glad looks at Lygia and Vinitius, who, white as two statues, stood among the cypresses in Linus's garden. Not a breeze stirred their garments. Twilight, lilac and golden, was falling upon the world as they held hands and conversed in the evening calm.

"May not some harm befall you," asked Lygia, "because you left Antium without Caesar's knowledge?"

"No, *carissima*. Caesar announced that he'd shut himself in for two days with Terpnos, to compose new songs. He often does this and then neither knows nor remembers anything else. Besides, what is Caesar to me, when I can be at your side, when I can look at you? I've been longing for you, and for several nights I've been unable to sleep. More than once, when weariness overcame me, I've been suddenly awakened, convicted that danger threatened you; at times, I dreamed that my relays of horses had been stolen, those horses that were to bear me from Antium to Rome, and that had already borne me from Rome to Antium with greater speed than any of Caesar's couriers. Besides, I couldn't live any longer without you. I love you too much for that, *carissima*."

"I knew you'd be coming," responded Lygia shyly. "Twice at my request, Ursus ran to the Carinae to inquire for you at your house. Linus laughed at me, and so did Ursus."

It was clearly evident that she had expected him, for instead of her usual dark dress, she wore a soft white *stola*,[1] out of whose graceful folds her head and shoulders emerged like primroses in snow. A few rose-colored anemones adorned her hair.

Vinitius pressed his lips to her hands; then they sat down on the stone bench amid wild grapevines and, inclining towards each other,

---

1 A long outer garment generally worn by Roman matrons.

gazed silently at the twilight as the last beams were reflected in their eyes. The mood of the quiet evening mastered them completely.

"How calm it is here," said Vinitius in a low tone, "and how beautiful the world is. The night is wonderfully still. I never felt happier in my life. Tell me, Lygia, the reason for this; never did I imagine that there could be such love—I assumed it to be a mere fire in the blood, a passion, but now I see for the first time that it's possible to love with every drop of one's blood and every breath, yet feel such sweet and boundless calm, as though sleep and death had put the soul to rest. For me, this is a totally new experience. I look at the stillness and serenity of the trees, and it seems to be within me. Now, for the first time, I understand that there may be a level of happiness that people have never known before. Now I begin to understand why you and Pomponia Graecina enjoy such peace. Yes, Christ gives it!"

"My dear Marcus—"

But she was unable to continue. Joy, gratitude, and the feeling that at last she was free to love deprived her of speech and filled her eyes with tears.

Vinitius, slipping his arm around her slender form, drew her towards him and said, "Lygia, blessed be the moment when I first heard His name."

"I love you, Marcus," was her low-voiced reply.

Both were silent again, their hearts too full for mere words. The last lilac reflection had faded away from the cypresses, and the crescent moon was now silvering the garden.

After a while, Vinitius said, "I know, barely had I entered here and kissed your dear hands, when I read in your eyes the question: Had I arrived at a full understanding of that divine creed that means so much to you, and had I been baptized yet? No, not yet. But do you know why, my flower? Paul said to me, 'I've convinced you that God came into the world and gave Himself to be crucified for its salvation, but let Peter wash you in the fountain of grace—Peter, who first stretched his hands over you and blessed you.' And I wish you, my beloved, to witness my baptism and for Pomponia to be my godmother. That's why I haven't been baptized yet, though I believe in the Savior and His teaching. Paul has convinced me and converted me—how could it be otherwise? How could I not believe that Christ came into the world when Peter, who was His disciple, says so, and Paul, to whom He appeared on the road to Damascus, testifies of Him? How could I not believe He is God when He rose from the dead?

He was seen in the city, on the lake, on the mountain—He was seen by men whose lips never knew how to lie. I began to believe all this the first time I heard Peter in Ostranium, for even then I said to myself, *I could believe any man on earth to be a liar before this one who declares 'I saw.'*

"But I feared your religion, convinced as I was that it would take you away from me. I thought that there was in it neither wisdom, nor beauty, nor happiness. But today, when I understand it, what sort of man should I be, were I not to wish truth to rule the world instead of falsehood, love instead of hate, virtue instead of license, constancy instead of unfaithfulness, mercy instead of vengeance? Your religion teaches all these things. Other religions also preach justice, but yours is the only one that makes man's heart just and, besides, makes it pure, like yours and Pomponia's, and faithful like yours and Pomponia's as well. I should be blind if I failed to see this. But if, in addition, Christ God has promised eternal life and happiness as boundless as only the might of God could bestow, what more could anyone wish? Were I to ask Seneca on what basis he enjoins virtue when wickedness brought me more happiness, he wouldn't be able to give me a logical answer. But now I know that I ought to be virtuous, because virtue and love flow from Christ and because when death closes my eyes, I shall find new life and new happiness, find myself and you, O *carissima.* Why not accept a religion that both speaks the truth and annihilates death? Who would not prefer good to evil? I had thought your religion opposed to happiness, but Paul has convinced me that it not only takes nothing away, but that it also gives beyond what one already has.

"Hardly yet does all this find room in my brain, but I know it's true, for I should never have been this happy had I taken you by force and possessed you in my house. For instance, but a moment ago, you said, 'I love you,' yet I couldn't have extorted those words from you with all the powers of Rome! Oh, Lygia! Reason declares this religion to be divine, to be far above all others; the heart feels it, and who could resist two such forces?"

Lygia, fixing on him her blue eyes, which in the light of the moon were like mystic flowers and bedewed like flowers as well, and nestling her head closer to his, said, "Yes, Marcus, that's true."

At that moment both felt supremely happy, for they understood that not only love but another power united them, at once sweet and irresistible, by which love itself became endless, not subject to change, deceit, treason, or even death. Their hearts overflowed with the certainty that come what may, they would not cease to love and to belong to each other;

for that reason an unspeakable peace filled their souls. Vinitius felt besides that not only was their love pure and deep, but it was also altogether new —such as the world didn't yet know and couldn't give. This love gathered all things into his heart: Lygia, Christ's teachings, the moonlight softly resting on the cypresses, and the still night—so that to him the entire universe seemed filled with it.

Then, after a while, in a low and trembling voice, he spoke again. "You'll be the soul of my soul, the dearest in all the world to me. Our hearts will beat together as one—one in prayer and one in gratitude to Christ. Oh, *carissima!* Together to live, together to honor the sweet God, to know that when death comes, our eyes will again open, as after a pleasant sleep, to a new light! What greater happiness could be imagined? I only marvel that I failed to understand this at first. You know what I think? I'm convinced that no one will be able to resist this religion. In two or three hundred years the whole world will have accepted it. People will forget Jupiter, and there will be no God but Christ, no other temples but Christian. Who would not wish to be happy? Ah! I heard Paul's conversation with Petronius, and do you know what Petronius said at the end? 'It's not for me.' He could give no other answer."

"Repeat Paul's words to me," requested Lygia.

"Well, it was at my house one evening. Petronius began to speak playfully and to banter, as he usually does, when Paul said to him 'How can you, O wise Petronius, deny that Christ existed and that He rose from the dead, when you weren't there in the world at the time, but Peter and John were and saw Him, and I myself saw Him on the road to Damascus? If your wisdom could prove us to be liars, then you might rightly deny our testimony.' Petronius replied that he had no intention of denying, for he well knew that many incredible things had happened and were confirmed by unimpeachable witnesses. 'But,' he said, 'it's one thing to discover a new foreign god and another to accept his teaching. I have no wish for anything that might spoil my life and mar its beauty. Be our gods true or false, they're beautiful, their rule is pleasant to us, and we live without anxieties.'

"Paul's reply was, 'You'd reject the teaching of love, justice, and mercy for fear of the anxieties and cares of life? But think, Petronius, is your life really free from anxieties? Behold, neither you, nor any among the richest and most powerful, knows when he falls asleep at night whether he may not wake to a death sentence. But tell me, if Caesar professed this religion that enjoins love and justice, wouldn't your happiness be more secure? You fear lest your pleasures be lost to you, but wouldn't life itself be more joyous in such case?

"'As to the beauty and the adornment of life, if we've raised temples and statues of such surpassing loveliness to evil, revengeful, adulterous, and false divinities, what might you not do in honor of one God of love and truth? You flatter yourself that your lot is a happy one, because you're wealthy and living in luxury, but you might just as easily have been poor and destitute, however highborn, and then indeed it would be better for you in this world if men professed Christ.

"'In Rome, even parents of high station, unwilling to assume the care of raising children, cast them out into the streets; those children are called *alumni*. You, master, might have been such an *alumnus*. But if your parents lived in conformity with our religion, that couldn't happen. Furthermore, if after reaching man's estate, you had married a woman whom you loved, you would have wanted her to remain faithful to you until death. But now look at what's going on among you! Behold what vileness and debasement, what shame, what abuse of marital faith. In fact, you're astonished yourselves when you hear of a woman whom you call a *univira*.[2] But I tell you, women who carry Christ in their hearts will not break faith with their husbands, just as Christian husbands will keep faith with their wives. But you're sure of neither your rulers, nor fathers, nor wives, nor children, nor servants. The whole world trembles before you, but you tremble before even your own slaves, for you know that at any hour they may begin a terrible war against your oppression, such a war as has already been fought more than once.

"'You're rich, but you don't know whether or not tomorrow you'll be commanded to surrender those riches. You're young, but who knows but you may die tomorrow. You love, but treason lies in wait for you. You're fond of villas and statues, but tomorrow you may be banished to the empty spaces of the Pandataria. You have thousands of servants, but tomorrow those servants may spill your blood. If all this is true, how can you possibly be calm and happy, how can you find pleasure in life? But I proclaim love. I proclaim a religion that commands rulers to love their subjects, and masters their slaves; slaves to serve from love; justice and mercy; and that promises, at the end, unlimited and eternal happiness. Therefore, O Petronius, how can you say that this creed ruins life, since it addresses its shortcomings and since you yourself would be a hundred

---

2 Of one husband only.

times happier and more secure were it to win the world as your Roman dominion has won it?'

"Such were Paul's words. Then it was that Petronius said, 'It's not for me.' Feigning weariness, he rose to go, and as he did so he added, 'I prefer my Eunice to all your creed, O little Jew, but I wouldn't care to be matched against you in debate.' As for me, I'd listened with all my soul, and when Paul spoke of our women I honored with all my heart that religion from which you were born—like a lily sprung from a rich soil in April. And I thought to myself then, *Take notice! There is Poppaea, who cast aside two husbands for Nero, there are Calvia Crispinilla and Nigidia, and almost all the women I know, save only Pomponia, who tromp on faith and vows. But she whom I love, she won't desert me nor deceive me nor quench the fire at my hearthstone, though all others in whom I placed my trust might desert and deceive me.* So I spoke to you in my soul, with these words: *How can I show my gratitude to you except by love and honor?* Did you feel that at Antium, I talked incessantly to you as though you were by my side? I love you a hundred times more for having escaped me en route to my house. And I no longer desire Caesar's palace nor its luxury nor its music, but you only. Speak but the word, and we'll leave Rome to take up our residence far away."

Without removing her head from his shoulder, Lygia thoughtfully raised her eyes to the silvered tops of the cypresses and answered, "Very well, Marcus, you've written me about Sicily, where Aulus wishes to settle in old age—"

And Vinitius joyfully interrupted her. "True, *carissima,* our lands adjoin. That's a wonderful coast, the climate is delightful, and the nights are still brighter than in Rome, fragrant and clear. There life and happiness are almost one and the same."

He paused to dream of the future.

"There we may forget all our troubles in groves; among olive orchards, we'll walk and rest in the shade. Oh, Lygia, what a life that will be! Loving each other, gazing together at the sea and the sky, honoring together a kind God, doing peacefully what is just and right."

Both paused, their thoughts intent upon the future. He drew her closer to him, the knightly ring on his finger glittering in the moonlight. In the quarter inhabited by the poor, toiling people, all were asleep; not a sound disturbed the silence.

"Will you permit me to see Pomponia?" asked Lygia.

"Yes, *carissima*, we'll invite them to our home or visit them ourselves. And if you wish, we can take in the Apostle Peter. He is bowed down by age and work. Paul will visit us also—he'll convert Aulus Plautius; and just as soldiers establish colonies in distant lands, so we'll establish a colony of Christians."

Lygia took his hand in hers and would have raised it to her lips, but he whispered, as though fearful that too loud a tone might frighten happiness away, "No, Lygia—no! It's I who honor and adore you. Give me your hands."

"I love you."

He pressed his lips to her hands, white as jasmine. For a time the beating of their own hearts was the only sound they heard. There was not the least stir in the air, and the cypresses were as motionless as if they, too, held their breath in suspense.

All at once, the silence was broken by an unexpected thunder, deep and as if coming from under the earth. A shiver ran through Lygia's body.

Vinitius stood up, saying, "Lions are roaring in the *vivaria*."[3]

Both listened intently. The first thunder was answered by a second, a third, a tenth, from all the various quarters of the city. There were often several thousand lions in Rome, quartered in different arenas, and frequently at nighttime they approached the gratings and, leaning their huge heads against them, proclaimed their longing for liberty and the desert. So it happened now. One answered the other in the stillness of the night, and the whole city was filled with their roaring. There was something so indescribably gloomy and terrible in those roars that Lygia, whose bright and calm visions of the future were now scattered, listened with a troubled heart and with wondering fear and foreboding.

But Vinitius encircled her with his arm and said, "Fear not, *carissima*, the games are at hand, and all the *vivaria* are crowded."

They entered the house of Linus accompanied by the thunder of the lions growing louder and louder.

---

3 A place where animals were kept.

Chapter XL

Meanwhile, in Antium, Petronius gained almost daily victories over the courtiers vying with him for Caesar's favor. The influence of Tigellinus had declined dramatically. In Rome, when it seemed desirable to put out of the way such men as seemed dangerous, to confiscate their estates, to settle public affairs, to prepare spectacles that astonished by their splendor and their barbaric taste, or generally to satisfy the monstrous caprices of Caesar, Tigellinus—crafty and resourceful—seemed absolutely indispensable. In Antium, however, among the palaces overlooking the azure sea, Caesar led a Hellenic life. From morn until night, poems were read, their metrical structure discussed, their subtlest graces pointed out. Music and the theater—in short, everything that Greek genius had invented for the enrichment of life—found ready appreciation. Petronius was more cultured than Tigellinus or the other courtiers, witty, eloquent, full of the most delicate tastes and feelings; thus he couldn't help attaining preeminence. Caesar sought his society, consulted him in all things, and accepted his advice when he was composing. His friendship was stronger than it had ever been.

To the courtiers it appeared that the triumph of Petronius was permanently assured. Even those who had hitherto looked askance at the exquisite Epicurean now surrounded him and sued for his favor. More than one was, in his inner soul, pleased at the victory of a man who always had a definite opinion, who accepted with a skeptical smile the flatteries of his erstwhile enemies, but who, either through indolence or a natural refinement, was not revengeful and didn't use his power to harm or destroy others. There were moments when he might have destroyed even Tigellinus, but he preferred to laugh at him and to expose his lack of education and culture.

The Senate in Rome took breath again. For a month and a half no sentence of death had been pronounced. True, both in Rome and in Antium, tales were whispered of the refinement of debauchery to which Caesar and

Petronius had attained; nevertheless, everyone preferred to be ruled by a refined Caesar than by one bestialized at the hands of a Tigellinus. Tigellinus himself lost his head and hesitated as to whether or not to acknowledge his utter defeat and discrediting. For Caesar repeatedly asserted that in all the Roman court there were but two true Hellenes, two souls that understood each other: himself and Petronius.

The astonishing adroitness of Petronius confirmed everyone in the opinion that his influence would outlast all others, for no one could explain how Caesar could live without him. With whom should he speak of poetry, of music, of racing? In whose eyes could he look to find out if his own creations were indeed perfect? Petronius, indifferent as ever, seemed to attach no weight to his position. As always, he was deliberate, indolent, witty, and skeptical. Often he produced upon others the impression of one who jested at them, at himself, at Caesar, at all the world. At times he even dared to criticize Nero to his face, and even when those around felt he'd gone too far and was asking for almost certain destruction, he instinctively seemed to know how to turn the criticism so that it resulted in his own gain. People marveled at his cleverness and began to think that there was no difficulty or position from which he could not triumphantly extricate himself.

A week after Vinitius's return to Rome, Caesar read to a small audience a passage from his *Troica*. When he'd finished, and the shouts of rapture had ceased, Petronius, in answer to a glance of Caesar, called them "bad verses, fit only to be cast into the flames."

The hearts of all present froze in terror. Never since his childhood had Nero heard such a sentence from the lips of anyone. The face of Tigellinus alone glowed with delight. Vinitius grew pale fearing that Petronius, who rarely got drunk, was now at last intoxicated.

Nero in a honeyed voice, tremulous nonetheless with deeply wounded vanity, inquired, "What defect do you find in them?"

Petronius didn't quail. "Don't believe them," he cried, pointing to those around him. "They know nothing. You asked me what fault I find in your verses. If you wish the truth, I'll tell you. They'd be good for Virgil, for Ovid, even for Homer, but not for you. You're not free to write such verses. The conflagration you described doesn't blaze enough. Don't pay attention to the flatteries of Lucan; had he written the verses, I should own their genius, but in your case it's different. Do you know why? You're greater than they are. From one so richly gifted by the gods, as you are, more is demanded. But you're slothful—you'd prefer to sleep after dinner than to sit yourself down to arduous labor. You have it in you to create a work such as the world has never seen; hence I tell you to your face, *write better ones!*"

And he said this carelessly, as if both bantering and chiding, but Caesar's eyes clouded over with a mist of delight. "The gods have given me a little talent," he said, "but they've given me also something still better—a true critic and a true friend, who alone knows how to tell me the truth to my face."

Saying this, he stretched out his fat hand, overgrown with rusty hair, to a gold candlestick plundered from the temple of Delphi, as if to burn the verses, but Petronius snatched them away from him before the flames had touched the papyrus.

"No, no!" said he. "Even as they are, they belong to mankind. Leave them to me."

"Then allow me to send them to you in a cylinder of my own invention," answered Nero, embracing Petronius.

"True," Nero continued after a moment. "You're right. My conflagration of Troy doesn't scald enough, but I thought it sufficient if I could merely equal Homer. A certain timidity and self-distrust have always hampered me, but you've opened my eyes. But do you know why it's as you say? When a sculptor wishes to create a statue of a god, he seeks a model, but never have I had a model—I've never seen a burning city; consequently there is a lack of truth in my description."

"Then I must tell you that only a great artist could appreciate that fact."

Nero grew thoughtful, and after a while he said, "Answer me one question, Petronius: Are you sorry that Troy was burned?"

"Am I sorry? By the lame husband of Venus, not in the least, and I'll tell you why. Troy wouldn't have been burned had Prometheus not given fire to man, nor the Greeks made war upon Priam. But had there been no fire, Aeschylus wouldn't have written his *Prometheus,* just as Homer, without the Trojan War, wouldn't have written his *Iliad.* I prefer the existence of *Prometheus* and the *Iliad* to the preservation of a small and probably unclean city, in the midst of which some paltry procurator might now be annoying you by his quarrels with the Areopagus."[1]

---

1   From the Greek court by that name on Mars Hill in Athens; later expanded to refer to any court.

"That's what I call speaking reasonably," replied Caesar. "For poetry and art, it's allowable, indeed it's necessary, to sacrifice everything. Happy the Achaians who gave a subject to the *Iliad;* happy Priam, who witnessed the destruction of his native city. As for me, I've never seen a burning city."

A moment of silence followed. Tigellinus was the first to break it.

"But I've already told you, Caesar: Say but the word and I'll burn Antium. Or, if you feel sorry for these villas and palaces, I'll order the ships in Ostia to be burned, or I'll build a wooden city for you beneath the Alban Hills, which you can set fire to yourself. Is that your wish?"

Nero cast upon him a glaı of withering contempt. "Am I to gaze on burning woodsheds?" he asked. "Your brains have left you, Tigellinus. Furthermore, I can see that you don't feel my talents are worth much, or my *Troica*, for that matter, since you don't feel it worthwhile to make a *real* sacrifice in order to make it possible."

Tigellinus drew back, abashed. Nero, as if wishing to change the conversation, added, "Summer is at hand. Oh, how Rome must stink by now! And I guess we'll have to return to it for the summer games."

Suddenly Tigellinus said, "O Caesar, when you dismiss the Augustinians, please permit me to remain a while with you."

An hour later, Vinitius, returning home with Petronius from Caesar's villa, said, "I had a moment's fright on your account, wondering if you were drunk and had irretrievably ruined yourself. Remember that you're playing with death."

"It's my arena," said Petronius carelessly. "I enjoy the feeling that I'm the best gladiator there. See how it ended? My influence has only grown greater. He'll send me his verses in a cylinder, which I wager will be as immensely rich in value as it will be immensely poor in taste. I'll order my doctor to keep laxatives in it. I have a second reason. Tigellinus, witnessing my success, will doubtless attempt to imitate me. I can imagine what will happen when he attempts a jest. It'll be as if a Pyrenean bear were to dance a tightrope—I'll laugh like Democritus.[2] If I willed it, I might easily ruin

---

2 Famous philosopher of Abdera (460–370 B.C.); called the laughing philosopher. Because of inherited wealth, he was able to travel extensively throughout Asia and Africa in search of knowledge; as a result, no one exceeded him in wisdom until Aristotle. He took the studies of Leucippus and evolved the atomic theory. The follies of mankind made him laugh; hence his nickname. According to tradition, he put out his eyes in order to be less disturbed by externals when he was studying the things that really mattered.

Tigellinus and succeed him as the Praetorian prefect. Then Ahenobarbus himself would be in my clutches. But I'm indolent, preferring my present life—even Caesar's verses—to trouble."

Admiringly, Vinitius said, "What adroitness to turn criticism into flattery! But tell me, are those verses so bad? I don't claim to be a judge in such matters."

"No worse than many others. Lucan has more talent in his little finger, yet Ahenobarbus is not entirely lacking. He has, above all, a great love for poetry and music. Two days from now we shall call upon him to recite his verses in honor of Aphrodite, which he'll finish today or tomorrow. There'll be only a small audience—myself, you, Tullius Senecio, and young Nerva. As for Nero's verses, it's not true what I once said—that I use them after feasting for the same purpose to which Vitelius devotes flamingo feathers. To be honest, they're sometimes eloquent. Hecuba's[3] words are touching: She complains of the pains of childbirth, and Nero found apt-enough expressions, perhaps because he himself gives birth to every verse in torment. At times, I feel sorry for him. By Pollux, what a marvelous mixture he is! The fifth stave was missing[4] in Caligula, but even he never did such strange things as Nero does. Caligula was insane, but he was not such a ridiculous creature."

"Can anyone foretell where Ahenobarbus's madness will lead?" asked Vinitius.

"No living man. Things may happen whose very remembrance may for entire centuries make the hair stand up on men's heads. That's just what interests me. Though I'm frequently bored, even as Jupiter-Ammon[5] in the desert, yet I believe that under any other Caesar, I should have been still more bored.

"Your Jewish friend is eloquent, I must admit. If his religion triumphs, then our gods must watch out, lest they be retired on the shelf. Of course, if Caesar were a Christian, we'd all feel more secure. But your prophet of Tarsus, in reasoning with me, failed to understand what it is that attracts

---

3 Priam's wife.
4 He was not quite all there.
5 The Greek and Roman conception of the Egyptian sun god, Amen-Ra. The Egyptians depict Zeus-Ammon (or Jupiter-Ammon) as having the head of a ram. The Oracle of Jupiter-Ammon was greatly venerated and consulted by the great of the world, including King Laomedon of Troy, Cepheus (father of Andromeda), King Croesus of Lydia, and the people of Sparta.

me most about life. He who never plays dice, will never lose his property; nevertheless, men play dice. There is in it some strange delight and oblivion. I've known knights and the sons of senators who voluntarily chose to become gladiators. You tell me I play with life, and it's true enough, but I do it because it amuses me. Your Christian virtues would bore me as much in one day as do the discourses of Seneca—that's why the eloquence of Paul was wasted on me. He ought to understand that men such as I can never accept his creed.

"With you it's different. A man of your disposition might either hate the very name *Christian* or might become one himself. Yawningly, I recognize the truth of their arguments. We *do* engage in madness; we *are* hurrying to the verge of an abyss; an unknown something *does* signal to us from the future; something *is* breaking under our feet; something *is* dying around us. So be it! But at least we'll be able to die. In the meantime, we have no desire to add a burden to life or to experience death before it arrives. Life exists for itself alone, not for death."

"Nevertheless, I'm sorry for you, Petronius."

"Don't be sorry for me, any more than I am myself. Once you felt glad to be part of us, and while campaigning in Armenia, you were always longing for Rome."

"And now, also, I long for Rome."

"Yes, because you're in love with a Christian vestal dwelling in the Trans-Tiber. I neither wonder at this nor reproach you for it. Rather I wonder that, in spite of a creed that you've described as a sea of happiness, and in spite of that love that will soon be crowned, sadness never leaves your face. Pomponia Graecina is eternally serious, and you, since you became a Christian, have ceased to smile. So don't try to tell me it's a joyous creed. You've returned from Rome more despondent than ever. If Christians love this way, by the yellow curls of Bacchus, I for one will not follow your example."

"Let me explain," replied Vinitius. "I swear to you, not by the curls of Bacchus, but by the soul of my father, that never before did I experience even a foretaste of that happiness in which I live at present. Nevertheless, I feel an endless longing for her, and what's even stranger, when I'm away from Lygia I have a foreboding that some danger is hanging over her. What it may be and when it may come, I know not, but I feel it in advance just as one feels a coming storm."

"In two days I'll try to obtain permission for you to leave Antium for as long a time as you please. Poppaea is a little more tranquil, and so far as I can see, no peril threatens either you or Lygia from that quarter."

"Yet today she asked me what I'd been doing in Rome, and my absence was supposedly a secret."

"Perhaps she gave orders to have your steps dogged by spies. But even she must reckon with me in the future."

"Paul," resumed Vinitius, "told me that God sometimes sends warnings, but forbids the belief in omens, so I struggle against this feeling but cannot ward it off. Let me tell you what happened, just to get this weight off my heart. Lygia and I were sitting side by side on a night as bright as this, laying out plans for the future. I can't begin to tell you how calm and happy we were. Suddenly the lions began to roar. It's no uncommon sound in Rome, but still, since that moment, I've had no rest. It seemed to me there was a menace in it, a presage of trouble. You know I don't frighten easily, but that sound filled all the night with terror. It came so strangely and unexpectedly that those roars still resound in my ears, and constant uneasiness unsettles my heart as though Lygia needed my assistance against something terrible—perhaps even against those very lions. I'm in torture. Therefore, please obtain permission for me to leave; otherwise I'll go without it. I can't remain here. I repeat: I cannot."

Petronius laughed. "Not yet," he said, "has it come to the point of throwing men of consular dignity or their wives to the lions in the arenas. Any other death may be in store for you, but not that. Of course they may not have been lions, for the German bisons roar just as loudly. As for me, I ridicule omens and fate. Last night was warm, and I saw stars falling like rain. More than one man would have grown uneasy at such a sight, but I thought to myself, *If my star is among them, at least I won't lack company.*"

Then he stopped short.

After a moment's thought, he added, "Look at it this way: If your Christ rose from the dead, He may be able to protect you both from death."

"He may," answered Vinitius, gazing upward at the star-strewn vault of heaven.

Chapter XLI

Nero played and sang a hymn in honor of the Lady of Cyprus, the words and music of which he'd composed himself. He was in good voice that day and felt that his music had really captivated his hearers. This feeling added such power to the sounds he produced that his own soul thrilled, and he actually seemed inspired. At last he grew pale from genuine emotion. For perhaps the first time in his life he turned a deaf ear to the praises of his audience, as he sat for a time with his hands leaning on the kithara and his head bowed.

Then, suddenly rising, he said, "I'm tired and need fresh air. Meanwhile, tune my kithara." Wrapping a silk kerchief around his throat, he turned to Petronius and Vinitius, who were sitting in the corner of the hall, and said, "Come with me. Give me your arm, Vinitius, for strength fails me. Petronius will talk to me of music."

They went out on the terrace of the palace, which was inlaid with alabaster and sprinkled with saffron.[1]

"Here one can breathe more freely," said Nero. "My soul is moved and sad, although I see that with the song I've just sung to you as a test, I can make my appearance before the public and gain a triumph such as has not fallen to the lot of any other Roman."

"You may appear here and in Rome and in Achaia. With all my heart and all my soul, I admire you, divine one!" replied Petronius.

"I know. You're too indolent to force yourself to flattery, and you're as sincere as Tullius Senecio, but you're a better judge than he is. Tell me, what do you think of the music?"

"Well, when I listen to a poem, when I gaze upon a quadriga driven by

---

1   From the saffron crocus. In Greece and Rome, it was strewn in halls, courts, and the-aters as a perfume; also in Roman baths. In Rome, the streets were strewn with saf-fron whenever Nero entered the city. From time immemorial, saffron has been asso-ciated with royalty and opulence.

you in the Circus or on a beautiful statue, temple, or picture, I feel that I embrace completely what I see in my own mind; but when I listen to music, especially yours, new beauty and new delight open up before me. I pursue them, I try to capture them, but before I can gather them in, new and newer ones flow in upon me like waves of the sea rolling on from infinity. So I say to you that music is like the sea: We stand on the shore and see boundless space before us, but we cannot see the other shore."

"Ah, what a deep judge you are!" exclaimed Nero, and they walked on for a time in silence, save for the saffron rustling under their feet.

"You've perfectly expressed my own thoughts," said Nero at last. "I've always said that in all Rome only you truly understand me. I think of music as you do. When I play and sing, I see things that I didn't even know existed in my own empire—or even in the whole world. Lo, I'm Caesar and the world belongs to me—I can do anything and everything. Yet music reveals to me new kingdoms, new mountains, new seas, new delights, all previously unknown to me. In most cases, I can't even understand them—I can only feel them. I feel the presence of the gods, I see Olympus. A certain breeze from beyond the earth blows on me; I behold, as in mist, some immeasurable greatness, calm and bright as the rising sun. The entire *spheros*[2] appears to me, and I must tell you"—here Nero's voice trembled with genuine wonder—"that I, Caesar and god, feel myself in such times to be as insignificant as dust. Can you believe that?"

"Yes; only a true artist can feel his insignificance in the presence of art."

"This is a night of sincerity; hence I spread out to you my soul as to a friend. Let me say more. Do you think I'm blind or bereft of reason? Do you think I'm unaware that in Rome, people write insults on the walls against me, call me a matricide, an uxoricide, consider me to be a monster and tyrant because Tigellinus obtained a few sentences of death against my enemies? Indeed, my dear Petronius, they call me a tyrant, and I know it. They have imputed to me such hideous cruelty that sometimes I ask myself whether I'm indeed a monster. But these people fail to understand that a man's deeds may be cruel, while he himself may not be. Ah, no one will believe—perhaps not even you, *carissime*—that at times when music sways my soul, I feel myself as innocent and joyful as a child in the cradle. By the stars that shine above us, I swear that I'm speaking the pure

---

2 Universe, the Infinite.

truth. People don't know how much goodness lies in this heart nor what treasures I can perceive there when music opens the door to them."

Petronius had no doubt that, for the moment, Nero was speaking sincerely and that music might bare to the light the nobler faculties of his soul hidden under the mountains of egotism, debauchery, and crime.

"It's too bad people don't know you as I do. Rome has never really been able to fully appreciate or understand you."

Caesar leaned more heavily on the arm of Vinitius, as if sinking beneath the burden of injustice.

"Tigellinus," he said, "has told me that in the Senate it's whispered that Diodorus and Terpnos play the kithara better than I do—they would deny me this! Now you, who always speak only the truth, tell me. Do they play better than I, or only as well?"

"By no means. Your touch is surer and has greater power. The artist is evident in you; in them one sees only skillful artisans. On the contrary, those who have already heard their music better understand what you are."

"If that be so, let them live. They will never guess what a service you've just rendered them. Of course, had I sentenced them, I'd be obliged to find others to take their places."

"And people would have said that for the sake of music you've destroyed music in the empire. Don't kill art for art's sake, O divine one!"

"How different you are from Tigellinus," replied Nero. "But, you see, I'm an artist in everything, and since music opens out to me new spaces that I hadn't even imagined, regions that are not under my rule, joys and delights that I hadn't known, I cannot live an ordinary life. Music reveals to me the extraordinary; therefore I seek it with all the powers with which the gods have dowered me. At times it appears to me that if I'm to reach those Olympian heights, I must accomplish something that no man has yet accomplished—in good and in evil, I must excel all humanity. I know, too, that the people suspect me of insanity, but I'm not insane—I'm seeking! And if I'm going mad, it's from weariness and impatience at my own failures. I *am* seeking! Do you understand me? I wish to be greater than a mere man, for only in this way can I be the greatest as an artist."

Here he lowered his voice so that Vinitius couldn't hear him, and placing his lips to the ear of Petronius, he whispered, "Do you know it was chiefly for this that I sentenced my mother and my wife to death? At the gates of the unknown world, I wished to lay the greatest sacrifice of which man is capable. Then I thought something would later happen, something that would open the doors behind which I could perceive the unknown. Let it be something marvelous or terrible beyond human conception, be it only great and uncommon! But the sacrifice was insufficient to open the door of the empyrean. Something still greater is necessary—and let it happen—as the Fates determine."

"What do you plan to do?"

"You'll see—and sooner than you imagine. Meantime, know that there are two Neros: one the Nero known to the world, the other an artist known only to you. If the artist is as pitiless as death or as full of folly as Bacchus, it's only because he's stifled by the flatness and the misery of common life, and he'd like to destroy it, even if he has to do it with fire or iron. Oh, how flat and savorless this world will be when I'm gone! No man has suspected—not even you—what an artist I am. But it's precisely because of this that I suffer so much, and I tell you sincerely that my soul sometimes grows as gloomy as those cypresses that loom up darkly before us. It's hard for a man to bear simultaneously the burden of supreme power and the burden of the greatest talent."

"I sympathize with you, O Caesar, with all my heart, and with me the earth and the sea, not to mention Vinitius, who idolizes you in his soul."

"I've always loved him," said Nero, "though he serves Mars and not the Muses."

"He serves Aphrodite before all," replied Petronius.

Suddenly the resolve came upon him to straighten out at one blow the affair of his sister's son and to eliminate all the dangers that threatened him.

"He's as enamored as Troilus was with Cressida. Permit him, O Lord, to return to Rome, for here he will wither. Were you aware that the Lygian hostage you gave him is found again? Vinitius, in setting out for Antium, consigned her to the care of one Linus. I didn't mention it to you, for you were composing your hymn, and that was the all-important thing. Vinitius would have made her his mistress, but when he found her to be as virtuous as Lucretia, he fell in love with her very virtue and now wishes to marry her. She's the daughter of a king and will bring no dishonor upon him. But he, like a true soldier, sighs and languishes, awaiting the permission of his imperator."

"An emperor does not select wives for his soldiers. Why, therefore, does he await my permission?"

"Lord, I've told you that he adores you."

"Then the more certain may he be of my permission. That's a beautiful maiden, but too narrow in the hips. Augusta Poppaea complained against her that she had cast an evil eye on our child in the gardens at the Palatine."

"But I told Tigellinus that the gods are not subject to evil charms. Remember, O divine one, how he grew confused before you and how you exclaimed, 'I have him!'"

"I remember." He turned to Vinitius. "Do you love her, as Petronius says?"

"Lord, I love her!" replied Vinitius.

"Then I order you to go straight to Rome tomorrow to marry her. Appear not before me without the wedding ring."

"From my heart and my soul, I thank you, O lord!"

"Oh, how pleasant it is," cried Caesar, "to make men happy! Would that I might do nothing else all the rest of my life."

"Grant us one favor more, O divinity," said Petronius. "Declare your will in the presence of Augusta. Vinitius wouldn't dare to wed a woman displeasing to the Augusta, but you, O lord, may with but one word dissipate her prejudices by declaring that you're commanding this marriage."

"Very well," said Caesar. "I can deny nothing to you and Vinitius."

He turned towards the villa, and they followed him, their hearts beating with triumphant joy. Vinitius could barely keep from embracing Petronius at the thought that now all obstacles had been overcome.

In the great hall of the villa, young Nerva and Tullius Senecio were entertaining the Augusta. Terpnos and Diodorus were tuning their kitharas. Nero, entering, took his seat in a chair inlaid with tortoiseshell and whispered something in the ear of a Greek lad standing beside him. The lad disappeared and soon returned with a golden casket.

Nero opened it and, taking out a necklace of large opals, exclaimed, "These are gems worthy of the evening!"

"The light of Aurora glitters in them," said Poppaea, assuming the necklace was intended for her.

Caesar dangled, now raising, now lowering, the necklace in the air. At last he said, "Vinitius, you shall give this necklace, from me, to her whom I command you to marry, the youthful daughter of the Lygian king."

Poppaea's eyes, glittering with wrath and sudden amazement, passed from Caesar to Vinitius and finally rested on Petronius. But he, leaning carelessly on the arm of a chair, passed his hand up and down the fingerboard of the harp as though wishing to fix its form firmly in his mind.

Vinitius, after having thanked Caesar, approached Petronius and said, "How can I ever repay you for what you've done for me today?"

"Sacrifice a pair of swans to Euterpe,"[3] answered Petronius, "praise Caesar's songs, and laugh at omens. I trust that the roaring of lions will no longer disturb your sleep, nor that of your Lygian lily."

"No," answered Vinitius. "Now my fears are all gone—how could they not be!"

"May fortune favor you! But now be careful, for Caesar is again taking up his kithara. Hold your breath, listen, and shed tears."

And, in fact, at this moment, Caesar had taken the kithara and raised his eyes. In the hall, all conversation ceased, and men stood still as if petrified. Terpnos and Diodorus, who were to accompany Caesar, looked on, gazing now at each other, now at Caesar's lips, waiting for the first notes.

Suddenly, in the vestibule arose a tumult and alarm; from behind the curtain Caesar's freedman Phaon and the consul, Lecanius, burst upon the scene. Caesar frowned angrily.

"Forgive me, O divine Emperor!" cried the panting Phaon. "Rome is on fire! The greater part of the city is in flames!"

At this news, all leaped to their feet.

Nero laid down the kithara and cried, "Oh, gods! I shall see a burning city and be able to finish my *Troica.*" Then he turned to the consul. "If I set out at once," he asked, "will I be in time to see the conflagration?"

"Lord!" replied the pallid-faced consul, "a sea of fire floats over the city; smoke suffocates the citizens; the people faint in their delirium or throw themselves madly into the fire. Rome is perishing, lord!"

There was a moment of silence, broken by a cry from Vinitius: *"Vae misero milhi!"*[4]

And the young man, casting aside his toga, clad only in a single tunic, rushed out of the palace.

Nero raised his hands towards heaven and cried: "Woe to you, holy city of Priam!"

---

3   The muse of harmony—appropriately for this occasion!
4   "Woe is me!"

Chapter XLII

Vinitius took time only to command a few slaves to follow him. Then springing on his horse, he galloped at full speed through the deserted streets of Antium towards Laurentum. The awful news had thrown him into a state of frenzy and utter bewilderment. His brain in a whirl, he felt only that the black specter of misfortune was perched on his shoulders, shouting into his ears, "Rome is burning!" and that it was lashing both him and his steed to the utmost possible speed. Laying his bare head on the horse's neck, he rushed blindly on, taking no note of the obstacles that might stand in his way.

In that silent and calm night, the horse and its rider loomed like phantoms in the moonlight. The Idumean stallion, lowering its ears and stretching out its neck, shot on like an arrow past the motionless cypresses and white villas hidden among them. The trampling of hooves on the flagstones roused the dogs here and there. Some barked and chased after the apparition; others, startled by its suddenness, howled their dismay to the moon. The slaves, following behind Vinitius on slower horses, soon fell far in the rear. When he'd whirled like a tempest through sleeping Laurentum, he turned towards Ardea, in which—as in Aricium, Bovillae, and Ustrinum—he'd kept horses from the time of his arrival at Antium, so as to cover the distance between that city and Rome in the shortest possible time. Remembering these relays, he didn't hesitate to tax his horse's strength to the utmost.

Beyond Ardea to the northeast it seemed to him that a rosy reflection was mounting in the sky. It might be the dawn, for in July day broke early, but he couldn't restrain a cry of rage and despair when he recognized that it was probably the glare of the conflagration.

The words of Lecanius rang in his ears: "The city is a sea of flames."

For a time he felt the threat of madness in his brain, for he'd lost all hope of saving Lygia or even of reaching the city before it became a heap of ashes. His thoughts outsped his horse and flew before him like a flock of dark birds, monstrous and despairing. Although he didn't know in which quarter of the city the flames had started, he assumed that the Trans-Tiber, packed with tenements, lumberyards, and wooden sheds serving as slave markets, would become the first victim to the flames.

Fires were not infrequent in Rome and were usually accompanied by looting and pillaging, especially in the quarters inhabited by the poor and the semibarbarous. What, therefore, could be expected to occur in the Trans-Tiber, where was concentrated the rabble that flooded into Rome from all over the world? The thought of Ursus and his superhuman strength flashed into his mind, but what could one man do, even a titan, against the overwhelming force of a fire?

The fear of another slave uprising had hovered over Rome for years. From lip to lip had passed the report that hundreds of thousands of these people still cherished the dreams they'd inherited from the time of Spartacus[1] and waited but for the first opportune moment to take up arms against their conquerors and against Rome. And now the moment had come! Even now battle and slaughter—as well as fire—might be raging in the city. Perhaps the Praetorians had hurled themselves on the city and were slaughtering at the command of Caesar.

At that thought, terror raised the hair on his head. He recalled the tales of burning cities so persistently repeated at Caesar's court and Caesar's complaints that he was forced to describe a burning city without ever having seen one, his contemptuous retort when Tigellinus offered to burn Antium or an artificial wooden city, and finally his invectives against Rome and against the pestilent alleys of the Suburra. Yes, Caesar had ordered the burning of Rome! He alone could give such an order, as Tigellinus alone could carry it out. And if Rome were burning at Caesar's command, who could be sure that he wouldn't order that the people be slaughtered as well? The monster was fully capable of such a deed.

Conflagration . . . a revolt of the slaves . . . a slaughter of the citizens. What hideous chaos! What an unleashing of popular fury and of the forces of destruction!

And Lygia was in the midst of it all!

The groans of Vinitius were mingled with the snorting and wheezing of the horse, which, scaling the hill towards Aricium, was expending its last breath.

---

1 Gladiator who led Rome's most famous and terrible slave revolt (73–71 B.C.); he was defeated by Crassus.

Who could rescue her from the burning city? Who could save her?

Vinitius, almost lying upon the horse, thrust his fingers into his hair, ready to gnaw the horse's neck in his agony. Just then, a horseman, riding like a hurricane from the opposite direction, shouted as he passed, "Rome is perishing!" and raced on.

The ears of Vinitius caught but one more word, "Gods." The rest was drowned in the thunder of hooves, but that word sobered him: *gods!*

He raised his head and, stretching out his hand towards the star-strewn heavens, began to pray.

"I call not to you whose temples are burning, but to You! You've known suffering! You alone are merciful! You alone can understand human pain and suffering! You came into the world to teach people mercy, so show it now. If You are such as Peter and Paul describe, rescue my Lygia. Take her in Your arms, and carry her out of the flames. You have the power to do it! Restore her to me, and I'll give You my blood. And if You won't do this for my sake, do it for hers. She loves and trusts You. You promised life and happiness after death, but she doesn't want to die yet. Let her live. Again, Lord, I beg, take her in Your arms, and carry her out of Rome. You can do it, unless it isn't Your will."

He stopped, for he felt that further prayer might change into threats; he feared offending God at the very moment when he most needed His pity and mercy. He was terrified at the very thought of that, and so, to banish all rebellious ideas, he once more applied the whip to his horse. He whipped all the more eagerly as he saw the white walls of Aricium, marking the halfway point on the journey to Rome, now gleaming before him, lit by the rays of the moon.

A moment later, he passed at full speed the temple of Mercury that stood in a grove before the city. It was evident that news of the disaster had already reached here, for there was strange excitement in front of the temple. While passing, Vinitius noticed throngs of men on the steps and between the columns, bearing torches and imploring the protection of the deity. Moreover, the road was no longer deserted and free, as it had been beyond Ardea. Though the crowds were hurrying to the grove through the byways, nonetheless, on the main road, people yielded before the onrushing horseman. From the town came the sound of voices.

Vinitius burst into Aricium like a hurricane, overturning and trampling a number of people who stood in his way. Shouts went up from all sides: "Rome is burning! The city is on fire! May the gods rescue Rome!"

The horse stumbled and fell, but reined in by the strong hand of the rider, it raised up on its haunches in front of the tavern where Vinitius had another steed. Slaves awaited their master's commands before the tavern and, at his command, hastened to bring on a fresh horse.

Vinitius, seeing a detachment of ten Praetorian cavalry, evidently bearing news from the city to Antium, sprang towards them eagerly.

"What part of the city is on fire?"

"Who are you?" asked the decurian.

"Vinitius, a military tribune; an Augustinian. Answer me or pay with your head."

"Lord, the fire broke out by the Circus Maximus. By the time we were sent out, the center of the city was already in flames."

"And the Trans-Tiber?"

"The flames haven't reached there yet, but with irresistible force, it's spreading rapidly on all sides. People are perishing from heat and smoke, and no rescue is possible."

A fresh horse was now led out. Vinitius jumped on its back and galloped away. He directed his course towards Albanum, leaving Alba Longea and her beautiful lake on his right. The road from Aricium now led up a mountain; thus, he could see neither the horizon nor the town of Albanum on the other side. Vinitius knew that when he reached the summit he would see not only Bovillae and Ustrinum, where fresh horses were awaiting him, but Rome itself. For beyond Albanum, on both sides of the Via Appia, stretched the low Campania, along which ran only the arches of the aqueducts, so that the city would no longer be hidden from sight.

From the top I'll see the flames, he said to himself and again applied the whip. Before he reached the top, however, the wind was in his face and the odor of smoke in his nostrils. Suddenly a golden gleam lit up the hilltop before him.

The fire! thought Vinitius.

The night had long since paled, the dawn had given way to day, and on all the near mountains shone golden and rosy gleams that might come either from burning Rome or from the rising sun. When at last he reached the summit, a terrible spectacle burst upon his sight: The entire lowland was covered with smoke, as if a gigantic cloud overlay the earth. It engulfed the towns, the aqueducts, the villas, the trees. And beyond this ghastly mass of gray, loomed the burning city.

But the fire didn't have the shape of a column of fire, as it does when a single great building is burning, but rather that of a long ribbon resembling the dawn. Above that belt rose a wavering billow of smoke—black in some places, rosy in others, blood-colored in still others—writhing like a snake that first withdraws then attacks. The monstrous wave seemed at times to cover even that belt of fire, so that it became as narrow as a tape, but at times it was illuminated from beneath, and its lower convolutions changed into waves of flames. Both the belt and the tape extended from one side of the horizon to the other, shutting it out at times as a belt of forests might shut it out. The Sabine Hills were utterly lost to view.

Vinitius's first thought was that not only the city, but the whole world as well was on fire, and that no human being could be rescued from this ocean of flame and smoke. The wind now blew still stronger from the fire, spreading the smell of burning matter and the mist that had begun to envelop even the nearest objects.

Daylight had now come bright and clear. The sun lit up the crests of the hills around the Aqua Albana, but its golden rays shone a pale and sickly red through the mist. Nearing Albanum, Vinitius rode into smoke still denser and more impenetrable. The town itself was completely engulfed, and the terrified citizens crowded into the streets. It was fearful to think what Rome must be like when in Albanum it was almost impossible to breathe.

Fresh despair gripped him, and terror once again raised the hair on his head. He sought to comfort himself as best he could.

It's utterly impossible, he thought, *that the whole city can burn at once. The wind blowing from the north drives the smoke this way only. There is none on the other side. The Trans-Tiber, divided by the river, may be entirely safe. In any case, Ursus has but to take Lygia through the Porta Janicula to save them both. Equally impossible is it that the whole population should perish and that the world-ruling city should be swept away with all its inhabitants. In cities that have been stormed and captured, when slaughter and fire are doing their worst, some few of the inhabitants always manage to escape. Why then should Lygia perish? May God protect her—He who conquered death Himself!*

Again he began to pray, and, according to the custom in which he'd been raised, he made vows to Christ of offerings and sacrifices.

When he'd passed Albanum, where most of the inhabitants swarmed onto roofs and trees for a better view of the conflagration, his terror subsided somewhat. He remembered too that Lygia was protected not merely by Ursus and Linus, but by Peter the Apostle. This was an added solace, for to him, Peter was a mysterious and almost supernatural being. From the time that he'd first heard him in Ostranium, a strange feeling had come over him. Of this he'd written to Lygia while in Antium: "Every word of this old man is truth or must become truth." The closer his acquaintance had grown with the Apostle during his sickness, the more this impression had deepened, until at last it had become unshakable faith. So since Peter had blessed his love and promised Lygia to him, Lygia couldn't perish in the flames. The city might burn, but not a spark would fall upon her garments.

Under the spell of sleeplessness, furious riding, and wild emotions, Vinitius now felt a strange exaltation. Everything seemed possible in this mood. Peter would make the sign of the cross over the flames, would part them by a word, and he and they would pass through unhurt. Moreover, the future was known to Peter; hence he'd doubtless foreseen the calamity and had warned the Christians and led them forth from the city—Lygia, whom he loved as his own child, would surely be among the saved. A stronger and stronger hope entered his heart. Were they fleeing from the city, he might find them in Bovillae or meet them on the way. At any moment the beloved face might emerge from the smoke that was spreading still wider over the whole Campania.

This seemed the more probable, since he now began to meet more people who, leaving the city, had sought the Alban Hills to escape from the fire and the smoke. Before he'd reached Ustrinum, he was compelled to slacken his pace because of the crowding on the road. Besides pedestrians with bundles on their backs, he met horses with packs, mules and vehicles laden with household effects, and litters in which slaves conveyed the richer citizens.

Ustrinum was so crowded by the fugitives from Rome that he found it difficult to pass through them. In the marketplace, under the columns of the temple, and in the streets were vast swarms of fugitives. Here and there people were erecting tents, under which entire families were seeking refuge. Others camped under the open sky, shouting invocations to the gods or cursing fate.

In the general panic, it was difficult to obtain any information. The people whom Vinitius addressed either made no reply or cried out with fright-crazed eyes that the city and the world were perishing. Every moment brought fresh crowds of men, women, and children from the direction of Rome, which increased the uproar even more. Some, having lost their dear ones in the crowds, were now desperately searching for them. Others fought for a camping place. Crowds of savage herdsmen from the Campania rushed onward to the town, urged by curiosity or the hope of easy plunder. Already the slaves and gladiators had begun to plunder the houses and villas in the town, fighting with the soldiers who'd been summoned to the defense of the citizens.

In a tavern, surrounded by a crowd of Batavian slaves, a senator named Junius provided Vinitius with the first detailed story of the conflagration. The fire, it seemed, had begun where the Circus Maximus bordered upon the Palatine and Caelian Hills but had spread with incomprehensible speed until it had engulfed the entire heart of the city. Not since the conquest of Brennus[2] had such a catastrophe befallen the city.

"The entire Circus," said Junius, "has gone up in flames, together with the adjacent stores and houses. The Aventine and Caelian Hills are on fire, and the flames from the Palatine have reached the Carinae."

Junius, who possessed a magnificent palace on the Carinae, groaned. But Vinitius shook him by the shoulder. "I also have a house on the Carinae," he said, "but when everything is perishing, let that perish, too."

Then, recalling the advice he had given to Lygia—to go to the house of the Auli—and fearing she might have followed it, he asked, "How about the Patrician Quarter?"

"On fire!" replied Junius.

"And the Trans-Tiber?"

Junius cast on him a look of amazement.

"Why should you care about the Trans-Tiber?" he asked, pressing his aching temples with his hands.

"The Trans-Tiber is more important to me than the whole of Rome!" exclaimed Vinitius furiously.

"You can reach it only by the Via Portuensis, for the heat on the Aventine would suffocate you. The Trans-Tiber? I know not. The flames hadn't yet reached it when I left; whether they've reached it now, the gods alone can tell."

Junius hesitated for a while, then continued in a low voice. "I know that you won't betray me, so let me tell you that this is no common fire. We were not allowed to save the Circus. I heard for myself. When the

---

2 Leader of the Gauls who defeated the Romans in 390 B.C.

surrounding houses began to burn, thousands of voices shouted, 'Death to the rescuers!' Certain men ran through the city and hurled burning torches into the houses. People are revolting and crying out that the city is burning by Caesar's command. I will say nothing more. Woe to the city, woe to us all, and woe to me! What is happening there, no human tongue can say. People are rioting in the flames or slaying one another in the confusion. This is the end of Rome."

And again he fell to wailing. "Woe to the city, and woe to all of us!"

Vinitius leaped on his horse and hastened on by the Via Appia. He now found that his difficulty was to force a passage through the torrent of men and vehicles pouring out from the city. That city extended before him as on an outstretched palm, enclosed in a monstrous conflagration. From the sea of fire and smoke came an awful heat, and the shrieks of human beings could not drown the hissing and the roaring of the flames.

Chapter XLIII

A s Vinitius drew nearer he realized that it was easier to get *to* Rome than to get inside the walls. He could barely force his way through the struggling multitudes on the Via Appia. In the temple of Mars, near the Porta Appia, the throng broke through the doors to find shelter for the night. In the cemeteries, the larger tombs had all been commandeered through severe fighting, often accompanied by bloodshed.

The disorder in Ustrinum gave but a mild foretaste of what was happening under the walls of the city itself. All regard for authority, for rank, for family ties, for differences of classes, had ceased to exist. Slaves were seen cudgeling citizens. Gladiators, intoxicated with the wine they'd plundered in the Emporium, gathered in large groups and, with wild cries, ran through the square, chasing people, trampling upon them, robbing them.

A number of enslaved barbarians, exhibited for sale in the city, had fled from the booths of their vendors. The conflagration and destruction of the city were for them the end of slavery and the hour of vengeance. While the citizens who'd lost all their property in the fire were lifting supplicating hands to the gods, these slaves, with howls of joy, fell upon them, dispersed the crowds, tore the clothing from the shoulders of the people, and carried off the younger women. Slaves who'd served long years in Rome, tramps with no clothing save woolen rags on their loins, terrible figures from the alleys who were rarely seen on the streets in daytime—whose very existence would have been unsuspected—joined in these acts of violence. Among them were Asians, Africans, Greeks, Thracians, Germans, and Britons shouting in all the languages of the earth, wild and dissolute, maddened with the thought that the hour had come when they could compensate themselves for years of suffering and misery.

Amid that awful crowd, in the glare of the sun and fire, glittered the helmets of the Praetorians, whose protection was sought by the more peaceful citizens and who were forced into frequent hand-to-hand conflicts with the bestialized rabble. Vinitius had seen many cities stormed, but never had he

337

The young tribune risked his life at every moment.

witnessed a spectacle in which despair, tears, pain, groans, barbaric joy, madness, rage, and license mingled together in so monstrous a chaos.

The fire roared above this weltering, maddened crowd, blazing on the hilltops of the greatest city on earth, scattering confusion with its fiery breath, and enveloping it in smoke that shut out the blue of the heavens. The young tribune, with the greatest effort, risking his life at every moment, at last gained the Porta Appia, but there he found that he couldn't reach the city through the quarter of the Porta Capena, not just because of the crowd, but also because of the terrible heat that from beyond the gate made the very air tremble. At that time the bridge at the Porta Trigenia, opposite the temple of Bona Dea,[1] hadn't yet been built. Therefore, to cross the Tiber, Vinitius would have had to force his way to the Sublicus, passing around the Aventine through a part of the city that was now a sea of flames. This was impossible. Vinitius understood that he must return towards Ustrinum, turn from the Via Appia, cross the river below the city, and reach the Via Portuensis, which led directly to the Trans-Tiber. This was no easy task on account of the still greater uproar on the Via Appia. Had he taken the time to grab his sword before rushing away from Antium, he'd now be able to force a passage through the crowd, but he was unarmed.

At the fountain of Mercury, however, he recognized a centurion of the Praetorians, who, at the head of a few score men, was defending the approaches to the grounds of the temple. Vinitius ordered him to ride behind him. Recognizing a tribune and an Augustinian, the centurion dared not disobey. Vinitius himself took command of the detachment. Forgetting for the moment Paul's precept of love for one's neighbor, he cut and slashed through the crowd with murderous effect. Curses and stones were hurled at him as he pressed onward to the less obstructed spots.

His advance was slow, for the people who'd already encamped themselves refused to yield but with angry oaths reviled Caesar and the Praetorians. In some places the crowd assumed a threatening aspect. Vinitius's ears were assailed by accusations that Nero had set fire to the city. Open threats of death to Caesar and to Poppaea were uttered. Shouts of "*Sanio!*"[2] "*Histrio!*"[3] "Matricide!" came from all sides. Some cried that

---

1 Roman goddess of fecundity, worshiped only by women.
2 Buffoon.
3 Actor.

Nero ought to be dragged down to the Tiber, others that Rome had shown patience enough. These threats might at any moment turn into open riot—only a leader was lacking.

Meanwhile the mob's rage and despair turned against the Praetorians, who couldn't extricate themselves from the crowd because the road was obstructed by huge piles of goods rescued from the conflagration (cases and barrels of provisions, more costly furniture and utensils, children's cradles, beds, wagons, and litters). Here and there, fistfights broke out. At last the Praetorians vanquished the unarmed mob and hurled them back.

Overcoming all obstacles along the Viae Latina, Numitia, Ardea, Lavinia, and Ostia, and passing on the way gardens, villas, temples, and cemeteries, Vinitius reached at last the Alexandrian Quarter, beyond which he crossed the Tiber. There was more space now and less smoke, but there was no lack of fugitives even here. From them he learned that only a few alleys of the Trans-Tiber had been invaded by the fire, but that in these nothing could escape. Burning torches had been hurled into the houses, and the bearers allowed no one to extinguish them, shouting that they were acting under orders.

The young tribune had no doubt that it was Caesar who had given the orders, and the vengeance clamored for by the crowds seemed to him right and just. What worse had been done by Mithridates[4] or the most fiendish enemies of Rome? The measure was more than filled. Nero's madness had grown too monstrous, and the security of human life was impossible while he lived. Vinitius believed that Nero's hour had struck, that the falling ruins of the city should and must overwhelm the monstrous jester and all his crimes. If a man was found brave enough to place himself at the head of that desperate mob, that might bring about his removal at once.

Daring thoughts crowded upon Vinitius. Suppose he should be that man? His family, which up to recent times had included a series of consuls,

---

4 Mithridates VI (also known as the Great, d. 64 B.C.), king of Pontus, one of Rome's deadliest enemies. In 88 B.C., having made himself the master of all the Roman possessions in Asia Minor, Mithridates ordered a general massacre of Roman citizens in the region (nearly 100,000 people, maybe more). He also assisted the Greeks in their revolt against Rome. For a time he threatened the very survival of the Roman state. Pompey the Great finally defeated him in 66 B.C. Mithridates then tried to poison himself, but he had deliberately taken so many poisons during his lifetime that he was virtually unpoisonable. Finally, he compelled a mercenary soldier to kill him so he could avoid being tortured or killed by Pompey.

was renowned in Rome. The mob needed but a man. Not long before, because of a death sentence inflicted upon the four hundred slaves of the prefect Pedanius, Rome had nearly been plunged into riot and civil war. What might not happen today in the face of this terrible disaster, which surpassed all disasters inflicted upon Rome in the last eight centuries?

Whoever summoned the Quirites to arms, thought Vinitius, *would certainly overthrow Nero and clothe himself with the purple.*

Why shouldn't he be the one? Not one of all the Augustinians was stronger, bolder, or younger. True, Nero commanded thirty legions stationed on the frontiers of the empire, but would not those very legions and their commanders rise at the news of the burning of Rome and of its temples? Then he, Vinitius, might become Caesar. He'd heard whispers among the Augustinians that a soothsayer had predicted that Otho would wear the purple. Was he Otho's inferior?

Christ Himself might help him with His divine power. Perhaps this very inspiration came from Him. *Would it were so!* said Vinitius to himself. He would avenge himself on Nero for the peril into which Lygia had been thrown and for his own sufferings. He would introduce the reign of justice and truth, would spread the creed of Christ from the Euphrates to the mist-enveloped coasts of Britain, and would clothe Lygia in purple and make her the empress of the entire world. These thoughts, bursting in his head like sparks from a burning house, died like sparks.

No, he couldn't do both at once: His first priority must be to rescue Lygia. He could now view the conflagration from close quarters. New fears assailed him. In the face of that sea of fire and smoke, in face of the terrible reality, the hope that Peter the Apostle would save Lygia died away in his heart. Despair fell upon him once more when he reached the Via Portuensis.

Not till he arrived at the gate did he recover himself. Here he heard again what the fugitives had already told him: The greater part of the quarter had not yet been reached by the flames, though in some few places the fire had already crossed the river. Nevertheless, the Trans-Tiber was already clogged by smoke and fleeing crowds. The streets were more impassable than ever, because the people in this area, having more time, carried out and rescued more of their property. The main street was, in many places, completely choked with people, and around the Naumachia Augusta, great piles were stacked. The narrower alleys were so constricted with even denser smoke that they were completely impassable. The inhabitants were fleeing by the thousands.

Terrible sights met his eyes. More than once, two rivers of people, flowing from opposite directions, met in a narrow passage, crushed together, fought hand to hand, struck and trampled each other, and fought to the death. Families lost one another in the uproar, and mothers called despairingly for their children. Vinitius shuddered at the thought of what might be going on nearer to the fire. Amid the noise and the confusion, it was difficult to ask questions or to hear replies.

Rolling across the river came new billows of smoke, so black and heavy that they followed one another along the ground, covering houses, people—everything—with the darkness of night. And then again, the wind from the conflagration would disperse them, and Vinitius would move further towards the alley where stood the house of Linus.

The sultry warmth of July, increased by the heat from the burning quarters, became unbearable. Eyes smarted from the smoke, breath failed in human breasts. Some inhabitants had remained in their houses, hoping that the flames wouldn't cross the river; now they, too, began to leave. Every hour the crowd grew.

The Praetorians following Vinitius lagged behind. Someone in the crowd wounded his horse with a hammer; the beast threw up its bloody head, reared, and refused further obedience. Someone in the crowd recognized by his rich tunic that he was an Augustinian, a member of Nero's inner circle. Immediately shouts arose of "Death to Nero and his incendiaries!" A moment of terrible danger followed, for hundreds of hands were raised against Vinitius, but his frightened horse carried him away, trampling the crowds on all sides.

And now came a new billow of black smoke, filling the street with darkness. Vinitius, seeing that further progress was impossible, leaped to the ground and continued his flight afoot, slipping by the walls and at times waiting till the pursuing crowd had passed him before moving on. He admitted to himself that, most likely, his efforts would be in vain. Lygia might already be out of the city, might already have saved herself by flight—it would be easier to find a pin on the seashore than to find her in this tumult and chaos. Even at the price of his life, however, he determined to reach the house of Linus. At times, he stopped and rubbed his eyes. With a piece torn from his tunic he covered his nose and his lips and ran on. As he neared the river, the heat grew more intense. Knowing that the fire had begun at the Circus Maximus, his first thought was that the heat came from its burning debris or from the ox market or from

Velabrum. Their proximity to the Circus would make them all a ready prey to the flames.

But now the heat became unbearable. One old man on crutches, the last fugitive Vinitius saw on this stretch of road, shouted as he passed, "Don't go near the bridge of Cestius! The whole island is on fire!" It was impossible to deceive himself any longer. At the turn towards the Jewish Quarter, where stood the house of Linus, the young tribune saw flames and clouds of smoke. Not only was the island burning, but the Trans-Tiber also—or at least the further end of the alley in which Lygia lived.

And now he recalled that the house of Linus stood in the middle of a garden, and between the garden and the Tiber was an open clearing. This thought encouraged him, for the fire might be halted at the clearing. He ran on, though every blast of wind now enveloped him not merely in smoke, but also in thousands of sparks that might reach the other end of the alley and cut off his retreat. At last, through the smoky curtain, he caught sight of the cypresses in Linus's garden. The houses beyond the clearing were burning like piles of wood, but Linus's little *insula* stood untouched as yet. Vinitius cast his grateful eyes towards heaven and raced forward, though the very air was burning. The door was shut; he pushed it open and rushed in. Not a soul was in the garden. The house seemed equally deserted.

They may have fainted from the smoke and the heat, thought Vinitius. He began to call, "Lygia, Lygia!"

The only reply was the roar of the distant conflagration.

"Lygia!"

Suddenly his ears were struck by the ominous sounds that once before he'd heard in this garden. The vivarium near the temple of Aesculapius on the neighboring island had evidently caught fire. Here lions and beasts of all kinds roared out their terror. Vinitius shivered from head to foot. Now for a second time, when all his thoughts were concentrated on Lygia, those terrible roars resounded in his ears as a herald of misfortune, an ominous prophecy of future woe.

But this impression was only momentary, for the roar of the fire, more terrible even than that of the beasts, forced him to turn his thoughts elsewhere. Lygia hadn't answered, but she might have fainted from the heat or been overcome by the smoke.

Vinitius rushed inside. The little atrium was empty and dark with smoke. Feeling for the doors that led to the *cubiculums*, he perceived the light of a small lamp and, approaching, saw a *lararium* where instead of

heathen lares, there was a cross. Beneath the cross burned a firepot. The
first thought of the young Augustinian was that the cross had sent him
this light to aid him in his search. He seized it and looked around for the
cubiculums; finding one, he lifted the curtain and peeped in.

The room was empty. Vinitius, however, was certain that he'd discovered Lygia's bedchamber, because her garments hung along the wall on
nails; on the bed lay a *capitium*. Vinitius grasped the garment, pressed it
to his lips, then throwing it over his shoulder, he continued his search.
The house was small, so that in a short time he went through every room
and even descended into the cellar, but search as he would, he found no
one. It was only too evident that Lygia, Linus, and Ursus, with other
inhabitants of the quarter, must have sought safety in flight.

I must look for them in the crowds beyond the gates of the city, thought
Vinitius.

It had not greatly surprised him that he'd not met them on the Via
Portuensis, for they might have left the Trans-Tiber from the opposite
side, in the direction of the Vatican Hill. In any case, they'd escaped
destruction from the fire. Vinitius was greatly relieved. He appreciated, it's
true, the terrible dangers that they'd escaped, but the thought of the superhuman strength of Ursus was a comfort to him.

I must flee from here, he said to himself, *across the gardens of Domitius
into the gardens of Agrippina. I'll surely find them there. I need not fear the
smoke there, because the wind is blowing from the Sabine Hills.*

The hour had now come when he was forced to think of his own
safety, for waves of flames were coming nearer and nearer from the direction of the island, and clouds of smoke almost entirely enveloped the alley.
The firepot that had lighted his way was extinguished by a gust of wind.
Rushing into the street, Vinitius ran at full speed towards the Via Portuensis. The flames seemed to pursue him with their fiery breath, now
enveloping him in fresh clouds of smoke, now pouring sparks upon him,
which fell on his hair, neck, and clothing. His tunic began to smolder in
spots, but he paid no attention to it and rushed on lest the smoke suffocate him. His mouth was choked with soot; his throat and lungs seemed
on fire. The blood rushed to his head, so that at times everything about
him seemed red, even the smoke itself.

Then the thought assailed him: *This is a living fire. Perhaps it's best that
I should throw myself down and perish.*

The running exhausted him more and more. His head, neck, and shoulders streamed with perspiration that scalded him like boiling water. Had it not been for Lygia's name, which he repeated over and over, and for her *capitium*, which he'd bound across his mouth, he would have fallen to the ground. A few moments later, he could no longer recognize the streets through which he ran, and he was gradually losing consciousness, remembering only that he must rush onward, for in the open field Lygia was awaiting him—Lygia, whom Peter the Apostle had promised to him. Suddenly he was struck by a strange conviction, half feverish like a vision before death, that he must see her, wed her, and then die.

On and on he ran, staggering like a drunken man from one side of the street to the other. And now, without warning, a dramatic change occurred in the terrible conflagration sweeping over the city. Places that had been merely smoldering now burst forth into one great sea of flame; the wind no longer bore smoke along with it. The smoke that had already accumulated vanished in a mad eddy of heated air. That onrush now drove millions of sparks ahead of it so that it seemed to Vinitius as if he were running through a cloud of fire. However, he could see ahead of him clearer than before, and just as he was ready to fall with exhaustion he beheld the end of the street, a sight that gave him new courage and strength. Passing the corner he found himself in the street that led to the Via Portuensis and the Campus Codeta. The sparks ceased to pursue him. He knew that if he could reach the Via Portuensis, he'd be safe, even if he fell and lost consciousness.

At the end of the street he saw a cloud that veiled the exit.

If that's smoke, he thought, *I won't be able to pass through it.*

He gathered up all his strength and rushed onward. As he ran he threw away his tunic, which had caught on fire from the sparks and was burning like the shirt of Nessus,[5] and he ran onward, naked save for Lygia's *capitium* wound about his head and over his mouth. As he approached the cloud, he perceived that what he'd taken for smoke was only dust, from which rose human cries and shouts.

The mob is pillaging the houses, said Vinitius to himself, but he ran in the direction of the voices nevertheless.

---

5   A centaur killed with an arrow shot by Hercules. In a very complicated story, Hercules dies from Nessus's flaming shirt.

In any case, people were there who might give him help. In this hope
he shouted for help at the top of his voice. But this was his last effort; lurid
lights danced before his eyes, the breath left his lungs, strength failed him,
and he fell.

He was overheard, however, or rather, some people saw him. Two men
ran to his assistance with gourds full of water. Vinitius, exhausted though
he was, hadn't lost consciousness. He seized a gourd with both hands and
eagerly drank its contents.

"Thank you," he said. "Please help me to my feet. I can walk on alone."

The other workman poured water on his head, then the two raised him
from the ground and carried him to their fellows, who immediately surrounded him and questioned him as to whether he'd suffered any serious
hurt. Their solicitude astonished Vinitius.

"Good people, who are you?" he asked.

"We're pulling down the buildings so that the fire may not reach the
Via Portuensis," answered one of the toilers.

"You aided me when I'd fallen. I thank you."

"We're not allowed to refuse to help," answered a chorus of voices.

Vinitius, who all morning had seen brutal crowds plundering and
murdering, now looked more attentively at the faces around him and said,
"May Christ reward you."

"Praise to His name," exclaimed a chorus of voices.

"Linus?" inquired Vinitius.

But he was unable to finish the question or hear the answer, for he
fainted from emotion and exhaustion.

He came to in the Campus Codeta, in a garden, surrounded by a
crowd of men and women, and asked, "Where's Linus?"

There was a pause, and then a voice well known to Vinitius said, "He
went out by the Porta Nomentana two days ago. Peace be with you, O
king of Persia."

Vinitius raised himself to a sitting posture and beheld Chilo.

"Your house, O master," said the Greek, "must have been destroyed,
for the Carinae is in flames, but you'll always be as rich as Midas. Oh,
what a misfortune! The Christians, O son of Serapis, long ago foretold
that fire would destroy the city, but Linus, with the daughter of Jove, is in
Ostranium. Oh, what a disaster to this city!"

Vinitius grew faint again. "Have you seen them?" he asked.

"I saw them, O master. Praise be to Christ and all the gods that I can repay your favors with good news. But Osiris, I'll repay you more, I swear by this burning Rome."

The shades of evening had fallen, but it was light as day in the garden, for the conflagration had increased. It now seemed that not just more sections of the city were burning, but rather that the entire city was enveloped in flames. The heavens were red as far as the eye could see, and a red light closed down upon the world.

PART III

Chapter XLIV

The flames of the burning city filled the sky as far as the eye could reach. The full moon, ng behind the hills, took on the hue of molten brass from the glare that pervaded the atmosphere and seemed to be staring with bewildered wonder at the perishing conqueror of the world. Rose-colored stars glittered in the rosy depths of the heavens, but reversing the conditions of the normal night, the earth was brighter than the sky. Rome, like a gigantic funeral pyre, lit up the whole Campania. The blood-colored light fell upon faraway mountains, cities, villas, temples, and monuments. On the aqueducts, which extended from the neighboring mountains into the city, crowds of people gathered for safety or for a vantage point from which to gaze upon the burning city.

Fresh districts of the city were being lapped up by tongues of fire. That criminal hands were adding fuel to the flames was evident from the fact that more fires broke out here and there, far from their original center. From the seven hills whereon Rome was founded, the flames flowed down like waves into the densely populated settlements in the valley—into five- and six-story houses, full of shops and booths; into movable wooden amphitheaters built for all sorts of public diversion; into storehouses for olives, wood, grain, nuts, and pinecones whose seeds were eaten by the poor, and into storehouses filled with clothing that through the generosity of Caesar were periodically distributed among the starving rabble that huddled into the narrow alleys. Here the fire, finding an abundance of inflammable materials, became almost a series of explosions and took possession of whole streets with astonishing rapidity. Spectators who were encamped outside the city or who stood upon the aqueducts could determine by the color of the flames what was burning. The enraged wind clawed out of the fiery whirlpools thousands—no, *millions* of burning walnut and almond shells, which shot upward into the sky like brilliant butterflies, to burst with a crackling report, or which were carried by the malevolent wind into the remotest parts of the city, or upon the aqueducts, or the fields in the outlying country. All hope of stopping the conflagration had been abandoned; thus confusion increased with every moment that passed, for on one side, the fleeing population poured out the city gates, while on the other, the peasants and villagers and semisavage shepherds of the Campania came rushing towards Rome, lured by hopes of plunder.

Here, there, and everywhere rose the cry, "Rome is dying!" The ruin of the city resulted in the termination of all the laws and controls enacted to protect the individual rights of Rome's citizens.

What cared the mob, consisting largely of slaves and aliens, about the sovereignty of Rome? Destruction of the city could but free them; thus violence and plundering continued to increase. It appeared that only the riveting spectacle of the burning city restrained for a moment the outbreak of slaughter that would begin with the city's death. Hundreds of thousands of slaves, oblivious of the fact that Rome was not merely a locality but the master of legions all over the world, awaited but a signal and a leader. The name of Spartacus flew from mouth to mouth. But Spartacus was dead.

Meanwhile, citizens began to assemble, seizing what arms they could find. At all the gates monstrous rumors gained credence. Some asserted that Vulcan, at the command of Jupiter, was hurling destruction from the bowels of the earth; others, that Vesta was avenging Rubria.[1] Those who thought so made no effort to save anything from the wreck, but flocked to the temples and besought the mercy of the gods. The most general belief was that Nero had ordered the burning of Rome to rid it of the stenches that arose from the Suburra and to erect upon its ruins a new city that he would call Neronia. The very thought of this enraged the populace, and had a leader but taken advantage of that outburst of hatred, as Vinitius feared one might, Nero's hour would have come much sooner than it actually did.

It was also rumored that Caesar had gone insane, that he had ordered an indiscriminate slaughter of the people by Praetorians and gladiators. Others swore by the gods that the wild beasts of the vivaria were to be let loose at the command of Ahenobarbus. Lions with burning manes, elephants, and bisons crazed with fear had been seen hurling themselves upon the struggling crowds of men and women. Nor was this without some foundation in truth. In some places elephants, scenting the

---

1   For her violation at the hands of Nero.

approaching danger, had burst the barriers of their pens and had crashed through the streets away from the fire, carrying destruction with them in their flight.

By this time it was estimated that tens of thousands of citizens had already perished in the cataclysm. In fact, this was no exaggeration. Many, distracted by the loss of property or dear ones, had cast themselves despairingly into the flames; others were suffocated by the smoke. In the center of the city, with the Capitol on one side, the Quirinal, the Viminal, and the Esquiline on the other, and also between the Palatine and the Coelian Hills, where the streets were most densely thronged, the flames burst out simultaneously in so many places that people fleeing this way or that unexpectedly found themselves engulfed by a new wall of fire and perished terribly in a deluge of flame.

In terror, confusion, and bewilderment, the people knew not which way to turn nor where to flee. The streets were obstructed by great mounds of possessions left behind by their frantic owners; some of the narrower ones were hopelessly blocked. Refugees who found their way to the squares and markets—near the place where subsequently arose the Flavian Amphitheater, near the temple of the earth, near the Porticus of Silvia, or, higher yet, near the temples of Juno and Lucinia, between the Clivus Vibrius and the old Porta Esquilina—were completely surrounded by a sea of fire and died a dreadful death. In places not reached by the flames were found afterward hundreds of bodies burned to a crisp, though here and there unfortunates had pried out stone slabs and half buried themselves in a vain attempt to escape the blasting heat. Hardly a family in that portion of the city remained intact. Hence along the walls, at the gates, and on the highways outside were heard the wails of women vainly calling out the names of dear ones who had been burned or trampled to death.

Thus, while some were imploring the gods for mercy, others blasphemed them, holding them responsible for this awful disaster. To the temple of Jupiter Liberator streamed old men who cried with outstretched arms, "If you in truth are a liberator, save your altars and this city." But their despair was turned chiefly against the ancient Roman deities, who were expected to protect the city from catastrophes like this. Since they'd failed in the hour of need, they were now openly ridiculed. On the Via Asinaria,[2] a procession of Egyptian priests happened to be carrying the

---

2 Asses' Gate.

statue of Isis, which they'd rescued from the temple near the Porta Cae-limontana. The mob scattered the priests, seized the chariot, drew it to the Porta Appia, and placed the statue in the temple of Mars, beating back the priests of that deity who sought to restrain them. In other places, the names of Serapis, Baal, and Jehovah were invoked, whose confessors swarmed out of the alleys near the Suburra and the Trans-Tiber, filling the fields outside the walls with their cries and wails.

A triumphant note was sometimes heard above the clamor; while some of the populace joined in a chorus glorifying the Lord of the World, others were incensed and sought to repress them by violence. Hymns floated upward from some places—sung by men in the prime of life, by old men, by women, and by children—wonderful and solemn hymns, whose meaning the listeners didn't understand, but in which rose continually the refrain: "Behold the Judge comes in the day of wrath and disaster!" Thus this deluge of restless and sleepless people encircled the burning city like a tempest-driven sea.

But neither despair nor blasphemy nor hymn was of any avail. The destruction seemed to be as irresistible, as absolute, and as merciless as predestination itself. Stores of hemp caught fire around Pompey's Amphitheater, together with ropes and all variety of machines used in the circuses and arenas; then followed barrels of pitch used for smearing the ropes, which were stored away in adjoining buildings. In a few hours all that part of the city, beyond which lay the Campus Martius, was burning with such a bright yellow flame that to the spectators, only half conscious from terror, it seemed that the order of day and night had been reversed and that they were looking at sunshine. But in the end, a monstrous bloody gleam extinguished all other colors of flame. From that sea of fire, gigantic fountains and pillars of flame shot up into the heated sky, spreading at their summits into fiery branches and feathers; then the wind bore them away, turned them into golden threads, into hair, into sparks, and swept them on over the Campania towards the Alban Hills. The night grew brighter; the air itself seemed saturated, not only with light, but also with flame. The Tiber flowed on as living fire. The doomed city was changed into hell, as the insatiable dragon seized more and more space, took hills by storm, flooded level places, drowned valleys, raged, roared, and thundered.

Chapter XLV

Vinitius had been taken to the house of Macrinus, a weaver, who washed him and nourished him; upon recovering his strength, the young tribune declared his intention of searching for Linus that very night. Macrinus, who was a Christian, corroborated Chilo's statement that Linus had gone with the high priest, Clement, to Ostranium, where the Apostle Peter was expected to baptize a large number of new converts. It was known to Christians in that section of the city that two days earlier Linus had entrusted the care of his house to a man named Gaius. To Vinitius this indicated that apparently neither Lygia nor Ursus had remained in the house but had left for Ostranium as well. This gave him great comfort. As Linus was an old man, too old to walk every day from the Trans-Tiber to the far-off Porta Nomentana and back again, it was almost certain that he had lodged for the past few days with one or more of the Christians encamped outside the walls. Lygia and Ursus would be with him, thus escaping the fire that had barely touched the other slope of the Esquiline. In all this Vinitius saw a special dispensation of Christ, who had watched over him, and his heart was filled with even more love than before—he vowed to repay God for this with the devotion of the rest of his life.

But all the more anxious did he become to reach Ostranium to find Lygia, as well as Linus and Peter. He'd take them away with him to one of his estates, perhaps to Sicily. Let Rome burn; in a few more days it would be but a mere heap of ashes. Why should they remain in the midst of such disaster and an enraged population? On his estates were troops of willing slaves, more than enough for protection, and there they'd be surrounded by the quiet of the country and live in peace under the protection of Christ and the blessing of Peter. If only he could find them!

But that was no easy task. Remembering the difficulty he'd experienced in getting from the Via Appia to the Trans-Tiber, especially the time wasted in circling around to reach the Via Portuensis, he decided that this

355

time he'd go around the city in the opposite direction. Going by the Via Triumphatoris, he could reach the Aemilian Bridge by going along the river, then passing the Pincian Hill along the Campus Martius, by the gardens of Pompey, Lucullus, and Sallust, and finally make his way through to the Via Nomentana. Although this was the shortest way, both Macrinus and Chilo advised him not to take it. True, the fire hadn't reached that part of the city, but it was more than likely that all the market squares and streets would be blocked by people and furniture. Chilo suggested that he go across the Vatican Hill to the Porta Flaminiana, cross the river at that point, and push on outside the walls beyond the gardens of Acilius to the Porta Salaria. Vinitius, after a moment's hesitation, accepted the advice.

Macrinus had to remain behind to look after his house, but he provided two mules, one of which Lygia might use if she were found. He'd have added a slave, but Vinitius demurred as he expected that the first detachment of Praetorians whom he met on the way would pass under his command.

And so, with Chilo, the young tribune set out across the Janiculum Hill to the Via Triumphatoris. In open spaces were camps, but they made their way through them with less difficulty, as most of the inhabitants had fled by the Via Portuensis in the direction of the sea. Beyond the Porta Septima they rode between the river and the magnificent gardens of Domitius, where huge cypresses were reddened by the conflagration, as by a sunset. The road became freer, but at times they had to struggle against the current of the flowing peasantry. Vinitius urged his mule onward. Chilo, in the rear, kept muttering to himself the whole way:

"So we've left the fire behind, but it's burning our shoulders. Never was seen so great a light upon this road after nightfall. O Zeus, unless you send a torrential rainstorm to quench that fire, it's clear you have no love for Rome! Human power will never extinguish this fire. And *such* a city—a city before which Greece and the whole world bowed in submission! And now the first Greek who comes along may roast his beans in its ashes. Who would have expected it? And there will be no more Rome, nor Roman patricians! When its ashes grow cold, whoever wishes to may walk over them and whistle[1]—and whistle without danger. Ye gods! To think of whistling over a city that ruled the world. No Greek or even barbarian

---

1   Whistling was a form a derision.

would have dared to hope for this. Yet now they may whistle—for ashes, whether those of a herdsman's fire or of a burned city, are only ashes, which the wind will blow away sooner or later."

Saying this, he turned at times towards the conflagration with a face filled at once with malice and delight.

"It's dying! It's dying! It will perish completely and will completely and utterly cease to exist. Where now will the world send its grain, its olive oil, and its money? Who'll squeeze gold and tears from it? Marble doesn't burn, but it crumbles in fire. The Capitol will turn into dust, and the Palatine into dust. O Zeus! Rome was like a shepherd and the other nations were the sheep. When the shepherd was hungry, he slew a sheep, ate the flesh, and offered the skin to you, O father of the gods. Who, O cloud-compeller, will now do the slaughtering, and into whose hands will you put the shepherd's whip? For Rome is burning, O father, as truly as if you had fired it with a thunderbolt."

"Hurry up!" cried Vinitius. "Why are you lagging behind?"

"Master, I'm weeping over Rome, the city of Jupiter."

For a time they rode on in silence, listening to the roar of the fire and the noise of birds' wings. Doves, vast numbers of which nested in the villas and small towns of the Campania, and every kind of bird from the sea and the surrounding mountains, evidently mistaking the glow of the conflagration for sunlight, were flying—whole flocks of them—blindly into the fire. Vinitius was the first to break the silence.

"Where were you when the fire broke out?"

"Master, I was on my way to my friend Euritius, a shopkeeper near the Circus Maximus, and was pondering over the teachings of Christ when the cry of 'Fire!' arose. Crowds flocked to the Circus, some for rescue, some through curiosity, but when the flames surrounded the Circus itself and broke out in other places, each had to look out for himself."

"And did you see people throwing torches into houses?"

"What haven't I seen, O grandson of Aeneas? I saw people fighting their way through the crowds with drawn swords. I saw pitched battles, the entrails of men and women scattered on the pavement. You'd have thought the barbarians had captured the city and were putting it to the sword. People cried out that the end of the world had come. Some lost their heads completely and, forgetting to flee, waited stupidly for the flames to devour them. Some were bewildered, some howled in despair— I also saw some who howled from joy. O master, there are many bad people who fail to appreciate the many benefits of your gentle ruling and those just laws, by virtue of which you take from everyone what they have and appropriate it for yourselves. How sad that people find themselves unwilling to accept the will of God."

Vinitius, preoccupied with his own thoughts, failed to catch the sarcasm and irony in Chilo's words. A shudder ran through him at the thought that Lygia might be in the midst of that weltering chaos, in those terrible streets whose pavements reeked with human entrails. Though ten times, at least, he'd asked Chilo to tell all he knew, he once more turned to him. "And you're *absolutely* sure you saw them with your own eyes in Ostranium?"

"I saw them, O son of Venus! I saw the maiden, the worthy Lygian, the saintly Linus, and the Apostle Peter."

"Before the fire broke out?"

"Before the fire broke out, O Mithra!"

Vinitius couldn't suppress a doubt that the old man was lying. Reining in his mule, he looked threateningly at the old Greek and asked, "What were you doing there?"

Chilo was confused. Like many others, he assumed that the destruction of Rome meant the destruction of the Roman Empire. But face-to-face with Vinitius, at that moment, he remembered that the young tribune had forbidden him, under pain of some terrible penalty, to spy on the Christians, *especially* Linus and Lygia.

"Master," he replied, "why don't you believe that I love you? I was in Ostranium because I'm already half a Christian. Pyrrho has taught me to esteem virtue more than philosophy; therefore, more and more I cleave to godly people. And I'm poor. Many a time, O Jove, when you were at Antium, I've starved over my studies. Therefore, I sat on the walls of Ostranium, for the Christians, poor though they be, distribute more alms than all the rest of the Romans taken together."

Vinitius was softened by this plausible answer.

"And you don't know," he asked in a milder tone, "where Linus is now living?"

"Once you punished me terribly for curiosity, master," reminded the Greek.

Vinitius rode on in silence.

"Master," said Chilo, after a while, "but for me you'd never have found the maiden, and now, if we find her again, you won't forget the needy philosopher?"

"I'll give you a house with a vineyard at Ameriola."[2]

"I thank you, O Hercules! With a vineyard? Thanks to you! Oh yes, with a vineyard!"

They had now reached the Vatican Hill, gleaming ruddy red from the fire. Gaining the Naumachia, they turned right, so that when they'd passed the Vatican Hill they could reach the river and, crossing it, reach the Porta Flaminiana.

Suddenly Chilo reined in his mule and cried, "Master, I have an idea!"

"Speak!" answered Vinitius.

"Midway between the Janiculum and the Vatican Hill, just beyond Agrippina's gardens, are quarries from which stones and sand were taken to build the Circus. Listen to me, master! Recently, the Jews, who as you know live in vast numbers in the Trans-Tiber, have begun to persecute the Christians. You'll remember that during the time of the godlike Claudius, there were similar disturbances that forced Caesar to banish the Jews from Rome. But now that they've returned and feel safe under the protection of the Augusta, they've waxed ever more insolent in their attacks on the Christians. I know this! I myself have witnessed it. True, no edict has been issued against the Christians, but the Jews defame them to the prefect of the city, accusing them of murdering infants, of worshiping an ass, of preaching a religion not approved by the Senate. Likewise they waylay them or attack them in their houses of prayer with such ferocity that the Christians are obliged to hide."

"Well, what are you trying to say?"

"This, master. That synagogues exist openly in the Trans-Tiber, but the Christians, to evade persecution, are forced to pray in secret and assemble in deserted sheds outside the walls or in the sandpits. The Christians of the Trans-Tiber chose the quarry that was formed by taking sand for the building of the Circus and various houses along the riverfront. Now while Rome is burning, doubtless the Christians are praying. Beyond a doubt we'll find countless numbers of them in the quarries, so my advice is to go there on the way."

"But," was Vinitius's impatient retort, "you told me that Linus went to Ostranium."

"But you promised me a house with a vineyard in Ameriola," answered Chilo guilelessly. "Therefore, I wish to seek the maiden wherever there's a

---

2 A town in Umbria.

chance of our finding her. Who knows but they may have returned to the Trans-Tiber since the outbreak of the fire! They may even have gone around the city as we're doing. Linus owns a house; perhaps he wished to find out whether the fire had reached that portion of the city. If they *have* returned, I swear to you by Persephone that they would be praying at the quarry. If not, at least we'll be able to get news of them."

"You're right. Lead on!" said the tribune.

Without a moment's hesitation, Chilo turned to the left towards the hill. As they passed it, they lost sight of burning Rome. For a while the slope of the hill concealed the conflagration so that, though the neighboring heights were in the light, they were in the shade. Having passed the Circus, they turned again to the left and entered a kind of ravine that was completely dark. Through that darkness, Vinitius beheld the gleam of many lanterns.

"Here they are," said Chilo. "There'll be more today than ever, for their other houses of prayer are either burned down or filled with smoke, as is every house in the Trans-Tiber."

"True!" said Vinitius. "I hear singing."

And, in fact, voices were wafted to them from the dark opening, and into that opening lanterns disappeared one after another. But from all sides new lantern bearers appeared, so that in a short time Vinitius and Chilo found themselves part of a multitude, all streaming towards the opening.

Chilo slipped from his mule and beckoned to a youth who sat near.

"I'm a priest of Christ and a bishop," he said. "Hold our mules, and you'll receive my blessing and forgiveness of sins."

Then, without waiting for an answer, he thrust the reins into his hands and, with Vinitius, joined the advancing throng.

Finally reaching the quarry, they pushed through the dark passage by the aid of the lanterns until they reached a spacious cave, evidently formed by the recent removal of stone, for the encircling walls all looked freshly cut.

Here it was somewhat brighter than in the passage, for besides the fire-pots and lanterns, torches were also burning. By their light Vinitius saw a throng of people kneeling with upraised hands. He couldn't see Lygia, nor the Apostle Peter, nor Linus; instead all around him were solemn and expectant faces. Fear was depicted on some, hope on others. The light glowed on the whites of their raised eyes; perspiration trickled down their foreheads, pale as chalk. Some were singing hymns, others feverishly repeated the name of Christ, others were beating their breasts. It was apparent that they expected something extraordinary at any moment.

Meanwhile, the hymn ceased and, above the assembly, in a niche made by the removal of an immense stone, appeared Vinitius's old acquaintance Crispus. His face was half delirious, pale, stern, and fanatical. All eyes turned to him as though waiting for words of consolation and hope. After he'd blessed the assembly, he began to speak in hurried, almost shouting tones.

"Repent your sins, for the hour has come! Behold the Lord has sent down devouring flames on Babylon, on the city of crime and debauchery. The hour of judgment has struck, the hour of wrath, the hour of universal calamity. The Lord has promised to return, and soon you'll see Him— but He won't come as the Lamb who offered His blood for your sins, but as a terrible Judge who in His justice will hurl sinners and unbelievers into the pit. Woe then to the world! Woe to the sinners! There'll be no mercy for them. Lo! I see You, Christ! Showers of stars are falling to the earth, the sun is darkened, abysses yawn in the earth, the dead rise from their graves, but You are moving amid the sound of trumpets and legions of angels, amid thunder and lightning. I see You, I hear You, O Christ!"

Here he became silent, and lifting up his face, he seemed to gaze into something distant and terrible. At that moment a muffled rumble was heard from underground. Once, twice, a tenth time. In the burning city, whole blocks of partly consumed houses began to fall with a terrible crash, but most Christians took these noises as tokens that the terrible hour was at hand, for a belief in the second advent of Christ and the end of the world was common among them. Now the destruction of the city confirmed that belief.

Terror seized the assembly. Here and there voices called out, "Lo! The day of judgment! Behold it is coming!" Some of the people covered their faces with their hands, believing that the earth was about to be shaken to its very foundation and from its fissures hellish monsters would emerge and hurl themselves upon sinners. Others cried aloud, "Christ have mercy on us! Savior, have pity!" Some confessed their sins aloud; others threw themselves into one another's arms, to have a dear one in their arms during their last moments.

But there were also some whose faces shone with joy, with smiles radiant with a happiness not of this earth, and who showed no fear. In some places were heard voices; those were from people who in their religious exaltation uttered strange words in unknown tongues. There was one in a dark corner who called out, "Awake, you that sleep!" Above all that commotion the voice of Crispus was heard: "Watch! Watch!"

At times, however, there was silence, as if all were holding their breath, waiting for whatever would come next. And then they'd hear the distant thunder of falling buildings, followed by renewed groans and cries: "Oh, Savior, have mercy!"

Then Crispus lifted up his voice and cried, "Cast away all earthly goods! Soon there won't be earth enough beneath your feet for standing room. Cast away all earthly love, for God will destroy those who value above Him wife or child. Woe to him who loves the creature more than the Creator. Woe to the powerful, woe to the oppressors, woe to the dissolute, woe to man, woman, and child!"

Suddenly a roar, louder than any previous one, shook the quarry. All fell to the ground, stretching out their arms crosswise as a protection against evil spirits. A hush followed, in which nothing was heard save panting breath, whispers full of terror, "Jesus! Jesus! Jesus!" and now and then, the weeping of children. At that moment, a certain calm voice spoke above the prostrate multitude.

"Peace be with you!"

It was the voice of Peter the Apostle, who had entered the cavern just moments before. At the sound of his voice, terror passed at once, as it passes from a flock when its shepherd appears. People rose from the earth; those who were nearer gathered at his feet as if seeking protection under his wings. He stretched his hands out over them.

"Why are you troubled in heart? Who among you can foretell the future? God has smitten Babylon with fire, but don't forget for a moment that God's protective hand remains over you whom His blood has redeemed. Remember that death is for you not an end but a beginning. In that journey, the Lamb, in His loving-kindness, will give you the strength and courage to die with His name on your lips. His peace be with you!"

After the terrible and merciless words of Crispus, the words of Peter fell like balm on those assembled. Instead of God's wrath, it was God's love that he held up before them. The hearers realized that it was the Christ whom they'd learned to love through the teachings of the Apostles, hence not a pitiless Judge, but a sweet and patient Lamb, whose loving-kindness and mercy surpasses man's wickedness a hundredfold.

People…gathered at his feet as if seeking protection under his wings.

A feeling of solace and relief descended upon all hearts, along with a feeling of gratitude towards the Apostle. Voices called from all sides, "We are your sheep! Feed us!" Those who were closest cried, "Don't leave us in the days of our trouble!" They fell at his knees.

At this Vinitius approached, grasped the edge of Peter's mantle, bent his head, and said, "Master, save me! I've searched for her in the flames, in the smoke, and among the people, and I haven't found her. But I believe that you can restore her to me."

Peter laid his hands upon the young tribune's head. "Have faith!" he said. "And come with me."

Chapter XLVI

The city burned on. The great Circus Maximus fell in ruins. In those parts of the city that first started to burn, whole blocks of buildings had now fallen, but still buildings and blocks continued to collapse. After each fall, pillars of flame shot into the sky. The wind now changed and blew a storm from the sea, bearing down waves of flame and brands and cinders upon the Caelian, the Esquiline, and the Viminal. The authorities were now providing means of rescue. By order of Tigellinus, who three days before had hurried in from Antium, they began to pull down houses on the Esquiline Hill so that the fire might die by itself when it reached empty spaces. It was a vain attempt, undertaken solely to preserve a remnant of the city, since those sections already in flames were hopelessly doomed. It was deemed necessary, however, to prevent further spreading of the calamity. Incalculable wealth had perished, and continued to perish, in the city, most of the inhabitants having lost virtually everything they'd owned. Hundreds of thousands wandered about outside the walls in utter destitution. As early as the second day, hunger began to torment the multitudes, for the immense stores of provisions amassed within the city had all been consumed by the flames. In this universal chaos, amid the dissolution of all authority, no one thought of furnishing new supplies. Only after the arrival of Tigellinus were emergency orders dispatched to Ostia. But the people, in the meantime, had grown more and more threatening.

The house at Aqua Appia, where Tigellinus lived, for the moment was surrounded by crowds of women who clamored from morning till late in the night for "bread and roof." The Praetorians who were brought from the great camp situated between the Via Salaria and the Via Nomentana vainly strove to maintain some semblance of order. Here and there they met with open armed resistance. Elsewhere, defenseless groups pointed to the blazing city and urged the soldiers to finish the job, saying, "Go ahead and kill us!" They cursed Caesar, the Augustinians, and the Praetorian soldiers. The tumult increased every hour, so that Tigellinus, gazing at night on thousands of fires spread around the city, declared that they might as well have been the fires of enemy camps.

Besides flour, as large a quantity as possible of baked bread was rushed in at his command, not only from Ostia, but also from the surrounding towns and villages. But when the first convoy reached the Emporium at night, the people stormed the chief gate leading towards the Aventine and seized the supplies. Then followed a terrible uproar as, in the light of the flames and amid the battle for loaves, some of the mob were trampled to death. Flour from torn sacks whitened as with snow the entire space from the granary to the arches of Drusus and Germanicus. The tumult lasted until the soldiers regained control of the buildings and dispersed the mob with arrows and missiles.

Never since the invasion of the Gauls under Brennus had Rome experienced such a disaster. In despair, the mob compared the two conflagrations. In the earlier there had remained, at least, the Capitol. But now the Capitol was encircled by a terrible wreath of flame. Marble, it's true, couldn't burn; yet at night, when the wind turned the smoke aside for a moment, rows of columns of the lofty sanctuary of Jove were visible, red and glowing like burning coal. Again, in the time of Brennus, Romans had been a patriotic and harmonious people, attached to the city and their altars. But now mobs speaking various tongues, mostly slaves and freedmen, roamed nomadlike around the walls of the burning city, unmanageable, unruly, and ready under pressure of destitution to turn against Caesar and the city.

But the very magnitude of the catastrophe, which terrified every heart, disarmed the crowd to a certain degree. After the scourge of fire might follow famine and disease, and to complete the misfortune, the terribly hot days of July had set in. It was impossible to breathe air inflamed by both the fire and the sun.

Night not only brought no relief, but it also made a hell of the city. In the daytime, an awful and ominous sight was before them, for the very center of the gigantic city upon the hills changed into a roaring volcano, and around it, reaching to the Alban Hills, was a single endless camp composed of booths, tents, huts, wagons, wheelbarrows, packs of merchandise, and fires, all clouded by the smoke and dust. Everything was lighted by the beams of the sun, which, owing to the smoke, shed a weird bloodred light on the whole, full as it was of noise, threats, hatred, and terror. A monstrous crowd of men, women, and children held possession. Mingling with the Quirites were Greeks, Africans, Asians, and shaggy, blue-eyed and light-haired people from the north. Among the citizens were slaves, freedmen, gladiators, merchants, tradesmen, peasants, and soldiers—a veritable sea of humanity flowing around the island of fire.

Various rumors stirred this sea, just as the wind raises waves in the real one. Some were favorable and others unfavorable. It was reported that immense stores of food and clothing were on their way from the Emporium to be distributed gratis. It was also rumored that, at the command of Caesar, provinces in Asia and Africa would be plundered of their riches, and the treasure thus gained would be divided among the inhabitants of Rome, so that everybody might build his own house. Another story had it that the water in the aqueducts was poisoned and that Nero intended to destroy the city and annihilate all the inhabitants, so that he might move to Greece or Egypt and rule the world from there. Each report spread with lightning speed, and each was received by the rabble as fact. So these various reports produced outbursts of hope, indignation, terror, and rage. Finally, these encamping thousands were attacked as by a fever, as the Christian belief—that the end of the world by fire was at hand— spread itself even among the followers of the gods and increased daily. By this time, many were numbed by all these multiple shocks. Others lost their minds: Gazing into the firelit sky, they saw gods looking down at the ruin of their world—then the people stretched their hands up to them, imploring pity or cursing them.

Meanwhile soldiers, assisted by a number of citizens, continued to tear down houses on the Esquiline and the Caelian, also on the Trans-Tiber, thus saving much of these sections of the city. But in the city perished the accumulations of ages of conquest, priceless works of art, magnificent temples, the most precious treasures of Rome's past and Rome's glory.

The public perception was that when the fire was finally out, only a few buildings on the outskirts of the city would be left standing and that hundreds of thousands of people would be left without any shelter. A report spread that the soldiers were tearing down the houses, not to stop the fire, but to make sure that nothing was left of the city. Tigellinus implored Caesar, in every letter, to return so that by his presence the despairing people might be calmed. But Caesar refused to move until his own palace was on fire and then hastened back so as not to miss the period when that part of the fire should reach its hottest point and highest flames.

Chapter XLVII

Meanwhile the fire had reached the Via Nomentana but turned from it at once, due to a sudden change of wind, towards the Via Lata and the Tiber. It surrounded the Capitol, spread along the Forum Boarium, destroyed everything it had missed the first time, and again approached the Palatine.

Tigellinus, gathering all the Praetorian forces together, dispatched courier after courier to the approaching Caesar, notifying him that he would miss nothing of the great spectacle, since the conflagration was increasing.

But Nero elected to arrive during the night, so that he might have a better view of the dying city. With that object, he halted near the Aqua Albana. Then he summoned the tragedian Aliturus to his tent and with his help determined how he would pose, look, and express himself. He learned appropriate gestures and argued with the actor whether at the words, "O sacred city that seemed to be more lasting than Ida,"[1] he should raise both hands or, holding in one hand a kithara, drop it by his side and lift the other. This question seemed to him at that time more important than any other. Starting at last about nightfall, he sought counsel from Petronius as to the verses that were to be dedicated to the conflagration. Might he insert some magnificent blasphemy against the gods? From an artistic point of view, wouldn't such expressions have been spontaneously uttered by any man like himself who was losing his ancestral home?

About midnight, he and his splendid court, composed of whole detachments of nobility, senators, knights, freedmen, slaves, women, and children, approached the city. Sixteen thousand Praetorians were posted along the roadside in battle array, to guard the safety and peace of his entrance and to keep the excited people at a proper distance. The people

---

1 A mountain in Crete, where Jupiter was nursed.

cursed, shouted, and hissed as they caught sight of the retinue, but dared not attack them. In many places, however, the rabble applauded. Since they were destitute to begin with and they had no home to lose, they hoped that because of their applause Caesar would bestow a more bountiful than usual distribution of grain, olives, clothes, and money. Finally, the shouting, hissing, and applause were drowned in the blare of the trumpets and horns that Tigellinus ordered to be blown.

When Nero arrived at the Porta Ostia, he halted and said, "Oh, houseless ruler of a homeless people, where shall I lay my unfortunate head tonight?"

After passing the Clivus Delphini, he ascended the steps prepared for him on the Appian aqueduct. He was followed by the Augustinians and a choir of singers bearing kitharas and other musical instruments.

All held their breath, waiting to see if he would say something profound, which for their own safety they would be forced to remember. But Nero remained solemn and speechless in a purple cloak, with a wreath of golden laurels on his head, staring at the raging of the mighty flames. When Terpnos handed him a golden kithara, he lifted his eyes towards the flame-illumined city, as though waiting for inspiration.

The people pointed at him from far off as he stood in the bloodlike light. In the distance, dragons of flame were hissing, devouring the oldest and most sacred monuments: the sacred temple of Hercules built by Evander; the temple of Jupiter Stator; the temple of Luna built by Servius Tullius; the house of Numa Pompilius;[2] and the sanctuary of Vesta with the penates of the Roman people—all were on fire. Through the soaring flames the Capitol could be seen from time to time—the past, the very soul of Rome, was burning. But Caesar stood, kithara in hand, his features set like those of a tragedian, caring not in the least about the destruction of his city, but intent on the right posture of his body and the pathetic words by which he would describe the greatness of the catastrophe, elicit the most admiration, and provoke the most enthusiastic applause.

He detested that city, and he detested its inhabitants. He loved only his songs and his verses; hence he inwardly rejoiced that at last he beheld a tragedy worthy of the one he was writing. The poet was happy, the declaimer felt inspired, the dramatist was jubilant at the appalling sight and rhapsodized that the destruction of Troy was nothing compared to that of this great city. What more could he wish for? There lay world-ruling Rome in flames, while he stood on the arches of the aqueduct, with a

---

2   Second king of Rome (715–678 B.C.); a beloved monarch.

"O nest of my fathers! O cherished cradle!"

golden kithara in his hands, conspicuous in purple, admired, magnificent, and poetic. But his thoughts were racing.

Down below in the darkness, the people are muttering and storming. But let them mutter! Ages will pass, thousands of years will go by, but mankind will remember and glorify the poet who on such a night sang about the fall and burning of Troy. What was Homer compared to him? What was Apollo, with his hollowed-out forminga, *compared to him? None could be compared to him!*

Here he raised his hands, and striking the strings, he sang the words of Priam: "O nest of my fathers! O cherished cradle!"

His voice in the open air, against the roar of the fire and the distant noise of a crowd of thousands, seemed astonishingly feeble, trembling, and weak; the sound of the accompanying instruments was like the buzzing of flies. But senators, dignitaries, and Augustinians gathered together on the aqueduct, bowed their heads and listened in apparent rapture. Nero sang long, and his subject gradually became sadder. At intervals, when he stopped to catch his breath, the chorus of singers repeated the last verse, then Nero would cast the *syrma*[3] from his shoulders and, assuming a tragic gesture that he'd learned from Aliturus, would strike the kithara and continue his song. When at last he finished his composition, he began to improvise, seeking grandiose comparisons in the spectacle unfolding before him. His face began to change. While inwardly unmoved by the terrible destruction of his capital city, he was so intoxicated and moved by the pathos of his own words that his eyes suddenly filled with tears. He dropped the kithara to his feet with a clatter and, wrapping himself in his *syrma*, stood as if petrified, like one of those statues of Niobe that graced the court of the Palatine.

After a short period of silence, a storm of applause followed, but the multitude in the distance answered it by unappreciative howling. Now there could no longer be a doubt that Caesar had ordered the burning of the city so as to provide himself with a spectacle that might move him to perform.

When Nero heard the cry of hundreds of thousands of voices, he turned to the Augustinians with a sad smile of resignation, such as men wear when suffering from injustice, and said, "See how the Quirites value poetry and me?"

"Scoundrels!" snarled Vatinius. "Lord, command the Praetorians to fall on them."

---

3   A long, trailing robe, frequently worn by tragic actors.

Nero turned to Tigellinus. "Could I count upon the loyalty of the soldiers?"

"Yes, O divine one!" replied the prefect.

But Petronius shrugged his shoulders. "On their loyalty you can count, but not on their numbers. Remain for the present where you are, for this is the safest place, but there is need to pacify the people."

Seneca and the consul Licinus were of the same opinion. Meanwhile the tumult below was increasing. The people were arming themselves with stones, tent poles, boards from the wagons, planks, and pieces of iron. Not long afterward some of the chiefs of the Praetorian Guard arrived. They reported that their cohorts, threatened by the multitudes, maintained their position only with extreme difficulty, and as they had no orders to attack, they knew not what to do.

"Gods, what a night!" said Nero.

On one side was the conflagration, on the other a raging sea of people. He began to look for more poetic expressions, so that he could better describe the peril of the moment. But belatedly noticing pale faces and alarmed looks around him, he became frightened himself.

"Give me the dark cloak with the hood," he called out.

"Must we really resort to battle, lord?" hesitantly asked Tigellinus. "I've done everything that I could, but danger is threatening. Speak, O lord, to the people and offer them extravagant promises."

"Must Caesar speak to a rabble? Let somebody else do it in my name. Who will undertake it?"

"I," said Petronius calmly.

"Go, my friend! You are always my most loyal friend. Go, and spare no promises!"

Petronius turned to the retinue with a careless, sarcastic expression. "Senators here present," he cried, "and also Piso, Nerva, and Senecio, come with me."

Then he descended slowly from the aqueduct. Those whom he had summoned followed him, not without hesitation, but with a certain confidence that his calm courage had given them. Petronius, halting at the foot of the Arcades, ordered a white horse to be brought to him. He mounted it and, followed by his companions, rode through the deep ranks of the Praetorians towards the surging dark mass of people. He was unarmed save for a light ivory cane that he habitually carried.

When he reached the howling mob, he pushed his horse into its midst.

All around, clearly visible in the flame-lit night, were upraised arms clutching every manner of weapon, inflamed eyes, perspiring faces. Roaring and foaming like madly surging waves, the masses surrounded him and his followers. On every side was a sea of heads, moving, pushing—a dreadful scene.

The shouts of indignation increased and changed into an unearthly roar. Poles, pitchforks, even swords, were brandished above Petronius. Clutching hands were stretched towards him his horse's bridle, but he kept riding on ever deeper into the midst of the crowd. Cool, self-possessed, and contemptuous, at times he struck the most audacious on their heads with his cane as though he were opening a road for himself through an ordinary throng, and that self-confidence of his, that calmness, dumbfounded the tumultuous mob. At last the people recognized him, and numerous voices began to shout. "Petronius! *Arbiter elegantiarum!* Petronius! Petronius!" was heard on all sides.

At the repetition of that name, the crowd became less turbulent, the faces less agitated, for that brilliant, splendid patrician, though he'd never tried to gain the favor of the people, was nevertheless their favorite. He was considered to be both humane and magnanimous, and his popularity had increased since the affair of Pedanius Secundus, when he pleaded for the mitigation of the ruthless edict condemning all the slaves of that prefect to death. Especially did the slaves feel a boundless affection for him, loving him as the unfortunate tend to love those who show them even the slightest sympathy. Apart from this they were curious to hear what Caesar's message might contain, for nobody doubted that Caesar had specially commissioned him to speak.

Petronius removed his white, scarlet-bordered toga and waved it over his head as a signal that he wished to speak.

"Silence! Silence!" shouted voices on all sides. In a moment the mob was quieted.

Petronius straightened himself on his horse and spoke in a calm and collected voice. "Citizens! Let those who hear me repeat my words to those who stand at a distance. Let all of you behave like men and not like beasts in the arena."

"We listen! We listen!"

"Then hear me. The city will be rebuilt. The gardens of Lucullus, Maecenas, Caesar, and Agrippina will be opened to you. Tomorrow the distribution of grain, wine, and olives will begin, so that everybody may fill his belly up to his throat. After this Caesar will prepare spectacles for you such as the world has never seen. During these games, banquets and gifts await you. You'll be richer after the fire than before."

He was answered by murmurs that spread from the center to all directions, as waves spread when a stone is cast into the water. Those who were near repeated the words to those at a distance, but here and there were shouts of anger and applause, which finally turned into a universal cry: *"Panem et circensus!"*[4]

Petronius wrapped himself in the toga and for some time listened motionless. In his white apparel he resembled a marble statue. The noise from all sides so increased in volume that it even drowned out the roaring of the fire. But the messenger evidently had something more to say, for he waited. At last, once more with upraised hands, he commanded silence.

"I promise *panem et circensus* to you, so now let's hear a shout in honor of Caesar, who feeds and clothes you. Then go to sleep and cease to be an unruly mob, for dawn will break soon."

So saying, he turned his horse, touched lightly with his cane upon the heads and faces of those who stood in his way, and slowly proceeded to the Praetorian lines.

Soon he arrived under the aqueduct. Above, there was something like panic, for they hadn't understood the shout, assumed it to be a new outbreak of rage, and didn't expect Petronius to escape alive. So when Caesar saw him, he hastened to the steps to meet him and, with his face pale from excitement, asked, "Well, what happened? What are they doing? Are they going to attack us?"

Petronius drew a long breath and replied, "By Pollux, they sweat—and such a stench! Somebody give me *epilimna*[5] or I'll faint."

Then he turned to Caesar.

"I promised them," he said, "grain, olives, the opening of the gardens, and games. They worship you anew and are bellowing in your honor. Gods! What a foul odor these plebeians emit!"

"I had the Praetorians ready," blustered Tigellinus, "and had you not quieted them, the shouters would have been silenced forever. It's a pity, Caesar, that you didn't allow me to use force."

---

4 "Bread and games!"
5 A kind of perfume.

Petronius looked at Tigellinus, shrugged his shoulders, and said, "That chance may come—and is not lost yet. You may have to use it tomorrow."

"No, no!" cried Caesar. "I'll order the gardens to be opened to them and grain to be distributed. Thanks to you, Petronius! I'll have spectacles prepared, and the song that I sang before you today, I'll sing in public."

This said, he placed his hand on Petronius's shoulder and asked, "Tell me truthfully, what did you think of my performance?"

"You were worthy of the spectacle as the spectacle was worthy of you," answered Petronius.

Then Nero turned to the fire. "Let's look at it again," he said, "and bid farewell to old Rome."

Chapter XLVIII

The words of the Apostle inspired the Christians with fresh hope. While the end of the world seemed to them always close at hand, they now began to realize that the terrible final judgment had been postponed. The first thing that might happen would be the end of Nero, whose reign they considered as that of the Antichrist and whose crimes cried out to God for vengeance. Thus strengthened in their hearts, they dispersed after the prayer and departed to their temporary habitations and even to the Trans-Tiber, for news had reached them that the conflagration, set there in some twenty places, had turned again (with a change of the wind) towards the riverside and, after devouring here and there what it could, had ceased to spread.

The Apostle, in company with Vinitius and Chilo, also left the quarry. The young tribune didn't venture to interrupt him in his prayers, so he walked on in silence, imploring only with his eyes for pity and trembling from worry and excitement. But many came to kiss Peter's hands and the hem of the Apostle's garment. Mothers held up their children to him. Men knelt in the long, dark passage, holding up tapers and begging a blessing. Others moved by on both sides of them, singing, so that there was no appropriate moment either for question or for answer.

Only when they came out in the open, where the burning city could be seen, did the Apostle bless them three times, then turn to Vinitius and say, "Don't be afraid. Not far from here is the hut of a quarryman, in which we shall find Lygia and Linus, as well as her faithful servant. Christ, who predestined her for you, has preserved her."

Vinitius reeled and only kept himself from falling by leaning against a large rock. The ride from Antium, the events along the wall, the search for Lygia among the burning houses, the sleepless nights, and the unceasing worry about whether or not she was still alive had depleted nearly all his physical reserves; thus the news that the most precious person in the world to him was not only safe, but also near, was more than he could handle.

He suddenly dropped to the Apostle's feet, embraced his knees, and was unable to say so much as one word.

The Apostle, warding off all thanks and honor, declared, "Not to me— but to Christ."

"What a good God!" said the voice of Chilo from behind. "But what shall I do with the mules that are waiting here?"

"Rise and come with me," said Peter, taking by the hand the young man who'd been holding the mules.

Vinitius rose. By the light of the flames, tears were seen to trickle down his pale face, and his lips trembled as though he were praying. "Let's go," he said.

But Chilo once more repeated, "Master, what shall I do with the mules that are waiting? This worthy prophet probably prefers riding to walking."

Vinitius himself didn't know how to answer, but since Peter had told him that the hut of the quarryman was near, he said, "Lead the mules to Macrinus."

"Excuse me, sir, if I remind you of the house in Ameriola. In the shadow of this horrible fire, it's quite natural to forget such trifling things."

"You'll get it."

"O grandson of Numa Pompilius! I was always sure of it, but now hearing the promise and knowing that this magnanimous Apostle has also heard it, I won't even remind you again of my promised vineyard. *Pax vobiscum.* I shall find you, master. *Pax vobiscum.*"

Peter and Vinitius replied, "And with you."

Then they turned to the right towards the hills. Along the way, Vinitius said, "Master, wash me with the waters of baptism so that I may call myself a true confessor of Christ, for I love Him with all my soul. Wash me soon, for I'm ready in my heart, and I'll do whatever you command me to. Just tell me all I ought to do."

"Love everyone as though they were your brothers," answered the Apostle, "for only with love can you serve Him."

"Yes, I already understand and feel that. When I was a child, I believed in the Roman gods, although I didn't love them. But this God I love so much that I'd gladly give my life for Him." He looked towards the sky and repeated with exaltation, "For He is one; for He only is good and merciful; therefore even if not only this city, but also the whole world, should perish, Him alone will I acknowledge, Him alone will I confess."

"And He will bless you and your house," concluded the Apostle.

Meanwhile, they entered another ravine, at the end of which a faint light was visible. Peter pointed to it and said, "That is the dwelling place of the quarryman who sheltered us when we were returning from Ostranium with Linus, who was sick, and we couldn't make it to the other side of the Tiber."

Soon they reached it. The cottage was in reality a cave formed in the slope of the hill and was faced with a wall made of clay and reeds. The door was closed, but through an opening, which served for a window, the interior was visible, lighted by a fire. A dark giant figure rose to meet them and inquired, "Who are you?"

"Servants of Christ," Peter replied. "Peace be with you, Ursus."

Ursus bowed down to the Apostle's feet; then, recognizing Vinitius, he seized his hand by the wrist and raised it to his lips. "And you, master," he said. "Blessed be the name of the Lamb for the gladness you'll bring to Callina."

Saying this, he opened the door and they entered. Linus was lying on a bundle of straw, with an emaciated face and a forehead as yellow as ivory. By the fire sat Lygia, holding in her hand a string of small fish, evidently intended for supper.

Busily occupied with removing the fishes from the string and assuming it was Ursus who had entered, she didn't raise her eyes. But Vinitius softly stepped to her side and said but one word, her name, and extended his arms to her. Springing to her feet, her face lit by surprise, joy, and relief, without a word, as a child who after long days of fear and sorrow finds its father or mother, she ran into his open arms.

He gathered her into his arms and just held her there for some time in rapture—for he'd feared her lost in the fire. Now here was this miracle! Then, withdrawing his arms, he gently placed his hands on her head, kissed her forehead and her misty eyes, pulled back, embraced her again, repeated her name, kissed her hands, and just looked at her in adoration.

At last he told her how he'd hastened in from Antium, how he'd searched for her at the walls and in the smoke in the house of Linus, how great his sufferings were, how much he'd gone through before the Apostle showed him her hiding place. "But now," he said, "now that I've found you, I won't leave you near this fire and these raging crowds. People are murdering one another under the walls; slaves are rebelling and pillaging. Only God knows what miseries are yet to fall on Rome. But I'll protect you and yours, *carissima!* Let's go to Antium; we'll find a ship there and sail for Sicily. My land is your land, my house is your house. Listen to me! In Sicily we'll find Aulus. I'll restore you to Pomponia, and after that I'll take you from her hands as my wife.

"But, *carissima*, have no further fear of me. I'm not yet baptized, but ask Peter if I haven't expressed my desire to become a true confessor of Christ, if I didn't ask him to baptize me, even in the quarryman's cave. Believe, and let all believe in me."

Lygia's face was radiant as she listened to these words.

Christians, first because of Jewish persecution, and now because of the conflagration and consequent confusion, could only live in uncertainty and alarm. A removal to peaceful Sicily would put an end to all this trouble and open a new epoch of happiness in their lives.

Had Vinitius determined to take Lygia alone, she would certainly have resisted the temptation, as she would have been unwilling to leave Peter and Linus. But Vinitius said to them, "Come with me! My land is your land, my houses are your houses."

At this Lygia bowed to kiss his hand, as a mark of obedience, saying, "Where you are, Caius, there am I, Caia."

Then, ashamed that she'd spoken words, which according to Roman custom, were repeated by wives only at the marriage ceremony, she blushed deeply and stood in the light of the fire with drooping head, uncertain whether he would misunderstand. But in his face was only heartfelt adoration. He turned to Peter.

"Rome," he said, "is burning at Caesar's command. He complained at Antium that he'd never seen a great fire. If he shrank not from such a crime as this, think what may yet come to pass. Who knows if he may not now mass his troops in the city and order a general massacre of the inhabitants; who knows what persecution may follow, and who knows whether after the calamity of fire, the calamity of civil war, murder, and famine may not follow? Hide yourselves, and let's also hide Lygia. In Sicily you can wait in peace until the tempest passes and, when it's over, return anew to sow the good seed."

From the direction of the Vatican, as though to confirm the fears of Vinitius, distant cries now arose, cries of rage and terror. At that moment the owner of the hut entered and hastily shut the door behind him.

"Near the Circus of Nero," he cried, "the people are killing one another. Slaves and gladiators are attacking the citizens."

"I baptize you in the name of the Father."

"Do you hear that?" asked Vinitius.

"The measure is filled," said the Apostle, "and disasters will follow, one after another, without limits, controls, or boundaries—like the sea."

He turned to Vinitius and, pointing to Lygia, said, "Take the maiden and save her, together with Linus and Ursus. Let them go with you."

Vinitius, who had come to love the Apostle with all the power of his impetuous soul, exclaimed, "I swear to you, my teacher, that I won't leave you here to die!"

"The Lord bless you for that," answered the Apostle, "but haven't you heard that Christ, when on the lake, three times repeated to me, 'Feed my lambs'?"

Vinitius was silent.

"Moreover, if you who aren't responsible for me, declare that you won't leave me behind to be destroyed, how can you ask that I should abandon my flock in the day of calamity? When we were on the stormy lake and were troubled in heart, He didn't forsake us. How much more should I, a servant, follow the example of my Master?"

Then Linus raised his emaciated face and asked, "And why should I, O representative of the Lord, why should I not follow your example?"

Vinitius pressed his fingers into his forehead as though wrestling with himself or struggling with his thoughts. Then he grasped Lygia by the hand and spoke in a voice quivering with the energy of a Roman soldier.

"Listen to me, Peter, Linus, and you, Lygia. I spoke according to the dictates of my human reason, but you have another reason, which regards not your own danger, but only the commands of the Redeemer. I didn't understand this, and I erred, for the scales haven't yet been removed from my eyes, and the old Adam is not yet dead within me. But since I love Christ and wish to be His servant, and though it's a question for me of something more than my life alone, I kneel here before you and swear that I, too, will fulfill the commandment of love and will not forsake my brethren in the day of trouble."

This said, he knelt down, and suddenly transported into a state of ecstasy, he raised his eyes and hands and called out, "Do I understand You now, O Christ? Am I worthy of You?"

His hands trembled, his eyes glistened with tears, his body shook with faith and love—and Peter the Apostle took a clay amphora full of water, approached him, and solemnly said, "Behold! I baptize you in the name of the Father, the Son, and the Holy Ghost."

Then a spiritual ecstasy seized all present. It seemed to them that the cottage was filled with heavenly light, that they heard heavenly music, that the cliffs had opened above their heads, that choirs of angels floated down from heaven, and that far above, they beheld a cross and pierced hands blessing them.

Meanwhile the riotous shouts of fighting and the roar of flames from the burning city were heard outside.

Chapter XLIX

People camped out in the magnificent gardens of Caesar and in the former gardens of Domitius and Agrippina. On the Campus Martius, in the gardens of Pompey, Sallust, and Maecenas, they occupied the porticos, the ball courts, the comfortable summerhouses, and sheds erected for wild beasts. Peacocks, flamingos, swans; ostriches, gazelles, and antelopes from Africa; stags and deer—all served to ornament the gardens, and all fell under the knives of the mob. Provisions arrived from Ostia in such abundance that one could walk from one side of the Tiber to the other on a bridge of rafts and boats. Grain sold at the unheard-of low price of three sestertia, and to the poor it was distributed free. Immense stores of wine, olives, and chestnuts were brought in. From the mountains, sheep and cattle were driven daily into the city. Beggars, who before the fire hid themselves in the alleys of the Suburra in a starving condition, now lived a pleasant life of ease. Although the fear of famine had entirely vanished, it was more difficult to suppress murder, robbery, and abuses. A vagrant life insured impunity to malefactors, especially since they proclaimed themselves admirers of Caesar and were unsparing of applause whenever he showed himself.

When all authority was suspended and there was not enough power to keep order in a city inhabited by the scum of the world, unspeakable crimes were committed. Every night there were fights, murders, and abductions of women and children. At the Porta Mugionis, where there was a station for the herds driven in from the Campania, there were daily fights in which hundreds of people perished. Every morning the banks of the Tiber were covered with drowned bodies that nobody buried and that, decomposing quickly because of the heat, which was intensified by the fires, filled the air with an almost unbelievably foul stench. Sickness broke out in the encampments, and many feared a great epidemic.

Meanwhile, the city continued to burn. By the sixth day, however, it at last reached the empty space on the Esquiline, where an enormous number of houses had been purposely demolished—only now did the flames slacken. But the piles of burning coals produced so powerful a light that the people refused to believe that the calamity had come to an end. And indeed, on the seventh night, the fire burst out anew in the buildings belonging to Tigellinus, although it soon subsided for lack of fuel. But burned houses collapsed in all directions, which in their fall threw up towers of flame and pillars of sparks. Slowly the glow from the burning began to darken, and the sky after sunset ceased to gleam with a bloody haze, and only during the nighttime could the blue tongues leaping up from the black cinders be seen.

Of the fourteen divisions of Rome there were only four left—including those on the Trans-Tiber; all the others had been destroyed by the fire. When the heaps of cinders were at last reduced to ashes, one could see, from the Tiber to the Esquiline, an immense, gray, dead, and melancholy expanse, upon which stood rows of columns like so many tombstones in a cemetery. Among these columns, crowds of gloomy people moved about during the daytime, some searching for loot, others for the bones of those who were dear to them. In the night, dogs howled above the ashes and ruins of their former homes.

All the bounty and assistance showered on the mob by Caesar didn't keep them from pouring out their wrath and indignation in speech and imprecations. Only the host of robbers, cutthroats, and homeless ruffians, who were now free to eat, drink, and steal, were content. But people who'd lost family members and all their possessions couldn't be appeased by the mere opening of gardens, nor by distribution of grain, nor by promises of games and gifts—the catastrophe had been too great and unprecedented. Others, in whom still glimmered a spark of love for their city and fatherland, were reduced to despair at the news that the old name of Rome was to disappear from the face of the earth and that Caesar intended to raise upon its ashes a new city under the name of Neropolis. A flood of hatred rose and swelled every day in spite of the adulations of the Augustinians and the calumnies of Tigellinus. Nero, more dependent than any of his predecessors on the favor of the rabble, trembled lest he lose mob support in his underhanded efforts to destroy the power of both patricians and the Senate. The Augustinians themselves were not less apprehensive, for any morning might bring destruction upon them. Tigellinus thought of drawing several legions from Asia Minor; Vatinius, who laughed even when slapped in the face, now lost his sense of humor; Vitelius lost his appetite.

Others now talked openly with each other about how they might avert total disaster. It was an open secret that in case of any uprising that would remove Caesar, with the possible exception of Petronius, not a single Augustinian would escape death. Nero's madness was ascribed to their influence; all the crimes he committed, to their suggestion. The hatred of them was almost stronger than that towards Nero. Desperately, they now searched for a way of shifting the responsibility for all those fires away from themselves to some hapless scapegoat. But in clearing themselves, it was also necessary to clear Caesar; otherwise no one would believe that they weren't responsible for the calamity.

Tigellinus sought counsel on this subject with Domitius Afer and even with Seneca, whom he detested. Poppaea, too, understanding that the ruin of Caesar meant also her own, turned to her confidants, the Jewish priests. For some years it had been noised about that she acknowledged the faith of Jehovah. Nero himself found methods of dealing with the crisis that were uniquely his own, varying from the horrible to the foolish, and reeled back and forth between outright terror and maudlin childishness—but with one constant: He was continually complaining.

On one occasion a consultation was held in Tiberius's house, which had escaped the flames. It was a long but fruitless conference. Petronius's advice was to leave the seat of the troubles and depart for Greece, and from there to Egypt and Asia Minor. This voyage had been planned before; why then delay it when it was so dangerous in Rome?

Caesar accepted the suggestion eagerly, but Seneca, after he'd thought a while, objected. "It would be easy to go, but to return would be more difficult."

"By Hercules!" replied Petronius. "We may return at the head of the Asian legions."

"I'll do it!" cried Nero.

But Tigellinus objected. He couldn't think of any solution himself, and had Petronius's idea come into his head first, he would have unhesitatingly declared it to be the safest one. But his chief objective was to prevent Petronius from posing as the one man who could be successfully appealed to in an emergency.

"Listen to me, O divine one," he said. "This advice is ruinous. Before you got as far as Ostia, civil war would break out. Who knows whether one of the still-living descendants of the divine Augustus may not proclaim himself Caesar, and what then shall we do if the legions declare for him?"

"This we can do," answered Caesar. "We can see that there remain no descendants of Augustus. Since there aren't many of them left, it won't be difficult to get rid of the rest of them."

"This can be done. But are they the only ones? Only yesterday, my people heard murmurs in the crowd that Thrasea ought to be Caesar."

Nero bit his lips. After a moment's thought, he raised his eyes and said, "Insatiable and ungrateful! They have plenty of grain, and coal on which they can bake cakes. What more can they want?"

"Vengeance!" exclaimed Tigellinus.

Again there was silence. Suddenly Caesar rose, raised his hand, and began to declaim. "Hearts call for vengeance, and vengeance calls for sacrifice." Forgetting everything, his face brightened, and he called out, "Hand me a tablet and stylus so that I may write this verse. Lucan could never have composed one like it. Did you notice that I conceived it in the twinkling of an eye?"

"O incomparable one!" cried several voices.

Nero wrote down the verse and said, "Yes, vengeance demands a victim." He cast a glance on those who surrounded him. "Suppose we were to spread the news that Vatinius commanded the burning of the city and deliver him to the furious people?"

"O divinity! Who am I?" exclaimed the terrified Vatinius.

"True, one greater than you is needed—Vitelius?"

Vitelius grew pale but began to laugh. "My fat," he said, "would be apt to start the fire again."

But Nero was looking for something else: a victim who could fully appease the fury of the people—and he found him. "Tigellinus," he said after a while, "it was *you* who burned down Rome!"

A shiver ran through those present, for they understood that this time Caesar was in earnest and that a momentous decision was about to be made.

The face of Tigellinus wrinkled up like the jaws of a dog ready to bite. "I burned Rome at your command!" he snarled.

They glared at each other like two demons.

A silence followed so deep that the buzzing of flies could be heard through the hall.

"Tigellinus!" said Nero. "Do you love me?"

"You know, lord."

"Sacrifice yourself for me."

"O divine Caesar," answered Tigellinus. "Why do you offer me the sweet cup that I'm not permitted to raise to my lips? The rabble are muttering and conspiring—would you want the Praetorians to rise as well?"

A feeling of terror swept through those present. Since Tigellinus commanded the Praetorian Guard, beneath his words was an open threat. Nero's face paled as he realized that these were no idle words.

While this was going on, Epaphroditus, Caesar's freedman, entered and made it known that the divine Augusta wished to see Tigellinus, as she was holding audience with people whom the prefect ought to hear.

Tigellinus bowed to Caesar and left with a calm but contemptuous face. They'd wished to strike him and he'd shown his teeth, letting them know who he really was. Knowing the cowardice of Nero, he was confident that the ruler of the world would never dare to raise a hand against him.

Nero sat for a while in silence, then seeing that those present expected some answer, he said, "I've nourished a serpent in my bosom."

Petronius shrugged his shoulders, as much as to say that it was easy to tear off the head of such a serpent.

"What are you trying to say? Speak! Advise!" cried Nero, who'd observed the gesture. "In you alone I trust, for you have more understanding than all of them, and you love me."

Petronius had already on his lips, "Appoint me prefect, and I'll deliver Tigellinus to the people and pacify them in one day," but his natural indolence prevailed. To be prefect meant to bear on his shoulders Caesar's person and a thousand public affairs. Why take upon himself such labor? Was it not preferable to read poetry in a spacious library and look at vases and statues, besides holding the divine body of Eunice on his lap and arranging her golden hair with his fingers and pressing his mouth to her coral lips?

"Then," he said, "I counsel the journey to Achaia."

"Ah!" sighed Nero. "I expected something better from you than that. The Senate detests me; who will guarantee, if I depart, that it will not revolt against me and proclaim someone else Caesar? The people were formally loyal, but now they'll follow the Senate. By Hades! I wish that the people and the Senate had one head."

"Permit me to tell you, O divine one, that if you desire to preserve Rome, you need to preserve a few Romans also," returned Petronius smilingly.

But Nero renewed his complaints. "What are Rome and the Romans to me? In Achaia I should be obeyed. Here nothing but treason surrounds me; all abandon me. You yourselves are getting ready for treason. I know it! I know! You don't even think what future ages will say of you if you forsake such an artist as I am."

He struck his forehead suddenly and cried aloud, "True! In the midst of these troubles, even I myself had forgotten who I was."

He turned a radiant face upon Petronius. "Petronius," he said, "the people murmur, but if I take the kithara and go with it to the Campus Martius, if I sing to them that song that I sang to you at the conflagration, don't you think that I'd move them with my song as Orpheus once moved wild beasts?"

Tullius Senecio, impatient to return to his slave women who'd just arrived from Antium, now broke in. "Beyond doubt, Caesar, if they permit you to begin."

"Let's go to Hellas!" cried Nero with displeasure.

At that moment Poppaea entered, and with her, Tigellinus. The eyes of those present turned to him unconsciously, for never had a victor entered the Capitol with such pride as he stood before Caesar. He began to speak slowly and impressively, in tones through which the bite of iron, as it were, was heard. "Listen to me, O Caesar, for I can tell you what I've found! The people want vengeance and victims—not one victim but hundreds, thousands.

"Have you, lord, heard of Christus, who was crucified by Pontius Pilatus? And do you know who the Christians are? Haven't I told you of their crimes and their infamous ceremonies, of their prophecies that fire would bring about the end of the world? The people hate and suspect them. Nobody has ever seen them in a temple at any time, for they consider our gods to be evil spirits. They are not at the Stadium, for they despise our games and races. Never have the hands of a Christian applauded you. Never has any one of them recognized you as a god. They are the enemies of the human race, enemies of the city and of you. The people murmur against you, for *you* ordered the burning of Rome, not I. The people are thirsting for vengeance; let them have it. The people are thirsting for blood and games; let them have them. The people suspect you—let their suspicion be directed elsewhere."

Nero at first listened with amazement, but as Tigellinus progressed, his actor's face altered and assumed a look of anger, of sorrow, of sympathy, and of indignation. Suddenly he stood up, threw down his toga, which fell at his feet, raised both hands, and remained in that attitude for a while.

At last he exclaimed in the voice of a tragedian, "Zeus, Apollo, Hera,

Athena, Persephone, and all you immortal gods, why didn't you come to our assistance? What has this unfortunate city done to those cruel people that they so inhumanely burned it?"

"They are the enemies of mankind and of you," said Poppaea.

And others began to cry, "Deliver a sentence! Punish the incendiaries! The very gods cry for vengeance!"

Nero sat down, dropped his head on his breast, and was silent again as though stunned by such an atrocity.

But after a while, wringing his hands as though in despair, he said, "What punishment and what tortures should be meted out for such a crime? But the gods will inspire me. Assisted by the power of Tartarus,[1] I'll give my poor people such spectacles that for ages they'll remember me with gratitude."

Petronius suddenly became pale. He thought of the danger hanging over Lygia and Vinitius, whom he loved, and over all those people whose doctrine he rejected, but of whose innocence he was convinced. He also thought of the bloody orgies that would soon take place, against which his aesthetic sense revolted. But above all he said to himself, *I must save Vinitius, who will go mad if that maiden dies.*

This thought outweighed all others. Petronius fully understood that he was attempting something far more perilous than anything he'd ever before ventured. Nevertheless, he began to speak freely and carelessly, as was his custom when criticizing and ridiculing subjects insufficiently aesthetic with Caesar and the Augustinians.

"So you've found victims! Good! You may send them to the arena or dress them in tunics of torture. Good also! But listen to me. You have authority, you have Praetorians, you have power. Deceive the people, but deceive not yourselves. Give the Christians to the mob. Condemn them to whatever torture you please; but have the courage to acknowledge to yourselves that they didn't burn Rome. Fie upon you! You call me *arbiter elegantiarum.* As such I declare to you that I cannot stomach bad comedies. Fie! How all this brings to mind the theatrical booths near the Porta Asinaria, where actors play the parts of gods and kings to amuse the gaping suburban mobs and, when the play is over, wash their onions down with sour wine or submit to a clubbing. Be indeed gods and kings, for you're entitled to the honor.

---

1 Infernal regions, the Furies.

"As to you, O Caesar! You've threatened us with the verdict of coming ages, but remember that the future will also pronounce judgment against you. By the goddess Clio! Nero, ruler of the world—Nero, a god—burned Rome, for he was as powerful on earth as Zeus in Olympus. Nero, a poet, loved poetry so much that to it he sacrificed his country! From the beginning of the world nobody ever did the like—no one ever ventured to do the like. I conjure you in the name of the Muses, do not renounce such glory, for your songs will resound to the end of the ages. Compared with you, what will Priam be? What will Agamemnon be, what Achilles—no, the very gods themselves? It matters not whether the burning of Rome was a good thing, if it was great and out of the common. For this reason, I tell you that the people will not raise their hands against you. Have courage. Keep yourself from acts unbecoming to you, for this only can you fear: that future ages will be able to say, 'Nero burned Rome, but, being a cowardly Caesar and a small-souled poet, he denied the great act out of fear: and cast the blame on the innocent.'"

The words of Petronius made their usual powerful impression on Nero. Nevertheless, Petronius was not deceived as to the fact that his speech was a desperate last-ditch attempt to stave off disaster for the Christians, recognizing at the same time that the speech might well seal his own doom. However, he hadn't hesitated so much as an instant, for the matter concerned Vinitius whom he loved—besides, games of chance had always amused him.

The die is cast, he said to himself. *We shall see how far the fear of death outweighs the love of glory in this ape.*

In his soul, Petronius scarcely dared to doubt that fear would gain the day.

Silence followed his words. Poppaea and all present looked in Nero's eyes as in a rainbow. He pursed up his lips so that they were drawn up to the very nostrils, as he was accustomed to do whenever he knew not what to say. At last wretchedness and anxiety were visible on his face.

"Lord," cried Tigellinus when he saw this, "permit me to go, for when anyone seeks to expose your person to destruction and, besides, calls you a cowardly Caesar, a small-souled poet, an incendiary, and a comedian, my ears cannot suffer such words."

I've lost! thought Petronius. But, turning towards Tigellinus, he measured him with his eyes, in which shone the contempt natural to a great and elegant personage contemplating a knave. Then he said, "Tigellinus, it was you I called a comedian, for you are one this very minute."

"And why? Because I won't listen to your insults?"

"No. It's because you are now professing boundless love for Caesar, yet only a moment ago you threatened him with the Praetorians. All of us understood this as well as he!"

Tigellinus hadn't expected that Petronius would be so daring as to throw such a cast of the dice on the table. He turned pale, lost his head, and became speechless.

But this was the last victory of the *arbiter elegantiarum* over his rival, for at that moment Poppaea broke in: "Lord, how can you permit that such a thought should pass through the head of anybody and especially that anybody should have the temerity to speak it aloud in your presence?"

"Punish the insolent one!" cried Vitelius.

Nero again raised his lips to his nostrils. Turning towards Petronius his nearsighted, glassy eyes, he said, "Is this the way that you reward me for the friendship I had for you?"

"If I'm mistaken, point out my mistake," answered Petronius. "But know that I only speak that which my love for you dictates."

"Punish the insolent one!" repeated Vitelius.

"Punish!" echoed a number of voices.

In the atrium there rose a murmuring, a stir, as the Augustinians began to draw away from Petronius. Even Tullius Senecio, his once steadfast friend, and young Nerva, who up to this hour had shown him the greatest affection, withdrew. Soon Petronius was left alone on the left side of the hall. With a smile on his face he arranged the folds of his robe and awaited what Caesar might say or do.

Caesar said, "You wish me to punish him, but he's my companion and friend. Though he's wounded my heart, let him know that this heart has for its friends only forgiveness."

I've lost! I'm ruined! thought Petronius.

Caesar rose—the consultation was ended.

Chapter L

Petronius returned to his house. Tigellinus accompanied Nero to Poppaea's hall, where people awaited them by appointment with the prefect. There were two rabbis from the Trans-Tiber, in long robes and miters, a young scribe, their assistant, and Chilo. At sight of Caesar, the Jewish priests paled from excitement, stretched out their arms, and bowed their heads.

"We salute you, O monarch of monarchs and king of kings!" cried the elder. "We salute the ruler of the world, the protector of the people, and Caesar, lion among men, whose dominion is like the light of the sun and like the cedars of Lebanon, like a spring, like a palm tree, and like the balm of Gilead!"

"You refuse to address me as a god?" asked Caesar.

The priests grew paler, but the older one continued to speak.

"Your words, O lord, are sweet as a cluster of grapes and as a ripe fig, for Jehovah has filled our hearts with your kindness. Your father's predecessor, Caius Caesar, was a tyrant. Nevertheless, our ambassadors didn't address him as a god, preferring death to a breach of the law."

"And Caligula, didn't he command them to be thrown to the lions?"

"No, Lord; Caius Caesar feared the wrath of Jehovah."

Here they raised their heads, for the name of the almighty Jehovah restored their courage. Trusting in His might, they were emboldened to look straight into Nero's eyes.

"Do you accuse the Christians of setting fire to Rome?"

"Lord, we accuse them only because they are public enemies of the human race, the enemies of Rome and of yourself. Long ago they threatened the city and the world with fire. This man will tell the rest. He is a truthful man, for in the veins of his mother flowed the blood of the chosen people."

Nero turned to Chilo. "Who are you?"

"Your admirer, Osiris! And besides, a poor Stoic."

"I detest the Stoics!" cried Nero. "I hate Thrasea. I hate Musonius and

393

Cornutus. Their sayings I cannot bear, their contempt for art, their voluntary squalor, and their filthiness."

"Lord, your teacher, Seneca, has one thousand tables of lemon wood. If it pleases you, I will have twice as many. I'm a Stoic because of necessity. Dress my stoicism, O radiant one, in a garland of roses, put a pitcher of wine before it, and it will sing Anacreon[1] in such strains as to deafen every Epicurean."

"I'm pleased with you."

"This man is worth his weight in gold," exclaimed Tigellinus.

Chilo answered, "Lord, fill my weight with your liberality, or my weight will be blown away by the wind."

"He wouldn't weigh more than Vitelius," said Caesar.

"Eheu! Silver-bowed Apollo, my wit is not of lead."

"I notice that your law doesn't hinder you from addressing me as a god."

"O immortal one, my faith is in you. The Christians blaspheme against this faith, and therefore I hate them."

"What do you know about the Christians?" asked Poppaea a little impatiently.

"Will you permit me to weep, O divinity?"

"No," said Nero. "It annoys me."

"You are triply right, for eyes that have seen you ought forever to be free from tears. Oh, lord, defend me against my enemies."

"Tell us of the Christians," said Poppaea, with more than a shade of impatience in her voice.

"It will be as you command, O Isis," answered Chilo. "Since my youth I've dedicated myself to philosophy and have searched for truth. I searched for it in the ancient divine philosophers, in the academies of Athens, and in the schools of Alexandria. When I heard of the Christians, I presumed that they formed some new school wherein I might find some grains of truth, and unfortunately I made their acquaintance. The first Christian that I met was a physician from Neapolis, Glaucus by name. From him I learned in due course that they worship a certain Christus, who promised them that he would exterminate all people and destroy all the cities of the world but would spare them should they assist him in stamping out the children of Deucalion. For this reason, lady, they hate people and poison fountains; for this reason in their meetings they heap

---

1   A Greek lyric poet of Teos who wrote around 540 B.C.

curses on Rome and on all sanctuaries in which homage is given to our gods. Christus was crucified, but he promised them that when Rome was destroyed by fire he would come again into the world and give them dominion over the universe."

"Now men will understand why Rome was destroyed by fire!" said Nero, affecting outrage.

"Many understand that already, O lord," answered Chilo, "for I visit the gardens and the Campus Martius and teach. But if you listen to the end you'll understand why I demand vengeance. At first Glaucus didn't reveal to me that their religion taught them hatred. He told me, on the contrary, that Christus is a good God and that the foundation of their religion is love. My tender heart couldn't reject such truth; therefore I loved Glaucus and trusted him. I divided with him every morsel of bread, every coin. Lady, how do you think he repaid me? On the road from Neapolis to Rome he stabbed me with a knife, and my wife, the young and beautiful Berenice, he sold to a slave trader. Oh, that Sophocles knew of my story! But what do I say? One better than Sophocles is listening."

"Poor man!" said Poppaea.

"Whoever has seen the face of Aphrodite is not poor, lady, and I see her at this moment. But at that time I sought consolation in philosophy. Coming to Rome I tried to reach the Christian elders, in order to obtain justice against Glaucus. I thought that they'd force him to give up my wife. I became acquainted with their high priest. I know another, Paul by name, who was a prisoner here but was liberated. I made the acquaintance of the son of Zebedee, of Linus, and Clitus, and many others. I know where they lived before the conflagration, and I know where they meet. I can show you an underground grotto on the Vatican Hill and a cemetery beyond the Porta Nomentana where they celebrate their abominable ceremonies. I saw the Apostle Peter. I saw Glaucus killing children so that the Apostle might have something to sprinkle on the heads of those present. I saw Lygia, the ward of Pomponia Graecina, who boasted that though she was unable to bring the blood of a child, she had caused the death of an infant by bewitching the little Augusta, your daughter, O Osiris, and yours, O Isis!"

"Do you hear, Caesar?" cried Poppaea.

"Can this be so?" exclaimed Caesar.

"I can forgive wrongs done to myself," continued Chilo, "but hearing of yours, I wanted to stab her. I was unfortunately stopped by the noble Vinitius, whom I love."

"Vinitius? How can that be? Didn't she run away from him?"

"She did flee, but he searched for her, as he couldn't live without her. For a pittance I helped him in his search, and I pointed out to him the house where she lived among the Christians on the other side of the Tiber. We went there together, and with us your pugilist Croto, whom the noble Vinitius hired for protection. But Ursus, the slave of Lygia, killed him. He is a man of enormous strength, O lord, who could wrench off the head of a bull as easily as the head of a poppy from its stalk."

"By Hercules!" cried Nero. "The man who choked Croto is worthy of a statue in the Forum. But you are mistaken or inventing, for Croto was killed by the knife of Vinitius."

"That's the way in which people lie against the gods, O lord! I myself saw how the ribs of Croto were crushed in the hands of Ursus, who then fell upon Vinitius. He would have killed him, were it not for Lygia. Vinitius was afterward sick for a long time, but they nursed him, hoping that by their kindness he would become a Christian—in fact, he *did* become a Christian."

"Vinitius?"

"Yes."

"And perhaps Petronius also?" inquired Tigellinus.

Chilo squirmed, rubbed his hands, and said, "I admire your penetration, master. It may be so."

"Now I understand why he defended the Christians!"

But Nero laughed. "Petronius a Christian? Petronius an enemy of life and comfort? Don't be fools and ask me to believe it—I'm prepared to believe anything but that!"

"But the noble Vinitius became a Christian, lord. I swear by the radiance that emanates from you that I speak the truth and that nothing disgusts me so much as falsehood. Pomponia is a Christian, and Lygia and Vinitius are Christians. I served them faithfully, but at the request of Glaucus, they recompensed me with a flogging, in spite of my advanced age and though I was suffering from hunger and sickness. I've sworn by Hades that I'll never forget it. Oh, lord, avenge my wrongs, and I'll deliver to you the Apostle Peter, the elders Linus, Clitus, Glaucus, and Crispus, as well as Lygia and Ursus. I'll point out to you where hundreds, indeed thousands, of them meet. I'll point out their houses of prayer and their cemeteries—all your prisons together will not be enough to hold them all. Without me you'd be unable to find them. Up to this time, when I was poor, I sought consolation in philosophy. Let me find it now in the favors that will be showered upon me. I'm old, but I haven't enjoyed life—let that enjoyment now begin!"

"You wish to be a Stoic before a full plate," quipped Nero.

"Whoever renders service to you will be paid just as generously."

"You're not mistaken there, O philosopher."

Poppaea never forgot her enemies. Her attraction to Vinitius was but a momentary passion; the result was jealousy, anger, and injured self-love. The coldness of the young patrician stung her and filled her heart with stubborn offense. The mere fact that he dared to prefer another over her seemed to her a crime calling for revenge. As for Lygia, she'd hated her from the very first moment, when the beauty of the northern lily caused her uneasiness. Petronius, who spoke of the too-narrow hips of the girl, could say what he pleased to Caesar, but not to the Augusta. The knowing Poppaea understood at a glance that in all Rome, Lygia alone could rival and even surpass her. From that moment on she'd sworn her ruin.

"Lord," she cried, "avenge our child!"

"Hasten!" cried Chilo. "Hasten! Otherwise Vinitius will hide her. I'll point out the house to which they returned after the fire."

"I'll give you ten men, and go there instantly," commanded Tigellinus.

"Master, you didn't see Croto in the grips of Ursus. If you give me fifty men, I'll point out the house from afar—but if you fail to imprison him, I'm lost."

Tigellinus looked at Nero with veiled malevolence.

"Would it not be fitting, O divinity, to rid yourself at once of both the uncle and the nephew?"

Nero thought for a moment, then answered. "No, not now. People wouldn't believe that Petronius, Vinitius, or Pomponia Graecina fired Rome. Their houses were too beautiful. Today other victims are needed. Their turn will come next."

"Then, lord, give me soldiers as a guard," said Chilo.

"See to this, Tigellinus."

"You will, meanwhile, live with me," said the prefect.

Joy beamed from the face of the Greek. "I'll betray every last one of them! Only hurry! Hurry!" he shouted with a hoarse voice.

Chapter LI

After leaving Caesar, Petronius had himself carried to his house on the Carinae, which, surrounded as it was on three sides by a garden and having in front the small forum of Cecilia, had miraculously escaped the conflagration. Other Augustinians who'd lost their houses with all their treasures and works of art dubbed Petronius a lucky man. For a long time past they had spoken of him as the firstborn son of Fortune, and Caesar's growing friendship had seemed to confirm this opinion.

But the firstborn of Fortune might now meditate on the fickleness of his mother, or rather on her likeness to the god Cronus,[1] who devoured his own children.

Had my house been burned, he said to himself, *together with my gems, my Etruscan vases, Alexandrian glass, and Corinthian bronze, Nero might have forgotten his anger. By Pollux! And to think I had the opportunity to be prefect to the Praetorians! At this moment I might have held the power to brand Tigellinus as the incendiary, which he is in fact. I'd have placed him in the tunic of torture, delivered him over to the mob, saved the Christians, and rebuilt Rome. Who knows but that a happier period might not have arisen for honest men? I ought to have done that, were it only for Vinitius's sake. If the work had proved too hard, I could have surrendered the office of prefect to him. Nero wouldn't even have attempted opposition. Then Vinitius might have baptized all the Praetorians and even Caesar himself for all I cared. What harm could that have done? Nero pious, Nero virtuous and merciful— that would indeed be an amusing spectacle!*

He couldn't help but laugh at this improbable, if not impossible,

---

1 Father of Zeus. Before their sixth child was born, Cronus's wife Rhea was said to have fled to Arcadia and entrusted her baby Zeus to Gaea for safekeeping. When Zeus grew up, he and Metis (daughter of Oceanus) got Cronus to swallow a potion that caused him to disgorge Hestia, Demeter, Hera, Hades, Poseidon, and the stone dressed in baby clothes that had been substituted for the baby Zeus. Together, the children then defeated Cronus.

development. But after a while his thoughts flowed into another channel. He was in Antium and Paul of Tarsus was speaking. *"You call us enemies of life, but answer me, Petronius, if Caesar were a Christian and acted according to our doctrines, wouldn't your lives be more secure?"*

Remembering these words, he continued to muse. *By Castor! Even if they were to murder all the Christians here, Paul would find new ones, for unless the world can stand upon knavery, he's right. But who knows, perhaps knavery may not triumph after all! I who've learned not a little, clearly didn't learn enough to be a great enough scoundrel—because of that I may have to open my veins. But in any event this would most likely have been the end anyhow, or something much like it. I'm only sorry for my Eunice and my goblet. Eunice, however, is free and the vase will go with me. At least Ahenobarbus won't get it. I'm also sorry for Vinitius.*

Since recently I've been bored less often than before, I'm ready. There are many beautiful things in the world, but people are generally so vile that life is just not worth living. Though I belong to the Augustinians, I was freer than they supposed.

Here he shrugged his shoulders.

Quite likely, at this very moment, they assume I'm so trembling with terror that my hair is standing straight up. But when I reach home, I'll take a bath in violet water; then my golden-haired lady will herself anoint me, and after refreshment we'll command the singing aloud of that hymn to Apollo which Anthemius composed. I remember saying once that it's a waste of time to think much about death, because it thinks about us all the time, whether we think about it or not.

Wouldn't it be a wonder if there really were such a thing as Elysian fields, and in them the spirits of the departed? If that were true, Eunice would at once come to me, and together we'd wander over asphodel meadows. We should find, too, better company there than here. What buffoons and tricksters! What a vile herd without taste or polish! Tens of arbiters elegantiarums *couldn't change those Trimalchions[2] into respectable people. By Persephone, I've had enough of them!*

He noticed with surprise that something had already separated him from that world. He had known it well and had known therefore what to

---

2 A central (fictional) character in Petronius's *Satyricon*, Trimalchio is a former slave who achieves great wealth and power—but not taste. Thus he is ludicrous when he pretends to be cultured.

think of it, but now a greater contempt than ever came over him. Surely he'd had enough of it all!

But afterward he began to reflect on his position. Thanks to his acute reasoning powers, he felt confident that no destruction was threatening him directly—yet. For Nero had seized an appropriate occasion to utter a few select and lofty phrases about friendship and forgiveness, thus binding him for the moment. He would now be obliged to search for a pretext, and in the search, time must surely elapse.

The first thing he'll do is send the Christians into the arena, thought Petronius. *Only then will he think of me. If so, it's not worthwhile to trouble myself about it nor change my mode of life. Vinitius is in far more immediate peril.*

And from then on he thought only of Vinitius, whom he was determined to save. Four sturdy Bithynian slaves bore his litter through ruins, ash heaps, and chimneys, with which the Carinae was yet filled, but he commanded them to run swiftly so as to reach Vinitius as quickly as possible. Vinitius, whose *insula* had been burned, now lived with him and fortunately was at home.

"Have you seen Lygia today?" asked Petronius as he entered.

"I've just returned from her."

"Listen to what I tell you and lose no time in questions. It was decided today to lay the blame for burning Rome on the Christians. Terrible persecutions and tortures await them. Pursuit may begin at any moment. Take Lygia and flee instantly, be it to beyond the Alps or to Africa. Hurry, for the Palatine is nearer the Trans-Tiber than this place."

Vinitius was too much of a soldier to lose time in asking questions. He listened with knitted brows and with a face intent and terrible, yet fearless. It was obvious that his first impulse was to defend himself and give battle. "I go," was all he said.

"One word more. Take a purse of gold, take weapons, and a few of your Christian people. In case of need, rescue her!"

Vinitius was already at the door of the atrium.

"Send me news by a slave!" Petronius called out.

When left alone, Petronius began to walk along the columns that adorned the atrium, thinking about all that had happened. He knew that Lygia and Linus had returned after the fire to their former home, which, like the greater part of the Trans-Tiber, had been spared. It was unfortunate, for otherwise it wouldn't have been easy to find them among the crowds of people. Petronius hoped, however, that nobody in the Palatine

knew where they lived, so that Vinitius could get there before the Praetorian Guard. It also occurred to him that Tigellinus, wishing to capture as
many Christians as possible at one time, would extend his net over all
Rome; to do so, he'd have to divide the Praetorians into small divisions.

If they send no more than ten men for her, he thought, *that Lygian giant
will break their bones, and think of the combined resistance when Vinitius
arrives with his forces!*

This thought reassured him. Surely armed resistance to the Praetorians
was tantamount to war with Caesar. Petronius also knew that if Vinitius
hid himself from Nero's vengeance, that same vengeance might fall on
himself, but he cared little about that; on the contrary, he rejoiced at the
thought of the plans of Nero and Tigellinus and determined to spare neither men nor money in the struggle. Since, in Antium, Paul of Tarsus had
converted most of Petronius's slaves, he might be sure that in defending
the Christians he could count on their zeal and devotion.

The entrance of Eunice interrupted his thoughts. At sight of her, all his
cares and troubles vanished without a trace. He forgot Caesar, the disfa-
vor into which he had fallen, the degradation of the Augustinians, the persecution that threatened the Christians, and Vinitius and Lygia, but only
looked upon her with the eyes of an aesthete enamored of wonderful
forms and of a lover who breathed love through such a form. Arrayed in
a transparent violet robe through which shone her rose-colored body, she
was in truth as beautiful as a goddess. Conscious of the admiration she
excited, loving Petronius with her whole soul, and ever ready for his
caresses, she now began to blush for joy as though she were not a concubine but an innocent maiden.

"What have you to say to me, Charis?"[3] asked Petronius, stretching out
his hand to her.

Inclining her golden head, she answered, "Anthemius has arrived with
his choristers. He asks if you wish to hear him today."

"Let him stay and sing to us during dinner. Surrounded by the burning ashes, we shall listen to the hymn to Apollo. By the groves of Paphos!
When I see you in this Coan[4] gauze, it seems to me that Aphrodite, veiled
with a portion of the sky, stands before me."

---

3 According to Homer, one of the Graces and the wife of Hephaestus (one of the twelve
   Olympians).
4 From the island of Coa.

"Oh, master!" said Eunice.

"Come here, Eunice, embrace me with your arms—and give me your lips. Do you love me?"

"I couldn't have loved Zeus more."

She pressed her lips to his mouth, trembling in his arms from happiness.

After a while Petronius said, "Suppose the time has arrived when we have to separate?"

Eunice looked into his eyes with fear. "How so, master?"

"Fear not! But who knows whether I may not have to set out on a long voyage."

"Take me also."

Petronius suddenly changed the conversation and asked, "Tell me, are there any asphodels in the grass plots in the garden?"

"The cypresses and the lawns are withered from the fire, the leaves have fallen from the myrtles, and the entire garden seems dead."

"All Rome seems dead, and soon it will be a real graveyard. Do you know that an edict is about to be issued against the Christians and that a persecution will begin, during which thousands of people will perish?"

"Why should they be punished, master? They are good and quiet people."

"Just for that very reason."

"Then let's go to the sea; your divine eyes don't like to look on blood."

"True, but meanwhile I must bathe. Come to the *elaeothesium* to rub unguents on my arms. By the girdle of Cypris, never have you seemed so beautiful to me! I'll order a bath to be made for you in the form of a shell, and you'll seem like a costly pearl within it. Come, golden-haired one!"

They went out. An hour later both of them, their heads wreathed with roses, their eyes covered with mist, rested at a table spread with vessels of gold. They were served by youths attired as cupids; they drank wine from ivy-covered goblets and heard the hymn to Apollo sung to the music of the harp under the direction of Anthemius. What did they care that around their villa rose chimneys like funeral pyres of the ruined houses and gusts of wind scattered the ashes of burned Rome in every direction? They were happy, thinking only of love, which made their lives like a divine dream.

But before the hymn was ended, a slave, the *atriensis*, entered the hall.

"Master," he said in a voice trembling with alarm, "a centurion with a detachment of the Praetorian Guards stands below and, at Caesar's command, wishes to see you."

The song and the music ceased. All present were alarmed, for Caesar was not accustomed to sending Praetorians on friendly errands to his friends; thus their presence in those days forebode no good. Petronius alone showed not the slightest emotion but said, like a man annoyed by too frequent callers, "They might have let me dine in peace." Then turning to the *atriensis* he said, "Let them enter."

The slave disappeared behind the curtain. A moment later, heavy steps were heard and an acquaintance of Petronius, the centurion Aper, armed and with an iron helmet on his head, entered the hall.

"Noble lord," he said, "here's a letter from Caesar."

Petronius extended his white hand deliberately, took the tablet, read it, and handed it with the greatest composure to Eunice. "He reads a new book on the *Troica* this evening and commands my presence."

"I have only the order to deliver the letter," said the centurion.

"Yes! There'll be no answer, but perhaps you'd like to rest a while with us and empty a goblet of wine?"

"Thanks, noble lord. Gladly will I drink a goblet of wine to your health, but I can't remain long, for I'm on duty."

"Why did Caesar send the letter by you and not by a slave?"

"I know not, master. Perhaps it was because I was sent in this direction on another duty."

"I know," said Petronius, "against the Christians?"

"True, master."

"Is it long since the pursuit began?"

"Some divisions were dispatched to the Trans-Tiber before noon." Thus saying, the centurion spilled out a little wine in honor of Mars, quaffed it, and said, "May the gods grant you, lord, what you wish!"

"Take the goblet and keep it," said Petronius. Then he signaled to Anthemius to finish the hymn to Apollo.

Ahenobarbus is beginning to play with me and Vinitius, he said to himself as the harps sounded again. *I can guess his purpose. He wants to frighten me by sending his summons through a centurion. In the evening, the centurion will be asked in what manner I received him. No! No! You will not amuse yourself overmuch, O malicious and cruel monkey. I know that you won't forget the offense, I know that my destruction is certain, but if you think that I'll look into your eyes beseechingly, that you'll discover in my face either terror or humility, you're most mistaken.*

"Caesar writes, master, 'Come if you wish,'" said Eunice. "Will you go?"

"I'm in excellent health, so I can listen even to *his* verses," answered Petronius. "I'll go, the more so since Vinitius can't."

After dinner and his usual promenade, he placed himself in the hands of his slaves, hairdressers, and attendants, who arranged the folds of his garments, and in an hour's time, beautiful as a god, he had himself borne to the Palatine.

It was late. The evening was calm and warm. The moon shone so brightly that the *lampadarii* preceding the litter extinguished the torches. On the streets and among the ruins meandered drunken crowds, adorned with garlands of ivy and honeysuckle, carrying branches of myrtle and laurel procured from Caesar's gardens. An abundance of grain and the expectation of splendid games had filled the hearts of the people with joy. Here and there songs were heard, magnifying the divine night and the power of love. Here and there people danced in the moonlight. The slaves had to shout for more room for the litter of the noble Petronius, and the mob fell back and shouted in honor of their favorite.

He thought of Vinitius and wondered why he hadn't received any news from him. He was an Epicurean and an egotist, but through his association with Paul of Tarsus and with Vinitius, and hearing daily of the Christians, he'd changed a little without being aware of it. A breeze, as it were, had wafted upon his soul an unknown seed. Other people besides himself began to interest him. Also, he'd always been attached to Vinitius, for in his childhood he had greatly loved his sister, the mother of Vinitius. Now, therefore, when he was taking an interest in his nephew's affairs, he looked upon them with as much concern as he would have looked upon a tragedy.

He didn't lose hope that Vinitius had arrived before the Praetorians and fled with Lygia or, in the worst case, had rescued her. But he'd have preferred to be certain, since he foresaw that he might have to answer various questions for which it would be well to be prepared.

Halting in front of the house of Tiberius, he alighted from his litter. After a while he entered Caesar's hall, already filled with courtiers. His friends of yesterday, clearly astonished that he'd been invited, attempted to ignore him. But he mingled among them, handsome, independent, careless, and as self-confident as though he still had the power to distribute favors. Seeing this, some were alarmed, lest their coldness towards him might prove to have been premature.

Caesar, however, pretended not to see him and made no response to his bow, being apparently occupied in conversation.

But Tigellinus approached and said, "Good evening, *arbiter elegantiarum*. Do you still assert that Rome was not burned by the Christians?"

Petronius shrugged his shoulders and clapped Tigellinus on his back as he would a freedman. "You know as well as I what to think of that."

"I don't dare to compare myself with you in wisdom."

"For once you're right. For when Caesar reads us a new song from the *Troica*, you'll be obliged, instead of screaming like a peacock, to say something that's not pointless."

Tigellinus bit his lips. He wasn't overjoyed that Caesar had decided to read a new song, for that opened up a field in which he couldn't compare favorably with Petronius. In fact, at the time of the reading, Nero involuntarily, from old habit, turned his eyes towards Petronius with careful scrutiny as if to read his face. Petronius, as he listened, raised his brows, approved at times, and at others intensified his attention as if he wanted to be sure he had heard correctly. Some parts he praised, others he criticized, recommending modifications or corrections. Nero couldn't fail to recognize that others in their fulsome praises thought only of themselves, while Petronius occupied himself with poetry for its own sake, he alone understanding it. When he happened to praise, one could be certain that the verses were good. Little by little he was drawn into a discussion with him.

Finally, when Petronius questioned the fitness of a certain expression, he said, "You'll see in the last song why I used it."

Ah! thought Petronius, *then we shall wait for the last poem.*

Many in the audience thought to themselves, *Woe is me! Petronius, having ample time, may return to favor and even overthrow Tigellinus.*

They began to flock around him. But the close of the evening was less fortunate. When Petronius was taking leave, Caesar asked suddenly, with blinking eyes and a face full of malicious delight, "Why did Vinitius not come?"

Had Petronius been certain that Vinitius and Lygia were already beyond the gates of the city, he might have replied, "He was married, with your permission, and left." But observing the odd expression of Nero, he answered, "Your invitation, O divine one, did not find him at home."

"Tell him that I'll be glad to see him," answered Nero, "and tell him from me not to miss the games in which Christians will appear."

These words alarmed Petronius, for it seemed to him that they contained a direct allusion to Lygia. Seated in his litter, he gave orders for even greater speed than in the morning. But this was no easy task, for in front of Tiberius's house stood a dense and tumultuous crowd, drunk as before, but not singing and dancing, and clearly excited about something.

Cries were heard from a distance that Petronius at first couldn't comprehend, but these increased in volume, until at last they merged into one savage roar: "The Christians to the lions!"

Splendid litters of courtiers hustled through the howling rabble. From the depths of the burned streets poured in new crowds, who, hearing the cries, repeated them. The news flew from mouth to mouth that the pursuit had been continued since noon and that already a great number of incendiaries had been rounded up.

Along the new streets and the old, through alleys lying among the ruins near the Palatine, along all the hills and gardens, through the length and breadth of Rome, rang ever-increasing shouts of swelling rage: "The Christians to the lions!"

Asses! thought Petronius with contempt. *The people are worthy of their Caesar.*

And it struck him that a people propped up by force, by cruelty such as even barbarians had no conception of, mad and dissolute, couldn't long endure. Rome dominated the world, but it was also its ulcer. The putrid odor of a corpse was rising from it, and over its decaying life the shadow of death was descending. More than once had this been spoken of, even among the Augustinians. But never before had the truth come so clear to Petronius that the laureled chariot, upon which stood the statue of triumphant Rome dragging behind it a chained herd of nations, was hastening on to a precipice. The life of the world-ruling city appeared to him a sort of mad dance, an orgy which must soon end.

He now perceived that the Christians alone had a new foundation for life. But, alas! Before long not a vestige would be left of the Christians. And what then? The mad dance would continue under the lash of Nero. When Nero was gone, another would be found like him, or one even worse, since among such people and such patricians there was no hope for a better one. There would be a new orgy, viler and fouler than ever. But the orgy couldn't last forever. Sleep must eventually terminate it, even if for no other reason than total exhaustion.

While thinking of this, Petronius felt greatly troubled. Was life worthwhile if spent in uncertainty, with no aim save to gaze upon a world of this sort? The god of death was no less beautiful than the god of sleep,[5] and he also had wings on his shoulders.

The litter stopped in front of his door, which was opened at once by the ever-watchful *atriensis.*

"Has the noble Vinitius returned?" asked Petronius.

"Yes, lord, a moment ago," answered the slave.

So he failed to rescue her! thought Petronius, and casting aside his toga, he hurried into the atrium.

Vinitius was sitting on a three-legged stool, his head bent almost to his knees and his hands on his head. At the sound of steps, he raised his stonelike face, in which his eyes shone with a feverish gleam.

"Did you arrive too late?" asked Petronius.

"Yes! They seized her before noon."

A moment of silence followed.

"Did you see her?"

"Yes."

"Where is she?"

"In the Mamertine prison."

Petronius shuddered and cast an inquiring glance on Vinitius.

"No," said the latter, comprehending his meaning, "they didn't thrust her down in the *tullianum,*[6] nor in the middle prison. I paid the guard to surrender his own room to her. Ursus took his place at the threshold and now watches over her."

"Why didn't Ursus defend her?"

"They sent fifty Praetorians, and Linus prohibited him."

"But Linus?"

"Linus is dying; that's why they didn't take him."

"What do you propose to do?"

"To rescue her or die with her, for I also believe in Christ."

Though Vinitius spoke quietly, his voice betrayed such heartbreak that the heart of Petronius responded in empathetic pity. "I understand," he said, "but how do you think you can save her?"

---

5 Both the Roman god of death (Mors or Thanatos) and the Roman god of sleep (Hypnos or Somnus) were winged. In art, the two were portrayed as young men, often sleepy or carrying inverted torches.

6 The lowest part of the prison, lying entirely underground. It had only one opening: in the ceiling.

"I paid large sums to the guards; first, to protect her from indignity; second, to make no effort to impede her flight."

"When will that be accomplished?"

"They replied that they couldn't deliver her up to me at once, as they feared responsibility. As soon as the prison is crowded and the register of the prisoners becomes confused, they'll deliver her to me. But this is a last resort! Save her and me! You are Caesar's friend; he himself gave her back to me. Go to him and save us!"

Instead of replying, Petronius called a slave and commanded him to bring two dark cloaks and two swords, then he turned to Vinitius.

"On the road I'll answer you," he said. "Meanwhile, take the cloak, take the sword, and we'll go to the prison. There, give the guards a hundred thousand sesterces—give them twice, or even five times, as much—if they agree to free Lygia immediately. Otherwise it will be too late."

"Let's go!" cried Vinitius.

"Now listen to me," said Petronius as they reached the street. "We must lose no time. From today on I'm in disgrace. My own life hangs suspended on a hair; therefore I can get nothing from Caesar. Worse still, I'm certain that to spite me he would refuse my request. Were it not for this, would I have counseled you to flee with her or to rescue her? If you should succeed in escaping, the wrath of Caesar will fall upon me. He might concede your request today, but not mine, so don't count on it. No other option remains for you. Get her out of the prison and flee! If this doesn't succeed, then there'll be time for other remedies. Meanwhile, keep in mind the fact that Lygia is a prisoner not only because of her belief in Christ, but also because Poppaea's anger is against her and you, and she hates you both. Have you forgotten that you gravely offended the Augusta by rejecting her? She knows that Lygia was the cause of the rejection and has thus hated her from the first time she laid eyes on her. Once before she tried to destroy Lygia by attributing to her the death of her child by witchcraft; thus the finger of Poppaea is in all that's now happening. Otherwise, how can we explain why Lygia was the first to be imprisoned? Who could have pointed out the house of Linus? But I can confirm that she's been shadowed for some time. I know that I wring your soul and tear the last shred of hope from you, but I say all this on purpose, for if you fail to free her before they scent your intentions, then you're both lost."

"True. I now understand!" answered Vinitius in a broken voice.

Owing to the lateness of the hour, the streets were deserted. Further conversation was interrupted by a drunken gladiator. He reeled against Petronius and placed his hand on his shoulder. Breathing into his face the odor of wine, he shouted in a hoarse voice, "The Christians to the lions!"

"*Mirmillon*,"[7] was Petronius's quiet answer, "listen to good advice: Hurry on your way."

The drunken gladiator seized Petronius by the other hand.

"Shout instantly 'The Christians to the lions!' or I'll break your neck."

Petronius's nerves had stood about as much as they could from this rampaging rabble. From the time he'd left the Palatine they had continually assailed him like an endless nightmare, so when he saw the uplifted hand ready to strike him dead, the measure of his patience was filled.

"Friend," he said, "you smell of wine and impede my way."

So saying, he ran the short sword with which he'd armed himself up to the hilt in the man's breast. Then, taking Vinitius by the arm, he moved on as though nothing had happened.

"Caesar said to me today, 'Ask Vinitius in my name to be present at the games in which the Christians will appear.' Do you fully understand what that means? They wish to make a spectacle of your anguish. It's a settled affair and may be the reason why you and I haven't yet been imprisoned. If you're not able to get her out of prison . . . I don't know! . . . Perhaps Acte might intercede in your behalf. But could she do it? Your Sicilian lands might also tempt Tigellinus. It's at least worth trying."

"I'll give him everything I own!" answered Vinitius.

From the Carinae to the Forum was not far, hence they arrived quickly. Night was already paling, and the outlines of the walls of the castle could be discerned.

Suddenly, as they turned towards the Mamertine prison, Petronius stopped and said, "Praetorians! Too late!"

In fact, the prison was surrounded by a double row of soldiers. The dawn silvered their iron helmets and the points of their javelins. Vinitius's face became as pale as death.

"Let's go," he said.

After a while they halted before the line. Gifted with an uncommon memory, Petronius knew not only all the officers, but also nearly all the

---

7 A kind of gladiator, generally matched with a *retiarius*, a gladiator with a net to entangle an opponent.

Praetorian soldiers. He soon discovered one of his old acquaintances, the leader of a cohort, and nodded to him.

"What does this mean, Niger?" he asked. "Did they order you to guard the prison?"

"Yes, noble Petronius; the prefect feared lest attempts might be made to rescue the incendiaries."

"Have you an order to refuse admittance?" inquired Vinitius.

"No, master, we have none, for friends will visit the prisoners, and thus we'll be able to seize more Christians."

"Then let me in," said Vinitius. Pressing Petronius's hands, he said to him, "See Acte. I'll come to you for her answer."

"Come," replied Petronius.

At that moment, from beneath the ground and beyond the thick walls, was heard the sound of singing. A hymn low and faint at first, by degrees it swelled in volume. Voices of men, women, and children formed together a harmonious chorus. The whole prison began to resound like a harp in the quiet dawn. But these were not voices of anguish or despair, but on the contrary, of joy and triumph!

The soldiers looked at one another in amazement. In the sky appeared the first golden gleams of the dawn.

Chapter LII

"The Christians to the lions!" was heard increasingly in all parts of the city. From the first, not only did no one doubt that the Christians were the incendiaries, but also no one wished to doubt, since their punishment would yield amusement for everyone. Nevertheless, it was assumed that the punishment wouldn't have been so severe were it not for the anger of the gods. For this reason, *piacula*[1] were commanded in the temples. After consultation of the sibylline books, the Senate ordered solemnities and public prayers to Vulcan, Ceres, and Proserpina. Matrons laid offerings before Juno; a great many of them, in fact, went in procession to the seashore to draw water and besprinkle the statue of the goddess. Married women prepared feasts for the gods and night watches. All Rome purified itself from sin, brought offerings, and placated the immortals.

Meanwhile, broad new streets were laid out through the wreckage of what had once been Rome. Here and there foundations were already being laid for spacious buildings, palaces, and sanctuaries. But first of all was constructed, with unprecedented speed, an enormous wooden amphitheater, in which the Christians were to die. Immediately after the consultation in the house of Tiberius, orders were sent out to the proconsuls to procure wild beasts. Tigellinus emptied the *vivaria* of all Italian cities, not excepting the smallest. At his command, gigantic hunts were ordered in Africa, in which the entire local population was forced to take part. Elephants and tigers were brought in from Asia, crocodiles and hippopotami from the Nile, lions from the Atlas Mountains, wolves and bears from the Pyrenees, savage dogs from Hibernia, Molossian dogs from Epirus, bisons and gigantic wild bulls from Germania. Because of the great number of prisoners, the games would surpass in magnitude any spectacle ever seen before. Caesar wished to drown the memory of the conflagration in blood, to make Rome drunk with it; hence the flow of blood would be staggering.

1 Purifying sacrifices.

The people were eager to help the guards and the Praetorians in their hunt for Christians. It was not a difficult task, for large groups of them camped among the people in the gardens and openly made known their faith. When surrounded, they knelt and, singing hymns, permitted themselves to be led away without resistance. Their patience only increased the anger of the mob, who, not understanding its source, looked upon it as stubbornness and a hardened persistence in crime. Madness seized the populace. Often the rabble wrested Christian captives from the Praetorians and tore them to pieces. Women were dragged to prison by their hair; children's heads were smashed against stones. Thousands of howling people ran wildly through the streets, day and night, searching for victims among the ruins, in chimneys, and in cellars. In front of the prisons, around fires and casks of wine, bacchanalian feasts and dances were celebrated. In the evening, the noise of the drunken crowd, like the roar of thunder, reverberated through the entire city. The mob and the Praetorians brought in new victims daily. Pity ceased to exist. It appeared as though the citizens in their wild frenzy had forgotten everything except one clamor: "The Christians to the lions!" The days and nights were more stifling than anything ever known before in Rome. The very air seemed to be filled with madness, blood, and crime.

This appalling lust for cruelty was met by an equally intense desire for martyrdom. The confessors of Christ went willingly to their death; in fact, they even sought death, until they were held back by the command of their elders, who ordered them to assemble only outside the city, in subterranean places[2] near the Via Appia and in the suburban vineyards belonging to patrician Christians, who had so far escaped imprisonment. It was known perfectly well on the Palatine that among the Christians were numbered Flavius Domitilla, Pomponia Graecina, Cornelius Pudens, and Vinitius. Caesar, however, feared that the crowd wouldn't believe such patricians could possibly have been incendiaries. Since it was, above all, necessary to convince the people, punishment and vengeance against these were deferred until later. Those who thought that the patricians' safety was owing to Acte's influence were mistaken. Petronius, after parting with Vinitius, had gone directly to Acte to ask help for Lygia, but she could only offer him tears, for she lived in suffering and neglect and was tolerated only so long as she hid herself from Poppaea and Caesar.

---

2 What became known as the catacombs.

Nevertheless, she visited Lygia in prison and brought her clothing and food, and at the same time protected her from insults at the hands of the prison guards who were already bribed.

Petronius couldn't forget that had it not been for him and his scheme for taking Lygia from the house of Aulus, the maiden would almost certainly not be in prison now. He was eager, moreover, to win the game against Tigellinus; so he spared neither time nor expense in his efforts. In the course of a few days he interviewed Seneca, Domitius Afer, Crispinilla (through whom he wished to reach Poppaea), Terpnos, Diodorus, and the handsome Pythagoras, and finally Aliturus and Paris, to whom Caesar seldom refused anything. With the help of Chrysothemis, now the mistress of Vatinius, he tried to gain his aid. In all cases he was unsparing of his promises of favors as well as his money.

But all these efforts were fruitless. Seneca, uncertain of his own morrow, argued that the Christians, even if they hadn't burned Rome, ought to be exterminated for the good of the city. In a word, he justified the slaughtering for political reasons. Terpnos and Diodorus accepted money but did nothing in return. Vatinius reported to Caesar that an effort had been made to bribe him. Aliturus alone, who at the beginning of the persecution was hostile to the Christians, took pity on them and dared to remind Caesar of the imprisoned maiden and to intercede in her behalf.

Yet he obtained nothing but the answer, "Do you think I have a soul inferior to that of Brutus, who for Rome's welfare didn't even spare his own sons?"

When Aliturus repeated that reply to Petronius, the latter said, "Now that Caesar has compared himself to Brutus, there's no saving her."

He was sorry for Vinitius and dreaded lest he might try to take his own life in utter despair. *For the present,* he said to himself, *he's supported by his efforts to save her, by the sight of her, and by his own sufferings. But when all plans fail and the spark of hope is extinguished, by Castor, he won't survive; he'll throw himself on his sword.*

Petronius could understand a death of this sort better than he could the love and suffering of Vinitius.

Meanwhile Vinitius was doing his best to save Lygia. He visited the Augustinians and unbent his pride to beg their assistance. Through Vitelius, he offered Tigellinus his Sicilian lands and all he might ask. But Tigellinus, apparently not wishing to offend the Augusta, refused. To go to Caesar himself, kneel down before him, embrace his knees, and implore him, would lead to nothing.

Vinitius, it's true, wished to do this, but Petronius, learning his purpose, asked, "Suppose he should refuse you or answer you with a jest or with a foul threat, what would you do then?"

At this the face of the young tribune contracted with pain and rage, and between his set jaws his teeth gritted together.

"Yes," said Petronius, "I advise you against this, because it would close all other roads of rescue."

Vinitius checked himself and, passing his hand over his forehead, wiped off cold perspiration. "No, no!" he cried. "I'm a Christian."

Chapter LIII

A nd everything failed. Vinitius had humiliated himself even to the
extent of seeking supp⟨ ⟩ from the freedmen and the slaves of both
Caesar and Poppaea. He paid enormous sums for empty promises; by rich
gifts he won only their goodwill. He found the first husband of Poppaea
and secured a letter from him. He made a present of a villa in Antium to
Rufius, her son by her first marriage; in so doing, he only succeeded in
angering Caesar, who intensely disliked his stepson. He dispatched a special courier to Poppaea's second husband, Otho, in Spain, offering him all
his possessions. At last he realized that he was but the plaything of these
people and that if he had shown less anxiety about the imprisonment of
Lygia, he might have freed her sooner.

Petronius also realized this. Meanwhile, day followed day, and the
amphitheater was finished. The *tesserae*[1] to the *ludus matutinus*[2] were
already distributed. But now the *ludus matutinus*, on account of the
unheard-of number of victims, were to continue for days, weeks, and even
months. They didn't know where to lodge the multitude of Christians.
The prisons were crammed, and fever was raging among them. Sanitary
facilities were nonexistent, as was medical care of any kind. The *puticulli*[3]
became overfilled, and it was feared that an epidemic might break out and
spread across the whole city; therefore it was decided to hurry.

All these reports came to the ears of Vinitius and extinguished the last
spark of hope. While there was yet time, he could delude himself that he
might obtain her release, but now that time had passed, the games were
about to begin. Lygia might be brought any day into the *cuniculum*[4] of the
Circus; the only way out led to the arena. Vinitius, knowing not where

---

1 Entrance tickets.
2 Morning games.
3 Common pits in which slaves were kept.
4 Dungeon.

fate or the cruelty of violence might throw her, visited all the circuses,[5] bribed the guards and the *bestiarii*, and proposed to them plans that they couldn't execute. In time, he recognized that the utmost he could hope for was to lessen the horrors of her death—then he would feel that instead of brains, burning coals filled his skull.

He had no intention of outliving her but resolved to perish with her. His worst fear, however, had to do with himself: Pain might burn the life out of him before the dreadful hour for Lygia should come. Petronius and all their friends concurred, feeling that any day might open to him the kingdom of shadows. His face darkened and resembled those waxen masks that were kept in the sanctuaries of the *lararia*. In his face, astonishment and disbelief had frozen into hard lines, as though he'd long since lost the power of understanding or being surprised by anything. He seemed unconscious of all that was going on around him. If someone spoke to him, he raised his hand mechanically to his head and, pressing his temples with the palms of his hands, looked at the speaker with inquiry and dismay. He passed whole nights with Ursus at Lygia's door in the prison. When she ordered him to leave and seek rest, he returned to Petronius and paced back and forth all night in the atrium, contemplating how he might try to rescue her.

"You have a right to destroy yourself, but not her. Remember what Sejanus's daughter suffered before her death," said Petronius.

But speaking thus, Petronius was not altogether sincere, for he loved Vinitius more than he did Lygia. Still he was wise enough to know that nothing could restrain Vinitius more effectively from such a dangerous course than the certainty that such action on his part would doom Lygia. Moreover, he was right, for on the Palatine they'd counted on such a visit from the tempestuous tribune and had made precautions against such an attempt in advance.

However, the suffering of Vinitius surpassed all that even strong men can endure. Ever since her imprisonment and the glory of imminent martyrdom had fallen on her, not only did he love her a hundred times more than before, but he also began to pay her in his soul almost religious honor, as though she were a heavenly being. And now at the very thought that he'd lost this being—both beloved and holy—and besides, that tortures more horrible than death might befall her, the blood froze in his veins, his

---

5   The smaller circuses all fed into the Circus Maximus.

thoughts grew confused, and his soul remained in a state of torment. At times it seemed as though his skull were filled with living fire that would either scorch it or burst it. He couldn't understand why Christ, the merciful and the divine, failed to come to the rescue of His followers, why the dingy walls of the Palatine didn't sink into the earth, and with them Nero, the Augustinians, the Praetorian Guard, and that vast wicked city. He didn't see how it could end otherwise, and all that his eyes gazed upon and all that was breaking his heart had to be but a dream rather than reality. But the roaring of wild beasts disabused him of that delusion; the sound of axes beneath the rising arena, the howling of the uncontrollable mob, and the overflowing prisons—all this confirmed the grim reality that it *was* true.

Then his faith in Christ was shaken, and that was a new torture, probably the most awful of all. It was at this moment that Petronius had said to him, "Remember what Sejanus's daughter suffered before her death."

Slaves often found him kneeling with his hands raised or lying prostrate, praying to Christ, for He was his last hope. Everything had failed. Lygia could only be rescued by a miracle, and that she might be saved by a miracle, he prayed fervently. Vinitius beat the stones of the floor with his forehead.

But there remained to him yet the perception that Peter's prayers were of more value than his own. Peter had promised Lygia to him; Peter had baptized him; Peter himself performed miracles—let him now provide help and assistance.

One night he couldn't take it anymore, and he left his house in search of the Apostle. The Christians, of whom only a few remained at large, had hidden him carefully, even from one another, lest the weaker among them betray him unwittingly or unintentionally. Vinitius, in the midst of general confusion and terror, occupied only with his efforts to get Lygia out of prison, had lost sight of the Apostle. Since the time of his baptism he'd seen him but once, and that was before the beginning of the persecution. But from the quarryman in whose hut he'd been baptized, he learned that there would be a meeting of Christians in Cornelius Pudens's vineyards just outside the Porta Salaria. The quarryman promised to guide him to the vineyard, assuring him that he'd find Peter there. When darkness fell, they started, passed beyond the walls, walked through hollows overgrown with reeds, and reached the vineyard, which lay in a wild and lonely place. The meeting was held in a wine shed. As Vinitius neared the place, the murmur of praying reached his ears. On entering he saw, by the dim light of a lantern, several scores of kneeling people absorbed in prayer. They recited a kind of litany, a chorus of voices, male and female, repeating each moment, "Christ have mercy on us." Deep and heartrending sorrow was expressed in those voices.

Peter was present. He was kneeling in front, near a wooden cross fastened to the wall of the shed, and was lost in prayer. Vinitius recognized him from a distance by his white hair and uplifted hands. The first thought of the young patrician was to advance through the kneeling people, cast himself at the feet of the Apostle, and cry, "Help!" But either out of a sense of the decorum due to prayer or because of a weakness that buckled his knees under him, he began to repeat, groaning and clenching his hands, "Christ have mercy on us!"

Had he been fully conscious he would have realized that his prayer was not the only one with a groan in it, and that he wasn't the only supplicant who brought pain, sorrow, and grief. There was not one person present in that meeting who hadn't lost dear ones at a time when the most zealous and boldest believers were already prisoners, when every moment brought news of new insults and tortures inflicted on them in prison. The magnitude of the calamity so far exceeded anything anyone could have imagined that now, when only a pitiful handful of Christians remained free, not one of them wasn't terrified, didn't ask doubtingly, "Where is Christ? Why does He tolerate evil so that it becomes mightier than God?"

Meanwhile they despairingly implored Him for mercy, since {each soul harbored a lingering spark of hope that He would come, destroy evil, throw Nero into the abyss, and rule the world. They still looked towards the sky; they still listened; they still prayed with trembling. Vinitius also, as they repeated "Christ have mercy on us!" was overcome with the same ecstasy he'd experienced before in the quarryman's hut. Then, from the depths of their sorrow, they called on Him, and then Peter called on Him. At any moment the heavens might open, the earth be shaken to its foundations, and He appear in infinite glory with stars at His feet, merciful but terrible. He would resurrect His faithful ones and command the abyss to swallow up their persecutors.

Vinitius covered his face with both hands and dropped to the ground. Suddenly a silence encircled him as though fear had hushed the voices of all present. It seemed to him that now at last something must surely happen, that the moment for a miracle had arrived. He was certain that when he rose and opened his eyes, he would see a light blinding to mortals and hear a voice from which hearts would grow faint.

But the silence remained unbroken until interrupted by the sobbing of the women. Vinitius rose and looked with dazed eyes around him. In the shed, instead of heavenly glory, flickered the dim glow of the lantern. The moon penetrated through an opening in the roof, filling the shed with a silvery light. The people kneeling around Vinitius raised their tearful eyes in silence towards the cross. Here and there sobbing was heard, and from the outside came the careful whistling of the watchmen.

Then Peter rose, turned towards the congregation, and said, "Children, lift up your hearts towards our Redeemer and offer Him your tears." Then he was silent.

Suddenly from the midst of the congregation, the voice of a woman, sorrowful and wracked with pain, was heard. "I'm a widow. I had only one son, and he supported me. Return him to me, O Lord!"

Silence reigned again. Peter was standing near the kneeling group, old and full of care. In that moment he appeared to them the personification of decrepitude and weakness.

Then another voice began to complain. "Executioners violated my daughter; Christ permitted it."

Then a third voice: "I remain alone with the children, and when I'm taken, who will give them bread and water?"

Then a fourth: "Linus, whom they spared at first, they've taken again and put to torture, O Lord!"

Then a fifth: "When we return home, the Praetorians will seize us. Where can we hide?"

"Woe to us! Who will protect us?"

And in the silence of the night rose plea after plea. The old fisherman closed his eyes and shook his white head over the pain and suffering of humanity.

Silence reigned again, broken only by the watchmen's low whistles beyond the shed.

Vinitius sprang up so as to push through the group to the Apostle and demand help from him. But suddenly he saw in front of him a precipice, a sight that took the strength from his feet. What would happen if the Apostle should confess his own weakness and affirm that the Roman Caesar was mightier than Christ of Nazareth? Terrified at that thought, he felt that in such a case not only would the remainder of his hope fall into the precipice, but also he and Lygia, his love for Christ, his faith, and everything for which he lived. Nothing would remain save death and a night like a boundless sea.

Meanwhile, Peter began to speak in a voice so low that one could barely hear him. "My children, I've seen how on Golgotha men nailed God to the cross; I heard the sound of the hammers and saw how they raised the cross so that the mob might revel in the death of the Son of Man.

"And I saw them slash open His side; I saw how He died. And when I returned from the cross, I cried out in anguish as you are now crying: 'Woe! Woe! Lord! You are God. Why have You permitted this? Why have You died? Why have You tormented our hearts when we believed that Your kingdom would come?'

"But He, our Lord and our God, rose from the dead on the third day and was among us until He entered His kingdom in great glory. And we, conscious of our little faith, were strengthened in heart, and from that time we've been sowing the seed."

Turning to the side that the first complaint had come from, he spoke in a stronger voice. "Why do you complain? God surrendered Himself to torture and death, and yet you wish that He would shield you from it? Oh, people of little faith! Have you received His teaching? Has He promised you nothing but life? He comes to you and says: 'Come, follow in My path.' He raised you to Himself, and you clutch the earth to your heart and call, 'Lord help!'

"In the presence of God I am but dust, but before you I am the Apostle of God and His vicar. I say to you in the name of Christ: There's not death before you, but life; not torture, but endless joy; not tears and groans, but singing; not slavery, but dominion! I, an Apostle of God, tell you, O widow, that your son will not die but will be born into glory, into everlasting life, and you will rejoin him! I promise you, O father whose chaste daughter has been violated by the executioners, that you'll find her whiter than the lilies of Hebron! To you mothers, bereaved of your children; to you who've lost fathers; to you who complain; to you who must witness the death of your beloved ones; to you who are careworn, unfortunate, timid; to you who have to die—in the name of Christ, I tell you that you will awake as from sleep to a happier condition and as from night to the light of God. In the name of Christ, let the scales fall from your eyes, and let your hearts be glowing."

He raised his hands as though in command, and his hearers felt new blood coursing through their veins and a quivering in their bones, for before them was no longer standing a careworn and feeble old man, but a mighty one who had aroused their souls and lifted them up from dust and terror.

"Amen!" cried several voices.

The light from Peter's eyes was constantly increasing, and power and holiness radiated from him. When the amens ceased, he continued. "You sow in weeping so that you may reap in joy. Why, then, fear the power of evil? Above the earth, above Rome, above the walls of the cities, is the Lord who dwells with you. The stones will be wet from tears, the sands will be steeped with blood, the pits will be filled with your bodies; but I say to you, You are the victors! The Lord will conquer this city of crime, oppression, and haughtiness, and you are His legions. And as He has redeemed with blood and torture the sins of the world, so He wishes that you should redeem with torture and blood this city of iniquity. This He announces to you through my lips!"

And Peter opened his arms and fixed his eyes heavenward. The hearts of the people almost ceased to beat, for they felt that he gazed upward because he beheld something invisible to their mortal eyes. His whole face had changed; a serene light illuminated it. For a while he was silent, as if speechless through rapture, but after a moment they heard his voice.

"You are here in this room, O Lord. If it be Your will, point out to me the way." A long silence followed, so long that Vinitius wondered if the Apostle had fallen asleep. But no; in a tone of incredulity, Peter continued, as though completely unaware of anyone but his Lord, "How can this be, O Christ? Not in Jerusalem but in this city of Satan, You desire to establish Your church? Do you really mean that it's Your intention to build Your church upon the tears and blood of these martyrs? Here, where Nero rules today?" Another long silence followed, and this time, when his prayer resumed, Peter appeared to be conscious of the believers in the room. "O Lord! Lord! So it's true that You commanded these timid ones to sacrificially lay the foundation of the new holy Zion on their bones? And You command me to assume the leadership of Your church...until my time shall come?" Yet another long pause followed, and this time, when he spoke again, power, resolution, and triumph filled his voice. "And You are pouring the fountain of Your strength upon the weak, so that they are made strong; and You command us to feed Your sheep from here until the consummation of the ages. Oh, be praised in Your decrees whereby You have ordained victory. Hosanna! Hosanna!"

The timid arose; in the doubters new streams of faith flowed. Some voices shouted "Hosanna!" others, "*Pro Christo!*"[6]

Then came silence. The bright summer lightning illuminated the interior of the shed and the faces that were pale from emotion.

Peter, in the midst of his vision, prayed for a long time, but at last he turned upon the group his inspired face, radiant with light. "Now, as the Lord has vanquished doubt in you, you will go out to victory in His name!"

And though he knew that they would conquer, although he knew what would spring from their tears and their blood, still his voice trembled when he began to bless, comfort, and encourage them by the Cross. "And now," he said, "I bless you, my children, as you go to torture, to death, to eternity!"

They gathered around him, calling out, "We're ready, but guard your holy head, for you are the vicar of Christ, performing His office."

With these words they grasped his mantle. He then placed his hands on their heads and blessed each one individually, just as a father blesses children whom he sends out on a long journey.

And immediately they began to leave the shed, for they had to hurry to their houses, knowing full well that most of them would soon be hauled off to the prisons and the arenas. Their thoughts were separated from the world, their souls soared towards eternity, and they walked as though in a dream or in ecstasy, opposing with all the force that was in them, the force and cruelty of the Beast.

Nereus, the servant of Pudens, took the Apostle and led him through a secret path to his house. But in the clear night, Vinitius followed them, and when they finally reached the hut of Nereus, he suddenly threw himself down at the Apostle's feet.

The Apostle recognized him and asked, "What do you wish, my son?"

But Vinitius, after all that he'd heard in the shed, didn't dare ask anything. He only embraced the Apostle's feet with both hands and pressed his lips to them, sobbing, seeking only Peter's compassion.

"I know," said Peter, "they've taken from you the maiden whom you love. Pray for her."

"Lord," groaned Vinitius, embracing his feet even more convulsively. "Lord! I am but a worm. I'm totally unworthy, but you've known Christ.

---

6   "For Christ!"

Please implore Him on her behalf."

From anguish, he trembled like a leaf. He beat his forehead against the earth. Knowing the Apostle's power, he knew that he alone could restore her to him.

Peter was moved by that anguish. He remembered how once Lygia herself, attacked by Crispus, lay at his feet in the same manner, asking for mercy. He remembered, also, that he'd lifted her and comforted her. So now he raised Vinitius.

"My dear son," he said, "I will pray for her, but remember what I told those doubting ones: God Himself passed through torture upon the cross. And remember that after this life, another begins—an everlasting one."

"I know! I heard!" replied Vinitius, breathing heavily through his pale lips. "But you see, master, that I cannot accept Lygia's death! If blood is required, ask Christ to accept mine. I'm a soldier. Let Him torment me doubly—no, make that triply—what is prepared for her! She's still a child, master, and I believe that our Lord's mightier than Caesar—mightier! You love her yourself and blessed her! She's yet an innocent child!"

Again he bowed and, pressing his face against Peter's knees, repeated, "You've known Christ, master, you've known Him. He'll listen to you. Please take her part!"

Peter closed his eyes and prayed earnestly.

The summer lightning once more flashed in the sky. By its illumination Vinitius gazed on the Apostle's lips, waiting for the verdict of life or death. The silence was broken only by the calling of the quails in the vineyard and the distant, dull noise of the treadmills near the Via Salaria.

"Vinitius," said the Apostle at last, "do you believe?"

"Master, were it otherwise, would I be here?" answered Vinitius.

"Then believe to the end, for faith moves mountains. Even though you were to see the maiden under the sword of the executioner or in the jaws of a lion, believe yet, for Christ is able to save. Believe and pray to Him, and I will pray with you." Then, raising his face towards heaven, he cried aloud, "O merciful Christ, look down on this aching heart and console it! O merciful Christ, temper the wind to the fleece of the lamb. Merciful Christ, who begged the Father to turn away the bitter cup from Your lips, turn it away from the mouth of this Your servant. Amen!"

But Vinitius, stretching his hands towards the stars, said, groaning, "O Christ, I'm Yours—take me instead of her!"

The sky began to grow pale in the east.

Chapter LIV

Vinitius, on leaving the Apostle, went to the prison with a heart strengthened by hope. Somewhere in the depths of his soul, terror and despair still clamored for utterance, but he stifled those voices. It seemed to him impossible that the intercession of the vicar of God and the power of prayer should be without result. He feared to hope; he feared to doubt.

I will believe in His loving-kindness, he said to himself, *even if I see her in the jaws of the lion.*

At this thought, though his heart trembled within him and cold sweat drenched his temples, he nevertheless believed. Each throb of his heart was a prayer. He began to perceive that faith indeed moves mountains, for he felt within himself a certain living strength, which he'd never before known. It seemed to him that he could now do things that yesterday would have appeared impossible. At times he almost convinced himself that the danger had passed. When despair revived in his soul, he recalled that night and that holy gray face raised to heaven in prayer.

"No! Christ won't refuse His first disciple and the shepherd of the flock! Christ won't refuse him! And I will not doubt!"

And he ran to the prison as a herald of good news.

But there an unusual thing awaited him. All the Praetorian guards at the Mamertine prison knew him, and usually they didn't raise the slightest objection to his entering. This time, however, the lines didn't open.

The centurion approached him, saying, "Your pardon, noble tribune, but today we have an order not to admit anyone."

"An order?" repeated Vinitius, growing pale.

The centurion looked at him in pity and answered, "Yes, master, an order from Caesar. There are many sick people in prison, and possibly it's feared that visitors might spread infection throughout the city."

"But did you say that the command was for today only?"

"The guards change at noon."

424

Vinitius silently uncovered his head. It seemed to him that the pileus he wore was made of lead.

Meanwhile, the soldier came nearer and said in a low voice, "Be at ease, master. The guard and Ursus are watching over her." As he said this, he bent and quickly drew on the flagstone with his sword: the outline of a fish.

Vinitius looked at him keenly. "And you're a Praetorian?"

"Until I'm in *there*," replied the soldier, pointing at the prison. "I also worship Christ."

"Praised be His name! I know, master, that I cannot admit you to the prison, but write a letter and I'll give it to the guard."

"Thanks to you, brother."

Vinitius pressed the soldier's hand and went away, the pileus ceasing to weigh as heavily upon him. The morning sun had risen over the walls of the prison, and with its bright splendor, hope once again crept into his heart. That Christian soldier was to him a new witness to the power of Christ. After taking a few steps, he halted. Gazing at the multihued clouds above the Capitol and the temple of Jupiter Stator, he exclaimed, "I haven't seen her this day, O Lord, but I have faith in Your mercy."

Petronius had been waiting for him at home. As usual he'd been turning night into day and so had returned but a little while before. He'd succeeded, nevertheless, in taking his bath and anointing himself for sleep.

"I have news for you," he said. "I was with Tullius Senecio today; Caesar was likewise there. I know not how it entered the mind of Augusta to bring little Rufius with her. It may have been to soften the heart of Caesar by his beauty. Unfortunately the child, overpowered by drowsiness, fell asleep during the reading, as once did Vespasian. Seeing this, Ahenobarbus hurled a goblet at his stepson and seriously wounded him. Poppaea fainted. All heard Caesar exclaim: 'I've had enough of this brood!' And that, you know, means the same as death."

"God's punishment was hanging over the Augusta," said Vinitius, "but why do you tell me this?"

"I tell you because the wrath of Poppaea is ever pursuing you and Lygia. But now, occupied by her own woes, she may lay aside her vengeance and be more easily influenced. I'll see her this evening and talk with her."

"Thanks to you. You've brought me good news."

"Now bathe and rest. Your lips are blue, and only a shadow of you remains."

But Vinitius, his mind elsewhere, asked, "Was it announced when the first *ludus matutinus* would take place?"

"In ten days, but they'll empty other prisons first. The more time we can gain, the better. All is not yet lost."

But he didn't believe his own words, for he knew perfectly well that Caesar's high-sounding reply to Aliturus, when he compared himself to Brutus, had closed all hope of rescue for Lygia. Also, he compassionately held back what he'd heard at Senecio's: Caesar and Tigellinus had resolved to select for themselves and their friends the most beautiful Christian maidens and defile them before the torture. The others were to be given, on the day of the games, to the Praetorians and *bestiarii*. Believing that Vinitius wouldn't survive Lygia, he had purposely strengthened hope in his heart. For, first, he sympathized with him deeply; second, he desired that if Vinitius must die, he should die beautiful and not with a face emaciated and darkened by pain and sleeplessness.

"Today I'll speak to Augusta," he said, "somewhat like this: 'Save Lygia for Vinitius, and I'll save Rufius for you.' Truly, I'll think up some plan. One word spoken at the right moment to Ahenobarbus may save or destroy anyone. At the worst, we'll gain time."

"Thank you," repeated Vinitius.

"You'll thank me better after you've eaten and rested. By Athena, Odysseus in his greatest misfortunes took thought about sleep and food. You must have spent the entire night in prison."

"No!" answered Vinitius. "I tried to visit the prison a moment ago, but I was met by an order to admit no one. Find out, dear Petronius, if the decree is only for today or until the day of the games."

"I'll find out this evening, and tomorrow morning I'll tell you for how long the order was given and for what reason it was given. But now, even were Helios to plunge himself into Cimmerian regions[1] from mourning, I must go to sleep, and you should follow my example."

They separated, but Vinitius went to the library and wrote a letter to Lygia. When he finished, he took it himself to the Christian centurion, who bore it at once into the prison. He returned shortly with a greeting from Lygia and a promise to secure an answer from her that day. Vinitius, not caring to return home in the interim, sat down on a stone, waiting for the return letter. The sun had risen high in the heavens, and through the

---

1 The underworld of darkness.

Clivus Argantarius to the Forum, hucksters called out their wares, fortune-tellers offered their services to the passersby, and citizens leisurely strolled to the rostra to hear the orators or to discuss news of the day. As the heat increased, crowds of idlers found shade under the porticos of the temple. Above them flew, in clusters and with great rustling of wings, flocks of doves whose white feathers glistened in the bright sun and deep blue sky.

From excess of light, bustle, heat, and immense fatigue, Vinitius's eyes began to close. The monotonous shouts of boys playing *mora* and the measured tread of the soldiers lulled him to sleep. Several times he roused himself and stared at the prison for a time. Finally, leaning his head against a slab and sighing like a child drowsy after long weeping, he fell asleep.

Dreams came.

In the middle of the night he was bearing Lygia in his arms through an unknown vineyard. Before him walked Pomponia Graecina with a lamp in her hand. A voice like the voice of Petronius called to him from a distance.

"Turn back!"

But he paid no attention to the call and continued to follow Pomponia. At last they reached a cottage, on the threshold of which stood Peter the Apostle.

He showed Lygia to Peter and said, "Master, we come from the arena. We cannot resuscitate her. Please wake her!"

Peter answered, "Christ Himself will come to awaken her."

Then the visions grew confused.

He saw Nero and Poppaea holding little Rufius, whose head was bleeding. Petronius was washing the boy's head, and Tigellinus was sprinkling ashes on tables laden with costly dishes. Vitelius was devouring these dishes, while a multitude of Augustinians were sitting at the feast. He himself was resting near Lygia, but between the tables walked lions whose yellow manes dripped with blood. Lygia begged him to take her away, but such a terrible weakness had seized him that he was unable to move. Then, in his vision, he perceived greater disorder, and finally everything fell into complete darkness.

He was roused out of his deep sleep by the heat of the sun and by shouts that proceeded from near where he was sitting. Vinitius rubbed his eyes. The street was swarming with people. Two runners in yellow tunics pushed aside the crowd with long canes, shouting and making room for a magnificent litter that was carried by four powerful Egyptian slaves.

In the litter sat a man dressed in white robes, whose face couldn't be seen well, for near his eyes he held a papyrus roll, in which he was deeply engrossed.

"Make way for the noble Augustinian," shouted the runners. But the street was so crowded that the litter halted for a moment.

Then the Augustinian put down his papyrus and stretched out his hand, crying, "Drive away these vagabonds! Hurry!"

Suddenly, noticing Vinitius, he drew back his head and raised the papyrus quickly to his face.

Vinitius shaded his forehead with his hand, thinking that he was still dreaming.

In the litter sat Chilo.

Meanwhile, the runners had opened a way, and the Egyptians were about to run forward. But suddenly the young tribune, who in one moment guessed many things that until then had been incomprehensible, approached the litter.

"A greeting to you, O Chilo!" he said.

"Young man," answered the Greek, with pride and haughtiness, striving to give his face an appearance of calm that was not in his soul, "I greet you, but don't detain me, for I'm hurrying to my friend, the noble Tigellinus."

Vinitius, grasping the edge of the litter, bent towards him, and looking him straight in his eyes, inquired, "Did you betray Lygia?"

"Colossus of Memnon!" cried Chilo in terror.

But seeing that in the eyes of Vinitius there was no threat, the terror of the old Greek quickly disappeared. He remembered that he was under the protection of Tigellinus and Caesar himself—before whom all must tremble—and that he was surrounded by stalwart slaves. He then noted that Vinitius stood before him unarmed, his face emaciated, his form bowed by suffering.

At this, all his insolence returned. He fixed his red-lidded eyes upon Vinitius and said in a low voice, "And you, when I was dying of hunger, commanded me to be flogged!"

Both remained silent for a moment.

Then in a dull voice, Vinitius said, "I wronged you, Chilo!"

The Greek raised his head and, snapping his fingers as a sign of slight and contempt, said in a loud voice that everybody could hear, "Friend, if you have a petition to make, come to my home on the

Esquiline early in the morning. I receive guests and clients after my bath."

And he waved his hand. At that sign the Egyptians who carried the litter brandished their staffs and shouted, "Make way for the litter of the noble Chilo Chilonides! Make way! Make way!"

Chapter LV

L ygia, in a long but hasty letter, bade farewell to Vinitius forever. Well she knew that henceforth no one could enter the prison except the guards. Thus she wouldn't see him again until they sent her to her death in the arena. Therefore, she begged him to find out when her turn would come and to be present at the games, for she wished to see him once more before she died. There was no sign of fear in her letter. She'd written that she and others yearned already for the arena, where they'd find freedom from the degradations of imprisonment. Expecting the arrival of Pomponia and Aulus, she begged that they, too, might be present. Every word of hers showed the ecstatic contempt of life in which all the imprisoned lived and at the same time revealed an unshaken faith that the promises must be fulfilled beyond the grave.

"Whether Christ," she wrote, "frees me now or after death, He has promised me to you by the mouth of the Apostle; therefore, I'm yours."

She implored him not to grieve for her and not to permit himself to be overcome by suffering. She didn't regard death as a dissolution of marriage. With the trusting confidence of a child, she assured Vinitius that after the suffering in the arena, she would tell Christ that her betrothed, Marcus, remained behind in Rome, that he yearned for her with his whole heart. She felt that perhaps Christ would permit her soul to return for a while to assure him that she was living, that she did not remember her torment, and that she was happy. Her whole letter breathed happiness and intense hope. There was only one petition connected with earthly affairs—that Vinitius should remove her body from the *spoliarium*[1] and bury it as his own wife, in the same tomb where he himself would eventually rest.

He read this letter with a broken heart, but at the same time it seemed

---

1 The place in the amphitheater where the slain gladiators were stripped of their arms and clothing.

impossible to him that Lygia should perish under the claws of wild beasts and that Christ should fail to have compassion upon her. In that belief were hidden hope and trust. When he returned home he wrote her an answer. He promised to come every day behind the walls of the *tullianum* to wait till Christ crushed the walls of the prison and gave her to him. He commanded her to believe that He could deliver her to him even in the Circus. The great Apostle had confirmed him in that faith, and the moment of delivery was at hand. The converted centurion was to carry her this letter on the morrow.

When Vinitius went next morning to the prison, the centurion left the ranks, approached him, and said, "Listen to me, master! Christ, who enlightened you, has shown you His favor. Last night Caesar's freedmen and those of the prefect came to select the Christian maidens for violation. They asked for your betrothed, but our Lord sent her a fever from which prisoners are dying in the *tullianum*, and they left her. Last evening she was unconscious, and blessed be the name of the Redeemer, for the same sickness that saved her from dishonor may also save her from death."

Vinitius leaned heavily on the soldier's shoulder so that he might not fall. The other continued.

"Thanks to the mercy of God, though they took and tortured Linus, seeing that he was in the last agonies, they've given him back to his own. Perhaps they'll now return her to you, and Christ will heal her."

The young tribune stood for a while with drooping head; then he raised it and said in a whisper, "True, centurion. Christ who saved her from dishonor will also save her from death."

He sat at the wall of the prison until evening. Then he returned home to send his people for Linus and have him carried to one of his suburban villas.

When Petronius had heard everything, he also determined to act. First he called on Poppaea. At this second visit he found her at the bed of little Rufius. The child, his head badly injured, was suffering from fever. With anguish and terror in her heart, his mother was trying all possible means to save him. Yet she feared that if she did save him, it would be only for a more dreadful death.

Preoccupied with her own pain, she didn't even wish to hear of Vinitius and Lygia. But Petronius terrified her.

"You have offended," he said to her, "a new and unknown divinity. It seems that you, Augusta, are a worshiper of the Hebrew Jehovah, but the

Christians maintain that Christ is His Son. Think, therefore, whether the anger of the Father is not punishing you. Who knows but it's their vengeance that has struck you? Who knows but that the life of Rufius depends on this? How will you act?"

"What do you want me to do?" asked the terrified Poppaea.

"Appease the offended deities."

"How?"

"Lygia is sick. Seek to influence Caesar or Tigellinus to give her back to Vinitius."

She cried out in despair, "Do you think I have the power to do this?"

"You can do something else. When Lygia recovers, she must meet her doom. Go to the temple of Vesta and command that the head vestal be near the Mamertine at the moment the prisoners are led to death; she must then command that the maiden be freed. The head vestal won't refuse you."

"But if Lygia dies of the fever?"

"The Christians say that Christ is vengeful but just. Perhaps you'll soften His wrath by your intent."

"Let Him give me some sign that Rufius will be healed."

Petronius shrugged his shoulders. "I come not as His envoy, O divinity! I only say this: better to be on good terms with all the gods, Roman as well as foreign."

"I'll go," said Poppaea brokenly.

Petronius breathed deeply. *At last I've accomplished something*, he thought.

Returning to Vinitius, he said, "Implore your God that Lygia not die of the fever, for if she doesn't die, the chief vestal will order her freedom. The Augusta herself will ask her to do it."

Vinitius, looking at him with fever-bright eyes, replied, "Christ will save her."

Poppaea, who was ready to burn hecatombs to all the gods for the recovery of Rufius, went that same evening through the Forum to the vestals, leaving the patient in the care of her faithful nurse, Silvia, by whom she herself had been raised.

But on the Palatine the sentence had already been issued. Scarcely had the litter of Poppaea disappeared behind the great gate when two of Caesar's freedmen entered the room where little Rufius rested. One of them threw himself on old Silvia and covered her mouth; the other, seizing a bronze statuette of a sphinx, felled her with a single blow. Then they approached Rufius, who, insensible from fever, knew not what was going on around him. He smiled at them and blinked his beautiful eyes, as though trying to recognize them. But they, taking the girdle from the nurse, put it around his neck and began to strangle him. The child cried once for his mother, then died easily. They wrapped him in a sheet and mounted their horses, then galloped clear to Ostia, where they threw the body into the sea.

Poppaea, not finding the chief vestal, who was with the other vestals at the house of Vatinius,[2] soon returned to the Palatine. She found the empty bed—and beside it, the cold body of Silvia. She fainted, and when they restored her, she fell to sobbing, and her wild cries were heard during all that night and the following day.

But on the third day Caesar commanded her to appear at a feast. She arrayed herself in an amethyst-colored tunic and came and sat, beautiful, stone-faced, golden-haired, silent, and as ominous as an angel of death.

---

2 Implied violation of them by the Augustinians.

Chapter LVI

Before Flavius built the Colosseum, the Roman amphitheaters were mainly constructed of wood; hence nearly all of them were burned during the conflagration. Nero, however, ordered others to be erected in anticipation of the promised games. One among them, a gigantic structure started immediately after the fire, was built of large beams taken from the slopes of the Atlas Mountains and transferred to Rome by sea and by the Tiber. The structure was needed, for the games were to surpass all previous records in splendor and in the number of victims.

Large spaces were provided both for spectators and wild beasts. Thousands of men worked night and day, building and embellishing. Stories were told of wonderful pillars inlaid with bronze, amber, ivory, mother-of-pearl, and tortoiseshell from beyond the seas. Long canals filled with ice-cold water from the mountains were to run between the rows of seats in order to maintain an agreeable coolness through the building even during the most intense heat. A gigantic purple velarium was positioned so as to provide shelter from the rays of the sun. Between the rows of seats were censers for the burning of Arabian perfumes. Above the seats would be fixed contrivances to sprinkle the spectators with a decoction of saffron and verbena. The famous architects Severus and Celer employed their utmost skill in raising an unequaled amphitheater that should accommodate a greater number of spectators than any theater ever before built.

Therefore, on the day set for the first *ludus matutinus*, huge crowds waited from early dawn until the opening of the gates. They listened with pleasure to the roars of lions, the hoarse snarling of panthers, and the howling of dogs. For two days, food had been withheld from the beasts, though pieces of bloody flesh had been placed in their sight to increase their rage and hunger. At times such a storm of wild howling and roaring arose that the people standing near the Circus couldn't hear one another's voices. The timid grew pale from fear. With the rising sun came other sounds from within the Circus, loud yet peaceful, which were heard with

434

astonishment by the outside listeners, who repeated among themselves, "The Christians! The Christians!" In fact, many Christians had been brought to the amphitheater during the night, not all from one prison, as previously arranged, but a few from all. Though the crowd knew that the spectacles would continue for weeks and months, they disputed among themselves whether the great number of Christians intended for today's game could possibly be dispatched in a single day. Voices of men, women, and children singing morning hymns were so numerous that the knowing ones maintained that even if one or two hundred people were to be brought into the Circus at one time, the beasts would become wearied, sated, and unable to tear them all to pieces before nightfall. Others affirmed that the great number of victims would distract attention and therefore not permit them to really relish the spectacle.

As the moment drew near for the opening of the vomitorias leading to the interior, the people, in a joyous and animated mood, fell to discussing a thousand subjects concerning the spectacle. Parties were formed and took sides as to the relative strength, efficiency, and speed of the lions or tigers in ripping apart and devouring the victims. Here and there, bets were made. Others, however, turned their thoughts to the gladiators who were to appear in the arena in advance of the Christians. Thus yet other parties formed, some of whom favored the Samnites and others the Gauls; some the *mirmillons*, others the Thracians. Still others preferred the *retiarii*.

Early in the morning detachments of gladiators, under the command of masters called *lanistae*, began to arrive at the amphitheater. Not wishing to tire themselves out before the appointed time, they entered unarmed, many of them nude, often with green branches in their hands or garlands of flowers on their heads, young and handsome in the light of morning and full of life. Their bodies, glistening with olive oil, were massive as if chiseled out of marble. Their physical training was designed to develop bodies that would please the people, who were delighted with shapely forms. Many of them were known personally, and from moment to moment cries could be heard: "Greetings to you, Furnius!" "A greeting, Leon!" "Greetings to Maximus!" "Greetings to you, Diomed!" Young maidens gazed upon them with admiring eyes. The gladiators singled out the most beautiful and replied to them jestingly, as though no cares rested upon them, sending kisses and calling aloud, "Embrace me before death does!" Then they disappeared through the gates to prepare for the games, from which many would never return.

But new arrivals attracted the attention of the crowds. Behind the glad-iators came the *mastigophori*, who were armed with lashes and whose occupation it was to whip and urge on the combatants. Next, mules drew towards the side of the *spoliarum* long rows of wagons, upon which were piles of wooden coffins. At this sight, the people rejoiced, deducing from their number the immensity of the spectacle. After these followed people whose occupation it was to kill the wounded in the arena; they were dressed to resemble Charon and Mercury. Then followed people who kept order in the Circus and showed spectators to their seats; then slaves used for carrying food and cool drinks; and at last the Praetorians, whom every Caesar kept close at hand in the Circus.

At last the vomitorias were opened and crowds rushed to the railings. But the multitude was so great that it flowed in for hours—it seemed a wonder that the amphitheater could hold such a countless throng. The wild beasts scented the exhalations of humanity, and their roars grew louder. The people, too, as they took their places, made an uproar like waves crashing upon rocks in a storm.

Finally the prefect of the city arrived, surrounded by guards, and after him filed in an unbroken line of the litters of senators, consuls, Praetori-ans, public and imperial officers, elders, patricians, and exquisite women. Some litters were preceded by lictors bearing axes in bundles of rods,[1] while others were preceded by crowds of slaves. The gilt gleamed in the sunlight, as did the red and white liveries, the feathers, the earrings, the jewels, and the steel of the axes. From the audience loud shouts greeted the arrival of eminent personages. Small detachments of Praetorians con-tinued to arrive from time to time.

The priests of the various temples came later, followed by the vestal vir-gins and preceded by lictors. And now the appearance of Caesar was the only thing lacking for the games to begin. Unwilling to annoy the audi-ence by overmuch waiting, he arrived without delay, accompanied by Augusta and the Augustinians.

---

1   Lictors were freedmen who attended magistrates, each bearing fasces (bundles of rods with an ax bound in with them, blade protruding) signifying the power magistrates had over life and limb. Rank determined the number of lictors preceding you; a prae-tor had six, a consul twelve, and a dictator twenty-four. In modern times, dictators such as Mussolini used fasces as a symbol; hence that type of government became known as "fascist."

Petronius arrived among the Augustinians, with Vinitius in his litter. The latter knew that Lygia was sick and unconscious, but all access to the prison during recent days had been strictly forbidden, and new guards had been substituted for the old, with strict orders not to permit anyone to speak to the jailers, nor to communicate the least information about the prisoners. Thus, he couldn't be sure that she wasn't among the victims destined for the first day of the spectacle. A sick woman, even an unconscious woman, wouldn't be spared from the lions. The victims were to be sewn up in the skins of beasts and sent into the arena in groups. No spectator could be sure that this or that person might not be among them. Nor could any one of them be recognized.

The jailers and all the servants of the amphitheater had been bribed, however. It had been arranged with the *bestiarii* that Lygia should be hidden in some dark corner of the amphitheater and at night delivered into the hands of a servant, who should take her at once to the Alban Hills. Petronius, admitted to the secret, advised Vinitius to go openly with him into the amphitheater and then slip out and mix with the crowd. Then he should hasten to the vaults and, to avoid the possibility of a mistake, point out Lygia to the guards.

The guards admitted him through a small door through which they themselves had entered. One of them, Syrus by name, led him at once to the Christians. On the way, Syrus said, "I know not, master, if you'll find who you're looking for. We inquired for a maiden named Lygia, but nobody gave us an answer. It may be they don't trust us."

"Are there many of them?" asked Vinitius.

"Yes, master, but a number must wait until tomorrow."

"Are there any sick among them?"

"None who couldn't stand on their feet."

With these words, Syrus opened a door and entered a spacious room that was dark with low ceilings. Gleams of light penetrated only through grated openings. At first Vinitius could see nothing. He heard only the murmur of voices and the shouts of people coming from the amphitheater. But after his eyes had accustomed themselves to the darkness, he saw groups of strange beings in the guise of wolves and bears—Christians sewn up in skins of beasts. Some were standing, others praying on their knees. Here and there, by the long hair, one might discern that the victim was a woman. Mothers, resembling wolves, carried in their arms children sewn up likewise in hairy covering. But from beneath the skins appeared bright faces, eyes that in the darkness gleamed with delight or with fever. It was evident that one thought dominated the greater part of those people— a thought above all earthly considerations, so that, while still among the living, they were unmindful of all that happened around them or that might befall them. Some to whom Vinitius spoke looked on him with staring eyes, as if newly awakened from sleep, and answered nothing. Others smiled at him, placing a finger to their lips or pointing to the iron grating through which entered bright rays of light. Here and there, children were crying, terrified by the roars of the wild beasts, the howling of the dogs, the uproar of the people, and the likeness to wild beasts borne by their own parents. Vinitius, walking beside Syrus, scanned every face, searching, inquiring. At times he stumbled over the bodies of those who'd fainted from the suffocating heat. He pushed farther into the dark depths of the room, which seemed to be as spacious as the whole amphitheater.

Suddenly he stopped. It seemed to him that near the grating he heard a voice known to him. Listening for a while, he turned, pushed through the crowd, and approached the sound. The dim rays of light fell on the head of the speaker, and Vinitius recognized under the wolf skin the emaciated and inexorable face of Crispus.

"Mourn for your sins," thundered Crispus, "for the hour is at hand! Those who think that death will ransom sins commit a new sin and will be hurled into everlasting fire. With every sin you have committed in life you have renewed the suffering of the Lord. How dare you, then, think that the life that awaits you will ransom sin? Today the righteous and the sinner will die together, but the Lord will find His own. Woe to you! The claws of the lions will rip apart your bodies but not lessen your sins, nor square your accounts with God. The Lord showed sufficient mercy when He permitted Himself to be nailed to the cross; but from now on you must not expect Him to be other than a stern Judge.

"Moreover, whoever thinks that torture will blot out his sins blasphemes against divine justice and only sinks deeper into sin. Mercy is at an end. The hour of God's wrath has arrived. Soon you will stand before the awful Judge, before whom even the righteous can scarcely be justified. Bewail your sins, for the mouth of hell is open, and woe to you, husbands and wives! Woe to you, parents and children!"

Stretching out his bony hands, he shook them above the bent heads, unterrified and inexorable even in the presence of death, which in a little while all the condemned must meet.

After he concluded, voices were heard: "We bewail our sins!"

Then came silence, broken only by the crying of children and the beating of hands against breasts. The blood of Vinitius curdled in his veins. He, who'd placed all his hope in the mercy of Christ, now heard that the day of wrath was at hand and that mercy could not be obtained, even by death in the arena. Through his head flashed, quick as lightning, the conviction that the Apostle Peter would have spoken otherwise to those about to die. Yet the terrible fanaticism of the words of Crispus, the dark room with its grating—beyond which lay the field of torture—and the crowd of victims already destined for death filled his soul with terror. All these things taken together seemed to him terrible, a hundredfold more horrible than the bloodiest battles in which he'd ever taken part. The foul air and heat almost overpowered him. Cold perspiration bedewed his forehead. He feared he might faint like those he'd stumbled on earlier; but when he remembered that at any moment the grating might be opened, he began to call aloud for Lygia and Ursus in the hope that if not they, then someone who knew them, might answer.

And, in fact, a man wrapped in a bearskin pulled at his toga and said, "Master, they remained behind in the prison. I was the last whom they led out, and I saw her lying sick on the couch."

"Who are you?" inquired Vinitius.

"I'm the quarryman in whose hut the Apostle baptized you. They imprisoned me three days ago, and today I die."

Vinitius breathed more freely. When he'd entered, he'd expected to find Lygia, but now he was ready to thank Christ that she wasn't there and behold therein a sign of His mercy.

Meanwhile, the quarryman pulled at his toga again and said, "Do you remember, master, that I conducted you to the vineyard of Cornelius, where the Apostle preached in the shed?"

"I remember," answered Vinitius.

"I saw him later on the day before they imprisoned me. He blessed me and said that he would come to the amphitheater to bless the perishing. I should like to look at him as I am dying and see the sign of the cross; it would make it easier for me to die. If you know, master, where he is, tell me."

Vinitius lowered his voice and said, "He's among the people of Petronius, disguised as a slave. I know not where they've chosen to sit, but I'll return to the Circus and find out. Look then at me. When you enter into the arena, I'll rise and turn my head towards the side where he is. Then you'll find him with your eyes."

"I thank you, master. Peace be with you."

"May the Redeemer be merciful to you."

"Amen."

Vinitius went out from the *cuniculum* and set out for the amphitheater, where he took his place near Petronius in the midst of the other Augustinians.

"Is she there?" asked Petronius.

"She's not. They left her in prison."

"Hear what's occurred to me, but while you're listening, look at Nigidia, for example, so that it may appear as though we're talking of her headgear. Tigellinus and Chilo are watching us at this moment. Listen. Let them put Lygia in a coffin and carry her out of the prison as a corpse. You can guess the rest."

"Yes," answered Vinitius.

Further conversation was interrupted by Tullius Senecio, who, leaning towards them, asked, "Do you know whether they'll arm the Christians?"

"We don't know," answered Petronius.

"I wish that arms might be given to them," said Tullius. "If not, the arena will soon become like a butcher's shambles. But what a splendid amphitheater!"

Truly the scene was magnificent. The lower seats, crowded with senators in their togas, were white as snow. In a gilded box sat Caesar, wearing a diamond collar and a golden wreath; at his side sat the beautiful but gloomy Augusta. Around him were vestal virgins, great officials, senators with embroidered mantles, officers of the army with glittering weapons. In a word, all there was in Rome of power, brilliance, and wealth sat there. Knights sat in the higher rows. Even higher up were the common people. Above them, from pillar to pillar, hung garlands made of roses, lilies, ivy, and grapevines. People talked loudly, called to one another, sang, burst out in laughter at some jest sent from row to row, or stamped impatiently to hasten the beginning of the spectacle.

At last the stamping became like thunder and remained unbroken. Then the prefect of the city, who, with a retinue of brilliant followers, had already ridden around the arena, gave the signal with a handkerchief. It was answered from the amphitheater with exclamations of "Aaa!" escaping from thousands of throats.

In a gilded box sat Caesar.

The games usually began with lions or other beasts pitted against various barbarians from the north and south—but this time beasts were not considered of sufficient interest. The initial performance was given by gladiators called *andabates*,[2] who wore helmets without eye openings. Scores of them entered the arena and together began to shake their swords in the air while the *mastigophori* pushed them towards one another with long forks. The connoisseurs in the audience looked upon such proceedings with contempt, but the crowd was pleased with the awkward motions of the swordsmen. When the combatants happened to slam into each other backward, observers in the crowd laughed aloud, calling out, "To the right!" "To the left!" "To your front!" This was frequently and intentionally done to mislead the opponents. However, a number of pairs closed in, and the fighting grew bloody. Then the combatants cast aside their shields, and extending their left hands to one another so as not to be separated again, they fought to the death. Whoever fell would raise his fingers, begging mercy by that sign, but in the beginning of a spectacle the audience usually demanded death for the wounded, especially in cases where the combatants had their faces covered or who were relatively unknown. Gradually, the number of the combatants decreased. When at last only two remained and were pushed together so that they should meet, both fell on the sand and stabbed each other reciprocally. Then amid cries of *"Peractum est!"*[3] slaves removed the corpses, while boys raked away the bloodstained sand and spread a blanket of crocus leaves over the arena.

Now a more important combat followed, arousing the attention not only of the rabble, but also of the better class of spectators. Young patricians offered enormous bets, many risking everything they owned. From hand to hand were passed tablets upon which were written the names of the favorites and also the amount of sesterces that each bettor was willing to risk. The *spectati*, established champions who had already won their laurels, found the most backers. But among the bettors were many who posted considerable sums on new and unknown gladiators, hoping to win immense amounts in case of success. All bet, even Caesar. Priests, vestal virgins, senators, knights, and the people bet. Often, some in the crowd who had no money wagered their own freedom. Then they waited with

---

2 The word means "blindfolded."
3 "It's finished!"

agonized anxiety upon the issue of the fight, more than one loudly appealing to the gods for the protection of his favorite.

When the piercing sound of the trumpets was heard, silence reigned in the amphitheater. Thousands of eyes turned towards the great bolts of the gate, which a man dressed like Charon approached. Amid general silence, he knocked three times upon the gate with a hammer, as if summoning to death those hidden from view. Then the two halves of the gate opened slowly, revealing a black channel out of which gladiators poured into the bright arena. They came in divisions of twenty-five—Thracians, *mirmillons*, Samnites, Gauls, all heavily armed. In their rear followed the *retiarii*, holding in one hand a net and in the other a trident. At sight of them, applause broke out here and there on the benches. Soon the applause changed into one continuous storm. From top to bottom were seen excited faces, clapping hands, and open mouths, from which shouts burst forth.

The gladiators paraded the entire arena with even, springy steps, their weapons glittering in the sun. Before Caesar's box they halted—proud, calm, and brilliant. The shrill sound of a trumpet silenced the applause, and the combatants, lifting their right hands and turning their heads and eyes towards Caesar, chanted in a monotonous singsong: "*Ave, Caesar imperator. Morituri te salutant.*"[4]

Then they separated quickly, each occupying the place assigned to him in the arena. They were to fall on one another in whole sections, but first the most renowned combatants were permitted to engage in one-on-one combat, wherein strength, dexterity, and courage were best exhibited.

From among the Gauls appeared a champion well known to frequenters of the amphitheaters as the Butcher. He'd been a victor in many games. With a huge helmet on his head and a coat of mail shielding his torso front and back, he looked in the golden light of the arena like a giant gold beetle. The equally powerful *retiarius* Calendio appeared against him.

The spectators began to bet.

"Five hundred sesterces on the Gaul."

"Five hundred on Calendio!"

"By Hercules, a thousand!"

"Two thousand!"

Meanwhile, the Gaul had reached the center of the arena. He slowly

---

4 "Hail, Caesar emperor. We who are about to die salute you."

backed away, a pointed sword in his hand. Lowering his head, he carefully watched his opponent through the opening of his visor. The lean and well-formed *retiarius*, naked save for a belt around his loins, nimbly circled his antagonist, waving his net gracefully, lowering and raising his trident, and singing the customary song of the *retiari*:

> *Non te peto, piscem peto;*
> *Quid me fugis, Galle?*[5]

But the Gaul was not fleeing. He soon stopped and, standing in one place, began to turn slowly so as to keep his enemy always in sight. In his form and enormous head was hidden explosive power. The spectators fully understood that the heavy man encased in bronze was preparing for a sudden leap that would decide the battle. Calendio, meanwhile, sprang up to him, then sprang back, handling his trident so dexterously that the spectators had difficulty following his motions. The sound of the trident's teeth striking the shield was heard repeatedly. Yet the Gaul did not quail, thus demonstrating gigantic strength. All his attention seemed to be concentrated, not on the trident, but on the net continually circling above his head like a bird of ill omen. The spectators held their breath as they followed the masterly play of the gladiators. The Butcher bided his time, then rushed upon his enemy. The latter, with equal speed, shot past his sword, raised his arms, straightened himself, and cast the net.

The Gaul, turning where he stood, caught the net on his shield. Then both sprang aside. From the amphitheater thundered shouts of "*Macte!*" On the lower rows, new bets were made. Caesar, who from the beginning had been talking to Rubria and up to this time had paid little attention, turned his head towards the arena. The combatants began to struggle again with such uniformity and precision that it seemed as though they cared not for life or death, but only for the exhibition of their skill. The Butcher escaped twice more from the net and again retreated towards the edge of the arena. Then those who had bet against him, not wishing him to rest, began to shout, "Attack!" The Gaul obeyed and attacked. The *retiarius's* arm was suddenly covered with blood, and his net dropped. The Gaul gathered up all his strength and leaped forward to deliver the finishing stroke. But at that instant, Calendio, who'd intentionally made it appear as though he could no longer manage the net, sprang aside, thus evading the thrust, and ran his trident between the knees of his opponent,

---

5 "I seek you not, I seek a fish; / Why flee from me, O Gaul?"

tripping him and bringing him down. The Butcher strove to rise, but in only seconds the fatal meshes closed over him, and with every movement he entangled still more his powerful hands and legs. Repeated stabs of the trident pinned him to the ground. Making one last supreme effort, he raised himself by his arm and endeavored to rise, but in vain. Lifting to his head his weakened hand, which could no longer hold the sword, he fell on his back. Calendio jammed the Gaul's neck to the ground with the teeth of his trident and, leaning with both hands on its hilt, turned towards Caesar's box.

The whole Circus trembled with the applause and the roar of the people. Those who'd bet on Calendio held him, at that moment, greater than Caesar himself; but this fact banished all hatred towards the Gaul, for at the cost of his own blood, their purses were to be filled. The wishes of the people were divided. On all the benches signs were shown; half of them were for death and half for mercy. But the *retiarius* looked only at Caesar and the vestals, waiting for their decision.

Unfortunately for the fallen gladiator, Nero disliked him, for at the last game before the fire he'd bet against him with Licinus and lost a considerable sum; hence he thrust his hand out of the podium and turned his thumb towards the ground. The vestals repeated the sign at once.

Calendio knelt on the breast of the Gaul, pulled out a short knife from his belt, drew aside the armor around the neck of his opponent, and ran the three-edged knife into his throat up to the hilt.

"Peractum est!" resounded from all sides of the amphitheater.

The Butcher quivered for a moment like a stabbed ox, dug the sand with his feet, stretched, and ceased to move. There was no need for Mercury to try with a heated iron to find out if he were yet alive. He was then disentangled from the net.

Other pairs appeared. After them, whole detachments fought in battles. The audience took part in them with soul, heart, and eyes. They howled, roared, whistled, applauded, and laughed. In the arena the gladiators, dividing into two companies, fought with the fury of wild beasts. Chest struck chest, bodies were intertwined in deadly embrace, strong bones cracked in their sockets, swords were driven into breasts and stomachs. Pale lips spat blood upon the sand. Towards the end, so terrified did some of the novices become that, tearing themselves from the turmoil, they fled—but the *mastigophori* drove them back again with lead-tipped lashes. On the sand, great dark spots were spreading; more and more naked and armed bodies lay stretched out like grain sheaves. The living fought on top of corpses, stumbled against armor and shields, cut their feet against broken weapons, and fell. The audience lost all self-restraint in their feverish excitement; intoxicated with death, they breathed it, sated their eyes with the sight of it, and drew into their lungs the exhalations of it.

Finally, almost all the conquered lay dead. A mere handful of the wounded knelt in the middle of the arena and tremblingly stretched out their hands to the audience, praying for mercy. The victors were rewarded with wreaths and olive branches; most of the losers with death.

A moment of rest followed, which at the command of the all-powerful Caesar changed into a feast. Perfumes were burned in vases. Sprinklers sprayed upon the people saffron and violet water. Cooling refreshments were brought—roasted meat, sweet cakes, olives, and fruit. The people ate, talked, and shouted in honor of Caesar, hoping to incline him to greater liberality. Then, when they'd appeased their hunger and quenched their thirst, hundreds of slaves brought baskets full of gifts, from which boys, dressed as cupids, took various items in both hands and threw them among the people.

With the appearance of lottery tickets in the distribution, a scuffle began. People pushed, tripped, and trampled one another. They cried for help, jumped over rows of seats, and throttled one another in the terrible melee. For whoever captured a lucky number might win a house and garden, a slave, costly clothing, or a wild beast that could be sold to the amphitheater. Distribution of lottery tickets typically resulted in such chaos that frequently the Praetorians were obliged to intercede and restore order. After each distribution, people were carried out with broken arms or legs, and some were trampled to death in the crowd.

But the rich took no part in the scramble for lottery tickets. The Augustinians now amused themselves with the sight of Chilo making vain efforts to show that he could look on fighting and bloodshed as undisturbed as anybody. From the beginning, the unfortunate Greek had begun to wrinkle his brow, bite his lips, and squeeze his fists so that the nails pierced his flesh. His Greek nature and personal cowardice unfitted him to endure such a sight. His face paled, his forehead grew wet with drops of perspiration, his lips turned blue, his eyes sank in, his teeth chattered, and his body trembled. At the end of each fight he recovered somewhat, but when finally they all jeered at him, he erupted with sudden anger and defended himself desperately.

"Ha, Greek! The sight of a torn human skin is unbearable to you," taunted Vatinius, yanking him by the beard.

Chilo bared his last two yellow teeth and snarled, "As my father wasn't a shoemaker, I can't do anything about it."

"*Macte! Habet!*"[6] answered several voices, but others continued the taunting.

"It's not his fault that instead of a heart he has a piece of cheese in his breast!" observed Senecio.

"Neither is it your fault that instead of a head you have a bladder," retorted Chilo.

"Perhaps you'll become a gladiator. You'd look great with a net in the arena."

"Should I happen to catch you with it, I should catch a stinking hoopoe."

"And how will it be with the Christians?" asked Festus of Liguria. "Wouldn't you like to be a dog so that you might bite them?"

"I wouldn't wish to be your brother."

"You Maeotian copper-nose!"[7]

"You Ligurian mule!"

"Evidently your skin is itching, but I don't advise you to ask me to scratch it."

"Scratch yourself. If you scratch your pimple, you'll destroy the best part of you."

In such fashion they attacked him, and thus he defended himself viciously, amid general laughter. Caesar, clapping his hands, repeated "*Macte!*" several times and urged them on.

Then Petronius approached. Touching the Greek's side with his ivory cane, he said, "Well done, philosopher. In one thing only you've blundered: The gods created you a pickpocket, but you've become a demon, and that's why you won't hold out."

The old man gazed at him with his reddened eyes, but this time he wasn't ready with an insulting reply. After a silence, he said lamely, "I'll endure!"

Meanwhile, the trumpets announced the end of the intermission. The people began to leave the passages where they'd assembled to stretch and talk.

---

6 "A solid hit!"
7 Crimean leper (copper substituted for nose eaten away by leprosy).

A general movement began, with the usual dispute over seats previously occupied. Senators and patricians hurried to their places. The noise ceased at last, and the amphitheater returned to order. In the arena was a crowd of people engaged in digging out, here and there, clumps composed of matted sand and blood.

It was now the Christians' turn. Since this was a new spectacle to the people, no one could foresee how they would comport themselves. All waited expectantly for these incendiaries of Rome, these destroyers of its ancient treasures! The Christians had drunk the blood of infants and poisoned the waters; they had cursed the whole human race and committed the most heinous atrocities. The cruelest punishments were not terrible enough for their crimes; in fact, what the people feared was that the tortures provided for the Christians might be inadequate for the enormity of their guilt.

Meanwhile, the sun had risen to the meridian, and its rays, passing through the purple velarium, filled the amphitheater with a bloody light. The sand assumed a fiery color, and in those gleams, in the faces of people as well as in the empty arena—which after a time was to be filled with the mangling of people and the rage of savage beasts—there was something terrible. Death and terror pervaded the air. The throng, usually joyous, grew sullen under the influence of their hate. Their faces clearly revealed their inner anger.

Now the prefect gave a sign. The same old man dressed as Charon who'd summoned the gladiators to death appeared. After walking with steady steps around the arena, amid perfect silence, he struck the door three times with a hammer. Throughout the amphitheater ran a deep murmur: "The Christians! The Christians!"

The iron gratings creaked. From the dark openings came the usual cry of the *mastigophori:* "To the sand!"

The next moment, the arena was peopled with men, women, and children covered with skins. All ran quickly, feverishly, and when they reached the middle of the Circus, they fell on their knees together and raised their hands. The spectators, conceiving this to be a prayer for pity and enraged by such evident cowardice, began to stamp, whistle, throw empty wine vessels and clean-picked bones, and shout, "The beasts! The beasts! Bring out the beasts!"

Then an unexpected thing happened. From the midst of the shaggy group, voices were heard in song. For the first time in the history of the

Roman Circus, there arose the hymn "*Christus regnat!*"[8]

Astonishment seized the people. The victims sang with eyes raised to the velarium. The spectators saw pale but inspired faces. It was plain enough now that these people were not begging for mercy. Apparently, they saw neither the Circus nor the people, neither the Senate nor Caesar. "*Christus regnat!*" rose even louder, and the spectators all the way to the topmost rows inquired of themselves, *What's going on? And who is this Christus who reigns, as is asserted by these people about to die?*

Meanwhile, another grating opened, and into the arena rushed madly barking dogs, great packs of dogs—huge yellow Molossians from the Peloponesus, pied dogs from the Pyrenees, and wolflike dogs from Ireland, all purposely famished. Lean, with bloodshot eyes, they filled the amphitheater with their barks and howls.

The Christians, having finished their hymn, remained on their knees, motionless as statues, repeating with doleful intonations, "*Pro Christo! Pro Christo!*" The dogs scented human beings beneath the animal skins. Surprised at their immobility, however, they didn't at first dare to attack the martyrs. Some leaned against the walls of the seating sections, appearing eager to attack the spectators; others ran around barking furiously, as if chasing some invisible enemy. The people were angry. A thousand voices shrieked, some roaring like beasts, others barking, others urging on the dogs in various languages. The maddened dogs would attack the kneeling Christians, only to draw back again, gnashing their teeth. Finally, one of the Molossians drove its fangs into the skin-covered shoulder of a woman kneeling in front and dragged her under it.

At this, a number of dogs pounced upon the Christians. The mob ceased its tumult to better observe. Amid the canine howling and snarling, the plaintive voices of men and women crying "*Pro Christo! Pro Christo!*" were still audible. The arena was now a quivering mass of dogs and people. Blood gushed from torn bodies. Dogs snatched from one another bloody pieces of flesh. The odor of blood and torn entrails drowned the Arabian perfumes and filled the whole Circus. At last, only here and there were to be seen kneeling forms. But even these were soon covered by the howling masses of vicious canines.

Vinitius, at the first entry of the Christians, had risen and turned his head, according to his agreement with the quarryman, to that side where

---

8 "Christ reigns!"

Peter sat among Petronius's people. He now sat gazing with glassy eyes at the ghastly spectacle. At first he feared that the quarryman might have been mistaken and that Lygia might be among the victims. The very thought numbed his heart. But when he heard the voices crying "*Pro Christo! Pro Christo!*"—when he witnessed the ripping apart of so many victims, who, dying, acknowledged their faith and their God—he couldn't drive back other feelings, which pierced him with the most poignant agony. If Christ Himself had died in agony, if thousands were following Him, if a sea of blood was to be poured out, what mattered one little drop more? Wouldn't it almost be a sin to ask for mercy?

That thought came to him from the hell of the arena, pervaded with the groans of the dying and the odor of their blood. Nonetheless he prayed on and repeated through his parched lips, "O Christ! O Christ! Your Apostle prayed for her."

Then he lost consciousness of his surroundings. It seemed to him that the level of blood in the arena was rising and would soon overflow the whole city of Rome. He was deaf now to everything—to the howling of the dogs, the clamor of the people, and the voices of the Augustinians, who suddenly called out, "Chilo has fainted!"

"Chilo has fainted!" repeated Petronius, turning towards the place where the Greek sat.

He really *had* fainted. He sat there, white as a sheet, his head thrown back, his mouth wide open, in corpselike immobility. At that very moment, new victims sewn up in skins were being driven into the arena.

They knelt immediately, in the same manner as their predecessors. But the worn-out dogs were loath to rend them. Only a few attacked those kneeling nearby. Others lay down, scratched their sides, and yawned wearily, opening wide their bloody jaws.

The audience, restless in soul but drunk and maddened with blood, began shouting with shrill voices, "Lions! Lions! Let loose the lions!"

The lions had been destined for the following day, but in the amphitheater the people imposed their will on everyone, even Caesar. Caligula alone, arrogant and fickle, had dared to oppose them. There were times when he gave orders to beat the crowd with clubs, but even he was often obliged to give way. Nero, however, to whom applause was dearer than anything else in the world, never opposed them. This time he was more lenient than ever because he wished to appease the angry crowd and lay upon the Christians the blame for the conflagration.

Therefore he gave the signal for the opening of the lions' *cuniculum*, an act that calmed the people immediately. The creaking of the gates was heard. The dogs, at sight of the lions, huddled together, whimpering, on the opposite side of the ring. The lions stalked into the arena, one after another. They were tawny monsters with shaggy heads. Even Caesar turned towards them his weary face and placed the emerald to his eye to see better. The Augustinians greeted them with applause. The crowd counted the lions, eager at the same time to note the impression that the lions would make on the Christians, who, kneeling in the center, again repeated, "*Pro Christo! Pro Christo!*"

But the lions, though hungry, didn't hasten towards the victims. The reddish gleam upon the arena had blinded them, so that they half closed their eyes as if dazed. Some stretched their yellow bodies lazily, others opened their jaws and yawned, as if to show the spectators their terrible teeth. But soon the odor of blood and the torn bodies, a number of which still lay in the arena, began to act on them. They became restless; their manes rose; their nostrils drew in the air with a snort. One of them made a sudden dash on the body of a woman with a torn face. Lying with his forepaws on the body, he licked the coagulated blood with his rough tongue. Another approached a Christian holding a child sewn up in a fawn's skin.

The child trembled and wept, convulsively embracing his father, who, wishing to prolong the infant's life, if only for a moment, endeavored to tear him away so that he might hand him over to those kneeling farther on. But the noise and movement excited the lion. Almost instantly, he growled a short, sharp roar; killed the child with one blow of his paw; and caught the father's head between his jaws and crushed it.

This was the signal for all the other lions to fall upon the Christians. Some women couldn't restrain cries of terror, but their cries were drowned in the applause. This soon ceased, the crowd's desire to see overcoming everything else. Then began nightmarish scenes. Heads disappeared entirely in the lions' jaws. Breasts were opened by one blow of a paw. Hearts and lungs were dragged out. The crunching of bones was heard. The lions, seizing the victims by the sides or backs, ran around with mad leaps, as though in search of hiding places where they might devour them undisturbed. Other lions fought each other, rearing on their hind legs, clasping one another with their paws like wrestlers, and filling the amphitheater with thunderous roars. Some of the audience stood up, others left their seats to rush towards the arena for a closer view, many being trampled to death in the process. It seemed as though the bloodthirsty spectators would leap into the arena themselves to join the lions in tearing apart the Christians. At times unearthly noises were heard, at others applause; then came roaring and rumbling, the gnashing of teeth, the howling of the Molossian dogs. And at intervals, only the groaning of the martyrs could be heard.

Caesar, holding the emerald to his eye, renewed his attention. Petronius assumed an expression of disgust and contempt. Chilo had already been borne out of the Circus. But from the *cuniculum*, fresh victims were driven out continually to replenish the supply.

From the upper tier of seats, the Apostle Peter looked on. No one saw him, for all had their heads turned towards the arena. He rose to his feet, and as before in the vineyard of Cornelius he'd blessed for death and eternity the hunted fugitives, so now he blessed with the sign of the cross those who were in the clutches of the wild beasts—blessed their blood, their agony, their dead bodies changed into shapeless lumps, their souls flying upward from the blood-soaked sand.

Some of the martyrs raised their eyes to him. Their faces grew radiant as they caught sight of the sign of the cross high above them.

But Peter's heart was torn as he prayed silently, *O Lord, Your will be done! For Your glory, for the testimony of the truth, these my sheep are perishing. You have commanded me to feed them. For this reason I give them to You. Count them, O Lord! Take them, soften their pain, let their recompense be far greater than their torture!*

And he blessed one after another, group after group, with loving compassion, as a father surrendering his own children into the hands of Christ. Then Caesar, spurred by madness or the desire that the spectacle should surpass all others ever seen in Rome, whispered a few words to the prefect of the city, who thereupon left Caesar's box and descended at once to the *cuniculum*. Even the populace was astonished when the next moment they heard again the sound of the opening of the gates. And now all kinds of wild beasts were let out—tigers from the banks of the Euphrates, panthers from Numidia, bears, wolves, hyenas, and jackals. The whole arena seemed turned into a sea of moving skins: striped, yellow, faded yellow, dark brown, brown, and spotted. Then followed chaos, in which the eye could distinguish nothing save the horrible turning and twisting of the backs of the wild beasts. The spectacle lost the aspect of reality and turned into an orgy of blood, a dreadful dream, a monstrous nightmare of a berserk imagination. All records were surpassed. Above the roars and howlings and yells rose the shrill, hysterical laughter of women in the stands whose nerves had given way at last under the strain.

People were horrified; faces grew dark, and voices were heard saying, "Enough! Enough!"

But it was easier to let loose the beasts than to beat them back. Caesar, however, found a means of clearing the arena and starting a new amusement for the people. In all sections, in the midst of the benches, appeared detachments of black Numidians, adorned with feathers and earrings, with bows in their hands. The people guessed what was coming and greeted the archers with shouts of satisfaction. The Numidians approached the arena, fitted their arrows to the strings, and shot them into that maelstrom of slaughter. That was indeed a new spectacle! Their shapely black bodies bending backwards, stretching the flexible bows, and dispatching shaft after shaft. The snapping of the strings and the whistling of the feathered darts mingled with the howling of the wild beasts and the shouts of admiration from the spectators. Wolves, bears, panthers, and such of the martyrs as were still living fell side by side. Here and there a lion, feeling an arrow in his side, turned suddenly with mouth wrinkled from rage, trying to snatch and break the shaft. Other lions groaned from pain. The smaller beasts, panic-stricken, ran aimlessly around the arena or thrust their heads between the gratings. Meanwhile, the arrows whizzed on till every living thing went down in the last agony of death.

Then hundreds of slaves streamed into the arena, armed with spades, shovels, brooms, wheelbarrows, baskets for carrying out entrails, and sacks of sand—crowd after crowd of them—in seething, feverish activity. The arena was soon cleared of corpses, blood, and refuse; was dug over, made even, and spread with thick layers of new sand. Cupids ran in, scattering rose leaves, lilies, and many other flowers. The censers were lighted again, and the velarium was removed. The sun was now dropping low in the western sky.

The crowd looked at one another with surprise, wondering what new spectacle was still in store for them. And indeed it was a spectacle that none had expected. Caesar, who some time before had left his box, appeared suddenly on the flower-strewn arena, arrayed in a golden mantle and crowned with a golden wreath. He was followed by twelve choristers, with kitharas in their hands. In his own hand he held a silver kithara.

Advancing with solemn step to the center, he bowed his head several times, raised his eyes towards the sky, and remained in that posture for a while, as though waiting for inspiration.

Then he struck the strings and began to sing:

> O radiant son of Leto,
> Ruler of Tenedos, Chios, Chrysos,
> Art thou he who, having in his care
> The sacred city of Ilion,
> Could yield it to Argive anger,
> And suffer sacred altars,
> Which blazed unceasingly to his honor,
> To be stained with Trojan blood?
> Aged men raised trembling hands to thee,
> O thou of the far-shooting silver bow,
> Mothers from the depths of their breasts
> Raised tearful cries to thee,
> Imploring pity on their offspring.
> These complaints might have moved a stone,
> But to the suffering people
> Thou, O Smintheus,[9] wert less feeling than a stone!

The song passed gradually into an elegy, plaintive and full of pain. In the Circus there was silence. After a while Caesar, himself affected, sang on.

> With the sound of thy heavenly lyre
> Thou couldst drown the wailing,
> The lament of hearts.
> At the sad sound of this song
> The eye today is filled with tears,
> As a flower is filled with dew,
> But who can raise from dust and ashes
> That day of fire, disaster, ruin?
> O Smintheus, where wert thou then?

9　Refers to Apollo. As mouse god, he controlled mice and thus helped to prevent mice-induced pestilence or plague.

Here his voice quivered, and his eyes grew moist. Tears appeared on the lids of the vestals; the people listened in silence before they burst into a long, unbroken storm of applause.

Meanwhile, from outside through the *vomitorias* came the sound of creaking vehicles on which were placed the bloody remnants of Christian men, women, and children to be taken to the pits called *puticuli*.[10]

And Peter held his trembling white head in his hands and groaned in spirit, *O Lord! O Lord! To whom have You given dominion over the world? And why will You establish Your capital in this terrible place?*

---

10 "Putrid pits."

Chapter LVII

Meanwhile, the sun continued to descend towards its setting, appearing to melt in the red of the evening. The spectacle was at an end. The crowd began to quit the amphitheater for the city, through the *vomitorias*. The Augustinians were the only ones who tarried, waiting for the sea-like crowd to pass. A large number of them left their seats and proceeded to the box, where Caesar showed himself anew, eager for their praises. The public hadn't applauded his song as much as he'd expected. He'd expected enthusiasm bordering on frenzy. In vain did the Augustinians' hymns of praise sound in his ears; in vain did the vestals kiss his divine hand while Rubria bowed so low that her red hair touched his breast. Nero wasn't satisfied and couldn't hide his chagrin. He was both astonished and disquieted because Petronius kept silent. Praises or favorable criticism from his mouth would have afforded great comfort at that moment.

Finally, unable to restrain himself, Caesar beckoned to him and said, "Tell me."

Petronius answered calmly, "I'm silent because I can find no words. You've surpassed yourself."

"So it seemed to me. But that crowd of people!"

"Can you expect mongrels to be judges of poetry?"

"So you also noticed that they didn't thank me as much as I deserved."

"Because you chose a bad moment."

"Why?"

"When their brains are affected by the odor of blood, they are unable to listen attentively."

Nero clenched his fists and answered, "Ah, those Christians! They burned Rome, and they hurt me now. What new punishment should I devise for them?"

Petronius perceived that he'd taken the wrong tack and that his words had produced an effect quite opposite to his intentions. To divert Caesar's mind into another channel, he bent to him and whispered, "Your song is wonderful, but I will venture one suggestion: In the fourth line of the third strophe, the meter left something to be desired."

Nero, blushing with shame, as though he'd been caught in an infamous act, looked alarmed and answered, also in a whisper, "You never miss anything! I know! I'll write it again. But has anyone else noticed it? No? I command you to tell it to nobody if life is dear to you."

Upon this Petronius furrowed his brow and answered as though he were vexed and disaffected. "Condemn me to death, O divinity, if I deceive you, but you won't terrify me, for the gods know best if I fear death."

Saying this he looked straight into Caesar's eyes, who, after a while, responded, "Don't be angry. You know that I love you."

A bad sign, thought Petronius.

"I wish to invite you today to a feast," continued Nero, "but first I must lock myself in and polish the cursed fourth line of the third strophe. Seneca, and perchance Secundus Carinus, may have noticed it as well as you; but I shall quickly rid myself of both."

He summoned Seneca and informed him that he would be sent with Acratus and Secundus Carinus to Italy[1] and to other provinces for money, which he was to draw from cities, villages, and famous sanctuaries. In a word, he was to get money wherever it could be obtained and by whatever means. Seneca, understanding that Caesar entrusted him with a work of plunder, sacrilege, and murder, flatly refused.

"Lord," he said, "I must go to the country and there await death, for my years are many and my nerves are shattered."

Seneca's Iberian nerves were stronger than those of Chilo and were hardly shattered, perhaps, but in general his health was poor. He looked like a shadow, and his hair had lately turned completely white.

Nero, studying him with remorseless eyes, determined that he wouldn't have to wait long for his death. "If you're really ill, I certainly wouldn't want to expose you to the perils of the journey, but because of my love for you, I wish to have you within call. Therefore, instead of going to the country, you'll stay in your own house and not leave it."[2] He laughed and added, "If I send Acratus and Carinus alone, it'll be like sending wolves after sheep. Whom shall I place above them?"

---

1 During the Roman Empire, Italy was only a province, and included about two-thirds of what is now Italy.

2 Putting him under house arrest was almost the same as imprisoning him and signified that a sentence of death for him could come at any moment.

"Put me above them," said Domitius Afer.

"No, I don't wish to bring upon Rome the wrath of Mercury, whom you would shame with your villainy. I need some Stoic like Seneca, or like my new friend, the philosopher Chilo."

Here Nero looked around and asked, "What's happened to Chilo?"

Chilo, who'd come to his senses in the open air and had returned to the amphitheater to hear Caesar's song, approached and said, "Here I am, O radiant offspring of the sun and moon. I was ill, but your song cured me."

"I'll send you to Achaia," said Nero. "Doubtless you know to a copper the amount in each temple."

"So be it, Zeus. The gods will grant you tribute greater than they've ever given before."

"I *would* send you . . . but I don't wish to deprive you of the sight of the games."

"O Baal!" said Chilo.

The Augustinians, overjoyed at Caesar's return to good humor, laughed and exclaimed, "No, lord, deprive not this brave Greek of the sight of the games."

"But preserve me, O lord, from the sight of these strident geese of the Capitol, whose brains all put together wouldn't fill a nutshell," retorted Chilo. "O firstborn of Apollo, I'm composing a Greek hymn in your honor, and I need to spend a few days in the temples of the Muses to beg for inspiration."

"Oh, no!" exclaimed Nero. "You're only trying to escape the next games, and that won't do."

"I swear, lord, that I'm composing a hymn."

"Fine! You can write it at night. Beseech Diana for inspiration. She's Apollo's sister."

Chilo dropped his head and gazed with malice on those present, who again burst into laughter.

Caesar addressed himself to Senecio and Suilius Nerulinus: "Just think—of the Christians allotted for today, we've hardly disposed of half."

Hearing this, old Aquilus Regulus, who was a great critic of all things pertaining to the amphitheater, thought for a moment and said, "Spectacles in which the performers are unarmed and without skill endure almost as long as the others and are less interesting."

"I shall command that the rest of the Christians be armed," replied Nero.

But the superstitious Vestinius, suddenly rousing himself from a reverie, inquired in a mysterious voice, "Have you noticed that, while dying, these people see something? They gaze upward, and one would say that they perish without pain. I'm certain that they see something."

He raised his eyes towards the opening of the amphitheater, over which night had spread its star-strewn velarium. But others laughed and jested at the mere thought that the Christians escaped pain and saw something at the point of death that others couldn't see. Then Caesar gave a signal to the torchbearers and left the Circus. After him followed officials, vestals, senators, and Augustinians.

It was a bright, warm night. In front of the Circus were crowds of people who'd remained to witness Caesar's departure. All were morose and silent. Occasional applause was heard, but it ceased immediately. From the *spoliarium,* creaking carts bore away the bloody remains of the last slain Christians.

Petronius and Vinitius made their way homeward in silence. Only when approaching his villa did Petronius inquire, "Have you thought about what I told you?"

"Yes," replied Vinitius.

"Do you understand that for me also this is an affair of the greatest importance? I must free her in spite of Caesar and Tigellinus. It's a battle wherein I must conquer, a game that I must win even at the price of my life. This day has only strengthened my resolve."

"May Christ reward you."

"You'll see."

They had now reached the door of the villa. As they left the litter, a dark figure confronted them, asking, "Is the noble Vinitius here?"

"Yes," answered the tribune. "What's your request?"

"I'm Nazarius, the son of Miriam. I come from the prison to bring you news of Lygia."

Vinitius laid his hand on the young man's arm. He looked in his eyes by the gleam of the torch, powerless to speak a word.

Nazarius answered the unasked question. "She's still alive. Ursus sent me to you, master, to tell you that she prays in her fever and repeats your name."

"Praise be to Christ, who may return her to me!" exclaimed Vinitius.

Then he led Nazarius to the library. Soon Petronius joined them.

"Her illness saved her from shame because the executioners were afraid," said the boy. "Ursus and Glaucus watch over her day and night."

"Are the guards the same?"

"Yes, master, and she's in their room. All the prisoners in the *tullianum* died of fever or from the foul air."

"Who are you?" asked Petronius.

"The noble Vinitius knows me. I'm the son of the widow with whom Lygia lived."

"Are you a Christian also?"

The boy cast an inquiring glance at Vinitius. Seeing that he was praying, he lifted his head and answered, "Yes, master."

"How is it that you're allowed access to the prison?"

"I was engaged, master, to carry out the bodies of the dead. I offered myself with the intention of aiding my brethren and bringing them news from the city."

Petronius carefully scrutinized the handsome face of the boy, his blue eyes and dark hair. Finally he asked, "Where are you from, my lad?"

"I'm Galilean, master."

"Would you like to see Lygia free?"

The boy raised his eyes. "Even if I died the next moment."

Vinitius finished his prayer and said, "Tell the guards to place her in a coffin as if dead. Find some helpers to bear her out in the night with you. Near the *puticuli*, you'll find men waiting with a litter. Give them the coffin. Tell the guards I promise them as much gold as each can carry in his mantle." As he spoke, his face lost its now-usual pallor, and the soldier awoke in him, for hope brought courage.

At Vinitius's words, Nazarius, overjoyed, raised his hands with the cry: "May Christ restore her health, for she'll be free."

"Do you believe the guards will consent?" asked Petronius.

"Yes, master, if they knew that they wouldn't meet with punishment and torture."

"True," said Vinitius, "since the guards would have consented to her flight, all the more will they let us carry her out as a corpse."

"There's a man," said Nazarius, "who discovers by means of a red-hot iron whether the bodies that we remove are really lifeless. But he'll take a few sesterces not to touch the face of the dead; for one gold piece he would touch the coffin and not the body."

"Tell him that he'll get a bagful of gold pieces," said Petronius. "But can you find trustworthy helpers?"

"I can find men who, for money, would sell their own wives and children."

"Where will you find them?"

"In the prison itself or outside of it. Once the guards are bribed, they'll admit anyone I wish."

"Then take me in the guise of a servant," said Vinitius.

But Petronius dissuaded him from this course. The Praetorians might recognize him even in disguise, and this would bring failure upon the enterprise. "Go neither to the prison nor to the *puticuli*," he said. "Everyone, including Caesar and Tigellinus, must be convinced that she has really died; otherwise they'd order immediate pursuit. We can allay suspicion only by staying in Rome while she's being removed to the Alban Hills, or even farther, to Sicily. A week or two later, you'll fall sick and summon Nero's physician, who'll prescribe for you the mountain air. There you'll join her, and afterward—" He thought a little, then, waving his hand, he continued, "Afterward, the times may change."

"May Christ have mercy on her," said Vinitius. "You speak of Sicily, while she's ill and may die."

"We can keep her nearer at first. The air alone will cure her, if we can but get her out of prison. Is there no one in the mountains whom you can trust?"

"Yes," replied Vinitius. "Not far from Corioli is a trustworthy man who used to carry me in his arms when I was a mere child and who loves me still."

Petronius handed him some tablets. "Write him to come here tomorrow, and I'll send a messenger at once."

Then he summoned the *atriensis* and gave him the necessary orders. A few moments later, a mounted slave left for Corioli.

"I'd like Ursus to accompany her on her journey," said Vinitius. "I'd feel safer."

"Master," said Nazarius, "he's a man of such superhuman strength that he'll break the grating and follow her. There's one window above a steep, high rock where no guard is stationed. I'll bring a rope to Ursus, and he'll do the rest."

"By Hercules!" exclaimed Petronius. "Let him break from the prison as he pleases, but not at the same time with her, nor within two or three days after, for they'd follow him and discover her hiding place. By Hercules! Do you wish us all to perish with her? I forbid you to mention Corioli to him, or I'll wash my hands of the whole affair."

The others silently acknowledged the prudence of his remarks. Nazarius prepared to take leave of them, promising to come back the next morning at dawn.

He hoped to strike a bargain with the guards that night, but he wished first to see his mother, who, on account of the terrible times, was very anxious about him. After some reflection he resolved not to seek an assistant in the city, but to bribe one of his comrades among the corpse bearers.

Before leaving, he took Vinitius aside and whispered, "Master, I'll mention our plan to no one, not even to my mother. But Peter the Apostle promised to come to our house from the amphitheater, and to him I'll tell everything."

"In this house you may speak openly," said Vinitius. "The Apostle Peter was in the amphitheater with the people of Petronius. But wait—I myself will go with you."

He ordered a slave to bring him a cloak, and they went out.

Petronius drew a deep breath. *I hoped that she would die of the fever,* he thought, *since that would be less terrible for Vinitius. But now I'm willing to offer a golden tripod to Aesculapius for her restoration to health. Ah, Ahenobarbus, you wish to make a public spectacle out of the agony of a lover! You, Augusta, were jealous of the beauty of this girl, and now you would destroy her because your child Rufius is no more! You, Tigellinus, would ruin her just to spite me! We shall see. I tell you that your eyes will not see her in the arena, for either she'll die a natural death, or I'll wrest her from you as from the jaws of dogs . . . and in such a fashion that you won't be aware of it; and afterward every time I look at you I'll think,* These are the fools I outwitted.

And satisfied with himself, he went into the *triclinium,* where he sat down to supper with Eunice. During the meal, a lector read to them the idylls of Theocritus. Meanwhile, outside a sudden storm broke the calm serenity of the summer night as it swept down from Mount Soracte. From time to time thunder reverberated through the seven hills, while they, lying side by side at the table, listened to the pastoral poet, who, in the singing Doric dialect, celebrated the loves of shepherds. Soothed and lulled, they later prepared for sweet repose.

But before this, Vinitius returned. Petronius, learning of his return, went out to meet him and asked, "Well, is everything going as planned? Has Nazarius already gone to the prison?"

"Yes," replied the tribune, running his hands through his soaked hair.

"Nazarius has gone to bribe the guards, and I've seen Peter, who commanded me to pray and to have faith."

"Good. If everything goes well, we can carry her off tomorrow night."

"My steward from Corioli should be here at dawn with his men."

"The road is a short one, so go and get all the rest you can before he
arrives."

But Vinitius knelt in his *cubiculum* and prayed.

At sunrise, Niger, the steward, arrived from Corioli. In accordance
with the instructions of Vinitius, he brought with him mules, a litter, and
four trusty men selected from among his British slaves. To avoid attract-
ing attention, he'd left them at an inn in the Suburra.

Vinitius, who hadn't slept the whole night, stepped out to meet him.
The steward, greatly moved at sight of his young master, kissed his hands
and eyes and exclaimed, "My dear master, are you ill, or has sorrow sucked
the blood from your cheeks? At first glance, I hardly recognized you."

Vinitius led him to the interior colonnade, and there admitted him to the
secret. Niger listened with close attention. On his dry, sunburned face, great
emotion was evident, an emotion that he made no attempt to suppress.

"She's a Christian then?" he cried, with an inquiring glance at the face
of Vinitius.

Guessing what that look meant, Vinitius replied, "I also am a Christian."

Tears filled Niger's eyes. He was silent for a while; then, raising his
hands, he said, "Thanks be to Christ for having removed the scales from
the eyes that are dearest to me on earth." Then he embraced Vinitius and,
weeping from sheer happiness, kissed his forehead.

A moment later Petronius appeared, accompanied by Nazarius.

"Good news!" he cried from afar.

It was good news indeed. First, Glaucus vouched for Lygia's life,
though she was down with the same prison fever of which, in the *tullianum* and other dungeons, hundreds were dying every day. As to the jailers and the man who tested the corpses with a red-hot iron, there hadn't
been the slightest difficulty; his assistant, Attys, had also been enlisted on
their side.

"We made holes in the coffin so that Lygia could breathe," said
Nazarius. "The only danger is that she may groan or speak as we pass the
Praetorians. She's very weak and lies the whole day with closed eyes. Glaucus will give her a sleeping potion prepared from herbs that I'll bring to
him. The lid won't be nailed to the coffin, thus you'll be able to lift it easily

and transfer the maiden to the litter. We'll substitute in the coffin a long bag of sand that you'll have ready."

Vinitius, as he listened, grew pale as a sheet, but listened so intently that he seemed to anticipate all Nazarius had to say.

"Will there be other bodies removed from the prison?" asked Petronius.

"Nearly twenty people died last night, and before evening more will die," said the boy. "We'll have to join the rest, but we'll delay and drop to the rear. At the first turn my companion will begin to limp. In this way we shall fall considerably behind the others. Wait for us at the small temple of Libitina. May God give us the darkest possible night."

"God will do so," said Niger. "Last evening that sky was clear and cloudless, but later a sudden storm blew in. Today the sky is clear again, but it has been sultry since early morning. Mark my words, every night for a time there'll be wind and rain."

"Are you going without torches?" asked Vinitius.

"The torches are carried only in front. In any case, wait in the vicinity of the temple of Libitina as soon as it is dark, though we normally don't remove the dead bodies until about midnight."

Silence fell. Only the ragged breathing of Vinitius was heard.

Petronius turned to him. "I said yesterday," he remarked, "that it would be the best plan if we both remained at home. But I see now that I couldn't possibly remain behind. Besides, were it a question of flight, we'd have to be more careful, but since she'll be carried out as a corpse, it seems to me that not the slightest suspicion will be aroused."

"True, true!" agreed Vinitius. "I must be there, too. I'll take her out of the coffin myself."

"Once she's under my roof at Corioli, I'll answer for her," said Niger.

This ended the conference. Niger returned to the inn to rejoin his men. Nazarius, after slipping a heavy purse of gold under his tunic, went back to the prison. For Vinitius, a day filled with uneasiness, excitement, fear, and hope began.

"The undertaking ought to succeed, for it's well planned," said Petronius. "The matter couldn't have been arranged better. You must feign suffering and wear a dark toga. But don't miss the performances at the Circus. Let the people see you. Everything is so arranged that failure is impossible. But—are you absolutely sure of your steward?"

"He's a Christian," answered Vinitius.

Petronius looked at him in astonishment, then, shrugging his shoulders, said almost as if to himself, "By Pollux, how it spreads, and how it takes possession of human souls! Under its powerful influence, people renounce all the gods—Roman, Greek, and Egyptian. It's amazing! By Pollux! If I believed that any of our gods had power, I'd sacrifice six white bulls to every one of them, and to Jupiter Capitolinus, twelve. But forget not to make an offering to your Christ."

"I've given Him my soul," quietly answered Vinitius.

Then they parted.

Petronius returned to his *cubiculum.* Vinitius, however, desiring to take a look at the prison from a distance, wended his way up the slope of the Vatican Hill to the cabin of the quarryman, where he'd received baptism at the hands of the Apostle. It seemed to him that Christ would more readily listen to his petition in this hut than in any other place; consequently, when he found it, he threw himself upon the floor and so poured out his suffering soul to God, begging His mercy, that he forgot himself entirely and recalled not where he was or what he was doing.

Not until the afternoon was he aroused by the sound of trumpets that came from the direction of Nero's Circus. He then left the hut and looked about him as if just awakened. It was hot and perfectly still, the silence broken only from time to time by the sound of trumpets and the chirping of crickets. The air remained sultry, the sky above the city was still clear, but near the Sabine Hills, dark clouds were gathering across the horizon.

Vinitius returned home. At the entrance Petronius was waiting for him. "I've been on the Palatine," he said. "I showed myself there purposely and even sat down to a game of dice. Anicius gives a banquet tonight; I promised to go but not until after midnight, because I must sleep a little before that hour. And I shall go, and it would be well if you could be present as well."

"Any news from Niger or Nazarius?" inquired Vinitius.

"No; we won't see them before midnight. Have you noticed that a storm is coming?"

"Yes, I have."

"Tomorrow there's to be an exhibition of crucified Christians, but rain might prevent it." Then coming closer to Vinitius and taking his arm, he said, "But you won't see her on the cross, only in Corioli. By Castor! I wouldn't exchange the moment in which we free her for all the gems in Rome. The evening is almost here."

And indeed the evening was approaching rapidly. Darkness began to envelop the city earlier than usual, on account of the clouds that now covered the entire horizon. With night came a heavy rain, which, falling on the heated stones, turned into steam and filled the streets of the city with a mist. Then followed a lull and, after that, intermittent showers.

"Let's hurry," said Vinitius at last. "Because of the storm, they may carry the bodies away from the prison earlier than usual."

"It's time," agreed Petronius. And taking Gallic mantles with hoods, they passed through the garden gate out into the street. Petronius had armed himself with a *sica*, as always when he went out at night. The streets of the city were deserted due to the storm. From time to time, lightning rent the clouds, illuminating with lurid flashings the newly built walls of houses just completed or under construction and the wet flagstones with which the streets were paved. By one of these lightning flashes they descried, at last, the hill whereon stood the little temple of Libitina. At the bottom of the hill was a group of mules and horses.

"Niger!" called Vinitius in a low voice.

"Here I am, master," a voice answered out of the rain.

"Is everything ready?"

"Yes, dear master, we were here immediately after dark. But get yourself under cover or you'll be completely soaked. What a storm! I think that it's going to hail."

Niger's apprehension was well founded. Soon hail began to fall. The hail was, at first, small, but then became larger. The storm swept down with real speed and the air grew cold. Having found shelter and protection from the wind and hail, they conversed in low tones.

"Even if someone should discover us," said Niger, "suspicion wouldn't be aroused, for we look like people who are waiting for the storm to pass over. But I fear lest the removal of the bodies should be postponed until tomorrow."

"This storm won't last long," said Petronius, "but at any rate, we must wait here until daybreak."

They waited, eagerly straining their ears to catch the sound of the procession. It ceased hailing, but immediately afterward rain poured down. At times the wind rose, and from the *puticuli* wafted a dreadful odor of decaying bodies that had been interred carelessly near the surface.

All at once Niger exclaimed, "I see a faint light through the mist! One, two, three—those are torches." Turning to his men, he said, "Make sure that the mules don't snort."

"They're coming," said Petronius.

The lights were growing more and more distinct. Soon it was possible to discern the flames of the torches wavering in the wind.

Niger made the sign of the cross and began to pray. Meanwhile the dismal procession came nearer and at last drew up before the temple of Libitina and halted. Petronius, Vinitius, and Niger pressed up against the rampart, not knowing the meaning of this halt. But the men had stopped only for a moment to cover their faces and mouths with cloths to ward off the stench, which at the edge of the *puticuli* was simply unendurable. Then they lifted the coffins and moved on.

Only one coffin remained in front of the temple. Vinitius hurried towards it, followed by Petronius and Niger and two British slaves with a litter.

But before they reached it, the voice of Nazarius was heard saying, in tones of anguish, "Master, they took her with Ursus to the Esquiline prison. We're carrying another body, for she was removed before midnight."

Petronius, returning home, was as gloomy as the storm itself and didn't even attempt to console Vinitius, knowing full well it would be impossible to rescue Lygia from the Esquiline prison. He assumed that she'd probably been transferred from the *tullianum* lest she die of fever and thus escape the destined arena. For this reason, she was being watched and guarded more carefully than were the others. From the very bottom of his soul, Petronius pitied her and grieved for both her and Vinitius. But he was also tormented by the realization that, for the first time in his life, he'd been beaten in a struggle.

Fortune appears to have deserted me, he said to himself, *but the gods are mistaken if they think I'll consent to such a life as his.* Here he looked at Vinitius, who in turn gazed at him with wide-staring eyes.

"What's the matter with you? Do you have a fever?" asked Petronius.

But Vinitius answered with a strange, broken, and slow voice, like that of a sick child, "I still believe that He'll restore her to me."

Above the city, the last thundering of the storm had ceased.

Chapter LVIII

The spectacles were interrupted by three days of rain—rare in Rome during the summer season—and hail, which, contrary to the natural order of things, fell not only during the day and evening, but even at night. People were growing alarmed. Failure of the year's grape crop was predicted. When, at noon one day, a thunderbolt melted the bronze statue of Ceres on the Capitol, sacrifices were ordered in the temple of Jupiter Salvator. The priest of Ceres spread a report that the wrath of the gods had been poured out on the city because the Christians hadn't been punished enough. People then began to demand that, irrespective of weather, the spectacles should take place; thus great rejoicing greeted the news that the *ludus matutinus* would begin again after an interval of three days.

Meanwhile fair weather returned. The amphitheater was already filled by daybreak with thousands of people. Caesar arrived early with the vestals and the court. The spectacle was to commence with a battle among the Christians, arrayed for the purpose as gladiators and supplied with all the various weapons used by gladiators for offensive and defensive warfare. But here the spectators were doomed to disappointment, for the Christians threw the nets, darts, javelins, and swords down upon the ground, and instead of fighting, they embraced and encouraged one another to persist in the face of torture and death. At this unexpected development, the spectators became angry and indignant. Some accused the Christians of cowardice and baseness of mind; others asserted that the real reason they refused to fight was because of their hatred of the people and their desire to deprive them of the enjoyment of a display of courage. Finally, at Caesar's command, real gladiators were summoned, who then made short work of the kneeling and unresisting Christians.

When the bloody bodies were removed, the spectacle was changed to a series of mythological representations conceived by Caesar himself. Hercules appeared, blazing in living fire on Mount Oeta. Vinitius had trembled at the thought that perhaps Ursus had been selected for the part

468

of Hercules. But evidently the turn of Lygia's faithful servant hadn't yet come, since there perished at the stake some other Christian quite unknown to Vinitius.

In the next display, however, Chilo, whom Caesar refused to excuse from attendance, was forced to watch people whom he knew well. The deaths of Daedalus and Icarus were represented. The role of Daedalus was taken by Euritius, the old man who had first explained to Chilo the symbol of the fish. The role of Icarus was forced on his son, Quartus. Both were hoisted in the air by means of cleverly contrived machinery and then hurled from an immense height down upon the arena. Young Quartus fell so near the imperial box that his blood spattered not only the external ornaments, but even the purple seat. Chilo didn't witness the fall, because he'd closed his eyes, hearing only the sickening thud of the body. When, after a time, he opened his eyes and noticed all that splattered blood near him, he came near fainting again.

The tableaus changed rapidly. The rabble were next entertained by the shocking rape of Christians violated before death by gladiators in the guise of wild beasts. Priestesses of Cybele and Ceres were to be seen, and the Danaides[1] and Dirce[2] and Pasiphae.[3] Finally, little girls were tied to wild horses and torn apart when the horses were set off running in opposite directions. The people applauded every new device of Nero, who, proud of his inventions and immensely pleased by the applause, didn't take the emerald from his eye for an instant while gazing upon the convulsive anguish of the victims and their white bodies mutilated by iron weapons and animals.

Tableaus representing the history of the city were next. Musius Scaevola's[4] hand, fastened to a tripod over a fire, filled the amphitheater with the odor of burning flesh. Like the real Scaevola, he stood there silent, without emitting a groan, his eyes raised and the murmurs of a prayer on his blackened lips. When death had ended his torments, and his body had been removed, the usual noonday interlude took place.

---

1 Fifty daughters of Danaus. Apparently, fifty Christian girls were slain during the scene.

2 Wife of King Lycus of Thebes, punished by being bound to a bull.

3 Daughter of Helios, mother of the half-bull Minotaur. Most likely a woman was mutilated and gored to death by a bull in this scene.

4 Roman general who, when caught attempting an assassination, thrust his hand into a bonfire—thus becoming left-handed.

Caesar, with the vestals and the Augustinians, left the amphitheater and entered a scarlet tent erected for the occasion, in which a magnificent *prandium* had been prepared for him and his guests. The spectators, for the most part, followed his example. They streamed out, scattered into picturesque groups, gratefully stretched themselves, and disposed themselves near the tent to enjoy the food that through Caesar's favor was lavishly served to them by slaves. Only the more curious among the spectators stepped down into the arena itself, touching the sand clotted with blood and discussing as connoisseurs the performances that had taken place and those that were to follow. Soon even they left the arena, lest they should miss the banquet. Only a few remained, and these not through curiosity but out of compassion for the coming victims. These hid themselves in compartments or beneath the lower seats.

Meanwhile the arena was leveled, and slaves began to dig pits in rows throughout the entire circle so that the last row was but a few steps from the imperial box. From outside the Circus came voices, shouts, and applause, while within, everything was being prepared with feverish haste for new tortures. The *cunicula* were all opened simultaneously, and through all the passages leading to the arena, groups of Christians were driven, naked, with crosses on their shoulders, until the great amphitheater was filled with them. Old men, bent under the weight of wooden crosses, ran forward. Alongside them were vigorous men in the prime of life; women with loosened hair, under which they strove to conceal their nakedness; and little children. Most of the crosses, as well as the victims, were decorated with flowers. The servants beat the unfortunates with whips and clubs, then forced them to place their crosses beside the pits prepared for them and to stand beside them. In this way were to perish all those who had not on the first day of the games been driven out as food for dogs and wild beasts. Black slaves seized the victims and, laying them upon the wood, nailed their hands and feet rapidly to the arms of the crosses so that after the intermission, the people should find the crosses already standing.

The noise of hammers reverberated through the whole amphitheater and, echoing among the higher tiers of seats, reached the area immediately outside the amphitheater and even the tent where Caesar was entertaining his retinue and the vestals. There he quaffed goblet after goblet of wine, bantered with Chilo, and whispered into the ears of the priestesses of Vesta. But in the arena the workers rushed: Spades moved quickly, filling with earth the pits into which the crosses had been dropped.

Among the victims awaiting their turn was Crispus. Since the lions hadn't had time to tear him to pieces, he'd been sentenced to die on the cross. Always ready for death, he rejoiced that his hour was near. Today he seemed like another man, for his withered body had been entirely stripped—his clothing replaced with an ivy wreath encircling his loins, and on his head, a garland of roses. But in his eyes there shone that same unsubdued energy; that same stern and fanatical face looked out from beneath the garland of roses. Nor had his heart changed. As before in the *cuniculum* he'd threatened with the wrath of God his brethren sewn up in hides, so now standing beside his cross, instead of consoling them, he thundered forth.

"Thank the Redeemer that He permits you to die the same death that He Himself died! Perhaps some of your sins will be forgiven on this account, but tremble, for justice must be fulfilled, and there cannot be one reward for the wicked and the good!"

He spoke to the accompaniment of hammers driving the nails into the feet and hands of the victims. Every moment more crosses were rammed into the pits. Nonetheless, turning to those who still stood by their crosses, he continued.

"I see heaven open before me, but I see also an open abyss. I don't know what account I'll give the Lord of my life, though I believed and hated evil. I fear not death, but the resurrection; not torture, but the Judgment, for the day of wrath is at hand."

At that moment, from among the nearest tiers of seats, came a voice, calm and solemn. "Not the day of wrath, but of mercy—day of salvation and joy, for I tell you that Christ will gather you in, will comfort you, and will seat you on His right hand. Be of good courage, for heaven is opening before you."

At these words, all eyes were turned towards the benches; even those already fastened to the crosses raised their pale, anguished faces and looked in the direction of the speaker.

Then the man who had spoken strode to the barrier surrounding the arena and blessed the victims with the sign of the cross.

Crispus stretched out his hand, as if to expostulate, but when he saw the speaker's face, he dropped his hand, his knees bent under him, and his lips whispered, "Paul the Apostle!"

To the amazement of the servants of the Circus, all those who were not yet nailed to the crosses fell upon their knees.

Paul of Tarsus turned towards Crispus and said, "Crispus! Threaten them not, for this day they'll be with you in paradise. You assume that they may be damned, but who will condemn them? Will God condemn them, He who gave His Son for them? Will Christ, who died to save them, just as they die now in His name? And how is it possible that He who loves them could condemn them? Who will accuse the chosen of God? Who will say of this blood, 'It is cursed'?"

"Master, I have hated evil!" cried out the old priest.

"Christ laid more stress upon His command to love men and women than to hate evil, for He taught love, not hatred."

"I've sinned in the hour of my death!" cried Crispus, beating his breast.

Suddenly the manager of the benches approached the Apostle and demanded of him, "Who are you who dares to speak to the condemned?"

"A Roman citizen," Paul replied calmly. Then turning to Crispus, he said, "Be confident, for today is a day of grace. Die in peace, O servant of God!"

Two Africans approached Crispus at this moment to place him on the cross, but he looked around once more and exclaimed, "My brethren, pray for me!"

His face had lost its usual severity; his features had assumed an aspect of sweetness and mildness. He stretched his arms out upon the cross so as to facilitate the work and, looking straight upward to the sky, began to pray earnestly. He seemed insensible to pain, for when the nails entered his palms not the least tremor shook his body, nor did the slightest contortion of pain appear upon his face. He prayed while his legs were being nailed and continued to pray when they raised the cross and the earth was being beaten down about it. Only when the rabble began to fill the amphitheater with shouts and laughter did the brows of the old man contract, as if in anger that a pagan people were disturbing the peace of a sweet death.

By this time all the crosses had been raised, so the arena bore the appearance of a forest with people hanging on the trees. On the arms of the crosses and on the heads of the martyrs fell the rays of the sun, but engulfing the arena was a thick shadow, like a black, tangled grating, through which gleamed the golden sand. The entire pleasure of this spectacle consisted in the delight taken by the audience in watching a lingering death. Never before had there been such a vast forest of crosses. In fact, so jammed with crosses was the arena that the arena servants squeezed between them only with difficulty. On the crosses closest to the seats hung women, but Crispus, as a leader, was placed close to the imperial box on an enormous cross wreathed at the bottom with honeysuckles.

None of the victims had as yet died, but a few of those who'd been crucified first had fainted. Yet no one groaned or cried for mercy. Some were hanging with their heads fallen upon their shoulders or dropped upon their breasts as if overcome by sleep; some seemed in meditation; some, looking towards heaven, moved their lips silently. There was something ominous in that fearful array of crosses, in those crucified beings, and in the silence of the victims. The people, sated with the banquet and in a pleasant state of mind, had returned to the Circus with joyful shouts; but now they grew silent, not knowing upon which body to fix their eyes, nor what to think of the performance. The nakedness of the women seemed to excite no interest. They even refrained from betting as to who should die first, a thing usually done when smaller numbers of criminals appeared in the arena. Even Caesar appeared to get little enjoyment from the spectacle, for he turned his head in indolent and drowsy fashion to arrange the costly necklace dangling from his fat neck.

Suddenly Crispus, who was hanging opposite, and who for a time had closed his eyes like a man fainting or dying, opened them and gazed at Caesar. His face assumed an expression so pitiless, and his eyes blazed with such fire, that the Augustinians began to whisper among themselves, pointing him out with their fingers until at last Caesar himself turned his attention towards that cross and sluggishly raised the emerald to his eye.

Perfect silence followed. The eyes of the spectators were fixed upon Crispus, who strove to move his right arm as if to tear it from the cross. After a while his chest rose, his ribs stood out, and he cried, "Matricide, woe to you!"

The Augustinians, hearing this mortal insult flung publicly into the very face of the lord of the world, scarcely dared to breathe. Chilo came near fainting. Caesar shuddered and let his emerald fall. The people, too, held their breath. Then the voice of Crispus reverberated once again, with rising power, throughout the entire amphitheater.

"Woe to you, murderer of wife and brother! Woe to you, Antichrist! The abyss is opening beneath you; death is stretching out its arms to embrace you; the grave is waiting for you! Woe to you, you living corpse, for you will die in terror, and you will be damned for eternity!"

Unable to wrench his hand off the cross, Crispus strained himself

frightfully. He was terrible—a living skeleton, inexorable as predestination. He shook his white beard at Nero's box, and with every motion of
his head, the rose leaves fell from the garland that decorated it.

"Woe to you, murderer! Your measure is surpassed, and your time is
near at hand!"

Thus speaking, he made a supreme effort; for a moment it seemed that
he actually would wrench his hand from the cross and extend it in menace towards Caesar. But suddenly his emaciated arms extended still more,
his body slipped downward, his head dropped upon his breast, and he
died.

Among the forest of crosses, weaker victims also began to drop into the
sleep of eternity.

Chapter LIX

"Lord," said Chilo, "the sea is like oil, and the waves seem to sleep; let us go to Achaia. There the glory of Apollo awaits you, there crowns and triumph await you, there people will worship you, and the gods will receive you as one of their own, whereas here, O lord—" He stopped, for his lower lip began to tremble so feverishly that his words were reduced to meaningless sounds.

"We'll go only when the games are over and not before," replied Nero. "I'm fully aware that even now some call the Christians *innoxia corpora*.[1] Were I to leave, everyone would repeat this. What are you afraid of, you dog of a coward?"

Then he frowned, looking inquiringly at Chilo as if awaiting an answer, but he only pretended to be at ease. During that last spectacle, he'd been so frightened himself by the words of Crispus that when he'd returned to the Palatine, he'd been too tormented by anger, shame, and fear to be able to sleep.

Suddenly the superstitious Vestinius, who'd listened in silence to the conversation, looked cautiously about and said in a solemn voice, "Listen, O lord, to the words of that old man! There's something strange about these Christians. Their god grants them an easy death, but he may have vengeance in store for their enemies."

Nero retorted quickly, "It wasn't I who organized these games—but Tigellinus."

"True indeed! Of course I'm responsible for organizing the games," bragged Tigellinus, who heard Caesar's answer, "and I jeer at all Christian gods! Vestinius is nothing but a bladder full of superstitions, and this heroic Greek is likely to die of terror at the mere sight of seeing a hen bristling up in defense of her chickens."

"Well said," said Nero. "But from this day on, send out orders that the

---

1 An innocent group of people.

475

tongues shall be torn out of the mouths of the Christians, so that they may be silenced."

"Fire will silence them, O divinity!"

"Woe is me!" groaned Chilo.

But Caesar, whose courage was restored by the arrogant confidence of Tigellinus, burst out laughing and exclaimed, pointing a scornful finger at the old Greek, "Behold this offspring of Achilles!"

Chilo indeed appeared to be a wreck of his former audacious self. What hair remained on his head had become white; on his face was fixed an impression of some immense dread, fear, and inner disintegration. At times he appeared to be stupefied, and he failed to answer questions; sometimes again he became so angry and insolent that the Augustinians preferred to let him alone. Such a moment came to him now.

"Do what you please with me," he cried in desperation, "but I absolutely refuse to attend any more games!"

Nero regarded him intently for a while, then turning to Tigellinus, he icily commanded, "See to it that this Stoic is near me in the gardens. I want to see what impression the torches have on him."

Chilo was frightened by the cold threat in Caesar's voice. "Lord," he said, "I won't be able to see anything, for I can't see well at night."

But Caesar, with a terrible mirthless laugh, retorted, "The night will be as bright as day."

Then he turned towards the Augustinians, with whom he talked about some races that he intended to arrange at the end of the games.

Petronius approached Chilo and, touching his arm, said, "Didn't I tell you that you wouldn't be able to hold out?"

Chilo merely answered, "I'm thirsty." But though he stretched out his trembling hand for a goblet of wine, he was incapable of raising it to his lips.

Seeing this, Vestinius took the goblet from him and, drawing near to him, inquired with a curious and frightened face, "Are the Furies pursuing you? Tell me."

The old man stared at him for a time, with mouth wide open, as if unable to comprehend the question.

Vestinius then repeated, "Are the Furies pursuing you?"

"No," replied Chilo, "but the night is yet to come."

"How is that? The night? May the gods have mercy on you! What do you mean?"

"A night terrible, ghastly, and midnight dark, in which something moves and comes towards me. I don't know what it is—but I'm terrified of it."

"I've always believed in sorcery and witchcraft. But do these things come to you in dreams?"

"No, because I can't sleep. I never imagined that they'd be punished like this!"

"Are you sorry for them?"

"Why do you shed so much blood? Didn't you hear what that man said from the cross? Woe to us!"

"I've heard," answered Vestinius in almost a whisper, "that they are incendiaries."

"Not true!"

"And enemies of mankind."

"Not true!"

"And poisoners of water."

"Not true!"

"And murderers of children."

"Not true!"

"How so?" inquired Vestinius in amazed disbelief. "You said so yourself! And wasn't it you that delivered them into the hands of Tigellinus?"

"And because I did, night engulfs me, and death comes towards me. At times it seems to me that I'm dead already, and you are too."

"No! They're the ones who die, and we remain alive. But tell me, what is it they see as they are dying?"

"Christ."

"Their god? Is he a powerful god?"

But Chilo answered with a question instead. "What kind of torches are to be lighted in the gardens? Did you hear what Caesar said?"

"I heard and I know. They are called *sarmentitii* and *semaxii*. They are made by clothing men in painful tunics steeped in pitch. After that, the victims are bound to posts and set on fire. May their god not revenge us by unleashing some dreadful calamity upon the city. *Semaxii!* That's a horrible punishment."

"I prefer it, because there'll be no bloodshed," replied Chilo. "Command a slave to hold the goblet to my lips. I'm thirsty, but I spill the wine, my hand trembles so from old age."

Meanwhile, others also were talking about the Christians. Old Domitius Afer scoffed at them.

"There is such a multitude of them," he said, "that they might incite a civil war if they wished; but they die like sheep."

"Let them just *try* to die any other way!" snapped Tigellinus.

To this, Petronius replied, "You're mistaken; they *do* defend themselves."

"With what?"

"With patience."

"Well, *that's* certainly a new weapon."

"True. But can you say that they die like common criminals? No! They die as if the criminals were those who put them to death—that is, we and the whole Roman people."

"What nonsense!" exclaimed Tigellinus.

"Hic Abdera!"[2] replied Petronius.

But others, struck with the truth of his remark, began to look at one another in astonishment and repeat, "True! There's something strange and peculiar in their manner of dying."

"I tell you that they see their god!" cried Vestinius, whereupon several Augustinians turned to Chilo.

"Eheu, old man! You know them well. Tell us what they see."

The Greek spat wine upon his tunic and answered, "The resurrection."

And he began to tremble so much that the guests who sat nearest to him burst into loud laughter.

---

2   A native of Abdera, which had the reputation of being peopled by dunces.

Chapter LX

Vinitius had been away from home for several nights now. Petronius surmised that perhaps ˙ ʼd made some new plan for liberating Lygia from the Esquiline prison, but he didn't want to question him lest he bring misfortune upon his efforts. The skeptical exquisite had become, in a certain sense, superstitious; for from the moment he'd failed to deliver Lygia from the Mamertine prison, he'd ceased to believe in his own star.

Besides, he didn't really expect much from the efforts of Vinitius either. The Esquiline prison, constructed in a hurry upon the foundations of houses torn down to check the conflagration, was not, it's true, so terrible as the old *tullianum* near the Capitol, but it was a hundred times better guarded. Petronius understood very well that Lygia had been transferred there so that she might not die and thus escape the arena. It was obvious to him that they were now guarding her as though their lives depended on it.

Evidently, he said to himself, *Caesar and Tigellinus are reserving her for some singular spectacle more horrible than the others, and Vinitius is more likely himself to perish than to rescue his loved one.*

Vinitius, too, had lost hope that he'd be able to rescue Lygia. Christ alone could save her. But the young tribune longed to visit her in prison.

For some time, the fact that Nazarius had succeeded in entering the Mamertine prison disguised as a corpse bearer had given him no peace. Finally, he resolved to try this method himself.

The overseer of the *puticuli*, whom he'd bribed with an immense sum of money, finally placed him on the list of those servants whom he sent every night to bear the corpses from the prison. The danger of discovery was slight. The night, the dress of a slave, and the meager light in the prison were good allies. Besides, who would even imagine that a patrician, the grandson of one consul and the son of another, could be found among hirelings, exposed to the foul air of prisons and of the *puticuli*, and that he'd accept a work to which men were forced by slavery or by direst penury.

When the longed-for evening came, he joyfully wound rags saturated with turpentine around his loins and his head to combat the terrible stench and, with a throbbing heart, accompanied a crowd of others to the Esquiline. The Praetorians made no trouble because all the corpse bearers possessed the proper *tesserae*, which the centurion scrutinized by the light of a lantern. After a while, the great iron gates swung open, and they entered.

Vinitius saw before him a vast vaulted cellar, through which they passed to a number of others. Tapers dimly lighted the interiors to reveal rooms crowded with prisoners. Some of these were lying on the floor, sunk in sleep or perhaps dead. Others crowded around large vessels of water that stood in the middle of the vaults and from which they gulped as do people tortured by fever; still others sat upon the floor, their elbows on their knees and their heads upon the palms of their hands. Here and there children nestled close to their mothers, fast asleep. All about were heard groans, the accelerated breathing of the sick, weeping, whispered prayers, hymns in an undertone, and the curses of the jailers. The air of the dungeon was heavy with the odor both of those still living and those now dead. In its gloomy depths, dark figures moved here and there; closer to flickering flames could be seen pale faces, terrified, emaciated, and hungry, with eyes lifeless or burning with fever, with lips blue, with streams of sweat on their foreheads, and with clammy, matted hair. In corners the sick moaned loudly, some begging for water, others to be led to death. Yet, this prison was not so horrible as the old *tullianum*.

At the ghastly sight, the legs of Vinitius trembled beneath him, and his breath almost failed him. The thought that Lygia was in the midst of this horror and misery raised the hair on his head, and a cry of despair died in his heart. The amphitheater, the teeth of wild beasts, the cross—anything was better than this horrible dungeon, full of putrid air, from every corner of which rose imploring human cries: "Lead us to death!"

Vinitius drove his nails into his palms, for he felt that he was growing weak, that his consciousness and presence of mind were leaving him. All that he'd suffered heretofore, all his love and pain, changed into one intense yearning for death.

Just then the overseer of the *puticuli* asked, "How many corpses do you have today?"

"About a dozen," replied the prison guard, "but by morning there'll be more, for there next to the walls, some are already in their last agony."

He complained about the women, that they concealed their dead children so as to keep them as long as possible and not to yield them to the *puticuli.* The corpses, he further pouted, could only be discovered by their odor, and this rendered the foul air still more baleful and poisonous.

"I'd rather be a slave in a rural *ergastulum,*" he whined, "than to be here guarding these dogs that rot while still alive."

The overseer of the *puticuli* consoled him, declaring that his own work was no easier.

By this time Vinitius had regained his senses, and he began to search the dungeon; but he sought for Lygia in vain, fearing that he might never see her alive again. Several cellars were connected by new passages; the corpse bearers entered only those from which dead bodies were to be removed. Vinitius feared that all his efforts might prove useless. Fortunately his patron came to his aid.

"The bodies must be removed immediately," he said to the guard, "for infection spreads mostly on account of the corpses. If you aren't careful, you'll die with the prisoners."

"Only ten men are allotted for all the cellars," said the watchman, "and we must sleep sometime!"

"Then I'll leave these four of my own men to patrol the cellars during the night and report all cases of death."

"We'll drink to your health tomorrow. Every corpse must be tested. We have an order to pierce the neck of each corpse and then to take it at once to the *puticuli.*"

"Very well then, but we must have our drink," muttered the overseer. He selected four men, Vinitius among them; the rest he took to load the corpses upon the biers.

Vinitius drew a long breath, now certain that he'd be able to find Lygia. He began by examining the first dungeon. He looked into all the dark corners and examined the figures who slept beside the walls under rags, and he examined the most grievously ill, who were dragged to a special corner; but still he couldn't find Lygia. His search through the second and third dungeons was also without result.

In the meantime, the hour had grown late; all the bodies had been carried out. The guards went to sleep in the corridors adjoining the dungeons; the children, weary of crying, were silent; nothing was heard but the breathing of the weary and, here and there, the murmur of prayers.

Vinitius carried his torch into the fourth dungeon, which was much smaller, and raising the torch, he began to search. Suddenly he trembled, for it seemed to him that he could make out the gigantic figure of Ursus close to a grating in the wall. Then extinguishing his light, he approached and said, "Is it you, Ursus?"

The giant turned his head, asking, "Who are you?"

"Don't you recognize me?"

"You blew out the light. How can I recognize you?"

Vinitius at that moment discovered Lygia lying on a cloak near the wall, so without another word, he knelt beside her. Ursus then recognized him and said, "Glory be to Christ, but don't wake her, master."

Vinitius, kneeling, gazed at Lygia through his tears. Despite the darkness, he could distinguish her face, pale as alabaster, and her emaciated arms. At that sight, he was overwhelmed by an agony of love that shook his soul to the utmost depths. At the same time, that soul was so full of compassion, respect, and homage that, falling upon his face, he pressed to his lips the hem of the cloak upon which rested the head dearer to him than all else on earth.

Ursus looked at him for a long time in silence. Finally he tugged at his tunic.

"Master," he asked, "how did you get here, and have you come to save her?"

Vinitius rose and for a time struggled with his emotions. "Show me a way," he said.

"I thought you'd find it, master."

"I know of one way only."

Here Ursus turned his eyes towards the grated opening in the wall and then, as if in answer to himself, he said, "Yes, but there are soldiers outside."

"A hundred Praetorians," answered Vinitius.

"We can't get by, then?"

"No."

The Lygian rubbed his forehead and asked again: "How did you get in?"

"I have a *tesserae* from the overseer of the *puticuli.*" Suddenly he stopped, as if a new thought had struck him. "By the torture of the Savior!" he said quickly. "I'll remain here; let her take my *tesserae*, cover her head with a cloth and her shoulders with the mantle, and pass through.

Among the gravediggers' slaves, there are a few striplings. The Praetorians won't recognize her, and when she reaches the house of Petronius, he'll guard her."

The Lygian dropped his head upon his breast and sighed, "She'd never consent to this, for she loves you. Besides, she's ill and couldn't even stand up unassisted. If you, O master, and the noble Petronius can't save her from prison, who can?"

"Christ alone!"

Then both were silent. In his simple mind the Lygian thought, *Christ undoubtedly could save all of us, but since He doesn't do so, the hour of agony and death has evidently come.* For himself he bowed to the decree, but he grieved for the dear child who'd grown up in his arms and whom he loved above all things.

Vinitius knelt once again beside Lygia. The pale beams of the moon stole through the grating in the wall and gave better light than the solitary candle now flickering over the entrance. Lygia opened her eyes and, laying her fever-ish hand on that of Vinitius, said, "I see you. I knew you'd come."

He took her hands, lifted them to his forehead and his heart, raised her somewhat, and pressed her to his breast. "I have come, my dear one," he said. "May Christ watch over and save you, *carissima!*"

He could say no more because his heart was breaking and he didn't wish to betray his anguish in her presence.

"I'm sick, Marcus," said Lygia, "and I must die, either here or in the arena. I've prayed to see you before I die, and you've come. Christ has heard my prayer."

Unable to utter a word, Vinitius pressed her to his breast, and she continued, "I saw you through the window in the *tullianum,* and I knew that you wished to come in and find me. And now the Savior has granted me a moment of consciousness so that we may say farewell. I'm going to Him very soon, but I love you, Marcus, and I'll love you forever."

By a great effort Vinitius controlled himself, stifled his pain, and spoke in a voice that he kept calm only with difficulty. "No, dear one, you won't die. The Apostle commanded me to have faith, to believe, and promised to pray for you. He knew Christ. Christ loved him and won't refuse his request. If it was ordained that you should die now, Peter wouldn't have ordered me to be confident—but he said, *'Have confidence.'* No, Lygia, Christ will have mercy. He doesn't desire your death. He won't permit it. I swear by the name of the Savior that Peter is praying for you."

Silence followed. The candle hanging over the doorway went out, but the moonlight streamed through the opening. In a corner of the cellar a child cried, then was silent again. From outside came the voices of Praetorians, who after their watches, played *scriptae duodecum*[1] under the wall.

"Oh, Marcus," replied Lygia, "Christ Himself called to the Father, 'Let this bitter chalice pass from Me,' but still He drank it. Christ Himself died on the cross, and now thousands perish for His sake. Why then should He spare me alone? Who am I, Marcus? I heard Peter say that he also would die in torture, and what am I compared to him? When the Praetorians came for us, I was afraid of death and torture, but I dread them no longer. See what a terrible prison this is? But I'm going to heaven. Just think of it: Here is Caesar, but there is the Savior, kind and merciful; and with Him there is no death. You love me; think then how happy I'll be. Oh, Marcus, *carissime*, just to think that you'll soon follow me."

Here she paused for breath and then raised his hand to her lips. "Marcus?"

"What, dear one?"

"Don't weep for me, and remember this: You'll come to me. I've lived only a short while, but God gave your soul to me; hence I'll tell Christ that though I died and you remained behind in sorrow, yet you didn't blaspheme against His will and that you'll love Him always. And will you, dear Marcus, love Him and bear my death patiently? For then He'll reunite us. I love you, and I wish to be with you forever."

Here again she paused for breath, and in a barely audible voice, she continued: "Promise me this, Marcus!"

Vinitius embraced her with trembling arms and replied, "By that sacred head, I promise."

Her pale face grew radiant in the sad light of the moon, and raising once more his hand to her lips, she murmured softly but with deep feeling, "I am your wife!"

Beyond the wall, the Praetorians, in the midst of their game, were disputing loudly; but these two, for a moment, forgot the prison, the guards, and the world. Feeling themselves in the presence of angels, they began to pray.

---

1   A game, involving writing something twelve times.

Chapter LXI

For three days, or rather three nights, nothing disturbed their peace. After the usual prison work—which consisted of separating the dead from the living, and those who were very ill from those who were moderately ill—had been completed, and after the tired guards had gone to sleep in the corridors, Vinitius would enter the dungeon in which Lygia was and remain there until dawn. She would put her head on his breast, and in low voices they would talk about love and death. By degrees, their thoughts and conversation, even their desires and hopes, turned more and more away from life, and they lost even their awareness of life outside the prison. Both were like people who, having put out to sea in a ship, seeing the shore no more, gradually sink into infinity. Both were transformed by degrees into sad spirits in love with each other and with Christ and ready to fly away.

Only at times did pain, like a storm, rush into the heart of Vinitius. At times, like lightning, there flashed through him a hope born of love and faith in the mercy of the crucified God; but more and more he turned his mind away from the world, and his thoughts towards death. Each morning when he emerged from the prison, he viewed the world—the city, his friends, and all the affairs of life—as though but a dream. Everything seemed to him strange, distant, vain, and transitory. Even torture ceased to terrify him, since it might be passed through with thoughts and eyes fixed on other things. Both he and Lygia felt as though they were already entering eternity; they talked about how they would love each other and live together beyond the grave. If their thoughts occasionally returned to earth, it was much like the thoughts of people who, setting out for a long journey, discuss preparations for the road. Moreover, they were enveloped by a silence such as might envelop two columns standing forgotten in the solitude of a desert. They desired only that Christ should not separate them; and as every moment strengthened the faith of both, they loved Him as a link uniting them in endless happiness and peace. Though still

485

on earth, the dust of earth fell from them, their souls becoming pure as tears. With death staring them in the face, in the midst of misery, suffering, and prison filth, heaven had begun, for she'd taken him by the hand and led him, as one already saved and among the saints, towards the Source of eternal life.

Petronius was astonished to see on the face of Vinitius an expression of calmness and wonderful serenity never seen there before. At times, he wondered whether Vinitius had devised some plan of rescue, and Petronius was piqued that his nephew hadn't confided in him.

Finally, he could stand the suspense no longer and said, "You look like a totally different man. Keep no secrets from me, for I'm willing and anxious to help you. What's your plan?"

"I do have a plan," answered Vinitius, "but you can't help me anymore. After her death I'll confess I'm a Christian, and then I'll follow her."

"Have you then no hope?"

"On the contrary, I do have. Christ will give her back to me, and afterward I'll never be separated from her again."

Petronius paced up and down the atrium with an air of disappointment and impatience. "No Christ is needed for that," he said at last, "for our own Thanatos can render the same service."

Vinitius smiled sadly and said, "No, my dear friend, you don't understand."

"I am both unwilling and unable to. This isn't a time for argument, but do you remember what you told me after we failed to rescue her from the *tullianum?* I'd lost all hope, but after we returned home, you declared, 'Still I believe that Christ will restore her to me.' Let Him restore her then to you now. Should I cast a costly goblet into the sea, none of our gods could restore it to me. If yours is no better, I fail to see why I should honor Him above the ancient ones."

"But He *will* restore her to me," said Vinitius.

Petronius shrugged his shoulders. "Are you aware," he said, "that tomorrow Caesar's garden will be illuminated by Christians?"

" *Tomorrow!*" repeated Vinitius. In view of this near and dreadful reality, his heart trembled with pain and fear as he thought, *This may very well be the last night I share with Lygia.* So, taking leave of Petronius, he hastened to get his *tesserae* from the overseer of the *puticuli.* But a disappointment was in store for him, for the overseer refused to give it to him.

"Pardon me, master," said the overseer. "I've done what I could for you, but I can't risk my life. Tonight they'll take the Christians to the gardens of Caesar. The prison will be filled with soldiers and officials; should they recognize you, my family and I would perish."

Vinitius understood that it would be vain to insist. He hoped, however, that the soldiers who'd seen him before might admit him without the *tesserae*. When night approached, he disguised himself in the tunic that he'd formerly worn and, with covered head, wended his way towards the prison, only to find that on this day the *tesserae* were scrutinized with particular care. What was more, the centurion Scevinus, a strict disciplinarian devoted soul and body to Caesar, recognized Vinitius. But evidently in his heart, beneath his steel armor, there yet beat some compassion for those suffering misfortune. Instead of striking his spear against his shield as an alarm, he led Vinitius aside and said, "Master, return home. I recognize you, but not wishing your death, I'll keep silent. Since I cannot admit you, go on your way, and may the gods console you."

"I understand that you can't admit me," countered Vinitius, "but is there any reason I couldn't just stand here and watch those who are led out?"

"I have no orders against that," said Scevinus.

Vinitius stood before the gate and waited. At last, about midnight, the gates were thrown open and there appeared long lines of prisoners: men, women, and children surrounded by armed detachments of Praetorians. The night was very bright, for the moon was full, and it was easy to identify not only the figures, but even the faces of the unfortunates. They marched in pairs, in a long, dismal procession, amid silence broken only by the clatter of armor and weaponry. So many were led forth that it seemed as if all the dungeons had been emptied.

At the end of the procession, Vinitius caught a glimpse of Glaucus, but neither Lygia nor Ursus was among the condemned.

Chapter LXII

E vening had not yet come when crowds of people began to flow into the gardens of Caesar. They were decked in holiday attire, crowned with floral wreaths, and joyously singing; some of them were already drunk. All had come to see the new and magnificent spectacle. Cries of "*Semaxii! Sarmentitii!*" echoed in the Via Tecta, on the Aemilian Bridge, and, from the other side of the Tiber, on the Via Triumphatoris, around the Circus of Nero, and far off on the Vatican Hill. People had been burned at the stake before in Rome, but never had there been such a vast number of victims.

Caesar and Tigellinus, in order to have done with the Christians and to suppress the plague that was spreading from the prisons into the city, had ordered all the dungeons to be emptied so that there remained in them only a handful of people—perhaps fifty—destined for the close of the spectacle. Consequently, when the crowds had passed the gates of the gardens, they were struck dumb with astonishment. All the main and side alleys, which led through dense groves and along lawns, thickets, ponds, and dales strewn with flowers, were studded with mastlike pillars smeared with pitch, to which the Christians were fastened. In higher places, where the view was not obstructed by trees, whole rows of pillars were to be seen, and bodies decked with flowers and ivy leaves. These rows extended over the hills and dales so far that, whereas the nearest looked like the masts of ships, the farthest off seemed like colored lances or staffs thrust in the earth. The sheer number of them surpassed all expectations. It was as though an entire nation had been lashed to the pillars for the amusement of Rome and Caesar. Groups of spectators stopped before individual posts when the form, the sex, or the age of the victims attracted them. They looked at the faces, the wreaths, the garlands of ivy, and then went on to other posts, asking themselves in amazement how there could be so many guilty, or how children scarcely able to walk unaided could have set fire to Rome. This astonishment changed gradually into an uneasy fear.

Meanwhile, darkness fell, and the first stars appeared in the sky. By the side of every victim appeared a slave with a lighted torch in his hand. When from various parts of the gardens came the sound of trumpets as a signal for the commencement of the performance, each slave stooped down near the base of the pillar and extended his torch.

The pitch-covered straw, concealed under flowers, at once caught fire. The flames increased rapidly, withered the garlands, and leaping upward, licked the feet of the victims. A hush fell upon the spectators. The gardens echoed with one vast groan and with cries of excruciating pain. Many of the victims, however, lifted their faces towards the starry heavens and sang hymns in praise of Christ. The people listened, but even the stoniest hearts among them were touched with pity when from the smaller posts children began to shriek with shrill voices, "Mama! Mama!" A shiver ran through even the spectators who were drunk, when they saw the little heads and innocent faces distorted with pain or choking in the smoke that was stifling them. But the flames rose and seized new crowns of roses and ivy every instant. The main and side alleys were illuminated; the groves of trees, the lawns, the flowery squares were illuminated; the water in pools and ponds was gleaming; the trembling leaves on the trees had grown rose-colored—and everywhere it was as bright as day.

The odor of burning bodies filled the gardens, but immediately slaves sprinkled aloes into incense burners placed among the poles. Here and there among the people shouts were heard—but whether of compassion, intoxication, or delight, who could tell? The cries rose with the flames, which embraced the pillars, climbed to the breasts of victims, shriveled with burning breath the hair on their heads, licked their faces until they were black and charred, and then shot up higher as if to display the victory and triumph of the power at whose command they had burst forth.

At the beginning of the spectacle Caesar had appeared in a magnificent Circus quadriga drawn by four white steeds. He was dressed as a charioteer in the color of the Greens, the party to which he and the court belonged. After him followed other chariots with courtiers in brilliant costumes, senators, priests, and naked bacchantes with wreaths on their heads and pitchers of wine in their hands, half drunk and uttering wild cries. By the side of these were musicians disguised as fauns or satyrs, who played on kitharas, flutes, and horns. In other chariots rode drunk and half-naked Roman matrons and maidens. Around the quadrigas ran men who shook thyrsi decorated with ribbons; others beat drums or scattered flowers.

The brilliant pageant moved onward, shouting, "*Evoe!*"[1] along the widest road of the garden, amid the smoke and the living torches. Caesar, keeping near him Tigellinus and Chilo, whose terror he reveled in, drove the steeds himself and, proceeding slowly, looked at the burning bodies and listened to the cries of the populace. Standing on the high, golden quadriga, surrounded with the wreath of a Circus victor, he was a head taller than the courtiers and seemed to be a giant. His monstrous arms stretched out to hold the reins and seemed to bless the people. A smile played over his face and in his blinking eyes. As a sun or a god, he shone above the throng—terrible, but splendid and mighty.

At times he stopped to look closer at some maiden whose bosom had begun to smolder into flame or at the face of a child distorted by agony and convulsions; and then he continued to ride on, leading a wild and frenzied retinue. At times he bowed to the people, and then, again bending backward, he drew in the golden reins and conversed with Tigellinus. Finally, when he'd reached a great fountain at the crossing of two roads, he alighted from the quadriga and, nodding to his companions, mingled with the throng.

He was greeted with shouts and applause. The bacchantes, the nymphs, the senators and Augustinians, the priests, the fauns, the satyrs, and the soldiers surrounded him in an excited circle while he, with Tigellinus on one side and Chilo on the other, walked around the fountain, about which were burning some fifty torches.

Stopping before each one, Nero made remarks about the victims or ridiculed the old Greek, whose face betrayed horror and utter despair. At last he stopped before a tall pillar decked with myrtle and ivy. The red tongues of fire had reached to the knees of the victim, but it was impossible to see his face, for it was veiled with smoke from the green wood. In a little while, however, a breeze blew aside the smoke and unveiled the head of an old man with a white beard falling over his breast.

At sight of him, Chilo suddenly writhed like a wounded snake, while from his lips escaped a cry more like a raven's croaking than a human voice. "Glaucus! Glaucus!"

It was indeed the face of Glaucus that looked down at him from the burning post.

The physician was still alive. His face revealed terrible pain and was

---

1   Usual shout of Bacchantes.

inclined forward as if he wished to look closely for the last time at his tormentor—to look upon the man who had betrayed him, who had robbed him of wife and children, who had hired an assassin to kill him, and who, after all this, had been forgiven in the name of Christ and yet had delivered him into the hands of the executioners. Never had any one man inflicted more terrible and bloody wrongs on another. And now the victim was dying at the burning stake and the perpetrator was standing at his feet.

The eyes of Glaucus were riveted on those of the Greek. At times smoke hid him, but when the breeze blew this away, Chilo saw again those eyes staring directly at him. He rose and tried to flee but couldn't. All at once his legs seemed made of lead; an invisible hand seemed to hold him at that burning pillar with superhuman force. He was petrified, powerless. He felt that something had given way within him, that he'd had a surfeit of blood and torture, that his end was approaching, and that everything was vanishing—Caesar, the court, the throng—and around him was only a kind of bottomless, dreadful black abyss with no visible thing in it, only the fiery eyes of the martyr, which summoned him to judgment. Glaucus, bending his head still lower, continued to stare fixedly at him.

Gradually those nearby sensed that something unusual was taking place between the two men. Laughter died on their lips, for in Chilo's face there was something terrible. So distorted was it by fear and pain that it was as if tongues of fire were scorching his own flesh. Suddenly he reeled, and, stretching imploring arms upward, he cried in a terrible and heartrending voice, "Glaucus! In the name of Christ! *Forgive me!*"

A deep silence fell all around him; a shiver ran through the spectators, and all eyes were raised involuntarily. The head of the martyr moved slightly, and then from the top of the mast there came a voice like a groan: "I forgive!"

Chilo fell down upon his face and howled like a wild beast; gathering earth in both hands, he sprinkled it on his head. Meanwhile the flames shot up and licked the breast and face of Glaucus. The myrtle crown upon his head began to burn, as well as the ribbon on the top of the pole, all of which now blazed with leaping flames.

Chilo rose after a time with a face so changed that to the Augustinians he seemed like another man. His eyes flashed with an extraordinary light, and joy spread over his wrinkled forehead. The Greek, who but a minute before had appeared to be a craven wreck of a man, now took on the stature and authority of an Old Testament priest or prophet, inspired by God to deliver a message to His people.

"What's the matter? Has he gone crazy?" asked a number of voices.

But he turned towards the multitude and, raising his right hand, shouted in a voice so loud that not only the Augustinians, but even the multitude, heard it.

"Oh, Roman people! I swear to you that the innocent are perishing here! *There* is the one who burned down Rome!" And he pointed his finger at Nero.

Silence followed. The courtiers were numbed with shock. Chilo continued to stand with arm outstretched and with finger pointing at Nero. All at once a tumult broke out. The people, like a wave urged on by a hurricane, rushed towards the old man to get a better view of him. Here and there were cries of "Seize him!" and "Woe to us!"

Among the crowds rose hisses and shouts: "Ahenobarbus!" "Matricide!" "Incendiary!" Disorder increased every instant. The bacchantes, screaming in heaven-piercing voices, sought the shelter of the chariots. Then some of the pillars, having burnt through, crashed to the ground and, scattering sparks about them, increased the confusion. A blind, half-crazed wave of people engulfed Chilo and swept him into the depths of the garden.

The pillars of fire began to burn through in every direction and to fall across the roads, filling the alleys with smoke, sparks, and the smell of burnt wood and human flesh. The nearer lights went out. It grew dark. The terrified crowds pressed towards the gates. News of what had taken place spread rapidly and was changed and augmented as it passed from mouth to mouth. Some said that Caesar had swooned, others, that he'd confessed that he'd ordered Rome to be set on fire, still others that he'd been taken seriously ill and had been borne out in a chariot, dying.

Here and there were heard voices of compassion for the Christians: If they hadn't burned Rome, why, then, all this blood, torture, and injustice? Wouldn't the gods avenge the innocent, and what *piacuda*[2] could possibly appease their wrath? The words *innoxia corpora* were repeated oftener and oftener. Women expressed aloud their pity for the children, so many of whom had been thrown to wild beasts or crucified or burned in those cursed gardens!

---

2 Atonement, sacrifices.

Finally, compassion changed into maledictions against Caesar and Tigellinus. There were some who, stopping suddenly, asked themselves or others, "What kind of a God is this who gives such strength to meet torture and death?" And they returned to their homes deep in soul-searching.

Chilo, however, roamed about the gardens, not knowing where to go or what to do. Again he felt himself an impotent, weak, and sick old man. Now he stumbled over half-burned corpses; now he trod on embers that sent after him a shower of sparks; now he sat down and gazed about with a vacant stare. Already the gardens were becoming dark. The trees no longer stood out in a red glare. Only the pale moon lighted the alleys, the dark pillars fallen across them and the partly consumed victims reduced to something no longer human. But it seemed to the old Greek that in the moonlight he could still see the face of Glaucus, with eyes that never left him—unable to rid himself of that eerie sensation of being watched, he fled the light and hid himself among the shadows. Finally, however, he emerged again and, as if led by some hidden force, directed his steps towards the fountain beside which Glaucus had breathed his last. Suddenly, a hand touched his shoulder.

The old man wheeled and, perceiving an unknown figure before him, cried out in terror, "Who's there? Who are you?"

"Paul of Tarsus."

"I'm cursed. What is it you want?"

"I wish to save you," answered the Apostle.

Chilo leaned against a tree. His legs trembled beneath him, and his arms hung down by his sides.

"There's no salvation for me," he said despairingly.

"Have you not heard that Christ forgave the thief upon the cross?" asked Paul.

"Don't you know what I've done?"

"I saw your suffering and heard your testimony."

"Oh, master!"

"The servant of Christ forgave you in the hour of agony and death. Why then shouldn't Christ forgive you?"

Chilo put his head in his hands, clearly bewildered. "Forgiveness! Forgiveness! For *me?*"

"Our God is a God of mercy," said the Apostle.

"For *me?*" repeated Chilo, and he began to groan like a man who is too feeble to control the pain and torment wracking him from within.

"Take my arm and come with me."

And taking him upon his arm, Paul went towards the crossing of the roads, guided by the voice of the fountain, which seemed to weep in the night stillness over all those martyrs who'd died such a horrible death.

"Our God is a God of mercy," repeated the Apostle. "Were you to stand on the shore and cast pebbles into the sea, could you fill up its depths? I tell you that the mercy of Christ is like the sea, and the sins and transgressions of men will sink into its depths just as stones dropped into a bottomless abyss. I tell you that it's like the sky that covers land and mountains and seas, for it's everywhere and is without limit and without end. You've suffered at the stake of Glaucus, and Christ beheld your anguish. Regardless of what might happen to you on the morrow, you bravely pointed out the true incendiary to the crowd. Christ will remember your words, for your depravity and falsehood are gone. In your heart there remains only contrition. Come with me and listen to what I have to say. I am he who hated Christ and persecuted His followers. I didn't want Him and didn't believe in Him until He appeared before me and called me into His service. Since that time, I've come to love Him. And now He's permitted you also to travel that same road of anguish, grief, and suffering, in order to call you to Himself. You hated Him, but He loved you even then. You delivered His followers to torture and death, but He wishes to forgive and save you."

Great sobs shook the breast of the wretched man and ripped his soul to its depths. But Paul embraced him, comforted him, and led him away as a soldier leads a prisoner.

After a time the Apostle spoke again.

"Follow me, and I'll lead you to Him, for why else would I have come to you? He commanded me to gather souls in the name of love, and I obey His command. You believe yourself to be damned, but I say to you, 'Believe in Him and salvation awaits you.' You believe yourself to be hated, but I repeat that He loves you. Before I had Him, I had nothing but the wickedness and malice that dwelt in my heart, but now His love takes the place of father and mother, of riches and power. In Him alone is refuge. He alone will take note of your sorrow, will understand your despondency and wretchedness, will free you from fear and raise you to Himself."

So speaking, he led Chilo to the fountain, where the silvery spray gleamed in the moonlight. Complete silence reigned in the deserted gardens, for slaves had already removed the fallen pillars and charred bodies of the martyrs.

Chilo fell upon his knees with a groan and, hiding his face in his hands, remained motionless. But Paul raised his face towards the stars and prayed, "O Lord, behold this wretched man, his sorrow, his tears, and his agony! O Lord of mercy, who did shed Your blood for our sins, forgive him through Your own torment, Your death, and Your resurrection."

Then he was silent, but for a long time he looked towards the stars and prayed. Meanwhile, at his feet arose a cry like a groan.

"O Christ! Christ! Forgive me!"

Then Paul approached the fountain and, cupping water in his hands, he returned to the kneeling penitent. "Chilo! I baptize you in the name of the Father, and of the Son, and of the Holy Ghost. Amen."

Chilo raised his head, opened his arms, and remained motionless. The moon shone full upon his white hair and upon the equally white face, which was as motionless as if dead or chiseled out of stone. The moments passed one after another. From the great aviaries in the gardens of Domitian came the crowing of cocks; but Chilo remained in his kneeling posture, like a monument.

Finally he arose and said to the Apostle, "What shall I do before death?"

Paul, roused from his reverie, meditating on that measureless power that even villainous souls such as this Greek could not resist, answered, "Have faith and bear witness to the Truth!"

They went out together. At the gates of the garden, the Apostle blessed the old man once more, and then they parted. Chilo insisted upon this, because he foresaw that after what had happened, both Caesar and Tigellinus would give orders that he should be pursued.

In this, he wasn't mistaken. When he returned home, he found the house surrounded by Praetorians, who seized him and, under the command of Scevinus, took him to the palace.

Caesar had retired, but Tigellinus was waiting. As soon as he saw the unfortunate Greek, he greeted him with a calm, ominous face.

"You are guilty of treason," he said, "and your punishment will be sure. But should you confess tomorrow in the amphitheater that you were drunk and insane and that the instigators of the conflagration were the Christians, your punishment will be reduced to flogging and exile."

"I can't do that," said Chilo.

Tigellinus approached him with a slow step and said in a low but terrible voice, "What's that I hear, that you *can't*, you dog? That you weren't drunk and don't understand what's waiting for you? Look there!" He pointed to a corner of the atrium, where, beside a long, wooden bench, stood four Thracian slaves with ropes and pincers in their hands.

But Chilo replied, "I cannot."

Tigellinus, though infuriated, yet restrained himself. "Haven't you seen," he asked, "how Christians die? Do you wish to die in the same way?"

The old man raised his pale face. His lips moved silently for a time; then he said, "I, too, believe in Christ."

Tigellinus looked at him in astonishment. "Dog! You've completely lost your reason!" Suddenly the rage that had accumulated in his breast burst forth. Springing at Chilo, he caught his beard with both hands, threw him to the floor, and stomped on him, repeating, with foam upon his lips, "You *will* retract, you *will!*"

"I cannot," answered the prostrate and battered Chilo.

"Take him to the rack."

At this order, the Thracians seized the old man and laid him on the bench, then fastening him to it with ropes, they began to squeeze his lean legs with pincers. But when they were tying him, he kissed their hands with humility; then he closed his eyes and seemed dead.

He was alive, however, for after a time, Tigellinus bent over him and asked him once more, "Will you retract?"

The old Greek's pale lips moved slightly, and a barely audible whisper escaped them: "I cannot!"

Tigellinus ordered the torture to be stopped. Helpless, his face distorted by fury, he strode up and down the room. At last a new thought brightened his mood. He turned to the Thracians and snarled, "Rip out his tongue!"

Chapter LXIII

The drama *Aureolus* was usually performed in theaters or amphitheaters that were set up with two separate stages. But after the spectacle in Caesar's gardens, this device was discarded; for in this case it was essential that the greatest number of spectators enjoy the death of a crucified slave who, in the drama, is devoured by a bear. In the theater, the role of the bear was played by an actor sewn up in a bearskin, but this time a real bear was to appear upon the scene. This was a new device of Tigellinus. At first Caesar announced that he wouldn't come, but at the urgent request of his favorite he changed his mind. Tigellinus convinced him that after what had happened in the gardens, he ought to show himself to the people. He also guaranteed Nero that the crucified slave wouldn't abuse him, as had Crispus. The people were becoming sated and tired of bloodshed; consequently, a new distribution of lottery tickets and gifts was announced, as well as a banquet, for the performance was to be given at night in a brilliantly illuminated amphitheater.

By dusk the whole amphitheater was packed. The Augustinians, with Tigellinus at their head, came in a body—not so much for the sake of the performers as to show their devotion to Caesar and their opinion of Chilo, about whom all Rome was talking.

It was rumored that Caesar, after his return from the gardens, had fallen into a frenzy and couldn't sleep, that terrors and strange apparitions tormented him, in consequence of which he announced the next morning that he would depart for Achaia earlier than originally planned. But others denied this, declaring that he would now be all the more pitiless to the Christians. Cowards also were not lacking; they predicted that the accusation that Chilo had flung into Caesar's face might have the worst possible consequences. Finally, there were others who petitioned Tigellinus to stop further persecution for humane reasons.

"Behold what's happening!" said Barcus Soranus. "You wished to satisfy the anger of the people and to convince them that the guilty were being punished, but the result is just the opposite."

"That's true," added Antiscius Verus. "All now whisper to one another that the Christians are innocent. If that be cleverness, then Chilo was right in saying that your brains wouldn't fill an acorn's cup."

Tigellinus turned to them and said, "Barcus Soranus, people also whisper that your daughter Servilia concealed her Christian slaves from the justice of Caesar. The same thing they say also of your wife, Antiscius."

"That's not true!" exclaimed Barcus, his face paling under this veiled threat.

"Your divorced women," said Antiscius Verus, with equal apprehension, "wished to ruin my wife because they're envious of her virtue."

But others talked of Chilo.

"What's the matter with him?" asked Eprius Marcelus. "He himself delivered the Christians into the hands of Tigellinus. He was a beggar who became wealthy; it was possible for him to live out his days in peace, to have a grand funeral and a fine tomb, but now look what's happened! All at once he chooses to lose everything and ruin himself—without doubt he must be insane."

"He's not insane, but he's become a Christian," said Tigellinus.

"Impossible!" said Vitelius.

"Have I not said," remarked Vestinius, "that you may butcher Christians if you like, but believe me, you can't war against their deity! It's no joking matter, either. See what's taking place. I certainly didn't set Rome on fire, but should Caesar permit me I should immediately sacrifice a hecatomb to the Christian god. And everyone else should do the same thing, because, I repeat, it's no joking matter. Mark my words."

"And I said something else," said Petronius. "Tigellinus laughed at me when I asserted that the Christians were defending themselves, but now I shall say more: They are conquering."

"How is that? What do you mean?" asked a number of voices.

"By Pollux! If such a man as Chilo couldn't resist them, who can? If you think that after every spectacle the number of Christians doesn't increase, then you'd better become coppersmiths or begin to shave beards, for then you'll really find out what people think and what's going on in the city."

"He speaks the truth, by the holy garment of Diana!" cried Vestinius.

But Barcus turned to Petronius and posed the question, "What would *you* do?"

"I conclude where you began—there's been more than enough blood-shed."

Tigellinus looked at him scornfully, and said, "Eheu! Yet a little more!"

"If your head collapses, you've another on your cane," retorted Petronius.

The arrival of Caesar interrupted the conversation. Caesar took his place, with Pythagoras next to him. The performance of *Aureolus* began immediately, but nobody paid much attention to it, for the minds of the audience were fixed on Chilo. The people, accustomed now to scenes of blood and torture, began to hiss and to shout out remarks distinctly unflattering to the Augustinians and to call for the bear scene, which was the only thing they cared to see. Had it not been for the promised gifts and the hope of seeing Chilo, the spectacle wouldn't have held the crowd.

Finally the anticipated moment came. The Circus servants first brought in a wooden cross, low enough to allow the bear, standing on his hind legs, to reach the chest of the victim; then two men dragged in Chilo, for as the bones in his legs had been shattered during his torture, he couldn't walk. He was nailed to the cross so quickly that the curious Augustinians had no opportunity for a good look at him, and only after the cross had been fixed in the pit prepared for it did all eyes gain a view of the victim. But few indeed could recognize Chilo in this naked old man. After the tortures that Tigelli-nus had commanded, not a drop of blood remained in his face, and only on his beard was to be seen a red spot, caused by the bleeding from having his tongue ripped out. It was almost possible to see his bones through the trans-parent skin. He seemed to have grown much older also, and decrepit. His eyes formerly had cast glances filled with malice and ill will, his face had before reflected alarm and uncertainty; but now, though it was drawn with pain, it was as calm and serene as the faces of the sleeping or the dead.

Perhaps he was comforted by the memory of the crucified thief whom Christ forgave, or perhaps he said in his soul to the merciful God, *O Lord! I bit like a venomous worm, but all my life I was unfortunate. I was hungry, people trampled upon me, beat me, and jeered at me. I was poor and very unhappy, and now they torture me, and I'm hanging on a cross! But You, O merciful One, will not reject me in the hour of my death.*

Evidently peace came to his broken heart. No one laughed, for in this crucified man there was something pathetic. He seemed so old, so defenseless, so feeble, and his humility invited compassion, so that invol-untarily each spectator wondered why men should be crucified and nailed to crosses who would soon die in any case.

The crowd was silent. Among the Augustinians, Vestinius, looking to right and left, whispered in a terrified voice, "See how they die!" Others were looking for the bear and wishing a speedy end to the spectacle.

The bear at last entered the arena and, swaying his drooping head from side to side, looked about as if seeking something. When he saw the cross with the naked body upon it, he approached and stood on his hind legs. After a moment he dropped down and, sitting beneath the cross, began to growl as if in his heart there were pity for this poor remnant of a man.

The servants of the Circus urged the bear on, but the people were silent. Meanwhile Chilo slowly raised his head and for a time let his eyes glide over the audience. At last his eyes rested somewhere among the highest tiers of the amphitheater; his breast began to heave, and then appeared something that caused wonder and astonishment, for his face became radiant with a smile, a ray of light seemed to encircle his forehead, his eyes were uplifted, and after a while two great tears that had risen between the lids flowed slowly down his face.

Then he died.

And at the same moment a man's voice rang out clearly from under the velarium: "Peace to the martyrs!"

In the amphitheater, deep silence reigned.

Chapter LXIV

After the spectacle in Caesar's gardens, the prisons were almost empty. New victims, indeed, suspected of the Oriental superstition, were still seized and imprisoned; but fewer and fewer people were captured—barely enough for coming exhibitions, which were to follow quickly. The people had become sated with blood, and they evinced growing weariness and increasing alarm on account of the unparalleled conduct of the victims. Fears like those of the superstitious Vestinius spread among thousands of people. More and more the people talked of the vengefulness of the Christian God. The prison typhus, which had spread all over the city, increased the general dread. Funerals were frequent. It was reported that fresh *piacula* were necessary to appease the unknown God. In the temples, sacrifices were offered to Jove and Libitina. Finally, notwithstanding all the efforts of Tigellinus and his followers, the conviction spread rapidly that the city had been set on fire at the command of Caesar and that the poor Christians were innocent of the crime after all.

For this very reason, Nero and Tigellinus continued the persecution. To placate the people, fresh orders were issued to distribute corn, wine, and oil. New rules were proclaimed to facilitate the rebuilding of houses, and these rules granted special privileges to the owners. New ordinances were passed determining the width of the streets and the materials to be used for building, so as to avoid fires in the future. Caesar himself participated in the sessions of the Senate and counseled with the city fathers about the welfare of the people and the city—but not a shadow of a favor fell on the doomed. The ruler of the world desired to impress upon the people the conviction that such cruel punishment could be inflicted only upon the guilty. In the Senate, no voice was raised in behalf of the Christians, for no one dared to risk Caesar's wrath. Besides, those who looked into the future asserted that the very foundations of the Roman Empire were threatened by this new creed.

The dead and dying were given to their relatives, as the Roman law took

501

no vengeance on the dead. Vinitius consoled himself to some extent with the thought that when Lygia died, he would bury her in his family vault and himself rest alongside her. He no longer had any hope of saving her from death. Half separated from life and absorbed in Christ, he didn't now dream of any union save an eternal one. His faith had become so strong that eternity seemed to him something incomparably more real and true than the fleeting existence that he had lived up to that time. His heart overflowed with joy. Though yet alive, he'd been transformed into an almost immaterial being, which, desiring a complete deliverance for itself, desired it even more for another. He imagined that, when freed from earthly bondage, he and Lygia would go hand in hand to heaven, where Christ would bless them and allow them to live forever in a light as calm and brilliant as the dawn. He implored only one gift from Christ: to save Lygia from the torments of the Circus and let her fall asleep in the prison, feeling that he himself would die at the same time. In view of the enormous amount of blood that had been shed, he couldn't hope that she alone would be spared. He'd heard from Peter and Paul that they, too, must die as martyrs. The sight of Chilo on the cross had convinced him that death, even that of a martyr, could be sweet. Hence, he wished it for both himself and Lygia, as a change from a sorrowful and wretched fate to something better.

At times he experienced a foretaste of the afterlife. The sadness that hung over his soul, and that of Lygia, was gradually losing its former burning bitterness and changing into a peaceful and heavenly submission to the will of God. Vinitius, who formerly had battled against the current and had struggled and tortured himself, now let himself drift, believing that the stream would bear him into eternal rest. He sensed also that Lygia, as well as he, was preparing for death; that in spite of the walls of the prison that separated them, they were going on together, and at this thought he smiled.

In fact, they were acting in such harmony that it was as if they continued to exchange thoughts every day. Lygia had no desire or hope save the hope of an afterlife. She looked upon death not only as a deliverance from the terrible walls of the prison, from the hands of Caesar and Tigellinus, but also as the hour of her wedding day with Vinitius. In view of this unshakable certainty, all else lost importance. After death, great happiness awaited her in heaven; thus she waited for it as a betrothed longs for her wedding day.

And that immense current of faith, which swept thousands of believers away from life and bore them beyond the grave, bore away Ursus as well. He, too, for a long time hadn't been able to resign himself to the thought of Lygia's death. But when every day, through the prison walls, came news of the terrible things that were going on in the amphitheater and in the gardens, when it became increasingly clear that death would be the almost inevitable lot of all the Christians (and that it would bring each of them into a higher happiness than anything earth could provide), Ursus no longer dared to ask Christ to save Lygia from the common fate of all the rest of the believers. In his simple barbarian soul he thought, also, that the daughter of the Lygian king would be entitled to more of those heavenly delights than the common crowd to which he himself belonged and that she would sit nearer to the Lamb than would others. Though he'd heard that before God all are equal, still a conviction lingered at the bottom of his soul that the daughter of a king, the king of all the Lygians, was much better than a servant. He hoped, also, that Christ would allow him to continue to serve her.

His one secret wish was to die on the cross like the Lamb, but this he considered bliss so great that he didn't dare to pray for it, though he knew that in Rome even the lowest criminals were crucified. He assumed that he'd almost certainly be condemned to die under the teeth and claws of wild beasts, and this was his one sorrow. From his childhood on, he'd roamed through forests in pursuit of wild animals. While still a youth, thanks to his superhuman strength, he'd become famous as a hunter among the Lygians. In fact, hunting brought him so much joy that afterward, when in Rome, he visited the *vivarias* and the amphitheaters just to look at beasts, known and unknown to him. The sight of these always roused within him a great desire for struggle and killing. So now he feared that when he should meet the beasts in the arena, he would be possessed by thoughts unbecoming a Christian, whose duty it was to die piously and patiently.

But he committed himself to Christ and found other more agreeable thoughts to console himself. Hearing that the Lamb had declared war against the powers of hell and evil spirits, which, according to the Christian creed, included the pagan gods, he felt confident that in this conflict he might be of considerable service to the Lamb and serve Him all the better, for he couldn't help but believe that his soul must be stronger than those of other martyrs. He prayed through entire days, rendered service to the prisoners, helped the guards, and consoled his princess, who regretted at times that in her short life she hadn't been able to perform as many good deeds as had the famous Tabitha, of whom the Apostle Peter had told her. Even the prison guards, who feared the great strength of the giant, since neither chains nor bars could restrain him, took a liking to him for his gentleness. Amazed at his serenity, they asked him more than once how he achieved it. He spoke with such firm certainty of the life that awaited him after death that they listened with astonishment, seeing for the first time that happiness might come even into a dark dungeon where the sun's rays could never penetrate. And when he urged them to believe in the Lamb, it occurred to more than one of them that their own service was but that of a slave and their lives those of the wretched, and more than one fell to thinking over his lot, the end of which was death.

But death brought new fear and promised nothing, whereas the giant and the maiden (who resembled a flower cast upon the straw floor of the prison)—these two went towards death with delight, as towards the gates of happiness.

Chapter LXV

On a certain evening Scevinus, a senator, called upon Petronius and conversed with him at length about the grievous times in which they lived and also about Caesar. He spoke so openly that Petronius, though friendly, thought it best to be on his guard. Scevinus complained that the world was becoming mad and that all must end in some calamity more terrible even than the burning of Rome. He said that even the Augustinians were discontented; that Fenius Rufus, second prefect of the Praetorians, endured only with the greatest effort the vile rule of Tigellinus; and that Seneca's entire family had been driven to the utmost despair by the conduct of Caesar towards his old master and towards Lucan. Finally, he began to hint of the dissatisfaction of the people, and even of the Praetorians, a considerable part of whom had been won over by Fenius Rufus.

"Why do you speak this way?" asked Petronius.

"Out of concern for Caesar," replied Scevinus. "I have a distant relative among the Praetorians, whose name is also Scevinus; from him I learn what's going on in the camp. Discontent is growing there also. Caligula was mad, and see what happened—Cassius Chaerea appeared. It was a terrible deed, and none of us applauded it; but still Chaerea freed the world from a monster."

"Or, in other words," dryly remarked Petronius, "is this your meaning: I do not praise Chaerea, but he was an excellent man, and would that the gods gave us more like him."

Scevinus changed the subject and began of a sudden to praise Piso, glorifying his family, his generosity, his attachment to his wife, and finally his intellect, his calmness, and his wonderful gift for winning over people.

"Caesar is childless," he said, "and all see his successor in Piso. Doubtless everyone would help Piso to ascend the throne. Fenius Rufus loves him, the family of Annaeus is entirely devoted to him, Plautius Lateranus and Tullius Senecio would go through fire for him. Equally devoted to

him are Natalius, Subrius Flavius, Sulpicius Asper, and Atranius Quinetianus—and even Vestinius."

"The latter won't be of much help to Piso," said Petronius. "Vestinius
is afraid of his own shadow."

"Vestinius fears dreams and spirits," said Scevinus, "but he's a brave
man, who, rumor has it, will be nominated for consul. If in his heart he's
opposed to persecuting the Christians, you mustn't blame him for it, for
it concerns you also that this madness should cease."

"Not me, but Vinitius," said Petronius. "On his account, I'd like to
save a certain girl, but I can't, because I've lost favor with Caesar."

"How's that? Don't you see that Caesar wishes to be friendly with you
again? And I'll tell you why. He's preparing to return to Achaia, where he'll
sing Greek songs of his own composition. He's crazy about the trip, but
trembles at the thought of the jeering disposition of the Greeks. He imag-
ines that either the greatest triumph awaits him, or the greatest failure. He
needs good advice, and he knows that no one can counsel him as well as
you. That's the reason why you're returning to favor."

"Lucan might take my place."

"Ahenobarbus hates Lucan and destines him for death. He's awaiting
but a pretext, for he always seeks pretexts. Lucan understands that it's necessary to make haste."

"By Castor!" said Petronius. "This may be. But I have still another way
to regain favor."

"What is it?"

"To repeat to Ahenobarbus what you've just told me."

"I've said nothing," said Scevinus, aghast.

Petronius laid his hand upon the other's shoulder.

"You've called Caesar a madman, you've predicted the succession of
Piso, and you've said Lucan understands that it's necessary to make haste.
What would you hasten, my dear friend?"

Scevinus grew pale, and for a moment the two looked at each other.

"You won't tell anyone what I said?"

"By the hips of Cypris, I won't! You know me well; no, I won't repeat
it. I haven't heard anything, and I don't wish to hear anything. Do you
understand? Life is too short to deliberately seek out trouble. I beg of you
only to visit Tigellinus today and talk with him as long as you've talked
with me, about anything that may please you."

"What for?"

"So that should Tigellinus someday say to me, 'Scevinus was with you,' I might retort, 'You mean, the same day he came to see you?'"

Scevinus, hearing this, broke the ivory cane that he held in his hand and said, "May an evil spell fall on this cane! I'll be with Tigellinus today and afterward at Nerva's feast. Will you not be there too? But, in any event, we'll see each other the day after tomorrow in the amphitheater, where the remainder of the Christians will appear. Farewell."

"The day after tomorrow," repeated Petronius when alone. "There's no time to lose. Ahenobarbus will need me in Achaia; hence he may show some regard for my wishes." And he determined to try the last means open to him for obtaining Lygia's release.

At Nerva's banquet, Caesar himself asked that Petronius occupy the seat opposite him because he wished to ask his advice about Achaia and about what cities he might appear in with the greatest chances of success. He feared most the Athenians. Other Augustinians listened to the conversation with attention, to retain in their memory the opinions of Petronius and repeat them afterward as their own.

"It seems to me as if I hadn't lived until this time," said Nero, "and that I'll be born only in Greece."

"You'll be born to new fame and immortality," declared Petronius.

"I trust that it will be so and that Apollo will not be jealous. Should I meet with success, I'll offer to him a hecatomb such as no god has ever before had."

Scevinus began to repeat the lines of Horace:

> *Sic te diva potens, Cypri,*
> *Sic frates Helenae, lucida sidera,*
> *Ventorumque regat Pater.*[1]

"The vessel is waiting at Neapolis," said Caesar. "I should like to set out even tomorrow."

Petronius rose and, looking straight at Nero, said, "Permit me, O divine one, first to celebrate a wedding feast, to which I shall invite you before any others."

"A wedding feast! What wedding feast?" inquired Nero.

---

1 "May the powerful Cyprian goddess, with Helen's brothers (now stars) and the father of the winds, escort you on this journey."

"The wedding feast of Vinitius with your hostage, the daughter of the king of the Lygians. Though she's now in prison, as a hostage she isn't subject to imprisonment. You yourself ordered Vinitius to marry her; and as your decrees, like those of Zeus, are unchangeable, you'll command her to be set free, and I'll give her to the bridegroom."

The cool and calm self-possession with which Petronius spoke impressed Nero, who was always impressed by this method of addressing him.

"I know," he said, with eyes cast down. "I've thought of her, and of the giant who choked Croto."

"Then both are saved?" asked Petronius quietly.

But Tigellinus came to the rescue of his master.

"She's in prison at the command of Caesar, and you yourself have said, Petronius, that his decrees are unchangeable."

All present, knowing the history of Vinitius and Lygia, understood the situation well, and they preserved silence, curious to see how the affair would end.

"She's in prison against the will of Caesar, through your mistake and through your ignorance of the law of nations," replied Petronius, laying stress upon his words. "You are a naive man, Tigellinus, but even you dare not assert that she set Rome on fire, for Caesar wouldn't believe you."

But Nero had recovered himself and begun to half close his nearsighted eyes with an expression of indescribable malice.

"Petronius is right," he said after a while.

Tigellinus looked at him with astonishment.

"Petronius is right," repeated Nero. "Tomorrow the gates of the prison will be opened for her. As to the wedding feast, we'll talk it over the day after tomorrow in the amphitheater."

I've lost again, thought Petronius.

When he returned home, he was so certain Lygia's fate had been decided that he sent a trustworthy servant to the amphitheater to make arrangements with the overseer of the *spoliarium* for the delivery of her body, which he wished to entrust to Vinitius.

Chapter LXVI

During Nero's reign, evening exhibitions in the Circus and amphitheater had become common; but before his reign, such nocturnal exhibitions had been rare and had been used only for exceptional occasions. The Augustinians liked them because they were often followed by feasts and revels that lasted until morning. Though the people had had enough of bloodshed, still when the news was spread that the end of the games was approaching and that the last of the Christians were to die during the night performance, great crowds filled the amphitheater. The Augustinians appeared in a body, for they understood that this would be an unusual performance, and they knew that Caesar had determined to make a production out of the anguish of Vinitius. Tigellinus had not revealed what kind of torture was intended for the betrothed of the young tribune, but that merely served to increase the suspense. Those who'd seen Lygia at the house of Plautius and in the palace of Nero extolled her beauty to the skies. Others were mainly concerned with the question as to whether they would actually see her in the arena that night, because many of those who'd heard the reply of Caesar to Petronius were uncertain about what he really meant. Some believed that Nero would deliver, or perhaps had already delivered, the maiden to Vinitius (remembering that she was a hostage and hence could worship any god she pleased, and that the law of nations didn't allow her to be punished).

Uncertainty, expectation, and curiosity characterized the vast audience. Caesar arrived earlier than usual, and immediately after his arrival, conjectures were whispered that something unusual would happen, for besides Tigellinus and Vatinius, Caesar had with him Cassius—a centurion of enormous size and gigantic strength—whom Caesar took with him only when he needed a defender, such as on his night escapades to the Suburra. During these excursions, he enjoyed an amusement called *sagatio*, which consisted of tossing on a soldier's cloak every maiden he met on his way. It was noted, also, that precautions had been taken in the amphitheater itself: The detachment of the Praetorian Guard was increased, and it was commanded, not by a centurion, but by the tribune Subrius Flavius, known for his blind attachment to Nero. It was generally understood that Caesar wished in any case to secure himself against an outburst of despair from Vinitius, and this added to the suspense.

All eyes were turned upon the seat occupied by the unfortunate bridegroom. He was very pale, and his forehead was covered with drops of sweat. He was as uncertain about Lygia's fate as were the other spectators and was both alarmed and despondent. Petronius, ignorant himself of what would happen, had said nothing to him, except that when he'd returned from Nerva's banquet he'd asked Vinitius whether he was prepared for *everything*, and then whether he'd be present at the spectacle. To both questions Vinitius answered yes, but he couldn't restrain a shudder, for he surmised that Petronius wouldn't have asked those questions without reason.

For some time now he'd been only half alive—sunk in death—for he'd reconciled himself to Lygia's death, perceiving it as both a deliverance and a marriage. But now he realized that it's one thing to meditate over the last moment as though it were but a peaceful falling asleep, and quite another to behold the torment of a person dearer than life. All his former sufferings came flooding back upon him. The despair that he'd repressed began again to engulf his soul; he felt again the old desire to save Lygia at any price. He'd tried all morning to enter the *cuniculum* of the prison just to see if she was still there, but the Praetorian Guard watched all the entrances, and the orders were so strict that even the soldiers whom Vinitius knew personally didn't dare succumb to either entreaties or bribes. It seemed to Vinitius that uncertainty would kill him before the spectacle ever came off. In his heart there still lingered a faint hope that Lygia wasn't in the amphitheater, and thus all his fears would prove groundless—at times he clung to this hope with all his strength. At other times, he reveled in the thought that perhaps Christ Himself would step in and remove her from the prison, not permitting her to be tortured in the Circus. Formerly he'd submitted in everything to the divine will, but now, when turned away at the doors of the *cuniculum*, he returned to his seat in the amphitheater, and from the curious eyes directed towards him, he sensed that his most nightmarish fears might prove true. He began to implore Christ for help with such passion that it bordered on a threat.

You can! he repeated, clenching his fists convulsively. *You can!* Before, he hadn't realized that the reality of this long-feared moment could be so terrible. Now, in his frenzied state of mind, he felt that if he should see Lygia tortured, his love for God would turn into hatred and his faith into despair. He was terror-stricken at the same time, for he feared to offend Christ, whom he was imploring for mercy and miracles. He prayed no longer for her life, but only that she might die before being led into the arena. With unspeakable anguish, he bargained with the Lord. *Refuse me not this one request, and I'll love You more than I ever loved You before.*

His thoughts raged like waves tossed about by a hurricane. A desire for blood and vengeance arose in ˙ ˙ n; in fact, he was seized with a mad desire to swoop down upon Caesar and strangle him in the presence of all the spectators—yet, at the same time, he felt this desire was an offense against Christ and His commandments. At times flashes of hope whirled through his brain that an almighty and merciful hand would turn away all that his soul feared; but they were quenched at once, as if in measureless sorrow that He, who could destroy the Circus with one word and save Lygia, had abandoned her, though she trusted in Him and loved Him with all her pure heart. And then the horrible thought that even now she was lying in the dark dungeon, weak, defenseless, deserted, dependent upon the mercy of the brutal guards, drawing perhaps her last breath, while he had to wait in that horrible amphitheater, not knowing what torture was destined for her or what the next moment might bring forth! Finally, as a man who, falling down a precipice, grasps at everything that grows on the edge of it, so did he clutch with both hands at the thought that faith alone could save her. For only this was left! Peter had said that faith could move the earth to its very foundations.

So it was that he regained his equilibrium, crushed his doubts, and compressed his entire being into one thought: "*Fide.*"[1]

But just as a cord stretched too tightly may break, so he was broken by the strain. The pallor of death could be seen in his face, and his body began to stiffen in the strange assumption that Christ had answered his prayer already by bringing about his own death; thus he could now rejoin Lygia (who might have died already) in that ultimate release, and together Christ would call them home. The arena, the white togas, the countless spectators, the light of thousands of lamps and torches, all vanished from his sight.

---

1 "I believe."

But this momentary weakness and mistaken assumption quickly passed. In a moment he awoke, or rather, was awakened by the stamping of the impatient crowd.

"You're ill!" said Petronius to him. "Command your slaves to take you home."

Regardless of what Caesar might say, he rose to support Vinitius and leave with him, his heart full of compassion; moreover, he was vexed beyond endurance by the fact that Caesar was gazing through the emerald at Vinitius and scrutinizing his agony with sadistic satisfaction, perhaps in order to describe it afterward in pathetic strophes and so win the applause of his audiences.

Vinitius shook his head. He might die in the amphitheater, but he could not leave it. Moreover, the spectacle might begin at any moment.

Indeed, at that very instant, the prefect of the city waved a red hand-kerchief; upon this signal, the hinges of the great doors opposite Caesar's box creaked, and out of the *cuniculum*, into the brightly illuminated arena, came Ursus.

The giant blinked, evidently dazzled by the brightness of the lamps and torches; then he moved towards the center, looking around to see what or who it might be he was to face. All the Augustinians, and most of the spectators, knew that this was the man who'd strangled Croto; hence, at his appearance murmurs rose from all the benches.

In Rome, there was no shortage of gladiators larger in stature than ordinary men, but Roman eyes had never seen the like of Ursus. Cassius, who stood by Caesar, appeared puny in comparison. Senators, vestals, Caesar, the Augustinians, and the people gazed with the delight of connoisseurs at his mighty legs, as large as tree trunks; at his massive chest, large as two shields put together; and at his great arms, worthy of Hercules himself.

The murmurs grew louder every moment. For such multitudes as these, there could not exist greater delight than to see such muscles in play, in strain, and in combat. The murmurs changed to shouts and eager questions: "Where do the people live who produce such giants?"

Ursus just stood there in the middle of the amphitheater, naked, more like a stone colossus than a man, calm and self-controlled, appearing both barbaric and melancholy. Glancing around the empty arena, he gazed wonderingly with his childlike blue eyes, now on the spectators, now on Caesar, now on the grating of the *cuniculum*, whence he expected his executioners to come.

At the moment he stepped into the arena, his simple heart was throbbing with the hope that death on the cross might be awaiting him. But when he saw neither a cross nor a pit in which it might be put, he concluded that perhaps he didn't really deserve such favor, and that he would have to perish in some other way—most likely from wild beasts. He was unarmed and had resolved to die as became a confessor of the Lamb, peacefully and patiently. Meanwhile, he wished to pray once more to the Savior, so kneeling, he folded his hands and raised his eyes to the glittering stars.

This attitude displeased the crowd. They'd had enough of those Christians who died like sheep; and they fully understood that should the giant refuse to defend himself, the spectacle would be a failure. Here and there hisses arose. Some cried for the *mastigophori*, whose office it was to whip combatants who refused to fight. But soon silence followed, for no one knew what awaited the giant, nor whether or not he would choose to fight when he looked death in the face.

Indeed, they didn't have long to wait. Suddenly the shrill sound of brass trumpets broke the silence, and at this signal a grating opened opposite the imperial box. Into the arena rushed, amid the shouts of the people, an enormous German aurochs, bearing on its head a naked woman.

"Lygia! Lygia!" cried Vinitius. Then he seized his hair near the temples, writhed like a man wounded by a spear, and in a hoarse voice cried out, "I believe! I believe!" Then, "A miracle, O Christ!"

It seemed to him that death or anguish had closed his eyes. He wasn't aware that Petronius, at that moment, had covered his head with a toga. He didn't look, he didn't see. A feeling of awful emptiness swept over him. No thought remained in his head, but his lips repeated, as if in delirium: "I believe! I believe!"

Suddenly the amphitheater became silent again. The Augustinians rose in their seats as one man, for something extraordinary was happening in the arena. The Lygian, submissive and ready to accept death without lifting a hand to defend himself, seeing his princess attached to the horns of the wild beast, sprang up as if burned by fire and, leaning forward, rushed towards the raging animal.

Cries of astonishment were heard on all sides; then again there was breathless silence. The Lygian had now overtaken the rampaging bull and seized him by the horns.

"*Look!*" cried Petronius, snatching the toga away from Vinitius's eyes.

Vinitius raised his face, pale as a sheet, and he looked into the arena with a glassy, vacant stare.

Everyone in the arena ceased to breathe—in the amphitheater a fly might have been heard. No one could believe their eyes, for in the entire history of Rome, no one had ever seen anything like this.

The Lygian held the wild beast by the horns. His feet were dug into the sand beyond his ankles, his back was bent like a drawn bow, his head was hidden between his shoulders, the muscles swelled on his arms so that the skin threatened to crack under the pressure, but he stopped the bull on the spot. The man and the beast remained so motionless that the spectators felt they were looking at a picture representing a deed of Hercules or Theseus or a group chiseled in stone. But in that apparent repose was evident the terrible exertion of two struggling forces. The bull also dug his hooves deep into the sand, and his dark, shaggy body was so curved that it resembled a gigantic ball. Which of the two would fail first, would fall first?—that was the question spectators enamored over such struggles always asked. This was the question that at the moment was of greater importance to the spectators than their own fate, than that of Rome and its rule over the world. The Lygian, in their eyes, was a demigod, worthy of admiration and statues.

Caesar himself stood up, as did the others. He and Tigellinus, hearing of the strength of this man, had purposely prepared the spectacle and, laughing to each other, had jeeringly said, "Let the slayer of Croto even *try* to vanquish the bull we've chosen!"

But now they looked with disbelief at the picture before them, hardly believing that it could be real.

There in the amphitheater, people could be seen who had raised their arms and remained in that posture. Sweat poured down the faces of others, as if they themselves were struggling with the beast. In the Circus nothing was heard save the hiss of the flames in the lamps and the rustle of pieces of coal falling from the torches. Words died in the throats of the spectators, but their hearts beat against their breasts as if to split them. It seemed to all that the struggle was lasting for ages.

But the man and the brute continued motionless in their terrible struggle. They seemed rooted in the earth.

Suddenly there reverberated through the arena a muffled roar resembling a groan, after which a brief shout was wrested from every breast, and then once again there was silence. As in a dream, the people saw that the monstrous head of the bull was twisting around in the iron grasp of the

The man and the brute continued motionless in their terrible struggle.

barbarian. The Lygian's face, neck, and arms grew purple; his back bent still more. He was evidently rallying the rest of his superhuman strength. But he couldn't stand the strain much longer.

Duller and duller, hoarser and hoarser, more and more wracked with pain, grew the groans of the bull, mingling with the exhausted whistling breath of the giant. The head of the brute was twisted more and more, and from its jaws a long, foaming tongue hung out. But a moment more . . . and the crack of breaking bones reached the ears of the nearest spectators; then the beast fell to the earth with a broken neck.

Almost instantly, the giant slipped the cords from the horns of the bull and, panting, raised the maiden in his arms. His face had paled, his hair was matted with sweat, his arms and shoulders were wet as though flooded with water. For a moment he stood as if only half conscious, then he raised his eyes to look at the spectators.

The amphitheater went wild.

The walls of the great structure trembled from the shouts of tens of thousands of people. Since the beginning of the games no such enthusiasm had ever been known. Those who occupied the higher tiers left them and crowded down the aisles between the seats to get a better view of the giant. From all sides came cries for mercy, passionate and insistent, which soon turned into one unbroken thunder. The giant was now the darling of the people, who above all things worshiped physical strength—for the moment, he was the greatest personage in Rome.

The Lygian understood that the mob was demanding his pardon and freedom, but his thoughts were not upon himself alone. For a time he looked about him, then he approached the imperial seat and, holding the maiden on his outstretched arms, he raised his eyes in supplication as if to say, "Have mercy on her! Save her! For her sake I have done this!"

The spectators understood perfectly what he asked for. The sight of the unconscious maiden, a mere child in comparison with the gigantic Lygian, had its effect upon the crowd and the soldiers and senators. That slender figure, white as if cut from alabaster, her swooning condition, the awful peril from which the giant had rescued her, and finally her beauty, moved every heart. Some assumed that the Lygian was a father begging mercy for his child.

Pity burst forth suddenly like a flame. Enough of blood and death and tortures. Mercy for them both! On every side arose entreaties for mercy from voices broken by sobs.

Ursus, still carrying the girl in his arms, moved around the arena and, by eye and gesture, begged mercy for the girl. Then Vinitius started up from his seat, leaped over the barrier that separated the front seats from the arena, and, running to Lygia, threw his toga over her naked body. Then he tore open his tunic and exposed the scars of wounds received in the Armenian war and stretched out his arms towards the people.

The excitement of the crowd now surpassed anything ever seen in a circus before. The mob began to stamp and howl. Voices demanding mercy grew terrible in their insistence. People not only took the part of the athlete, but also rose in defense of the maiden and the soldier. With flashing eyes and clenched fists, thousands of spectators turned towards Caesar. He, however, demurred and hesitated. True, he cherished no hatred for Vinitius, and the death of Lygia was of little importance to him; but he would have much preferred to see the lovely body of the maiden gored by the horns of the bull or ripped apart by the claws of fierce beasts. His cruelty and his innate sadism found demonic pleasure in such sights. And now the people wished to deprive him of one. This thought angered him. Wrath burned red on his bloated face. His self-love didn't permit him to yield to the will of the people; but on the other hand he dared not, because of his inborn cowardice, oppose it.

So he looked around among the Augustinians to see if he could discover thumbs pointing downward to give the verdict of death. But Petronius held up his hand and looked almost defiantly into Caesar's face. Vestinius, superstitious yet enthusiastic, who feared ghosts but not the living, also gave the sign for mercy. So did Scevinus the senator; Nerva, Tullius Senecio, and the famous warrior Ostorius Scapula; Antiscius, Licinianus Piso, and Crispinus; Minucius Thermus, Pontius Telesinus, and most important of all, Thrasea, who was adored by the people.

In view of this opposition, Caesar dropped the emerald from his eye with an expression of contempt and offense.

Tigellinus, who wished above all things to spite Petronius, turned to him and said, "Yield not, O divine one! We have the Praetorians at our command."

Then Nero turned to the place where Subrius Flavius stood in command over the Praetorians, and here he saw something totally unexpected: The face of the old tribune, hitherto always devoted heart and soul to him, was now set and stern, though bathed in tears, and his hand was raised in the sign of mercy.

Meanwhile the masses had become enraged. Clouds of dust rose from beneath the stamping feet and filled the amphitheater. Mingled with the shouts for mercy were cries of "Ahenobarbus!" "Matricide!" "Incendiary!"

Nero became terrified. In the Circus, the people were absolute lords. Former Caesars, especially Caligula, had ventured sometimes to withstand the popular will, and the consequent disturbances sometimes ended in bloodshed. Nero's position was different. Not only as a comedian and a singer did he need the favor of the people, but also as a bulwark against the Senate and the patricians. Since the burning of Rome, he'd striven to win it by every means possible and so had turned the anger of the people against the Christians. He understood that further opposition would be perilous. A riot begun in the Circus might sweep across the city and produce incalculable results.

Once more he looked at Subrius Flavius, at Scevinus the centurion, at the soldiers, and, seeing everywhere frowning knitted brows, moved faces, and stern eyes fixed upon him, he gave the sign for mercy.

Then a thunder of applause was heard from the highest seat to the lowest. The people were now certain of the lives of those condemned, for from that moment on they came under the people's protection—and not even Caesar would dare to pursue them any longer with his vengeance.

Chapter LXVII

Four Bithynian slaves bore Lygia to the house of Petronius, Vinitius and Ursus walking at her side, hurrying to place her as soon as possible under the care of their Greek physician. They walked in silence, for after the experiences of the day, speech seemed to have forsaken them. Vinitius was scarcely conscious. Again and again he repeated to himself that Lygia was saved, that neither imprisonment nor death in the Circus menaced her any longer, that their misfortunes were ended once and forever, and that now he was carrying her home and would never part from her again. All this seemed, in a surreal sort of way, to be the beginning of some other life rather than reality.

From time to time, he bent over the open litter to look at the face of his beloved, which in the moonlight appeared still as if in sleep, and he repeated to himself, *This is she! Christ saved her!* He remembered also that, while he and Ursus were carrying her away from the *spoliarium,* an unknown physician had assured him that the girl was living and would surely recover. This assurance filled him with such delight that he grew weak and was obliged to lean upon the arm of Ursus, who was looking up at the star-studded sky and praying.

They advanced hurriedly along streets where newly erected buildings gleamed white in the moonlight. The streets were deserted save where here and there they came upon groups of ivy-covered people who sang and danced before porticoes to the accompaniment of flutes, thus taking advantage of the marvelous night and the holiday season, unbroken since the beginning of the games.

Only when they were near the house did Ursus cease praying and, in a low voice, as if he feared to waken Lygia, say, "Oh, master, the Savior preserved her from death. When I saw her on the horns of the aurochs, I heard a voice in my soul saying, *Defend her!* And this I know was the voice of the Lamb. The prison had robbed me of my strength, but in that moment He restored it to me, and He inspired the cruel multitude to take her part. His will be done!"

519

And Vinitius answered, "Magnified be His name!"

But he could speak no further, for tears choked him. He felt an uncontrollable desire to fall down upon the earth and thank the Savior for the miracle and His mercy.

They'd now reached the house. The servants, informed by a slave who'd been sent ahead, swarmed out to meet them. Paul of Tarsus had converted the greater part of these people while in Antium. Since they were so familiar with the misfortunes of Vinitius, great was their joy at sight of the victims rescued from the malice of Nero. It increased still more when Theocles, the physician, after examining Lygia, pronounced that she'd suffered no serious injury and that when the weakness resulting from the prison fever had passed, she would surely recover.

During the night she regained consciousness. Awakening in a splendid *cubiculum*, lighted by Corinthian lamps and fragrant with the scent of verbena and nard, she knew not where she was or how she'd come to be there. The last coherent thing she could remember was the terrible moment when she'd been stripped and tied to the horns of a fierce chained bull. So now, not surprisingly, beholding above her the face of Vinitius, lighted by the pale glow of the lamp, she imagined that she was no longer on earth. Her thoughts were confused in her weakened state. It seemed somehow natural to be detained somewhere on the way to heaven because of her weariness and weakness. Not feeling any pain, she smiled at Vinitius and attempted to ask him where they were but could speak only in a low whisper, so that Vinitius could scarcely understand a single word.

He knelt beside her and, laying his hand softly on her forehead, said, "Christ saved you and restored you to me!"

Her lips moved again in an unintelligible whisper, then closed after a moment; her bosom heaved with a sigh, and she fell into a deep sleep, which the physician was expecting, and after which he foresaw her return to health.

Vinitius remained on his knees by her side, deep in prayer. His soul was transported with so mighty a love that he forgot himself entirely. Theocles now returned to the chamber, and from behind a lace curtain the golden head of Eunice appeared a number of times. At last the cranes outside in the garden announced the dawn of day with their cries, but Vinitius still knelt, embracing in imagination the feet of Christ, neither seeing nor hearing what was going on about him. His heart, full of thanksgiving, burned like a sacrificial flame, and he was carried away by his ecstasy to the very portals of heaven.

Chapter LXVIII

After Lygia was liberated, Petronius, lest he should offend Caesar, went to the Palatine with other Augustinians. He wanted to hear what they were saying, especially to find out whether Tigellinus was still determined to destroy Lygia. True, both she and Ursus were now under the protection of the people, thus no one could molest them without creating a tumult. But Petronius, knowing how the powerful prefect of the Praetorians hated him, thought it likely that Tigellinus, powerless to injure him directly, would now try to revenge himself upon his nephew.

Nero was angry and irritated because the games had ended in a way quite different from what he'd planned. At first he wouldn't even look at Petronius, but Petronius, preserving his composure, approached him with all the freedom of the *arbiter elegantiarum* and said, "Do you know, O divine one, what has struck me? Compose a song about the maiden, who, at the command of the ruler of the world, was rescued from the horns of a wild bull and returned to her lover. The Greeks have sensitive hearts, and I'm certain that such a song will enchant them."

Despite his irritation, Nero was pleased with the suggestion for two reasons: In the first place, it was a good subject for a song; and second, he could glorify himself as the magnanimous ruler of the world.

For a few moments, he stared at Petronius in silence; then he said, "Yes! You may very well be right, but would it be becoming for me to celebrate my own goodness?"

"There's no need to give names. In Rome, everybody will know the true hero of the song, and from Rome the news will spread all over the world."

"And are you certain that this will please them in Achaia?"

"By Pollux, it will!" cried Petronius.

And he took his departure, feeling certain that Nero, who loved to weave reality into his literary inventions, would retain unaltered that theme; thus the hands of Tigellinus would be tied.

But this didn't alter his plan for sending Vinitius away from Rome as soon as Lygia's health would permit it. So when he saw his nephew the next day, he said, "Take her to Sicily. As things have turned out, you need fear Caesar no longer, but Tigellinus is perfectly capable of poisoning you both, if not out of hatred for you, out of hatred for me."

Vinitius smiled and replied, "She was on the horns of a wild bull, and yet Christ saved her."

"Sacrifice then a hecatomb to Him," said Petronius impatiently, "but don't expect Him to save her a second time. Do you remember how Aeolus received Ulysses when he asked him a second time for favoring winds? Gods don't like to repeat themselves."

"As soon as she's restored to health," said Vinitius, "I'll take her to Pomponia Graecina."

"All the better, since Pomponia is very sick; Antiscius, a cousin of Aulus, told me so. Meanwhile, things will happen here that will make people forget about you—and in these times the forgotten are the happiest. May fortune be your sun in winter and your shade in summer."

Then, leaving Vinitius to his happiness, he sought out Theocles to find out how Lygia was doing.

Theocles pronounced her out of danger. Debilitated as she was by fever, had she remained in the putrid air of the Esquiline prison, unquestionably she would have lost her fight for life and died; but now she was surrounded by everything she needed to enable her to reverse that long and so nearly fatal slide. After two more days had passed, the good doctor ordered them to carry her out to the gardens of the villa, and there she remained in the sunshine for a number of hours. The treatment was continued during the days that followed.

Vinitius decked her litter with anemones but with even more irises, to remind her of the atrium in the house of Aulus. More than once, screened from the world in the grove of far-spreading trees, they spoke of past sufferings and fears, holding hands all the while. Lygia told Vinitius that Christ had led him through the dark valley of suffering to change his soul and raise it up to Himself. Vinitius acknowledged that this was true, convinced, in fact, that there was little in him of the former patrician who had recognized no law save his own unbridled passions.

There was no bitterness in these memories, however. It seemed to them both that whole years had rolled over their heads and that the terrible past lay far behind. A feeling of great peace came to them such as they'd never experienced before. A new life and great happiness lay before them. In Rome, Caesar might rage and fill the world with terror; but they, knowing they were under the protection of a far mightier power, no longer feared either Caesar's rage or his malice—it was as though Caesar had ceased to be master of their lives.

Once, about sunset, they heard the roar of lions and other wild beasts coming from the direction of a distant vivaria; formerly those roars would have filled Vinitius's heart with terror and dread, but now he and Lygia merely smiled in remembrance at each other and turned their eyes on the sun setting beyond the seven hills. At times Lygia, still very weak and unable to walk unaided, fell asleep in the quiet of the garden. At such times, Vinitius watched over her; at times, as he tenderly looked down at her sleeping face, the thought would come to him that this wasn't the same Lygia whom he'd met at the home of Aulus. Indeed, the prison and the sickness it had brought had somewhat diminished her beauty. When he first saw her at the house of Aulus, and when he came to take her from Miriam's house, she'd been as beautiful as a statue. Now her face was almost transparent, her arms were thin, her body emaciated by illness, her lips pale, and even her eyes seemed less blue than formerly. The golden-haired Eunice, who brought her flowers and costly rugs to cover her feet, seemed like a Cyprian deity in comparison. The aesthetic Petronius searched in vain to find that beauty that had once overpowered him; shrugging his shoulders, he concluded that this frail shadow from Elysian fields wasn't worth the struggle, pain, and torture that had almost cost Vinitius his life. But Vinitius, now in love with her spirit, loved her all the more—and when he watched her as she slept, he felt as if he were watching over the whole world.

Chapter LXIX

T he news of Lygia's miraculous rescue spread rapidly among those scattered Christians who'd escaped death. Believers came to look at her to whom the grace of Christ had been so manifestly shown. First came Nazarius and Miriam, at whose house Peter was concealed; after them came others. All of them, together with Vinitius, Lygia, and the Christian slaves of Petronius, listened with rapt attention to the narrative of Ursus as he related how a voice had spoken to his soul and commanded him to struggle with the wild bull. Each departed much consoled, now confident that Christ would not permit His followers to be exterminated on earth before His returning for the Day of Judgment—and this hope sustained them, for the persecution continued.

The Roman people no longer believed that the Christians had caused the conflagration, but still they were denounced as enemies of humanity and the state; thus the edict against them remained in full force. Whoever was declared to be a Christian by a citizen of Rome was immediately seized and thrown into prison by the Praetorian Guard. Though the games were over, the newly arrested were preserved for future games or punished at once. The number of victims was growing fewer, however, because the majority of the faithful had already been seized and tortured to death. The Christians who survived had either left Rome to wait out the storm in distant provinces or were concealing themselves in hiding places, not daring to assemble for common prayers, except in *arenariae*[1] outside the city.

It was a long time before the Apostle Peter dared to leave his place of hiding and come to visit Lygia and Vinitius, but at last one evening, Nazarius announced his arrival. Lygia, who was now able to walk unaided, and Vinitius hurried to meet him and embraced his feet. He greeted them with all the greater emotion because so few sheep remained in the fold

---

1 Sand pits.

Christ had entrusted to him, and the fate of these sheep filled his great heart with tears.

Consequently, when Vinitius said to him, "O master, because of your intercession, the Savior returned her to me," he replied, "He returned her to you because of your faith and so that not all the lips that praise Him would grow silent."

Clearly he was thinking then of the thousands of his lambs who'd been torn to pieces by wild beasts, of those crosses that had filled the arena, and of those fiery pillars in the gardens of the Beast, for he spoke with great sorrow. Vinitius and Lygia couldn't help but notice that his hair had grown quite white, that his body was bent, and that his face mirrored so much sadness and suffering, it was as if he himself had endured the anguish and tortures unleashed by the malevolent Nero. But they both understood that as Christ had delivered Himself to torture and death, no one else could hope to avoid such suffering. Nevertheless, the sight of the Apostle, bent by age and pain, almost broke their hearts. So concerned was Vinitius, in fact, that he urged the Apostle to leave Rome with them when in a few days they'd go to Neapolis to meet Pomponia, and then proceed to Sicily.

But the Apostle placed his hand on the tribune's head and replied, "I hear in my soul the words of the Lord, which He spoke to me on the Sea of Tiberias:[2] 'When you were young, you took care of yourself and were free to go wherever you wished to, but when you become old, you'll stretch out your arms and another will take care of you, and you'll follow, whether you really wish to or not.' Because of this, I must therefore follow my flock."

And when they grew silent, not fully understanding what he said, he added, "My toil is nearly over; I shall find refuge and rest only in the house of the Lord." Then he turned towards them and said, "Remember me, because I have loved you as a father loves his children; and whatever you do in life, do it for the glory of God."

With these words he raised his trembling hands and blessed them; they, in turn, clung to him, feeling that this might very well be the last blessing they would ever receive from him.

But it was destined that they would see him once again. A few days later, Petronius brought dreadful news from the Palatine. It had been discovered

---

2 Sea of Galilee.

that one of Caesar's freedmen was a Christian, and on him were found letters of the Apostles Peter and Paul, and also letters of James, John, and Judas.[3] Peter's presence in Rome had been known to Tigellinus, but he'd assumed that the Apostle had perished with the thousands of other believers. Now it was evident that the two leaders of the new faith were still alive and that they were in Rome. It was determined that they must be found and captured at any price, because it was believed that only with their deaths could the hated sect be eradicated. Petronius learned from Vestinius that Caesar himself had issued an order to lock up Peter and Paul in the Mamertine prison within three days and that whole detachments of Praetorians had been sent to search every house in the Trans-Tiber.

The moment he heard this, Vinitius resolved to warn the Apostle. That very evening, he and Ursus put on Gallic mantles and made their way to the house of Miriam, where Peter was living. The house was at the very edge of the Trans-Tiber section of the city, at the foot of the Janiculum Hill. On the way they saw houses surrounded by soldiers led by unknown persons. Everyone in this part of the city was, quite naturally, alarmed; thus here and there groups of curious people had assembled. Within the prisons, centurions interrogated prisoners, seeking to gain information about Simon Peter and Paul of Tarsus.

Ursus and Vinitius, being in advance of the Praetorians, arrived safely at the house of Miriam, where they found Peter surrounded by a handful of the faithful. Timothy, Paul's assistant, and Linus were at the side of the Apostle.

On hearing of the approaching danger, Nazarius led all by a hidden passage to the garden gate and then on to some deserted quarries a few hundred yards from the Porta Janicula. Ursus was obliged to carry Linus, whose bones, broken by tortures, hadn't yet knit together. But when they'd entered a quarry, they felt safe, and by the light of a torch that Nazarius lit, they consulted in low voices as to the best means of saving the life of the Apostle who was so dear to them.

"Master," said Vinitius to Peter, "let Nazarius at the break of day guide you to the Alban Hills. We'll find you there and take you to Antium, where a vessel waits to transport us to Neapolis and Sicily. Happy will be the day and hour when you enter my house and bless my hearth."

All the others approved this plan and urged the Apostle to accept, saying,

---

3 Judas, son of James, author of the New Testament book of Jude.

"Take refuge, O shepherd. Stay not in Rome. Preserve the living truth so that it may not perish with us and with you. Hear us, for we implore you as our father."

"Do this in the name of Christ," cried others, clinging to the Apostle's garments.

Peter answered, "My children, who but the Lord can know when the end of his life will be?"

But he didn't refuse to leave Rome, and he hesitated as to what course to pursue, for uncertainty, and even fear, had for some time been gradually stealing into his soul. His flock was scattered, his work had come to naught, the Church that, before the burning of the city, had flourished like a great tree, had almost been annihilated by the power of the Beast. Nothing remained save tears and the memories of torture and death. The sowing had yielded an abundant crop, but Satan had trampled it into the earth. The angelic legions hadn't come to rescue the perishing, and Nero still sat upon the throne of the world, terrible and more powerful than ever, lord of all seas and all lands. More than once, God's fisherman had stretched his hands heavenward in his loneliness and asked, "Oh, Lord, what am I to do? How can I, a feeble old man, wage war against the invincible power of evil, which You've permitted to rule and have victory?"

From the depths of his anguish, he cried out in his soul: *The sheep that You commanded me to feed are no more. Your Church is no more. In our capital are only loneliness and mourning. What do You command me to do now? Am I to stay here, or shall I lead forth the remnant of the flock to glorify Your name in secret somewhere beyond the sea?*

And he hesitated. He still believed that the living truth could not perish, that it must prevail. But at times he thought that the hour hadn't yet come, that it would come only when the Lord should descend upon earth on the Day of Judgment, in glory and power greater a hundredfold than that of Nero.

Often it seemed to him that if he left Rome, the faithful would follow him, and then he would lead them far away to the shady groves of Galilee, to the quiet waters of the Sea of Tiberias, to throw in their lot with shepherds as peaceful as doves or as the sheep that feed there among thyme and pepperwort. And an increasing desire for peace and rest, an increasing longing for the lake and Galilee, filled the heart of the old Apostle. His eyes were frequently full of tears.

But the moment he made up his mind to leave, sudden fear and anxiety took possession of him. How was he to leave that city whose sacred soil had drunk the blood of martyrs and where so many dying lips had given witness to the truth? Should he alone shrink from his fate? And what answer could he make if the Lord reproved him, saying, "They've suffered death for the faith, but you fled for your life"?

Nights and days passed for him in anxiety and suffering. Others whom lions had torn to pieces, who had died on crosses, who had been burned in the gardens of Caesar, now slept in peace after their moments of torture. But he couldn't sleep and suffered greater tortures than any of those invented by executioners for victims. Often the dawn whitened the roofs of houses while he was yet crying from the depths of his suffering heart: *O Lord, why did You order me to come here and found Your capital in the den of the Beast?*

During all the thirty-four years since the death of his Master, he'd known no rest. With staff in hand, he'd traveled over the wide world to spread the good news. His strength had been exhausted by his journeys and toils, and when he'd at last established the work of his Master in this city—the capital of the world—the fiery breath of malice had burned it. And his tired old heart saw that the struggle must begin all over again. And against what impossible odds! On one side, Caesar, the Senate, the people, the legions encircling the world with chains of iron, lands innumerable, and such power as was never seen before; and on the other side— he, so weakened with age and toil that his trembling hand could barely hold on to his staff. Often he admitted to himself that he was no match for the great Caesar and that Christ alone had the power to stand against him.

All these thoughts passed through his careworn head as he listened to the entreaties of the last handful of his faithful followers, who, surrounding him in an ever-narrowing circle, pleaded with him, "Hide yourself, O Rabbi, and lead us away from the power of the Beast."

Finally, Linus himself bowed before him his tortured head. "Master," he said, "the Savior commanded you to feed His sheep, but they're here no more or will be gone by tomorrow. Go, therefore, to where you may still find them. The word of God still lives in Jerusalem, in Antioch, in Ephesus, and in other cities. What will you gain by staying in Rome? If you fall, you'll merely swell the triumph of the Beast. The Lord hasn't foretold the limit of John's life. Paul is a Roman citizen and cannot be condemned without a trial. But if the powers of hell prevail against you, Teacher, those who've already lost heart will ask: 'Who is greater than Nero?' You are the rock upon which the church of the Lord is founded. Let us die, but don't permit the Antichrist to prevail over the vicar of God—and return not to this city until the Lord has crushed him who shed the blood of innocents."

"Look at our tears," repeated all those present.

Tears flowed down Peter's face as well.

After a while he arose and, stretching his hands over the kneeling people, said, "May the name of the Lord be magnified, and may His will be done!"

Chapter LXX

At dawn the following day, two dark figures could be seen moving down the Via Appia towards the plains of Campania. One of them was Nazarius, the other the Apostle Peter, who was leaving Rome and his distraught flock.

The eastern sky was tinted a pale green, which gradually coalesced into saffron. Silver-leafed trees, villas of white marble, and the arches of aqueducts stretching across the plain towards the city crystallized out of the mists of dawn. In the sky, green had given way to gold as night gave way to day. Then the east began to turn scarlet and ignite the Alban Hills, which flamed into rose of such heart-stopping beauty it seemed not of this earth. This resplendence was mirrored in drops of dew trembling on the leaves of trees. The mist began to dissipate and unveil wider and wider vistas of the plain, the houses that dotted it, the cemeteries, towns, and groups of trees, all crowned by the white columns of temples.

The road was empty. The villagers who brought vegetables to the city apparently hadn't yet harnessed their horses. No sound disturbed the morning silence save that made by the travelers' wood-soled sandals meeting the blocks of stone with which the road was paved all the way to the mountains.

Just as the sun burst through an opening between the mountains, something wonderful happened to the old Apostle—a vision that stopped his step almost in midair—for it seemed to him that the golden disk, instead of rising higher and higher into the sky, descended and advanced to meet him on the blazing Via Appia.

Peter, standing stock-still, asked, "Do you see that brightness approaching us?"

"I see nothing," replied Nazarius.

Peter, shading his eyes with his hands, continued, "Some figure is approaching us in the radiance of the sun."

But not the slightest sound of footsteps reached their ears. Although no breath of air stirred in the dawn stillness, Nazarius could plainly see that the trees ahead of them were trembling as though someone were shaking them, and the light was spreading wider and wider across the plain. He stared in disbelief at the Apostle.

"Rabbi, what's wrong with you?" he cried, thoroughly alarmed.

The pilgrim's staff fell from Peter's hand, his eyes stared forward, his mouth was open; on his face was depicted in succession astonishment, jubilation, rapture. He fell upon his knees with his arms stretched out and cried, "O Christ! O Christ!" Then he fell with his face to the earth, as though kissing someone's feet. A silence that seemed to last forever was broken by the voice of the old man, interwoven with tears, asking, "*Quo vadis, Domine?*"[1]

Nazarius didn't catch the answer, but to Peter's ears came a sad, sweet voice that said, "As you are deserting My people, I go to Rome to be crucified a second time."

The Apostle lay on the ground, his face in the dust, motionless and silent. It seemed to Nazarius that he'd fainted, or perhaps even died. But suddenly Peter rose and, without a word, seized his pilgrim's staff with trembling fingers and turned back towards the City of the Seven Hills.

The boy, seeing this, repeated like an echo, "*Quo vadis, domine?*"

"To Rome," replied the Apostle.

And he returned.

— — —

Paul, John, Linus, and all the faithful greeted Peter with consternation in their eyes. Their alarm was all the greater because, at daybreak, just after his departure, the Praetorians had surrounded the house of Miriam and searched it for the Apostle. But to all questions he simply answered, in a voice radiating joy and peace, "I've seen the Lord." That same evening he went to the Ostranium Cemetery to teach and baptize those who wished to bathe in the water of life.

And from that day on, he went there every day, followed by ever-larger crowds. It appeared that out of every martyr's tear new believers were born, and that every sob in the arena found an echo now in thousands of receptive hearts. Caesar wallowed in blood; Rome and the entire pagan world raged. But those who'd had enough of the crime and bloodshed, those who

---

1 "Where are You going, Lord?"

were trampled upon, those whose lives were a succession of misery and oppression—all the weighed-down, all the sorrowful, all the unfortunate—came to listen to the wonderful tidings of that God who, out of love for mankind, had given Himself to be crucified to redeem their sins.

When they found a God they could love, they found that which the world couldn't give—happiness born of love.

Peter understood now that neither Caesar nor all his legions could crush the living truth, that neither tears nor blood could drown it, and that now it would emerge victorious. He understood now why the Lord had turned him back on the road, for that city of pride, crime, dissolution, and power, was now becoming His city, and the capital from which would come a different kind of government: a rule not merely of flesh—but of the spirit.

Chapter LXXI

At last, the hour of both the Apostles had come. But, as if to complete his work, it was given to the fisherman of the Lord to rescue two souls even in prison. Two soldiers, Processus and Martinianus, who guarded him in the Mamertine prison, were baptized by him. Then came the hour of torture. Nero not being in Rome at the time, sentence was passed by Helius and Polythetes, two freedmen to whom the government of Rome had been entrusted.

The aged Apostle was first flogged, according to law, and the next day was taken outside the city walls towards the Vatican Hill, where he was to suffer death on the cross. The Praetorians were astonished by the crowds that gathered before the prison, for they couldn't understand how the death of a common man, and a foreigner besides, could possibly arouse such interest. They weren't aware that this retinue was composed not of the merely curious, but of believers who wished to accompany the great Apostle to the place of his execution.

At last, in the afternoon, the gates of the prison were thrown open, and Peter appeared in the midst of a detachment of Praetorians. The sun was already slanting towards Ostia; the day was calm and clear. Out of consideration for his venerable age, Peter wasn't required to carry his cross. It was supposed that on account of his years he wouldn't be able to support its weight; neither had they put the fork[1] on his neck, which would have slowed his progress. He walked without hindrance; thus the faithful could see him perfectly.

When his white head showed itself amid the iron helmets of the soldiers, weeping could be heard in the throng, but it ceased almost immediately, because the face of the old man was so serene and shone with such

---

1 A yoke placed on defeated enemies and prisoners to emphasize their forced submission to the power of Rome.

joy that it seemed to all that this was not a victim going to his execution, but a victor celebrating his triumph.

And thus it was. The fisherman, usually humble and stooping, now walked erect, taller than the soldiers, and full of dignity. Never before had anyone seen such majesty in his bearing. He looked like a monarch attended by the people and soldiers.

From all sides came voices: "There's Peter—going to the Lord!"

All seemed to forget that he was going to torture and to death. The crowd walked in solemn concourse, feeling that since the death on Golgotha, nothing so great had taken place, and that as the first death had redeemed the world, this was to redeem the city.

Along the road, people stopped, gazing with astonishment on the scene. Believers in the crowd often stopped and, after placing a hand on a bystander's shoulder, would say, "Just look and see how a just man goes to his death—one who knew Christ personally and proclaimed His love to the world." And those who'd halted to gaze upon the Apostle walked away, saying, "Truly, this man couldn't possibly be a criminal!"

Along the way, the usually noisy streets were strangely silent. The procession wound its way past newly built houses and the white columns of temples, above which hung the deep blue sky, calm and serene. The silence was broken only by the occasional clatter of Praetorian armor or weapons, or murmured prayers. Peter heard the prayers, and his face grew bright with increasing joy, for his eyes could barely take in all those thousands of believers. He now felt that his work had been completed after all, and that the truth that he'd proclaimed all his life would overwhelm everything like a sea—that nothing could stop it.

Thinking thus, he raised his eyes heavenward and said, "O Lord, You commanded me to preach the good news to this city that rules over the world, and I have done so. You commanded me to found Your capital in it, and I have done so. It is Your city now, and I am coming to You, because my work is done."

As he passed before temples, he proclaimed, "You will become temples of Christ!" Studying the throngs of people that surrounded him, he said to them, "Your children will be servants of Christ."

And he walked on with the consciousness of victory achieved, of the service he'd been able to render, of the power restored to him for this hour. He was calm and—to those who watched him—great.

The soldiers took him across the Pons Triumphalis, as if unwittingly testifying to his triumph, and led him on towards the Naumachia and the Circus. The faithful from the Trans-Tiber now joined the procession and swelled it to such an extent that the centurion who commanded the Praetorians belatedly realized that he was escorting a high priest surrounded by believers and grew alarmed because of the smallness of his force. But not a single cry of indignation or rage rose from the crowd.

All felt the solemnity of the moment, and the faces of the believers were grave and expectant. Some of the faithful, recalling that at the death of the Savior the earth opened and the dead rose from their graves, wondered now whether or not similar portents would appear, so that the death of the Apostle would not be forgotten for ages to come. Others said to themselves, *Perhaps the Lord will choose the hour of Peter's death to descend upon the earth as He promised and judge the world.* With this possibility in mind, they committed themselves to the mercy of the Savior.

And the quietness continued. The hills appeared to be resting and basking in the sun. At length, the procession stopped between the Circus and the Vatican Hill. Some of the soldiers began now to dig a hole; others placed the cross and the hammers and nails upon the earth, waiting till all the preparations should be finished. The crowd, hushed and solemn, fell upon their knees.

The Apostle, his head glorified by the sun, turned for the last time towards the city. Far away below them, the gleaming Tiber could be seen; beyond was the Campus Martius; higher yet was the mausoleum of Augustus; below, the great baths that Nero had just begun to build; still lower, Pompey's theater; and beyond these, partly visible and partly screened by other buildings, were the Septa Julia, a multitude of porticoes, temples, columns, great edifices; and finally, far away in the distance, were the hills studded with houses whose roofs faded away in the blue haze. This was an abode of crime, but also of power; of madness, but also of order. It had become the center of the world, and the world's oppressor, too—yet at the same time its laws and its peace seemed all-powerful, invincible, eternal.

Peter, surrounded by the soldiers, gazed over this scene as a ruler or king looks upon his dominions, and thus he addressed it: "You are redeemed and mine!" And no one present—not merely among the soldiers digging the pit in which the cross was to be planted, but even among the faithful—could divine that the real ruler of that city stood among them, that Caesars would pass away, that waves of barbarians would come and go, that ages would vanish, but that this old man would hold there uninterrupted sway.

The sun sank farther towards Ostia and became large and red. The entire western sky had begun to glow with intense brightness. Then the soldiers approached Peter to strip him of his garments.

But he, who'd been bowed in prayer, now suddenly stood erect and stretched forth his right hand. The executioners stopped as if intimidated by his action. The faithful scarcely dared to breathe, thinking that he desired to speak. Unbroken silence prevailed.

But he, standing on an elevated spot, with his right hand extended, made the sign of the cross, blessing in the hour of his death *"urbi et orbi!"*[2]

——— ——— ———

On that same beautiful evening, another detachment of soldiers led Paul of Tarsus along the Via Ostia towards a place called Aquae Salviae. He also was followed by a band of the faithful whom he'd converted. Whenever he recognized a friend, he stopped and talked with him, for the Praetorians treated him with greater consideration because he was a Roman citizen.

Beyond the Porta Tergemina, he met Plautilla, the daughter of the prefect Flavius Sabinus, and noticing that her youthful face was wet with tears, he said, "Plautilla, daughter of eternal salvation, depart in peace. Only lend me your veil to cover my eyes as I go to the Lord." Taking the veil, he went on with a face as full of joy as that of a laborer returning home after a day's toil.

His thoughts, like those of Peter, were as calm and serene as the evening sky. He gazed in thoughtful contemplation over the plain that extended before him, and upon the Alban Hills, bathed in light. He recalled his journey, his pains and labors, the trials he'd overcome, the churches he'd founded, in all lands and beyond all seas, and he felt he'd earned his rest, that he'd finished his work. He was convicted that this time the seed he'd sown wouldn't be blown away by the wind of malice. He was leaving this life with the certainty that the conflict against the world, which the spreading of the truth had occasioned, would result in its victory, and an immense peace filled his soul.

The road to the place of execution was long, and thus after a time the

---

2 "The city and the world!"

shades of evening began to fall. The mountains became purple and were gradually veiled in shadows. Flocks wended their way homeward. Here and there, groups of slaves walked along with their tools upon their shoulders. Children playing in front of houses on the road looked with curiosity at the procession. On that evening the balmy air seemed filled with peace and harmony, which, as it were, rose from the earth and floated heavenward. And Paul felt this, and his heart was filled with joy at the thought that to this harmony of the earth he'd added a note that hadn't existed before, but without which the whole earth was like sounding brass or a tinkling cymbal.

He remembered how he'd taught people to love—how he'd told them that though they should give all they possessed to the poor, and though they learned all languages, all mysteries, and all sciences, they would be nothing without love, which is kind and patient, which does not return evil, does not crave honor, suffers all things, believes all things, hopes all things, and endures to the end.

His whole life had been spent in teaching people this truth. And now he said to himself, *What power can equal it? What power can conquer it? Can Caesar suppress it, though he had twice as many legions, twice as many cities and seas and lands and nations?*

And like a conqueror, he moved on to his reward.

The procession finally left the main road and turned eastward along the narrow path leading to the Aquac Salviae. The red sun was now lying low on the heather. The centurion halted the soldiers at the fountain, for the time had come.

Paul placed Plautilla's veil over his arm, intending to cover his eyes with it, and for the last time he raised those eyes, filled with indescribable peace, towards the eternal light of the evening and prayed.

Yes, the hour had come; but now he saw before him a great road of light ascending to heaven, and in his soul he repeated the words that he'd written, now in the consciousness of duty done and of the end at hand: *I have fought the good fight; I have finished my course; I have kept the faith; henceforth there is laid up for me a crown of righteousness.*

Chapter LXXII

In Rome madness still reigned, so that the world-conquering city seemed ready at last to tear itself to pieces for want of leadership. Even before the last of the Apostles had died, there came the conspiracy of Piso and after that, such a merciless decapitation of the most prominent heads in Rome that even those who looked upon Nero as a god began to perceive him as a god of destruction. Mourning fell upon the city, and terror reigned in its houses and in all hearts. Yet the porticoes were decorated with ivy and flowers because it wasn't permitted to show sorrow for the dead. When the people awoke each morning, their first concern had to do with whose turn would come next. The retinue of ghosts following Caesar increased every day.

Piso paid with his head for his conspiracy; after him a like fate befell Seneca, Lucan, Fenius Rufus, Plautius Lateranus, Flavius Scevinus, Afranius, Quinetianus, Tullius Senecio (the dissolute companion of Caesar's madness); Proculus, Araricus, and Tugurinus; Gratus, Silanus, Proximus, Subrius, Flavius (once entirely devoted to Nero), and Sulpicius Asper. Some perished on account of their villainy, some due to fear, some on account of their opulence, some because of their courage. Caesar, terrified by the number of conspirators, covered the walls with Praetorians and held the city as if in a state of siege, every day sending out centurions bearing decrees of death to houses under suspicion. The condemned humiliated themselves in cringing letters filled with flattery, thanking him for his sentences and bequeathing to him a part of their fortunes in a bid to salvage at least something for their children. It seemed at last that Caesar was overstepping all bounds to discover to what depths the people had degenerated and how long they would suffer his bloody rule.

After the conspirators were put to death, their relatives, friends, and even mere acquaintances, suffered the same fate. Dwellers in the magnificent palaces constructed after the conflagration, when they went out on the street, were sure to see a whole succession of funerals. Pompeius, Cornelius,

Martialis, Flavius Nepos, and Statius Domitius died because they were accused of not loving Caesar enough; Novius Priscus, because he was a friend of Seneca; Rufius Crispus was deprived of the right of fire and water because he was the former husband of Poppaea. The great Thrasea lost his life simply because he was virtuous rather than corrupt. Many were put to death on account of their noble descent. Even Poppaea fell victim to the fury of Caesar.[1]

The Senate groveled before the terrible potentate, erected temples in his honor, made votive offerings on behalf of his voice, placed wreaths upon his statues, and appointed priests for him as though he were indeed divine. Senators, in fear and trembling, ascended the Palatine to magnify the song of the Periodonices and to go mad with him amid orgies of naked bodies, wine, and flowers.

But meanwhile, in the field soaked in the blood and tears of the martyrs, the seed that Peter had sown silently grew, ever stronger and stronger.

---

1 In a fit of rage, Nero kicked her so viciously that she died.

Chapter LXXIII

VINITIUS TO PETRONIUS:

We're kept well informed, *carissime*, of what's going on in Rome, and what we don't know we learn from your letters. When a stone is cast in the water, the waves go farther and farther in a widening circle, and so a wave of madness has reached even here from the Palatine. Carinas, sent by Caesar into Greece, stopped here on his way. On his march, he plundered cities and temples to refill the empty treasury. From the sweat and tears of the people will be built the Domus Aurea[1] in Rome. It's possible that the world has never before seen such a house, but neither has it seen such injustice. You know Carinas—Chilo was like him until he redeemed his life with death—but his men haven't come yet to towns lying in our immediate vicinity, for the reason, perhaps, that they have neither temples nor treasures.

You asked whether or not we were out of danger. I answer that for now we are "out of mind," and let that suffice for an answer. At this moment, from the portico under which I write these words, I see our peaceful bay, and on it Ursus in a boat, letting down a net into the clear water. My wife sits beside me, spinning red wool, and in the gardens, under the shade of almond trees, our slaves are singing. What peace and quiet, my *carissime!* What a contrast to our old-time fear and suffering! But it's not the Parcaea,[2] as you

---

1 The Golden House.
2 Fates.

asserted, but Christ, our Lord and our God, who blesses us. We're not strangers to tears and to sorrow, for our religion teaches us to grieve over the afflictions of others, but these tears hold within them a consolation unknown to you, for when our lives are ended, we shall find again the beloved ones who are dying or have already died for the truth of God. Peter and Paul aren't dead to us, but are merely reborn into glory. We see them with our souls, and though our bodily eyes may weep, yet our hearts rejoice with their joy. Oh yes, *carissime*, we're happy with a happiness that can know no end, since death, which for you is the end of everything, is for us only a passage to greater peace, greater love, and greater joy.

So the days and the months pass here in perfect peace. Our servants and slaves believe as we do in Christ, and in Christ's gospel of love, so we all love one another. Often, when the sun is setting or when the moon glistens on the water, Lygia and I talk about the past, which today seems but a dream to us. But when I remember how near was that beloved head, which now I hold on my breast, to torture and death, I glorify God with my whole soul, for He alone could have rescued her from the arena and returned her into my arms. Oh, Petronius! You've seen what comfort and fortitude that religion can give in the midst of afflictions, what courage in the face of death. Now come and witness the joy it can give in everyday life. The world has not hitherto known a God whom it could love, consequently people did not love one another, and from that arose all manner of afflictions. For just as light proceeds from the sun, so does happiness proceed from love.

Neither lawgivers nor philosophers have known this truth; it had no existence in Greece or in Rome— by Rome, I mean the whole world. The dry, cold philosophy of the Stoics, which appeals to so many who'd like to be virtuous, does indeed temper the heart as steel is tempered, but it makes them indifferent rather than better.

But why do I write this to you who are more learned and more clever than I? You've known Paul of Tarsus and have spoken with him more than once; thus you know better than I if, in comparison to the truth that he taught, all the teachings of your philosophers and rhetoricians are not a vain and empty jingle of words without meaning. You may recall the question he asked you: 'If Caesar were a Christian, would you not all feel safer, more secure in your possessions, freer from alarm, and more certain of the morrow?'

You have told me that our creed was an enemy of life. I tell you now that if from the beginning to the end of this letter I simply repeated, "I'm happy," I still could not have sufficiently expressed that happiness to you. You may report that my happiness is Lygia. Yes! There's truth in that, *carissime*, but that's because I love her immortal soul, and each of us loves the other in Christ. Such love can know neither separation, nor disloyalty, nor alteration, nor age—nor death. Even after youth and beauty have passed away, and our bodies wither, and death touches us, love will remain, for the spirit remains.

Before my eyes were opened to the light, I would have burned down my own home for the sake of Lygia; but now I admit that I didn't know what love was until Christ showed me the way. He's a fountain of happiness and peace. It's not I who say this, but truth itself. Contrast your luxuries, shadowed by fear and dread; your delights, but yet uncertain of the morrow; and your orgies, like funeral feasts—compare all these with the lives led by Christians, and an answer must at once be forthcoming. But for a better comparison, come to our hills, fragrant with thyme; come to our olive groves and ivy-covered shores. A peace such as you've never experienced awaits you here, as do the hearts that love you sincerely. You, having a noble soul and a good one, should be happy here. Your quick mind will be able to distinguish the truth and, seeing it, will learn to love it. Men like Caesar and Tigellinus may hate it, but none can be indifferent to it. Oh, Petronius! Lygia and I find solace in the thought that you'll soon be with us. Be well, be happy, and come to us.

Petronius received Vinitius's letter in Cumae, where he'd gone with other Augustinians in the company of Caesar. His struggle of many years against Tigellinus was nearing its end. Petronius knew already that he must be beaten in the end, and he understood the reasons. Caesar was now lost to him, for Nero daily slipped lower, down, down through comedy, buffoonery, charioteering into the muck of sick, foul, and bestial dissipation. Given that state of affairs, the *arbiter elegantiarum* must of necessity become nothing more than a nuisance to him. Even in the silence of Petronius, Nero now read disapproval; when the arbiter praised, Nero saw only ridicule. The brilliant patrician offended his self-love and awakened his jealousy. His riches and his magnificent works of art had become objects of desire both to the sovereign and to his all-powerful minister. Petronius had been spared with a view to this journey to Achaia, in which his taste and his knowledge of everything Greek might prove useful, but Tigellinus never let up for an instant in his long campaign of undermining the ground upon which Petronius walked. It wasn't hard, in Nero's current condition, to persuade Nero that Carinas quite probably might equal, or even surpass, Petronius in taste and knowledge—and in terms of which of the two would be best at arranging games, receptions, and triumphs in Achaia, it was no contest. From that moment, the doom of Petronius was certain. But Caesar hadn't the courage to send him his sentence in Rome. Both Caesar and Tigellinus knew that this indolent aesthete, who turned day into night and was interested only in art and banquets and luxury, had nevertheless shown great power of work and energy when he was proconsul in Bithynia and afterwards when consul in the capital. He commanded great respect in Rome, where he possessed not only the love of the people, but also of the Praetorians. None of Caesar's advisors could foresee exactly how Petronius would act, so it seemed wiser to lure him out of the city and to strike at him in a province.

Consequently, Petronius received an invitation to go with other Augustinians to Cumae. Though he suspected treachery, he went along, in order, perhaps, not to display open resistance and to show once more to Caesar and to the Augustinians a face joyful and free from care and so gain one last victory, before death, over Tigellinus.

Meanwhile, Tigellinus accused him of friendship with Senator Scevinus, who'd been the soul and organizer of Piso's conspiracy. Servants of Petronius remaining in Rome were imprisoned, and his villa was surrounded by the Praetorian Guard.

When Petronius received this news, he showed no alarm or concern but, with a smile, said to such Augustinians as he was entertaining in his own splendid villa in Cumae, "Ahenobarbus doesn't like direct questions, so you'll see how confused he'll be when I ask him whether it was he who gave the command to imprison my 'family' in the capital."

Then he invited them to a feast "before the longer journey" and had just made preparations for it when the letter from Vinitius arrived.

On studying it, Petronius grew somewhat thoughtful, but in a little while his face resumed its usual serenity. During that evening, he answered as follows:

> I rejoice at your happiness and admire your good heart, for I hadn't thought that two lovers could remember a third person at such a distance. Not only have you not forgotten me, but you also wish to persuade me to go to Sicily so that you may share with me your bread and your Christ who, as you write, has brought you so much happiness.
>
> If this be true, then honor Him. I think, however, *carissime*, that Ursus had something to do with saving Lygia, and the Roman people had a little to do with it, but since you're convinced that Christ accomplished it, I won't contradict you. Were Caesar a different man, I might conclude that they'd ceased to persecute her out of consideration for your kinship with him through the granddaughter who, at the proper time, was given by Tiberius to one of the Vinitiuses. Yes! Spare no offering to your Christ! Prometheus also sacrificed himself for man, but—alas!—apparently Prometheus is merely an invention of poets, while trustworthy people have told me that they saw Christ with their own eyes.

Together with you, I agree that He's the most worthy of all gods.

I remember well the question of Paul of Tarsus and agree that if Ahenobarbus lived in accordance with the teachings of Christ, I might find time to visit you in Sicily. Then, in the shade of trees and near fountains, we could talk about all the gods and all the truths discussed by all the Greek philosophers at any time. Today, however, I must give you a brief answer.

Two philosophers only do I respect; the name of one is Pyrrho, and Anacreon is the other. The rest I'll sell you cheap, together with the whole school of Greek Stoics, as well as our own. Truth abides somewhere so high that the gods themselves cannot see it from the heights of Olympus. To you, *carissime*, your Olympus seems still higher, and, standing upon it, you call down to me, "Ascend, and you'll see such sights as you hadn't dreamed of before!" Perhaps. But I answer, "I have no feet for the journey!" And when you reach the end of this letter, you will acknowledge, I think, that I'm right.

No, happy husband of the Princess Aurora! Your religion isn't for me. Am I to love the Bithynians who carry my litter, the Egyptians who heat my bath? Am I to love Ahenobarbus and Tigellinus? By the white knees of the Graces, I swear to you that even if I desired to love them, I couldn't! There are in Rome at least one hundred thousand persons who have crooked shoulders or big knees or thin thighs or staring eyes or heads too large for them. Do you command me to love them also? Where can I find that love if I don't feel it in my heart? And if your God wishes me to love such people, why in His omnipotence did He not endow them with, for example, the shapes of Niobe's children, whom you've seen on the Palatine? Whoever loves beauty can't, for that very reason, love ugliness. One may disbelieve in our gods, but it's possible to love them as did Phidias, Praxiteles, Myron, Scopias, and Lysias.

Even should I desire to go where you'd like to lead me, I couldn't. You believe, like Paul of Tarsus, that sometime beyond the Styx, in some Elysian fields, you'll see your Christ. Well! Let Him tell you whether He'd accept me with my gems, my goblet, my editions of Sozius, and my golden-haired Eunice. I smile at the thought of this, my friend, for even Paul of Tarsus declared to me that, for Christ's sake, it was necessary to renounce rose garlands, feasts, and luxuries. True, he promised me other kinds of happiness, but I replied that I was too old for new joys, that roses will always delight my eyes, and that the odor of violets will always be sweeter to me than the stench of some dirty neighbor from the Suburra.

These are reasons why your happiness cannot be mine. But there's one more reason, which I've saved for last: Thanatos summons me. For you, life is just beginning to dawn; but for me, the sun is already set, and twilight is descending upon my head. In other words, I must die, *carissime!*

It's not worthwhile to speak at length about this. It had to end this way. You, who know Ahenobarbus, will understand what I'm trying to say. Tigellinus has conquered, or rather, my victories reached their end. I've lived as I pleased and will die as I please.

Don't take this to heart. No god has promised me immortality; therefore, I won't be taken by surprise. But you're mistaken, Vinitius, in affirming that only your God teaches men to die peacefully. No. Our world knew, before you were born, that when the last cup is drained it's time to go, to rest, and it knows yet how to do this serenely. Plato declares that "virtue is music, and the life of a sage is harmony." If this is true, I'll die as I've lived: virtuously.

I'd like to say farewell to your divine wife with the words I once spoke to her in the house of Aulus: "Many persons and nations have I seen, but never your equal."

So if the soul is something more than what Pyrrho thinks, mine will fly to you on the way to the edge of the ocean and will alight at your house in the form of a butterfly or, as the Egyptians believe, in the form of a sparrow hawk. Otherwise, I cannot come.

Meantime, may Sicily take the place for you of the gardens of Hesperides; may the goddesses of the fields, woods, and fountains scatter flowers on your path; and may white doves build their nests in every acanthus of your house.

Chapter LXXIV

Petronius was not mistaken. Two days later young Nerva, who'd always been friendly and devoted to him, sent his freedman to Cumae with the news of all that had happened at Caesar's court.[1]

The death of Petronius had already been determined. On the morning of the following day, a centurion was to be sent to him with the command to remain in Cumae and wait there for further instructions; another messenger was to bring the death sentence a few days later.

Petronius received the news brought by the freedman with unruffled calmness and said, "You'll take to your master one of my vases that will be handed to you before you leave. Say to him in my name that I thank him with all my heart, for now I'll be able to anticipate the sentence."

And suddenly he began to laugh like a man who's just conceptualized a brilliant idea and enjoys beforehand its fulfillment.

That same evening, his slaves ran about inviting almost all of the Augustinians, with their ladies, to come to a banquet at the beautiful villa of the *arbiter elegantiarum*.

Petronius spent the afternoon hours writing in his library, then he took a bath, after which he commanded the *vestiplicae*[2] to dress him. Splendid and adorned like a god, he went to the *triclinium* to cast a connoisseur's eye upon the preparations and then to the gardens, where youths and Greek maidens from the islands were weaving garlands of roses for the banquet.

Not the slightest anxiety was visible on his face. The servants knew only that the banquet would be something out of the ordinary, for he'd ordered unusual rewards to be given those with whom he was satisfied and some light blows to those whose work shouldn't please him or to those who'd previously deserved blame or punishment. He directed that the

---

1 Apparently the court had moved on to a town in proximity to Cumae.
2 Robe dressers/folders.

kithara players and the singers should be generously rewarded ahead of time. Finally, seating himself in the garden beneath a beech, through whose foliage the sun made bright spots upon the ground, he called Eunice to his side. Gently touching her lovely forehead, he gazed at her with the admiration of a connoisseur looking upon a statue fresh from the chisel of a master.

"Eunice," he questioned, "do you know that for a long time you haven't been a slave?"

She raised her calm, heavenly blue eyes to his and shook her head in denial. "I'm yours always, master."

"But perhaps you don't know," continued Petronius, "that this villa and those slaves weaving garlands and all that's here—the fields and the herds—belong to you from this day on."

Eunice, when she heard this, drew away from him quickly and asked in a voice filled with sudden apprehension, "Why do you tell me this, master?" Then she approached him again and stared at him with eyes that missed nothing. After a while, her face grew as pale as linen.

He still smiled, and said only one word—"Yes."

There was a moment of silence, broken only by the rustling of the wind in the leaves of the beech trees. Petronius might almost have imagined that he had in front of him a statue cut from white marble.

"Eunice," he said, "I wish to die calmly and peacefully."

And the maiden, looking at him with a heartbroken smile, whispered, "Master, I obey you."

In the evening, the guests arrived in large numbers. They'd been at many of Petronius's banquets and knew that, in comparison, even Caesar's feasts seemed dull and barbarous. To no one did it occur that this might be Petronius's last symposium. Many knew well that the clouds of Caesar's displeasure hung over the *arbiter elegantiarum,* but this had happened so many times, and so many times had Petronius known how to disperse the clouds with a clever word or a daring act, that no one actually believed any grave danger threatened him now. His joyful face and customary carefree smile confirmed that assumption. The beautiful Eunice, to whom he'd expressed his wish to die in peace and to whom his every word was as the word of an oracle, preserved perfect serenity of expression, and there was in her eyes a wondrous radiance, which might have been taken for inner joy. At the door of the *triclinium,* youths with hair in golden nets put wreaths of roses on the heads of the guests, warning them, as the custom was, to step over the threshold right foot first. A slight fragrance of violets pervaded the hall; lights burned in colored Alexandrian glass. Beside the couches stood Greek maidens, whose office it was to anoint the feet of the guests with perfumes. The walls were lined with kithara players and Athenian singers, waiting for a signal from their leader.

The table service gleamed with splendor, but that luxury didn't offend or oppress; it seemed so natural, so appropriate for the occasion. Joy and freedom from restraint spread through the hall with the fragrance of violets. The guests as they entered felt that neither compulsion nor menace was hanging over them, as was the case in Caesar's palace, where insufficient or unsatisfactory praise for a song or poem might be paid for with one's life. The sight of the lamps, the goblets entwined with ivy, the wine cooling on banks of snow, and the exquisite dishes cheered the hearts of the guests. The conversation became as lively and vibrant as the buzzing of a swarm of bees over an apple tree in blossom. Now and then it was interrupted by an outburst of joyous laughter, a murmur of praise, or too loud a kiss imprinted upon a bare white shoulder.

As they drank their wine, the guests spilled from their goblets a few drops to the immortal gods, to gain for their host both their protection and their favor. It mattered not that many of them didn't believe in the gods; custom and convention commanded it. Petronius, reclining beside Eunice, talked of Rome, of the latest divorces, of love affairs, of the races, of Spiculus—who'd recently earned fame in the arena—and of the newest books that had appeared at the shops of Atractus and Sozius. When he spilled some wine, he explained that he spilled it only in honor of the Lady of Cyprus, the oldest and greatest among all the gods, the only immortal one, enduring from the beginning and taking precedence over all.

His conversation was like a sunbeam that lights up every new object, or like a summer breeze that rustles the flowers in the garden. At last he nodded as a signal to the leader of the music; the soft sounds from the kitharas were heard, accompanied by fresh young voices. Then maidens from Cos, the birthplace of Eunice, danced, their rosy young bodies shining through translucent robes. Finally, an Egyptian soothsayer began to tell the future of each guest, based on the movements of rainbow-colored fish in a crystal vessel.

When they'd had enough of these amusements, Petronius lifted himself slightly from his Syrian cushion and said carelessly, "Friends, pardon me if I ask a favor from you at this feast. It's this: Will every guest accept from me as a gift the goblet from which he spilled wine in honor of the gods and for my well-being."

The goblets of Petronius glittered with gold and precious stones and the carving of renowned artists; thus, although gift-giving was common in Rome, joy and disbelief filled the hearts of the revelers. Some of them thanked him and praised him loudly; others declared that Jupiter himself had never honored the gods in Olympus with such precious gifts. There were even some who hesitated about accepting them, since these gifts were of such unprecedented value.[3]

Petronius, lifting up a goblet resembling an iridescent rainbow in brilliancy, said, "This is the goblet from which I spilled wine in honor of the Lady of Cyprus. Henceforth, let no lips touch it, and let no other hand pour out wine from it in honor of any other deity."

He cast the precious vessel down upon the floor, which had been strewn with lilac-colored crocuses, and when it shattered into small pieces, he said, in answer to the general astonishment, "My dear friends, be merry and not astonished. Old age and debility are sad comrades for the last years of life, so I will give you a good example and good advice. As you have the power not to wait for old age, you can depart before it comes— as I do."

"What are you planning to do?" cried a number of voices at once.

"I intend to be merry, to drink wine, to hear music, to gaze at these divine forms that you see around me, and then to fall asleep with my head crowned with flowers. I have already taken leave of Caesar, and would you like to hear what I wrote him in parting?"

From beneath the purple cushion he took a letter and read it aloud:

> O Caesar, I know that you anxiously await my coming and that your loyal and friendly heart yearns for me day and night. I know that you're ready to rain gifts upon me, make me the prefect of your Praetorian Guard, and command Tigellinus to become that for which the gods created him—a mule driver in those lands that you inherited after poisoning Domitius.

---

3 These goblets represented perhaps Petronius's greatest treasure, comparable to the fabulous Faberge eggs of the Russian czar.

Pardon me, however, for I swear to you by Hades and by the shades of your mother, your wife, your brother, and Seneca, who are all there, that I cannot come to you. Life is a great treasure, and I've known how to select the most precious gems from that treasure. But in life there are many things I can no longer endure.

Do not suppose, I pray, that I'm offended because you killed your mother, your wife, and your brother, or because you burned down Rome and send to Erebus all the honest men in your empire. No, grandson of Cronus, death is the common doom of humanity, and thus one could expect nothing else from you.

But to lacerate my ears year after year with your singing; to see your fat belly of Domitius whirled around on scrawny legs during a Pyrrhic dance; to listen to your playing, your declamation, your doggerel verses, O wretched poet of the Suburbanus,[4] would be too much for my strength and has aroused in me a wish to die. Rome stuffs its ears to keep from listening to you; the world derides you; I can blush for you no longer, I simply cannot. The howling of Cerberus,[5] *carissime*, though resembling your singing, will be less trying to me; for having never been the friend of Cerberus, I need not be ashamed of his howling.

Farewell, but do not sing; commit murder, but do not write verses; poison, but do not dance; be an incendiary, but do not play the kithara. This is the wish and the last friendly counsel sent to you by the *arbiter elegantiarum.*

The guests were struck dumb with terror. They knew that the loss of the empire would have been a less cruel blow to Nero; they knew also that the man who wrote that letter must die—at the same time, pallid fear seized them for their own sakes, because they'd been present at its reading.

---

4 An estate outside of Rome. We get the word "suburban" from it.
5 The three-headed dog who guards the entrance to Hades.

But Petronius burst into a laugh so genuine and so joyous that it seemed as if the whole matter were merely an innocent joke.

Then he glanced around at his Augustinian companions and said, "Be merry, and cease your fears. No one need boast that he heard this letter read. I myself will boast of it only to Charon, when he ferries me over the river."[6]

He beckoned then to the Greek physician and stretched his arm out to him. The skillful Greek quickly bound it with a golden ribbon and opened the vein at the bend of the elbow. Blood spurted out upon the cushion and onto Eunice, who, supporting the head of Petronius, bent over him and said, "Master, did you think that I would let you leave without me? If the gods promised me immortality, and Caesar were to give me the rule of the whole world, I would follow you still."

Petronius smiled. Raising himself a little, he touched her lips with his and answered, "Come with me." Then he added: "You have truly loved me, my goddess!"

And she stretched out her rosy arm to the physician, and soon her blood began to flow and mingle with his.

He then signaled the leader of the music, and again the voices and kithera players were heard. First they sang "Harmodius," then the song of Anacreon—that song in which the poet complains that having found under the tree the frozen and weeping child of Aphrodite and having brought him in, warmed him back to life, and dried his wings, the ungrateful child returned his kindness by piercing his heart with an arrow. Thus ever since that time, all peace had left the poet.

Petronius and Eunice, reclining against each other, beautiful as two gods, listened as they smiled and grew paler. When the song was ended, Petronius ordered more wine and fresh dishes to be served and commenced a discussion with the guests seated near him about all those pleasant things that are usually mentioned at feasts. Finally, he summoned the Greek to bind up his veins for a moment, explaining that drowsiness was overpowering him, and he wished to yield himself to Hypnos before Thanatos put him to sleep forever.

Indeed, he fell asleep. When he awoke, the head of Eunice was lying upon his breast like a white flower. He gently placed that beloved head on a cushion so that he might look upon her one last time. Then his veins were opened again.

---

6 Over the Styx.

At his signal, the singers began to sing the song of Anacreon again, and the kithara players accompanied it gently so as not to drown the words. Petronius grew paler and paler. When the last sounds died away, he turned once more to the guests.

"Friends, confess that with us perishes—"

But he had not the power to finish; his arm with its last movement embraced Eunice, his head fell on the cushion—and he died.

But the guests, gazing at those two white bodies, like two wondrous statues, well knew that with them had perished all that was left to their world at that time—its poetry and beauty.

Epilogue

At first the revolt of the Gallic legions under the leadership of Vindex didn't seem very serious. Caesar was barely thirty-one years of age; thus no one dared to hope that the world would soon be free from the nightmare he represented. It was remembered that many revolts had occurred during previous reigns without resulting in any change of rule. Thus, in the time of Tiberius, Drusus had crushed the revolt of the Pannonian legions, and Germanicus, that of the legions upon the Rhine. "And who," asked the people, "could possibly succeed Nero, now that all the descendants of the divine Augustus have been put to death?" Others, looking at the colossus, imagined him to be a veritable Hercules and assumed that no known force could possibly break his power. There were even those who, after his departure for Achaea, longed for his return, since Helius and Polythetes, to whom he'd relegated the government of Rome and Italy, governed even more murderously than he did.

Nobody was sure either of life or property. Law ceased to protect. Human dignity and virtue perished. Family bonds existed no longer. Hope had all but disappeared. From Greece came rumors of the unparalleled triumphs of Caesar, of the thousands of garlands he'd won and of the thousands of competitors he'd vanquished. The world seemed to be one vast orgy, bloody and farcical. The perception prevailed that since virtue and human dignity were passé, the time had thus arrived for dancing and music, for debauchery, for blood, and that the future trend of life would be in this direction. Caesar himself, to whom rebellion opened the way for renewed plundering, didn't pay much attention to the rebelling legions and Vindex; in fact, he frequently expressed his delight over the revolt. Neither did he wish to leave Achaea—only when notified by Helius that further delay might result in the loss of his empire did he set out for Neapolis.

There he again played and sang, paying little attention to the seriousness of the reports coming in. Vainly did Tigellinus warn him that former rebellions of the legions had no leader, whereas now there stood at their head a descendant of the ancient kings of Gaul and Aquitania, a tried warrior of great renown.

Nero's answer was, "Here: the Greeks listen to me—they who alone know how to listen and who alone are worthy of my singing," declaring that his first duty was owed to art and glory.

But when he learned that Vindex had proclaimed him to be a wretched artist, he sprang up in rage and at last set out for Rome. The wounds that Petronius had inflicted upon his self-love had been partially healed by his stay in Greece, but now they opened anew, and Nero was determined to seek justice and restitution from the Senate for such unparalleled calumny.

On the road, he came across a bronze statuary group, representing a Gallic warrior vanquished by a Roman knight, and took this as a favorable omen. From that time on, if he bothered to even mention the mutinous legions and Vindex, it was only in jest. His entrance into the city surpassed any comparable event ever known. He drove the very chariot that Augustus had used in his triumph. One arch of the Circus was destroyed in order to open a passage for the procession. The Senate, the knights, and an immense multitude came out to greet him. The walls trembled from shouts of "Hail Augustus!" "Hail Hercules!" "Hail the divine one, the unconquerable one, the Olympian, the Pythian, the immortal!" Behind him were borne the wreaths that he'd worn and tablets inscribed with the names of the cities where he'd triumphed and of the champions he'd defeated.

Nero himself was intoxicated with his triumph and, with deep emotion, asked the Augustinians surrounding him, "What was the triumph of Julius Caesar compared to this?"

The thought that any mortal would dare to raise a hand against such a demigod didn't even enter his head. He felt himself to be truly an Olympian and therefore safe. The enthusiasm and the madness of the crowd stirred up answering madness within him. In fact, on that day of triumph, it seemed that not only Caesar and the city, but also the whole world had gone mad.

The flowers and the piles of garlands hid the abyss that yawned beneath. Yet that very evening the columns and walls of the temples were covered with graffiti denouncing the crimes of Nero, threatening him with coming vengeance, and ridiculing him as an artist. From lip to lip passed the words: "He sang until he awakened the cocks."[1] Alarming news circulated throughout the city and was exaggerated with each retelling. The Augustinians were filled with terror. The Roman people, uncertain what the future might bring, dared not express wishes or hopes, dared not even feel or think.

Meanwhile, Nero lived only in the theater and in music. He *was* interested, however, in some newly invented instruments and a new water organ, of which trials were made on the Palatine. Childishly incapable of thought or action, he imagined that he could avert all danger by promises of spectacles and exhibitions reaching far into the future. Those nearest to him—seeing that instead of providing means and an army, he was exerting himself only to find apt expression for depicting the panic around him—began to lose all confidence in his leadership. Others, however, thought that he was deafening himself and others with his poetic compositions to hide the alarm and disquietude of his soul.

His acts became confused and feverish. Every day thousands of fresh plans passed through his head. At times he sprang up to rush out against the danger, commanding that his kitharas be packed in wagons and that his young slave women be armed as Amazons, saying that he planned to lead his forces to the west. At times he thought that he'd conquer the rebellious legions, not by war, but by song. And he laughed within himself as he conjured up in his imagination the spectacle of the soldiers yielding to his music. They would surround him with streaming eyes. He would sing to them an *epinicium*,[2] after which a golden epoch would begin for him and for Rome. At times he called for blood; at others he declared that Egypt alone would satisfy him. He recalled the soothsayers who had promised him rule over Jerusalem. Or he would be moved to tears by the thought that, as a wandering minstrel, he'd earn his own livelihood and be honored in far-off cities and countries—honored, not as Caesar, the sovereign of the world, but as a poet whose like had never yet been seen in the world.

And so he struggled, fumed, played, sang, changed his plans, changed his quotations, changed his life and that of the whole world into an absurd dream, fantastic and horrible—a mad drama of bombastic expressions, pompous verses, groans, tears, and blood. Meanwhile, the cloud in the

---

1   In Latin this involves a pun upon Gallus, a cock.
2   Hymn of victory.

west was growing larger and darker every day. The measure was exceeded; the insane tragicomedy was nearing its end.

When news came that Galba and all Spain had joined the rebellion, Nero fell into maddened fury. He smashed goblets, overturned the tables at a banquet, and gave orders that neither Helius nor Tigellinus dared to carry out: Murder all the Gauls residing in Rome; let loose the beasts from the vivaria; transfer the capital to Alexandria. Each of these seemed, to his diseased mind, to be sublime and astonishing deeds that could easily be accomplished. But the great days of his power had passed, and even those who shared the responsibility for his former crimes began to look upon him as a madman.

The death of Vindex and the consequent discord that arose in the mutinous legions seemed for a moment to tip the scales in his favor. Already new feasts, new triumphs, and new decrees were intended for Rome. But one night a courier, mounted on a foaming horse, came dashing in from the camp of the Praetorian Guard with the news that within the city itself, the soldiers had raised the banner of revolt and had proclaimed Galba as Caesar.

Nero was asleep when the courier arrived. On waking, he called vainly for the guards who at night watched the doors of his chambers. The palace was already deserted. Slaves were plundering in the remote quarters whatever could be carried away in a hurry. But the sight of Nero frightened them away. He wandered through the empty halls, filling them with wails of terror and despair.

At last his freedmen Phaon, Sporus, and Epaphroditus answered his calls. They urged him to flee, declaring that there wasn't a moment to be lost, but he continued to delude himself. Suppose he arrayed himself in his mourning robes and appealed to the Senate; could the Senate resist his tears and his eloquence? Suppose he used all his oratory, his rhetoric, and his talent as an actor; could anyone in the world resist him? Wouldn't they at least give him the prefecture of Egypt?

Accustomed only to flattering him, his freedmen dared not even now to contradict him. All they could do was warn him that before he could reach the Forum, the mob would tear him to pieces, and they threatened that if he didn't mount his horse at once, they too would desert him.

Phaon offered him a hiding place in his own villa beyond the Porta Nomentana. After a while they mounted upon their horses and, covering Nero's head with a mantle, galloped off towards the edge of the city. The

So passed Nero.

night was waning. The streets were already in motion, and there could be no doubt that change was in the air. Praetorians, sometimes singly and sometimes in detachments, were scattered throughout the city. Not far from the camp, Nero's horse shied suddenly at sight of a corpse. When the mantle slipped from his head, a soldier who happened to be passing recognized the emperor. Confused by the suddenness of the apparition, he could only give a military salute.

On passing the Praetorian camp they overheard thunderous cheers for Galba. Only now did Nero fully realize that the hour of his death was near. Filled with terror and smitten by his conscience, he cried out that he saw in front of him darkness in the form of a cloud—and from that cloud came forth the faces of his mother, wife, and brother. His teeth chattered from fright, but even now his comedian soul found a certain pleasure in the very terror of the moment. To be absolute lord of the earth and lose it all now seemed to him the height of tragedy. True to himself, he continued to play the leading role in it. Feverishly, he coined new quotations, in the passionate hope that those around him would preserve them for posterity. There were moments when he cried out for death and called for Spiculus, the most skilled killer of all the gladiators; there were other moments when he declared, "Mother, wife, brother, call me to death!" Flashes of hope rose in him from time to time—hopes that were vain, deluded, and childish. Though he knew that death was approaching, he still couldn't bring himself to believe it.

Finding the Via Nomentana open, they galloped through and passed by Ostranium, where Peter had taught and baptized. At daybreak they reached Phaon's villa. There the freedman hid from him no longer the fact that it was time to die. Nero commanded them to dig a grave; then he lay down on the ground so that they might take his exact measurement. But at the sight of the earth turned up by the spades, he was filled with mortal terror. His fat face became pale, and clammy drops of sweat, like morning dew, stood out upon his forehead. He began to delay. In a voice at once abject and theatrical, he cried out that his hour had not yet come. Then he began to quote again. Finally, he asked them to burn his body after his death. "What an artist is now perishing!" he declaimed, as if in amazement.

Meanwhile, a messenger arrived for Phaon, announcing that the Senate had already pronounced sentence: The parricide should be punished according to ancient custom.

"What's the ancient custom?" inquired Nero with whitened lips.

"They'll place your neck in a fork, flog you to death, and hurl your corpse into the Tiber," replied Epaphroditus curtly.

Nero bared his breast.

"It's time, then," he said, looking upward at the sky; and he repeated: "What an artist is now perishing!"

The clatter of horses' hooves was heard. It was the centurion, coming with his soldiers for the head of Ahenobarbus.

"Hurry!" cried the freedmen.

Nero placed the knife to his neck, but he only pricked himself with a timid hand. It was clear that he would never have the courage to drive in the blade. Suddenly Epaphroditus grasped Nero's hand, pushed hard, and the blade slid in to the hilt. Nero's eyes turned in his head, horrible, immense, terrified.

"I bring you life!" shouted the centurion as he galloped into their presence.

"Too late," answered Nero in a hoarse voice. A moment later he added, "This is faithfulness for you!"

Death came quickly. Blood from his huge neck spurted in a thick stream upon the flowers of the garden, his feet kicked the ground, and he died.

On the morrow, the faithful Acte wrapped his body in costly stuffs and burned it on a funeral pyre drenched with perfumes.

— — —

And so passed Nero, as passes a whirlwind, a storm, a fire, a war, or a plague. But even now the basilica of Peter rules over the city and the world from the heights of the Vatican.

Near the ancient Porta Capena stands to this day a little chapel with an almost obliterated inscription: *Quo vadis, Domine?*

Afterword

DISCUSSION WITH PROFESSOR WHEELER

(For Formal School, Home School, and Book Club Discussions)

First of all, permit me to define my perception of the role of the teacher. I believe that the ideal teaching relationship involves the teacher and the student, both looking in the same direction, and both having a sense of wonder. A teacher is *not* an important person dishing out rote learning to an unimportant person. I furthermore do not believe that a Ph.D. automatically brings with it omniscience, despite the way some of us act. In discussions, I tell my students beforehand that my opinions and conclusions are no more valid than theirs, for each of us sees reality from a different perspective.

Now that my role is clear, let's continue. The purpose of the discussion sections of the series is to encourage debate, to dig deeper into the books than would be true without these sections, and to spawn other questions that may build on the ones I begin with. If you take advantage of these sections, you will be gaining just as good an understanding of a book as you would were you actually sitting in one of my classroom circles.

As you read this book, record your thoughts and reactions each day in a journal. Also, an unabridged dictionary is almost essential in completely understanding the text. If your vocabulary is to grow, something else is needed besides the dictionary: vocabulary cards. Take a stack of three-by-five-inch cards, and write the words you don't know on one side and their definitions on the other, with each word used in a sentence. Every time you stumble on words you are unsure of—and I found quite a number myself!—make a card for it. Continually go over these cards; and keep all, except those you never miss, in a card file. You will be amazed at how fast your vocabulary will grow!

The Introduction Must Be Read Before Beginning the Next Section.

— — —

QUESTIONS TO DEEPEN YOUR UNDERSTANDING

PART I
Chapter I

1. Petronius was a real person, and Sienkiewicz fairly accurately describes him as he was. Most critics feel he comes close to running away with the book. Gradually construct a character portrait of him—three-dimensional—with all his strengths and weaknesses. How does Sienkiewicz make him seem real to you? Follow the same procedure with each other major character.

2. Note the argument that took place at Nero's feast, having to do with the question: "Do women have souls?" With that as a starting point, begin to develop a picture of the role of women in Roman society. Start with Petronius's female slaves.

3. Contemporary America is often compared to Rome. Do you feel that's a fair comparison? Begin piecing together a mosaic of Roman life and morals during the reign of Nero. From a sexual standpoint, how does it compare to society today as you know it?

4. What was the Romans' general attitude towards their many gods? Did they take them seriously?

5. Sienkiewicz often writes about wealthy individuals and connoisseurs of art, whose love of beauty and aesthetics takes the place of worship of a Higher Power. There's much of that in *Quo Vadis*. Keep studying it. Have you known people like that?

6. Petronius submits that the Romans had lost the ability to differentiate between that which was moral and that which was not. Do you think he was right? Give reasons.

7. Why is it that the boss's jokes are always funny, even when they're not? Are we really that insincere where highly placed people are concerned? And what about the other side: One day your jokes are funny, your poetry great, your music moving—then the day after you retire, no one cares anymore. What lessons can this teach us?

8. Notice Vinitius's initial love for Lygia. Or would you classify it as lust? What makes him love her? Does he really care whether or not she loves him? Is that sort of thing typical among people you know? Discuss.

9. What's the attitude of Petronius and Vinitius towards virtuous women? Reactions?

10. Tigellinus is another historical figure. Begin building a dossier on him. He'll play a major role in this book.

11. Rome didn't have the media we have today, but it had activities that came close. Have you noticed any yet? Which ones?

12. Pay particular attention to the slave Eunice. What are your first impressions of her?

Chapter II

13. Even today in hot Latin countries, the siesta is part of the fabric of life. Do you think it would be a good thing to have in this culture? Why?

14. Why is it, do you think, that great love leaves us speechless? Have you ever experienced such a thing?

15. Are you familiar with the sign of the fish? Discuss what it is and how you learned about it.

16. How does Sienkiewicz make you feel like you're in ancient Rome? What devices does he use to accomplish that? Have you read other books about Rome that help you here? If so, which ones? Compare them.

17. What had Petronius learned about popularity in Rome? About his own personal popularity? Was he apprehensive about it? Why?

18. What surprises Petronius most about the house of Aulus? What impresses him most?

19. Why and how does Pomponia seem unique to Petronius?

20. What impresses Petronius most about Lygia? Why?

21. How effective is Vinitius in his courtship of Lygia? How does she respond initially? Continue constructing character portraits of Lygia, Vinitius, Petronius, Aulus, and Pomponia (flesh them out, and don't forget to factor in such things as how they play and personality quirks).

Chapter III

22. Note how astutely Petronius goes about bringing Vinitius into line, how he erodes the credibility of Plautius and Pomponia in Vinitius's eyes. What reasoning does he use?

23. Note that Vinitius's love is almost totally self-centered. He yearns for Lygia, but he seemingly cares little if she deeply loves him; neither does he at any time ask himself what he can do to make her happy. He threatens to murder Aulus and Pomponia just so he can run off with Lygia. Do you see any indication that he even considers whether such a crime would cause Lygia *not* to love him? Or is he so self-centered he doesn't even care?

    Note, too, that Vinitius is ready to marry Lygia—if he can't get her any other way. Petronius, proud Roman that he is, doesn't consider even princesses worthy of Vinitius or himself, if that royal lineage isn't Roman. Thus Petronius determines to find a way to deliver Lygia to his nephew without having to go through the bother of a marriage. What are your reactions to this?

24. Chrysothemis is a key prototype in the book: Petronius once loved her, but now is merely amused by her obvious unfaithfulness to

him. But the basic assumption here is: *In Rome, everybody is unfaithful.* This is why Pomponia and Aulus stand out. Where along this spectrum of behavior is Lygia going to fall? What do you think?

Chapter IV

25. What would it be like to fear the kind of knock on the door that the Praetorian Guard represented? Describe how it makes you appreciate living in a free nation.

26. The way to really appreciate or love someone is to realize you're in danger of losing that person. How is this fact of life reflected in the words and acts of Aulus and Pomponia in this chapter?

27. Study carefully Pomponia's counsel to Lygia regarding the temptations that will assail her in Caesar's palace. Do you agree? What, if anything, would you have added or deleted?

28. There's much in these chapters about the dangers inherent in marriages where one is a Christian and the other is not. What points, in this respect, is Sienkiewicz making? How valid are they?

Chapter V

29. The study of history adds spice to all of life. At the minimum, you should read the appropriate entries in the encyclopedia (a full-sized one); if possible, other sourcebooks and biographies on this period ought to be studied as well. What do you think reading such supplementary material would add to your enjoyment of *Quo Vadis?*

30. What's the effect of stirring real historical figures into a novel? What new dimensions result? Keep track of the real historical figures in the book.

31. There appears to be a divinely ordained rule incorporated into the very fiber of our universe: What goes around, comes around. Notice how Nero treats people; now watch to see if things go full circle by the end of the book. Have you noticed such cause and effect fallout in the lives of others? Discuss.

32. It's said of Petronius that he's lost the ability to differentiate between right and wrong. Would you agree? What gives you that impression? What are the effects of such a loss?

33. Do you think many people today would prefer death to disgrace? Or do you think our tell-all talk shows have conditioned us to prefer notoriety to honor, celebrity to integrity? Discuss.

Chapter VI

34. Vinitius so far is depicted as the prisoner of his passions, acting on caprice, without first finding out what the truth of the matter might be. Have you known such firebrands? What kind of a price have they paid for such reckless actions and words?

35. How does Petronius use psychology against Nero? Obviously, he learned much from Socrates and Plato. Have you ever consciously used such an approach to gain a desired end? Discuss.

36. Strange, isn't it, that even an acknowledged murderer such as Nero should find it necessary to justify his evil acts to those he rules over. Comment on Petronius's statement: "What a strange involuntary homage vice pays to virtue!" What do you think he meant by it?

Chapter VII

37. Acte not only was a real historic figure, she plays a central role in this book. Study her carefully. What's her effect on Lygia? How might things have gone for Lygia had not Acte been there to counsel her?

    Do you feel Acte was right when she declared that she was the only person who truly loved Nero? Why do you think she loved him still?

38. Chronicle Lygia's response to the evening and to Vinitius, from beginning to end. How do her responses change? What causes them to? Note that Sienkiewicz begins with abstract description, then circles back with actual actions and words. What's the result?

39. What was your reaction to the description of Acte's preparation of Lygia for the banquet? How would preparation for a similar event differ today?

40. Petronius clearly fears that Nero will violate Lygia. What psychological game does he play with Nero to get him off that particular track?

41. Who does Domitius Afer remind you of? Are his concerns valid? Are they still being voiced today?

42. At the end of this chapter, update your character portrait of Vinitius. It's not likely to be a pretty picture, but it's important as a way-station snapshot, to be looked at as a referent later on.

Chapter VIII
43. How heartbreaking to realize that to return to the only home you've ever known would unquestionably result in the death of those you love most! That's what Lygia now realizes. How would you respond to such a situation?

44. Ursus is worthy of a character sketch of his own. He's a person who acts rather than thinks very much; nevertheless, he can be surprising. Is it true that giants are often unexpectedly gentle? Might it be because, if they weren't, they'd leave a long trail of maimed and dead people in their wake?

Chapter IX
45. Lygia, like many other Christians through the centuries, welcomed the thought of suffering for her Lord, just as He'd suffered on her behalf. Have you ever felt that way? Discuss.

46. How does Acte's brief association with Lygia change her? Was Acte more content or less content to stay in the palace now? Why? Why was it difficult for her to understand Lygia's refusal to become Vinitius's concubine?

47. What's your opinion of Poppaea *now?* Give reasons.

48. Note that at no time—even when Atacinus is sent to get her—does Vinitius ask Lygia if she desires to come to his house as a concubine. What does that tell you about him?

Chapter X

49. Do you get the feeling that Petronius no longer feels the same about his uncontrollable nephew? How does he feel about Vinitius's behavior at Nero's feast?

50. One must pity Atacinus and the other slaves. Atacinus was beyond help, but the others must return to a monster. Each chapter we think we have seen the worst of Vinitius, and always the next disabuses us of that conclusion. Can you possibly justify his behavior at the end of this chapter? Discuss.

Chapter XI

51. In this watershed chapter, Sienkiewicz slows the pace so that reflection can finally take place—*especially* in act-first-think-later Vinitius. Study the chapter carefully; then ask yourself, What did the author intend to accomplish in these pages?

52. Had you been in Acte's shoes, how would you have responded to Vinitius's wild and ugly words?

53. What does Vinitius not understand about Pomponia's sad opening words to him? Why wouldn't he?

Chapter XII

54. Notice that Vinitius is still incapable of using his mind effectively in his search for Lygia. Petronius alone knows how to make things happen. Have you ever known people with this kind of gift? Describe them and compare them to Petronius.

55. The story of Eunice is a special one. Continue to develop a portrait of her.

56. Petronius had just that day noticed wrinkles in the corners of

Chrysothemis's eyes. Horrors! She was getting old! Have you noticed this deification of youth in America, in our advertising? Discuss.

Chapter XIII

57. Study Chilo Chilonides carefully, for he's one of the consummate villains in all literature. On the basis of this chapter, construct a character sketch of him, and then build on it as you read. Questions to ask include: Is Chilo totally corrupt, or is there good in him somewhere? Would he sell out his own mother for money? Is nothing in the world sacred to him?

58. Next, approach Chilo from Lygia's vantage point. With Chilo on the trail, her life has just become a lot scarier, for he'll stop at nothing, will tell all the lies he needs to, just to find out how to reel her in. Don't the chills go up and down your spine at the thought that a totally unscrupulous sleuth such as Chilo could be on one's trail?

59. Informer, stool pigeon, rat fink—our dictionary has words for the likes of Chilo, and none of them is nice. Why do you think people like him sell out—even friends—for the money it will bring them? Would money be adequate compensation for ostracism from the community? Discuss.

Chapter XIV

60. Petronius's life was hanging in the balance, but he risked everything on his knowledge of Nero's nature. What were your reactions to his verbal sparring matches with Nero and Tigellinus? How close a call was it?

61. Who's better able to stand up against Chilo, Petronius or Vinitius? Have you ever known anyone like Chilo (with such a gift of getting money out of people)? Compare, if you have.

62. How important to Vinitius was Chilo's news? When the Christians' very lives depended upon each other, how significant to them was Chilo's false profession of Christianity? What might be the price Christians would have to pay down the line? Later on in the book, come back to this and ascertain how close to the mark you were here.

Chapter XV

63. Letters are one of the oldest forms of communication we know. How effective is the use of letters in this chapter? Could the information contained in them have been communicated as effectively in another way? How?

64. Petronius doesn't say too much about Nero and the imperial court, but from what he does say, how would you sum up the gist? What's his opinion of it? What kind of odds does he give himself in terms of his life-or-death battles with Tigellinus for Nero's favor? Why?

65. Vinitius is still obsessed with finding Lygia and has grown ever more dependent upon the unscrupulous Chilo. Do you like Vinitius or Chilo any more than you did before? Why?

Chapter XVI

66. Is Vinitius, in this part of the story, teetering on the edge of insanity? If so, what would be the key contributing factor?

67. How did you react when Chilo so glibly proposed assassinating Glaucus, a man he professed to love? Did you expect Vinitius to agree to this murder so quickly, expressing no compunctions whatsoever?

68. Notice that even in the midst of planning murder, Chilo's number one priority is to get his hands on the thousand sesterces. What does that tell you about the extent to which he's let greed take control of his life?

Chapter XVII

69. Chilo has worked energetically to construct a pious reputation for himself in the Christian community. But evil compounds itself. Once having started on that slippery slope, Chilo could no longer stop—even at murder. After murder, mere lies were easy. Have you noticed this sad truth in real life? Discuss.

70. Chilo is too much of a coward to do the actual killing himself, thus he must find an accomplice, not caring at all that his patsy

will have murder upon his conscience for the rest of his days. In the process, he accuses an innocent man of the very crime (turning traitor) that he's contemplating himself. Interesting, isn't it, that the very frailty gossips revel in talking about in others is the one they secretly have a weakness for. Have you seen this truth in action? Discuss.

71. Testimonials—our society lives on them. Few of us are ever hired without someone who's known and trusted by the hiring person vouching for us. Chilo, recognizing this fact of life, uses such a testimonial from the innocent Quartus to validate his credibility with "Urban," and so sets up a secondhand murder. Does this mean that we should be wary of testimonials? Are there other things we ought to consider? Discuss.

72. Notice Chilo weaves truth and lies together so brilliantly that he can deceive even good people. Which do you personally feel are most dangerous: unadulterated lies or truth mixed with lies? Which would be more difficult to detect? Why?

Chapter XVIII

73. Petronius is clearly concerned that Vinitius has let his obsession with Lygia warp him so that he no longer is a part of the stream of life. Do you feel he has a valid point? In what way?

74. Some critics have accused Sienkiewicz of going too far in portraying Nero as a buffoon; others maintain that, in general, he's correct in his assumptions. Perhaps the truth is somewhere in between. From this vantage point, we laugh and ridicule all those who openly pandered to him. However, were our lives and the lives of all those we loved most at stake, which of us would have volunteered the truth? How about you? How would *you* have responded?

75. Petronius knows it's a mad world, yet he's fascinated by it, and he doesn't know how to get out alive, so he continues his mental juggling act. Do you sometimes feel that way about life? In what ways?

Chapter XIX

76. Notice Chilo's announcement to Vinitius that Christians give women equal status to men. That was revolutionary indeed in that time! Perhaps this is why romance is unique to cultures where Christianity is predominant, for reciprocity of love cannot exist where the partners are unequal, where one is forced to do the other's bidding. Had you ever thought about this aspect of human love between a man and a woman? Discuss.

77. Chilo comforts himself with the thought that Christians wouldn't take revenge on anyone. What about Christians today—would *they* consider revenge if someone had wronged them terribly? Discuss.

78. Why does Chilo consider Christianity to be a rich man's religion? Do you agree with his reasoning? Why?

79. Had Vinitius not kept Chilo's bag of silver as security, do you think Chilo would have returned before departure time? Why? Why do you think Chilo was reluctant to go?

Chapter XX

80. How did the music of the assembled Christians affect Vinitius? How was it different from all other religious music he'd ever heard? He was most affected by its yearning. Do you think that if Vinitius walked into Christian churches today, he'd recognize that same yearning? Why?

81. What changes of emotion and attitude did Vinitius go through in listening to the Apostle Peter speak? What impressed him most? Why?

82. What effect did this chapter have on you? Was it different from reading the same account in Scripture? How? Did this account make you feel that you were *there,* listening to Christ's disciple speak? What methods does Sienkiewicz use to create this response in you?

83. How did Vinitius feel the Apostle compared to priests of other religions he'd known and heard? Compare all dimensions.

84. Why did Vinitius consider the Apostle's message to be revolutionary and almost impossible to practice?

85. What impresses us most about listening to an eyewitness tell a story (as opposed to hearing the story secondhand)? Are Matthew, Mark, Luke, and John's accounts of an eyewitness nature? If so, should we respond to them as we do to Sienkiewicz's? Discuss.

Chapter XXI

86. Notice that Vinitius, while deeply moved by the words of Peter, is determined to abduct Lygia still. Even though he knows Lygia would rather die than become his mistress, he refuses to change course. Can you provide valid reasons for this refusal to court her kindly and lovingly?

87. When Chilo isn't being repulsive, devious, mercenary, vindictive, or evil, he can be awfully funny. What kind of comic relief does he provide in this chapter? Quite likely, had Vinitius not been there for protection, Croto would have slain the whining Chilo.

88. What does Vinitius realize, watching the soldier kneeling before the Apostle, about the size and impact of the Christian faith?

Chapter XXII

89. Once again, impulsiveness and acting without due deliberation wrecks the plans of Vinitius and saves Lygia and Ursus. Do you know others who also possess this fatal flaw? Have they learned how to conquer such self-defeating behavior? Discuss.

90. Chilo is clearly a prisoner of his past; thus he knows it would be dangerous to go to the authorities. He'd fully understand the ancient aphorism: "The wicked flee when no man pursueth." A modern version is this: "A clear conscience is the softest pillow." Have you ever been prisoner to such guilt or known people who were? How was that guilt dealt with?

PART II
Chapter XXIII

91. This is a pivotal chapter. Even Vinitius realizes that he's about to lose Lygia again—this time, in all likelihood, for good. He has no Petronius to think for him now; if he doesn't use his mind instead of emotions this time, he'll regret it the rest of his days. So what does he do? What logic does he bring into play? Do you feel he's sincere? Give reasons.

92. Describe Lygia's feelings through all this. Does she seek revenge or retaliation for the way he's treated her? Why?

93. How does Vinitius respond to the reversal of roles (he helpless, at her mercy)? Does that surprise you? Why?

94. One of the oldest fallacies in history is the tendency for a good woman to assume that if she marries a bad man, reform would come naturally. In real life, is it likely that a bad man would achieve a total change in behavior just because of biological attraction? In *Quo Vadis,* if Vinitius's attraction to Lygia had been unaccompanied by a conversion experience of his own, do you think his change in behavior would have lasted? Give reasons.

Chapter XXIV

95. Chilo is to be feared because he speaks truth only when lies would prove less effective. What can be the impact of a person so unprincipled that he has lost all conception of what right is—or what evil is?

96. In the battle of wits between Chilo and Ursus, who wins? How?

97. Chilo is a master of manipulation and using words as weapons. Study his methodology and how he's able to box Ursus in rhetorical corners. Have you ever known anyone in real life who was manipulative to such a degree? If so, compare the person with Chilo. Which one was the more effective? Why? Is it possible to be manipulative yet remain honest and kind? How?

98. Isn't it funny to listen to Chilo's righteous indignation at Croto? Chilo, the most despicable of rogues himself, feels compelled to ride a white horse, metaphorically speaking. Could that be true of most men and women who permit evil to become dominant in their lives? Discuss.

99. Chilo discovers to his chagrin that it isn't easy to stay true to an assumed belief or identity, for sooner or later, slips will inevitably occur and one's true character will flash through. Have you known such people who lead double lives? How effective were they in either of them? Were they happy? Why or why not?

100. Chilo now faces his worst nightmare: being unmasked as the destroyer of Glaucus's family and as the ruiner and would-be murderer of Glaucus. The Roman code doomed him to death for such acts, and he expected no less from those he'd wronged. But what was the Apostle saying? Chilo couldn't believe his ears. If someone had stolen everything you owned and tried to kill you twice, would you forgive that criminal? Or would you call the police? Are those words of Christ (about how many times we should forgive) perhaps not operative anymore? What do *you* think?

101. Does Vinitius come to his accomplice's rescue? Why? Does his behavior here make sense to you? In what way?

Chapter XXV

102. How different would this world be if both individuals and nations outlawed revenge and retribution? Be specific. Is such a development likely to occur? Why or why not?

103. Note Sienkiewicz's method of revealing truth to Vinitius: having him overhear the Apostle's words from his cot. How effective is this approach to inner understanding? Vinitius is a mighty tough nut to crack; isn't it probable that anything less than a firsthand telling of the crucifixion story might have left him unconvinced?

104. Describe the inner turmoil of Ursus as the Apostle Peter tells the story of Christ's seizure. Would you have felt the same? Why or why not?

105. Have you ever experienced half-waking dreams, such as the ones experienced by Vinitius? Do you feel such dreams can be a way for a Higher Power to communicate with us? What about real dreams?

106. Even today, we find it difficult to separate love from lust, selfless agape love from raging hormonal eros. Far too often it's belatedly discovered that eros was all there was—and inevitably eros alone burns itself out. This great truth Vinitius learns gradually, even though he was thoroughly aware that without the extra dimension that Christianity brings into a marriage, no contemporary Roman marriage was likely to long endure. With this in mind, what's your marriage ideal?

Chapter XXVI

107. Note that, according to Roman law, a slave wasn't even recognized as a human being; the same was sadly true in American history. Why is it, do you think, that human beings find it necessary to treat certain individuals and people as though they are outside the human race and thus can be treated as brutally as inclination dictates? Even supposed Christians buy into this mind-set. How do you think they justify such actions?

108. Once again, Vinitius unleashes on Lygia the full battery of his passions. Helpless as he is, submissive to her care, with every glance filled with ardor, this young patrician, handsome as a Greek god, proved to be more than a handful to the pure maiden. She felt herself to be teetering on the rim of an abyss, felt that an evil force was boring its insidious way into her soul's inner sanctum. What does Lygia realize about herself by the chapter's end? Would you have felt the same had you been in her shoes?

She assumes his changed manner towards her mirrors a changed attitude towards her God; is she right in this assumption? If not, how does she discover her error?

109. How has Vinitius changed? How has he remained the same? Had Lygia given in to him now—even in marriage rather than in concubinage—do you think he'd have become a sincere Christian? Why or why not? Give reasons.

Chapter XXVII

110. Is pity enough, as a basis for marriage? Why or why not?

111. Is it dangerous for a man and a woman to be together day after day? Even if that person isn't the right one, is there a danger that the wrong choice will be made just because of propinquity? Discuss.

112. Can there be much headier feelings than being loved and adored by an attractive member of the opposite sex (loved to the exclusion of all others)? Discuss.

113. Jealousy, the green-eyed monster, has probably destroyed millions of relationships. If Vinitius had a *real* rival for the affections of Lygia, do you feel he could have made peace this quickly?

114. Vinitius cannot see how a world ruled on Christian principles could work. Lest we be too smug on this issue, just picture what would occur if we attempted to operate our own government on this basis (forgiving everyone *everything*, total honesty in all things, no subterfuge, absolute equality, etc.). Would you welcome the opportunity to be the one to set up such a government? Given our sinful tendencies, do you feel you could make it work? Discuss.

115. What lessons had Lygia learned from the marriage of Pomponia Graecina and Aulus? Would those lessons still be applicable to us today? In what way?

116. What realization came to Lygia after her one moment of ecstasy with Vinitius? Do you agree with her decision? Why or why not?

117. Kindness—is it possible that there can exist a more crucial character trait than this? What is ability without it? Eloquence without it? Friendship without it? Love without it? In this respect, what can we learn from the interchange between Crispus and the Apostle Peter?

Chapter XXVIII

118. We now find Vinitius stretched over two worlds: the Christian world of values worth living for and by, and the pleasure-driven society that had satisfied him before. Why do you think he's now restless and unsatisfied?

119. This is a profoundly moving chapter. Had the mouthing of the Christian creed come first, we'd have doubted both Vinitius's sincerity and intentions. But it wasn't so—what came first was totally foreign to his arrogant nature: compassion and kindness! These were impossible to account for, separate from his association with Lygia, the Apostle Peter, and the other Christians. What kind of a turning point do you believe this to be? What kind of a turning point to refrain from rage and retribution when he caught the slaves carousing in his living quarters?

120. What does the long letter to Petronius reveal about changes in the life of Vinitius? What effect has Lygia's running away had on him? What effect the cross she made for him?

121. What does the ordering of a stone monument for Gulo reveal about Vinitius's inner thought processes?

122. What did the Apostle Paul mean when he said, "Love is a stronger hoop than fear"?

Chapter XXIX

123. Even when one *knows* she or he is loved, there remains a strong desire to hear that fact confirmed secondhand. Have you ever noted that in your experience? Discuss.

124. Intriguing, isn't it, how Petronius, considered one of the wisest men of his age, is unable to marshal his reason to provide an acceptable substitute for Christianity? Rather, he's forced to attack it, unsubstantiated by reason or documentation. Is that true even today? How?

But notice how Petronius, failing in one approach, tries others: the lust of the flesh, the lure of travel and strange places, the fear of incurring Caesar's wrath, turning the positive traits of Christians into negatives, and evoking Roman pride. It's a devastating attack from every direction of the compass and accomplishes his objective. Is it not a perfect example of how logic can be used to discredit and destroy almost anything?

Chapter XXX

125. Whatever else one might think of Petronius, the last two chapters reveal how almost impossible to resist are his seductive arguments. Just as individual drops of water form rivers that carve canyons through granite mountains, so the words of Petronius accumulate to smash through anything that stands in their way. Imagine yourself in Vinitius's place: Could *you* have held out against them?

Petronius is true to his philosophy of life: *Live only for pleasure, sensation, and beauty.* And his portrait of the Rome of Nero rings equally true. Note that marriage has almost ceased to exist; sexuality is viewed as a skill, much as is true today as depicted by media and advertisers; divorce is accepted as the norm; and virgins are openly seduced by those in power. After completing this chapter, draw comparisons between the world depicted in these pages and the world we live in today. What are the similarities? What are the differences? What are the implications? What are the alternatives?

126. How is the cult of youth and beauty described in these pages similar to or different from its counterpart today? Is there any room for the aging or unattractive in Nero's court? Discuss.

Chapter XXXI

127. How did you feel when the full realization hit you that Nero had violated the most sacred being of his time? That he'd thereby given his wife the pretext to consort with whomever she chose; thus, her next child might not even be his. Are the events depicted here that far removed from what we see and experience all around us today? In reality, is our age that far removed from Rome's?

Chapter XXXII

128. Notice how quickly Petronius's arguments change when Caesar demands Vinitius's attendance in Antium. Where are all the freedoms he boasted about earlier? Nero's chains may be golden ones, but they are chains nonetheless. In truth, are any of us free from chains of one kind or another? What chains can you think of that fetter us into submission of one kind or another? Do we perhaps even put on chains voluntarily? In what way?

129. Chilo has clearly not changed his spots. In spite of the incredible act of forgiveness by those he'd wronged most, he remains at heart unbelievably slimy and ungrateful. Is such ingratitude even conceivable to you? Discuss.

Do you feel his punishment by Vinitius was justifiable? Was Vinitius justified in beating a man almost to death who had merely followed his orders? Why do you feel Vinitius was so enraged at Chilo? Given Chilo's last words and gesture, do you expect retaliation down the line? Why or why not?

130. Did you expect Vinitius to give in to the great temptation? Why doesn't he? In what respect has he changed since his last abduction attempt?

Chapter XXXIII

131. Compare the scene in this chapter to what it would have been had Vinitius attacked the house and taken Lygia away by force. What would have been lost had he done so? Compare this love to what Vinitius encountered at Caesar's feast. What were the differences?

132. In generations past, even in America, no man could marry a woman without the consent of her father. Today, when permission is asked, it's generally considered a mere formality. Do you feel the old way was better in this respect or today's? Why?

Chapter XXXIV

133. This chapter is an idyll stolen from the oncoming holocaust; as such, it's even more fragile and beautiful, seen against the backdrop

of all that follows. Did you sense the imminence of a storm? What are the roles of the Apostles Peter and Paul in the love story found in the last two chapters?

Chapter XXXV

134. Ah love! What a difference it makes to Vinitius—to know Lygia loves him and that she'll soon be his of her own free will. Belatedly he's learned a great truth: Nothing that we clutch or hold by force is truly ours; only as we let go and eliminate all constraints can anything be truly ours. Had you noted this principle of relationships? Discuss.

135. What surprises Vinitius about Petronius's calm acceptance of his engagement to Lygia? Do you think Eunice's love has mellowed or changed Petronius? In what ways?

136. What does Vinitius's freeing of his older slaves say about his changing values and attitudes? Where do you think he got the idea for doing it?

137. Note Petronius's reaction to Vinitius's having had Chilo flogged: that he should have either rewarded him or killed him. As it was, Chilo would never forget it, and should the wheel of fortune raise him to eminence, he'd be an unforgiving enemy indeed. This is a tough principle, far removed from turning one's other cheek to an enemy. How would you have responded to that observation?

Chapter XXXVI

138. This is a wondrous chapter for all who love history. What a treasure trove of information it has about what it was like to watch the imperial court move from one location to another! What have you learned about the ancient world in these pages?

139. Perhaps saddest of all the procession was the description of beautiful children from all over Greece and Asia Minor, snatched out of their loving parents' arms and brought to Rome as sexual toys for the Augustinians. Child abuse and child pornography have long been with us, as this section proves, but the destruction of a child's

innocence is perhaps the ultimate crime one could commit. What are your thoughts on this matter?

140. First we have the apparently invincible imperial court, more than 12,000 strong, pass by—then the Apostle Peter, who sighs at the daunting task ahead of him. How could he possibly stand up against such might, such evil? And there, passing by him, is Nero, the personification of all that was evil in the world. What were your thoughts as you envisioned those two men looking at each other? What were the implications?

141. Would the Vinitius of old have "lowered" himself to publicly stop his retinue to pay attention to an apparent slave? What could possibly have happened to him?

142. Pay particular attention to the concluding sunset scene in this chapter. Did it strike you as being prophetic? As symbolic? Why do you feel Sienkiewicz incorporated it into the fabric of this chapter conclusion?

Chapter XXXVII
143. Vinitius finds himself on a razor's edge in Antium with Poppaea. In the boat with her, only the quick wit of Petronius saves him and Lygia from disaster. Is Vinitius tempted by Poppaea? Why or why not? Is he afraid of her? As much afraid as Petronius is? Why or why not?

Chapter XXXVIII
144. I once read a true story titled "To See It Fall." It had to do with the largest, and possibly the oldest, tree in the nation—a sequoia in California around the time of the Gold Rush. As the early settlers gaped at it, one of them muttered, "Wonder what it would be like to see it fall?" So they decided to fell it for that one reason, no matter how much work or time it would take. Nero is much like the men in that story: wanting to burn Rome just so he could watch the excitement of it all. Have you ever known anyone to commit a similar action with a similar motive? Tell us the story of it. What eventually happened?

145. For thousands of years transportation and the speed of life essentially stood still. A ruler in ancient China or Egypt who wished to deliver a message quickly could accomplish it only by utilizing swift horses or fast sailing ships. Thousands of years later, man could still travel no faster than a horse or sailing ship. Compare that world to ours, accelerated constantly by our computers, faxes, E-mail, telephones, air travel, and so on. Which world do you prefer? Why?

Chapter XXXIX

146. Vinitius has been unable to sleep: first because he longs for Lygia, and second, because a sixth sense tells him that danger threatens his beloved. Have you ever experienced this sort of thing yourself? A strange conviction that something was wrong or threatening, in either your own life or the life of someone you loved dearly? Or perhaps, a prickly feeling in the scalp accompanied by a conviction that you should take a different route than the one you'd planned? Call it intuition, call it extrasensory perception, call it an impulse delivered by a guardian angel, call it what you will, but don't you agree that such a strange, unexplainable force exists and operates in this world? Discuss.

147. Vinitius is now at peace—at last—because he's committed himself to God, as Lygia did long before. Is it possible to live at peace without such a commitment? What kind of reasons did he give her for the seismic changes he'd made in his spiritual life?

148. What arguments did the Apostle Paul use in trying to convince Petronius to accept Christianity? Were they effective? What was Petronius's response?

149. What do you feel the symbolism was of the concert of roaring lions? Was it an omen? If so, of what?

Chapter XL

150. Lord Acton postulated long ago that "power corrupts, and absolute power corrupts absolutely." Nero had that absolute power, and even though still young—in his twenties—he'd permitted corruption to

seep into every fiber of himself and society; as a result, Rome lost the qualities that made it great in the first place.

One of the liabilities attached to one-person rule, whether in a monarchy or in a corporation, is that there's no one to stop bad decisions before it's too late. Nero is surrounded with yes-men and yes-women; consequently he realizes full well that truth is in short supply. Only Petronius dares to tell him the truth, and even he mixes it with considerable untruth in order to remain popular—and alive—with Nero. Have you noticed the effects of one-person decision-making yourself in everyday life? What are the results you've noticed?

151. One of the most fascinating things about this book has to do with the number of windows it opens to the past. Our language has a heavy Latin base, as you've no doubt already learned. Once you understand what a base Latin term means, you can then expand that knowledge to grandfather in a host of derivative words. Have you enjoyed developing a smattering of Latin knowledge as you've read this story? What do you consider to be the most valuable result of this?

152. Sienkiewicz was fond of inserting omens into his books—omens that served as foreshadowing—so take them seriously as you read on. What omens have you noticed? How much reliance should we place on omens?

Chapter XLI

153. One of the reasons for the worldwide popularity of *Quo Vadis* is the depth and breadth of its characterization. Watch movies made from it and you'll miss the character development, for celluloid portrayals tend to border on the stereotypical—*especially* in portrayals of Nero. It would be easy to oversimplify the bloody ruler and make of him an archetype of evil, but Sienkiewicz avoids this trap and makes him multidimensional, develops his human foibles, arouses our empathy for him. Although the most powerful man in the world, Nero is yet a man, with all the frailties and insecurities flesh

is heir to. He's more than just the buffoon Petronius calls him in private, and much less than the divinity he calls him in public. What do you think? Are you beginning to gain a clearer perception of this complex emperor? Is it becoming more difficult to perceive him one-dimensionally? Discuss.

154. Do you agree with Petronius and Nero in their philosophical discussion about the effects of music? How does music affect you in comparison?

155. How unstable is life! Almost the very moment Vinitius's problems with Lygia and Poppaea are settled, and he feels that he's home free, so to speak, the roof caves in. The burning of Rome will change *everything*—for Vinitius and Lygia, for Petronius and Tigellius, for Nero, for the Christians, for the world itself. Nothing will ever be the same!

Look back at the great scenes in the book (the ones you find impossible to forget), then prepare yourself for one of the most unforgettable in all literature, comparable to the burning of Atlanta in *Gone with the Wind* (which perhaps owed much to this antecedent). As you read, jot down responses: What's the effect of each scene? Do they give you new understanding and empathy with the people of that time? In what ways?

Chapter XLII

156. Have you ever noticed that in moments of great stress, your brain thinks differently? That you enter into a foggy, surreal world in which nothing seems distinct? Compare that to what you read in these pages.

157. Disasters—what makes us so fascinated by them? Does the description here make you feel you were actually there? In such a life-or-death situation, do mere *things* mean much (compared to those people dearest to us)? Compare other disasters you've known or experienced to the one portrayed here.

Chapter XLIII

158. Have you ever experienced a disastrous fire? A city out of control? A complete breakdown of law and order? How do they compare to this?

159. What causes Vinitius to turn a deaf ear to the temptation to become the next Caesar?

160. How were the Christians treating people during the conflagration, compared to most of the others? Would they do this today?

PART III
Chapter XLIV

161. It's easy to forget how thin the veneer of civilized law and order really is and take it for granted. Remove that protective hand, even for moments, and the amoral criminal element is at the site immediately, ready to destroy and plunder. In such a throwback, everyone is on his own, with no one to protect him but himself. That, of course, is what happened in Rome. Have you ever experienced, or known of, such experiences? Describe them.

162. What an epic scene this chapter is! One would swear Sienkiewicz was an eyewitness to the cataclysm! Interesting, isn't it, what a difference a word or two can make in such a visual panorama. Study it, and write down your favorite lines or passages. What made you single them out? What can one learn from your choices (what it takes to write vividly, unforgettably, persuasively, etc.)?

Chapter XLV

163. In our time, American military, ideological, and financial might is felt around our world in the same way that Rome's was. Should catastrophe strike America—the world's greatest market and financial power—the resulting shock waves could plunge the entire planet into a worldwide economic depression. That's an aspect of life Chilo fails to consider in his premature funeral of Rome. What additional similarities between our two cultures do you notice here?

164. It's funny, isn't it, to listen to Chilo speaking out of both sides of his mouth about the condition of Rome? But do we do that—speak

one way when alone or with close friends and another way when we are trying to impress or make points? Is that honest? Why or why not?

Is some of what Chilo says tongue-in-cheek? Which lines? Why do you feel that way?

165. The Jews persecuting the Christians, one minority persecuting another; why do you think this happens? One would think that those who had themselves been mistreated would be the last to pass on such treatment to others. Have you noticed this situation in real life? What are your reactions to it?

166. Crispus remains true to form in his preaching the *letter* of the law (terrorizing people into heaven); true to form in another way is the Apostle Peter, preaching the *spirit* of the law (loving people into heaven). Even today, we still have both kinds. Are both kinds really needed? Would some respond to one approach and not the other? Which approach do you feel more comfortable with? Which approach would stroke the ego the most? Why?

Chapter XLVI

167. If indeed Nero caused this fire, as many historians contend, just think of the loss of irreplaceable art, sculptures, buildings, and so on, not to mention precious manuscripts and historical and genealogical records. Should the owner of such treasures be allowed to destroy them on a mere whim? Discuss.

168. Rumors—they're always with us, aren't they—and it's amazing how many unsubstantiated ones are taken for truth by those who hear them. How should each of us respond to unsubstantiated rumors? What about spreading them ourselves?

169. Courage—neither Nero nor Tigellinus had it—but Petronius did. Courage enough to ride unprotected into what would have been almost certain death for many of his peers. Courage and belief in his persuasive powers and "presence." What's this thing called "presence"? Why is it that some people command by their mere presence

in the room and others do not? Is there a magical ingredient to account for it? Is it something one is born with, or is it acquired?

Chapter XLVII

170.   We have little to go on, other than the New Testament accounts, as to how the early Christians treated the Apostles Peter and Paul. Sienkiewicz, heir to the Greek Orthodox, Byzantine, and Roman Catholic traditions, may have assumed that their current practice mirrored earliest practice—this we cannot either confirm or deny. Obviously, this is an issue likely to be raised any time a novelist uses poetic license in recreating history. Without question the early Apostles were greatly revered, but in what form that respect came, we can only speculate. After studying the New Testament for yourself, ask: How closely do I agree with Sienkiewicz in his portrayals of the Apostles? Why?

171.   "Predestined her for you." Those are powerful words, are they not? Do you believe that God sometimes preordains who it is that we marry? On what do you base your belief? And if we reject His choice for us, what then?

172.   Chilo never for a second permits anyone to forget what's owed him. Does this greed grate on you? Have you ever known anyone like him in this respect? If so, compare the two.

173.   Can there be much greater happiness than to find someone you believed was lost to you forever? Someone beloved to you above all others—and whom you had searched for vainly and without much hope? Have you ever experienced such a thing? How did it compare to Vinitius's relief at finding his Lygia at last?

174.   It's one thing to *say* one trusts in God for protection, and another to turn down a safe haven in favor of a place full of great danger. This is the dilemma facing Vinitius here. He knows he can get Lygia to escape with him to comparative safety, but at the price of deep regrets at leaving her surrogate father, the Apostle Peter, behind. Does life often get this complex? Are decisions often this difficult to make? Why or why not?

Chapter XLVIII

175. Belatedly, Nero now learns the fallacy of his assumption that he was totally in control of his empire. Too late, he discovers that by his open pandering to it, he's empowered the mob to control him instead of his having the power to control it. Can you think of parallels to this in our society?

176. Notice how power corrupts: To retain it, Nero is not only willing but even eager to murder every last one of the descendants of his predecessors—plus, for good measure, anyone else who could possibly be viewed as a threat to him. Have you noticed this same principle at work in our time? Reactions?

177. Petronius—at least at the end—loves his nephew so much that he risks his own life on his behalf, knowing even as he does so that the odds are against him this time. Had the battle been just between him and Tigellinus, the odds would have been much more even, but once Poppaea enters on Tigellinus's side with all of her malevolence, only a miracle could save him and those he loved. How did you respond to this particular portrait of Petronius? Why?

Chapter XLIX

178. Did it surprise you to see Chilo testifying against his supposed fellow believers? Or would you have been surprised *not* to see him in that role? Note that he lies with a completely straight face: ascribing to Glaucus the very atrocities he himself committed! He knows so much about the private lives of Vinitius and the Christians that he represents the worst enemy Christians could have had. Was Petronius right earlier on when he told Vinitius he might later rue the day he didn't finish the flogging job with Chilo? Why?

179. Notice that Chilo includes just enough truth to give his fiendishly clever stories credibility, and that he slays even those he pretends are his friends. Essentially, the entire diatribe could be chalked up to a massive settling of old grudges and returning evil for good, death for life. Why is it that half-truths are harder to deal with than outright lies?

180. A number of times, Petronius had Tigellinus's life in his hands: One word to Nero, and it would have been all over for the unprincipled panderer. Does Tigellinus now return the favor? Why or why not?

Chapter L

181. It now becomes clear how different the scenario would have been had Chilo not turned traitor to the Christians. How would the beginning sequence of events probably have played out without the involvement of Chilo?

182. Unlike Acte, Eunice isn't even a freedwoman when this story begins; thus she has no rights whatsoever. Now, unbeknownst to her, she does have rights, but she lives only for Petronius. She's one of the only faithful non-Christians in the book. As beautiful as her relationship with Petronius may appear, were she to lose her beauty, to get old, do you feel Petronius would remain faithful to her? Why or why not? Does this likelihood change the picture?

183. Here now, as the sands of his life are running out, Petronius belatedly begins to reevaluate his erstwhile life of pleasure and pursuit of beauty. How is he changing? How is he different from what he once was?

184. Petronius and Vinitius now feel that since they're living on borrowed time, they've nothing to lose by taking extreme measures. If the worst is going to happen to you and those you love anyway, what difference could anything else you do make? Have you ever been in such a dead-end situation? Describe it.

Chapter LI

185. Mob mentality—what causes people to lose their sense of reason and do unthinkable things in groups, when they'd never do such things alone? Only an exceedingly brave person will dare to stand against a crowd. In our own country, lynch mobs have been known to slay innocent people. All this was now happening in Rome. And people *assumed* the Christians had burned Rome, but didn't want to know for sure. Have you ever been part of a mob (remembering that a mob mind-set can control large groups or groups as small perhaps as three people)? Describe it.

186. Of all questions we humans are forced to deal with, perhaps this is the hardest: How can a just and kind God permit great evil, atrocities, and massacres to take place? Certainly the Jews are still asking that question of God about Hitler and the Holocaust. There are indeed no easy answers, are there? Evil exists and so do its effects. Have you found reasons or solace for such agonizing questions? What solutions or answers have you found?

187. Does it surprise you that the early Christians were so willing—even eager—to die? To what do you attribute that? Would Christians today be that willing? Would you?

Chapter LII

188. Each generation since Christ lived, died, and was resurrected on earth has lived in daily expectation of Christ's imminent return. The same was true of this Age of Nero. Did this surprise you? How does such a conviction affect one's daily walk and actions? Any perceived difference between then and now, in this respect?

189. How often, when we place our faith in a mere mortal, we are disappointed or disillusioned! Vinitius has built the foundation of his faith on one frail old man, the Apostle Peter. Is he afraid Peter will fail him? Does Peter? In what ways does this section remind us just how important or significant our example may be?

190. Is Sienkiewicz being ambivalent in having the Apostle Peter call the church in Rome eternal, or is he reminding us that God's church is indeed eternal and lives on in heaven after the Second Coming? Why do you think that?

191. Some blessed people are caregivers and bring strength and encouragement to all they interact with—as was true with the Apostle. Have you known such caregivers? How do they do it? Who ministers to *them?* Or does anybody even think about ministering to the needs of apparently strong men and women?

Chapter LIII

192. To the Christian women now came another terror: violation before

death—a fate to them worse than the death that followed. Such treatment is a matter of historical record and is thus not mere speculation.

What follows during the rest of the book is difficult to read without tears; nevertheless we're reading about what actually took place in Rome during the reign of Nero. Do you think that such an age, such atrocities, is likely to be imitated in our time? Has it been already? Discuss.

193. Seeing Chilo in the regalia of an Augustinian, Vinitius at last understands many things. What do you think they were? Had the flogging paid compound dividends? Was the satisfaction Vinitius gained from it worth the cost? Why? Had Petronius's prophecy come true in this respect?

Chapter LIV

194. What do you think of Lygia's contention that her death wouldn't dissolve what she considered equivalent to marriage: betrothal? If we really believed that today, would our partners of marriage and remarriage be different? In what ways?

195. Although almost totally evil, Poppaea still retained a mother's love for her child. And who among us can read of the murder of that innocent without empathy and pity? There's an old saying: "To know all is to forgive all." In what ways does this scene change your view of the desperate empress?

Chapter LV

196. Is Crispus true to character all the way to the end? How would you describe him and his role in the book? Is he at heart a sadist, a shepherd, or something else?

197. Did it surprise you that the victims came into the arena covered with animal skins rather than in clothes? Why do you think this was done?

198. You will most likely recognize, in the gripping ceremony during which the gladiators salute Caesar with that famous couplet, lines

that have trickled down into our popular culture. In songs, dramas, films, and novels, these words have developed a life of their own, almost achieving cult status. Have you ever noticed them, used them, or wondered about them? Discuss.

199. This is *not* a chapter for children—or even the faint of heart! The sights and sounds are almost more than we wish to experience, even vicariously—yet they happened, and happened this way. What were your responses to the crowd, the Christians, and comparisons between the two?

Chapter LVI

200. Meanwhile, Vinitius is suffering terribly. Have you ever noticed that in times of trauma and tragedy, it can almost be worse to be the one left behind, worrying and not knowing what's happening? Have you experienced such a situation? Describe it.

201. Niger now loves his master. Would that have been likely before Vinitius became a Christian? Why or why not? How can Christianity make such a difference? Does it today? If not, why not?

202. We human beings may, after a great deal of time and effort, come up with what we regard as failure-proof plans, yet they can and do fail, just as happens with the elaborately planned rescue of Lygia. What lessons can we learn from this?

203. The letdown from prolonged stress or anticipation can leave us absolutely limp, for the body can literally drain itself of all its reserves in such instances. Thus when the period of trauma ends, there are no healing, regenerating reserves to fall back on. Have you ever experienced this? What was it like? How did it compare with Vinitius's experience?

Chapter LVII

204. A pleasure-driven, sensation-driven society! Does reading about this fixation on live gore and slaughter remind you of any parallels in our modern society? What is there about tragedies that fascinates us? Are people today superstitious enough to believe that slaughtering

innocent human beings would propitiate forces that bring on atmospheric disasters? Discuss.

205. There's an aspect of the perversely funny in the tantrum the Roman spectators throw when the Christians refuse to entertain them by putting up a futile fight before they're killed. Lest we wax too self-righteous in our judgment of them, how far removed are we today when we trash a stadium when our team has lost or torch and loot a city when our cause has suffered? Do some things, after all, never change? Why?

206. Do you wonder with horror at the Roman delight in observing death, saying to yourself, *How could an apparently civilized people do such a thing?* Yet the undeniable truth is that it was standard custom, up until about a hundred years ago, in much of Western society, for entire regions to throng a town or city whenever a criminal was being hanged or decapitated. Entire families, from the oldest to the youngest, would make a picnic of the spectacle, and hawkers and venders sold them food, drinks, and souvenirs of the event! Study our televised coverage of the news and see if we really have changed. Or might it be that we have merely become more-anonymous voyeurs of violence and death? If so, what are the implications?

207. These Christians were crucified in deliberate mockery of their belief in the crucified Christ—but they counted it an honor to die as Christ had. Crispus, at the end, attains both the ultimate in religious zeal and the ultimate in repentance. Only someone like him would have dared to so address the ruler of the world! What were your reactions to this moving scene? Had you been there, on a bench or on a cross, how might *you* have responded?

Chapter LVIII

208. Chilo found it easy to betray in private, but finds it anything but easy to watch the bloodbath his words made possible. To know in theory that your actions will harm someone is one thing; to see the actual results, with the eyes of the world on you, is something totally different. What are your thoughts on this? Was it not true also in

the Holocaust (no one taking responsibility for his actions, but only following orders from above)? Discuss.

209. Are the Roman Furies merely synonyms for what we label "conscience"? Discuss.

210. What do you think Sienkiewicz intended this short interim chapter to accomplish? Was he successful? Why or why not?

Chapter LIX
211. There's a haunting beauty about Vinitius and Lygia's profession of love for each other in such an unromantic spot—in fact, it would be mighty difficult to imagine one less conducive to such a thing! How did you respond to it?

How do their perceptions of the future differ? Which do you personally lean towards? Why?

Chapter LX
212. May we today experience a sense of bridging into eternity, even while still alive, as did Vinitius and Lygia? Or does it take the imminence of death to accomplish this? What does such a bridging mean?

213. Petronius is totally incapable of understanding how his cruel firebrand of a nephew could turn into a new creature, characterized by serenity rather than rage, peace rather than torment. None of the Roman gods could have accomplished that! Is such a change, for such reasons, still possible today? Discuss.

Chapter LXI
214. "Burning at the stake" may be a quaint term to most of us, but I daresay no one who reads this chapter will ever again be able to say those words, or listen to them, without remembering the graphic imagery in these pages: man's inhumanity to man. What was the impact on you? Which portions especially affected you?

215. Chilo had been forgiven once before, but now, when it seemed no

one but God could possibly forgive him, beyond all human reason, Glaucus, the one he'd wronged most, *forgives* him in the name of Christ. Could you have possibly done the same? Why or why not?

216. Chilo's transformation from a craven coward to a fiery denunciator was the work of but moments—or was it really the work of years? Might it be more accurate to say that repeated hammer blows had rained down on the anvil of his corrupt soul, all with no apparent effect. Yet each had made a difference. Crispus and Paul had weakened the anvil; Glaucus represented the final stroke that smashed through the weakened structure, opening up room for God to come in and begin the process of rebuilding. Might this be the reason why Christ enjoins us to forgive—not just seven times—but seventy times seven (symbolic of placing no limits on the number)? Do we sometimes give up too easily, failing to realize that some nuts are harder to crack than others?

What if it had been the Apostle Peter who spoke to Chilo in the garden? Would his words have been as effective as those of the Apostle Paul, who also had persecuted and caused the death of many Christians—and yet been forgiven? Does God use our failures in positive ways? Explain.

217. How does Tigellinus respond to Chilo's new fearlessness? Do you feel Tigellinus has any redeeming qualities? Or do you perceive him as totally evil? Why?

Chapter LXII

218. What do you think Tigellinus expected to get out of Chilo's death? Did he? If not, what do you feel the effect was?

219. Was the tide at last beginning to turn? If so, what was causing it to?

220. Excess demands ever greater excess—thus, what could Tigellinus possibly do to exceed the impact of his previous entertainments? Did the live bear help in that respect?

Chapter LXIII

221. The priorities of Vinitius have certainly changed. Earlier on, he was obsessed with rescuing Lygia from Nero in order to enjoy the good life with her. Now he spends more time thinking about the afterlife than the earthly one. True, that often occurs among us as well—but not usually until we are old and the quality of our days has begun to decline. Might it be that Nero's hell had something to do with this? Discuss.

222. Ursus is indeed a gentle giant. What about quick thinking—do we normally associate that trait with giants? Or with those much smaller? Why?

Chapter LXIV

223. Petronius had long ago learned to be wary of those who appeared to be disloyal to the emperor, for in an autocracy, even the walls have ears, and one careless word can mean a death sentence. Might the same principle be true of an employee in the corporate world today? Might not the habit of undermining leadership become so deeply grooved that one would lose the ability to be positive? Is a negative person ever likely to accomplish much? Why or why not?

224. Petronius is always quotable. Have you ever noticed, in this respect, that only a rare few speak and write original thoughts? Are your thoughts generally uniquely your own? Explain.

225. Petronius is a master at skating on thin ice, so he knows when the ice is so thin under him that he could break through at any moment. Isn't that true of his verbal sparring in this chapter? Are you that daring? Have you known others that are? Discuss.

Chapter LXV

226. Vinitius discovers that it's one thing to conceptualize what might be done to Lygia and quite another to have to watch those things actually happen. Oftentimes, anticipation can be worse than reality; but is it not also possible that reality may sometimes be worse than anticipation? Have you ever experienced such instances? If so, discuss.

227. Sadism doesn't have to be overt; oftentimes it's a subtle thing: inwardly reveling over pain someone else is experiencing. Sometimes it's revealed only through one's tone, inflections, or body language. In Caesar's case, of course, it's blatantly obvious: Few things made him happier than to inflict pain on others. Have you ever known people like Nero? Compare. Have you ever experienced it yourself (on either the receiving end or the delivering end)? Describe.

228. Fascinating, isn't it, the difference one word can make, the right choice separating the memorable from the forgettable. Case in point is the scene in which Lygia is borne into the arena on the head of an aurochs—naked. Had the word "nude" been used, the connotative effect might have been sensual or suggestive—not so the word "naked," the same word used to describe Adam and Eve in Eden, when sin caused them to be aware for the first time that they had no clothes on. "Naked" thus carries with it a sense of being embarrassed, even of shame. Once you notice the difference a word can make, you're on your way to becoming a writer. How can you become more of a wordsmith?

229. The scene at the end of this chapter is truly one of the most moving in all literature—all the more so as it follows so many other memorable ones. Which passages moved you most, and why?

230. The slaughtering of innocent Christians in the arena, seen and approved by the mob, was Nero's brainchild. In the end he learns a sobering truth: A mob is a most unstable and unreliable creation— as likely to devour you as to eat out of your hand. What other parallels to this can you think of in history?

Chapter LXVI

231. Joy after sorrow, peace after pain, restoration from the very jaws of death—all this Vinitius now experiences, and with it an overwhelming love for his Lord. How would you compare Vinitius's ability to love here to its counterpart earlier in the book?

Chapter LXVII

232. How astutely Petronius plays on Nero's petulance! Even though his verbal sparring matches with Nero and Tigellinus are a life-or-death matter, Petronius never strays from the high road, never loses his composure, never permits himself to be cowed; if humiliated, he doesn't admit it in public. How about yourself? Ever played such a game? With what kind of stakes?

233. Vinitius and Lygia, having emerged from the crucible as pure gold, now have different assumptions, different priorities, different goals. Can trauma refine and restructure us as well? Is it possible for us to grow, set down deep roots, and stand against any tempest that may assail us when we live as hothouse plants? Or do we have to face the elements in order to achieve such strength, seasoning, and stature? If that be so, are prolonged good times to be wished for? Should we pray for trouble? Why or why not?

Chapter LXVIII

234. A misperception many of us share is our conviction that great men and women of faith—such as the Apostle Peter—remain strong all the time. We forget that each of us is subject to weakness. Even Elijah, after his great triumph over the priests of Baal, so feared for his safety that he blindly fled into the wilderness to hide from Jezebel and Ahab's wrath. So here we have the Apostle Peter, also fearing for his life, also afraid of an earthly potentate. Does this make us respect him less? Or empathize with him more? Why?

235. From a human point of view, the odds against the old Apostle were ludicrously lopsided. Peter, a defenseless, weak old man, was facing the most powerful ruler on earth, a man responsible for slaughtering thousands of innocent people. Surely the Lord was jesting when He told the Apostle to stay in Rome, awaiting the victory. Victory indeed!

What about us: Do we, too, assume sometimes that the odds against us are hopeless and so completely discount the forces God can call into action at any moment? And, lest we be unduly smug, had we endured all that Peter had endured, and seen all that he'd seen, would we, too, have decided to get out while there was still time? If not, what approach do you think would have been a wise one to take? Why?

Chapter LXIX

236. Sunrise on the Appian Way! It would be difficult to envision a lovelier work of art than these words setting the stage for the "*Quo vadis*" section of the book. Rare is the writer with the power to so paint a scene in words that it's preserved forever after, framed in all its loveliness, on the walls of the reader's mind. Sienkiewicz was such a writer. What kind of impact did this opening scene have on you? How did it compare with similar descriptive prose you've read?

237. Few passages in all literature have moved me as much as this one. According to early Christian tradition, it actually took place. It's Peter's personal Road to Damascus experience—and it changes the direction of his life and that of the early church. At this point, I suggest that you try to complete a character description of the Apostle Peter—not as a mere biblical cardboard stereotype, but as a real flesh and blood creature. Sadly, more often than not, men and women of the Bible fail to achieve three-dimensionality to us. How do these scenes involving Peter change your perception of him (keeping in mind that Sienkiewicz skillfully interweaves fact and supposition)?

238. If Peter hadn't returned, certainly the rebirth of the early church would have been more difficult, for he returned to Rome not as a fugitive, but as a conqueror. The seed had been sown by thousands of martyrs—now it was harvesttime. Do we, like Peter, sometimes surrender too soon? Discuss.

Chapter LXX

239. **Historical Note:** Sienkiewicz's portrait of Peter is a complex one. On the one hand, he portrays him as a humble man, fully aware of his many frailties; on the other, as a proud monarch who ascribes the victory represented by the huge crowds of new believers to himself rather than to the seed planted by thousands of martyrs and to God. It's a difficult synthesis of opposites to swallow. With the

advantage of almost nineteen centuries of history, Sienkiewicz is free to safely wax prophetic.

Harper's Bible Dictionary scholars both confirm and refute Sienkiewicz on various points: (1) They confirm that both Peter and Paul were incarcerated in the Mamertine prison by Nero during the same time period (ca. A.D. 67–68).

(2) Sienkiewicz stops short of describing the last moments of both Paul and Peter; *Harper's* scholars feel confident that Paul, as a Roman citizen, met his death by the sword (which is implied by Paul's wrapping Plautilla's veil over his eyes during his last moments). Tertullian of Carthage (ca. A.D. 198–200) declared that Paul was beheaded. Peter was crucified head down, at his own request, not considering himself worthy to die as his Lord had. Apparently Peter was martyred at the site of the Egyptian obelisk in today's Piazza of the Basilica of St. Peter. According to Eusebius, "The graves of Paul on the Ostian Way and Peter in the cemetery near Nero's Circus were extant ca. A.D. 200."

(3) According to *Harper's* scholars, Peter was indeed the most charismatic and powerful of all the Twelve: Even his shadow was thought to bring healing with it, and he was treated by many early believers with a veneration bordering on worship.

(4) *Harper's* scholars point out that the belief that Peter, the man, was the rock upon which the Church was built "has no support among Protestant scholars. . . . It's difficult to determine what words Christ actually spoke on this occasion, and what he meant."

(5) Sienkiewicz's *"Quo vadis?"* story is confirmed by *The Acts of Peter* (A.D. 200–220). (Information in preceding sections from Madeleine S. Miller and J. Lane Miller's *Harper's Bible Dictionary* [New York: Harper & Brothers, 1952], 529–34, 541–42.)

It appears that Sienkiewicz was generally on target with his account—much more so than is the case with many historical novelists, especially those writers prior to the middle of the twentieth century. Given the information above, what are your reactions to the Sienkiewicz portrayals of the Apostles Peter and Paul?

Chapter LXXI

240. The people of Rome had deliberately turned a deaf ear to injustice and the massacre of innocent Christians. Consequently, when their turn came, just as was true in Hitler's Third Reich, there was nobody left to stand up for them. If you fail to stand up for injustice today, tomorrow you may be the one being treated unjustly, and there may be nobody left to defend you. How relevant is this principle of action today?

Chapter LXXII

241. While not likely to ever become a philosopher, Vinitius has indeed come a long way from his act-first-think-later days. He's found peace at last and only wishes his dear uncle, who risked his life over and over on his behalf, might find this peace, too. Which of his arguments do you feel are the strongest? Why?

242. In the end, Petronius recognizes—in theory—Vinitius's God; recognizes, too, the truth of Paul's words. But Petronius, having experienced no conversion, remains the aesthete to the last. He came close to surviving Nero, but like so many of his time, especially the elite and the noble, he fell to Nero's bloody scythe. However, he chose to die, not like a craven, but like a man.

Why do you feel Petronius was constitutionally unable to love the unbeautiful? Have you ever known such a person? Discuss.

243. What sort of an afterlife does Petronius expect?

Chapter LXXIII

244. What do you think of the Roman custom of wearing fresh rose wreaths on their heads? Obviously, they didn't view it as a feminine thing. Wouldn't it be interesting to see men in a boardroom, at a football game, at a concert, so attired? Reactions? What does this custom say about Roman society?

245. When people have lived together for a long time, words are often unnecessary: They can read each other's body language and eyes so perfectly that they frequently know what the other is going to say

before it's said, and they often finish each other's sentences. Thus Eunice, having known and loved Petronius for years, knows him like the proverbial book; knows without even asking what was going to happen to him. Have you noticed this kinship of minds in people you know? In yourself? Discuss.

246. Putting on a dinner is just as much an art form as painting, sculpting, or writing. Few such dinners during our lifetimes approach perfection, but those few we never forget! What are the contributing factors to the success of Petronius's last dinner? How does the dinner compare to special evenings you've known?

247. Had Petronius shared the dramatic news at the beginning of his dinner instead of at the end, how would the effect have been different? Would there have been a refusal to eat, indigestion, fear of staying for the rest of the evening? So could timing also be an art form? Discuss.

248. Isn't Eunice's love story a moving one? Though Petronius never treated her as an equal, as Lygia was treated by Vinitius, she nevertheless proves to be a dramatic exception to the norm for the time. What are your final evaluations of her and Petronius?

249. Imagine you are Nero opening this last sizzling letter—what might your reactions be?

250. *Before going on to the Epilogue, I strongly urge you to stop here and think about the book and its impact on your philosophy of life. The true ending of the book occurs here with the death of Petronius and Eunice. What follows is probably necessary, but I personally would rather have read it much later, after I'd had time to really savor the book up to this point. So, before reading on, please answer these questions:* Just how has the book affected you? Has it changed your philosophy of life in any way? How? Has it made you stronger? Has it made you want to learn more about the ancient world? The Roman Empire? What do you feel are the most valuable insights you have gained from reading the book?

Who do you feel are the most memorable characters? Why? Which characters have provided you with the deepest insights into life? In what way?

Does this book make you want to read more books by Sienkiewicz?

Epilogue

251. As I read Sienkiewicz's historical account of Nero's last days, I couldn't help but think that had he not been so incredibly inept, he could have ruled and continued to bathe the empire in blood for much longer! Perhaps Providence intervened here as well. Would you have liked to live during such a bloody period of history? To have been a Christian then? Discuss.

252. Why are we all so fascinated by bad men and bad women? Because Nero was so horrible and despicable, actors always love to play him on the stage or in the cinema. Why do you think that is? Aren't good people interesting, too? Discuss.

About the Editor

Joseph Leininger Wheeler's earliest memories have to do with books and stories—more specifically, of listening to his mother read aloud both in public and to him at home. Wheeler recalls that, as soon as he was able to read, he followed his mother around the house, relentlessly reading his storybooks to her.

Shortly after Wheeler turned eight, his parents moved from California to Latin America as missionaries. From the third through the tenth grade, he was home-schooled by his mother. Of those years, he says today, "I was incredibly lucky and blessed. My mother, a trained teacher and elocutionist, was a voracious reader of books worth reading and had memorized thousands of pages of readings, poetry, and stories. All of that she poured into me. Wherever we went, she encouraged me to devour entire libraries."

At 16, Wheeler returned to California to complete his high school years at Monterey Bay Academy near Santa Cruz. Because of his inherited love of the printed word, Wheeler majored in history at Pacific Union College in the Napa Valley, completing both bachelor's and master's degrees there. After completing a master's in English at California State University in Sacramento, Wheeler attended Vanderbilt University, where he obtained a Ph.D. in English.

Today, after 34 years of teaching at the adult education, college, high school, and junior high levels, Wheeler is Professor Emeritus at Columbia Union College in Takoma Park, Maryland. The world's foremost authority on frontier writer Zane Grey, Wheeler is also the founder and executive director of Zane Grey's West Society and Senior Fellow for Cultural Studies at the Center for the New West in Denver, Colorado. He is editor/compiler of the popular *Christmas in My Heart* series (Review & Herald; Doubleday; Tyndale House); editor/compiler of the *Heart to Heart* story anthologies (Tyndale House and Focus on the Family); and editor/compiler of Focus on the Family's *Great Stories Remembered* and *Great Stories* series (Tyndale House). Along the way, Wheeler has established nine libraries in schools and colleges, as well as building up his own collection (as large as some college libraries).

Joe Wheeler and his wife, Connie, are the parents of two grown children, Greg and Michelle, and now make their home in Conifer, Colorado.

IF YOU LIKED *QUO VADIS*, YOU'LL LOVE THE OTHER BOOKS FROM FOCUS ON THE FAMILY'S® "GREAT STORIES" COLLECTION!

The Best of Times

There was a time when stories were read aloud, remembered, and passed on. Now discovered tales from the golden age of story writing have been woven into one heartwarming collection: *The Best of Times*. These beautifully crafted stories honor the virtues we all hold dear: love, courage, loyalty, and sacrifice.

Great Stories Remembered II

Families love this forgotten collection of touching accounts, warm narrations, and exciting adventures dating back to the turn of the century. Each classic tale highlights timeless virtues and inspiring morals. Great gift book!

Ben-Hur

In an unforgettable account of betrayal, revenge, and rebellion, a nobleman learns the grace of God when he falls from Roman favor and is sentenced to life as a slave.

Little Women

Despite the Civil War, four sisters discover the importance of family and manage to keep laughter and love in their hearts—even through illness and poverty, disappointment, and sacrifice.

Little Men

In this exciting sequel to *Little Women,* Jo and her husband open their hearts and home to school a handful of rowdy boys—then the fun, adventures, and lessons begin!

(continued on next page)

Anne of Green Gables

When Matthew goes to the train station to pick up a boy sent
from an orphanage, he discovers a *girl* has been sent instead!
Not having the heart to disappoint her, he agrees to take her
home, and their lives are changed forever.

A Christmas Carol

When the miserly Scrooge retires for the day on Christmas Eve, he is
visited by the ghost of his long-dead partner, who warns him
of what surely will be if he doesn't change his stingy ways.

The Christmas Angel

After throwing all other reminders of her childhood away, Miss Terry
decides to keep the Christmas Angel, after all. When the angel comes
to life, it reminds the bitter, lonely woman of a family's value
and the joy of reconciliation.

Robinson Crusoe

A shipwreck's sole survivor struggles to triumph over crippling fear,
doubt, and isolation as a castaway on a lonely island—and learns
the amazing revelation that God is always with us.

The Farther Adventures of Robinson Crusoe

Daniel Defoe's faith-filled *The Farther Adventures of Robinson Crusoe*
finds Crusoe back on the high seas, returning to the island
he left years before. Readers will be captivated by this sequel,
which is every bit as engaging as the original.

The Twenty-fourth of June

Grace Richmond's *The Twenty-fourth of June* is rich with romance, suspense,
and a deep love for the home. To prove himself worthy to Roberta,
Richard Kendrick undertakes the greatest challenge of his life—one
that makes this novel almost impossible to put down.

(continued on next page)

David Copperfield

A captivating tale of an innocent orphan in an indifferent society.
David encounters memorable characters that shape his world and the
paths he takes. A message of hope and determination
amid a harsh reality makes this a perennial favorite.

Heart to Heart: Stories of Friendship

This engaging short-story collection, celebrates the richness friendships
bring to our lives. For anyone who has known the special bond friends
share, these moving stories will bring back fond memories and
remind us to treasure the friends we hold close to our hearts.

Heart to Heart Stories for Moms

A mother's love knows no bounds—no sacrifice or effort is too much
for her children. Joe Wheeler pays tribute to the love that lasts
for a lifetime in this short-story collection.

Heart to Heart Stories for Dads

A father's impact on his children is undeniable. In *Heart to Heart
Stories for Dads,* Joe Wheeler has gathered stories that celebrate
the legacy fatherhood leaves in our lives.

Christmas in My Heart (#8)

It seems nothing is impossible at Christmas . . . relationships mend,
miracles happen, and our spirits are renewed. Celebrate the season by reading
Christmas in My Heart, a poignant collection of holiday stories that bring
back the hope and meaning of the most wonderful time of the year.

• • •

**Call 1-800-A-FAMILY or write to us at Focus on the Family, Colorado Springs,
CO 80995. In Canada, call 1-800-661-9800 or write to Focus on the Family,
P.O. Box 9800, Stn. Terminal, Vancouver, B.C. V6B 4G3.
Or, visit your local Christian bookstore!**

FOCUS ON THE FAMILY®

Welcome to the *Family!*

Whether you received this book as a gift, borrowed it from
a friend, or purchased it yourself, we're glad you read it! It's just
one of the many helpful, insightful, and encouraging
resources produced by Focus on the Family.

In fact, that's what Focus on the Family is all about—providing inspiration, information, and biblically based advice to people in all stages of life.

It began in 1977 with the vision of one man, Dr. James Dobson, a licensed
psychologist and author of 16 best-selling books on marriage, parenting,
and family. Alarmed by the societal, political, and economic pressures
that were threatening the existence of the American family, Dr. Dobson
founded Focus on the Family with one employee—an assistant—
and a once-a-week radio broadcast, aired on only 36 stations.

Now an international organization, Focus on the Family is dedicated
to preserving Judeo-Christian values and strengthening the family
through more than 70 different ministries, including eight separate
daily radio broadcasts; television public service announcements;
11 publications; and a steady series of award-winning books,
films, and videos for people of all ages and interests.

Recognizing the needs of, as well as the sacrifices and important
contribution made by, such diverse groups as educators, physicians,
attorneys, crisis pregnancy center staff, and single parents,
Focus on the Family offers specific outreaches to uphold and
minister to these individuals, too. And it's all done for one purpose,
and one purpose only: to encourage and strengthen individuals
and families through the life-changing message of Jesus Christ.

• • •

For more information about the ministry, or if we can be of help to your
family, simply write to Focus on the Family, Colorado Springs, CO 80995
or call 1-800-A-FAMILY (1-800-232-6459). Friends in Canada may write
Focus on the Family, P.O. Box 9800, Stn. Terminal, Vancouver, B.C. V6B 4G3
or call 1-800-661-9800. Visit our Web site—www.family.org—
to learn more about the ministry or to find out if there is a
Focus on the Family office in your country.

We'd love to hear from you!

IN REMEMBRANCE

Sadly, the martyrdom of Christians did not end with the death of Nero or of the Roman Empire. In fact, some experts are convinced that more Christians were martyred in the twentieth century than in all the previous centuries combined. For information about how you can help, please contact the following organizations:

Christian Freedom International
15 Chester Street
Front Royal, VA 22630
(800) 323-2273
E-mail: cfi@rma.edu   Web site: www.christianfreedom.org

The Voice of the Martyrs

P.O. Box 443
Bartlesville, OK 74005-0043
(800) 747-0085 (orders only)
(918) 337-8015
E-mail: thevoice@vom-usa.com
Web site: www.persecution.com

P.O. Box 117, Port Credit
Mississauga, Ontario L5G 4L5
(905) 602-4832
E-mail: VOM @planteer.com
Web site: www.persecution.net

International Christian Concern
2020 Pennsylvania Avenue, NW, #941
Washington, DC 20006
(800) 422-5441
(301) 989-1708
Fax: (301) 989-1709
E-mail: icc@persecution.org   Web site: www. persecution.org

Freedom House
1319 18th Street, NW
Washington, DC 20036
(202) 296-5101
Fax: (202) 296-5078
E-mail: fh@freedomhouse.org   Web site: www.freedomhouse.org

OPEN DOORS with Brother Andrew
P.O. Box 27001
Santa Ana, CA 92799
(949) 752-6600
Web site: www.opendoorsusa.org